THE LEGEND OF
ZERO

FORGING ZERO

SARA KING

ISBN-13: 9781492333203
ISBN-10: 1492333204

Published by
Parasite Publications

DISCLAIMER

(a.k.a. If You Don't Realize This Is A Work Of Fiction, Please Go Find Something Else To Do)

So you're about to read about a kid getting abducted by aliens and life on other planets. In case you're still confused, yes, this book is a complete work of fiction. Nobody contained within these pages actually exists. If there are any similarities between the people or places of *The Legend of ZERO* and the people or places of Good Ol' Planet Earth, you've just gotta trust me. It's not real, people. Really. Yet.

BOOKS IN THE LEGEND OF ZERO SERIES:

Listed in Chronological Order
(because nothing else really makes sense):

Forging Zero
The Moldy Dead (short story)
Zero Recall
Zero's Return
Zero's Redemption
Zero's Legacy
Forgotten

DEDICATION

These are the people most responsible for The Legend of ZERO:
Tom Brion.
My first exposure to storytelling.
Fortunately for me, I learned from the very best.
Chancey King.
His gift for brainstorming was instrumental in creating so many aspects of this world, and his genius is surpassed only by his humility. Thanks, bro.
Logan Brutsche.
The devious mastermind behind Forgotten.
Kyle Brutsche.
It all started with his homework assignment.
Stephen Buchanan.
If 'moral support' were a job description, he'd have the Ph.D.
Sarah Liu.
My supremely talented editor on these books.
She has the eyes of an Ueshi and the brain of
a Geuji. (Well. At least a small Geuji.)
Patricia Brion.
She taught me to read. That kinda trumps it all.

AUTHOR'S NOTE

Forging Zero is the darkest book I've ever written. Not by desire,
but by necessity. Because, at the heart of every great epic, there is
something awful happening, something that demands change.
Forging Zero tells that story.

THE PARASITE PUBLICATIONS GLOSSARY
(BECAUSE SOMEBODY'S GOTTA TELL YOU THIS STUFF!)

Character author – That rare beast who lets his or her characters tell the story. (And often run completely wild.)

Character fiction – Stories that center around the characters; their thoughts, their emotions, their actions, and their goals.

Character sci-fi – Stories about the future that focus on the characters, rather than explaining every new theory and technology with the (silly) assumption that we, as present-day 21st centurians, know enough to analyze and predict the far future with any accuracy whatsoever. I.e. character sci-fi is fun and entertaining, not your next college Physics textbook.

Parasite – The Everyday Joe (or Jane) who enjoys crawling inside a character's head while reading a book; i.e. someone who enjoys character fiction.

Furg – Anyone who believes the best fiction makes your eyes glaze over. (Unless, of course, the glazing happens because you stayed up all night reading it and you can't keep your eyes open the next day. Then you're a parasite, not a furg.) ;)

TABLE OF CONTENTS

1

AN ALIEN MISTAKE

Joe Dobbs was fourteen when Congress discovered Earth.

The day they set their ships down in Washington, Joe found it hard to move from the TV. His whole family, from his little brother Sam to his great-aunt Lucy…even his dad's old Marine buddies who came over for beer on Fridays…all of them huddled together in his parents' living room, attention locked on the broadcasts from all over the world. Outside Joe's house, there was relative silence. Nobody was driving. Nobody was playing football or going to the zoo or having picnics in the San Diego sun. Everybody was inside their homes, watching the invasion. Joe's dad had gotten a huge TV for Christmas, so his house had twelve bodies packed in the room like sardines, filling all the empty space, breathing and rebreathing the same stuffy air, leaning forward in their chairs and sofas in silence, watching the live feeds from the frantic mass of reporters surrounding the capital with the total, rapt attention of the condemned.

Pundits took over the news channels, talking nonstop, twenty-four hours a day, debating the endless pictures of aliens, alien ships, and alien weaponry. They said that their squat, tentacled forms were semi-aquatic, and the flipping gills that fluttered in the sides of their head were an evolutionary throwback, like an appendix in humans. Sudah, they were called. Humanity knew that because a reporter's autistic kid was killed for touching them during a press conference, and the live alien tirade that followed included the word 'sudah' about three hundred times as the alien screamed at the bleeding, dismantled corpse of the kid, his parent, and two otherwise innocent bystanders.

Sam, however, disagreed. As usual.

"That's stupid," Sam snorted loudly, once when it was just him and Joe in the room and they were listening to yet another lecture about the cultural importance of 'sudah.' "It's not an evolutionary throwback. It's obvious they're using them to breathe. That means they came from a planet with something in the air. They're *filters*. They keep stuff *out*. They just don't like someone touching them there 'cause it's like putting your hand over someone's mouth and nose. Cutting off your air, you know?"

All the adults had left to discuss whether it was safe enough to attempt driving out to Uncle Davvie's place for some meats and vegetables—which had quintupled in price since the aliens had landed—leaving just Joe and his ten-year-old brother Sam to watch the aliens in the living room.

With just Joe in the room, Sam didn't have to pretend to be 'kiddy' for the adults. The skinny turd actually liked showing off to Joe. He got out a pencil and walked up to the screen like an indignant college professor. "See that?" Sam asked, slapping the pencil to the picture of a tentacled creature's thick, ropy arm. "So what if they're boneless? That right there is built like a *snake*. There's no aquadynamics. It's meant for swinging through trees. Like an orangutan. They're land-dwellers."

"Just shut up, Sam," Joe muttered. He tried to peer around his brother.

Sam, however, had other ideas. He turned to face the TV. "And they're *not* a hundred fifty pounds," he snorted, speaking directly to the bald, sweating Talking Head on the other end of the live news feed who was lecturing them on body size. He crossed his arms over his chest and sneered, as if the very idea was ridiculous. "They're *denser* than us, you dipshit. Look at the way it hit that car—" there was a famous video of a kamikaze attack by a drunken motorist on one of the aliens…which had resulted in a crumpled car, a dead motorist, and a very pissed off alien, "—it was obviously at least four or five hundred pounds. Just the impact *alone* should've told you that."

"Shut *up*, Sam," Joe muttered, irritated. "Get out from in front of the TV. I can't see through your scrawny ass."

Sam rolled his eyes and turned to face him, but remained firmly planted in front of the television. "Not like you're gonna learn anything new. They've been saying the same stuff for the last three days."

"*Now!*" Joe snapped. "Go find a coloring book or something."

Sam sighed deeply and went to check on the adults.

Joe watched him go, scowling. He hated the way his younger brother seemed so cocky about the whole affair; like he had everything completely under control.

Or, at least, Dad did.

Must be nice to be a kid, Joe thought, returning his attention to the aliens. Something about them seemed…familiar, and it was giving him a nagging sense of dread that he just couldn't shake. Almost like he'd had a bad dream like this a very long time ago and it was starting to unfold before his eyes.

…and there was nothing he could do to stop it.

More than once during his vigil, Joe found his hands sweaty, his skin broken out in goosebumps. As each new snippet of information came in from the White House, the feeling of dread intensified, congealing in his guts like a cold, hard rot. Unlike Sam, Joe knew what it meant for their family. For Dad. A few hours after the aliens first landed, Joe had heard Dad and Manny discussing the military's order to stand down. He had heard their furtive whispers about a group of Marines 'taking things into their own hands.'

Joe wasn't an idiot. He knew what that meant. He also knew his dad didn't stand a chance. Not against *that.*

Tens of thousands of massive, skyscraper-sized ships, their sleek black bodies gleaming like obsidian, had landed on whatever building, parking lot, shopping mall, or school that got in their way. The news helicopters that hadn't been shot down had caught live pictures of the masses of aliens that came marching out of each ship, looking like glossy black ants marching in perfect synchronicity.

There were too many of them. Some experts said they'd unloaded a tenth of the population of Earth from those ships, and each one a hardened warrior sporting advanced weaponry and glistening black suits that seemed to be utterly impenetrable to anything humans had to throw at them.

Dad didn't stand a chance. Nobody did.

Thus, Joe ignored Sam's know-it-all bullshit and clung to every scrap of information, listening to the same tiny tidbits replayed over and over until he could repeat them by heart, praying to God that it was a bad dream and his Dad wouldn't have to go to war.

God wasn't listening.

The invasion wasn't a game, wasn't a huge hoax, wasn't a dream. It was real, and the longer the aliens stayed camped out in the headquarters of every major government on the planet, secretly talking to world leaders behind closed doors, the more agitated the populace got. A thousand different debaters on television had a thousand different opinions. They claimed the aliens were invaders, there to take humans as slaves. Or liberators, there to raise human consciousness, end war, and give humanity great new technology. Or diplomats, there to invite them into a vast alien democracy.

In the end, they were all right.

They called themselves Ooreiki. When they weren't encased in inky black suits and bulbous ebony helmets, they were squat brown creatures with huge, glistening eyes, tentacles protruding from their heads and bodies, and four parallel slits along each side of leathery necks that fluttered like gills, though they breathed air as well as any human. They also lived a really long time. Some said four, even five hundred years.

The Ooreiki claimed they were not alone. They said they came from an immense alien society, one that spanned the entire universe, swallowing whole galaxies and all the species within. Earth was only one of hundreds of thousands of planets to fall under its dominion, the latest in its ever-expanding search for the ends of space.

And, in their very first press-release, translated by a terrified-looking woman in a rumpled business suit, they told humanity what would be expected of it, now that it had been tested and accepted as a sentient race and given a seat in Congress. The woman's mascara-smeared eyes darted continually to something behind the camera as she listed out new law after new code after new regulation. It was the end, however, that made every hair on Joe's body stand on end.

These are your rights and responsibilities during your probationary period, as your formal rights have not yet cleared Congressional committees. In summary, you will do as you are told. Do not attack, confront, or in any way impede the movement or actions of Congressional forces. Relinquish all of your projectile weapons to our collection stations, which will be set up in every major city by the end of the day. For a full list of prohibited weapons, see the local collection center. Anyone found with a weapon on this list will be killed as a saboteur. We say again, anyone who stands in our way will be annihilated.

The matter-of-fact way the aliens spoke of Earth's submission was accentuated by the way the government did nothing to stop them. There were no brilliant aerial battles, no brave last stands. Jets remained grounded, guns remained quiet, missiles remained siloed. As Joe agonized over every news clip, Earth simply gave up without a fight.

With no one to challenge them, all that was left was to listen to their demands. Endless demands, ranging from the mundane; a few odd souvenirs for individual aliens to bring home to their families as gifts, to the outrageous; a global meeting to pick a single representative to speak for Earth. And still their demands came. Rules for living, rules for government, rules for population...

Joe's mom kept getting distracted watching the news and burned so many nightly meals she ended up screaming, throwing pots of spaghetti and burnt Brussels sprouts across the kitchen. She didn't cook after that.

His father's troubled heart was not as obvious, but Joe could see it. His dad had a lot of the old Celtic blood in him, blood that left him smiling and constantly at play, even when things went wrong. He wasn't playing now. The way he held his broad shoulders, the constant tension in his muscular body, the way he looked at Joe and Sam when he thought they were distracted—together, these things were even more disturbing than their mother's spaghetti-fest.

For once, Joe was glad he was still a kid. He was glad this was somebody else's problem.

And yet, he couldn't stop watching the newsfeeds, his lungs aching from holding his breath for too long. He knew something bad was happening inside the White House, that the worst of the aliens' demands was yet to come. Something about the way the aliens stood guard on the lawn, their onyx suits matching their sleek obsidian guns like they were stone statues in a museum of freaks, left Joe sick with apprehension.

Then they murdered a Secret Service Agent on live TV.

The young man had been trying to get the President to safety through a secret tunnel out of the White House when the aliens caught him. As Joe watched, they dragged him out onto the lawn and shot him in the face with some flesh-dissolving bluish goo that made his bloody neck look like it was oozing purple snot, then went right back into the White House without saying a word, pushing the president ahead of them like a criminal. The picture of the grinning young man that the news crews flashed all over TV only a few minutes later showed him holding a baby, wearing a Marine uniform in front of an American flag. Seeing it reminded Joe of similar pictures of his dad and he quietly locked himself in the bathroom until his queasiness went away. He knew the worst was still to come.

When CNN broadcasted the aliens' final list of demands, it read like something the conquistadors might have dictated to the South Americans. They wanted allegiance. They wanted hostages. They wanted supplies.

And they wanted children.

Ninety-eight percent of the healthy ones. Boys and girls. Everyone five to twelve. To start a human section of their vast alien army.

And, just that suddenly, Sam wasn't such a smartass anymore. He actually got kind of quiet—a first for Sam—and spent a lot of time in his room. Their mom spent a lot of time with him, crying.

All over the world, riots broke out at the news, and suddenly the reporters had something else to talk about. The Crips and the Bloods and the Hells Angels were taking a stand right alongside disbanded soldiers, National Guard, and Marines. People everywhere were dying in swaths, the aliens obliterating whole city blocks if too many people tried to fight. Joe stayed glued to the TV, only eating when his stomach distracted him from the aliens marching across the screen. They were so precise, so perfect...like the old World War II videos of Nazi soldiers. It triggered something primal that made him want to crawl under his bed and hide.

But not his dad. When they finally announced that the alien collection crews would be sweeping through their neighborhood, Joe's father pulled out his old military work cammies and started getting dressed. They were the desert ones, the ones Joe had associated with war back when Joe had to stand in a crowd with his mom and watch his dad get on a ship to go overseas.

What Joe remembered most about that first night was his father's sleeves. He took hours to get them right, ironing them so flat they wrapped around his biceps like Celtic armbands. His dad prided himself on having the most tightly rolled sleeves in his unit, tighter than the captains and majors and generals themselves. Joe could always tell his father from a distance just by looking at his sleeves.

"A Marine takes pride in his job, Joe. Even if it's rolling sleeves." It was what his father had said a thousand times before when he labored over his uniform. Now he said nothing. Joe and Sam watched him, neither able to dredge up the courage to ask him why he was getting dressed in the middle of the night. The silence was ominous.

When their mother saw what her husband was doing, she ushered Joe and Sam to their rooms and made them lock the doors. Through the cracks, Joe heard her argue with his father, plead with him, and cry, but finally she retreated and sequestered herself in the other end of the house. Joe crept back out to watch his father iron his cammies, his anxiety growing like a hard lump in his throat. Sam followed him, his skinny ten-year-old body hunched close behind Joe as they came to a stop beside their father's ironing board.

For long moments, the three of them just stood there watching the iron in silence. Then, softly, without looking up, their dad said, "Sometimes you've gotta stand up for yourself, even when you know you ain't got a chance." Outside, they heard shouts and helicopters and car alarms.

"What are you doing, Dad?" Sam whispered.

"Yeah, Dad," Joe said softly. "They disbanded the Marines. You heard the TV."

The iron stopped, settling over the sleeve. Their father stared down at it, his muscular arm no longer moving. When he looked at them, Joe was stunned to see tears. Their father settled his gaze on Sam. "You get yourself in MIT, Sam. You're gonna be a big guy like your brother and me, but brute strength ain't gonna win this. It's gonna be someone with a brain like yours, and you ain't no warrior. You're a scholar, kid. Stay here and figure out a way to beat these bastards." The iron started to move again.

Sam's chest caught in a sob. "I'll go. Stay here, Dad. I'll go with them."

"No." Their father's tone brooked no argument.

Sam, the idiot, argued anyway. "But—"

"Go back to your room." Their father's voice was filled with warning.

"But Dad—"

"*Go, Sam.*"

Giving Joe an agonized look, Sam went.

Joe's father finished ironing in silence and then tugged his cammi jacket over his wide shoulders. The sleeves rested just above his biceps, crisp and perfect despite the chaos outside. Seeing it on his father for the first time in four years, Joe felt a cold chill. When their eyes met, there was a sadness in his father's face, a recognition that Joe could not understand. He watched his dad pick up the three guns he'd left by the front door, his throat burning with the need to say something.

"Take care of your brother, Joe." Then his father opened the door and disappeared into the chaos of black smoke, gunfire, and screaming.

That was two months ago.

Joe was still fourteen, but he felt older now. Compared to the other kids in the hazy red light of the obsidian dome, he was ancient.

I'm not supposed to be here. Sam is.

Joe closed his eyes and let his head touch the wall behind him. The black substance depressed slightly at his touch, cradling his skull with its eerie, alien perfection. Like everything else on the ship, the wall seemed alive. It seemed to move with a soul of its own, like a billion little ants covered the surface. Sometimes his hair stuck, just enough that it was uncomfortable, but not enough to pull it out. The cloth under his butt and against his shoulder-blades likewise fused to the stuff.

Behind closed eyes, an image blazed in Joe's mind. His dad, stepping into the whirling smoke outside, sleeves rolled for war.

Joe immediately fought the surge of anger twisting in his gut. The government had ordered the Marines not to get involved. They'd *told* everyone to stay in their homes, to do whatever the aliens told them. Yet Joe's father had rallied his old friends anyway. Why? Why couldn't they just hide Sam? Why did Dad have to fight?

The children trapped in the room with Joe had long since stopped crying. Some were sleeping, snot and tears leaking down their faces. Many were huddled in whimpering groups, wide-eyed, clutching their knees or whatever relics of home they had managed to salvage before the sweeps. One little girl had a sooty cloth doll, one half of its head singed from the fires.

The stench of smoke still stung the insides of Joe's nostrils. In the weeks that followed the start of the Draft, burning houses had cast the subdivision in a putrid black haze. Along the sidewalks, cars had smoldered, adding spent gasoline and plastic fumes to the choking smog. Constant gunfire had rattled the glass in the windows. Armed looters had followed behind the Congies, taking stuff from the homes and bodies of people who had resisted the aliens' collection efforts.

But now all Joe cared about was food. He hadn't eaten in so long that his stomach was a constant pain to him, keeping him awake. They had water, piped in from the walls in constant-supply tubes that looked a lot like the bottles on a gerbil tank, but that was it. Worse, the water tasted funny, almost like algae. Joe guessed it had been days since their capture, but like the other kids that the aliens had kidnapped and herded in here like cattle, Joe had spent most of his time sleeping. It had been so quiet since their abductors had shoved them in here that several times, Joe had wondered if they had been forgotten in their prison to starve.

I'm not supposed to be here. It should have been Sam.

Joe took a deep breath and released it angrily, then pushed himself to his feet. The living black walls gripped his damp palms like frozen metal. Joe yanked his hands away and rubbed his palms together to rid himself of the sensation.

Everywhere, little kids were watching him. Joe tried to ignore them, but he was head and shoulders taller than anyone else in the room and his size drew their anxious gazes.

They wanted his help. He could see the fear and desperation in their eyes. They wanted him to do something, like their parents would have done something for them, and for days Joe had resented them for it. He hated their stares. Their need. Who did they think he was? What made them think he could help them? He wasn't their *dad*. He was just a kid, just like them, and they were captured by *aliens*. A *big* kid, but still just a *kid*.

I'm not supposed to be here.

The thought wrenched at Joe's spirit, just as it had a thousand times already. He hated his brother. It was Sam who was supposed to be on this ship, listening to children whimper and smelling kiddie pee as they wet themselves. It was Sam who'd been strung out in a line of kids bound for the ship. And it was Sam who'd run away while Joe got caught.

His mother's words from the day of his capture still haunted him.

Go to Hell, Joe.

The agony of that moment was still raw in his chest, so raw it hurt to breathe. His mom had begged him. *Begged* him not to go after Sam. *"You're all I have left,"* she kept saying, through tears. *"Please, Joe. Please don't do this. You can't help Sam…"*

And Joe had turned his back to her and walked out the door.

Go to Hell, Joe, had been his mother's last teary words she shouted after him as she stood there, shaking, on the front porch, watching him go. *I hope you go to Hell.*

She'd gotten her wish.

Miserable, he got up and stumbled over to one of the tiny holes spaced along the circular edge of the room. He pissed in it, then zipped up and looked out over the ocean of children. He saw one kid in fake cammies, the kind you could buy at the PX to dress your kid up like a soldier. It even had cute little rolled sleeves, though they were flat and lifeless from mechanical pressing. Nothing like his father's.

Stupid kid.

Joe tore his attention away from the boy, his eyes stinging. He let his gaze wander around the edges of the obsidian dome, looking once again for an exit, a seam, a lock, *any* indication that they weren't trapped here forever.

The silky black surface of the room was flawless. Two feet out of reach, a scarlet globe protruded from the ceiling and cast the space in an eerie red haze, but there were no doors, no windows, nothing but hundreds of little kids watching him.

Joe's angry, frustrated scowl fell once again upon the little groups of children huddled against the walls. The boy who was brave enough to meet his gaze flinched and looked at the floor between his legs. Moments later, his thin shoulders began quaking in tiny sobs.

In that moment, Joe felt like he'd been slapped. Watching the kids whimper and cringe away from his angry look, he realized that they all just wanted someone to tell them they'd be okay. Just like Joe had wanted, back when his world was falling apart. When Dad disappeared, and nobody would go looking for him. When he found Dad's friend Manny, slumped against a bent parking meter in a pool of blood, Dad's knife in his hands. When they came for Sam.

Though Joe's nerves were screaming at him to curl up against the wall somewhere and pretend they didn't exist, he went over to the boy and squatted in front of him. The kid glanced up, the hope in his eyes so strong it was painful.

Swallowing hard, Joe said, "How you doing?"

The kid blurted, "Do you know when they're gonna let us go home?"

Hearing the innocent desperation in the kid's voice, Joe felt a tiny part of him die. Nobody had told him. Nobody had even bothered to even tell him.

I can't help these kids, Joe thought, in despair. What the hell did he say to them? Who the hell was he, Joe Dobbs, to tell them they were never going to see their families again?

But he had to tell him *something.* Looking into his eyes, Joe knew he couldn't just walk away and go back to sulking. But he couldn't tell him the truth, either.

"I don't know when they're gonna let us out," Joe said, "but I do know they're not gonna leave us in here forever." *Not by a long shot.*

The kid began to shake. "I don't want them to come back. They scare me."

They're gonna do a lot worse than scare us. Joe reached out and put a hand on the boy's thin shoulder, enveloping it with his palm. "Look, kid, they're just big squid. You find scarier stuff in your kitchen sink."

"They don't look like squid," the kid whimpered.

He's right. They're goddamn aliens, you insensitive son of a bitch. "Prunes, then. Big, butt-ugly prunes."

The kid laughed, a relieved half-sob. Joe patted his shoulder and stood up.

"Aren't you too big to be here?" an older girl behind Joe said, accusation strong in her voice.

Joe flinched. "Yeah, I'm fourteen," he offered reluctantly. Two years older than the aliens' max collection age. What was worse, Joe was a freak. At fourteen, he was built like a professional NFL linebacker and already over six feet. To these kids, he probably looked eighty.

"So why'd they take you?" another nearby girl demanded.

"I was stupid," Joe said, grimacing.

"Stupid how?"

"I did something they didn't like," Joe said, tensing his fists with the memory, wishing he had somewhere he could hide from all of their piercing stares. *Every* eye in the room was on him. He probably looked like a lot of their dads.

"Like what?" a kid insisted.

Joe grimaced. "Look, uh…guys. I really don't want to talk about it."

"You should tell them you're fourteen," a girl said sagely.

"Yeah," a little boy piped up. "You can't be here if you're older than twelve." He was probably seven or eight, and he looked perfectly sure that if Joe were to walk up to the aliens right now and tell them he was fourteen, not twelve, he would receive a Get Out Of Jail Free card and everything would be all right.

Obviously, none of them had seen what Joe had done to get into this place. Or the look in the aliens' eyes when they'd first shoved him into this huge room, alone, more than a day before the other kids.

None of them understand. Joe felt an overwhelming urge to get away from them, to get back to his empty spot against the wall and be alone, but he forced himself to smile, instead. "Maybe I'll do that." Yeah, right about the time they pulled out a gun and blew his head off for being too damn old.

Feeling the pressure of their stares, Joe slunk back over to his 'corner' and turned to partially face the wall. It was the only way he could pretend they weren't watching him.

I want to go home. God, please just let me go home.

There were no heavenly choirs, no celestial trumpets, no parting of the skies. Just hundreds of desperate little kids, watching him like he had all the answers.

2

LITTLE HARRY SIMPSON

Without warning, the obsidian wall dripped open beside Joe, and a group of aliens rushed inside in a wave. They weren't wearing the glistening black suits that they had worn on the White House lawn, the ones that deflected bullets. For the first time, he could see the sticky brown skin up close, the four slender tentacles protruding from each boneless arm, the big snakelike eyes that reminded him of wet gummi bears, the two tentacles wriggling from their heads like worms had burrowed into their brains.

In the chaos that followed—aliens shouting, kids screaming, children scattering—Joe ducked out the door and ran for it.

At six-foot-one, with all of his spare time before the Draft spent practicing for football season, Joe was faster—much faster—than his boneless five-foot captors. He peeled out of the room and down the closest red-lit hall. The aliens shouted at him through their translators for him to come back.

Joe ignored them and kept running.

Soon, he was alone. He stopped and glanced down two equally long corridors, wondering which way was the way out.

They hadn't left Earth yet. The ship hadn't so much as jiggled since they'd shoved Joe inside the prison with the others only days before.

He still had a chance.

Joe chose a corridor and hurtled down it, praying that he could find his way out. He charged down two more hallways—and then abruptly hit a dead end. The corridor terminated in a sleek black wall. It was too abrupt, however, obviously the entrance to another room or hall. Joe desperately searched the wall, looking for some sort of control pad or lock—something that would let him inside. Feeling the beginnings of panic, Joe swept his fingers across the wall, digging at the sticky blackness seeking a button or catch, but he could find no irregularities to indicate an entrance.

Behind him, Joe heard the muffled pounding of boots as his pursuers caught up with him. Adrenaline scoured his chest and his breath began to come in quick, labored pants as he frantically slapped at the corridor's unyielding surface, still to no avail. Heart thundering a roaring staccato in his ears, Joe gave up on the door and turned to backtrack.

Five aliens blocked his path like wormy brown turds. They had small-ish black guns out, grunting to themselves in their harsh alien language, pointing at him and nodding their heads.

Joe didn't need their translators to know they were laughing at him.

The alien in front, his wrinkled brown face streaked with light orange highlights, was the loudest of the bunch. The little device around his neck even managed to interpret the amount of scorn in his voice. *"The pathetic creature is too stupid to open a door. We should leave it here to starve. It's not going anywhere."*

Joe tensed. "Back off! I'm fourteen. I'm too old to be a soldier."

Although the translators around their necks didn't repeat Joe's words, the pale, scarred alien in the back gave him an appraising glance. Seemingly having no trouble at all understanding him, it said, *"You're right. Commander Lagrah has something else in mind for you."*

The alien with the orange facial features made another grunting laugh. *"You're too kind, Kihgl. Just tell the Human we're gonna kill it."*

"Be silent, Tril." The words rang from the translator of the same alien in the back, the one called Kihgl. Kihgl seemed to be a lighter color than the rest, with droopier folds of skin and a startling cross-hatching of black scars across his neck and face disappearing under a crisp black uniform.

Tril wrinkled his orange-tinted face. *"It's already caused us enough trouble…I don't see why we can't extract a little payment before we kill it."*

"He's faster than you, Commander Tril. He's gonna be even harder to control if you panic him."

"We can fix that." Tril raised his gun, aiming at Joe's leg. The other aliens grunted with laughter as Joe hopped out of the way in a panic.

"Commander Tril." The warning in the pale, deeply-scarred alien's tone was clear.

Tril immediately tucked the little black gun under his belt and said to Joe, *"Lower yourself to the ground and place your arms behind your back."*

"No." Joe's heart was hammering like gunfire against his ribs. He desperately scanned the hall behind them, trying to judge whether or not he could make it past their barricade of bodies before they shot him.

Commander Tril stepped closer to Joe and held both four-fingered tentacles spread wide, narrowing his escape route. On either side of him, his friends were also moving forward, ready to surround Joe. They moved slowly, with no sudden movements, like horse trainers trying to calm their animals.

"I said back off!" Joe screamed. He backed up two feet, until he ran out of hallway. The aliens laughed again and kept coming.

"Look at it," Tril said. *"It's as terrified as a Takki."*

Joe ducked and rammed himself into the speaker, intending to knock him over and keep on going. Instead, like a five-hundred-pound lineman, Commander Tril never budged. He garbled a curse and wrapped stinging tentacles around one of Joe's arms, tightening them like miniature pythons, depressing the muscle and making the fingers in that hand instantly numb. Joe gasped and tried to jerk away, but the alien remained rooted in place, watching Joe writhe with its sticky brown eyes narrowed in a satisfaction that did not need to be translated.

With his free hand, Joe yanked the little black gun out of his aggressor's belt. The tentacles strangling his arm loosened suddenly and Joe wrenched himself free. He had the gun in both hands and was desperately trying to figure out how to fire it when an alien grabbed his throat from behind.

The gun went off, an echoing *burp* that made every alien in the hall jump.

The glowing blue shot hit the scarred alien in the neck, dissolving one of the writhing tentacles that dangled from either side of its head. With a roar of rage, an alien wrapped its snakelike arm around Joe's neck, tightened its stinging grasp, and shook him like a toy. Joe dropped the gun, the edges of his vision going black.

"The burning furg shot Kihgl!"

The alien holding Joe by the throat wrenched him forward and, between the grip on his throat and his forward momentum, almost snapped Joe's neck. Joe dropped to one knee, his lungs burning for air, his vision closing to tiny, blurred windows. Other aliens converged on him, grasping his arms, pinning him down.

All too quickly, Joe's world shrank to an inch of the glossy black floor under his face, then faded to total darkness.

Then, out of the void, he heard the scarred one speak. *"Stop, you Takki! It was just a hahkta. Give the ignorant creature some air."*

The stinging tentacle around Joe's throat loosened just enough to allow him to breathe. Joe gasped in a desperate lungful of air, coughing in frantic, whooping breaths as his vision slowly started to come back into focus.

When his mind began to register shapes again, the alien he'd shot was staring down at him, his sticky brown gaze unreadable. A clear, brownish liquid was dripping from the dissolved tentacle on the side of his head, landing in little spatters on Joe's jeans, but Joe couldn't have moved if he'd tried. The three aliens holding him down seemed bent on trying to pull him apart, and the bones in Joe's arms were screaming, on the verge of snapping from the pressure. Joe closed his eyes and felt the welling of a sob in his chest. He struggled against it, forcing it back down. He wasn't gonna cry. Not for them.

"Commander Tril, until we kill him, fit him with a modifier. I don't want to have to chase the asher down again."

The grip on Joe's arm released suddenly.

Then the alien behind him was yanking him onto his back, holding him down as Commander Tril fitted a bluish band around his ankle. Once it was secured, they all released him at once.

Panicked, confused, Joe dove away from them and ran.

He was maybe fifty feet down the hall when, all at once, his body stopped responding. Streaks of pain lanced up from his ankle, into his stomach, chest, and eyes, balling him up, emptying his lungs in a scream.

He fell into an awkward, shrieking tumble on the floor, unable to think or feel anything but the awful pain consuming him from the inside out.

Then, as quickly as it had started, the pain was gone. Joe felt a warm wetness on his stomach and realized he had vomited bile and algae-flavored water down his chest. He panted on his back, staring up at the domed scarlet light above him as he gripped the sticky black floor beneath him with both trembling hands.

The pale, scarred alien he'd shot came into view as he lay there, panting. For a long moment, they just stared at each other.

"Are you finished?" the scarred alien finally asked. In his tentacled hand, he held a small device made of the same bluish metal as the band around Joe's ankle.

Joe shuddered and turned away, the pain still raw in his mind. He spat out the leftover bile that had accumulated in the back of his throat, shuddering. He wanted to run, but now he was terrified to actually do so.

As soon as he realized that, he stiffened.

Dad would fight them, Joe thought. *Dad wouldn't give in. He wouldn't just lay here.* Still, though, he couldn't force himself to make his muscles move, knowing the torment would come again.

"There's no shame in it, Human. There's nowhere for you to go." Kihgl's voice held a note of kindness to it, one that made Joe sick.

Unable to hold still for the alien's pity, Joe lunged to his feet and ran again.

This time, he only got a couple yards before he tumbled back to the floor, agony tearing through his body in relentless, unending waves. Somewhere in the thrashing that followed, his bladder loosened and he peed himself. He hurt like his whole body was being thrown into a furnace, inside and out, and every breath was a nightmare he wished would end him. All he wanted, at that point, was to die.

The aliens left him in pain longer this time. By the time he could finally breathe without crying, Joe lay there, panting, as the aliens casually strolled up to him, his entire body still shaking with the aftereffects.

Realizing he wasn't lying in a pool of blood and guts, and that the pain wasn't actually hurting him, Joe shakily got back to his feet.

Someday these assholes are gonna wish they'd killed me, he thought, shaking as he stared them down.

Commander Tril was laughing again. *"Think the furgling sooter will try for three?"*

Joe straightened his spine and stared back into the orange-streaked Ooreiki's sticky brown eyes. *You're dead,* he thought. *Soon as I figure out how to use that gun. You're dead.* When Kihgl saw he wasn't going to run a third time, the scarred Ooreiki wrenched his arms behind his back and led him down the hall. They came to a mass of children milling in the corridor with their alien guardians, where Kihgl and his companions shoved Joe into the group, switched off their translators and said a few words in rattling, grunting Ooreiki, then abruptly left.

Both aliens and children gave Joe questioning looks. He could feel the aliens' gazes settling on the metal band around his ankle and he reddened.

I'm gonna get back home. As soon as they give me the chance.

This time, Joe gave no resistance as they herded them down another tubular black hall and into an enormous room with blinding white lights. His eyes were no longer aching with the strain of trying to distinguish shapes and shadows, but his skin began to crawl when he got a good look at the ship in this new light. Every surface seemed alive with glossy liquid energy. For the first time, he realized that the ship surfaces didn't look like stone or metal or glass or anything else Joe had ever seen. With the way the gloss seemed to ebb and flow in ebony waves, it almost looked like it was *breathing.* Seeing that, Joe had to fight down a moment of panic, suddenly wondering if he were trapped in the belly of a space-going monster.

It's not alive, he had to tell himself. *It can't be.* Besides, he'd seen the outsides of their sleek black ships. They were *ships.*

Still, watching the gloss shift in waves, like wind against a field of grain, Joe started to back towards the far wall, his hair standing on end.

The other kids didn't seem to notice. They were more interested in clinging to each other and running from the couple dozen aliens that were herding them around like cattle. Within minutes, the aliens had pushed hundreds—if not *thousands*—of children into the room, their fearful voices rising in tides, drowning out all other sound.

Joe reached down and tugged on the bluish band around his ankle in increasing panic. Like the doors that melted into walls, it was seamless—a paper-thin ring that had no give whatsoever. He wrenched on it in frustration, but eventually gave up and went to hide his wet crotch in a corner, plotting how he was going to kill his kidnappers for making him pee himself in front of thousands of kids.

About an hour passed as more and more kids were added to the panicked mass. The aliens packed them into one half of the room until there was barely space to breathe, let alone move, before dozens more aliens began pouring inside and a fearful hush descended on the kids. Joe, taller than anyone else in the room by almost a head, was able to see the aliens line up in nine rows against the opposite wall. He recognized the group of five that had chased him down and caught the pale, scarred one's eyes, the one called Kihgl.

The pale alien and eight others moved forward and began sorting the kids like captains on a playground team, barking orders to each other in their harsh, guttural language while other Ooreiki hurried to obey. Joe felt a twinge of fear when he realized the aliens had turned off their translators. He ducked low and moved as far to the back of the group as he could, his gut instincts telling him that, whatever was about to happen, it was not good.

Eventually, the nine 'captains' had all but Joe and a few others standing in groups behind them. Joe noticed with growing concern that, aside from himself, the remainders all looked weak or sickly in some way. One of the kids had an angry red gash in his leg that ran from his knee to the base of his calf, laying open a deep section of muscle and skin tissue. A wound from the hellish days of the Draft. The kid had long ago given up on standing on it and instead, the boy sat on the floor, his red-rimmed eyes watching the aliens nervously.

Joe's breath caught when he recognized him. Little Harry Simpson. He'd seen him a dozen times a week, riding his tricycle out in the road at the end of his subdivision. The boy always leaned on the fence when Joe, Sam, and their dad played football in the front yard, sucking down a Freeze-Pop, acting as the ref when they had a foul.

Now Harry looked like a skeleton with skin. The little fingers that had offered Joe popsicles were now bony protrusions bunched in his shorts as he fought off pain and fever. He had dark hollows under his eyes and his cheeks were wet from crying.

Seeing the discolored pus oozing from Harry's wound, Joe knew he needed to go to a hospital. Joe had read about wounds festering. If he didn't get help, Harry was going to die.

Joe sucked in a breath as an alien with orange features stepped toward them. The last thing he wanted was to be chosen by Commander Tril. Already, Joe's arm was turning into a huge purple bruise where Tril had held him down.

Tril walked up to Harry and gestured at him, looking back at his alien companions as he spoke in his alien tongue. None of them moved. Tril gestured again and Harry looked up at him with hopeful, pain-brightened eyes.

Why isn't Tril taking him back with him? Joe wondered, dread beginning to form a cold knot in his gut.

Commander Tril activated the translation device hanging his neck and turned to speak to the entire gathering.

"The battalion leaders have made their decision. Twice I requested a place for this one, and twice I was denied. No Congressional soldier will take him into his fold. Thus, he has no place in the Army."

The alien pulled his gun from his belt and shot Harry in the face.

For a long moment, Joe was too shocked to move. Then a primal yell erupted from the pit of his gut and he jumped to his feet. Heart hammering in terror, he began backing away from the scene.

Harry's emaciated corpse slumped to one side, oozing purple slime down its Sesame Street T-shirt, half his head missing. Joe stared at the body, beginning to hyperventilate. *They're going to kill us all,* he realized. The other twelve kids in the center of the room began to scream. The aliens quieted them ruthlessly, slamming several of them into the glossy black floor to shut them up. One sat up bleeding from his ear, blinking desperately.

Tril waited for silence, then spoke to his companions, the translator once again switched off. An alien had to hold a freckled kid in place in front of him while he screamed and writhed to get away as they made their exchange.

"Stop it!" Joe lunged forward to help the kid.

Before he had taken three steps, an Ooreiki grabbed him and yanked him back.

"Don't!" Joe said, "Don't do it!"

Tril ignored him and turned back to the freckled kid. Like he'd done with Harry, he said, *"The battalion leaders have made their decision. Twice I requested a place for this one, and—"*

"Please don't shoot him!" Joe cried. "He's just a—" The alien holding him wrapped a tentacle around his throat and tightened it, silencing him.

Tril cast Joe a dark look. *"—and twice I was denied. No Congressional soldier would take him into his fold. Thus, he has no place in the Army."*

Joe kicked his aggressor and struggled free. "Don—"

The little boy's scream ended in a wet *burp*.

"You son of a bitch!" Joe screamed at Tril. "You evil son of a bitch!" Three aliens converged on Joe and dragged him to the ground, their stinging tentacles biting into his skin, leaving bloody welts in their path as he struggled against them.

The third child, an extremely small toddler, was claimed before Tril could shoot her. Joe looked up to see Kihgl pushing her into his group. The tentacle Joe had shot off ended in a dark brown stain on one side of his head, making him appear lopsided.

Joe couldn't watch the rest. He closed his eyes and slumped his head against the floor, waiting for it to end.

The next two children were claimed by another scarred alien, though this one was paler than Kihgl. Upon seeing his pale face, Joe had an instant of recognition that left him cold.

Smoke wafted from the burning street. Joe stared at a black boot, his head and stomach on fire, the night exploding in bright, beautiful colors all around them. Sam was gone…escaped with the others. The alien stared down at him through its sleek black helmet with the cold fury of a wasp. "How old do you think it is?"

"Sixteen, is my onboard's guess, Commander Lagrah," one of the glossy, black-suited aliens said. "Maybe fourteen, with growth irregularities."

There was cruel purpose in the alien's pale brown eyes as he said, "I'm sorry, Gokli. What did you say his age was?"

There was a long pause. "Twelve, sir."

Lagrah. His name is Lagrah.

Then the aliens holding Joe wrenched him to his feet, shattering the memory. When he looked up and saw Commander Tril standing in front of him, all Joe could hear was his own frantic heartbeat thudding in his ears. Tril was looking at him, his sticky brown face a picture of satisfaction.

"Go to Hell," Joe said.

Tril made a guttural rapping in the base of his neck—an alien laugh. Languidly, his big, gummy eyes on Joe, Tril made an alien garble at its companions.

Scanning their squashed, indifferent faces, Joe knew he was going to die.

Tril asked again, looking back on his fellows where they stood with their selected groups. None of them moved. Joe could feel the gunman's satisfaction as he snaked a tentacle to the small black device around his neck and switched it on.

Tril waited until the room had fallen silent, until every eye single was on him. "The battalion leaders have made their decision. Twice I requested a place for this one, and twice I was denied. No Congressional soldier will take him into his fold. Thus, he has no place in the Army."

Joe lifted his head and stared at a point on the wall across the room as Commander Tril raised his gun, determined not to let them see his fear. He knew that begging was worthless. They could have left all of the sickly kids back on Earth, but instead they brought them aboard to use as a warning to the others.

The sickly kids…and the kids who'd pissed them off.

Joe felt his bowels churning and he absurdly hoped he didn't shit himself in front of all the little kids. Most of the kids had shit themselves. Even then, little Harry Simpson had a brown stain running down his twitching, skeletal leg.

In the silence that followed, Commander Kihgl made a guttural noise that sounded like more laughter.

Get on with it, you assholes, Joe thought, his fists clenching despite his guards' tight grips cutting off the circulation in his forearms. What were they trying to do? Make him cry?

The pale, scarred alien called Kihgl spoke again. Tril turned to face him, an unmistakable look of irritation on his wrinkled, orange-brown face. His weapon never wavered from where its muzzle aimed between Joe's eyes.

Joe stared at it. Odd, how it looked like the tip of the gun was rippling like a desert mirage. It reminded him of swirling water, like the meandering stream that ran through his friend's back yard.

Joe's eyes snapped back to the aliens as a flurry of brutal alien words erupted between Tril and Kihgl. Several other aliens joined in, all team 'captains,' most of whom seemed to side with Tril. Joe realized the alien he'd disfigured was bargaining for his life.

He was surprised, knowing that alien, of any of them, had the most reason to kill him. Joe allowed himself an instant of hope, but it quickly faded as he realized that the other battalion commanders were winning the argument. Joe looked at the floor, wondering how long they would drag it on.

An authoritative tone rose above the fray and the argument stopped with an unmistakable note of finality. Joe recognized the speaker and he suddenly felt his blood coagulate in his veins. Lagrah. The one he had humiliated. The one who had taken him, alone, back to the ship in Sam's place. The one who had intended to kill him as an example to the others.

Commander Tril put his weapon away, shoved Joe at Kihgl, and stalked from the room. Joe stared at Lagrah, utterly dumbfounded.

He took my side?

Joe could still feel the alien's malice towards him for what he had done back in the alley, every ounce of which Joe had earned. And yet, for some reason, the alien he had humiliated on the streets of San Diego had saved him on the ship.

Confused, Joe allowed Kihgl to push him into his group.

Lagrah moved to the front of the room to address them all. *"I am Prime Commander Lagrah of the Ooreiki Ground Force. Humans, you are standing here today because an Ooreiki commander saw something redeemable in you, something he could transform into a soldier. From this point on, you are all recruits in the Congressional Army. Look at the Ooreiki around you. These are the commanders and battlemasters that will be guiding you through your next three turns of service. Battalion commanders, step forward."*

Kihgl stepped forward and faced Joe's battalion.

"Do you accept these recruits?"

Joe felt Kihgl's eyes flicker towards him before, in unison, they said, *"In the name of Congress, we do."*

"Then you may take them to your pods and begin their training. We will break away in nine hundred tics. Dismissed."

The cavern erupted in barked orders as the Ooreiki took control of their new battalions. Kids screamed and ran in all directions, and black-clad Ooreiki grabbed them and hurled them viciously back into the terrified mass, herding them toward the exit like terrified cattle.

Then Joe realized what Lagrah had said. *We will break away in nine hundred tics.* They were leaving Earth. The sharp sting of adrenaline began to trace Joe's veins.

I've gotta get off this ship.

The thought kept pounding his brain as he stayed well in the center of the group while they were funneled awkwardly into a sleek black hall bathed in the eerie red glow. Every passing second felt like a knife in his chest.

I gotta get off now.

The aliens spread out around the perimeter of the group, herding them like squat, brown, tentacled sheepdogs. They took it for granted that everyone would cooperate, spreading themselves thin over hundreds of kids. Seeing that, Joe drifted to the back, his panicked mind listening for the sound of the ship's engines.

When he saw his chance, he bolted.

The Ooreiki watching his section of kids gave a startled grunt of surprise, his see-through eyelids flicking startledly across his big, gummy eyeballs as he twisted to try and catch Joe. Joe, blessed with bones, was faster.

Joe quickly outdistanced his startled guard and barreled down the tube-shaped hallway, gaining more courage as the shock anklet failed to activate. Maybe he was out of range. The hall out of the domed cavern ended with suspicious abruptness and Joe slowed, scanning the surface for any indication of a door to the outside. Nothing. He kept going, choosing a smaller side-corridor. Nothing but gleaming black walls, no sign of a way out. Joe was anxiously turning a corner into another section of the ship when the anklet activated.

Joe cried out and tumbled to the floor, his momentum carrying him crashing into the wall. The aliens didn't end the brutal agony after a couple seconds this time, but instead let it continue for what seemed like excruciating hours. To his shame, he heard himself bawling like a baby. Somewhere along the line, he peed himself again.

Joe was curled in fetal a ball when Kihgl found him.

"I save your life and you act like a spoiled Takki." Kihgl kicked him. *"I should've let you die, furg."*

"Kill me, then," Joe moaned in a mixture of hatred and misery.

"Get up."

"Screw you."

A stinging tentacle wrapped around Joe's arm and brutally tore him from the floor. With his other arm, Kihgl grabbed him by the skull and forced his head down until they were eye-to-eye. *"You were supposed to die for what you did on Earth. You humiliated the Prime Commander himself. Robbed us of an entire battalion. Don't make me regret saving your sooty life, asher. I can make you wish we'd sold you to the Dhasha."*

Joe swallowed hard and Kihgl released him.

"Stop running," Kihgl commanded. *"We're three days out from Earth. You do it again and I'll toss you into space."*

Where they had once shown a bit of kindness, even compassion, Kihgl's sticky brown eyes were now hard with fury.

Cringing there, stared down by the only ally he had in this alien place, Joe realized he had made a mistake.

He wanted to apologize, but it was far too late. Kihgl shoved Joe and a few others inside a small room with triple-tiered shelves and left them there, the unnatural black doors oozing shut behind them. In the silence that followed, the kids clustered around Joe, waiting to see what he would do. The hazy red glow highlighted their faces, leaving their eyes looking huge and frightened.

"Where'd you run to?" a boy asked. "I thought we're on a ship. How you gonna get off a ship?"

Smartass. "I'll find a way out eventually," Joe muttered.

"Are you sick, too?" a freckled little girl asked, tugging on his T-shirt. "Why'd they make you stand out there with those sick kids they shot?" Like it was completely natural to shoot the sick kids because they were sick.

His gut twisting, Joe ignored her.

"That alien stuck a gun in your face," a little boy insisted. "Were you scared?"

"I don't get scared," Joe muttered, hoping it would shut them up. Even then, though, his bowels were still twisting with residual fear. He knew how close he had come to dying. Tril's sticky brown eyes had wanted death. He wondered how many more seconds it would have taken for him to blow his head off. One? Two? He got goosebumps thinking about it. And then Kihgl...

The cool resentment in his gaze still made Joe's throat hurt with regret. The one seemingly decent being on the ship and Joe had humiliated him just as thoroughly as he'd humiliated Lagrah. And Kihgl had just finished making it clear to Joe that he was going to make Joe pay for his transgressions with pain.

Of course Joe was afraid.

Apparently, though, the other kids didn't catch his lie. They seemed to take it for granted that the big kid hadn't gotten scared, and drew strength from it. Joe felt like shouting at them, *Of course I was scared! We're going to die here, can't you see that?!*

But they couldn't see that. They clumped around him like he was the designated soccer dad, with three of the littlest ones even clinging to his stinky, piss-covered leg. It was when silence began to hum in their prison that Joe realized that all the little kids were waiting for him to do something, so they could follow.

Grimacing, Joe took a good look at the huge, three-tiered, round, bunk-like objects lining the walls. They each had six sheets of what looked like folded tinfoil laid out on their surface and were shaped almost like bowls. He was pretty sure they were beds. Or industrial-sized microwaves.

Eventually, though, he broke away from the clingy, frightened kids and went over to inspect the apparent shelves of bowls. When he gave a test-push on the surface, he found it depressed easily, almost as if it were made of foam.

Beds, then, Joe thought, running his hand under the crinkly metallic blanket. Even from that brief contact, he could tell that the flimsy metal blanket was going to be warmer than anything he'd had back on earth.

The kids, still clinging to the far wall, were watching him nervously.

"They're just beds," Joe said, crawling into one of the big bowls on the bottom and pulling the metallic blanket over himself pointedly. Still, no one moved.

"My daddy works in a morgue," one of the older kids said, giving the beds a dubious look. "That looks like the incinerator."

"Or a packet of popcorn," another kid said. "Like you make on the stove."

Joe groaned. "Everyone just get in bed, okay? It's fine. See?" He stretched out over the bed, though the odd scooped slope felt strange on his back.

Most of the kids tentatively came over to check it out, but a few hunkered down by the wall and refused to get any closer. They just spent the rest of the night like that, huddled and whimpering by the door.

Joe lay staring at the bunk above him, stewing over his problems in exhausted, hungry silence. The other kids weren't so discreet. One kid huddled along the wall spent the entire night whining. It was a low, primal sound that grated on Joe's nerves until his every muscle was taut, his fists itching to plant themselves into the idiot's face.

What does he know about being scared?

Images of the days before Joe's capture returned to haunt him. Bodies had littered the streets like trash, their chests burned open or dripping purple glop. The constant whimpering reminded Joe of the sound Sam had made the night their father didn't come back—

Joe got out of bed and went over to the boy. He opened his mouth to tell him to shut up, just shut the hell up and stop whining, that everyone there was dealing with the same crap and he wasn't special, but the kid mistook his intentions and jumped up from the wall, wrapping his scrawny arms around Joe's torso. In a flood of tears, the little boy cried for his Mom.

Joe held him, startled, before he felt his own eyes start stinging. Awkwardly, he tightened his arms around the little boy in a hug. "It's okay," he finally said, though he knew it was stupid, that it wasn't okay, that they weren't going to see their families again for many years…maybe never. But he said it anyway and the boy eventually relaxed in his arms and stopped crying. It was at least an hour before his breathing quieted and his grip loosened enough to allow Joe to carry him over and tuck him into a bunk.

The boy didn't whimper again after that, but although Joe returned to his own bed to the perfect sound of silence, he couldn't sleep. Lying there, remembering how the aliens had executed *kids*, Joe didn't know if he would ever sleep again.

It was probably because of this that he was the only one who noticed the tiny tubes that emerged from the walls several hours later. One was a few inches from his head and Joe could hear the hissing of gas.

"Oh shit!" Joe cried, lunging away from the wall. "Everybody wake up! Wake up! They're gassing us! Shit!" He threw his shirt over his mouth and backed to the center of the room, heart hammering painfully in his ears.

All around him, kids on the beds were sitting up in wild-eyed confusion…

…Only to have their eyes roll up into the backs of their heads and their little bodies slump limply back to the beds.

They're gassing us, Joe thought on a surge of panic, watching the kids fall all around him like little lifeless puppets. *The aliens are gassing us…*

Though Joe tried to keep his mouth protected, he nonetheless caught an overpoweringly acrid tang that shot biting waves of acid through his lungs and up into his brain. He was dimly aware of the bitter tang turning to pounding waves of ice before his legs went limp beneath him and he surrendered to oblivion.

3

THE ORIGIN OF ZERO

"Commander Tril?"

Kihgl's voice at his door was soft, sympathetic.

"Not now, Commander," Tril said, barely able to keep his voice under control. "I need some time alone, please."

Tril's Secondary Commander remained in his doorway for long moments in silence. "This was your first time, wasn't it?" Kihgl finally asked.

Tril refused to look up. He was staring at his desk, where he had plucked his potted *ferlii* to pieces. It was a gift from Corps Director Niile from when he had left her service for the excitement of teaching a newly-discovered species to speak Congie. Somehow, in the last hour, he had snapped the stone-hard limbs into pebble-sized chunks without even knowing it. It confused him. Surely he would have heard himself doing it.

Kihgl came in, unbidden. "What you did today is unfortunate, but it must be done."

Of course it was. Tril knew that. It was a leftover tradition from the formation of Congress, when the Jreet had to teach the first Ooreiki the art of war. The Ooreiki, artists and craftsmen all, had refused to fight. The Jreet, pitiless warriors that they were, began executing ten percent of every incoming class on principle, keeping only the strongest, killing the weak as an example.

Yet, in forcing the peace-loving Ooreiki to adapt the skills of war, the Jreet had hit upon such an overwhelmingly successful tactic that it would be passed down from generation to generation of the Congressional Army for almost two million years. Kill the rebels and the sickly as a warning to the others. Show them the consequences of failure. Prove to them that it wasn't a game. Give them *incentive* to succeed.

As a former intelligence officer, Tril was well-versed in the psychology behind it, but he had still never thought it would be so hard. They were *aliens*. Why should it have bothered him to shoot *aliens*?

The answer was simple: The large Human. The one who almost scraped the low ceiling of the ship corridors with his head when he walked, and whose body should have been floating through space in their backwash, not protected by Congressional law as a recruit in his own unit. The Human's condemnation still rang in his ears, his disgust and disdain like acid against his soul.

"We've all got to do it, one day or another," Kihgl said softly.

Tril idly began to try and piece the *ferlii* back together. The fragments kept falling back to the desk with a stony clatter. As he stared at it, Kihgl moved forward and gently pushed the plant away. "It's never easy. I've done it too many times myself."

"That sooty Human didn't make it any easier," Tril managed. Abruptly, he picked up the remains of the *ferlii* and threw it against the wall, shattering what was left.

Kihgl watched the pieces settle on the floor. He looked apologetic. "I made a mistake. I shouldn't have taken him."

Tril said nothing, but he felt a pang of satisfaction at his secondary commander's admission.

"He ran again," Commander Kihgl offered. "Embarrassed me in front of the entire regiment."

Tril picked at the crumbled black stone littering his desk.

"Now I've got to deal with him for the next three turns."

Softly, Tril said, "There's plenty on this ship willing to get rid of him for you. Especially after what he did on Earth."

"I know." Kihgl brushed a few pieces of the *ferlii* plant into his balled fist. "But I chose him. I'll live with my decision."

"Even if the rest of the regiment thinks it's ridiculous?" Tril demanded.

"Especially then." Kihgl dropped the fragments into the waste system. "You should prepare for stasis. Ship's shutting the crew down for travel in an hour." He walked to the door, then hesitated at the jamb to turn back. "I'm sorry it was your turn today. It's never easy." He turned and left.

In the silence that followed, Tril stared at his empty desk.

• • •

they're gassing us…

Joe groaned as something lit up his brain on the inside, like a flashlight of God poking up against his eyeball.

"I think this one made it. Had a bit of a severe reaction to the forced metabolic stasis, but he's still showing life signs."

"This sooter's dead. Wonder if the other regiments had similar reactions.

"Damn. We got another corpse over here."

"These sooty things are so delicate."

The searing light in Joe's retina retreated and his eyelid slapped shut.

"These two are fine."

"Yeah, this whole section is good."

"That's it. Fourteen total. Not bad, for the first time shipping Humans. Grab the bodies, we'll let the sootbag furgs sleep while they can. They won't be getting much of it for the next three turns."

Joe groaned and felt himself slipping back into the deepest sleep he'd ever known.

A few hours later, he was woken in a disorienting rush of guttural alien shouting and sudden, blinding light. After Joe stumbled to his feet on strangely lethargic limbs, their Ooreiki captors bustled Joe and the other kids out of their room and into the same huge auditorium where they had shot Harry.

They had, Joe noticed, cleaned up the shit stains in the center of the room.

As the aliens lined them up, Joe concentrated on learning as much as he could about them. After enduring the ubiquitous crimson haze on the rest of the spacecraft, the glaring white light of the gymnasium was a welcome change for his aching eyes, and he was able to see them clearly for the first time since yesterday's slaughter. The aliens weren't wearing their glossy black suits again today, leaving the elephant-like skin of their brown bodies exposed along their necks and a V down their chests where their robe-like uniforms tied like a karate gi at the front. Though initial pundits' impressions suggested they were some sort of water-dwelling creatures by the gills and tentacles, Joe was beginning to think that Sam was right—they really looked like fat, squat monkeys with tentacles instead of arms.

Then, in front of three hundred other kids, the aliens made Joe strip.

Sure, they made everybody strip, but Joe felt his cheeks burn because he was one of the only kids with pubic hair, and he could *feel* a bunch of the little kids staring at it. He gritted his teeth and tried to ignore them. Didn't anyone nowadays teach their kids not to stare? It was *rude*.

Joe was folding his jeans on the floor in front of him as the aliens instructed when something metallic fell from his pocket, hitting his toe. Joe bent to snatch it up.

His dad's pocketknife. A cheap little Swiss Army deal that his dad had always carried with him, whether he was in the woods or at a business meeting. Joe had kept it in his pocket ever since he'd found Dad's friend Manny, strung up in a parking meter, half his chest blown apart, the knife clasped in the guy's dead fingers.

Joe glanced up to see if any of the aliens had seen the weapon. They hadn't—they were too busy forcing the kids that wouldn't strip out of their clothes. He straightened, one hand fisted around the knife, the other grasping his crotch, and he tried not to flinch when one of the Ooreiki took his clothes away.

After the kids who refused to strip had their clothes ripped off of them and discarded while the aliens taunted them and made them cry, the Ooreiki had them re-form into lines.

Commander Tril inspected them like this, walking among the naked ranks and peering at them with slitted brown eyes. He stopped at Joe and gave him a smug look.

In that moment, Joe wanted nothing more than to rip the alien's head off his shoulders. Instead, he was too humiliated to let go of his groin.

Tril turned away from Joe as the one called Kihgl went to the front of the room to address the entire gathering. Through the little black translator around his neck, Kihgl loudly said, *"Listen to me, frightened Takki scum. I am Secondary Commander Kihgl of the Ooreiki Ground Force. That Ooreiki over there is Small Commander Linin, and the one standing at the head of the ranks is Small Commander Tril. You are now a part of Sixth Battalion. Commander Tril, Commander Linin, and myself will be your commanding officers throughout training."*

Joe's stomach recoiled when Tril turned back to once again meet his eyes. *He's in my battalion?* Instinctively, he knew that wasn't good.

Commander Kihgl went on, heedless. *"It is my job to inform you that you are now property of the Congressional Army. Any injuries you incur, any damage you cause, any expense for your outfitting beyond standard costs, will be paid with extra service added to your contract. You all began with thirty-three Standard Turns of duty to look forward to. For all of you except one, that number is still in effect."*

Joe's gut twisted in fear. He knew which one.

"For the next three turns, until you graduate as a full member of the Congressional Army," Commander Kihgl went on, *"you will be referred to by numbers. My battlemasters will be passing among you, handing out temporary armbands with your recruit number on them. As soon as you get your number, strap it to your arm. Memorize it, because that's all you will be allowed to use for the next three turns."*

The aliens began passing out armbands. Joe held out his hand as the closest alien approached him, but it ignored him, giving an armband to the kid beside, behind, and in front of Joe. Reddening, Joe lowered his arm and stared straight ahead, refusing to let them bully him.

Commander Kihgl stopped in front of Joe. *"Why don't you have a number?"*

"You never gave me one," Joe said. *Asshole.*

"That's unfortunate." Kihgl's gaze was hard. *"We seem to have run out, as the battalion was only supposed to have room for nine hundred. You can be Zero."*

Joe's flush deepened. He knew some of the kids had died in travel. He'd woken up to missing faces. He'd heard the aliens talking. He knew they could give him a number.

One of the smallest kids in the room raised her hand.

"What?" the alien asked, eyes locked with Joe.

"Can I make him an armband?" she asked. "I know how to draw a zero."

"No," Kihgl said. *"Zero doesn't need an armband."* Kihgl cocked his head, looking up at him. *"After all, zeros don't exist. Do they, Zero?"*

Joe straightened over the alien, staring down at him. His every fiber was telling him to fight, to pound Kihgl's smug face in.

The alien leaned closer, its sticky, slitted eyes almost close enough to touch Joe's chin. *"Need another lesson, Zero? Didn't learn the first time?"*

Joe leaned down, until they were face-to-face. "Bring it on," Joe replied.

The slits along the sides of Kihgl's neck started to flutter. In an instant, a meaty, boneless arm lashed out, catching Joe in the jaw hard enough to crack teeth. Joe spun out of formation, landing in a daze on the floor, his face on fire.

"Do you need medical attention, Zero?" Kihgl demanded, walking up to him. *"We both know how deeply it would pain me to add another three turns to your service."*

Three turns? What the hell does that mean? Weeks? Months? Years? Joe pushed himself back to his feet, fists clenched. It took all his self-control not to swing at the snake-eyed bastard.

"So the ashy furg is smarter than its father. A shame. It would've been interesting if you'd followed in his footsteps. Congressional soldiers can always use more target practice."

In that instant, a switch flipped in Joe's head and all he saw was red. In an instant of madness, Joe tackled Kihgl and crawled on top of him as he fell, ramming his fists into the sides of his soft skull. Before he could open the pocketknife and use the blade on him, however, Kihgl threw Joe twenty feet across the room with one boneless arm.

Two seconds later, the other Ooreiki were on him, over twelve of them at once, and the beating that followed seared Joe's memory like a branding iron.

When it was over, they left him there in full view of the rest of the children, his arms and legs each shattered in multiple places by the Ooreiki's heavy arms. Joe's last thought before surrendering to oblivion was of the little red Swiss Army knife he'd found in Manny Hernandez's fingers, surrounded by a pool of blood.

• • •

"Give me control of the modification unit."

Commander Kihgl was scowling at the medical officers as they carted the Human away for repairs. Without looking at Tril, his secondary commander growled, "What for, Commander Tril?"

"He's in my platoon, sir," Tril replied. "He's my responsibility."

"We shouldn't even be using the modification unit," Kihgl muttered. "It's for prisoners, not recruits. It stays with me." Despite his words, Kihgl's sudah were fluttering in his neck, betraying his frustration. Tril understood—such a show of disobedience, in front of a third of the battalion, would make it harder to control the rest of the children.

"Why didn't you use it this afternoon? Why let the furg attack you like that?"

Commander Kihgl turned on him, anger in his eyes. "I didn't *let* him do anything, Commander," he snapped, startling Tril. "I deliberately provoked him. I took a lesson from the Jreet and used him as an example. If you could not see that, you're as daft as he is."

The disdain with which the *vkala* had spoken to him in front of other Ooreiki caste members made Tril tense. He glanced to the side and saw that several of his own subordinates were watching the exchange with interest. Struggling to regain composure, Tril said, "He's giving the other children ideas."

"No," Commander Kihgl said bluntly. "He's showing them that disobedience has consequences."

Tril decided to try a new tactic. "If I had the modification unit, I could—"

"No." Still watching the departing physicians, Kihgl made an irritated gesture at the naked, whimpering Humans. "Go give your recruits their vid time, Commander. I'll deal with Zero." At that, Tril's commander turned and followed the path the medics had taken.

• • •

When Joe woke up, he was surprised that they had patched him up as good as new. Every broken bone, every bruise, every cut was healed. A new anger rose in Joe's throat as he looked down at himself, flexing limbs that he had seen twisted back upon themselves earlier that morning. The evidence was unmistakable. They hadn't needed to kill the sickly kids. They could have healed them, just like they had Joe, and they would have been good soldiers out of gratitude for it. But they had needed to make examples out of them, so they blew their heads off, instead.

Spiritually and emotionally sick, Joe was barely paying attention when the alien medic told him they'd tacked another six turns onto his enlistment to pay for his medical treatment. The medic never mentioned finding a little red pocketknife, and Joe knew he wasn't getting it back. Somehow, that knowledge was worse than the extra time he'd have to serve. It was the only thing he'd retained of home, the only thing he had of Dad's. He wanted to grab the alien and shout at him, demand it back, fight until he had it, but Joe knew that the medics had probably dumped it into one of the trash holes as soon as they had found it.

Numbly, Joe put on the loose white shorts and matching T-shirt the medic gave him and followed him to a line of similarly-dressed kids standing in booths with little TVs inside them. The pictures were of people talking, and immediately Joe wondered if it was some sort of brainwashing session disguised as free time.

Only when the alien pushed him inside one of the booths did Joe realize the screen held his mother's image. It looked…older.

Thinking it was some sort of trick, Joe started to back out of the booth.

"Joe?"

Joe hesitated, staring down at her. Her hair was messy and her eyes were red from crying. She looked so real. How could she be there? Weren't they traveling a billion miles an hour through space? Was this some weird mind-trick the aliens were playing on them? Subliminal messages?

Joe turned to the alien outside the booth. "What's going on?"

The alien gave him a dispassionate look. Through its translator, it said, *"Congressional law states every recruit must have six tics to speak with its family before training begins."* The alien glanced at a group of moving squiggles under Joe's mother and its face scrunched. *"You have five left."*

Joe dove back into the booth. "Mom?"

"Joe!" She looked so relieved. So *happy*. So different from the last time he'd seen her, when she had thought it would be Sam leaving her, not Joe. "Thank God. Joe, I've been waiting so long to talk to you! Are you okay? What's happening there? Have they hurt you?"

Joe took a long look at his mother's face. It was lined with worry. She looked like she'd aged ten years since that first day the aliens landed in Washington. She was paler, almost gaunt. Her eye sockets were heavy and dark from lack of sleep. He decided she needed to hear good news. As much as he wanted to tell her his problems, beg her to find a way to help him, he said, "No, they haven't hurt me. I'm doing fine."

His mother's face momentarily slackened with relief. Then a line formed in between her brows. "That's not what the other parents are saying. They're saying the aliens are killing kids and—"

"They're not," Joe said. "They're just little crybabies. They don't understand."

His mom smiled and looked like she was crying. "You're so brave, Joe," she said. "You remind me so much of your father."

Joe had to look away from the screen, digging his fingernails into his palms to keep the tears at bay. "Has Dad come back yet?"

On the screen, his mother's face contorted. "You know he hasn't. Why do you keep asking?! You're not as young as Sam. You know he's—"

"Where is Sam?" Joe interrupted.

His mother's face softened. "Here," she whispered. "You saved him, Joe. You actually *saved* him." She sounded so stunned. And happy. Glad.

Glad that it was Joe on the ship, not Sam.

Joe bit his lip and looked at the wall beside the unit. "They didn't come back for him?" He'd been *wondering* why he hadn't caught sight of the know-it-all bastard in the panicked throng of kids.

"It was the last sweep, Joe." His mom sounded like she was close to sobbing. "Sammy made it back home and the aliens left. They've been gone for two years, Joe. Sammy's okay, Joe. You saved him."

Two...*years.* Joe felt oddly numb. Sam got to stay...and Joe was with the aliens.

Because he ran like a pussy and left me to die.

He must have said it out loud, because his mother's face hardened on the screen. "He was *ten*, you insensitive bastard." Sammy always had been a Momma's Boy. "You wanted him to fight *aliens*, Joe? At *ten*? Why, so he could get his face blown off like your father?" And her favorite. Sammy had always been her favorite.

"He left his own brother to *die*," Joe muttered. "They had guns to my head, Mom. And he just left."

"Seeing how you got him caught in the first place, Joe," his mother said, her voice cold and utterly even, like ice, "I'd say it's only fair you took his place." And it was obvious Sam was her favorite, seeing the fury in her face, the outrage at the idea that Sam should've risked his life to save Joe. Joe had always wondered, but had never worked up the balls to ask.

And here, plain as day, was his answer. Looking at him like she was disgusted he was still breathing. Joe, his father's son, the football jock, the C-student, the Marine wannabe who never really had any serious aspirations beyond retiring a USMC staff sergeant... Shoved aside for a skinny little math whiz who'd had a college recruiter from MIT come over to watch Sam do Joe's Trig homework for him while Sam chewed gum, played two MMORPGs, listened to Bach, and watched a pirated Star Trek re-run in the background.

Of course she wants him more than me, Joe thought. *Sam's a genius.* Joe was just...

Average.

Then the alien monitoring his call terminated the connection so the kid behind Joe could have a chance. Joe left the booth feeling like someone had poured acid over his insides.

4

JOE'S GROUNDTEAM

That night, after everyone had made their mandatory phone calls, Joe and the others were lined up once more in the brightly-lit gymnasium. This time, the aliens arranged them in groups of six. They put the tallest in front, the youngest in back.

"*You are now a member of Sixth Battalion,*" Commander Kihgl told them once they were arranged. "*It contains roughly nine hundred recruits, monitored by a single secondary commander—myself—two small commanders—Small Commander Tril and Small Commander Linin—and ten battlemasters, whom you will acquaint yourselves with personally as your training goes on. Normally, a battalion is led by a tertiary commander, but as one of the senior officers of this Takkiscrew, I was chosen to lead the brigade, as well. Likewise, Prime Commander Lagrah is in charge of both Second Battalion and the regiment as a whole.*" He stopped, letting that sink in.

When none of the kids interrupted him—and in fact stared at him in slack-jawed silence—Commander Kihgl gestured around the room. "*What you see here is your half of the battalion, called a company. You belong to First Company, Sixth Battalion of the Second Brigade, Eighty-Seventh Regiment of the Fourteenth Human Ground Force. But for the rest of your training, all you really need to concern yourselves with are battalion-level and below. Brigades, regiments, and ground forces are only brought together during ceremonies or times of war. Understand so far?*"

Nobody did, of course, but that didn't stop him from plowing onward. *"A company has four hundred and fifty members, arranged into seventy-five groundteams. A groundteam has six members. Because half of you ignorant Takki can't yet count, we've organized you into groups of six."* Commander Kihgl gestured at the lines behind them. *"Take a good look behind you. These are your groundmates for the next three turns."*

Joe glanced behind him. The kid in the back of his group was easily the smallest girl in the room—he had trouble believing she was five. It was the same little girl who had offered to make him a zero when Kihgl ran out of armbands. Remembering that, Joe grinned. She gave him a tentative smile around her thumb.

"From now on, the six of you will eat, sleep, bathe, and crap together. The recruit in front will make sure the rest of the group does this properly or he will be punished. Further—" Commander Kihgl cut off as five new Ooreiki strode into the room, a very pale, scarred alien at their lead. *"Battlemaster Nebil, take it from here. I'm late for a vid meeting with Lagrah."*

The much paler newcomer nodded and swiftly moved toward the front of the formation.

"Sir," Tril interrupted, stepping toward Kihgl, *"I'm the small commander of the Company. Perhaps I would be better suited to—"*

"Nebil, make sure they understand their responsibilities," Kihgl said, then departed. Commander Tril shot a furious look at Kihgl's back.

Battlemaster Nebil seemed to be of the same mold as Kihgl, with pale skin and drooping folds of flesh. His neck, arms, and head—every exposed *inch* of his rough brown skin—were likewise marred by horrible, gruesome claw-marks, mixing with the rumpled, circular marks Joe guessed were gunshots, though nothing as intense as Kihgl's. Still, compared to Tril's dark, unblemished skin, Nebil looked as if he'd been run through a meat grinder.

Nebil stood back to eye them, saying nothing. After several minutes of just staring at them, he twisted his tentacles behind his back and began walking in front of their ranks, looking them up and down like a warden in a Nazi concentration camp.

After several minutes of silence, one of the big kids tentatively raised his hand. At Nebil's grunt, the kid said, "How do we keep our groundmates in line?"

"*How do you keep them in line?*" Battlemaster Nebil snorted. "*However you burning feel like it.*" He started pacing again, watching them. His sticky brown eyes caught on Joe and paused there.

"*What he means is—*" Tril began.

Still looking at Joe, Nebil spoke over Tril with the unstoppable force of a locomotive running over a duck. "*But if they've gotta go to medical, it will be* you *who gets time added to your enlistment.*"

Joe actually got chills, getting the specific idea that Battlemaster Nebil was talking to *him*.

"So we can hit them?" a girl with a grotesquely large lower jaw insisted. She looked like some sort of piranha, with her chin jutting out past her nose. The child in the back of her group whimpered.

Nebil continued to hold Joe's gaze for a moment before he turned and looked her up and down, the silence filling the room absolute. "*You can do anything you want, as long as they can fight at the end of the day.*"

Inwardly, Joe groaned. Were they *trying* to turn everyone into bullies?

"*But,*" Nebil said, looking back at Joe, "*Keep in mind you'll have to rely on them in battle. They might end up saving your life—or not. It all boils down to trust, and if you squirming Takki break that confidence, they're not going to—*"

Tril interrupted him. "*We're running out of time. Group leaders, take a moment to get to know your teammates. You have three tics.*"

Nebil turned and gave Tril a silent stare, but did not contradict him.

Joe turned to face the five kids behind him. "Everyone get over here," he said, squatting. "Group huddle."

Only the youngest two moved. The older three glared at him.

Joe sighed and positioned himself closer, so he could see them all. "My name's Joe," he said, surveying them. "Look, we're in some pretty heavy crap, but I'm gonna do everything I can to get us out of here."

This got their attention.

The sniffling five-year-old shuffled forward and said, "I want Mom."

"We got the smallest kid in the whole room!" the oldest boy complained. He had a shock of red hair bright enough to make a leprechaun jealous.

"You also got the biggest," Joe said. He smiled at the little girl. "What's your name?"

"Maggie," the girl whimpered.

"You the one who wanted to draw me a Zero, Mag?"

She nodded, wiping snot from her nose with her sleeve.

Joe ruffled her hair. "I'd like that. Just as soon as we find something to write with okay?"

Maggie sniffled and nodded.

Joe turned to the oldest boy. The redhead was skinny—more Celtic than Nordic—and didn't even come up to Joe's chest. The kid looked like he had spent much of his life laughing before the Draft. Now his big, expressive face was strained with worry and the dimples were almost unnoticeable. He, like everybody else in the room, was gaunt and hungry-looking.

"I'm Scott," the redheaded kid said, his body tense, blue eyes wary.

"How old are you, Scott?" Joe said, looking him up and down.

"Ten."

Joe looked at the other groups in exasperation. Some had three, even four kids ten and older. Some of *those* didn't have anyone under eight.

"What about you?" he asked a skinny, freckled girl with big eyelashes.

"I'm Carol and I'm six."

Joe nodded and glanced at the older girl with a puff of curly African hair and bright brown eyes. "What about you?" he asked.

She stared at the floor, twining her fingers shyly. "Libby. I'm eight."

"That's some hair you got there, Libby."

Libby looked up and gave a tentative smile, displaying an unfortunate array of twisted front teeth. Feeling a pang of sympathy for her, Joe grinned back.

"And you?" he asked the last kid, who was somewhere in size between Libby and Carol.

The hazel-eyed boy grinned, making his big ears stick out even further. "Eric. But everybody calls me Elf." He had curly black hair that, coupled with the ears, made Joe immediately think of something he would've seen in Santa's Workshop.

"I can see why," Joe said. "How old are you, Elf?"

"Eight."

Carol held up her hand.

"You don't have to raise your hand," Joe said. "What is it?"

"If he gets to be called Elf, I want to be Monk."

"Why?"

"Because that's what my dad calls me."

"He calls you *Monk?*"

"Yeah, it's short for Chipmunk."

"Huh. Okay. Monk. I'm Joe."

Monk gave him a long look, peering up at him like an entomologist studying a funny-looking insect. "Are you really twelve, Joe?"

Joe blushed, feeling the others' attention immediately sharpen. "No," he admitted. "I'm fourteen."

Scott's eyes widened. "Then how—"

"He's bad," Monk interrupted. "Dad told me bad kids get sent to the Congies."

Immediately, Maggie's tiny chin began to quiver. Joe shot Monk an irritated look, then squatted and grabbed Maggie by the shoulders. "Look Mag, you weren't bad. It didn't have anything to do with that. They needed kids a certain age for their army, that's all."

"So why are you here?" Monk insisted. "You're too old."

Oh God, just shut up, Joe wished her, watching Maggie grow ever-closer to an all-out bawling session. He certainly recognized the look—he'd seen it on Sam enough times. "I was stupid," he muttered, hoping Monk would leave it at that.

"You mean you were bad?"

"No, I was stupid," Joe said, irritated. "Just drop it, all right?"

"I saw you try to beat up that alien," Elf said. "They kicked your butt." He grinned, flexing his ears with the force of his smile.

"That was *him?*" Scott's eyes widened. "I thought they killed that kid."

Joe glanced at the glossy black ceiling, willing himself patience. "Look, they're not gonna kill us. They'll just patch us up and put more time on our enlistments."

"What's an enlistment?" Maggie and Monk asked, at the same time, blinking up at him in innocent curiosity.

Oh crap, I can't do this, Joe thought, trying to figure out how to tell five little kids that they were about to spend half their lives as indentured servants to aliens who wanted to throw them into a meat grinder just to see what came out the other end. "Uh," he began, wincing, "it means time you owe to the army. I just owe a little bit more time for that fight earlier. No biggie."

"So that *was* you?" Scott asked, in awe.

Before Joe could answer, Commander Tril barked, *"Time's up. Get back in line!"*

Joe stood up and went back to the front of the group. Tril had taken up the head of the formation, with Battlemaster Nebil standing to one side, tentacles twisted in front of him in a formal posture, his bleached brown eyes betraying nothing of his thoughts.

Scott tugged on Joe's sleeve. "Maggie's not in line."

Joe turned around and cursed under his breath. Maggie was clutching Libby's skinny black leg, tears leaking down her cheeks. Her thumb was back in her mouth. Joe got out of line and ushered Maggie to the back. She refused to stay put.

He was pleading with her when Commander Tril snapped, *"Zero! Get up here!"*

Joe flinched and reluctantly turned to face Tril. Swallowing hard, he straightened and walked up to the squat orange-streaked alien, steeling himself. As expected, Tril slammed a heavy, boneless tentacle into Joe's gut, doubling him over.

"That's for taking too long. Now get back in line," Tril said. He waited, clearly wanting Joe to disobey. And, for a moment, Joe almost did. Fighting the urge to dismantle the Ooreiki's face, Joe straightened and limped back to his group. All five of the others were staring at him, wide-eyed. He winked at them.

"There are thirty-seven blue spheres behind me," Tril said once Joe was back in place. *"Approximately one for every two groundteams. Each groundteam that has a sphere in their possession nine tics from now will eat lunch this afternoon. Starting now."*

Joe frowned. *One for every two...* He froze, realizing Tril's intent. "Stay here!" Joe cried to his groundteam. He bolted forward for a ball and snatched it up as quickly as he could. A few others of the bigger kids moved with him, but most of the company just stared at the alien dumbly.

"Did I say stand there and *stare*?!" Tril demanded. "I said *fight*, you miserable Takki. Go get a ball!"

By the time Joe jogged back to his team, genuine panic was spreading throughout the room and mini battles began breaking out over the balls.

Joe hefted Maggie onto his shoulders and hurriedly gathered the others around him and backed them into a corner. With Joe holding the ball, no one challenged them, though others were not so lucky. In the end, one of the groups with a majority of twelve-year-olds had two balls and there were thirty-nine groups with none.

"Those of you who turned in balls may go to the chow hall," Tril said. *"The rest of you will run until they come back."*

He's going to starve them, Joe realized, disgusted. That must have occurred to the other kids, too, because their hungry faces were beginning to scrunch in sobs of loss and defeat. Seeing some of the less fortunate groups with a majority of toddlers, Joe almost felt sorry enough to toss them a ball.

Then he thought of Maggie, Monk, Scott, Elf, and Libby, and realized he had to worry about *them*, now. "Come on, guys," Joe said tiredly. "Let's go eat." He turned and led them after the flow of sphere-bearing teams, leaving the losers behind with Tril. An Ooreiki collected their balls as they exited, then funneled them down a corridor like cattle through a slaughter-chute.

Joe carried Maggie on his shoulders, her tiny fingers gripping tufts of his hair to hold herself steady as he bent low to keep from slamming her head into the low cafeteria doorframe.

The cafeteria itself was filled with rows of long ebony tables made of the same glossy black material as the rest of the ship. Ahead, dozens of kids stood in line to receive big white bowls of food an alien took from the nozzle of a humming metal box. The food machine was the first piece of furniture Joe had seen that wasn't made of the strange black stuff, but it was creepy in its own right. The blue metal had an iridescent sheen to it, making it shimmer and glow like ice. It reminded him of the thing around his ankle.

"Everybody here?" Joe asked, glancing behind him.

Scott made a face. "Might as well not be. This stuff is gross."

Joe eyed the alien serving the recruits their food. "I haven't tasted it yet." *Too busy racking up extra time on my enlistment.*

"It's *green*," Maggie said, atop his shoulders. "And it tastes like the dog bowl."

Elf wrinkled his nose. "Ewwww."

"Maggie drinks from the dog bowl!" Monk laughed.

"No she doesn't," Joe said, as they continued to shuffle slowly down the line towards the humming food-machine. He cocked his head up at her. "Do you, Mag?"

He could feel Maggie's pout when she said, "It tastes better than the fish bowl."

"*Ewwww!*" Elf screeched.

"Quiet!" Joe said, catching the eye of one of the aliens. "They're watching us."

That silenced the others immediately.

"Still think it's gross," Scott muttered under his breath.

When they reached the machine doling out their allotted meals, Joe realized the 'food' the aliens were trying to feed them was, to all appearances, pond scum. Nevertheless, Joe was at the point he would have eaten worms, had worms been offered to him. He accepted a bowl for himself and another for Maggie, then led the group over to an empty table.

"Where are the spoons for this stuff?" Joe asked, lowering Maggie to the bench.

"They don't give us spoons," Libby said. "We've got to use our hands."

The bastards. Joe looked at the pudding-like green slime for a moment, then scooped up a glob of the stuff with a finger and tasted it. Immediately, his stomach recoiled. It *tasted* like pond scum.

"Not that good, is it?" Elf asked, his green-brown eyes watching his expression. The other kids, too, were watching him, obviously waiting to take their cue from the big kid.

Joe smoothed his features and forced himself to eat some more. "It's good. Kind of tastes like sushi."

"Sushi's gross!" Monk cried.

"Then you haven't been eating the right sushi." Joe scooped a handful into his mouth and forced himself to swallow. It was like forcing liquid slime down his throat, and it was everything Joe could do not to gag in front of the kiddies. Struggling with every mouthful, Joe finished his bowl, then tried to get Maggie to eat. She stoutly refused. Instead, she began to cry, and no amount of soothing words would get her to stop.

Eventually, Commander Tril noticed. *"Silence that recruit, Zero."* The Ooreiki strode over to their table and hovered over him, anticipation in his sticky brown eyes.

Joe stiffened. The bastard had followed him to the cafeteria and was *looking* for reasons to punish him. Joe felt like tossing Maggie's bowl of scum into the alien's face. But that wouldn't be fair to Maggie. "I'm working on it," Joe said, as evenly as he could.

Tril hit him, a soft blow compared to what Joe had already endured, but it almost knocked him off the bench nonetheless. The alien actually looked pleased as he said, *"You will address me as Commander Tril or sir, Takki scum."*

Sir Takki Scum. Got it.

In Joe's arms, Maggie began to cry louder. Commander Tril drew back to hit her, too, but Joe pulled her out of the way, putting his body between her and the alien. He stood up so he could stare down at his aggressor. "Leave her alone—she's just hungry."

Tril glanced at the uneaten bowl of food, then at Maggie. *"She's not eating?"*

Seeing the eager look on Tril's face, Joe felt a lump of dread pool in his gut. "She'll eat it," he said quickly, not trusting his tone.

"See that she does," Commander Tril said. *"If she doesn't, she will be force-fed."* The bastard would probably enjoy it, too. Joe's heart began to pound as he wondered how he would get Maggie to eat.

Giving Maggie a last, parting look, the alien left them for another victim across the cafeteria.

Joe swiveled and tugged Maggie against his chest, patting her back as he watched the alien leave. After Tril was out of sight, Joe held Maggie out in front of him. "Mag. Listen to me. You've got to eat."

"I don't *want* to eat!" Maggie cried. "I want my *Mooooommmmm!*" She was hyperventilating, tears streaming down her face in force.

"That alien's looking at us again," Scott whispered.

Immediately, Joe switched tactics. "So you had a dog, Maggie? Was it yours?"

"It's my brotheeeeeerrrr's!" she wailed.

"You said you had a fishbowl. You have fish?"

She perked up a little. Sniffling, she said, "I've got guppies."

"Oooh! Guppies!" Joe cried. "They're pretty, aren't they?"

Maggie's teary gray eyes widened and she nodded. "Jabber's got spots."

"I always wanted guppies," Joe said. "What about you, Scott? Did you ever have guppies?"

Scott shot a glance at Commander Tril and shook his head.

"See? Not even *Scott* had guppies," Joe cried. "How many guppies did you have, Mag?"

"Five!" she said immediately, obviously having been drilled by her parents.

"Five, wow," Joe said. "Did you feed them?"

Maggie grinned, nodding. "One pinch." She put her tiny thumb and forefinger together and held it up to his face.

"Good," Joe said, grinning. "When I get guppies, I'll make sure to give them a pinch. I've got some food I keep at home, just for when I get guppies. You know what fish food tastes like, Mag?"

Maggie shook her head, enthralled.

"Sure you do. It's really good."

"Ew—" Elf began. Joe shot him a glare and he shut his mouth with a snap.

"Mom didn't let me eat the fish food," Maggie bemoaned.

"She didn't?! Well, that's too bad. You mind if I eat your fish food, Mag?"

Maggie frowned. "I don't have any fish food anymore."

"Then what's that right there?" Joe pointed to the uneaten glop in her bowl.

Maggie followed his gaze and her frown deepened. "That's yuck."

"No, that's fish food. They dry it out so it can fit in the canisters better. Sometimes they even dye it different colors so the guppies will have prettier spots."

Maggie's eyes widened and she looked back at the slop in her bowl. Monk rolled her eyes and Scott elbowed her in the side.

"But," Joe said, "When it's green like that, that's the special stuff. You ever heard of Popeye, Mag?"

Maggie's eyes lit up. "Popeye eats fish food?"

Joe couldn't have been more relieved. "Yeah. Loves it. It's just concentrated spinach. Makes you grow big and strong. So can I have your fish food, Mag?" He said the last and held his breath, knowing that everything was going to hinge on Maggie's answer.

Teary-eyed, Maggie glanced at him, then to her bowl, then back at him. Her little brow furrowed. "You don't need any more," she said, pulling her bowl away from him. "You're big enough."

"So you wanna give it to Elf, instead?" Joe demanded.

Maggie frowned at Elf, who grinned back at her. Possessively, she pulled the bowl away from Elf, too. "It's mine," Maggie said. She stuck a tiny finger into the slime and sampled it. Immediately, she wrinkled her nose. "Tastes bad," she muttered.

"That's all the good stuff they put in it," Joe said quickly. "For the guppies."

"And Popeye?" Maggie asked.

"And Popeye," Joe agreed.

Maggie gave the green goo an uncertain look, and for a moment, Joe thought she would shove it away again. Then, tears still glistening on her cheeks, she took a deep breath, visibly steadied herself, and proceeded to eat everything in her bowl. "I guess it's not so bad," she said, when she finished. Then she glanced down at herself. "I think I'm getting bigger already!" she cried, holding up her arm for Joe.

Monk snorted, but Joe obligingly pinched Maggie's bicep between thumb and forefinger. "What do you think, Scott?" he demanded, giving the little girl's arm a squeeze. "Show him your Popeye muscle, Mag."

Maggie flexed, looking up at Scott expectantly. Over her head, Joe shot him a warning glance.

Dimples looking like they were about to burst, Scott managed, "Soon you'll be picking fights like a pro, Maggie."

"I don't like to fight," Maggie said, deflating.

"Then you're in the wrong place, stupid," Monk said. "We're gonna be *soldiers*."

Looking at her excited face, Joe doubted Monk knew what a soldier was. None of them did. Because they were *kids* and they should be playing jacks and chasing butterflies and building tree-forts, not trapped on an alien ship, learning about war.

Once again, as one of the only ones in the whole room who truly understood what the aliens had in store for them, Joe felt the weight of responsibility suffocating him.

As his five groundmates argued the merits of soldiering, Joe suddenly felt ancient—an old man in a room full of children. This wasn't fair. They were just *kids*. He wanted to run up to someone who would listen and scream at them that this wasn't supposed to happen to *kids*.

A few minutes later, everyone's heads snapped around when Commander Tril suddenly shouted, "Now you've eaten, get out! Head back to the gym! Run!"

Joe snatched up Maggie and they ran. Back in Battlemaster Nebil's care, they joined the exhausted, sweaty-faced losers for three hours of physical exercise. By the time Nebil was finished with them and sent them back to their barracks room, the entire platoon looked like zombies, and everyone was too tired to cry.

5

EARLY BALDING

"You should have let me kill him."

The officers' hall fell silent at his words. Everyone had taken off the hated translation devices and had been engaged in the first real Ooreiki conversation they'd managed to enjoy since the choosing process began. Now they waited, every sudah fluttering in silent anticipation of Kihgl's next words.

Very slowly, Kihgl put down his meal and wiped his mouth. "Kill who, Commander Tril?" he asked, taking entirely too long to look up at him. Almost as if he were bored.

Tril scowled at his superior. Kihgl was a soot-loving furg. The bureaucrats had given him too much credit for his battle record. Anyone who looked him in the sudah could see he wasn't worthy of a brigade.

"You said yourself Lagrah planned on killing him," Tril continued. "Why else take him onto the ship? He's too old for our needs. The food is designed for younger recruits. It will wreak havoc on his system. Why spare him?"

"I changed my mind, Small Commander Tril," Kihgl said in that same, even, unhurried tone. "It is not your place to question me."

Hearing that, from a vkala still bearing the scars of his shame, made Tril's sudah speed up in anger. "Just as it wasn't your place to defy Lagrah?" he demanded, knowing that, as a *yeeri*, Tril's position would be heard amongst the other castes.

No one, however, raised a voice to support him. In fact, if anything, the others in the room seemed to be glaring at him. Commander Linin was carefully picking at his plate, looking like he wanted to sink out of sight. He could feel Battlemaster Nebil's ancient eyes on him, filled with disdain. His skin prickling, Tril ignored the aging Ooreiki. The furg had been a Prime Commander several times, only to keep getting repeatedly demoted to battlemaster just as soon as he gained a regiment of his own. Incompetents and jenfurglings. He was *surrounded* by them.

Holding his gaze, Kihgl gave him a long, cold glance. "I defied no one, Commander. I claimed a child slated for execution, as was my right. Commander Lagrah himself backed me."

Tril switched tactics. "He's a troublemaker—we knew that when Lagrah took him aboard. Next time he creates problems for us, we should get rid of him. It would give us back the respect we lost when we didn't kill him."

"He's a *recruit* now, Commander Tril," Battlemaster Nebil barked. "Protected by *Congressional law*. He was *entrusted to our care*." He looked him up and down, his pale brown eyes raking over him in pure disdain. "You would break the founding principles of our society to *save face*?"

A couple Ooreiki in the hall snickered and Tril felt his sudah flutter. "The Human lost all fear of us when I didn't shoot him," he retorted. "I saw it this afternoon, when I confronted one of his recruits who wasn't eating."

"Technically, making his recruits eat is his responsibility, Tril," Kihgl reminded him. "It is not your place to interfere."

Frustrated, Tril slapped a hand to the table. "Give me control of the modifier, sir. He will not respect us until—"

"Speaking of respect, Tril," Kihgl interrupted calmly, "I hear you took over the class after I specifically gave it to Nebil. Did you not respect my decision? Or was it Lagrah's personal order, commissioning me as Second Brigade's secondary commander, you did not respect? Or perhaps you simply have no respect for my authority as your commanding officer. What is it, exactly, that you failed to respect?"

Tril's eyes dropped to the seven-pointed star on Kihgl's chest and he could feel the heavy silence that followed suffocate the room like it had been stuffed with sand, the only sounds the whispers of his sudah as they fluttered in his neck. Sputtering, he said, "Of course I respect your decisions. Battlemaster Nebil was rambling. We were under a time constraint, and I decided I needed to cut him off before another battalion arrived to train."

"Battlemaster Nebil, were you rambling?"

"Not that I was aware of, sir," Battlemaster Nebil replied, the ancient Ooreiki's sudah absolutely still. Tril scowled at him.

Turning back to face him, Kihgl said, "He says he wasn't rambling."

Faced with the cold disapproval of his secondary commander, Tril swallowed. "Perhaps my…perceptions…were off. I do respect your decisions, sir."

"Then you will respect my decision to keep the modifier."

Frustration tightened Tril's every inner fiber. Never before had he experienced a vkala who did not bow to a yeeri's greater station when it came to decisions of politics. Glaring, he growled, "You had the bad grace to put him in my company. The least you can do is give me adequate means of controlling him."

"Nebil did not seem to have a problem controlling him," Kihgl noted.

Tril's sudah took off in his shame, becoming whirring blurs in his neck. "But *I* was the one with the gun, Kihgl," he insisted. "*I* was the one who failed to shoot him at the ceremony. Our scientists have consistently reported that the Human psyche is extremely primitive. If I don't reassert my authority, he will create more trouble within my company. Commander, you *must* allow me the tools I need to control my troops."

From across the table, Battlemaster Nebil gave him a flat look. "I was under the impression that the essence of becoming a small commander was demonstrating a marked ability to lead."

Tril bristled. "Careful, Nebil, or I shall have you thrown to the Dhasha for insubordination."

Battlemaster Nebil laughed. "Oh, you can try it, boy."

Tril's mouth fell open at his subordinate's blatant disregard for his station. Not only was Nebil a *battlemaster*, not even a commander—which should've meant he wasn't even technically supposed to be at the damn table—but he was *wriit*. A *worker* caste. That he dared to speak to Tril in such a manner without even the military ranking system to back him left Tril stunned.

In the long silence that followed, none of the others coming to Tril's defense, Battlemaster Nebil—the only battlemaster in the officer's hall—looked him up and down lazily. "You make me wonder if you gained those points on your star through your role as a Corps Director's interpreter and not by proving your merits in battle."

Tril had to contain his fury. "I fought for every rank. I did not have the advantage of being a *vkala*." He cast a disgusted look at Kihgl.

Battlemaster Nebil's eyes hardened. "Tril, you are blind."

Tril ignored the wriit, speaking to Kihgl, now. "You were recruit battlemaster in training. Two turns later, you were sent to Planetary Ops after only five turns in service. Should I question your ties to Commander Lagrah back then? He was an Overseer then, wasn't he? Two vkala must find each other companionable in a world filled with higher castes."

Kihgl's pupils tightened in anger. "Take a lesson from Battlemaster Nebil," he said. "Learn to control your company with approved means or I'll be forced to find you a less challenging task."

Outraged, Tril stood, feeling the eyes of every Ooreiki in the room. Their sudah were fluttering too quickly—they laughed at him.

A *vkala*, in front of *everyone*, had dared to threaten him. A *yeeri*. At first, Tril wanted to come across the table and grab Kihgl by the throat.

Putting every ounce of willpower into controlling his fury, Tril said, "This will be *your* mistake, Commander. Not mine." Then, before Kihgl had a chance to respond, he turned and stalked from the room.

Loudly at his back, Kihgl called, "Be sure you are prepared for your first class at 02:30." As if Tril were still a niish that needed to be reminded such things. His sudah fluttered madly as he strode from the room.

Fuming, Tril returned to his quarters to prepare for his lecture. He should have known they would favor Kihgl. After all, out of all twenty-one of the Ooreiki overseeing the training of Sixth Battalion, only Tril himself had not served with Kihgl sometime in the past. Of course they would side with Kihgl. He was much loved. Despite however much truth Tril's arguments held, he would always be an unknown to them.

• • •

After forcing the recruits to shower in a noxious chamber that reeked of alcohol fumes, Battlemaster Nebil sent them to a dark, amphitheater-style classroom.

A dark-skinned, orangish Ooreiki greeted them once they were settled. Joe felt a queasiness in his gut when he realized which alien it was.

"Hello. *Oonnai.* I am Small Commander Tril, two ranks under Secondary Commander Kihgl." He touched the five-pointed silver star on his chest with a tentacle. "You can tell our rank by these symbols. Ground leaders have a stripe, squad leaders have a triangle, battlemasters have a four-pointed star, small commanders a five-pointed star, and so on, all the way to Prime Commander Lagrah, whose star has eight points. From there, we get into Overseers and Directors, who you will not see until you get out of training. Soon we will give ground leaders their recruit rankings. Each ground leader will get a stripe, but recruits do not get the circle surrounding it until you graduate. The circle signifies your acceptance into the Army, and until you earn it, even the ten recruits we choose as recruit battlemasters will be outranked by the youngest grounder one day out of graduation. Do you all understand?"

Joe stiffened, realizing that Tril's translator had been turned off and the alien had somehow been able to form perfect English from his big, tongueless mouth. Hearing the utterly clean, *human-sounding* voice come out of the alien's fat face gave Joe goosebumps. It made him wonder how long the aliens had been in space before their attack, studying them.

"I'm a linguist with the Ooreiki Ground Force, Seventh Galactic Unit," Tril continued. "Usually I work as an interrogator, but right now I have the pleasure of teaching you youngsters to speak the Universal Language of Congress, affectionately called Congie." Commander Tril's eyes caught on Joe and an unmistakable look of irritation crossed his wrinkled alien face before he looked away again.

"Take this, for instance." An image of a wingless dragon flashed on the screen behind Commander Tril. It was breathtaking, with rainbow scales that shone like gems and black talons jutting from its stubby feet like polished scythes. It was in the process of ripping a spaceship to pieces. "This," Tril said, turning from Joe and jabbing a tentacle at the picture, "is a kreenit. If there's any word you'll need to know to save your life, it will be this one. Everyone please repeat after me. *Kree-nit.*"

Everyone repeated the word immediately, since Tril had beaten four children bloody that afternoon for being slow. When they were done, Joe raised his arm.

Tril ignored him.

Another kid on the other end of the room raised his hand.

"Yes?" Tril asked. "*Kkee?*"

Joe lowered his hand, glaring.

"Are you trying to say that dragon's *real?*" the kid asked.

"Very real. You'll learn more about them in your Species Recognition classes."

"It's tearing apart a *spaceship?*" another kid blurted.

"They're notorious for that," Tril said, wrinkling the skin over his head in what Joe recognized as his first look at an Ooreiki smile. "Sometimes they manage to shatter their collars, and when they do, even the Dhasha fear them."

Shatter their collars? Joe frowned down at the blue band of metal, wondering how much force it would take. Probably enough to pulverize his leg afterwards.

Tril was still answering questions, looking amused. Joe watched him closely, a little envious. He didn't seem to hate the other kids. Just Joe.

"What are Dhasha?" someone asked.

Commander Tril turned to glance at her. "Commander Linin will teach you more about different species. It is my job to teach you to speak Congie." Tril switched the image on the screen to a chart. "You Humans are uniquely talented in that you're natural linguists. If you look at the chart, you'll see how the different language sounds break down according to ability. Whereas most Congressional species can only physically pronounce seventy-five percent of the Universal language, you Humans can learn to pronounce all of it. Thus, I have a feeling many of you will be joining me as interpreters instead of scrambling down tunnels."

Tunnels? Joe's heart palpitated uncertainly. *Did he say tunnels?* Immediately, his skin grew clammy and his palms started to sweat. Joe hated tunnels. He couldn't even crawl through a culvert without utterly freaking out halfway and Sam having to go get Dad to pull him out.

Oblivious, Commander Tril changed the image to a group of nine pictures, each with a blocky scribble underneath.

"These are the first nine words I want you to learn. This one is food. *Nuajan*." He pointed his blue laser-light on the upper left picture of green slime. "It is fortified with everything your bodies need, and should increase your rate of growth by more than twenty times, so you'll all reach adult size in a few rotations. *Months*, to you ignorant ashy furgs. Or the closest approximate."

Joe froze. *Great,* Joe thought, glancing at the little kids around him, *Just freaking great.*

Maggie, however, was staring at the picture of goop in awe, mouthing *nuajan* to herself over and over.

Tril scanned them as he continued. "You'll quickly figure out basic measurements, but I'll give you a brief overview: A standard turn is 1.23 Earth years. There are six standard days to a standard week and thirty-six standard days to a rotation. Similarly, there are thirty-six hours to a standard day, and seventy-two standard tics to a standard hour. We measure distance in digs, rods, lengths, and marches. Digs are about the size of a large adult human foot. Rods are nine of those. Lengths are based off the height of ferlii on Poen, and are about four hundred and forty rods. Marches are nine thousand, nine hundred, and ninety-nine rods. I could try and explain that, but I have the feeling most of you are too young to understand, so you'll just have to learn along the way."

Indeed, most of the kids were staring at the alien in complete confusion.

Sighing, Commander Tril went on, talking about everything from aliens to Congressional politics, lapsing into Congie whenever it pleased him. Joe was finally beginning to relax when Tril's sticky brown eyes found him. "Zero. Recite for the class the nine words we learned today."

"*Nuajan,*" Joe began. "Uh…"

"A recruit must address every ranked Ooreiki member of the Congressional Army as *oora,*" Tril said harshly. "Either that, or address me by my caste title. *Uretilakki ni diirok Ooreiki oghis ni jreekil rrenistaba yeeri jare.*"

Joe stared at him stupidly.

Commander Tril looked pleased. "You cannot pick, Zero? Perhaps I should activate your modifier until you decide."

Joe's eyes fell to the shock collar on his ankle. *He's gonna do it anyway.*

He opened his mouth to tell the alien to go stuff himself, but caught the other kids in his team watching him, frightened. *It's their butts as well as mine, now,* Joe realized, uncomfortable. What would Tril do to *them* if Joe started mouthing off?

"*Oh-ra,*" Joe muttered.

"*Oora.*" Tril made it sound like the second O was a consonant.

"*Oh-oh-ra,*" Joe tried again.

"Your pitiful attempt will do for now. Recite today's words. Food, yes, no, left, right, commander, battlemaster, Congress."

Joe tried. He stumbled over every syllable until Tril took over. "Everyone repeat after me. Food. *Nuajan.* Yes. *Kkee.* No. *Anan.* Left. *Ki.* Right. *Po.* Commander. *Diirok.* Battlemaster. *Nkjanii.* Congress. *Jare.*"

Once they repeated to his satisfaction, Tril said, "Keep in mind you're now expected to use the words we learned. The translators will no longer interpret them for you. As an aside, I was impressed with your progress. I have faith you all will be speaking Congie within a rotation or two. Dismissed. *Haagi.*"

Battlemaster Nebil met them in the hall outside and took them to a clean white room that reminded Joe of the waiting area of a doctor's office. After the unyielding black of the rest of the ship, the white surfaces should have been a relief, but Joe felt a sense of dread as the Ooreiki instructed them to remove their crisp white shirts and fold them neatly at their feet.

The air in the room was cooler than the rest of the ship. It felt like they were standing in a refrigerator. Joe's skin prickled with goosebumps.

At the other end of the room, Battlemaster Nebil pulled a long-haired blonde girl out of formation and shoved her inside the door opposite the exit. Everyone waited, confused.

Three minutes later, the girl came back sobbing. She had a new scar on her abdomen and her long blonde hair was gone. Nebil pushed her back into line and led a black-haired boy into the room. The boy came out a minute later utterly bald, but otherwise didn't seem too worse for wear. The process continued, the girls returning from the door crying and bald, the boys just bald.

Joe started when someone tugged on his arm. Libby was looking up at him, her eyes wide and red. She was clutching a puff of her curly black hair.

"Libby?! Get back in line!"

"They're cutting off our hair," she whimpered.

Joe glanced at Nebil. "Libby, you're gonna get in trouble. Get back in line."

"I need my hair," Libby said, tears tracing her ebony cheeks.

"That's crazy, why?!"

"Because it's the only thing on me that's pretty!" she cried.

Behind them, Scott and Elf snickered. Joe rounded on them with a scowl. When they looked away, he said, "That's bull. Who told you that?"

"My mom," she whimpered.

Joe was taken aback. Her...*mom*? "Then your mom's a dumb bimbo who doesn't know her ass from her head," he blurted. "You're plenty pretty. Now *please* get back in line."

"You don't mean it," she whimpered.

Joe glanced at Battlemaster Nebil, who had finally noticed his group. He turned and squatted in front of Libby. "I mean it. You got pretty eyes, Libby. Dragon eyes."

"*Kreenit* eyes?" she whispered, her eyes widening. "But they're green."

"If *kreenit* had brown eyes, they'd look like yours." Joe said. "They're dragon eyes, sure as spit." He heard Battlemaster Nebil come up behind him and turned.

Joe flinched, but the blow did not come. "*You're next,*" Battlemaster Nebil said, calmly grabbing Joe by the hair. He tugged him out of line and through the little blue door. Nebil shoved him inside the blue door and slammed it behind him, startling the Ooreiki doctors inside. He hadn't waited long enough to let the last girl finish, so Joe had a first-hand view of what they were doing to the girls to make them cry.

A little bald-headed girl was in surgery. Ooreiki doctors were running a machine that slid back and forth over her abdomen, cutting into the skin with rapid, delicate precision while she struggled against the restraints holding her in place. The machine continued, heedless of her cries, and while Joe watched in horror, its mechanical tentacles reached into her stomach cavity and removed a bloody lump of flesh. This it tossed into a growing pile in a wastebasket to the side of the table. Then, as the girl screamed herself hoarse, the machine patched her up and the Ooreiki doctors injected a silvery solution into her arm. The wound stopped bleeding and began to mend before Joe's eyes.

The whole thing had taken less than a minute.

Then the girl was pulled off the table and shoved toward the exit, still crying.

Joe felt an involuntary wave of fear as the Ooreiki doctor grabbed him and shoved him down onto the chair. The doctor strapped his arms down and picked up a device that looked much like a gun. Joe started to panic.

"Don't breathe," the doctor ordered through his translator. Then he pressed the barrel of the gun to Joe's chest and pulled the trigger.

An instant flash of agony made Joe gasp. The pain was intense, like someone was jamming a knife deep into his flesh. He gritted his teeth and tried to yank his hands free, but the doctor was already moving away, replacing the gun on the table. Joe looked down.

A red mark about the size of a zit stood out to the right of his breastbone.

Then the doctor was back, this time with a syringe. The alien jammed the tip into Joe's arm and depressed the end, pushing the blue-silver liquid into Joe's body.

Almost at once, Joe was hit with a blinding headache. Joe groaned and closed his eyes as his vision started to swim. He doubled over against the chair's straps, feeling as if his brain was being ripped apart.

The doctor pulled the needle loose and set it beside the gun. Then he reached up and started rubbing Joe's head with his sticky brown tentacles.

Joe sat there dumbly as the alien gave him a scalp massage. It felt good, nothing like the painful, brute force that the other Ooreiki had used on him so far. Only as Joe saw his hair fall away in little tufts did he finally understand—the alien had injected him with something that made him go bald.

That made him struggle. He tried to jerk his head away from the alien, but it took his scalp in a stinging, tentacled grip and went on, heedless.

"Asshole," Joe said, watching his hair fall away. He had always feared going bald. His father had been bald as a cue ball at thirty and Joe had secretly harbored the hope that his dad was just a genetic freak and it wasn't inheritable. Now these aliens hadn't even given him the chance to find out.

The doctor rubbed the rest of Joe's hair from his head and tossed it into the same wastebasket as the bloody pieces of flesh.

"What'd you do to that girl?" Joe said.

The doctor looked him over, clearly considering whether it was worth his time to respond. Finally, he said, *"We removed her ability to breed."*

Joe felt a rising surge of fury.

The Ooreiki doctor found his anger amusing. *"Congress has no need of reproductive behavior in its soldiers. Be glad we only need to sterilize one sex in Humans."* At that, the alien released him from the chair. Without waiting for Joe to leave, the doctor swept up a few loose strands of his brown hair and dropped it in the bloody wastebasket.

Joe felt like he'd been hit with a hammer. "You don't have the right."

The doctor looked up at him and the skin on its head scrunched up in an imitation of Commander Tril's smile. *"I assure you, Human, we do."*

Joe stumbled back into the waiting room, numbed. He couldn't meet the others' gazes as he returned to the line.

"What happened in there?" Scott whispered.

Joe closed his eyes and wondered if he was ever getting home.

"Joe?"

"Just leave me alone," Joe whispered.

Everyone took their turns, and Joe never looked up. They were in Hell. All the churchgoers back home were wrong—it wasn't fire and brimstone; it was an Ooreiki troopship filled with little kids a billion miles from Earth.

Once everyone was bald, Nebil led them back to their rooms and locked them inside. Ignoring his teammates, Joe went over to a bunk, slumped into its concave surface, yanked the blanket over himself, and closed his eyes.

"I'm hungry, Joe," Maggie said, tugging on the blanket covering him.

"Me, too," Elf said. "Are they going to feed us, Joe?"

"I have to pee," Libby said. "Where do I go pee?"

"I don't wanna sleep in a bowl," Monk whined. "I want a *bed*."

"Why can't we have real blankets?" Maggie asked. "I want real blankets."

"So what are we supposed to do now, Joe?" Scott asked. "There's not enough beds for everybody. Do they want us to *sleep together*, Joe?" He scrunched his face and glanced at the girls.

"Yeah, I don't wanna sleep with him. Do I have to sleep with him, Joe?" Monk demanded.

"How the *hell* should I know?" Joe snapped, throwing the cover back and rounding on them all. "Start thinking for your own damn selves." He got out of bed, brushed past them, snatched up a metallic blanket, and lay down in a corner, his back to the five of them.

Back beside the bunk, Maggie began to cry.

"Oh shut up!" Joe shouted.

"*You shut up!*" Maggie screamed back.

And Joe did. Guiltily, he listened as the children climbed into the big round bed and began wrapping themselves up in the stiff, reflective blankets. They all lay down with their backs to Joe, snuggling together for warmth. Other groundteams did the same, leaving Joe the only one not in a bed.

Joe realized his feet were cold. He pulled them back under the blanket, tucking into a fetal position in order to keep his toes from being exposed. The blanket wasn't big enough to wrap around his scrunched-up body, so he ended up hugging his chest with his arms and wishing he was part of the dog-pile on the alien bed across the room.

After what seemed like an eternity, Scott said into the silence, "We aren't getting out of here, are we, Joe?"

For a long moment, Joe almost didn't respond. Then, softly, he whispered, "I don't think so, Scott."

6

BULLIES

It seemed like they'd been asleep only moments. Too soon, Battlemaster Nebil was kicking them awake, screaming, *"Rise and shine, lazy Takki scum! Get up and get in line, you miserable little janja turds! You have half a tic!"*

As Joe scrambled to line his groundteam up for the march to the gymnasium, Maggie ignored him completely, crossing her little arms over her chest and pouting. She was, Joe realized with frustration, still upset with him for sleeping on the floor.

What was worse, as the aliens counted down their allotted time to arrange themselves, no amount of desperate begging, pleading, or cajoling would get her to move. Joe finally had to bodily yank her into line, which she immediately fell out of the moment he let go of her arm. "Damn it, Maggie!" Joe snapped. He grabbed her by a chubby little arm and held her wrist tightly as she struggled, leading her back to formation. She responded by screaming and pounding her stubby fist against his leg in an all-out tantrum.

"Maggie, shhh," Scott hissed, eying Joe nervously.

Maggie ignored him and continued shrieking and slamming her fist into Joe's thigh. Thankfully, Nebil and the other aliens didn't seem to notice.

Grimacing, Joe endured her assault and dragged her down the hall and into the brightly-lit gymnasium in silence, knowing that, because Joe was under Tril's microscope, the rest of his groundteam had become targets of his wrath.

When they reached the gymnasium, Joe hesitated. Half of the kids that were milling in nervous groups, he realized with a sick feeling, had still not gone through the Hell behind the little blue door. They stared at the bald ones as they marched in, looking confused and smug. Some were even stupid enough to point and laugh.

The aliens lined them up in neat rows by group. When Joe released Maggie, she crossed her arms and turned her back to him, refusing to get in line. Joe had to pull her into her proper place and twist her around so she was facing forward. She refused to look at him, lifting her chin and sticking out her lower lip.

Sighing, Joe straightened and returned to his place at the front of his team. Once there, he noticed a black-clad alien walking around the edges of the room, placing blue spheres along the wall. He tensed, remembering the balls from last time. Frustration began building like a knot in his chest, knowing how many children were going to have to skip another meal. Other kids began to cry.

When Nebil strode into the room, the other battlemasters stomped their feet once in unison, silencing the room.

"*Did you backstabbing ashers sleep well?*" Nebil snapped.

No one dared respond.

"*Good,*" Nebil said. "*Tril isn't here, so today we do it differently. The recruit at the rear of each group, step out of line.*" When no one moved, Battlemaster Nebil added, "*Group leaders, get them moving.*"

Joe whirled and dragged Maggie out of the line, gritting his teeth when she smacked her little fists into his bicep and kicked him repeatedly in the shin. Once he got her away from the group, he left her there and went back to his own spot. Maggie, alone, stopped pouting and began to cry.

Others were bawling, having been hit by their leaders to get them to follow instructions. Joe overheard one leader threatening the youngest kid, telling him he'd get another beating if he didn't bring back a ball for their group.

"*Before we start, there is one sphere for every group. Still, I want you to run. A lazy Congie is a dead Congie. Now, each group member that stepped out of line, go claim a ball.*"

"Go, Maggie!" Joe ordered.

Maggie folded her arms over her chest and ignored him.

"Maggie, go get a ball!" Scott cried. "You have to run!"

Sniffing, Maggie shuffled to the wall and picked up a hard blue ball in two stubby fists. She brought it back at a walk, but Battlemaster Nebil did not seem to notice.

"*Now each child with a ball will choose four other group members,*" Battlemaster Nebil growled. "*The five of you will be the only ones to eat today.*"

Inwardly, Joe groaned. He already knew who was going to starve.

"Scott, Libby, Elf, Monk." There was no hesitation in Maggie's voice—she hadn't even had to think about it.

Every single group leader received the same treatment.

Nebil grunted. "*I've noted their choices. Those who weren't chosen will be punished if they take food from their own group members.*"

The twelve-year-old piranha-faced girl who had asked about hitting their groundmates raised her hand again. "Does that mean we can take it from other groups?"

"*You can unless they can stop you.*" Battlemaster Nebil's slitted eyes fell on Joe, then moved on. "*The other battlemasters and I are now going to give the ground leaders their recruit ranks. Hold still when your turn comes—it won't hurt.*"

Ooreiki began circulating through the hundreds of recruits, making every ground leader remove his or her shirt so they could touch a small black device to their chests. Those that still had their hair were overlooked, and could only watch in confusion as the Ooreiki approached those around them.

When it was Joe's turn, he flinched when the device touched his skin in approximately the same place the Ooreiki doctor had shot him in the chest. Nebil hadn't been lying when he said it wouldn't hurt, however. A moment later, the Ooreiki removed the device and allowed Joe to put his shirt back on. When he did, the cottony material shifted over the left side of his chest, thickening and hardening before his eyes. In seconds, the cloth had shifted into a hard whitish metal bar. It stood out on his shirt parallel to the floor, gleaming in the bright light.

Joe stared at it, mouth falling open. Everything he'd learned in school told him that it wasn't possible. Hesitantly, he touched the symbol. It was cold, hard metal. He touched the cloth. Stiff, pliable *cloth*. He looked at the symbol again and had the sudden realization that the single bar reminded him of a cattle brand stamped into the shaved skin of a fresh steer.

They're claiming me.

Joe wanted to tear his shirt off and throw it on the ground and stomp on it, but he knew they'd only make him put it back on. He forced himself to look away, but could feel it burning against his skin like the enemy stamp it was.

"Group leaders, take your groundteams into the cafeteria to eat."

Remembering Maggie's choice to let him starve, Joe sighed and said, "Come on, guys." He led them at a defeated walk back to the food line. The alien passing out the ladles of green goop looked up, but before Joe could indicate he should serve the other five, Maggie shoved Joe aside with her tiny body and stuck her bowl out for the alien to fill. "Don't give any *nuajan* to Joe," she said. "He doesn't get to eat today."

Grimacing, Joe went to the same table they ate at earlier and sat at one end. Maggie and the rest picked another table, pointedly ignoring him. Joe closed his eyes and put his head in his hands, trying to ignore the ache in his gut. He'd gotten pretty good at it since his capture, only having eaten once in…how many days had it been? He thought about home and what high school would have been like. Had Sam gone back to school yet? Would they even *have* school, now that there was nobody left?

Maggie's shrill scream broke him out of his thoughts, quickly followed by Elf's and Monk's. Joe's head snapped up.

Two big twelve-year-olds who wore their naked silver bars like badges of honor were arguing over three bowls of food they had taken from Joe's group. Joe grinned to himself and would have gone back to his thoughts when he saw that Libby, her fingers curled into fists, was getting out of her seat.

Against two twelve-year-olds twice her size, she would only succeed in getting brained. Sighing, Joe stood up and went to stop Libby from getting herself squished. Just as the eight-year-old was launching herself at the bullies, he grabbed her by the shoulder and pulled her back while the two big kids, oblivious, split the third bowl in half and threw the empty container on the ground as they walked away. Monk claimed it and started licking the sides.

"They're eating our food!" Libby cried, struggling desperately to get out of Joe's grip.

"I know," Joe said. "Let me take care of them, ok?"

Libby glared and tried to yank herself free as she watched the bigger boys depart with an anger that surprised him coming from a kid so young. "I don't need your help. I know taekwondo."

Joe grimaced, immediately envisioning the slap-happy play-fighting that was taught to anybody under twelve. "Just let me handle this, okay?"

Reluctantly, Libby looked up at him, but she stopped struggling to get free. "I do," she insisted. She looked him up and down. And, with complete, innocent contempt, she said, "I could kick *your* ass if I wanted to."

Joe inwardly rolled his eyes. *Sure, sweetie.* "Yeah, okay," Joe said. "But you're our secret weapon, okay? Which means you've gotta stay secret. Let me deal with this."

He thought he saw something move in her pretty brown eyes, and in the next moment, Libby just gave a tight nod.

Once Joe was sure she wasn't going to try and follow, he took a deep breath and followed the two big kids back to their table. He saw with disgust that one of them now had two and a half bowls of food in front of him. He and the other boy were eating and laughing, joking with the others about the group of babies.

Joe casually yanked one kid off of his bench, sending him sprawling. The other got up in a hurry and looked up—and *up*—and his eyes widened when he saw Joe looming over him. He backed up hurriedly, babbling apologies. Joe snatched up three bowls of food.

"There's always someone bigger," Joe said.

"We thought they were alone…" the kid babbled. Like he was apologizing for messing with Joe's kids, not apologizing for messing with kids that were weaker than them. The boy swallowed hard, obviously thinking Joe was gonna beat the crap out of him on principle.

Joe snorted and brushed past the boy who was just starting to get up, knocking him back to the floor. Meanwhile, all conversation in the room had stopped. He could feel all eyes in the cafeteria on him…*again*. Like he was a damn shark on the prowl in a pool of goldfish.

Which, really, is what he was. He had eight inches and eighty pounds on the next biggest kid in the room. Hunching his shoulders against their stares, Joe strode back to where his groundteam was sitting in a frightened cluster, watching him with eyes that were as big around as the rest of the kids in the cafeteria's.

"Here," Joe said, dropping the three bowls in front of his group. He sat down at the end of their table, to ward off any further attacks.

"Th-thanks J-Joe," Maggie said.

"You're welcome." Tiredly, he leaned his head into his hand, wondering how much longer they'd keep them all at lunch. He was surprised when Maggie got off the bench and carried her bowl of food over to him.

"You want some of mine, Joe?"

Joe gave the toddler a weak smile. "Sorry, Mag. I can't take any food from you. It's against the rules."

"She's *giving* it to you," Scott insisted, coming over with her. "You can have some of mine, too. Here. There's a little left in the bottom." The ten-year-old proudly offered up what remained of his meal.

Joe laughed, touched. "I don't think that'll fly."

"We won't tell anybody," Libby said, hurriedly scooping half of hers into Scott's bowl. "If you eat it real fast they won't know."

Joe looked down at Scott's bowl as the others added their portions, leaving him with more than he would have had if he had gotten his from the food line. He swallowed and glanced at Battlemaster Nebil, wondering if it was worth risking a beating to eat.

The Ooreiki was standing at one end of the cafeteria, fingers tangled behind him, calmly watching the tables with the acuity of a hawk.

Hunger eventually won out over fear. When Nebil's head was turned, Joe gulped down their offerings. When he was done, he shoved the bowl back in front of Scott and waited, nervous. He spent the next ten minutes tense, waiting for some blow, some bellow from the front of the room. Apparently, the alien hadn't seen. Joe perked up when he realized they had actually gotten away with it.

When everyone had finished eating—or not—Battlemaster Nebil took them to another dark, amphitheater-style classroom and made them sit down in the odd, scoop-shaped seats overlooking the stage. Commander Linin stood at the podium as they settled, looking bored.

"*This,*" Linin said, pointing to a picture of a stocky, bobcat-shaped animal with glorious rainbow scales dominating the screen behind him, "*Is a Dhasha. They're the deadliest fighters in the universe and they delight in taking multi-fingered sooters like you as slaves.*" The Ooreiki eyed them, his eyes as sharp as the five-pointed star set in a silver circle on his chest. "*I am Small Commander Linin. This is your Species Recognition Class and* that—" he jammed a boneless extremity at the screen, "—*is responsible for ninety-eight percent of the soot we gotta go through as Congressional soldiers. Dhasha. Males can withstand direct hits from laser and plasma fire. When we first found them on their sootwad planet, Dhasha warriors became our greatest asset. Congress sent them to colonize hundreds of planets, boosting our strength a thousandfold in just a few short centuries.*"

The Ooreiki made a face and turned to look back over the auditorium of students with depressing sobriety. "*But we made our own burning ashes. We should have left them eating themselves, digging holes in the dirt to survive. Hell, we should've wiped out their whole fire-loving solar system. See, the Dhasha began to rebel, and every time they do, Congress has gotta devote fifty percent of its fighting power to keeping those fire-loving monsters from carving out a chunk of a galaxy. As it is, it's been over a hundred turns since the last one, so the next Dhasha prince will probably get cocky sometime within your lifetimes. When he does, and Congress assigns you to fight him, you can all kiss your asses goodbye because you're not gonna survive it.*"

The Ooreiki changed the image and a wide swath of shredded meat appeared on the screen. Joe shifted uncomfortably, realizing that it was a field of dead Ooreiki.

"*This is what happens when you go to war against the Dhasha.*" He changed the picture again, giving them a close-up of a grotesquely mauled alien body, internal organs weeping through huge gashes along its chest. "*Notice the soldier's armor. The hardest material Congress can make and Dhasha talons slice through it like* nuajan."

Joe glanced around him. The other children were staring with wide eyes, their jaws hanging open. Many of them looked like they were about to cry.

Linin grunted. *"Lucky for you furgs, Dhasha rebellions are almost always contained in-species, or, if things get really ugly, they're put down by Jreet. Usually they don't have to get lesser fighters involved."*

Lesser fighter? Joe prickled, despite himself.

"If they do send you, at least it will end this charade. Once a few Human battalions get ripped apart, those jenfurgling ashsouls on Koliinaat will realize they shouldn't have forced us to dress you Takki up like soldiers. You aren't even good as beasts of burden. Hell, you'll probably end up crawling the slave tunnels to get torn to pieces in the Dhasha deep dens—you'd be good at that."

Joe's heart began to thud, his pulse racing in his limbs. *Tunnels?* It was the second time one of the Ooreiki had mentioned tunnels. Maybe they were just trying to scare them. Maybe they'd end up jumping out of planes, instead. Joe could handle that. He'd *love* to jump out of planes. *Oh please God let it be planes.*

The Ooreiki gave the room a disdainful look. *"Not that it'd be worth the trouble to fit you with a biosuit. Suited up, you charhead furgs couldn't even match an Ooreiki naked."*

Joe raised his hand. "Are they really sending us down tunnels?"

Linin's dark brown eyes came to rest on Joe. *"You were enlisted as part of the Ground Force. Of course they'll send you down the tunnels. Who else would do it? The Space Force?"* He made a derisive snort, expelling a rush of air through the frills in his neck. *"Those cowards don't even know what war is."*

Joe swallowed hard. His hands felt clammy. "Commander Tril told us we'd probably become interpreters."

"Commander Tril is a furg."

"Can I change to the Space Force, then?"

"No." The disgust in Commander Linin's eyes made Joe's throat burn. He looked at his fingers and closed them into fists to stop the shaking. Already, he could feel the pressure of the earth closing in on him. He felt queasy. *How much space will the tunnels have? Dhasha are big, so ten feet? I can handle it if it's ten feet. But didn't he say they were Takki slave tunnels?*

If Takki are the size of humans, that would only give me a couple inches… Thinking about that, Joe fought to control impending panic.

"So when do we get to see a Dhasha?" a girl asked excitedly.

"Pray you don't," the Ooreiki said. *"Even friendly ones eat their own troops, and all the War Commission does is slap 'em with a fine and give them an extra couple of turns before granting them another rank. To Congress, if we all died feeding a Dhasha warrior fighting under the Congressional banner, then our deaths would have been worthwhile. Here, let me show you furgs why."* Commander Linin lifted a black, circular briefcase-like box onto the table and opened it. Inside, nestled in a black, velvety substance, was an elongated, six-inch-wide metallic scale. Even in the reddish light, it gleamed with unearthly iridescence. Beside it lay a wedge-shaped black talon twice the length of Joe's middle finger.

Commander Linin used metal tongs to lift the talon from its bed, taking great care not to touch it. He held it up so they could see. It had a slight curve to it, like a scythe.

"A Dhasha claw." He motioned at Nebil. *"Battlemaster?"*

Nebil came to stand before him and held out a tentacle, looking bored.

"Dhasha claws are the perfect cutting device, their edges a perfect monomolecular surface able to cleave into any substance at an atomic level." Commander Linin held the tongs out two inches above Battlemaster Nebil's arm and released the talon.

Nebil grunted as the claw hit his arm and burrowed in more than halfway down the ebony tip. Thin, brown-tinted liquid began to leak from the wound, pattering upon the glistening black floor of the ship.

"As you can see," Commander Linin said, gently retrieving the claw from Nebil's arm with the tongs, *"Their own weight is enough to cleave flesh. Imagine thousands of pounds of muscle behind it and you are beginning to get an idea of how dangerous these creatures are."*

"Don't forget the scales," Nebil muttered, rubbing the wound on his arm. Already, it was healing.

Commander Linin returned the talon to its case and retrieved a scale. *"We will pass this around for you to examine. It's an outer scale from a Dhasha male. Utterly indestructible."*

"*What he means is,*" Battlemaster Nebil said, "*if every star in the universe suddenly decided to explode at the same time, these things would still be around a million years from now, after the dust settles.*"

Yeah, right.

But when Joe finally got his hands on the scale, he got goosebumps. It felt unnatural in his hands, gliding across his fingers like it was slick with water. It had absolutely no give whatsoever, and though it was only six inches across and nine inches tall, it weighed more than a sack of potatoes. It also stank like rotten fish.

Looking at the scale made Joe's eyes ache. It was never a single color at any time—the rainbow iridescence seeming to swirl across it unnaturally, pooling in yellows, reds, greens, purples, blues, oranges. Joe quickly passed it off to the next recruit and wiped his sweaty palms on his shirt.

Once they were finished examining the scale, Commander Linin went on. "*Takki,*" he said, flipping on a screen showing a short, bipedal purple lizard with pupiless, egg-shaped sapphire eyes similar to the Dhasha and kreenit's emerald. "*The ancestral Dhasha slaves, evolved on the same planet as the Dhasha and the kreenit.*" Linin's voice held an unmistakable note of disgust. "*Without them, the Dhasha would never have developed their own technology and would still be starving on Tenyuir where they belong.*" Abruptly, he switched the screen off. "*That's all you need to know about them.*"

"How big are they?" Joe asked, sweat slickening his palms and dampening his underarms.

Commander Linin eyed him carefully. "*Taller than Ooreiki. About your size, actually.*"

Oh shit, Joe thought. *Shit, shit shit…*

Commander Linin let that sink in, then changed the image to another picture of a male Dhasha, this one sitting on a pile of pillows like a smug cat. "*Now to discuss how to keep from getting killed when you're around Dhasha…just keep in mind you're Takki soot. As Takki soot, you must avoid eye contact. Dhasha find a lesser creature's gaze repulsive and they will eat you for it.*"

"Will we see Dhasha where we're going?" someone asked.

Linin grunted. *"When we left, Congress was still undecided. Your body composition might be too...tempting."* The Ooreiki glanced at the screen. *"But if they do decide to put you under a Dhasha commander, you'll see one as soon as we land on Kophat.*

Something about the word Kophat was familiar, as if he had heard it somewhere before. Joe sat up, desperate to drag his mind away from the thought of tunnels. "Kophat? That's where we're going?"

"Kophat is the training center for the Congressional Army. Of course that's where you're going, furgling." It sounded to Joe like the translator meant, 'moron.'

Giving Joe an irritated look, Linin went on, *"If you are given to a Dhasha Prime, this class will save your life. Never make eye contact, even in conversation. Always bow your heads when a Dhasha passes. If a Dhasha requests something of you, do it quickly, without question. Never speak to a Dhasha unless asked a specific question."* The Ooreiki's snakelike eyes came to rest on Joe and stayed there. *"And never show any insolence—you will be killed for it. Dhasha are not as merciful as certain Ooreiki Secondary Commanders."*

Joe flushed and suddenly found his lap fascinating.

Linin's scowl moved on. *"But, even if you follow all of these steps, many of you will get eaten anyway. Dhasha are prickly and unpredictable."* His face wrinkled in an Ooreiki smile. *"And each one of them is worth ten thousand of you, on a bad day."*

"Like Jreet," Nebil grunted.

"Yes," Linin said. *"Like Jreet."* He flashed a new picture onto the screen, this one of what looked like a crimson, scaly cross between a man, a bat, and an adder. It had two huge, muscular arms with bony, clawed fingers, and a long, twisted body like a snake. Most of its flat, diamond-shaped head was taken up with massive, predatory jaws and two huge, concave, ribbed depressions where a man's ears would have been. Though it didn't have wings, it was carrying a wicked-looking spear, tipped in what looked like milky glass, and was striking a tired pose, covered in blood and gore.

Joe frowned, unable to see why *that* would be worth ten thousand of *him.*

"*They can render themselves invisible at will, and just a scratch of the poison they carry in their chests will kill anything in Congress,*" Nebil said, when he asked. "*Instantly.*"

Oh.

Linin glanced at Joe again. "*But there are very few Jreet, so they are only used as Sentinels. They've only had three planets, in all of history. Their breeding habits are…less viral…and their training customs ensures only about one in a hundred actually survive to adulthood. Thus, if too many Dhasha princes rebel at one time, that's where you weaklings will come in.*"

Joe swallowed, suddenly not feeling very well.

At lunch, Nebil again let the youngest decide who ate. Again, Joe's team shared while the others squabbled. Again, they somehow evaded Ooreiki notice. Afterward, Joe watched the bullies move between the groups, taking whatever bowls of food pleased them, punching or hitting anyone who tried to resist, and a little ball of fury rose in his chest. He stood up before he really even thought about it. "Scott, Libby, come with me. Elf, Monk, you stay here and make sure Mag doesn't follow us." Then Joe was walking toward the last kid who'd had his meal stolen. Curious, Scott and Libby got off the bench and followed him.

"Hey," Joe said, touching the crying boy on the shoulder. "You're still hungry, right?"

Looking up with wide eyes, the boy nodded.

"Then follow me," Joe said, glaring at the big kids who were still roaming the tables. "We're putting an end to this."

Joe found a dozen more children that were too small to be bullies, but big enough to help him. He took them to the center of the room and got up on one of the tables. Nebil immediately noticed and started moving toward him at a run. Joe ignored him and shouted to the room, "Listen up, guys! The next shithead to take food from anyone gets his ass kicked."

Then Battlemaster Nebil had a stinging tentacle around his throat and was dragging him off the table. "*What in the Jreet hells do you think you're doing, boy?!*" Nebil demanded, shoving Joe away from the table.

"I'm stopping the bullies," Joe snapped. "Something you *should* be doing, anyway." Already, adrenaline was making his knees shake, and a good portion of him was screaming at him to bolt before Nebil could crush more bones, but he met Nebil's gaze stare-for-stare and refused to back down.

Battlemaster Nebil blinked his pale, sticky eyes up at him in obvious confusion. He glanced at the kids moving between tables, then back up at Joe, still looking stunned. *"Say that again?"* the alien asked.

"The bullies," Joe repeated. "They're taking kids' food and I'm going to stop them."

The Ooreiki stared at him so long that Joe began to think he might have somehow fried his tentacle brain. Then, in a gruff grunt, the Ooreiki muttered, *"Let them take care of themselves, Zero."*

Joe fisted his hands and glared down at Nebil stubbornly. "Some of them can't," he insisted.

"They've got to learn."

"They can't learn if they starve to death first," Joe retorted. He gestured at the roomful of kids. "You really think a *five year old* is going to be able to stand up to a gang of middle-schoolers?"

Battlemaster Nebil gave him a long look, his sticky, slitted pupils fixed on Joe's face. Then he warily turned and glanced in the direction Joe had pointed, his sticky eyes scanning the cafeteria with acute intelligence. He gave the bullies a long look before his gaze finally returned to settle on Joe. To Joe's surprise, Nebil twisted and barked something to the other battlemasters in the room. Immediately, all the Ooreiki that had taken up stations along the wall began walking from the room, leaving just Nebil to guard the kids in the cafeteria. The scarred, pale-skinned battlemaster leveled a long, calculating stare on Joe, then turned and followed the other Ooreiki from the room.

Joe felt a moment of triumph—until he realized the big kids hadn't listened to him. They were still out wandering, stealing food wherever they saw a weakness. The littler ones cowered, saying nothing, allowing themselves to be bullied.

Joe spotted a boy across the room taking bowls from a group of little kids just sitting down to eat. He walked over to him, yanked the bowls out of his hands, and shoved him to the ground so hard the kid started to cry.

Something about the bully having the audacity to cry after taking food from hungry little kids made Joe snap. He grabbed him by the white

T-shirt, dragged him to one side of the room, and slammed him against the wall. Into the boy's face, Joe shouted, "Do you think you're better than them? Is that why you take their food, you piece of shit?!"

The whole cafeteria went silent again.

The boy's blue eyes opened to wide circles of terror. "I won't do it again, Zero. Please." His fingers were half the size of Joe's where they feebly tried to loosen Joe's hold on his throat. Joe smelled fresh pee.

Realizing that, Joe felt sudden, overwhelming self-disgust. He pushed the kid away from him and turned away, wiping his palms on his pants. He felt dirty. Like he'd just helped his father dig up the septic tank and had accidentally fallen in.

He was halfway to his own table, shrinking under the accusation he saw in the hundreds of round, childlike faces around him, when Libby's voice made him turn back. She had hopped onto a table and was telling the kids how the new bully patrol was going to work. "From now on, anytime you see someone taking food, let us know. The bully patrol will come stop it. We've got twelve kids on the patrol so far, including Zero. Anyone else wanna join us?"

Three dozen hands went up.

Joe stared at Libby. Was she really eight? Up on the table, in front of all the kids, she seemed like she was five times that.

"From now on," Libby intoned, "You're all members of Zero's patrol. Any time you see someone stealing, shout, and the rest of the bully patrol will come help you."

"How are we supposed to eat if we can't take food?" a big kid asked.

"Share," Joe said, despite himself.

Libby glanced at him and jumped down from the table. Reluctantly, Joe took her spot. He peered over the sea of little faces and tried not to remember he had just made a sixth-grader piss himself. "*If* you're nice to your other group members, *maybe* they'll share," Joe said. "It's what you all learned in kindergarten."

Behind him, Maggie raised her hand. "Joe?"

"Yeah," Joe said, turning to her. "What is it, Mag?"

"I haven't been to kindergarten yet, Joe."

Joe sighed. "Can someone tell Maggie what it means to share?"

"I know what it means," Maggie said, puffing up. "It means everybody eats a little less so nobody starves."

Nebil came back ten minutes later to an entire cafeteria of kids all sitting down, eating or talking. His pale eyes flickered over to Joe once, finding him at a far table in the back of the cafeteria, before going back to silently scanning the tables from the front of the room.

After lunch, Nebil took them to the gymnasium to run laps for two hours. By this time, all of the children had bald heads and scars, and several were still red-eyed from crying. After everyone rinsed the sweat from their bodies in the noxious alcohol showers, Nebil herded them to another amphitheater-style classroom.

Joe's heartbeat quickened when he recognized the array of weapons upon the tables in the center of the room. Trying to look casual, he brought the others to sit in the very front row, as close as he could get to the guns, wondering if they were loaded.

The battlemasters moved to stand along the walls as an Ooreiki with a secondary commander's seven-pointed star emblazoned on its chest stepped into the room. Their eyes met and Joe knew that Kihgl immediately understood why Joe was sitting in the front row. The secondary commander gave Joe a baiting look, even stepping away from the table and gesturing to give him easier access.

When Joe remained in his seat, hands fisted, Kihgl made a derisive snort and began making his introduction. *"You know who I am. I'll be teaching your first class on Congressional weaponry, after which, Battlemaster Nebil will take over for me."* He scanned the children in the room with his sticky brown eyes. *"Believe me when I tell you we will not be able to teach you every single weapon and how to use it. We will only go over the basics, and if after you graduate your unit decides to, say, go after mud-dwelling janja slugs, then they will teach you then how to use the weapon that corresponds with that task—in that case a Viscous Burrowing Motionseeker, or an VBM. Because there are three thousand different species of soldiers in the Congressional Army and ten times as many different species Congressional Soldiers have to burn on any given day, Congressional troops have over thirty thousand different kinds of weapons in their arsenal. What you see here are just the most basic forms of Ooreiki Ground Force weaponry. These are specifically built for*

Ooreiki use, which are heavier than can be comfortably carried by Human hands. But don't worry, you Humans will receive your customized weapons once we reach Kophat. Until then, the concept is the same. We'll teach you to use these and more, though like Linin said, we're wasting our time training you. Humans are weak, stupid, and ill-prepared to fight what Congress has to throw at them."

The alien's four slender appendages caressed a gun. *"I know this because I'm an Ubashin veteran. That means I survived the last Dhasha rebellion."* Kihgl's fingers stopped and he looked up. *"Only two Ooreiki grounders made it off Ubashin alive. Does anyone know why the two of us survived?"*

Hesitantly, one girl suggested, "You're good shots?"

Kihgl snorted. *"Anyone else?"*

"You captured the Dhasha leader?"

"Are you an imbecile?" Kihgl snapped.

It was Libby who said, "You were really good at hiding."

Kihgl's face folded into wrinkles of pleasure. *"Exactly. The only reason I'm here today is because I was better at hiding than the rest of my Corps."*

"You *hid?*" a boy said. "I thought you were gonna teach us to *fight.*"

The little brown frills in Kihgl's neck began to flutter as he gave the boy an icy stare. *"You will learn soon enough, Human, that some things can't be fought."* He turned back to the rest. *"I survived. That's why Congress forsook me with this wretched job in the first place—they thought I might have some insights to keep you weaklings alive if we see another Dhasha rebellion."* Kihgl laughed, a guttural grunting sound that boomed across the room from the base of his stubby throat. It reminded Joe of a toad's croak. *"Well, I don't. None of this—"* he spread his tentacles over the equipment on the table, *"Will do you any good. It's all luck and wits, and, since Humans have neither, your survival will be up to the ghosts, not my teachings."*

Kihgl paused, scanning the room. *"Questions?"*

"Yeah," Joe said. "Are those guns loaded?"

Kihgl locked gazes with him before he lifted a gun and pointed to a black cylinder above the trigger. *"If it were loaded, it would have a glowing blue plasma charge in the chamber, here, and a plasma clip attached here."* Kihgl pointed to an empty notch settled in the top of the gun. Then he set the alien weapon down. *"Any other questions?"*

"How far can those things shoot?" Joe asked.

Kihgl gave him an irritated look. "*Accurately? Two ferlii lengths, if you've got a scope. The laser is much more, though it depends on particle and atmospheric interference.*" Kihgl touched a longer, lighter gun.

"Which is the better weapon?" Joe said.

"*Depends on what you want to do. Plasma packs a lot of punch, but laser is better for—*" The Ooreiki stopped and scowled at him. "*Why do you care, Human?*"

"I want to learn to fight." *So I can blow the rest of your head off.*

Kihgl stared at him for so long that Joe thought he was about to get clobbered. Abruptly, he said, "*I'm wasting my time. You're all Dhasha fodder, anyway.*" He gathered the guns into his boneless arms and strode from the room.

Joe was outraged. Kihgl hadn't even bothered to tell them the names of the weapons.

Joe led the others back to their quarters, ruminating on this. When they got back to the barracks room, black Congie gear lay in piles beside their beds, neat and new. Compared to the flimsy white skivvies they'd been wearing, the rugged black gear seemed…ominous. Joe, Scott, and Libby were the only ones who could even lift the rifles. After determining they weren't loaded, then determining there were no actual *clothes* to wear in the mess, Joe fiddled with the alien buckles, harnesses, and straps, trying to figure out how to put his gear on. Finally, he threw it aside in frustration, startling the other kids.

"They don't want to teach us," Joe said. "None of them do."

"Why not?" Scott asked.

Joe sighed and sat down against the wall. "Maybe they're afraid of us."

Libby looked up shyly from where she was fiddling with the piles of black alien gear. "They are. They're holding Earth hostage. That's why they took us kids—they did it to ruin the next ten years of our military."

Joe gave her a weary smile. "Even with our military at full strength, Lib, the government couldn't stop the Draft."

"Yeah," Libby said, gesturing at the other kids in the room, "But what about twenty years from now, when we've got our hands on their technology? It would be a different story, wouldn't it? We might not win, not with

Dhasha fighting for them, but we could give them a hard time. It works out better for them if they don't have to deal with our generation until Earth's had a chance to adjust. See, if we grow up here, in space, the little kids like Maggie won't remember anything except what the Congies tell them, so they'll be able to make us like them and forget about Earth. Then, if Earth rebels, they send us back to fight and Earth ends up being put down by *humans,* not *aliens,* so Congress isn't the bad guys, it's us, the kids who got brainwashed and turned traitor."

Joe stared at her.

Libby's enthusiastic expression suddenly disappeared, and she lowered her head and looked away. "Never mind. I'm probably wrong anyway." She went over to a corner and sat down, refusing to meet his eyes.

"I wanna go home," Elf whimpered. He looked terrified by the piles of gear. "Can we do that, Joe? I don't wanna touch the guns. I miss my dad. He told me not to touch guns."

Joe tore his eyes off of Libby, still a little stunned by what the eight-year-old had pieced together. He forced himself to smile at Elf. "We'll get you home. It might be a hundred years from now, at the rate they're adding time to our enlistments, but I'll make sure of it, okay?" He glanced at the alien rifles. "Until then, you need to do what the aliens tell us, all right?"

Elf's eyes widened. "A hundred *years*? You think we'll live that long?" He lowered his voice conspiratorially. "I thought only *Santa Claus* lived that long."

Monk frowned. "There is no—"

"With all the drugs they're feeding us?" Joe interrupted quickly and loudly, giving her a pointed scowl. "Hell, who's to say we wouldn't live three times that?"

"Somebody who shoots us," Libby muttered from her corner.

Joe glanced at her. "Yeah, I guess there's that."

Libby peered at the floor, the bald ebony dome of her skull soaking in the reddish light. Joe wondered what she was thinking, and why she constantly refused to meet his gaze. He still couldn't believe her mother had told her she was ugly. She was one of the cutest kids he'd ever seen, and had the pert chin and delicate features of a future supermodel. If it weren't for her teeth, she'd be beautiful—the type of eight-year-old they put in clothing magazines and on TV. And teeth could be fixed.

"Am I getting any bigger, Joe?" Maggie asked, flexing her bicep.

Joe turned away from Libby, suddenly feeling the injustices of the world as if they were leaden weights strapped to his shoulders. Halfheartedly, he said, "I'm not sure. We should start keeping track."

"Okay!" Maggie cried. "Mommy used to mark it on the door with a pen."

"Then we need a pen," Joe said, glad they didn't have one. The last thing he wanted to do was track just how freakishly fast the younger kids were growing.

In silence, Libby got up, went to her pile of gear, and rifled through it until she brought out a black marker. She handed this to Joe shyly, still not meeting his gaze.

He stared at her. *She memorized all of her gear already?* Then he realized that a marker would be the first thing an eight-year-old kid remembered seeing. "Thanks, Lib," Joe said, taking it reluctantly. He glanced around for something to write on, finally deciding on his blanket. "Okay, Mag, lay down. Right there. Hold still. Feet at the edge. Stop *wriggling*. Okay, we'll check it again in a couple days. I'll mark it Maggie Day One because I'm not sure how long we've been on this stupid ship already. What about you, Libby? You interested?"

Libby shook her head silently and looked away.

"I am!" Monk shouted, shoving her blanket at Joe. She was about five inches taller than Maggie. Maggie, meanwhile, had confiscated Joe's blanket as her own and was holding it up to Scott, who was sitting on the floor and rolling his eyes.

Joe finished with the others, who were already laying their blankets side-by-side, comparing them with serious looks, and looked back at Libby. "You sure?"

Quietly, Libby said, "I'm gonna be tall, Joe. I don't need to check."

Something about the way she said it made Joe believe her.

• • •

"Libby, get in the car. I forgot my eye kit."

Libby watched as her mother hurried back into the house, heels clicking loudly against the circular cobblestone driveway, leaving Libby standing alone beside the Ferrari. Libby stared at the little Barbie lunchbox her mom had packed her, which was dwarfed by the enormous pile of her mother's luggage that even then their housekeeper, Marcella, was trying to stuff into the trunk.

Something was wrong. Her mom always packed Libby more stuff than she could ever possibly use.

"Marcella," Libby said, "where's Mom going?"

Marcella's brown eyes widened, but instead of telling Libby what was going on, she abandoned the luggage and fled back into the house, rubbing her hands on her crisp white apron.

"Mom," Libby said when she returned, "Where are—"

"I said get in the *car,* Libby!" her mother interrupted, slamming the trunk down on what few bags Marcella had managed to pack for her. "I'm late as it is."

"Late for what?" Libby asked, still not moving from beside the little cherub fountain in the center of the courtyard. She eyed the Ferrari warily. Her mother never let her ride in the Ferrari. It always attracted too much attention.

"The *shoot.* Jean-Jean wants to do one in front of an alien ship. He got me a suite at the Hotel del Coronado and dinner at Donovan's. Now all we have to do is get there."

"Mom, why do I only have a lunchbox?" Libby asked.

Her mother wrinkled her perfect nose. "Because you're always complaining about me bringing too much luggage for you. Now get in the damn car or I'll tell your teacher you won't be needing karate lessons anymore."

Libby frowned. "It's taekwondo."

"Yeah, whatever." Her mother waved a perfectly manicured hand and yanked open the door on the driver's side. "Just get in the car, Libby. Don't make me tell you again." She slid inside, one long, perfect leg at a time. Libby heard her mutter, "Little brat," before the door slammed shut.

Feeling a weird pang of foreboding, Libby got in the passenger side and shut the door. The solid click of the door locking into place reminded Libby of a prison gate clanging shut. She hated road trips. Her mom would always be looking in the rearview mirror, primping, making sure her windblown look was perfect even though she would never put the top down and get the real thing.

Road trips, in general, were hell for Libby. The first thing her mom did upon reaching a shoot location was to hand her off to the staff. While her mother was out posing in new and exotic locales, Libby was often confined to a hotel daycare or the back of an RV. Libby would rather stay at the house with Marcella, but her mother liked to say that Libby needed to get out and "experience life."

Libby had figured out a long time ago that really meant her mom just didn't want to pay Marcella to watch her.

So it was with absolute boredom and a lot of resentment that Libby watched the lines of cars pass by on the freeway. Traffic had been crappy ever since the aliens showed up, but most of it was to get out of the city. There was almost nobody stupid enough to try getting *into* the city, where all the ships had landed. As far as traffic was concerned, their trip into San Diego was a breeze.

"Mom, can we *please* put the top down? It's hot."

"Then turn up the air conditioning," her mom said. She was dabbing at some mascara along the corner of her eye. "I don't want the stylist pulling out hair because I got it all snarled in the wind."

"Can we listen to the radio, then?" Libby asked.

"No. I'm driving. It'll distract me." *Dab, dab.* The applicator came back with a tiny clump of black, and her mother glanced down at it, then returned her attention to the mirror, leaning forward over the steering wheel to get a better look.

Something started to burn in Libby's chest as she watched her mom drive. "Doing your makeup doesn't distract you," she noted.

"If you were *pretty*, like me, makeup would come natural to you, so of course it wouldn't distract you." *Dab, dab.*

At her mother's words, the awful pain in Libby's gut returned, and she spent the rest of the trip curled up against the door, waiting to be released into a stranger's hands. When the car finally pulled to a stop, she sat up.

A huge obsidian sphere loomed over them, too close to be safe. It had landed in the middle of a playground, squashing the swingsets and monkey-bars flat. Libby stared up at it, suddenly finding her throat very tight, her hands sweaty and cold. The glossy black surface gleamed even more perfectly than her mother's pampered skin. A spiral staircase erupted from the bottom, the exit hole puckered and uneven like some sort of zit. An alien stood at the base of the staircase, watching them.

"Well, we're here," her mom said. *Dab, dab.* "Go on. Get out."

Libby reflexively grabbed the seat. "I don't want to get out. I want to stay in the car."

Her mother stopped dabbing at her makeup to give Libby a long look. She sighed, deeply. "They *told* us we've gotta give up our kids, Libby. You think I *want* to do this?"

Libby swallowed hard, looking at the alien. After years of being alternately ignored or used as a photo op, the thought had certainly crossed her mind. "Mom, I don't wanna—"

Her mother's award-winning features tightened in disapproval. "Are you seriously going to do this? Seriously? Do you know how *awful* it is for me, to have to give up my *kid*? Because they'll *kill* me if I don't?"

Libby bit her lip and looked at her lap.

"I don't have a *choice*, Libby," her mother went on. "What, you want me to *fight* the aliens for you? What, with my *purse*?"

"Sorry, Mom," Libby managed, remembering to reach for the calm Master Ryu had taught her. She was finding it difficult. "Maybe we could come back in a few days?"

Her mother grimaced. "We're here now, Libby. You want me to drive all the way back here just to do it all over again?"

Libby remained glued to the seat, tense. "Mom, I—"

With a huge, disgusted sigh, her mom got out of the car and slammed her door shut behind her. She stalked around to the side and wrenched Libby's door open, her delicate brows bunched in a scowl. As Libby cringed into the upholstery, her mother casually reached in, grabbed her daughter's wrist, and tugged her out of the seat.

Only the calm words of Sahyun Nim Ryu kept Libby from kicking her mother in her perfect nose as she dragged her out of the Ferrari toward the aliens. *Remember your peace, Libby,* he had said, while they practiced in a grassy area within her mother's perfectly manicured backyard gardens.

Center and find peace. Whatever happens, keep your mind still and at ease. A worried warrior makes mistakes.

"Be glad your Daddy isn't here to see this," her mother snapped. "The only thing he likes about you is you're not scared of anything. I wonder what he'd think if he saw you now."

Realizing it was true, Libby lowered her head in shame.

"Here." Her mother shoved her lunchbox at her. "Go up to that alien over there. Tell him you're here for the Draft."

Libby had heard about the Draft on the little TV Marcella kept on all the time in the laundry room, and suddenly it all made sense to her. She glanced up at her mom, both hurt and thankful. "You mean you pretended there was a photo shoot so I wouldn't get scared?"

Her mom snorted and pointed. "Jean-Jean's right over there." Indeed, the photographer's sleek gray RV sat backed over a hopscotch area. He was already setting up the lights. "I thought I'd get you out of the way first."

Libby looked. She saw the cameramen, the tripods, the flowing white tents, the beach towels spread over the playground sand. Six photographers, unbeknownst to her, had been taking pictures of them the whole time, the reflective black lenses of their cameras flashing in the sun as they clicked photo after photo of them together, in front of the ship. Libby took a deep breath. "Bye, Mom."

"Come here for a hug." Her mom wrapped her long, thin arms around her and squeezed gently to keep from damaging her expensive gauze dress. In that moment, she held Libby tighter and longer than she'd ever held her before, and for a moment, Libby thought her mother was showing the first real hint of love she'd ever gotten from her.

Then she heard the cameramen scramble in to get close-ups. "Just hold her right there," one of the guys said. "That's right. Perfect, *perfect!*" After another minute to give them their shots, her mother released her and went to begin rummaging through her luggage for her outfit bags. Now the photographers were focused on Libby, leaning in close, crouching upon the concrete in front of her for a better angle.

"You gonna be a hero, kid?" one of the photographers said, his face hidden behind the huge black eye of his camera. "You gonna go fight aliens?"

Gripping her lunchbox, surrounded by strangers, Libby lowered her head and bit her lip. She wanted to run to her mother and grip her leg, but her mom hated that.

"Poor kid's crying," one of the photographers called. "Be sure to get that." More clicking of their shutters. One leaned in close for face-shots. Libby twisted away, wishing she could drop her lunchbox and kick the guy in the head.

"Hey, kid," one of them prodded, "how about you look up for us, okay? Stop staring at the ground. Nobody gets on the front page of *People* staring at the ground."

Flushing, Libby took a deep breath and turned toward the alien ship. The alien standing guard was watching her. Swallowing hard, she walked up to the Ooreiki at the base of the staircase. It stared down at her through a black helmet that made his face look like some sort of wasp, utterly motionless. On its chest, a four-pointed star sat in a circular border, both made out of a bright, near-white metal that reminded Libby of her mother's wedding ring. Libby cleared her throat and glanced behind her. Her mom wasn't even looking, but the photographers used the opportunity to snap at least a thousand pictures, the flashes lighting up in waves. Libby turned back to the alien. In her strongest voice, she said, "I'm here for the Draft."

The alien made some guttural sounds in its chest. A little black ball hanging around its throat said, "*We don't start collections until tomorrow.*"

Libby lifted her chin. "I want to go now."

It gave Libby a long look. She couldn't see its eyes behind the helmet, but she stared back at it anyway. Finally, it said, "*You can't bring foreign objects on our ship.*" A slender tentacle snaked out to touch Libby's lunchbox.

"Fine," Libby said, throwing it aside. It clattered against the crushed jungle-gym and split open, spilling a dozen tiny bags of Cheetos out onto the sand. Out of the corner of her eye, she saw her mom walking away from the car, toward the mini city of the photo shoot. She could even make out Jean-Jean as he ran out and embraced her mother, then led her back to the site with an arm around her waist.

"*This way,*" the alien said.

Libby turned and followed him onto the ship.

7

AN UNEXPECTED GIFT

Now that Nebil's war classes had begun to give him a taste of what Congress could do to its enemies, Joe had begun to worry that the aliens would tire of the human resistance and simply blow Earth away.

It would be easy. Like popping a zit.

The more he learned about this alien army, the more the cold, hard truth settled into his guts like a cancer. Congress was too big. Utterly too big to be stopped. And it dealt with those who crossed it quickly, and with breathtakingly brutal efficiency. It wiped out whole cities, plunged planets back into the Dark Ages, then set up blockades to keep it that way.

And Earth was filled with groups of guys rolling their sleeves, planning out how to best take down the ship squatting in the parking-lot of their local strip-mall. Humans, Joe knew from agonizing experience, couldn't take a hint if it was splattered across live television.

Furthering his fears that Congress would simply decide that humans were more effort than they were worth and just blow up their whole solar system, every time Joe asked about Earth, the aliens completely ignored him. As if the idea wasn't fully off the table yet, but they didn't want to spook the nine hundred kidnapped kids so it would be easier to blow them away when the time came to abandon the farce.

Instead of giving them any news of Earth, the aliens filled their every waking minute with lessons about language, war, weapons, and culture.

And, despite Joe's aversion towards his captors, he learned everything they had to teach him and found himself craving more.

The military subjects especially fascinated him. When Battlemaster Nebil taught him to take his rifle apart and put it back together, Joe only needed to see the demonstration once before he could do it on his own. When taught the differences between laser and other energy weapons, Joe could identify them on sight from then on.

In fact, for the first time in his life, Joe actually found himself excelling in classes. He found himself putting together facts that the instructors didn't even mention, all of the pieces of the alien puzzle fitting together in his head. Joe knew he shouldn't enjoy learning what the enemy wanted him to know, but he couldn't help himself. It was as if everything was already in his brain, waiting to be brought to the surface.

Of all the other children, only Libby seemed to match him class-for-class. While Scott, Elf, and Maggie struggled with the knowledge and had to be told again and again, Libby complained that they were going too slowly. Actually looking somewhat pleased with that, Battlemaster Nebil gave Libby and a few other volunteers newer and harder things to learn, teaching this advanced class on weaponry himself.

It made Joe envious, but he felt like he would be betraying his home if he asked to join them, so he feigned ignorance, stuck with the slower class, and secretly listened to Libby's instruction from afar. After all, he didn't plan to stay with the Ooreiki. First chance he got, he still had to find a way back to San Diego.

Tril was the only alien who even came close to alleviating Joe's worries about Earth.

"Last I heard, they sent a Human Representative to Koliinaat," Tril said, when Joe asked. "If they did, they're safe, as long as they don't do something stupid. Sentient species have special protection from the Regency."

"What is Koliinaat?" Joe asked.

Commander Tril gave him a hard look. "Koliinaat is the seat of Congressional government. It's the largest artificial construction in the known universe, a product of millions of years of construction and care, an unparalleled masterpiece of technology. It houses the First Citizen, the

Tribunal, and the Regency. Over three thousand species' Representatives are quartered there."

Joe felt himself staring. "Three *thousand? Species?* But Small Commander Linin's only taught us about *five.*"

Tril scowled at him. "He chose the most important. It is impossible to pack your limited Human brains with that much information in just a few days."

"But there's three *thousand* different types of aliens?" Joe insisted.

"More," Tril said. "Some are slaves. Some are still evolving. And some are extinct. But once a species becomes a member of Congress, they will always retain a Representative at Koliinaat. The Watcher keeps them all alive even after their species dies off, in case their planets recover or a lost colony returns. There are even more species in galaxies so distant that it takes whole turns to visit or communicate with them, even with our advanced technology. Those races have smaller Regencies to rule them, which in turn bow to the wisdom of Koliinaat. Further, we plan on finding more. Koliinaat's Regency seats are only half full. Exploration of our universe is not even close to complete."

Joe again found the enormity of the problem staring him in the face. Earth was outnumbered, maybe millions to one. Humanity needed more than numbers to regain its independence. It needed weapons, ships, raw materials, science... It needed some kind of miracle.

Joe wondered if his dad had really understood what he was up against. Remembering the way he'd left that night, never to come home, Joe was pretty sure he had.

Yet, thinking of his father, Joe frowned. His father's face seemed fuzzy in his mind. In fact, everything about Earth felt vague, almost like they were feeding them some drug to make the memories just slip away. Joe was brooding over this when a tall, bony girl took him by the arm and pulled him out of the cafeteria line.

She looked twelve, but she already had a line in her brow. Joe recognized her as the piranha-looking girl who had asked Nebil if she could hit her groundmates.

"What?" Joe snapped. He was irritated because he could not recall his dad's favorite color. *What kind of son can't remember his dad's favorite color? I've heard it a hundred times before. I just need to concentrate harder...*

The girl jutted out her chin even further. "Well, if you're gonna be like that, maybe you don't want it."

"Want what?" Joe said, focusing his attention on the wiry girl. She had the cocky look of a bully, someone who was used to getting what they wanted.

"You sure? Maybe I'm having second thoughts." The girl pulled her fist away, hiding its contents, enjoying his confusion.

"Go screw with somebody else," Joe said. *What's Dad's color? I know this.*

The girl seemed to consider, then held something small and red out to him. "You dropped this, back on the first day when they beat you up."

Joe's breath sucked in. It was his Dad's Swiss Army knife. He snatched it out of her hand, unable to believe that it was real. The girl watched as he reverently pried open a blade, feeling the smooth red plastic in his fingers.

Red. Joe blinked. *His favorite color is red.* In a whisper, he said, "Thank you." He held out his hand. "I'm Joe. This is Monk." The other members of his groundteam were holding their spot in the cafeteria line.

The bony girl gave Joe a look like he had grown beetle antennae, ignoring his outstretched hand. "You use your real names?"

"Why not?" Joe asked.

"Because they'll *punish* you," the girl said. "They told us to use *numbers.*"

Joe shrugged. "Until they kill me, I really don't care."

The girl frowned at him. "Hasn't anyone told on you yet?"

"Like who?"

"Like *her,*" the girl said, jabbing a finger at Monk.

Monk's eyes darkened. "I'm not gonna tell."

"*They* tell on *me,*" she said, pointing at the kids behind her.

"Then you're a bad ground leader," Maggie said, helpfully.

Joe did not like the look the girl gave to Maggie. He stepped between them. "It was really nice of you to find my knife."

The piranha-girl snorted. "I only gave it back so you'd help me."

Joe prickled at her tone. "Help you do what?"

"We almost didn't get to eat last time Tril made us run for the balls. From now on, you can get a ball for my group first, then get yourself one."

Joe stared at her, wondering if the girl was from the special bus. "What's your name?"

"I'm Sasha." She sneered at him. "You're gonna help me if you wanna keep your knife, Zero."

"I'm not helping you."

"Then I'll tell the aliens about it," Sasha warned.

"Then we'll tell the aliens how you *hid* it from them," Monk said.

Sasha's eyes narrowed. "If you're not gonna help me, give me back my knife."

Joe's hand clenched reflexively over his father's knife. "*My* knife."

"It's mine. I found it," Sasha said. "Give it back." She made a grab for it.

"Screw off," Joe said, putting his back between her and the pocketknife.

Sasha kicked him in the side of the leg. It wasn't enough to tear tendons, but it bent his knee painfully sideways, making his leg collapse out from under him. He threw out his hands to catch himself and Sasha bent to take the knife from him as he fell. Instead of stopping his fall with his hands, Joe slammed all of his weight onto his knee and grabbed her collar, jerking her forward until her face was only inches from his.

"Back. Off." Every ounce of him wanted to smash her head into the wall for what she just tried to pull. "The knife is mine. You try to take it again and you'll wish the aliens had put you up there with me during the Choosing ceremony. Get me?"

The look of triumph drained from Sasha's face and she struggled against his fist, terror brightening her eyes. Joe let her squirm for a few moments before letting her go. She stumbled backwards, pale as a corpse. Her fear, however, was quickly replaced with angry promise on her piranha-like face. She sneered as Monk helped Joe to his feet.

"You won't always be the big one," Sasha said. "Someday I'll be big enough to beat you up, then I'll take my knife back and eat your food in front of you. Maybe if I'm really nice I'll let you lick the bowl."

"Maybe if Joe's really nice *right now,* he won't make you eat off the floor," Scott said.

"Yeah," Monk said, sticking out her tongue. Elf and Maggie laughed.

Sasha gave them another creepy sneer and strode off into the cafeteria.

"I don't like her," Scott said.

Joe watched Sasha go in silence. He felt bad, since she had given him back his knife, but somehow she reminded him of his Aunt Caroline. Lost in dementia, the woman delighted in hurting those around her with cruel words and underhanded, manipulative comments. Except Aunt Caroline had an excuse. She was old.

Sasha was just a bitch.

"They only had one boy, Joe," Libby said softly. "They're not gonna do good when we get bigger and Tril makes us fight for the balls."

So? Let that little psycho starve. Joe tightened his fist around his knife, reassuring himself of its presence. He still felt numb from the sheer amount of fury that had overcome him when Sasha had tried to take the knife back. *I almost killed her.* He stared down at the red plastic in his hand, wondering if he was going crazy.

"Girls are just as good as guys, Libby," Monk said. "My mom said so."

"Not in a fight," Scott said.

"Yes too in a fight!" Monk turned to face Scott with all six years of height. "I bet Libby could beat you up, Scott, and she's only eight."

Scott rolled his eyes. "Boys get bigger than girls. It's a fact of life. Isn't it, Joe?"

Still staring at his knife, he said, "Congress changed the facts of life." Libby frowned at him, then at his knife. Seeing her look, Joe stuffed it into his pocket.

Later, as they ate, Joe said, "Sasha's right. I'm not gonna be the big one forever. We gotta start planning for the future. Pretty soon—maybe just a couple months—we're gonna have to fight for our food like everybody else. Do any of you know how to fight?"

"I fought kids all the time in school," Elf said. "Bullies liked to pick on me, 'cause of my ears."

Looking at the elephant appendages that jutted from the sides of his head, Joe forced back a grin. "I'll bet. What'd you do to fight 'em off?"

Elf grinned at him proudly. "I stomped on their feet and punched them in the arm."

"Okay," Joe said, smiling. "I think we'll have to get a little more advanced than that." He glanced at the others. "I know a little about street fighting, mostly 'cause Sam was the biggest loser ever born and I ended up saving his ass every other day. When we get back to our rooms, I'm gonna teach you what I know. It's not too complicated. Even Mag should be able to do it."

"You're gonna teach me to fight?" Maggie cried gleefully.

Joe grinned despite himself. "You sound like I'm giving you a pony."

"She wants to be able to beat up that guy who took her food," Elf said. "She was drawing pictures of him in snot on the bench of that first class."

Joe's face twisted. "Snot? Mag, that's disgusting."

"The aliens wouldn't let me take my crayons," Maggie pouted.

"Well, you've got markers, now. You can use those."

"I can?" she cried, in enthusiastic glee. "Where can I draw, Joe?" She bounced in her seat, face full of childish excitement.

Joe thought about that. He didn't have any paper, and he doubted the Congies would be too impressed if he let her graffiti over her new white clothes. But, now the idea was in her head, he had to find *something* to draw on or that was just what she'd do. "You can draw on me," he said. "On my arm. You can give me an anchor like Popeye."

Maggie's eyes widened and she stood up to go.

Joe laughed. "We can't do it right now, Mag. We have to finish our classes, first." And he had to find someplace safe to stash his knife.

8

KIHGL'S PROPHECY

The next morning, Commander Kihgl stormed into the chow hall during their meal. He looked furious. The six battlemasters in charge stomped their feet in unison and everyone rose at once to stand at attention behind their bowls.

Kihgl stood at the front of the room, scanning the faces quickly. *"Prime Commander Lagrah just informed me that a spatial shift has occurred ahead of our pod. We will arrive in Kophat's system tomorrow, two weeks later than the rest of the regiment. Today's classes are on what to expect planetside. Understand?"*

As taught, the children shouted out, *"Kkee oora!"*

"Good. There's a good chance we'll be inspected by Representatives from Koliinaat once we arrive. If we are, you treat them like the gods they are, you understand? They are so far above you that if you fart, and they find the odor unpleasant, their Jreet will skin you alive if they so much as wrinkle their noses."

Kihgl scanned the kids' faces and his sticky brown eyes settled on Joe. The little frills in the base of his neck started fluttering rapidly. *"Zero. Get up here."*

Gut sinking, Joe reluctantly trotted to stand before Kihgl. He'd actually managed to go two days without getting pummeled, and the bruises were starting to heal.

"What is that?" Kihgl demanded.

"What is what?"

"Recruit Zero does not understand the question. Oora."

Joe flushed. "I don't understand the question."

Kihgl could have hit him, but he didn't. He pointed with a tentacle.

Joe stared down at his bicep in confusion.

Maggie's crude imitation of Popeye's anchor stood out in harsh black tones upon his pale skin and he felt a sudden settling of dread in his gut. "Oh."

"Well, Zero?" Kihgl demanded. *"What is it?"*

"A drawing," Joe said warily.

"Are you trying to say you defaced Congressional property?"

Knowing he was already in deep shit, Joe just straightened and got it over with. "'Defaced?' No, sir. That doesn't do it justice, sir. It took several *hours* to create this masterpiece." And it had, at that. Joe had fallen asleep while Maggie worked. He was lucky he hadn't woken up with a mustache.

Behind him, he heard several children giggle, Maggie among them.

Kihgl did not hit him, as Joe had expected. Instead, he turned to Nebil. *"Battlemaster, deal with them while I jettison this sootwad."*

Joe had just enough time to see Battlemaster Nebil's face scrunch in a fearsome alien smile before Kihgl's stinging python grip on his arm yanked him from the room. Joe tried to dig in his heels to slow him down, but the Ooreiki commander might as well have been a bulldozer for all the good it did him.

He was beating at the stinging coils around his forearm in desperation, knowing he was about to become flash-frozen, bulging-eyed space-debris, when Kihgl shoved him inside a small room with a desk and a huge round, scoop-shaped bed. It was more lavish than any other room Joe had seen, actually boasting two glowing pictures of Ooreiki on the walls. Obviously not an airlock.

Kihgl slapped his tentacles to the side of the door and it dripped shut. Then they were alone. Just Joe and Kihgl.

Commander Kihgl turned from the door slowly, making Joe back up until his calves hit the hard round bed.

"What is it?" Kihgl said, his pale brown eyes fixed on him in deadly seriousness.

"What is what?" Joe asked, wondering if he could outmaneuver Kihgl in the tiny room. Probably not. The Ooreiki's tentacles were at least four feet long when fully stretched. The room was only twelve-by-twelve, giving Joe a four foot window. Fat chance of escape.

"The drawing on your arm," Kihgl growled. *"What is it?"*

"You gave us markers," Joe retorted. "You never told us not to."

Kihgl lunged at him and within two startling seconds had a stinging grip around Joe's throat. The Ooreiki yanked him down until his unnaturally huge, sticky brown eyes were less than an inch from Joe's face. *"Listen to me very carefully, Human,"* Kihgl said, his voice low and deadly, *"I do not care about* why *you drew it. I want to know what it* means."

Choking, Joe managed, "It's…an…anchor."

Kihgl released him and stepped back. *"An anchor to what?"* he insisted.

Gasping, Joe collapsed to his knees, heaving in huge breaths of air. "It's from a cartoon. This guy wore it around, beating people up."

Kihgl cocked his head, his eyes staying on Joe's arm. *"So you believe you can act like this cartoon? Beat us up?"*

"No," Joe muttered. The truth of *that* had been made painfully clear the longer he stayed with his captors. Despite all the Hollywood movies about humanity kicking alien ass, Congress was just too *big*. Earth's independence—what so many phony movies celebrated when humans fought off their aggressors with projectiles and jets—wasn't going to happen. Not by force. "I don't."

Kihgl brushed past him, leaving behind the pungent scent of oregano as he moved to a smooth spot in the wall and slapped his tentacle against it. The aliens, Joe had noted, had taken an extreme interest in a couple of Earth's spices, and had begun wearing oils of oregano and rosemary as if it were some great honor. He had to snort, wondering if they knew they smelled like Sunday dinner.

A round cubby opened, revealing several odd-shaped alien artifacts, none of which were the standard black. It stunned Joe to see color again for the first time since they'd lost their clothes.

Kihgl drew out a little yellow-green sphere, only five or six inches in diameter. He brought this over to Joe and shoved it at him.

"Is it the same?"

Joe was not about to touch what looked like a globular ball of snot. "What?"

"The picture. I can't read Human script. Perhaps there is a detail I missed."

Reluctantly, Joe took the greenish sphere and immediately lost all interest in dropping it. It was wet and spongy, but when he peered into the gelatinous core, he saw a black-lined image floating in its center on a sheer white background. It looked exactly like the rough anchor Maggie had drawn on Joe's arm.

"Where did you get this?" Joe asked.

"Is it the same?" Kihgl snapped.

Joe peered at it, then examined the lines on his arm. They were exactly the same, right down to the stray line Maggie had accidentally drawn when he shifted in his sleep. "Yeah," he said, his skin puckering with goosebumps. "It's the same."

"Exactly?" Kihgl insisted.

"Yeah," Joe said, getting nervous.

Kihgl let out a sudden breath through the flaps in the side of his neck, looking like he had been punched. For a long moment, the Ooreiki just stared at the snot-ball. Then, slowly, he lifted his sticky brown eyes to Joe's face.

In that moment, Joe got the *distinct* feeling that Kihgl was thinking about killing him. Nervous, he took a step backwards, lowering the ball to his side.

His movement seemed to snap Kihgl out of his reverie, because, seeing Joe step away with his precious snot-glob in hand, his eyes hardened. He stepped forward and wrenched the spongy ball from Joe's grip and shoved it back into his cubby. Then, without another word, he went to the door to the hall and opened it, the incident apparently forgotten. *"Return to your platoon, recruit."*

"What was that thing?" Joe demanded.

"It's my concern, not yours, Human."

Joe didn't move.

The door dripped shut again as they stood there. When Joe made no motion to obey, Kihgl scowled. *"It's something that was given to me when I was a battlemaster."*

"Uh, by who?" Joe asked. From what he knew of the alien ranking system, battlemaster had been a *long* time ago, for Kihgl.

"By a damn Trith, that's who." Kihgl cursed. The way he said it, that was supposed to mean something.

Joe, however, had no idea what a Trith was. It certainly hadn't been mentioned in any of Linin's Species Recognition classes. "So what's it mean?" Joe asked.

"It means my destruction." Kihgl slapped the wall again and the door opened. *"Now get out."*

Joe's goosebumps returned, that weird nightmare-that-you-can't-stop feeling coming back in force. "What do you mean, 'your destruction?'"

Kihgl narrowed his slitted brown eyes. *"If I had wanted to tell you the intimate secrets of my life, Human, I would have done so. Now return. To your. Platoon."*

Joe stayed well out of reach, making no attempt to leave. "It's not fair for you to just whip that thing out, ask me about it, tell me it means your destruction, then expect me to go."

Kihgl slapped the door shut again, the tiny frills in his neck fluttering rapidly. *"You have no idea what 'fair' is, Zero."*

They stood facing one another in silence a moment before Joe tentatively said, "What did that picture mean? Come on, man. I'm the one with it on my damn arm."

For a long moment, Joe thought Kihgl was going to pummel him. He was actually surprised when Kihgl finally decided to answer him. *"It means the termination of my soul. The knowledge that I'll never walk the halls of Poen with my ancestors, adding my wisdom to that of every Ooreiki that has come before me. It means I will cease to exist, and can't stop it because the choice has been made."*

"The termination of your *soul*?" Joe said.

Kihgl looked like he wasn't going to respond, but then touched the baggy black Congie uniform covering his torso. *"Our souls live here, within our oorei. If the oorei is destroyed before it can be taken to a temple, the soul that lives inside it is released, its spiritual essence dissolving into the world around it. It is why we ban fire on all of our planets. It is one of the only things that can destroy our oorei and the souls inside it."*

"Is that what that little round thing was you showed me?" Joe asked, feeling a moment of awe. "An *oorei?*"

Kihgl's chest erupted in a froglike croaking sound. *"No, you furg. That was a mental image recorder. The oorei are tiny spheres we Ooreiki develop as we grow and live. They fit in your fist—on rare occasions they are bigger, if the bearer had a particularly long and emotional life. They're different colors according to the spiritual state of the Ooreiki who developed them. Mine, for instance, will probably be a dull brown or gray due to all the horrible things I've done in my life. A priest's oorei will glow a golden yellow or white. The priesthood on Poen collects them all and puts them in hallowed sites in the temples so that people may visit their ancestors."*

"Is this some technological thing?" Joe asked. "You record your lives?"

"No," Kihgl snapped. *"Ooreiki had oorei back when we wandered beneath the ferlii canopies, living in the dark, hunting draak with poisons. The temples on Poen still have many souls from that time, though visitors seeking them out have to spend days to find one, and when they do, they need a priest to translate. There's nothing technological about it."*

Joe squinted at him. "Are you telling me you've got dead people wandering around on your home planet? Zombies or something?"

"Ghosts," Kihgl said. *"Billions and billions of ghosts."*

Joe stared at the Ooreiki, not quite sure Kihgl wasn't utterly pulling his leg. After becoming Tril's scapegoat on everything from dirty floors to kids peeing themselves, Joe somewhat prided himself on being able to more or less judge an Ooreiki's mental state based on its scrunched brown face, and Kihgl looked utterly sober. "And you've *seen* them?" he asked carefully. "Ghosts?"

"Kkee. I make a pilgrimage to Poen after every war."

Joe didn't know what to say. Kihgl sounded serious. And afraid.

Tentatively, he moved closer and touched Kihgl's arm. The Ooreiki stiffened. Joe quickly withdrew his hand, realizing he had no idea what kind of alien etiquette he had just broken. He eyed Kihgl's python tentacles, knowing the alien could strangle him with ease. Clearing his throat, Joe motioned at Maggie's drawing. "It doesn't *mean* anything. It's just some five-year-old's scribble."

Kihgl's eyes grew sharp. "*Which five year old?*"

Hurriedly, Joe said, "The picture is just a bunch of lines. It doesn't mean anything. It's just a doodle."

"*You saw the picture I showed you, Zero. It was given to me by a Trith. Of all the species in the universe, the Trith are the only ones that haven't been swallowed by Congress. Do you know why?*"

Joe shook his head, confused. Until now, he'd never heard of a species to avoid Congress. Everyone had acted like it wasn't possible.

"*The Trith have avoided Congress because the Trith see the future. Every Congressional attack, every strategy Congress used against them, they thwarted it so thoroughly that Congress gave up after only three attempts. Three!*"

"They see the future?" Joe repeated. "Seriously? The whole race?"

"*Every single Trith can see every single detail of every moment from now until infinity. And a Trith told me that picture represents the destruction of my oorei.*"

Joe's lips formed an O.

"*So now you see.*" Kihgl's eyes shifted to Joe's arm.

Joe cleared his throat. "I think psychics are full of crap. There was one we went to at the Fair. She sucked."

Kihgl's neck-slits began fluttering with irritation. "*I told you about the Trith.*"

"I know," Joe said, "but why would he warn you unless he thought you could change it?"

Kihgl stared at him. The fleshy sudah in the side of the Ooreiki's neck fluttered almost to a stop.

"Why tell someone what's gonna destroy them unless they can do something about it?" Joe went on. "If he really sees the future, he had to know you were going to try and avoid it."

"*You realize you are advising me to kill you, don't you, Zero?*"

Joe swallowed. Quickly, he went on, "I'm just saying a lot of it's up to interpretation. I mean, shoot. We've got psychics on Earth that gaze into a crystal ball and tell your future. I had one tell me I'd end up living in a cave with a bunch of naked people who could slay dragons. She was supposed to be really good, a genuine psychic—"

Kihgl scoffed.

"Anyway, I didn't take it to heart. And look. Here I am. It wasn't a cave with naked people. It was a shipful of aliens with a bunch of little kids. Maybe she told me it would be naked people because kids are innocent and don't carry all of the burdens of adults. So maybe instead of destroying your soul, the Trith was telling you something's about to happen that's gonna be really emotional, earth-shattering. Like you lose your mom or something."

Kihgl stared at him so long Joe flushed and started to fidget.

"*Even if I cared about my mother, a Trith is not going to leave its planet and track me down to a sootbag bar out near the Line just to tell me she's going to die.*"

He had a point.

Kihgl slapped the wall again, once more allowing the door to drip open beside him. "*Go find Nebil. Let me deal with this in peace.*"

Joe didn't want to go. He wanted to dig that little snot-ball back out of the closet and get a really good look. It had to be some sort of mistake.

…Didn't it?

But then he caught the utterly serious—utterly *creepy*—look Kihgl was giving him. In that moment, Joe realized, again, that he was just an alien to this creature. An extra recruit. A cull.

Joe quickly backed to the door and left.

9

KOPHAT

"**K**ophat is an Ooreiki home planet. The air is low-oxygen and high in organic content, so you Humans will have to struggle a bit to breathe. That's what Ooreiki sudah are for." Small Commander Linin touched the little frills running down either side of his neck. "*Today's class will consist of Ooreiki anatomy, customs, and planets. Feel free to ask questions, because as soon as you step off of this ship, your training focus will become tunnel assaults.*"

Joe's heart spasmed. "Tunnel assaults?"

Ignoring him, Commander Linin and the battlemasters passed among the children, allowing them to examine them up-close for the first time. Continuing his lesson, he said, "*Aside from the Dhasha and the Ueshi, Ooreiki have the most planets in Congress—three thousand and twenty-three full members, six hundred and fifty-nine more applicants, all terraformed. We outnumber Humans ten thousand to one. Only the Ueshi are a more populous species.*"

"These are your fingers?" Maggie asked, tugging on the four little extensions of Linin's muscular arm, careful to avoid the prickly stinging growths on the bottom. "Why are they so soft?"

"They don't have bones, Mag," Joe replied.

"*We don't have bones,*" Linin said, casting Joe a glance, "*But we do have special fibers we can stimulate into rigidity with electrical impulses. That is how I am standing here in front of you instead of pooling at your feet.*"

"I heard you guys came to Earth a long time ago and evolved into apes."

Joe glanced at the kid who had spoken, wondering if he was an idiot.

The Ooreiki's slitted pupils narrowed. "*Whoever told you that was wrong.*"

"My dad told me that," the boy said defiantly.

Yep, Joe thought, *Definitely an idiot.*

"*Feel* his arm," Maggie said. "He doesn't have any hair, stupid."

"*Hair is a primitive trait,*" the Ooreiki agreed. "*More advanced species simply evolve ways to prevent evaporation and stave off freezing. Hair is not very effective, since only minor fluctuations in temperature can cause catastrophic damage.*"

"What are these?" Scott asked, touching the frills on the Ooreiki's neck.

The Ooreiki jerked back. "*Never touch those. Sudah are an Ooreiki's air supply. Many of my comrades would kill you for touching their sudah.*"

Battlemaster Nebil grunted his agreement.

"So you've got gills?" a girl said.

The Ooreiki stiffened. "*No, they are not gills.*"

"They sure look like gills," Joe said. "Hey, they even got the little red thingies!" He pointed.

Scott added, "You know, on *our* planet, it's the *fish* that are the primitive ones."

The Ooreiki scowled at Scott for so long that kids started to back away from him nervously.

"*This lesson is over,*" Small Commander Linin barked. "*Return to your rooms until your next class is ready for you.*" Then Linin turned and marched away, leaving the battlemasters to take charge.

"High five," Joe said, grinning. "That was kickass." Scott met his hand loudly, his impish face dimpling. Then they caught Nebil watching them with acute interest and their chuckles died in their chests. Scott cleared his throat and began to inspect the glossy black floor.

"*Fourth Platoon, form up,*" Nebil said, still watching Joe. "*Ground leaders, march your teams to the chow hall.*"

Joe could still feel Nebil's gaze itching at his shoulder blades long after they were out of sight.

• • •

Joe was running one of the numerous errands Tril had found for him that evening, errands that just happened to cut into his sleep time, when an Ooreiki tentacle touched his shoulder. Joe spun.

Battlemaster Nebil stood watching him, in one of his silent moods.

"*Kkee, oora?*" Joe asked nervously. The last thing he wanted tonight was to go back to his groundteam a mass of bruises so he couldn't get comfortable in the last hours he had to sleep before they docked at Kophat the next morning.

"*A battlemaster is never called 'oora,' Zero. Call us 'hiet' or 'rogkha,' but never that. 'Oora' means 'souled one.' Do you know why, Zero?*"

Joe found the conversation odd, especially since Battlemaster Nebil had rarely spoken more than two words at a time to him without cuffing him along with it. "No. Why?"

"*Battlemaster is 'nkjanii' in my language, which means 'evildoer.' Ooreiki had given up war by the time the Fire Gods went to the Jreet and helped form Congress. War,*" Battlemaster Nebil said softly, "*is evil, and since battlemasters are the ones who lead others into war, we are evildoers. Soulless. Thus you cannot call us oora. It is an insult. Every Battlemaster since the very first Draft has refused to allow themselves to be called 'oora' because we know we are betraying our own nature in doing what we do.*" Then Nebil lapsed back into silence, still watching him.

Joe fidgeted under the stare. He vaguely remembered Commander Tril saying something similar, but before this, he had never been called on it. "Sorry."

The silence stretched on, grating on his nerves, but Joe knew better than to move.

"*Why are you out of your room, Zero?*" Battlemaster Nebil finally said.

Joe held up the parcel Tril had given him. "Commander Tril wants this delivered to Commander Linin." The parcel appeared to be a perfect globe of rock with one flattened side. Joe still hadn't found a way to open it. "He said it was really important," Joe added, hoping Nebil would take a hint.

Battlemaster Nebil snorted. *"That's a paperweight. Tril bought it on Earth."*

Joe stared down at the thing in his hand. The bastard was keeping him awake…just because. Then, furious, he lobbed it against the wall. It hit hard, but did not give him the satisfaction of shattering.

Battlemaster Nebil made a froglike chuckle and picked it up. *"You'll still have to deliver it, since I'm sure he'll ask Linin about it in the morning, but first I have something important to ask you."*

More important than sleep? Joe wondered, perturbed. He took the paperweight back from Nebil and scowled at it. "Why's he hate me so much?" He said it to himself, so he was surprised when Nebil answered him.

"Each new recruit cycle, someone is chosen to dispose of the culls. It's a hard task and nobody wants to do it. This last cycle, it was Tril. It was his first time and you made it very difficult for him."

Joe digested that in silence.

"This morning Kihgl took you from the cafeteria," Nebil went on after a moment. His words were startlingly…tentative. *"What did he say to you?"*

Joe's eyes lifted from the paperweight. Battlemaster Nebil was watching him too closely. Joe opened his mouth to lie.

"Don't," Battlemaster Nebil said with an Ooreiki sigh. *"I ask out of curiosity, not spite. If you'd rather lie, I'll go."*

Joe scanned Nebil's face. Despite ruling his recruits with an iron fist, tossing Joe around whenever he didn't move fast enough, the alien now somehow felt…trustworthy.

When he didn't answer immediately, Nebil turned to go.

"He didn't like the drawing," Joe said, to his battlemaster's back.

Slowly, Nebil stopped and turned, his eyes dropping to the skin of Joe's bicep, where the image was mostly gone. Commander Tril had forced him to stand in the noxious baths and scrub it until it was raw and bleeding.

"Did he say why?" Nebil asked, almost softly.

"He's seen something like it before," Joe hedged.

"Ah." Battlemaster Nebil ran his snakelike fingers along the wall. *"Was it the one the Trith had given him?"*

Joe stared at him, stunned and wary.

Battlemaster Nebil's fingers stopped moving and he looked at Joe, saying nothing for a long time. Then, softly, he said, *"Then he made his choice. I wonder if you're worth it."* Without saying a word, he bent and touched the bluish ring around Joe's ankle. When Nebil squeezed, there was a click, and the anklet fell into two halves, clinking metallically upon the glossy black floor.

"I didn't see the catch," Joe said, feeling stupid.

Battlemaster Nebil picked up the pieces and tucked them into a pocket of his Congie robe-like uniform. *"You can't. It is on a different light spectrum, one Human eyes cannot register. All the controls on the ship are."*

At that, he left Joe standing in the hall, staring after him dumbly.

• • •

"Come on, Joe. Please? I'll pay you back."

"With what money?"

"She's only gonna be at the fair another day. Kyle went last night and he said she gave him the creeps."

"Why do you wanna go see someone who gives you the creeps? I'd rather spend the fifty bucks on a ride."

"You don't have to get yours done. Just me. That's only twenty-five dollars. I can get you that back in a week."

"Man, stop bugging me. I wanna see the knife shop. Dad's been wanting a Leatherman for Christmas."

"Mom said *to let me do what I wanted. It's for my birthday."*

"Your birthday was two weeks ago."

"Please?"

"Fine, but don't expect to get your money back when she turns out to be a hack."

"Thank you, Joe! I won't. She won't be a hack. I promise."

"Whatever. Can I go in with you?"

"Why?"

"So I can make sure she doesn't boil your bones and feed them to the ogre she keeps in her closet. Why do you think?"

"*Think she'd let us?*"

"*It's not like it's a goddamn doctor's office. I'm your brother. She'd better let me stay.*"

"*Okay, you pay her. She won't kick you out if you're the one who gives her the money... Look, that guy just came out. She's open! Let's go!*"

"*Calm* down. *Sheesh. Let go of my arm, I can get through the door by myself. Little shit. Hey, lady, you mind if I hang around while my brother gets his reading?*"

"*Does he want you to hear it?*"

"*He does if he wants twenty-five bucks.*"

"*Very well. Sit down in front of me, Sam.*"

"*You* hear *that? She knew my* name!"

"*It's on your T-shirt, dumbass.*"

"*Oh.*"

"*Joe, you're going to have to be silent if you wish to remain.*"

"*Uh, okay.*"

"*Sam, give me your hands, palms facing up. There. Now hold still while I peer into my crystal ball to—I will not say it again, Joe. Be silent or leave.*"

"*I was only coughing.*"

"*Shut* up, *Joe. Let her concentrate!*"

"*Yeah, whatever.*"

"*The crystal shows me you enjoy music.*"

"*I play the violin!*"

"*Hmm, yes. Practice. You will make a lot of people happy with that someday.*"

"*Really? That's great! Dad says I have to be an accountant because I'm good with numbers.*"

"*You will not be an accountant. You will be a thief and a gang leader. Now about this girl...*"

"*Wow, lady, isn't that, like, illegal to tell a little kid?*"

"*Ignore Joe. Focus on the girl.*"

"*Rosie?*"

"*That's the one. You have to stop letting her bully you. She's not your friend, Sam. She is only a selfish little girl who is growing up in her mother's* footsteps. Your lunch is for you, not her. Stand up for yourself at recess. Don't follow her around. Play with Wally, instead."

"Okay."

"Hmm. What would you like to know?"

"Is Wally my soul mate? Mom says everybody's got a soul mate and it doesn't have to be a girl. I don't want a girl for a soul mate. They're all stupid and play with dolls."

"Your soul mate's name is Leila. You will ensnare her with a pack of gum, then drag her home by her hair, much to your chagrin."

"Um…okay, but when? Like, sixth grade?"

"You will meet her in your attempt to take over the world, and once you find her, you will stop at nothing to obtain her."

"I don't want to take over the world."

"Yes you do. Deep down, you do."

"Hey, lady, that's really creepy, okay?"

"Shut up, Joe. So how do I take over the world? Wally says we need to make mind-control candy."

"Best-case scenario? You'll steal money from banks and large corporations, then dose yourself with experimental drugs that render you impotent because you're bored."

"Oh. Then will I at least get Starflight Jupiter for Christmas?"

"Your mother doesn't like video games."

"I know, but Wally's parents let him play."

"Don't worry about that. You'll get something nice for Christmas."

"You're not gonna tell me what?"

"And ruin the surprise? No, child. Ask me something else."

"This isn't very much fun. Kyle said it would be fun."

"The future's not always fun."

"Well, what about my dog? He's been sick. He ate some turkey bones at Thanksgiving."

"The bones punctured his intestines. Your dog is going to die in a week."

"…die? But we took him to the doctor!"

"The doctor didn't catch it in time. I'm sorry, Sam."

"You're a liar! Come on, Joe. I don't want to be here anymore. Let's go."

"Sure thing. Seeya, lady."

"Goodbye, Joe."

"Come on, Joe. I want to go home and see Max. That stupid psychic was wrong. He's not gonna die. Why did you stop? I want to go home."

"You go ahead. I'm gonna see if I can get your money back."

"I don't care about the money. I just want to go home."

"Just stay here. I'll be right back."

"Joe..."

"Stop whining. We did something you wanted to do, now just hold onto your horses for one damn minute and let me see if I can go get you a refund for that bullshit, okay?"

"All right."

"Good. Stay here."

"Welcome back, Joe."

"Hey, I want a refund. You really upset my brother. That's really crappy, scaring a little kid."

"What does the sign read above the door?"

"Don't Ask Unless You Seek The Answer? That Buddhist or something?"

"It's a warning."

"Huh. Uh. Yeah, well. I guess I can't get a refund?"

"No."

"Okay. I'll be seeing you. I just wanna know one thing before I go. How'd you know my name? You hear Sam say it outside the tent or something?"

"I knew it the same way I know your mother's name is Alice and your father's name is Harold."

"Huh. Uh. You think I could get the rest of the thirty minutes' worth? I mean, Sam isn't gonna use it."

"If you wish."

"Cool."

"Sit across from me and put your hands on either side of the crystal ball, palms up."

"You really need to do that? I mean, it looks really stupid."

"I certainly don't want to make you feel uncomfortable. Just get comfortable a moment. Ah. My. You're a difficult one to read. Most couldn't even do it."

"Oh no, it's clear...for now. I said most *couldn't do it. Let's see here. I'm going to go into a slight trance, and I want you to remain still, all right?"*

"Yeah, okay."

"While on Ko-fat, you will enter Congress into a new Age."

"Wait, what?"

"Shh. Be silent and listen. You will make friends with a White assassin, and at his command, a Jreet heir shall remove your still-beating heart from your chest and deliver it to strangers."

"Lady, you're really creeping me out."

"This is important. Shh. It has four parts, and you'll only ever hear this once, for no one else will be able to see through your vortex once it starts. Now, where was I? Ah, yes. After a battle the likes of which the universe has never seen, you shall have the cosmos' greatest mind helpless under your boot, and your mercy shall unmake him."

"Okay, how about we go back to talking about turkey bones. Seriously, are you on crack?"

"And while you shall die in a cave, shamed and surrounded by dragon-slaying innocents, your deeds will crush the unbreakable, and your name will never be Forgotten."

"That's...nice. You said Sam had a soul mate. What about me? I'm having a real hard time finding a girlfriend. Dude, why are you sighing? That's a legitimate question, okay? That crap about Sam being a gang leader and me being in Congress is stupid. I hate politics. And Sam's too smart to be in a gang."

"You will have a soul mate."

"Really? What's her name?"

"She doesn't have a name."

"O-kaaay. Uh. Where's she live?"

"She hasn't been born yet."

"Look, if you're just fooling around, I'm gonna leave."

"Go ahead. You already paid."

"Yeah. Well, shit. Okay. (cough) So I've got this...thing..."

"It's called claustrophobia."

"Uh. Yeah. That. It makes it a little hard to get in a car, you know? Dad says I'll get over it, but I don't really see how. Like, it's still just as bad as it was when I was little. I see blood. You know? Covering everything. I get in a tight space and I see blood everywhere. You think I'll get over it?"

"Of course. After you spend a few hundred hours screaming."

"…"

"I take your silence to mean you have no other questions?"

"That's really not cool."

"You asked."

"I'm really afraid of tunnels, lady."

"Of course you are. You're going to die in one."

"…"

"Out of questions, then?"

"What am I gonna do for a living?"

"You're going to invade enemy planets."

"Dude. I'm not five, okay? What the hell kind of reading is this, anyway? We haven't even been out of our solar system. How the hell are we going to invade other planets?"

"You'll find out soon enough."

"You're one hell of a psychic, lady. You take classes on being a pain in the ass?"

"I went to Harvard, if you must know."

"What'd you do, cheat on the tests?"

"I advise you to use the remaining time to focus on your own future."

"All right. After I'm done invading enemy planets, what's gonna happen to me?"

"I told you. You're gonna end up disgraced and impoverished, living in a cave with a group of naked innocents who can slay dragons, telling bedtime stories to little girls who make delicious cookies out of dirt."

"Okay, that's it. I've had enough. I think your drugs wore off, lady. Keep the money. You'll need it in the nuthouse. I hear if you're really good, you can bribe the guards to let you play with crayons."

"Enjoying your monthly visits to your Aunt Caroline, Joe?"

"Shut up. How'd you know that? Did Sam's stupid friend set us up? You know what, how about I go tell the fair manager that you're all drugged up? Won't that be funny?"

"Tell Max he's a good dog for me."

"Screw you, lady."

"Joe."

"I said *screw you*, lady!"

"Joe!"

"Bugger off!"

"Stop swearing! You want Maggie to learn to cuss? You stupidhead."

Joe sat up. The entire room was lit in shades of scarlet. He stared at Libby, wide eyed. "The dog died."

"What?"

"The dog died. A week later, just like she said."

"You're really creeping us out. What dog? There aren't any dogs here."

And she was right. There was nothing but a domed black room with a hazy red light and a few scared little kids wrapped in metallic blankets. Scott was holding Maggie, who was watching him with wide, teary eyes.

"Sorry," Joe muttered.

"What was that all about, Joe?"

"Nothing," Joe said. "Bad dream."

• • •

The next morning, Battlemaster Nebil woke them early. As soon as Joe opened his eyes, he realized that the silence of the ship had been replaced by a deep humming that seemed to reverberate through everything around him.

"Get up!" Battlemaster Nebil shouted. *"Collect your things and line up in the gymnasium. We're docking at Kophat."* Then he was gone, opening a door further down the hall to wake its occupants.

"I can't carry all this," Elf whined, tugging on his sixty pounds of gear.

"I can," Monk said, sticking out her tongue. With Scott's help, she shrugged herself into the shoulder straps of the pack, but within moments she had succumbed to the gear and was squatting on the floor, panting.

Joe watched her, worried. "Scott, can you carry yours?"

"Yep." Scott threw his rifle over his shoulder, only staggering a little as it settled atop the back of his pack.

"What about you, Libby?"

Libby, who was bigger than Elf, managed to get the pack over her shoulders by herself, but despite the determined look on her face, couldn't lift her gun along with it. She refused to let Joe have it, though, and held it by the shoulder-strap to drag it.

"All right," Joe said, glancing at Maggie. She was four or five inches taller than she had been when she left Earth, but she was still tiny. "I'll carry Mag's stuff. Scott, Libby, you think you can help Elf and Monk? We only have to get to the gymnasium."

Libby gave Elf's pack a doubtful look, but shrugged. She and Scott began unloading pieces from the younger two's gear and stuffing it into their own packs while Monk and Elf watched.

That left Joe a hundred and fifty pounds, between his gun, Maggie's gun, Elf's gun, and two packs. He pulled a large piece of equipment—some kind of a camp stove, he was told, *sans* fuel—from his pack and gave it to Maggie to carry, lightening his load by six or seven pounds. Still, he staggered when he got to his feet.

"Ready?" he managed.

Libby and Scott were likewise weighed down, Scott carrying two rifles himself, and Elf and Monk looked even worse.

"Let's hurry," Joe said. "Mag, lead the way. Make it fast."

Maggie, her eyes wide, rushed out the door, clutching the piece of gear to her chest. She led them to the gymnasium, where they gratefully dumped their equipment on the floor and lined up by group, waiting for Commander Kihgl. Those battlemasters who had gotten them from their rooms stood encircling the walls, gripping huge rings set in the metal ribbing with their long, boneless fingers.

They had been standing for almost thirty minutes when the continuous humming suddenly shut off. The silence felt ominous, and it was followed with a sudden jolt that threw the children off of their feet. Several kids screamed, and even Joe wondered if the metal screeching was truly part of docking procedures, or really some rogue asteroid tearing a hole in their hull.

The Ooreiki, however, did not seem to think anything was amiss. They began bellowing orders, hitting those kids who were not moving fast enough. "Hurry and grab your stuff," Joe said, helping Elf shrug back into his pack. "Looks like we're here."

The lines into the docking bay were endless. *Like cattle going down a slaughter chute,* Joe thought, looking over the untold thousands of bald, frightened kids in recruit white. Libby and Scott began to pant under their burdens, sweat trickling down their strained faces. The hall grew cramped and hot from all the bodies packed together, and tempers flared. Up ahead, two girls got into a shoving match, stopping up the meager flow of traffic completely. Eventually the battlemasters broke them up and shoved them back into the stream of kids to get the lines moving again. Following the flow, Joe and his groundmates filed out into an enormous, windowed room resembling an airport terminal. Beyond the windows above him, Joe saw space and moons and…

His gut clenched when he realized he was standing on his head, the planet under him.

"It's *purple,*" Libby whispered.

"And it's *big,*" Scott said. "That's bigger than Earth, right Joe?"

Joe had no idea, and he said as much.

"But they said we were weak because Earth's got weak gravity," Scott insisted. "My Science teacher told me that bigger planets have more gravity."

"Oh man," Joe groaned, taking another look at the purple planet. "Guys, we're not gonna be able to carry this stuff."

"I can carry it," Maggie insisted.

"You're barely carrying anything as it is," Scott said, peering through the domed ceiling at their destination. "Maaaaan…"

Even in the terminal, the going was slow. More kids spilled out of other doors on either side of theirs and the terminal began to reek of sweat and fear.

Alert Ooreiki battlemasters guided them towards the shuttles, cuffing children who stepped into the wrong lines. As time went on, Joe watched the shuttles fill up and depart, dropping down into the purple swirls of atmosphere before returning for more. Then Battlemaster Nebil was harrying them onto a shuttle—a constant, nerve-wracking barrage of, *"Keep moving! Find a row and sit down! Stop gaping and move, you slack-jawed Takki nitwits!"*

Once they secured their gear, they sat down on the benches, hands in their lap as Battlemaster Nebil marched up and down the aisles, still shouting. When the deck was full, Nebil slammed the hatch shut and stood by the door, glaring at them.

"What if I have to—" Maggie began.

"Shhhh," Joe said. "And sit up straight. Nebil's watching."

Maggie set her jaw into a pout, crossed her arms, and slouched.

Sighing, Joe glanced out the window. Filling the glass was a bird's-eye view of the purple planet. Orangish clouds swirled above the purple haze like whipped cream atop hot chocolate in some brightly-colored circus drink. Beneath that, he could just make out a deep, blood-red landscape that remained static under the roiling orange clouds.

Joe got a sick feeling in his stomach as he looked down on the alien planet. Was that air even *breathable*? What if Congress had transported them all this way to die gasping on some freak purple planet? They were, after all, the first humans to make the journey. What if Sam was right? What if there was something in the air? It looked thick, almost like cloudy purple water.

The shuttle left the dock with a jolt, knocking a few kids from their benches. The Ooreiki wandering the aisles found them quickly and shoved them back into their seats, shouting in their guttural, clicking language.

Joe's eyes were fixed to the window as they descended through the orange clouds and into the purple haze. Far below, the red landscape began to break up into black, perfectly circular city blocks, with six black roads radiating outwards from each city like spokes from a wagon wheel, creating six triangles of wild red growth around each city's circle.

The roads were perfectly straight, despite the enormous mountains and twisting purple rivers. The only development on the planet's surface was kept strictly inside the black city rings. It was obvious to even an idiot that the whole planet had been planned, and the mastery the Ooreiki had over their people to create such perfect symmetry left Joe in awe. On Earth, the woods would have been pocked with foresters' camps, or weekend vacationers, or squatters. Instinctively, Joe knew that *nobody* on Earth had that much control over the people, to keep them all neatly contained like that. It was more than a little frightening.

One thing was for certain—if the Ooreiki were going for sheer psychological intimidation, the perfect spoke-like cities certainly did the trick.

As they descended, the scarlet foliage reached up to greet them. The trees—if they could be called trees, as massive as they were—spread their limbs thousands of feet above the planet's surface. Their trunks were hundreds of feet in diameter, packed together like sardines. On the forest floor, mosses and shrubs the size of redwoods created a secondary mat of foliage that blotted out the light. As they lowered onto one of the landing pads on the outskirts of a city circle, Joe thought he saw one of the redwood-sized trees move, then snap back.

He had just enough time to glimpse the enormous white guard towers posted every quarter mile around the city, with turrets facing outwards, before Nebil threw the door open and ordered them outside. The gravity on the ship suddenly increased, and Joe felt himself struggling to stay on his feet. Everything—even his *organs*—felt heavier. Like someone had injected him with lead.

"Leave your gear," Nebil ordered. *"Takki will bring it to you later."*

Holding onto the chairs and walls for support, Joe and the others shuffled to the door of the shuttle.

Immediately upon reaching the opening, Maggie wrinkled her nose and covered her mouth. "Ugh!"

"We'll be fine," Joe said. "Just keep going, Mag. They wouldn't take us somewhere we couldn't breathe."

Still, at the first whiff of the putrid, almost rotten smell to the air, Joe held his breath and slapped his mouth against his sleeve. Despite the cloth protecting his face, when Joe breathed in, he gagged. The stench dribbled down into his chest and pooled there in disgusting rivulets.

And the air…

He began to feel lightheaded, the air thick in his lungs. It was almost like he was breathing water. *Septic* water.

"I can't breathe," Elf cried. He grabbed at his throat and made a rush to get back on the shuttle.

"Stop!" Joe called, grabbing at him. Elf slipped past his grip and tried to shove his way back onto the ship, but Nebil slammed a meaty limb into his chest, throwing him back down the stairs.

Elf collapsed on the top of the ramp, mouth wide and gasping. Joe could hear his hyperventilating from the base of the steps, and could see his wide eyes as he stared at the enormous trees surrounding them, and the purple sky beyond.

"Elf, get down here!" Joe shouted. "They're about to take off!"

The Ooreiki were hurling their gear out the door like they weighed no more than lunch sacks. Guns, blankets, packs—all fell into the same tangled mess.

"Elf!"

Elf ignored him. His breathing became worse, a rattling, gasping wheeze.

He's hyperventilating.

Battlemaster Nebil emptied the last pack overboard and shouted at Elf to get off the stairs. When Elf ignored him, he made a disgusted sound and descended, leaving him there. The ship's engines began to hum.

Joe took off at a jog up the stairs. Immediately, he regretted it. He was only halfway up when he fell to his knees, his head swimming, his chest burning for air. The sudden jump in heart rate made his lungs reflexively drag huge breaths of the putrid atmosphere into his chest, yet even so, he wasn't getting enough air. He felt himself sucking in the foul stuff faster and faster, his body panicking as it was denied the oxygen it needed.

Joe forced himself to slow his breathing, pouring every ounce of will-power into striking a balance between the dizziness and the sick burning in his chest. He felt himself sucking in the putrid air, felt it coagulating in his lungs. Above him on the stairway, Elf was turning as purple as the sky.

"Elf," Joe said, "Close your eyes and count to three between each breath. You've gotta slow down."

"I can't *breathe*," Elf sobbed. Snot was leaking from his nose, tears streaming from his bulging eyes. If anything, he breathed faster.

"Yes you *can!*" Joe snapped. He forced himself to stand. "Stop breathing so fast! You're gonna pass out."

Too late. Elf's eyes rolled into the back of his head and his body went limp.

Joe struggled the rest of the way up the stairs and grabbed Elf's arm. As he did, the shuttle began to rock and the engines started to hum, and it was all he could do to drag Elf off the ramp before the vessel took back to the sky.

Gasping, Joe managed to drag Elf a few yards before his knees gave out underneath him and he collapsed to the ground. It was some sort of crushed black stone, like sparkling concrete, and it was all he could see through the band of red that was his narrowing vision.

The air is bad.

It was all he could think. *The air is bad. They've dumped us on a planet where the air is bad. They couldn't know how we'd handle it. We're the guinea pigs and the air is bad.*

Joe felt his numb hands slide through glittering black stones. Behind him, the shuttle roared back into the sky.

Joe could feel the thick sewage on his tongue, running down his throat, puddling in his lungs. And, despite the putridity of the air, he couldn't breathe it fast enough. His eyes were open and he couldn't see. He was staring at the ground between his numb hands, he knew, but he couldn't see. He couldn't *breathe.*

The air is bad.

Joe whimpered for his dad. His lungs kept sucking the rotten stuff into his chest. He knew he was dying.

The hand that touched his shoulder was neither an Ooreiki's nor his dad's. It was cold and scaly, with hard, blunted claws. They dug into his skin, trying to pull him to his feet, but Joe couldn't move. Joe got a single glimpse of huge, pupil-less sapphire eyes as a violet lizard began hefting him over its shoulder.

God, that's a Takki, Joe thought, as his world narrowed. Immediately, he remembered the Takki tunnels that the Ooreiki kept talking about, and his heart began to slam in panic, hastening his descent into darkness.

10

KIHGL'S CHOICE

Joe woke in an inky room with a low ceiling, only about seven foot clearance. The walls were glittering black rock, the glassy waves and edges reminding him of obsidian as they gleamed in the deep scarlet light of the glowing red globes suspended in a straight line between rows of circular bunks to the open door.

Then the feel of the putrid air in his chest returned to Joe in full force, choking him. Joe sat up and dry-retched onto the rippled black floor. His lungs began to struggle again, his breaths coming in quick, ragged gasps.

"Careful," Libby said, grabbing his hand. "Breathe from this." She held a white cylinder over Joe's lips and Joe felt cool oxygen bathing his lungs.

Then, too quickly, Libby pulled the cylinder back.

"More," Joe gasped.

"No," Libby said. "Battlemaster Nebil said we only get one. Some of the other groups already used theirs up. Just try to breathe slowly. See? The rest of us can do it."

Joe forced himself to breathe despite the urge to gag, taking several minutes to prove to himself he wasn't drowning in his dad's septic tank. Once he had his itching lungs under control, he surveyed the sullen faces peering up at him from the fifteen alien bunks inside the room with him. The beds were sitting on low shelves set into the ebony rock, and most of the kids in the place were watching him expectantly. Maggie looked like she had been crying. Monk's lips were pressed together unhappily, her nose wrinkled. Scott looked almost green. Elf looked wide-eyed and scared, on the verge of hyperventilating again.

After scanning his face a moment, Libby drew her black, scabbed knees up and wrapped her arms around her long legs, setting her chin on her knees to watch him.

"Where are we?" Joe said, glancing around. The place appeared to be a cave, dug into a cliff-face.

"The barracks," Scott said, motioning to the other groups of kids in the room. They were all sitting on large circular beds, half-hidden by the niches of rock that cradled them. Chests made from the same icy blue metal as the shock collar sat at the end of each bed. Piled atop each chest were six stacks of black Congie uniforms. Beside the big round beds, tall, open niches had been dug into the rock. Their rifles hung inside, and their packs lay neatly on the floor beneath. Someone had even taken the time to fold their blankets.

"The lizards did that," Monk said, following his gaze.

"Those were *Takki*, Monk," Scott said. His voice almost carried the same disdain that Nebil and the other Ooreiki carried whenever they said the word, and Joe frowned.

"What about the canned air?" Joe was feeling a strong urge to gag again as the rancid atmosphere dribbled down his bronchial tubes and pooled in his lungs. Trying to fight down his desperation, he added, "Any idea how much is in here?"

"Not a lot," Scott said. "Those guys ran out in ten minutes." He pointed at the bed beside them, where all of its occupants were sprawled out, gasping piteously.

Joe took the device from Libby and peered into the tube. It appeared to be just that—a tube. When he depressed the red button in the side, however, he could feel a rush of cool air against his face. He quickly released the trigger.

"Battlemaster Nebil said they want us to adapt to this place," Libby said. "That we're gonna be living here for three turns."

Three…turns? "Why do these bastards do everything in threes?" Joe muttered.

"Maybe they think it's lucky," Elf said.

"Maybe that's how they count," Scott said. "We count by ten. Maybe they count by three."

"Maybe the first Congies only had three fingers," Elf said.

"Or six," Scott said. "Three on each hand."

"Ooreiki have four," Maggie said. "I can count to four, Joe."

"And that pretty purple lizard had six fingers on each hand," Monk added.

"That was a *Takki*, Monk," Scott said.

"At least I didn't pass out, *Scott*." Monk raised her chin proudly, "Joe, everybody but me and Maggie passed out, but Scott passed out first. The Takki had to carry him like a baby." She stuck her tongue out at Scott, who sighed.

But Monk went excitedly on. "Takki sorted us by number and stuffed us into this tower. Each battalion has a different level of the tower and there's nine levels and there's these circular stair thingies that go back and forth around each level like my mom's front deck that she made Daddy build her and there's a bunch of different doors, one for each platoon, and we got Fourth Platoon. I was listening to them and they said that only eight of the nine levels got filled and it's all your fault and they should gut you for it. Why's it your fault, Joe?" She paused, blinking at him expectantly.

Joe reddened as Libby and several of the other kids glanced up at him with curious looks. "Uh…" He swallowed, hard.

When he didn't answer immediately, Monk heedlessly went on, "This is all of Fourth Platoon. They were carrying kids away from the landing pad for hours, and they're still only now waking up. Battlemaster Nebil was mad. Said we're already behind the rest of the regiment and we don't need to sleep. Said we—"

"Wait," Joe said, "You're *sure* they were Takki? Like Commander Linin's pictures?"

The others nodded at him.

Joe's heartbeat quickened. He had been hoping it had been some sort of oxygen-deprived hallucination. If there were Takki nearby, then there might be Takki *tunnels* nearby. If there were tunnels nearby, they might want Joe to go down them. And that wasn't going to happen. Ever.

"You look scared," Maggie said. "Don't be scared. They're a little smaller than you, Joe. They don't even have really big teeth. And they're pretty. Like Mommy's necklaces."

Monk nodded vigorously. "They looked like big rubies."

"Rubies are red," Scott said. "Not purple. *Amethyst* is purple."

Monk glared. "*I* was the one that saw them, *Scott. You* were passed out."

Scott rolled his eyes. "If you knew anything, you'd know—"

His words were interrupted by a deep rumbling sound that sounded like someone gouging a chalkboard with an ice pick. Immediately, everyone grouped up closer to Joe, nervously looking at the open doorway.

"What is that?!" Joe said, standing. He could feel the vibrations in his lungs, the reverberations rattling his very bones. It sounded like an upended freight train screeching sideways down a highway.

"It's been doing that ever since we got here," Libby said.

"But what *is* it?" Joe asked.

"We don't know," Scott admitted. "But it's been coming from all over. And sometimes it's quiet, too, like it's a long ways off."

"I wanna go home," Elf said softly.

"I don't. *I* wanna see what's making that noise," Monk said, sticking out her tongue at Elf. Immediately, Elf looked like he was going to cry.

"Hey, guys," Joe said, "calm down. Be nice, Monk. I'm gonna go see what I can figure out, okay?" He stood, then caught himself on the wall as an immediate wave of dizziness hit. A sharp pain in his palm made him yank his hand back, however, and when he examined it, his hand was cut from where it had slid across the glassy black surface. Seeing himself bleed, Joe felt a surge of panic once again welling up from within. Since when did walls *cut* people?

Fighting his growing alarm, Joe took two deep breaths, trying to ignore the sickening way the putrid air clung to his lungs. When he was pretty sure he wasn't going to vomit all over himself, Joe opened his eyes and scanned the corridor of beds to the door. The exit was only a rounded hole in the wall, and yet it appeared to be several stories above the ground. Between the door and himself, the ridges and waves of the floor rose in deceptively elegant lines—enough to cut his feet to shreds.

"They give us boots and gloves for this?" Joe asked, eying the floor apprehensively.

"Yeah," Scott said, pointing to the pile of black gear atop the chest. "But Battlemaster Nebil told us not to put anything on until he teaches us to do it right."

Joe snorted. "I can dress myself." As the kids watched, he gingerly stepped across the floor and examined the pile. He found the largest outfit, pulled it loose, and unfolded it. His breath sucked in.

It was identical to a Marine cammi jacket. The material, the feel, the bagginess, the cut…the only thing that was different was that it was jet black.

Joe slipped his arms into the sleeves and settled it over his shoulders. It felt good to have something substantial on his body again. The flimsy white shorts and T-shirts from back on the ship had left him feeling exposed. *Probably their intention, the jackasses,* Joe thought, disgusted.

As he had seen his father do a thousand times before, Joe buttoned the jacket, then pulled up his pants and stuck his feet into the hard black boots. He laced them up, pulled the pant legs over the tops, and stood up. He didn't have any way to secure the cuffs of his pants like he'd seen his dad do because he had no bootbands, but he made do by tucking them into the tops of his boots. Then he pulled the heavy, leathery gloves over his hands, marveling at how the material seemed to mold to fit his fingers, almost like a liquid, yet remained tough and durable.

Once he was fully dressed, Joe took a moment to look himself over. It felt like he was missing something, but he couldn't put his finger on what was nagging at him. He glanced at the others. "So what do you think?"

"I think you're gonna get clobbered," Scott said. Libby nodded her agreement.

Joe scoffed and strode to the door. He could feel the eyes of the other children following him as he walked.

The Ooreiki hadn't even bothered to place a guard.

And why would they? Joe's heart began to hammer painfully as he stared out at the foreign landscape. They were a good fifty feet from the ground. Even from here, he could see the purple sparkles where the black rock of the plaza reflected the sky. It was a deep glassy ebony, apparently the same material the building was made of, but crushed.

Joe's stomach cringed when he glanced up. The buildings were huge onyx cylinders a thousand times bigger than any skyscraper. Framing the purple sky, they were so tall it seemed like they bent inward, creating a barred dome above him. Joe looked away before he fell over.

Out across the crushed black stone plaza, the massive bases of the huge obsidian buildings had stone stairways carved into the outer rims, snaking around the buildings and attaching to wide, railed balconies that encircled every story like the one upon which Joe stood. Black elevators moved up and down the sides carrying a flood of purple lizards and col-orfully-garbed Ooreiki. The glow of electricity lit up the windows of the enormous structures, reminding him of the office buildings back home. Massive, arched bridges hung between them, allowing four lanes of traffic in either direction.

Joe stared, feasting his eyes upon the skyscraper city. The Ooreiki, in particular, fascinated him. Instead of a constant, uniform black, these wore every color of the rainbow, their clothes shimmering oranges and reds and purples that fluttered around them in shawls and scarves and skirts and ribbons. Those that weren't walking along the highways encircling the buildings were traveling between the skyscrapers over the massive bridges with little open platforms that hovered over the ground without wings or any other visible means of keeping themselves afloat.

When Joe finally pulled himself back inside the barracks, Maggie said, "They made them from the trees."

Joe blinked at her. "Huh?"

"The buildings." Maggie tapped the wall behind the bed with a tiny knuckle. "They're *trees*."

Joe gave a derisive snort. "They're not tr—" Then his mouth fell open as he stared at the glossy, obsidian-like material. He glanced outside again, looking at the enormous circular skyscraper pillars in a new light. It was so obvious, once he thought about it. The buildings were the same size and shape as the massive white alien 'trees' surrounding the city.

From somewhere outside, the scraping sound came again, a distant rumble that seemed to come from beyond the city limits.

"I want to go home," Elf whimpered, cringing closer to the wall. "Can I please go home, Joe?"

"Scaredy-cat," Monk taunted. "Elf's a scaredy-cat, nie-ner nie-ner *nie*-ner—"

Joe scowled at Monk. "We'll go home, Elf. We just gotta find a ship to take us."

Elf's hazel eyes flickered up to Joe's face in wretched, painful hope. "Really?"

Joe winced, suddenly understanding *exactly* why none of those parents ever told their kids where the Congies were taking them. "Uh, yeah. We're just waiting for our ride. As soon as we find us a ship, I'll hotwire it and get us home, okay? No sweat." He patted Elf's shiny bald head.

Despite how stupid it sounded, Elf seemed to take that at face-value. "Okay, Joe," he said, giving him a shaky grin. He glanced outside at the huge skyscrapers and swallowed, taking visible courage from his lie. "A ship. Okay."

Joe turned and realized Libby was watching him much-too-closely, a small scowl of disapproval on her young face. He flushed and immediately dropped his hand from Elf's head. Feeling guilty, he cleared his throat. "Uh, yeah, Elf? There's really no way to—"

Joe was interrupted by the heavy boot tread of an Ooreiki behind him. When he turned, Secondary Commander Kihgl was standing in the corridor of big circular beds. The Ooreiki's sudah were fluttering, reminding Joe of the motion of the fins on a cuttlefish.

Kihgl motioned at the door. *"Come with me, Zero."*

Joe tensed, sensing that something was not quite right about the secondary commander's abrupt appearance. For one, he wasn't flanked by battlemasters and tertiary and small commanders. For two, Kihgl's stiff, almost nervous demeanor was sending warning signals through Joe's brain, his body language utterly opposed to the calm, confident— and always angry—façade the aliens put on for training their recruits. The normal Ooreiki reaction would have been to pound Joe senseless for disobeying orders and putting his clothes on. Kihgl, on the other hand, kept glancing over his shoulder like he was worried someone would see him.

"Where you going?" Joe asked, nervous that Kihgl hadn't called forth any of the other children. That was never good.

Kihgl's pupils narrowed on him in icy black slits. *"Today is not the day to question me, Zero. Come with me. Or don't."* The way the Ooreiki said it sounded almost…permanent. Then he turned and trod back down the hall, his booted feet clunking hard against the stone, giving Joe the option to follow or stay behind. Having heard something dangerous in Kihgl's voice, Joe reluctantly fell into step at a wary distance.

The Ooreiki led Joe to a small floating platform resting on the deck outside.

"Get on the haauk."

Kihgl climbed aboard the platform, then waited impatiently as Joe first nervously put one foot, then the other, on the inexplicably hovering device. It had no buzzing or whirring, no mechanics that he could see at all. When it began to slide sideways, Joe clenched the railing until his knuckles were white and he kept his eyes on the floor to keep from seeing how unnaturally the thing moved…almost as if gravity didn't even exist to it. Joe's stomach clawed its way toward his feet as the craft jumped over the banister and out into open air with the grace of a gazelle.

As the haauk dropped away from the barracks and skimmed above the plaza below, Joe nervously eyed the glittering black courtyard surface, knowing it would cut like shards of glass if the haauk tumbled them out onto it.

But it didn't. They shot smoothly across the plaza then dove between the first of the skyscrapers, Kihgl navigating the narrow roads between the massive buildings a little too quickly. Joe watched uneasily, but held his tongue thinking that the Ooreiki had a quicker reaction time than humans. When the craft scraped against a staircase hard enough to leave a streak of metal, however, Joe knew something was wrong.

"What the hell?" he shouted.

Kihgl ignored him.

"Hey!" Joe cried, touching Kihgl's arm. "Where are you taking me?!"

Without taking his attention from the road ahead, Kihgl lashed out viciously, nearly knocking Joe from the platform. Joe caught himself— barely—on the railing and backed away, his nerves giving rise to panic.

Oblivious to Joe's rising fear, Kihgl pulled onto a main avenue that shot between the enormous trees. The sixty-foot-wide road was strangely empty.

On either side, utterly mind-bendingly massive white trees towered above them, increasing Joe's anxiety. Unnatural black things that looked like barnacles clumped together on the surface of the white trunks, each one the size of a small car. Joe noticed a house-sized, turtle-like creature clinging to a trunk. As he watched it, the thing closed its jaws over a barnacle and its flat upper tooth scraped the surface of the protrusion. The screeching chalkboard sound that followed was enough to shatter glass. Joe slapped his hands over his ears, but Kihgl never even looked up, focused entirely on the road in front of him.

He's taking me out of the city, Joe realized, his heart beginning to thunder in his ears. *Where there's no witnesses.*

Kihgl flew for hours in silence, saying nothing, not even acknowledging Joe's presence on the skimmer. Joe had begun planning how he was going to try and make a break for it when Kihgl brought them to a halt in a huge, circular clearing with only a few jagged stumps where buildings should have been.

No, Joe realized, getting a better look. *They* were *buildings.* The clearing looked like it had been flattened by a bombing run. Shattered alien megaliths—the massive tree-like formations in which the Ooreiki made their homes—lay everywhere, honeycombed with caves and the remnants of sidewalks and bridges.

Kihgl veered from the road and took them across the ruined landscape, the destroyed buildings passing beneath them.

"Was there some sort of war?" Joe asked, watching the shattered ebony edifices over the edge of his skimmer. Everywhere, he could see pits of varying sizes whose shadowy entrances seemed to fade into darkness, almost like…

…tunnels.

Joe's fists clenched on the railing and he suddenly felt weak. *Please let it be some sort of war,* he thought. *Please let it be some sort of horrible war and those be bombing holes.*

"Training-ground," Kihgl grunted. It was the first thing he had said to Joe the entire trip.

Kihgl brought them to a halt at the edge of the ring of destruction, almost touching the root system of one of the massive alien trees. He put the haauk down between three of the ruined buildings, the stumps shielding the hovercraft from view of the distant roads.

This is where he kills me, Joe thought. His lungs began to labor for air and he grew painfully close to another gasping attack.

"Here." Kihgl shoved a white cylinder at him.

Joe stared at it. Would Kihgl really give him oxygen if he was going to kill him?

"Walk with me." Kihgl climbed off the hovercraft and started through the jagged forest of broken trunks, his gun gleaming on his hip. Reluctantly, Joe followed him.

"What's going on?" Joe asked once he caught up. He eyed the gun, wondering if he could take it before Kihgl broke a few more bones.

Remembering how fast the Ooreiki could move—and how violently—Joe quickly amended his plan.

"So, uh," Joe said, trying to break the ice as Kihgl marched them silently toward the undisturbed edge of the utterly enormous alien forest. "Where are we going?" There was something about Kihgl's mood that reminded Joe of his Aunt Caroline the day she bludgeoned her three dogs to death. The same week, they had put her into the mental institution.

Kihgl ignored his question and kept walking.

Nervously, Joe glanced up at the colossal pillars stretching to the sky above him. Because the silence was making him nervous and he'd never been good at keeping his mouth shut when his Dad gave him the quiet treatment, he babbled, "What are those things? Trees?"

Kihgl scowled, and for a moment, it looked like his secondary commander wouldn't answer him. Then, reluctantly, Kihgl turned his sticky brown eyes up at the canopy. *"Not trees. The closest approximation I can give you is a form of mold. The branches at the top are not there to consume light, like Earthling trees, but to spread spores. That is what makes the sky purple and the air sweet."*

"Sweet?" Joe snorted. "It stinks like my grandpa's porta-potty."

Kihgl immediately gave him an irritated glare. *"Your Human home was a rotting ball of biowaste and the air was as stale and tasteless as the inside of a ship. It's a pity our ferlii cannot grow on such a fetid mishmash, or I would have brought some along."*

The idea of Earth suddenly becoming a dark, sweltering, stinking ball of huge alien mold spores left Joe with a whole new respect for 'invasive species'. He swallowed, hard. "So, uh, ferlii? That's what they're called? What are they made of? Are these—" he rapped his knuckles on one of the black stone foundations of a fallen building, "—ferlii?"

"Yes."

"What is this stuff?" Joe asked, frowning at the black stuff. "It's like glass, but harder."

"It is a carbon composite. The ferlii deposit it on the inside as they grow. Hundreds of billions of them make up one tree. They draw carbon from the air and digest it."

Joe stared at the building, remembering his last geology class. Mostly-pure carbon, he knew, came in a few very useful forms: oil, coal, and diamond. The little hairs on the back of his neck started to raise as he considered that. "Wait a minute. That's too hard to be coal."

"It's not coal, furg."

"It's *diamond?*" Joe blurted. No way. Just no way.

"It's carbon. Diamonds are only valuable on your backward, carbon-poor planet. Congress controls whole planets made of diamond."

Joe squatted and touched the stone at his feet. It was crushed, as he had thought, a glittering mat of sharp black crystal. He stood up, bringing a diamond with him. When he held it up, he could see through it. It was at least ten carats, totally flawless except for the near-obsidian darkness to it. Enough to buy him a palace, back on Earth. Joe dropped it back to the ground.

Standing again, he hurried to catch up with Kihgl, who was still walking towards the multi-layered alien forest. "Where are we going?" he asked again.

Kihgl ignored him and kept walking. *"Ferlii are a blessing to a planet,"* he went on. *"They create ten times the living-space. If you look, the branches of ferlii are woven together so tightly that you cannot see the ground. Many species exist in the upper canopy that have not seen the underbrush in millions of years, when their ancestors decided to climb to the top to see what was up there. It was so with the Ooreiki, back on Poen."*

Nervous that he wasn't answering his question, Joe nonetheless asked, "And what *is* up there?"

"*Spores,*" Kihgl responded. "*The richest concentration of nutrients on the planet. It can be eaten raw or gathered by the shipload and distributed to factories for distillation. Any planet with ferlii will not starve.*"

"It won't see the sun, either," Joe muttered, "And it'll stink like crap."

Kihgl kept walking. Something about this little jaunt toward the woods was bothering him. Joe's palms grew sweaty and he watched Kihgl closely, planning out his next move. Humans could run a lot faster than Ooreiki. Almost twice as fast. At the first sign of Kihgl reaching for his gun, he was going to sprint back to the hovercraft and try to get it running before Kihgl caught up.

Still, when Kihgl stopped suddenly, swung around, and put the barrel of his gun in Joe's face, Joe could only stare at it. The tip was swirling with shimmering waves of heat, an indication that it was charged and ready.

"*Tell me why I shouldn't kill you, Zero.*" Kihgl said, his voice cold. "*What are you going to do that will make it worthwhile for you to exist and me to die? Why should you live when I'll lose everything?*"

Joe lifted his eyes from the gun to Kihgl's face. A million reasons flooded through his mind, but he could not pin down any one of them. He was a kid. He missed his family. He liked to play football. He hadn't said goodbye to his new friends. How would Maggie survive without him? Scott wasn't big enough to get them a ball whenever Tril made them race. They'd all starve until they grew up, and neither Scott nor Elf would grow up to be more than five-eight or five-ten from malnutrition.

"My groundteam," Joe said.

Kihgl's gun never wavered. Despairing that he had said the wrong thing, Joe waited for the shot to come, knowing that running would only make Kihgl pull the trigger faster.

Ages ticked by. Centuries. Millennia, and still Joe stared down the barrel of that gun, waiting. Then, slowly, Kihgl lowered his weapon. The moment of silence seemed to stretch into eternity, Kihgl not offering anything and Joe afraid to ask.

Finally, the Ooreiki said, "*I was going to kill you, Zero. I planned on it since the day I saw your mark. I planned out how I would hide your body,*" *how I would explain your disappearance to Lagrah, how I would take the penalty for losing a recruit. If you'd whined about your youth, about your family, about how you wanted to be a good soldier, I would have shot you."* He tucked the gun back into its holster.

Joe held his breath. *So that means he's* not *going to shoot me?*

Kihgl was silent for several more moments, picking rock dust from a gouge-mark in the black stone that almost looked like tooth marks in an apple. With his back to Joe, he said, *"I killed someone today."*

Joe felt goosebumps break out all over his body.

"A Peacemaker. He was just doing his job, researching what he had been ordered to research, but I had to stop him. I had to save your life, just in case the Trith was right."

"Right…about what?" Joe asked weakly.

Kihgl fixed him with an intent stare. *"About the fall of Congress."*

Joe did not know what to say.

"I made it look like an accident, but only time will tell if you evaded them. Whatever happens, I will be gone. My fate has already been decided."

"So you're not killing me?"

Kihgl continued to pick at the rock. *"For as long as anyone can remember, there's been a prophecy that spells destruction for Congress. The Fourfold Prophecy. Nobody tells it more than once, since the more times it is told, the more chances Peacemakers will hear it."* Kihgl turned to face him. *"So I will tell it to you."*

Joe felt goosebumps prickle his arms again.

"The prophecy arrived soon after the eight original species banded together to create the first Regency. It originated in four separate places at once, two of which Congress hadn't even discovered yet. It says a race will one day rise up against Congress and win its independence, and that Congress will smash its armies to pieces trying to bring it back. The Dhasha believe they are the ones, but their revolts always end in defeat. It makes the believers think that it will be one of the new species we discover. Some, like Nebil, are even foolish enough to believe it could be Humans."

Joe was unsure what to say. Kihgl still radiated a feeling of instability, like he was only a heartbeat from yanking his gun from his belt and blowing Joe away, despite what he had said. Carefully, Joe ventured, "You think it could be humans, too."

"Not Humans. You're too frail. I think it will be something else. Something new." Kihgl turned back to the wall. *"But it's hard to deny the power in a Trith's stare."* The Ooreiki looked like he wanted to say more, but didn't.

"Did you really save my life?" Joe asked.

"Kkee. The Trith said I would." Kihgl glanced at the horizon and seemed to steady himself. *"Every soldier must endeavor to avoid the Peacemakers, but now you must be doubly sure not to fall under their scrutiny. Along with the prophecy of my death, the Trith told me that the bearer of your mark would in all probability die. There was only one path you could take to save yourself, and out of the infinite possibilities in someone's future, it is not likely you'll choose it."*

"The Trith talked about *me?*" Joe asked, stunned.

"He did."

Caught completely off guard, Joe simply blurted, "What did he say?"

Immediately, the secondary commander's expression darkened. *"My fortune was for me to know, not you,"* Kihgl said harshly. *"If the Trith want you to know anything, they'll come to you personally. Just pray they don't. A Trith never gives the whole prophecy."*

"The whole…prophecy? They tell futures?"

Kihgl snorted. *"They* are *the future, boy. They walk in it as we walk in the present. If one comes for you, run. Don't listen to what he's got to say. Just get as far away as you can. Tell the Peacemakers you saw one—but never tell them it came for* you. *That's a death-sentence as surely as quoting the Fourfold Prophecy."*

Joe was getting more and more freaked out, realizing that he was finally recognizing the odd tone he'd first noticed to Kihgl's voice. The secondary commander was speaking as if he had already accepted his own demise… and was counseling Joe on how to avoid the same fate. "Okay," Joe said slowly, "What does a Trith look like? How do I avoid them?"

Kihgl flicked the rock chips from his fingertips and turned to him. *"Trith look like what Humans thought aliens looked like before Congress discovered your planet. Small and gray. Big heads, black eyes. Somehow, you knew. Nebil thinks it means you Humans are the ones."*

"But why would they visit us?"

Kihgl looked across the ruined city and seemed to think about it. *"To give you something,"* he finally suggested

Joe snorted. "If they gave anybody anything, they gave it to the government and the government hid it from us. That's so typical. They should have *told* us."

"Maybe it wasn't something to be told," Kihgl said, his pale brown eyes returning to him. *"Maybe it was something to be used."* And, in that moment, Joe almost thought he saw…hope…in his secondary commander's eyes.

Joe couldn't help but snort. "If they did, lot of good it did us when Congress attacked."

Kihgl stiffened as if he had personally insulted him. *"We didn't attack. If we'd attacked, your backwards planet would have been annihilated right down to its last insignificant iron atom."*

Which, Joe realized, was probably pretty damn close to the truth. He swallowed nervously, deciding a change of subject was appropriate. "Why was somebody investigating me? Was it for what I did on Earth?"

Kihgl snorted. *"Tril reported my collection of Prophecy-related artifacts. The Peacemakers are conducting an investigation. Soon they're going to find that ever since the Trith visited me, I've spent large portions of my life researching the Fourfold Prophecy. It's enough to have me executed, just like the Trith predicted. If they find a way to connect you to the drawing in my personal files, they'll execute you, as well. The Peacemaker I killed was sifting through the ship's files, examining the time I took you to my dormitory. I had to destroy his brain sac so they could not access his memories of the symbol on your arm."*

He really saved my life. Joe swallowed hard, dread thickening into an intestine-squeezing ball in Joe's gut. "You're serious, aren't you? You killed someone to save me?"

Kihgl made a croaking grunt. *"It's custom for a Trith to make four prophecies during a reading. He did so with me. Three of the four have come true. I don't have a choice. I never did."*

"Yeah, but prophecies can be vague. Like I said about the cave—"

"These weren't vague. These were precise, right down to the moment each would die."

"…each would…die?"

"Three very good friends. The Trith told me where and when I would watch each of them die."

"What was the fourth prophecy?"

Kihgl hesitated, his huge brown eyes showing his first hint of real fear. *"He said I will die frightened and alone on Kophat, with no one to carry my oorei to Poen because it will be destroyed."*

Joe felt a wash of goosebumps roll down his back and arms. He didn't know what to say. How did someone argue with a prophecy? It was like trying to argue politics or religion—it was no use because Kihgl was already convinced. And Kihgl looked…terrified. Clearing his throat anxiously, he said, "Poen's the place with all the ghosts?"

Kihgl looked away a moment, seeming to steady himself. *"If an Ooreiki does not get his oorei carried to Poen, he will haunt whatever place holds his oorei until he is taken home. Even a rebel Dhasha prince will gather up the oorei on a battlefield and return them to Poenian priests rather than risk the wrath of the dead."*

"So what happens when they're destroyed?" Joe asked softly.

It took Kihgl a long time to respond. When he finally did, he swept a handful of pulverized rock from atop a ruined building. *"They dissolve,"* he whispered, looking at the specks of obsidian he had collected into his hand. *"Like dust in the wind."*

"So what are you going to do?" Joe asked nervously.

Kihgl tossed his fistful of rock dust at the ground. *"I don't know. It's too late to kill you."* Kihgl started to head back the way they had come, then paused. *"Here."* He tugged a black circle the size of a large bracelet from his arm and held it out to Joe.

Joe gave it a wary glance. Another shock collar?

"It's not a modifier, you furgling," Kihgl growled. *"It's a kasja. Give it to Battlemaster Nebil so he knows of my choice."* Kihgl shoved it into Joe's hand. The thing was distinctly alien, though its black, utilitarian curves were unmistakably military in origin.

"Take off your shirt." Kihgl withdrew the small black ranking device from his vest and waited as Joe reluctantly unbuttoned his jacket. Joe got goosebumps as Kihgl reached forward, touching the cool metal to his chest.

He's marking me as one of them.

"I don't want it," Joe said suddenly. He threw the *kasja* on the ground between them and slapped Kihgl's rubbery tentacle away from his chest before he could finish. "I'm not fighting for Congress. I'm going home."

As soon as he said it, Joe knew Kihgl would kill him. As Kihgl's sudah began flipping like enraged hummingbirds' wings in his wrinkled neck, Joe backed up a pace nervously, tensing. Too fast to dodge, Kihgl whipped a heavy, stinging tentacle around Joe's neck and shoved him forward so that his face landed in the glassy dirt beside the black armband. *"Pick it up. You don't want battlemaster, that's fine. The kasja is a message for Nebil."*

Joe realized at that moment he would pick up the *kasja* or Kihgl would kill him. He picked up the *kasja*.

"Don't even think *about putting it on. You don't deserve it."* Kihgl's eyes glinted with rage as he spun and returned to the haauk.

Having the distinct feeling he could follow or be left behind, Joe struggled to catch up.

11

THE TRIBUNAL'S VISIT

When Battlemaster Nebil found Joe fully dressed, he was not amused. Joe tried to give him Kihgl's armband, but the Ooreiki stared at it so long Joe wondered if he'd done something wrong. Finally, Nebil said, *"You'll wear it. To remind yourself what he's done for you. I ever see you without it, I'll kill you."*

Joe stared. "But Kihgl told me not to—"

"Kihgl is dead," Nebil snapped.

Joe's heart skipped. "But I just talked to him."

"A day, a week, it won't matter. He's dead. And you're the cause. Let you remember that, when you live and he dies. Now put it on."

Biting his lip, Joe slid the armband over his wrist and up his forearm. It settled comfortably over his bicep, under the cloth of his uniform, though to Joe it felt like the thing had been made of cold, heavy lead. He wanted to get rid of it, to do anything except have it there, on his arm, strangling the muscle.

Apparently, Nebil did not mind the fact Joe had hid it under his sleeve, because he barely gave it a passing glance before launching into a tirade about his state of dress.

"Can't you follow one simple instruction, Zero? Tuck your shirt in. Pull your pants out of your boots. What do you think you are? An Overseer? Take it all off. No, not the kasja. *You'll wear that 'till you die. Start with*

your boots. You want to be dressed so badly, you can teach the others how to do it. Start over."

Battlemaster Nebil made Joe dress and undress eight times before allowing the others to begin putting their clothes on. By that time, after the stress and septic air sticking in his lungs, Joe was close to vomiting. He sat down on one of the groundteam beds to catch his breath, Kihgl's *kasja* tight on his arm.

"Zero, is my instruction so dull that you must sit down to endure it? Stand up! Where's your rank? Kihgl thought you were battlemaster material, yet all I see is a fat primate without a star. Why didn't he rank you, Zero? He must've changed his mind, eh? You do something to piss him off, you stupid janja turd? Get up and start sprinting up and down the aisle. As fast as you can. Don't stop until I tell you."

Joe, his lungs already struggling for breath, was in a near-panic. He knew he couldn't run without vomiting up the meager bowl of *nuajan* that he'd swallowed that morning. He started to shuffle along, desperately trying to keep his breathing under control. It felt like somebody was shoveling the contents of a porta-potty down his bronchial tubes, filling them until there was nothing left to absorb air.

Joe never knew Battlemaster Nebil had snuck up behind him until his casual blow sent him sprawling. *"You stinking puddle of shabba vomit! Run. Let's see how long it takes you to soil your shirt like a Jahul. Recruit battlemaster my ass. You've never excelled in anything. Your only strength is you were bigger than the rest of them when you were Drafted. I give you eighteen tics before you pass out like a Takki."*

Joe stood, fighting to keep his breathing under control. This was the first time Battlemaster Nebil had singled him out, and before this, Joe felt as if he had some sort of understanding with the Ooreiki.

At his hesitation, Nebil hit him again, sending him back to the floor. *"What makes you think you should be here instead of Kihgl? You don't deserve it. You can't even follow simple orders. Look at you. You're just a frightened Takki. Get up. Get up! You ferlii-eating primate get your Takki-loving ass off the floor before I puncture it with my foot."*

Joe sat up, struggling for air. The edges of his vision were fading again and Joe gripped the bed nearest him to keep from passing out.

Nebil reached down and wrapped a tentacle around his throat. Into his face, Nebil said, *"Kihgl thinks you're battlemaster material, but you're not. You're just ungrateful, selfish Human slime. You're not worthy of his sacrifice."*

Looking into Nebil's furious brown eyes, Joe knew he spoke of Kihgl's decision to let Joe live, not the lack of a battlemaster's star. *Nebil blames me. He thinks I should have died.*

Another Ooreiki had appeared in the doorway and used that moment to make his presence known.

"Did Kihgl really choose Zero as a battlemaster? Has he lost his Jreet-loving mind?"

Battlemaster Nebil wrenched around to glare at Small Commander Linin. *"If Kihgl wants to waste his recruit potential, that's his prerogative. It's gonna come from* his *hand, though. I'm not gonna attach my name to this sootbag."*

"Sometimes I think that seventh point sucks all the rationality out of them."

"Don't I know it." Battlemaster Nebil reached down to haul Joe off the floor. Before Joe was quite balanced, Nebil shoved him across the room, towards the others. *"Until Zero proves he's worth more than a wad of Takki soot, Kihgl can kiss my ass."*

Commander Linin gave an amused snort. *"Regiment formation in thirty-six tics. Commander Lagrah says the Tribunal arrived this afternoon and wants to inspect us. "*

Battlemaster Nebil froze, his sudah fluttering suddenly. *"Ghosts of Takki curse them! Don't they know we're two weeks behind?!"*

"And we haven't even met our Prime yet. Kkee, the fire-loving jenfur-glings know. But they've already inspected twenty other cities and don't want to delay, so whose ghost is our Prime to tell them to wait? Dhasha or no, they don't give a Takki soot."

"They didn't make Lagrah Prime?" Nebil demanded. *"He's already got the rank."*

"The planetary Overseer decided that every new Kophati regiment should be run by one of his sons. And apparently he's got enough sons. You ask me, the sooter's making a move to rebel. In the Old Territory, the damned furg."

The little gill-like *sudah* were fluttering ever-faster in Nebil's neck. *"Rethavn? I thought they convicted him and sent him to Levren."*

"Overturned the ruling," Linin said, with an Ooreiki grimace. *"When authorities went to pick him up, he'd gathered all of his sons together in his palace and the Peacemakers wouldn't touch the place."*

"The gutless Takki cowards." Battlemaster Nebil turned to the rest of his platoon. *"You heard him! Everyone outside. Form up at the base of the stairs. Zero, you'd better get off your ass or you'll be puking up your liver after I'm through with you. I'll be damned if I'll give a Takki bastard like you battlemaster. You're lucky I'm gonna give your unworthy ass squad leader. You! You look like you'd make a better battlemaster than this lazy charhead. Get up here and get them moving!"*

Sasha stepped forward like a startled deer, her jutting lower jaw hanging open in shock.

"Now, recruit!" Nebil bellowed.

"Everybody down the stairs!" the piranha-faced girl shouted. "That means you too, Zero!" Smug satisfaction oozed from her words, making them come out in a sneer.

Joe struggled to his feet and managed to follow everyone down the stairs and into one of the ragged lines on the crushed black glassy material of the plaza. Every step was an act of desperation. His gut was roiling and his vision was a narrow strip by the time they finally came to a stop.

Once they were together, Battlemaster Nebil led them across the plaza, their lines jerky and crooked. As they marched out across the obsidian gravel, Joe glanced up and his nausea returned. Overhead, the tall Ooreiki buildings seemed to close together in a cage above them, the buildings creating a dome of seemingly endless black poles against the violet sky.

We're never getting out of here, Joe thought. He had to fight the urge to run, to keep his steps short and fast to keep up with the kids around him. *We're on an alien* planet *and we're going to die here.* Never before had he felt so cut off from everything he had known, so utterly abandoned by humanity, than he did marching out between those enormous pillar buildings, surrounded on all sides by curious alien onlookers.

On the other side of the field of crushed rock, eight other battalions already stood in formation, their lines straight and symmetrical. The

Ooreiki in charge of each battalion were standing out in front, not even having to supervise their recruits, who stood straight and tall with their eyes forward and their hands clasped tightly in front of them.

Marching up to their place three spaces from the end, Joe realized how sorry Sixth Battalion appeared compared to the rest of them. Not only were the others physically bigger, almost fully-grown, but they actually looked confident. *How could we be this far behind?* Joe wondered. The last time he had seen the kids from those battalions, huddled together in the gymnasium, they had been toddlers and little kids, like Monk and Maggie. Now, they looked like *adults*.

We're in trouble, Joe thought, with a pang of unease. The other recruits actually looked like soldiers, not scared little kids with bald heads.

When Nebil's platoon tried to join up with the nine other platoons in Sixth Battalion, there was confusion as to where they should stand and how, and soon all the lines were broken and kids began milling in little groups, panic in their eyes.

The other Ooreiki noticed this and began converging on them, scattering amidst the ranks to help Kihgl rearrange his formation. Several Ooreiki's eyes caught the bulge under Joe's sleeve, but aside from giving him an odd look, they continued to usher kids into their assigned places. Joe began to sweat, not only because his platoon looked like garbage compared to the other battalions, but because the *kasja* caught the attention of every single Ooreiki that passed him, like they could see straight through his jacket.

Maybe it's glowing in another spectrum, Joe realized anxiously. *It could be shining under there like somebody turned on a damned flashlight. Damn it. Kihgl's going to* kill *me.* Joe wondered if there was some way to get rid of it without causing a scene.

A deep blast of a horn boomed out over the plaza, rattling the very air in his lungs. Kihgl's battalion jerked nervously, but the recruits from the other nine battalions stood absolutely still, unfazed.

After a few minutes, a commotion near the back of the formation made Joe turn. Of the three aliens walking along the back row, Joe only recognized one of them—the little blue-green Ueshi. It was even more rubbery in real life than it had looked in Commander Linin's pictures, its skin a translucent, ocean color that looked more like a type of plastic than living flesh. It waddled along beside an enormous blue abomination that looked like a freak experiment between a Smurf and a boar. The shambling monster had beady red eyes and shaggy, bright blue fur that hung around stubby, circular feet. It walked with the lazy grace of an elephant, and was about as big. Its sharp black tusks stretched ten feet out in front of it, threatening to skewer anyone who got in the way. Joe stared—until an Ooreiki yanked his head back to the front.

"*That's the First Citizen, asher. Keep your fire-loving eyes forward.*" Commander Linin's eyes fixed on the *kasja* and he froze. "*Where did you get that?*"

"Kihgl wanted me to give it to Nebil, but Nebil made me wear it. Would you give it back to—" Joe reached under his sleeve to pull it off his arm, but Linin stopped him.

"*Give it back to Kihgl your own jenfurgling self. A* kasja *like that should be in a temple on Poen, not my dirty fingers.*"

Linin looked like he wanted to say more, but he glanced at the inspecting aliens and moved to harass another child who was also staring at the blue monster. Joe returned his attention to the trio marching behind them.

Beside the shaggy blue alien, a slender creature with downy white fluff covering its body strode awkwardly on three tentacled legs. About its cylindrical torso flowed a paper-fine cloth-of-gold cape that glided over the ground as it walked. The creature had two enormous, electric-blue eyes that darted alertly from recruit to recruit inside a triangular, squid-like head that was indistinguishable from its neck. When its unnatural, ghostly gaze settled on Joe, his heart skipped and he quickly looked away, a flutter of fear in his gut. The First Citizen and the Ueshi were ugly, but something about this thing scared him.

When the three aliens moved closer, Joe was stunned to hear a human voice—an *adult* human voice—coming from one of the three. He turned back.

The creature with the golden cape was looking directly at him. Beside it, a full-grown human man had stopped and was frowning at Joe. He was balding and short of stature, with a sweaty, nervous aura about him. He was taking repeated puffs on the white cylinder he gripped in one hand. Joe's hopes soared. An adult! Maybe he was here to bargain for their release!

"No, your Excellency, none of them are above age."

The shaggy blue alien responded in a rough alien chatter and the glittering golden band around his left tusk translated it into English. *"That is good, Mullich. For a moment I feared you Humans were foolish enough to install spies in our great army."*

The downy white creature was still staring at Joe, its intelligent, lightning-bright eyes never moving from Joe's face. *"He has something around his arm,"* the downy creature's translator said.

"I don't see anything," the sweating man replied, frowning at Joe.

The downy creature stepped between the rows of children, toward Joe. Joe bit his lip and looked away, his back itching like it was on fire.

"The boy is probably wearing the wrong gear, your Excellency," the sweaty, balding guy replied. "This was the delayed shipment, after all."

"Perhaps." The word came from above Joe's shoulder. Joe flinched and turned.

The electric-blue eyes of the down-covered alien hovered inches from his face. Joe gasped and took a step back. The alien's arm snapped out, catching Joe's wrist in a flattened, stingless tentacle, the grip tight enough to break bones. It was all Joe could do to keep from crying out.

The alien pulled him back and held his gaze, the fishy, ostrich-sized eyes ethereal and penetrating, leaving him feeling like his brain was being scoured from the inside. It took Joe a moment to realize that the downy white hairs covering its body were writhing like filament-thin maggots, despite the fact that there was no breeze on the fetid planet. Watching the tiny white cilia twist and bend of their own accord made Joe's skin crawl. With its other paddle-like tentacle, the alien yanked up Joe's sleeve to reveal the armband.

"Who gave this to you?" the alien said, though it made no move to take it.

When Joe did not answer, it simply stared at him, waiting.

"Commander Kihgl," Joe whispered, wondering if the creature could bore into his mind with those strange electric eyes.

"What? What did he say?" the sweating man asked, mopping his brow.

"He said he found it," the alien said, dropping Joe's hand and allowing the sleeve to fall back into place.

"Can we move on?" the shaggy blue elephantine First Citizen demanded. *"This air is making me sick."*

"Of course, your Excellency!" the chubby bald man said, taking another puff on the white air tube and then hurrying to the tusked creature. "As you can see, human children are extremely intelligent and easy to train. They understand the great part they are playing for Earth's history and are pleased to serve the Congress. We haven't had a single escape attempt. They are honored to be here."

The downy alien standing beside Joe snorted. *"Honored? Who would want to escape on this disgusting planet? We spend much more time out here and I might require a respirator."* With one parting glance at Joe, the three-legged creature turned and threaded its way through the rows of children back to a spot beside the First Citizen.

To Joe's despair, the balding man followed the aliens further down the rows of children and none of them looked back.

He's leaving us. He's not even going to try to help. Joe turned back to the front of the formation and caught Commander Kihgl staring at him. Kihgl's sudah were fluttering, his eyes hard with fury. The armband felt like it was on fire where it touched his bicep under the cammi jacket. Joe swallowed down a lump of fear. *He told me not to put it on,* he thought, in agony.

Further down the formation, the three aliens and their human guide had stopped again, eyeing Second Battalion. Joe recognized Commander Lagrah at the head of the battalion, his scarred, pale, droopy-skinned body as still as stone as the Representatives discussed his recruits. Then they moved on. When they did, one of the little kids in the back row fell out of formation and ran towards them.

Before the child could reach the balding man, two enormous, serpentine aliens materialized out of nowhere, abruptly slamming the flat ends of their transparent, glassy spears into the child's gut and pushing her backwards, shouting in a language of clicks and pops completely different from anything Joe had ever heard before. The translators ringing their powerful scarlet arms said, *"Keep your distance from the First Citizen. Next time we take your head."*

With that dire warning, the two serpentine aliens vanished again, their scaled ruby bodies shimmering and then disappearing completely. Seeing that, Joe suddenly understood what Nebil had meant, back in their Species Recognition class. He was pretty sure those two Jreet could have annihilated all nine of the gathered battalions in Prime Commander Lagrah's regiment, Ooreiki and all, and nobody could have done a damn thing about it. They weren't *shadows* or *blurs* like Hollywood had portrayed invisible creatures in the movies. To all appearances, they weren't *there*. And they had to have been sixty feet long.

As the three Tribunal members went on, heedless, two Ooreiki battlemasters rushed from Lagrah's formation to pick the screaming child off the ground and spirit her off the plaza. The balding man wiped his brow and took another puff on his air tube, but then returned to his conversation with the enormous, shaggy blue beast.

The formation lasted another hour, giving the four Representatives a chance to circle the entire regiment three times before retiring from the plaza.

Once they were out of sight, Ooreiki barked orders and the eight other battalions began to move away from the plaza, their recruits moving as one. Joe and the rest of Sixth Battalion found themselves awed at the crisp movements, the sharp turns they made at the battlemasters' commands. Thousands of them, moving in perfect unison. It was awe-inspiring to watch.

Then Nebil grabbed Sasha by the collar and wrenched her violently out of formation. *"I said take them back to the barracks, you slithering wad of Takki waste! Are you deaf as well as stupid?"*

Sasha just stared at him.

"Now, janja scum!" Battlemaster Nebil bellowed. *"We already look like we've got our tentacles tied in knots."*

Sasha cleared her throat and did her best to imitate the Congie word for about-face. She was not loud enough, because only the kids nearest her complied. She tried again, a little louder. A full quarter of the platoon gave her a funny look.

"You sound like a Takki-loving spacer!" Nebil screamed into Sasha's ear. *"Say it like a* grounder, *recruit! I wanna hear the diamond rumble at the*

sound of your Takki-loving voice! I want to hear the ferlii crumble! I want to hear a spacer shitting himself in his plush little reclining chair all the way out in orbit!"

Sasha shouted again, and again Nebil shrieked into her ear that she wasn't loud enough. *"You sound like you've got a mouthful of Takki soot! Spit it out and try again! Zero, show this shabba turd how it's done before I use both your hides to decorate my shitter!"*

And just that fast, Joe became responsible for yelling the loudest, responding the quickest to commands, and making sure everyone else in the battalion did what they were told. Several times, Joe caught Sasha giving him a dirty look, but Joe knew it was a punishment more than anything else. Nebil had Joe at the front of the battalion the rest of the night, cursing him and yelling in his ear and kicking him if he did anything wrong.

And so it went on. All the lung-deep screaming left Joe dizzy and nauseous, but somehow he managed to keep from puking his guts out over the crushed black rock. Others were not so lucky. Nebil grabbed them and ruthlessly forced them back into formation. Then, while everyone was panting and struggling for breath, he made the battalion march endless laps around the enormous buildings, turning them at odd moments to head back in the other direction, forcing them to shout marching commands until Joe thought his lungs would burst.

Only after their feet were numb and their minds blurred with all the different commands Nebil had given them did their battlemaster allow them to return to the barracks. A few kids ran up the six flights of stairs in their enthusiasm to get back to their beds, only to end up gasping upon the steps, the putrid air overwhelming them.

It was then that Joe saw his second Takki. About a dozen of them crawled out of tiny side-tunnels that Joe had previously overlooked, gently scooping up those who had fallen.

The little lizards were covered in small round scales that, when Joe got close to them, gave the illusion of depth, making their whole bodies appear to be a multi-faceted gem. Joe found himself standing still, his mouth agape in wonder. *Maggie was right. They're beautiful.*

In seconds, they were out of sight, the fallen children cradled in their jeweled arms.

"Joe?" Scott called from several steps above. "You coming?"

Joe shook off his amazement and hurried after his group, a sense of hope rejuvenating him. *They're only five feet tall. Too small for Nebil to make us go down their tunnels.*

At the top of the stairs, Battlemaster Nebil was waiting for him. When Joe nervously tried to pass, Nebil blocked his path, the small black ranking device gripped in one tentacle. Nebil gave Joe a long, irritated look, his sticky brown eyes scanning his face in silence. Finally, he just shook his head. *"You're gonna need this, you stupid furg,"* he said, and grabbed Joe by the back of the neck in a stinging grasp. Holding him in place, Nebil snaked his arm under Joe's jacket and jabbed the small black device into the muscle of Joe's chest, in same place Kihgl had done when he tried to give him battlemaster.

Before he could start struggling, Nebil withdrew his arm and released him. *"Prove to me you can be a battlemaster. You're not getting it until you deserve it."*

Looking at his shirt, Joe realized that the silver bar of a ground leader was morphing into a triangle, though it still did not have the outside circle of a soldier. Nebil was already gone, stalking back down the stairs towards the plaza.

Joe stared after him, stunned.

Nebil had almost sounded...*pleased* with him.

12

REPRESENTATIVE NA'LEEN

oft, downy hands touched Joe's arm.

"Go back to sleep, Maggie," Joe mumbled. "It's not time to get up yet."

"Of all the Humans, Ko-Na'leen had to choose a stupid one."

Joe jerked awake and found himself staring into impossibly huge, electric-blue eyes. The tiny white hairs covering the creature's face were writhing on their own, like millions of microscopic worms protruding from its skin. Shouting, Joe leapt out of the covers and landed on the far side of the bed, cutting his feet on the glassy floor. He was naked except for his underwear and the *kasja*.

There were two of the three-legged, squid-like aliens watching him, one who had woken him and one waiting near the door. Both of them followed Joe impassively with their huge, white-blue eyes as he gingerly checked to see how badly he had injured himself. The cuts weren't deep, but they were enough to slicken the floor beneath him with his own blood. Once he was sure he wasn't going to bleed to death, Joe straightened and studied the aliens. They were easily six feet tall, dressed in glimmering shades of green trimmed with gold, not Congie black. Somehow that made Joe wary.

The alien closest to the door cocked its triangular head at Joe, its electric-blue eyes utterly unreadable. Like mirrors. *"Looks like it might be difficult. Use the tranquilizer."*

The one near the bed pulled a pen-shaped object from the vest it wore, the vertical slit above and between its eyes puckering together rhythmically, like a heartbeat.

Joe stiffened. Without boots to protect the soles of his feet from the glass, he wasn't going anywhere fast. "I'll come," Joe said.

"What did it say?"

"I'm not sure."

"Well, be sure to use the low setting. We don't want to kill it."

"I said I'll *come!*" Joe said, holding up his hands. "Don't you dare shoot me, you stupid squid bastards."

"Careful, that's a sign of aggression."

Joe frowned at the guard near the door. "No it's not." But he lowered his hands anyway.

Behind him, Elf whispered, "What do they want, Joe?"

Joe never took his eyes off the alien with the pen-shaped tranquilizer. "They want to recruit me for some obscene alien fornication ritual," he told him.

"What's that?" Maggie asked, wide-eyed.

"Don't worry about it, Mag," Scott said, grinning.

Slowly, to prove he wasn't resisting, Joe went to his clothes. To the aliens, he said, "I'm getting dressed. You try shooting me with that thing and I'll break you flimsy bastards in half. Understand me?"

The one with the pen-shaped object pointed it at Joe.

"Don't!" Joe snapped, picking up his boots and shoving his feet inside. He winced as the cuts in his soles stung from the rough treatment. "Dammit, I'm getting dressed. See?" He began to dress as quickly as he could.

The alien watched him a moment, then grunted and yanked a small translucent sheet of papery film from his chest. He ran the pen-shaped object across a slip of the clear blue film, leaving a squiggly mark. This it affixed to the wall above the bed.

At Joe's stunned expression, the white, squid-like alien gave him a flat electric stare and said, "In case anyone wonders where we are taking you for our obscene fornication rituals."

Joe's jaw fell open.

"You *talk!*" Maggie cried.

"A bit. Your vocal cords are easy to make, but hard to control." His voice was high-pitched and musical, like a eunuch in choir, almost too sing-song to understand.

"You can't *make* vocal cords," Monk said matter-of-factly from the bed. "Mom taught music. Your *vocal* cords make *sounds.*"

Unlike the Ooreiki, the downy creature showed no emotion in its flat face whatsoever. "Well, if we didn't reproduce the cords, how would we reproduce the sounds?" When Monk frowned at him, he added, "Hurry, please. We are wasting time."

"All right," Joe said, throwing his jacket over his shoulders reluctantly. "What do you want?"

The alien looked him up and down and took a moment to reply, obviously considering whether or not it was worth wasting the breath to tell him. Finally, with a condescending sneer, he said, "Our employer, Ko-Na'leen, Representative of the Huouyt, wishes to see you."

Joe froze. "That guy who inspected the regiment yesterday?"

The Huouyt closest to Joe glanced at his companion, clearly amused. "Ti'peth, if Ko-Na'leen does not want this one, I might have to claim him. He might liven up those long hours on the ship." He looked back at Joe, the amusement gone in an instant. "Do you realize that referencing one of the Tribunal members so casually would get you sold to the Dhasha if it were within a Jreet's hearing?"

Joe stiffened, remembering the huge serpentine creatures that had shoved the little girl to the ground. "The Jreet?" He nervously glanced at the door, wondering if any of the snakelike monsters had followed them inside.

It wasn't a question, but the Huouyt took it as one. "They're the bodyservants of the Representatives of Congress--the only species that can kill a Dhasha in true hand-to-hand combat. They train as Sentinels for their entire lifetimes before choosing their wards. Ko-Na'leen has had over two hundred pledge to him. More than twice that of any Representative in a thousand turns."

Joe's face twisted. "They're pricks."

"You should learn to guard your words," the closest Huouyt warned. "You never know when a Jreet is around, and if they hear you, they will claim you so they can torment you for years for your disrespect."

Joe recoiled. "*Claim* me? I'm a soldier."

"Not yet," the one guarding the door replied. "Right now you are fair game to any ranking citizen who shows any interest in you."

"*Wait* a minute!" Joe shouted. "They recruited us for the *army*. Not to be some ball-less snake's slave!"

"Then I advise you watch your tongue," the Huouyt said. "But the question is moot, anyway. Ko-Na'leen has already claimed you."

Joe's heart began hammering. It sounded like they were about to take him from his groundteam. Permanently.

"Now follow us, please." The Huouyt motioned toward the front of the building.

"No." Joe took a step backwards, toward the wall.

The Huouyt's electric-blue eyes sharpened predatorily fast. "You have no choice, boy."

"Actually, he does," Libby said from the bed. "The rules say a Congressional citizen can only claim recruits with no formal rank." She gestured at the triangle on Joe's chest. "He's not just a ground leader anymore. He's the squad leader for Fourth Platoon."

In that moment, Joe could have kissed Libby's feet.

To Joe, the two Huouyt looked like owls that had suddenly been defeathered, dumped in bleach, and electrocuted. They stared at the silver symbol on his chest and Joe could almost see their plans changing in their heads. They glanced at each other, obviously considering taking him anyway.

"Want us to get Battlemaster Nebil?" Libby said, getting up. "He's sleeping in the next room. All I'd have to do is yell." She held the aliens' eyes unflinchingly. Joe stared at her, wondering where she got the courage. They both knew Nebil couldn't hear them if they shouted, not with the wall of diamond separating them.

The Huouyt ignored her as if she didn't exist. His accusing electric eyes were on Joe, and he sounded angry. "When did this happen? You were a still ground leader yesterday afternoon when Ko-Na'leen saw you."

"Yesterday evening," Libby said.

"He marches good," Maggie added.

The Huouyt just gave him a flat, almost sociopathic stare. "Why?"

"Nebil decided he liked the way my butt looked in cammies," Joe said, crossing his arms. "If that's all you wanted, you should leave."

The downy cilia moved in sudden, vicious waves upon the Huouyt's body, then suddenly relaxed. "I was going to wait to tell you, but since you are being difficult, I'll tell you here. Representative Ko-Na'leen has questions about your age. He believes you were wrongly enlisted. He wants to send you home."

Joe tensed. They wanted to send him home?

"You're lying," Libby said. "You just said he wanted to claim him as a slave."

"For his own good," the closest Huouyt said. "If it was discovered that he was here illegally and then discharged, the Dhasha would take him before he even had a chance to exit the proceedings."

"Don't believe them, Joe," Libby said, her unwavering gaze leveled on the Huouyt. "They're lying."

"Ko-Na'leen is a believer in law, else he wouldn't be on the Tribunal," the closest alien said to Joe, still ignoring Libby. "If the Ooreiki broke the law when they took you, it is his way to put things right."

Joe ached inside at the thought of seeing his family again. He looked away.

"Joe!" Libby said. "They're just trying to get you out of the barracks." She was glaring at the aliens again, clearly waiting for Joe to back her up.

"I'll go," Joe whispered.

Libby flinched and turned to stare at Joe, looking stricken.

"What's going on?" Maggie asked, her small voice suddenly going high with worry. She was glancing from Joe to the aliens and back, fear in her eyes. "What's going on, Joe?"

"Don't worry about it, Mag," Joe said. He moved toward the aliens, leaving his groundmates staring after him in confusion. "Let's go." Behind him, he felt Libby turn away.

The two Huouyt quickly ushered Joe outside and to a very elaborate, palanquin-type metal platform parked outside, giving him no chance to change his mind. No sooner had he climbed aboard their haauk then they were airborne and moving at high speeds toward the civilian side of the city.

The building they aimed for was taller than any of those nearby, two or three hundred stories, easy. "Only the First Citizen gets higher quarters," the pilot said proudly as they approached. "It is a place of honor in the city."

Joe swallowed and closed his eyes. He'd never been afraid of heights, but the vast emptiness between him and the ground left his stomach weak and his skin sweaty.

The craft settled in a round indentation on the roof of the building. "This way," the Huouyt said, disembarking the platform and walking to a dark staircase cut into the glossy black stone.

This far up, the air was thinner and not as putrid. Still, Joe followed quickly, feeling as if the slightest gust of wind would whip him off the building and into the empty space beyond. As he stepped onto the staircase, Joe saw a brief crimson flash of a large serpentine body down below before it was gone again.

His guide saw it, too. The Huouyt's face remained utterly expressionless, but his voice held irritation when he said, "One of the new Jreet trainees. His commander will hear of his carelessness."

The Huouyt made Joe lead the way down the narrow passage. As Joe felt his way down the glassy black stairway, Joe got the sinking feeling he had made a mistake. Libby's look of betrayal haunted him, slowing his steps even further.

The hallway ended abruptly in a door. His guide pushed past him long enough to open it, then motioned Joe inside.

Behind the door, the first thing Joe noticed was the air. It was fresh and full of oxygen—such a relief that it took him a moment to realize his guide was locking the door behind them.

Before Joe could comment on it, though, his breath left him at the sight of the Representative's inner sanctum. He had been expecting a nice chamber for a member of the Tribunal, but the palace that unfolded in the hallway before him left his mind reeling. The black walls were alive with colorful tapestries, and elegant carvings of alien objects decorated every niche. Gold and silver and other colorful metals had been inlaid into the perfectly smooth, glassy floors in eye-boggling scenes of alien battles and scenic alien landscapes. A thirty-foot golden statue of the Huouyt who had examined Joe's *kasja* stood in the center of the hall, with things looking like fishing worms jutting from the slit above its eyes.

Everywhere, tables, floors, and corners were all piled with statues, carvings, rugs, paintings, and gemstone-encrusted vessels. It was enough wealth, in one place, to make a sultan or a pharaoh weep. Joe could only stare.

"Ooreiki are famous for their art," a translator from across the room said. *"Representatives will often debate for several turns to obtain the right to visit an Ooreiki planet, simply for the gifts they provide."*

Joe turned toward the sound of the voice.

The Huouyt with the cloth-of-gold cape stood in the corner, watching him, a small golden translator dangling from his shimmering metal clothing. His cigar-shaped chest was fitted with a swath of silver cloth that looked as if it weighed fifty pounds. Worked into the front in alternating colors of metal gleamed the symbol of the Tribunal—three red circles inside a silver ring, surrounded by eight blue circles formed into two sides facing off against each other. Joe could *feel* the power radiating from this creature, and it made his palms sweaty.

"Forgive the mess," Representative Na'leen said, giving the piles of treasure a dismissive gesture. *"My slaves are still sorting through my gifts."*

Joe flinched at 'slaves,' but he couldn't find the words to reply.

The alien behind Joe made a musical twitter and Representative Na'leen blinked his big fishy eyes and responded in kind. The two Huouyt then engaged in a long string of whale sounds until the assistant suddenly turned and departed.

When the Representative turned on his translator again, he was not happy. *"Ti'peth says I can't have you."*

Joe stiffened. "I'm a Squad Leader for Fourth Platoon."

"You must be very proud," Representative Na'leen said dryly.

Joe suddenly felt ashamed. After trying so hard to win Nebil's approval on the grounds the evening before, he *had* been proud. Proud of a pathetic alien rank that had been given to him by an enemy army, an insignificant skidmark on the seat of his brother's underwear compared to the power of the creature in front of him.

"You would enjoy being in my service, Human. Zol'jib and Ti'peth have gained much status in society, much more than they would have as Eelorian draftees."

"They said you might be able to get me home. That's why I came."

The Huouyt gave him a long, completely unreadable stare. *"Come with me,"* Representative Na'leen said.

Joe lost all sense of direction as the Huouyt led him down halls and passageways, through a silken curtain to a small room with a hovering blue orb in the far corner of the room. As Joe drew close, he could feel the warmth emanating from it and backed away, wary.

"It's the heating element," Representative Na'leen said. *"They ban fire on this miserable planet. Too many combustibles."* Na'leen mounted a large black pedestal in the center of the room and immersed himself in the pool of liquid it held, golden cloth cape and all, sloshing waves over the side of the bowl. *"What's your name, Human?"*

"Joe Dobbs." Joe hadn't intended to tell him, but something about the alien's electric-blue stare made him blurt out things he had meant to keep to himself. . It almost felt like Representative Na'leen could already read his mind and was just waiting to catch him in a lie.

Representative Na'leen removed the golden translator and set it on the lip of the pool beside him. Then he sank into the pool, submersing himself completely. The water began to click and vibrate and the translator on the lip of the pool said, *"Come up here where I can see you."*

Joe climbed the ramp in trepidation, the tread of his boots catching on the ribs carved into the black stone. As soon as he was at the top, he recoiled. Under the water, jutting from the slit above the creature's eyes, a blossom of hundreds of little red worms wriggled around like something on a coral reef. Joe felt his stomach lurch and he backed up a step.

"Are you hungry?" Still submersed, Representative Na'leen shoved a bowl of small, gummy orange discs toward him along the lip of the pool. When Joe declined, the Huouyt plucked one from the pile and delivered it to the wriggling worms protruding from his face. The worms locked

around it and dragged the morsel deeper into the Representative's body while Joe watched in horror.

"Do you know why you are here?"

Joe tore his gaze away from the writhing worms. He had to stare at Representative Na'leen's face a moment before he could remember. "They said you might be able to get me home."

Na'leen watched him. *"The kasja you are wearing is an Ooreiki war medal. Specifically crafted for a battlemaster who survived the fight on Ubashin. It is very valuable to collectors, since so few Ooreiki actually survived that fight, almost none of them of the rank of battlemaster or below. Those that received them guard them jealously, which is why I know you did not steal it. The only two Ubashin veterans in the city of Alishai happen to be in your Battalion. Both of them were watching me when I raised your sleeve."* Representative Na'leen paused, his electric gaze boring into Joe's skull. *"Why did Secondary Commander Kihgl give you his kasja, boy?"*

"I don't know," Joe said truthfully.

"He said nothing when he gave it to you?"

"He said to—" Joe cut himself off, realizing he didn't want to involve Battlemaster Nebil. "He said it was to show his decision."

Representative Na'leen assumed he was speaking of his new rank as a squad leader and quickly cut him off. *"A lie. Your uniform shows your rank, not a kasja you didn't earn."* Representative Na'leen pointed at the silver triangle on his chest. It was exactly like the one that Battlemaster Nebil wore except it lacked a fourth point and did not have the circle around it that Nebil's had. By itself, without the protective ring that signified a full-fledged soldier, Joe's rank looked naked. Childish.

"I was curious why he would do such a thing, so I examined his file. It seems Kihgl's personality underwent a radical shift after visiting Reuthos forty turns ago. His command even went so far to have him evaluated to make sure one of my kind hadn't assumed his identity, as some of us are wont to do." Representative Na'leen's flattened tentacle dropped another orange morsel into the water above the wriggling wormy appendage in his face. *"I find the fact that he was examined for a Huouyt to be especially telling—it had to have been something serious for his command to request a screening."*

The Huouyt paused, watching Joe unflinchingly as his wormy appendage slowly drew the orange morsel into its head.

Examined...for a Huouyt?

"What the hell is that supposed to mean?" Joe demanded.

The water moaned and clicked with Representative Na'leen's reply. *"Evolutionarily, before Congress discovered them, my kind were forced to mimic other creatures in order to survive."* Representative Na'leen dropped another gummy orange disc into the water. The Huouyt paused, watching Joe unflinchingly through his bath as his wormy appendage slowly drew the orange morsel into its head.

Joe frowned, both fascinated and disgusted by the display. "Mimic them how?" He couldn't see how this...*thing*...could mimic anyone. It looked like a cross between a jellyfish, a squid, and some odd new form of coral.

Still underwater, Representative Na'leen waved a paddle-like hand in dismissal. *"We were discussing Kihgl. Not only did he survive the Dhasha on Ubashin, but he also managed to capture a Huouyt assassin three days out of Planetary Ops training. Two great feats that have made him a sort of hero to the Ooreiki here. Some of his other traits fascinate me. He has at least two Congressional victories credited to his name, and is also of the* vkala *caste—a hardship among the Ooreiki like no other."* The Huouyt hesitated, peering up at Joe through the water. *"Do you know what that means?"*

Joe swallowed and shook his head, not really wanting to discuss Kihgl.

"Vkala are a stubborn remnant from an intentional genetic manipulation many eons ago, during the formation of Congress. They are the reason why genetic experimentation is now banned. Because the Ooreiki would not go to Vora otherwise, the Ayhi took the Jreet's immunity to fire and gave it to the Ooreiki delegates in order to broker a peace between the first eight nations."

Joe frowned. "They're immune to *fire*? Wouldn't that be, like, a *good* thing?"

The Huouyt made a sound of disdain. *"Not to the Ooreiki. To them, it is a symbol of their ancestors' betrayal. They throw all* vkala *children into a pen with* onen *and allow the beasts to eat them as penance for their ancestors' sins. About one in ten thousand survive that pit battle. And yet, not only did Kihgl survive the vkala cleansing, but he somehow rose to become a Congressional hero."* The Huouyt paused, watching Joe with his unnerving eyes. *"So why has he given you, a Human recruit, what most Ubashin historians would die to have?"*

"Kihgl—" Joe froze at the sudden sharpness in the alien's face. The utterly casual, friendly way the Representative was addressing him had almost overrode the nagging little voice in the back of his mind screaming that the conversation was headed into dangerous ground. Wariness winning out, Joe said, "—didn't give it to me."

If the Huouyt was disappointed with his response, he didn't show it. He just plucked another gelatinous orange disc from the tray and said, *"And yet he hasn't taken it away from you, either. I found this mystery even more intriguing once I discovered Kihgl is once again being investigated as a traitor. This time for owning relics of the Fourfold Prophecy."*

Joe felt his skin crawling. So this was what they had brought him to Na'leen for. They didn't want to send him home. They were trying to get at Kihgl.

Representative Na'leen continued to pick at his food, though his huge oblong eyes never left Joe's face. *"I find Kihgl's history fascinating. Almost as if he had a...destiny...if one were to make such...leaps."* The Huouyt hesitated, watching Joe through the water, and Joe got the unsettling idea that the alien was gauging his reaction carefully. After a moment, Na'leen went on, *"He was trained for Planetary Operations by one of the most famous generals of our day, a Dhasha prince by the name of Bagkhal. He has survived sixteen battles that he had no right to survive. He is extremely intelligent, with dozens of successful reconnaissance missions to his name. He is a gifted saboteur, and his tour on Ubashin proves he has a knack for survival."* The Huouyt paused, watching Joe with his unnerving eyes. *"So what interest does he have in you? Why didn't he simply disappear when this latest Peacemaker investigation began?"*

Joe knew how dangerous the conversation had become. He had seen the fear in Kihgl's eyes. He knew he was a single word from a death sentence, and every nerve was vibrating on edge. "Um," Joe said, trying to sound as confused as possible, "I'm a recruit. I don't see much of Commander Kihgl."

Na'leen's eyes narrowed for a fraction of a second, then he went back to his food. Moving on as if Kihgl's investigation did not matter to him, he said, *"When I saw you in formation, I noticed you wore no recruit number. I thought this was an error until I asked about it. Is it true that Kihgl calls you Zero, boy?"*

Joe gave a wary nod.

"Why is that, when it is Army custom to begin at One?"

"Kihgl hates me," Joe said.

"And yet he gave you the kasja. Fascinating, isn't it?"

Joe did not like the way the Huouyt was watching him beneath the water, so he said nothing.

"I found that contradiction curious," Representative Na'leen said. *"So I examined the ship's records. Do you know what I discovered? You seem to be bright. I'll wager you can guess."*

Joe waited, unsure.

"There was no Joe Dobbs on the passenger manifest. Someone had erased you from the rolls. Do you know what this means? Zol'jib could tell you. It's what someone does right before that unfortunate passenger goes missing."

Joe felt a cold chill trickle over his body, like all the blood was rushing out his feet. He took a step backwards, feeling suddenly vulnerable.

"Careful. The Jreet are watching you, boy." Na'leen lifted his paddle-like arm from the pool and motioned languidly at the empty room.

Joe swallowed hard, glancing at walls.

"How old are you, Joe?"

"Fourteen," he said, a flush of hope lightening his chest. It was the first time any of the aliens had asked him that all-important question.

"You weren't supposed to be on that ship, were you, Joe?"

Hearing that, from someone with enough power to do something *about* it, made Joe's heart ache. "No," he whispered.

"Why were you?" Na'leen asked, plucking at his food.

"I helped some kids escape," Joe said, remembering Sam. "Before Commander Lagrah could get them to the ship."

"And they took you aboard to use you as an Unclaimed?"

Joe nodded.

"*But Kihgl accepted you, instead. Gave you a place in his battalion. Why?*"

"I don't know," Joe said.

"*I could offer to send you home, with the Congress's apologies.*"

Joe's head snapped up, his heart thudding. "Will you?"

Representative Na'leen nudged the orange discs in the bowl with his paddle-like finger. "*That depends on what you can tell me of this Kihgl.*"

Joe wanted to shout that he would tell him whatever he wanted, anything to get him off the stinking purple planet. Instead, he waited, his nerves taut with wariness. He felt like there was something he was missing, a deeper message in the conversation that he couldn't quite put his finger on, and it left him feeling like someone had a shotgun aimed between his shoulder-blades.

"*As I told you, Kihgl is being investigated again. The Peacemakers have already submitted proof of his guilt to your regiment's Prime Commander, but they continue to investigate because they desire to know why he was hoarding tomes and artifacts relating to the Fourfold Prophecy. A self-made scholar on the end of Congress. Everyone on his ship knew it, too, but his reputation was such that he went unchallenged until now.*" Representative Na'leen's eyes suddenly seemed to crackle with intensity. "*Has Kihgl said anything to you about the Fourfold Prophecy?*"

"No," Joe lied.

Representative Na'leen's electric-blue gaze hardened. "A Huouyt can spot a lie, Joe Dobbs."

Joe swallowed hard and looked down at his hands, which were even then cut and scabbed from the ubiquitous diamond chips that covered the planet.

"*I know a few things about the Fourfold Prophecy,*" Representative Na'leen said, still watching him. "*Would you care to hear it, Joe Dobbs?*"

Joe swallowed hard. "I thought guys were put in jail for knowing stuff about the prophecy."

Representative Na'leen waved a dismissive hand. "*Kihgl's case was... unique. He had intimate knowledge of the Prophecy. What I would tell you, everyone already knows.*"

"Okay," Joe said nervously. He didn't really *want* to learn any more about it, but he also got the idea that if he didn't go along with the Huouyt's idle conversation, his assistants might do something nasty—like haul him outside and throw him off the roof.

Representative Na'leen visibly settled himself in the water. Then, taking another gummi disc, he said, "*The Fourfold Prophecy first appeared during the Second Regency, during a time of unrest between the first twenty members of Congress two million years ago.*" He cocked his head at Joe. "*I believe your people were still living in caves, yes?*"

Joe grimaced, trying not to feel utterly insecure that this creature's genes had been around long enough to watch man evolve out of apes. "Maybe."

"*It is nothing shameful,*" Na'leen said, apparently guessing the cause of Joe's displeasure. "*That your species is still evolving is exciting, indeed. You haven't reached your ideal genome, yet, which means your genetic code still allows for change. Most sentient races are fully evolved before we discover them. In fact, the scholars find your entire planet highly interesting.*"

Realizing the Huouyt was talking about Joe and his species as if they were an intriguing form of bacteria in a petri dish, he muttered, "You were saying something about a prophecy."

"*Ah, yes.*" The Huouyt made an amused sound. "*The Fourfold Prophecy seems to have originated in four places at once, at different corners of the galaxy. It is rumored that the Trith were involved, though no one has been able to verify that. What's important is that in each of the four prophecies, it is said that a new species will emerge that Congress will only crush itself trying to conquer. This species will have an 'extraordinary genetic makeup that tests the boundaries of science.' An obvious reference to Huouyt's ability to take other species' patterns.*"

Joe felt his curiosity piqued at yet another inference that the Huouyt could change shape. "You guys really transform?"

"*We do,*" Representative Na'leen said, gesturing enthusiastically. "*But that is not the most telling part of the prophecy. It is the fact that each of the Fourfold Prophecies uses these exact words… 'The new species will be a mixture of old and new, able to trade lives with a thought and sustain life without death.*"

"That's really vague," Joe said, remembering the stupid woman at the fair and her dumbass predictions about cave-people.

"*No, it's not,*" Representative Na'leen said, vehement. "*It describes the Huouyt perfectly. We trade lives with other species when we change form. And we are not bloodthirsty like the Dhasha or the Jikaln. Throughout our history, there has never been a war. We don't need to subjugate other races to thrive because we are other races. Any species out there, we can become.*"

"The Dhasha?" Joe asked.

Underwater, Representative Na'leen made a face. "*We can duplicate Takki genes, but it is true...the Dhasha are beyond our capabilities. They and the Jreet are some of the only ones. Our scientists believe that with the Dhasha, it is because of the chemical composition of their scales—if they are even a chemical at all. They certainly defy all logical explanation. They are almost as mysterious as an Ooreiki's oorei.*"

Joe was just starting to relax into the conversation when Representative Na'leen said, "*So did Kihgl mention any of this to you, before he disappeared? It would seem...odd...that you served underneath him and he never mentioned it.*"

Joe tensed all over again, not liking the way the Huouyt's excited exuberance seemed to slough away, leaving utter, rapt attention. Almost as if it were a switch that he had flipped, a mask he'd put on to put Joe at ease.

"Uh, Kihgl didn't say a lot," Joe lied. "He's an ornery old bastard."

"*Another lie!*" Representative Na'leen snapped, lunging up out of the bath. At his raised voice, Joe heard the dry slither of something invisible moving closer to the central pedestal. He swallowed, hard, his eyes flickering to the corners of the empty room.

"*I am your only way home, Joe Dobbs,*" Representative Na'leen continued, above-water, now. His flat, fishy blue-white eyes were once again mirror-hard. "*You please me and I need but say the word and you shall be escorted back to Earth with Congress's deepest regrets.*"

Joe hesitated, his heart pounding. More than anything, he wanted to go back home. He wanted to see his family. Even now, his fingers itched for the Swiss Army knife, which he had made smooth by rubbing it every night before bed as he thought of his family.

"*Perhaps a few more days in that putrid air will help you remember.*" Representative Na'leen flicked his paddle-shaped tentacle in an abrupt dismissal. Immediately, Joe could sense the Jreet in the room moving toward him.

"Wait," Joe said. "He did say something."

Na'leen's eyes sharpened to the steely-blue edges of razors. "*Tell me.*"

Joe, who had been planning on telling Representative Na'leen everything about Kihgl's odd behavior, saw something in the Huouyt's electric gaze that made him change his mind. "He said nobody tells the Fourfold Prophecy more than once."

"*Interesting,*" Representative Na'leen said. He did not sound interested. "*Come back if you remember more. If your information interests me enough, I might be able to find a way to bring your illegal recruitment to light. Until then,*" he motioned at the door and suddenly two massive, scarlet, serpentine Jreet appeared beside Joe, so close he could touch them, "*You have a squad to command.*" He said the last with a heavy dose of sarcasm.

Joe bristled with anger. The casual way Representative Na'leen dismissed the Army reminded him of adults back on Earth who had never had to sleep in a tent in their lives—people who got to take a shower every day and complained about the high price of steak when Joe's father was writing letters in a dusty, scorpion-filled ditch and eating his meals out of a sun-baked plastic pouch.

He doesn't want to help me, Joe realized. *As soon as he gets what he wants, he'll forget about me.*

…just like Libby had tried to tell him.

Still, a part of him was screaming to tell the Huouyt everything. He wanted to go home more than anything. He knew all he had to do was tell Na'leen about Kihgl's prophecies and Na'leen would be satisfied.

Then the two visible Jreet—which towered over him like forty-foot man-cobras with massive, diamond-shaped heads bearing those weird, ribbed hollows reminiscent of bat ears—slid into place beside the Representative's pool and forced Joe back with the butts of their spears. As Joe was stumbling backwards, a third Jreet took him roughly by the wrist and casually yanked him away from the pool with enough brutal force to tear his arm off, had he applied a fraction of an ounce more pressure.

The Ooreiki were strong. They could do things like crush the back ends of pickup trucks and hurl two-hundred-pound men twenty feet in a fit of rage.

Yet with that one, halfhearted motion, the Jreet had made Joe's Ooreiki kidnappers look like stunted infants in comparison.

Turning to face his new aggressor, Joe experienced an uncomfortable wave of vertigo when he stared at the place the creature should have been. He *knew* an alien stood there beside him, but he couldn't *see* it. The invisible Jreet gave him a violent shove and propelled him down the ramp and to the door of the chamber. A moment later, another invisible fist grabbed him by the throat—swallowing his entire neck in a single scaly hand—and began dragging him through the hall. Joe, disoriented and fighting panic, stumbled in the alien's grip, lurching through the silken drapery to the main hall, struggling to remain upright. The Jreet continued to hold him by the throat, casually towing Joe along, giving Joe no choice but to add his stumbling footsteps to the dry slithering sounds of the huge snake-body sliding on the glassy black floor directly beside and behind him.

Zol'jib was standing outside. The Huouyt made a curt sound to the invisible Jreet escorting Joe, and the scaly fist around his neck released him suddenly. The dry, whispery sound of the Jreet's scales on glass as it moved away left Joe's heart pounding.

They could be anywhere, he thought, his brain utterly balking at the idea that he *could not see* a creature obviously the size of an elephant.

"Come," the Huouyt said sharply, making Joe jump. Zol'jib then turned and led Joe back through the lavish apartments toward the staircase. Joe's lungs cringed once they stepped back through the doors and into the planet's natural air. The pilot had returned with the hovercraft by the time they climbed back out onto the rooftop.

The shape to Joe's left as he followed Zol'jib up the stairs caught his attention. A smallish Jreet was impaled, long-ways, on a stake on the roof, a pool of bluish fluid congealing beneath him. The creature's two powerful front limbs were tied together at each joint, its head yanked back and tied to its tail, the stake protruding from its cream-colored midsection.

"Jreet are much less forgiving teachers than the Ooreiki," Zol'jib said, noticing Joe's stare. "Even more so than the Huouyt. That's the one we saw earlier."

Remembering the brief flash of red that Joe had seen on the stairs, he frowned at the tiny Jreet. "What did he do?"

Zol'jib made a dismissive gesture. "He allowed his energy shield to drop within an outsider's vision. He was punished."

Joe stared at the corpse contorted on the stake and swallowed hard at the Jreet idea of 'punishment.' "That's…rough," he whispered, suddenly not feeling too good about his own training.

His escort seemed unconcerned. "That's *Jreet*. Be grateful Humans are too frail to serve under them." He motioned for Joe to hurry up and follow him.

The Jreet shuddered as Joe passed.

"Is it still *alive?*" Joe whispered.

Zol'jib scoffed. "Of course. He can live for days like that. If he survives long enough, the Sentinels might cut him down and allow him to return to duty." Zol'jib eyed the suffering creature and flicked a downy, paddle-like tentacle in dismissal. "Judging by how much blood he's already lost, though, I doubt he'll make it."

Joe swallowed down bile. "Why do they do that?"

Zol'jib looked unconcerned. "They're Jreet." As if that was the answer to everything. "Now get on the haauk. We're distracting him. The longer we stand here, the less likely he'll be able to save himself."

Already hating the idea that he was partially to blame for the Jreet's misfortune, Joe hurriedly climbed aboard the haauk, still staring at the unfortunate trainee. He could feel its small yellow eyes watching him as he departed with the Huouyt. In moments, they were out of sight, flying through the civilian side of Alishai.

The barracks appeared through the reddish haze, distinguishable from the civilian buildings by the lack of elevators running up the sides, as well as the fact it was only nine stories high when the buildings around it soared into the hundreds. No brightly-clad Ooreiki civilians ran errands along the balconies encircling it, and the only platforms nearby were the ones speeding over the top of it, going to other civilian towers.

The Huouyt lowered the ship onto the sixth story balcony.

Battlemaster Nebil saw them arrive and moved to intercept them.

"What are you doing with my recruit?" Nebil demanded of the Huouyt.

"Returning him to you," Zol'jib said, sounding absolutely unconcerned with the shorter, stockier Ooreiki.

Battlemaster Nebil turned his sticky brown stare on Joe, but said nothing more as the Huouyt unloaded him from their craft and took back to the air. He waited until the platform had disappeared before speaking again.

"What did they want?"

"Na'leen wanted me to tell him about Kihgl," Joe muttered, staring out at the city after them.

Nebil was silent so long that Joe turned to look at him. The Ooreiki was staring at Joe, his sudah deathly still.

"You spoke with a member of the Tribunal?" There was something akin to…fear…in the hardened battlemaster's rumpled brown face.

"Yeah," Joe said. "He was interested in Kihgl."

Nebil didn't stop staring. *"Congressional Representatives don't waste their time with secondary commanders. It's beneath them."*

"Well, that's what he wanted to talk about," Joe said, feeling smug that, for once, Nebil looked awed by him. "You don't want to believe me, you go ask him yourself. If they'll even let you in the door."

Battlemaster Nebil gave him an unreadable stare. Then, without taking his eyes from Joe, he held up the bluish film of paper that the Huouyt had attached to his bed. *"It says you've been claimed to serve out the rest of your enlistment at Representative Na'leen's discretion. It's signed by An'a Zol'jib, Na'leen's head assassin."* Joe thrust it against Joe's chest. *"If I were you, Zero, I'd be very careful how I step."*

Joe took the piece of film and stared down at it, feeling queasy. "He couldn't claim me because I got Squad Leader."

Battlemaster Nebil snorted. *"If Na'leen had wanted you, the Training Committee would've given you to him on a ruvmestin haauk. He just changed his mind."*

As Joe began to feel ashamed and sick, Nebil said, *"Get back inside. Since you're already up and dressed, you can polish the walls until I return to wake the rest of the platoon. The rag is behind the door in the bathing chambers.*" At that, Battlemaster Nebil shoved him inside the barracks and locked the door behind him. Joe heard a dull thumping on the other side as Battlemaster Nebil's boots thudded against the stone staircase switchbacking down the side of the building.

Feeling like he'd been hit with a truck, Joe went to his task. The glassy obsidian walls were already gleaming. A visitor had to lean in close to see the children's fingerprints marring the glossy surface in the areas near the beds.

Joe got the rag from the alcohol-stinking baths and went to the wall above his groundteam's bed. Maggie's tiny fingerprints were everywhere. Grimly, Joe began wiping them away.

"What happened?" Scott asked, and Joe realized he'd stayed up waiting for him.

"Go back to sleep," Joe said. "You've still got some time."

"Joe!" Maggie squealed. She lunged from the covers and grabbed his arm, tugging it away from the wall. "Libby said you were gonna leave us."

Joe was still feeling the urge to run back to the Huouyt and tell him everything he knew about Kihgl at the chance Na'leen would be pleased with him. Guilt stabbed at him and he avoided looking at her.

"They didn't give him the chance to leave," Libby said, glaring at him from the bed. "If they'd given him the chance, he wouldn't be here."

Before Joe could respond, Monk said, "Shut up, Libby. He's not gonna leave us. He said so. He's gonna help us all get home."

"Yeah," Maggie chimed. "You're just a big stupidhead, Libby."

Libby lowered her eyes, accepting their judgment. Seeing it, Joe felt ashamed of himself all over again. He set down his rag and cleared his throat. "Libby was right," he said softly. "I would've gone."

Libby's head jerked up and she stared at him, her brown eyes hurt and confused. It was obvious she had wanted to be wrong. Joe looked back at the rag he was holding.

For a moment, none of the others spoke. Elf's thin body shuddered and he coughed up a glob of red mucus. Joe went back to wiping the fingerprints from the walls.

"You were gonna leave us?" Maggie whispered. She was sitting apart from the rest, her arms wrapped around her knees.

"Come on," Joe said, "Any of us would leave if we got the chance."

"I wouldn't," Libby said, stiffening. "You're my friends."

"Well you're the only one," Joe said, getting angry now. "Hell, Elf can't stop talking about how he wants to go home. Mag misses her guppies. Monk misses her Dad. Scott looks like he hasn't smiled since he got on that ship...and I'm tired of babysitting five helpless little kids."

Libby looked away.

Joe let out a frustrated breath. "But none of us *can* leave, so it's stupid to even talk about it. Go back to sleep."

None of them spoke.

Disgusted with himself for hurting their feelings and disgusted with them for being naïve enough to let their feelings be hurt, Joe went back to work in silence until a soft touch on his arm made him turn.

Maggie was looking up at him, her eyes wet. "You wouldn't really leave us, would you, Joe?"

Joe opened his mouth to tell her to grow up, but hesitated at the looks the other recruits were giving him. He glanced from Maggie to Scott, to Libby, to Monk and Elf, each of whom were clinging to every word but desperately trying to pretend they weren't listening. It wasn't just his groundteam, either. Kids in nearby beds were watching, hanging on his answer. Seeing that, Joe felt something shift inside of him. *They need me,* Joe thought, stunned, looking back down at Maggie's desperate face. *They aren't going to survive without me.* He was their rock. Their strength. Their shelter from the storm.

If he left, their spirits were going to break apart like...

...*like dust in the wind,* Kihgl's words whispered to him.

Overwhelmed, Joe dropped to his knees and swept Maggie up in a hug. "No," he said against her scalp, "I wouldn't leave you guys. Never, Mag."

And he knew it was true.

13

TRAINED TO KILL

*P*imples. *I'm fourteen and I've got pimples.* Joe stared at his arms in disgust. He'd never even *heard* of anybody getting pimples on their arms before. That made having pimples on his face and back that much more humiliating, since he had no visible skin that wasn't affected. His face was a battleground, with bombs going off every day.

He sighed and went back to his task. Battlemaster Nebil had decided that he had done a pathetic job on the walls that morning and therefore Joe could spend the whole night cleaning the rest of the barracks in nothing but his underwear and the *kasja.*

I look like I've got the pox. If this was three hundred years ago, they'd wrap me in a blanket and catapult me into an enemy fort. Say-o-nara Joe, nice to know you, make sure to kiss a few girls before you succumb to your wounds. Not that you would know what it's like to kiss a girl, you bashful bastard. You had fourteen years to figure it out and now you're stuck with a bunch of toddlers for the rest of your li—

"*I told you not to wear it!*" Kihgl rammed Joe's face into the glassy stone, making his vision burst into dozens of bouncing stars. Joe gasped and dropped the rag he'd been using, the Ooreiki's seven-pointed star digging into his skin where Kihgl's chest pressed him into the wall. The day had been so brutal that Joe had been cleaning in a haze, too tired to notice Commander Kihgl's approach.

No one was there to witness as Kihgl wrapped a stinging tentacle around Joe's neck and pushed him deeper into the wall, choking off his air.

"Do you realize what you've done, you fire-loving Jreet?!"

"Nebil…told me…to," Joe said in a choked whisper.

"Na'leen knows," Kihgl snarled into his face. *"The other Representatives have moved on, but he's stayed in Alishai. It's only a matter of time before he puts it together."*

"I…can't…" Joe couldn't form the words through the grip the secondary commander had on his throat. He could feel himself passing out.

"I will not let you ruin things, you understand, Human?" He slammed Joe's head back against the stone wall, breaking Joe's world into thousands of tiny stars. *"You will do what the Trith foretold if I have to haunt you every step of the way."*

"Please…" his lips mouthed, no air escaping his lungs. Joe could not see, so quickly had his vision dimmed from the Ooreiki's vicious stranglehold.

Commander Kihgl released him suddenly, but stayed only inches from his face, so close Joe could feel the soft whispers of air moving from his sudah as he held him backed against a wall.

"Listen to me very carefully, Zero. A ghost without an oorei can haunt you for eternity. Even if you pathetic Humans have an afterlife, I can destroy it. If you reincarnate, I will be there. If you fail, I will give you no peace. I will allow you no happiness. I will bring you into my hell, Zero. I swear it with my very soul."

Joe was afraid to move, Kihgl's seven-pointed star digging into his chest.

"Go to bed," Kihgl said. *"And keep the kasja. Tell Nebil I authorized it."* At that, he turned.

"Wait," Joe said.

Kihgl paused, his gummy brown eyes hard.

"Why don't you run?" Joe asked. "You were in Planetary Ops. You could hide."

It took Kihgl a long time to respond. Finally, his pale brown eyes fixed on Joe, he said, "*I have hope that the Trith was right.*" At that, he turned and stalked off, leaving Joe in silence.

• • •

"*Lights are forbidden after dark on Ooreiki planets because they attract onen.*" Commander Linin scanned the platoon with a look of irritation. Kihgl and Tril had not shown up to formation that morning. "*So the ashers at medical finally decided to inform us that we gotta dose you weak-eyed sooters with nightvision if we want you not to shit yourselves when the sun goes down in twelve hours.*"

Joe had been wondering about that. He'd seen nothing but bright, purple sky ever since getting off the ship. The sun hadn't gone down in days.

Commander Linin started to pace. "*That puts Sixth Battalion even further behind. While the rest of the regiment is working on tactics in the tunnels this afternoon, we're gonna be standing around with our tentacles tangled while you worthless Humans sleep it off. Lagrah's gonna have Second Battalion shooting circles around us before we even get to our first hunt.*"

It was the first time the Ooreiki had mentioned tunnels since they'd been on the ship and Joe could not stop his heart from hammering a startled staccato. *They plan to have us go down tunnels...* His mind was screaming to ask about them, desperate to know their exact dimensions, but Linin was in a foul mood and Joe knew that he'd get pounded if he opened his mouth.

Instead of retiring the battalion and letting the ten battlemasters march their platoons to the medical center, Commander Linin took the whole battalion to the courtyard outside the medical center. *If they want you, they can come collect your bony Human asses themselves,* Commander Linin barked at them as he formed them into squads. *We have work to do.* Then, as if they were not in the middle of a busy civilian parking lot, he began drilling his recruits outside the hospital. The irritated medics came out every five minutes to claim another set of recruits, their sudah fluttering hotly.

The recruits under Linin's control dwindled steadily, since the ones the medics claimed did not return. As a squad leader, Joe was one of the last ones chosen. While he waited for his turn, Joe's world narrowed to the glassy crunch of gravel and the sound of Commander Linin's oaths as they fouled up the complex drills he gave them. When Joe was finally ushered into the dim red lights of the hospital, even the foreign black machines and the brusque Ooreiki medic were a relief from Linin's rage.

"Damn insane grounder," the medic muttered once they were inside. The Ooreiki was one of the higher-ranked medical officers, with the golden circle on his chest so big it almost filled its silver border. *"It's not our fault Kihgl got caught."* He shoved Joe into a small room and touched the wall. A black barrier dripped shut behind him, reminding Joe of the ship. With a prickle of goosebumps, he realized he had no way out.

"Drink this," the irritated medic ordered, offering him a clear vial. Inside, a reddish liquid sloshed around, looking slightly radioactive.

"What is it?" Joe asked.

The medic gave him a look that told Joe he would shove it down his throat, vial and all, if he gave him the slightest resistance.

Swallowing hard, Joe pulled the stopper off the vial and sniffed. It smelled even more rancid than the air. He wrinkled his nose and pulled his head away. "Man, what'd you do, create distilled ass? This *reeks*." The stench reminded him of the constant itch in his lungs and he reflexively coughed up a red gob of *ferlii* spores and phlegm. When he turned to spit it out on the floor, however, he caught the medic's glare and swallowed it convulsively.

"We can get a funnel and force-feed you if you aren't interested in drink-ing it willingly," the harried medic said pleasantly.

Realizing the Ooreiki was utterly serious, imagining choking on a fun-nel, Joe held his breath, tipped his head back, and emptied the vial of night-vision down his throat as quickly as he could gulp it down.

It was like swallowing sewage.

"Keep it down," the medic warned him. *"Waste it and we'll be forced to add another turn to your enlistment to pay the difference."*

Already knowing he had many more years of service than anyone else in his battalion, Joe was desperate to keep from vomiting the disgusting stuff back up. *Keep it down,* he chanted to himself, stumbling to grip the medic's desk in both fists. *Keep it down, keep it down…* Joe stood there, panting, a panicked moment, feeling the rancid potion work its way into his stomach and then try to claw its way out again. He swallowed hard to keep it where it belonged.

Then, as he felt the odd hot-cold heat spread through his stomach and chest, Joe began catching red, yellow, and blue flashes of color in the air all around him, almost like a northern aurora. He was frowning at that, squinting at the weird swaths of color beginning to drip from the walls, when an electrical spasm seemed to grab him by the back of his skull and dropped him to his knees. An instant later, he blacked out.

When he woke, the world was in shades of color that Joe had never imagined possible. The armband Kihgl had given him was laced with glowing gold designs beautiful enough to take his breath away. When he traced the patterns, they almost reminded him of Celtic knots…or crop circles. When he looked up, he realized the walls weren't actually black, but gleaming iridescent waves of color that reminded him of bird feathers. He could see blocky squiggles marking the doors and equipment like someone had taken a neon pink highlighter to the room. He got up and wove through the bodies of sleeping recruits to take a closer look.

Joe's excitement soared as he neared. The blocky squiggles were foreign, but he could recognize patterns—repeated symbols, common characters, rhythms to the words. And, as Coach Grimsley liked to say, recognizing your opponent's patterns was the first step to kicking his ass.

Joe peered harder, trying to locate exactly where the symbols began. He noticed a lot of numbers corresponding to the alien writing on the recruits' uniforms, but he couldn't locate a line or column to which the symbols were aligned. It was almost as if they were simply thrown into a jumbled mess on the wall. Joe traced the symbols with his fingers, perplexed. He could not conceive of an intelligent species using such a disorganized system.

Still, the alien writing was magic to Joe. The Ooreiki had made a mistake. *Seeing* the doors was the first step to stepping *through* them. For the first time since getting off the ship, Joe felt renewed hope that he could somehow get himself home.

Himself *and* his friends home. Joe glanced back, locating his groundteam amongst the sleeping recruits. Libby was the only one also awake. The rest were sprawled wherever the Ooreiki had left them, breathing peacefully.

Maggie's stubby toddler legs were already lengthening and losing their baby fat. She was probably about the size of a normal five-year-old now. Scott was approaching five and a half feet, and he was beginning to show signs of maturity—a widening jaw and more defined muscles. Libby, two years younger, was quickly catching up with Scott. Her long legs were growing longer and her limbs were beginning to sport pronounced muscle. She looked like a natural athlete. Joe wondered if it was the aliens' freakish drugs or good genetics from her parents, then decided it was probably a bit of both.

Elf was catching up to Monk, though it was obvious his growth spurt wouldn't last much longer. He had a small frame, the kind that lent itself to music or math. Sam had looked like that.

Monk was the enigma. She hadn't showed signs of growth like the others, not even a millimeter. Joe had panicked once he realized she wasn't growing, thinking she wasn't eating. Then she ate both her bowl and then his in front of him to prove she was, grinning all the while.

Joe had pretty much stopped growing after the first week. As far as he could tell, he was about six-three or six-four, a little taller than his dad. He was taking after his mom in body-type, though. Where his dad's family was filled with long-boned musicians and mathematicians, his mom's whole family was populated with squat, trollish athletes that took pride in pummeling little kids in touch football.

Joe eyed his arm. He would have given a front tooth to have access to a mirror. He was pretty sure he was gaining some muscle. He flexed a little to make the bicep stand out under Kihgl's *kasja,* trying to gauge how it compared to his father's. He was almost positive it was the same size, maybe even a little bigger.

Joe realized Libby was watching him from the cluster of little kids that made up his groundteam. Blushing, Joe dropped his arm and went over to her, trying to pretend he hadn't been flexing like a moron.

"Why can I see their writing?" Libby asked when he approached. She was frowning at the beautiful Ooreiki markings on the walls. "Was that there before?" she demanded.

"Beats the hell out of me," Joe said, relieved she hadn't noticed his preening. He followed her gaze back to the walls. "I don't think so. But we can use it to get away from here."

Libby immediately frowned at him. "I don't want to get away from here. I like it here."

"Yeah, well, you'll like it better on Earth," Joe said. "Whenever I get a chance, I'm gonna start exploring. Maybe find us a ship." Joe realized Elf was awake and he smiled, motioning at the walls. "See? We can read their writing now. Soon we'll be getting out of here."

"We can't read their writing until they teach us how," Libby said. "And you're being stupid, Joe. We're not going back home."

"I'll teach myself," Joe said. "I'm *going* to get us home."

Libby rolled her eyes, but Elf stared at him, enthralled. Joe winked at Elf, but immediately his enthusiasm began to ebb. Deep down, he knew Libby was right. Sure, he could see their writing, but he couldn't read it. And even if he could read it, it took pilots years to learn how to fly an airplane on Earth. How long would it take him to learn to fly a *spaceship*?

Sometimes, Joe, you're a real idiot. What's Elf gonna say when you don't take him home like you promised?

Grimacing, Joe sat down beside the nearest door and began trying to figure out how the Ooreiki thought. It baffled him that, with their sophisticated technology, they could present their words in such an unorganized manner. He felt a little smug, knowing that in at least one way, humans were more advanced than the aliens. He touched the blocky squiggles again, trying to memorize the shapes.

"They write in circles," Monk said behind him. Her voice was still groggy from just waking up.

"I know," Joe said, turning back to the blotch of alien symbols. "It looks like they threw darts at the wall and put a word wherever they landed."

"No," Monk said, brushing past him to place her finger at the center of the jumble. "They write in circles." She traced a spiral over the symbols, her finger following the curve of the words perfectly. Joe's jaw dropped.

"My parents are teachers," Monk said with a shrug. "My mom knows Chinese and German and my dad teaches gym."

"I thought your mom taught music," Joe said.

"She does," Monk replied. "And Chinese and German."

"What kind of elementary school teaches Chinese and German?"

Monk frowned at him. "She's a professor." Her look added, *Stupid.*

Joe blushed. "I just thought maybe she'd teach kids your age, since you're her kid and I thought teachers would teach their kids when they—"

"She makes more money at the university. My dad's the one who's gotta smell boys' stinky locker-rooms when she gets to listen to Chopin."

Joe frowned. "What's your last name?"

Monk frowned at him. "Grimsley-Biggs. My dad's name comes first only because he won the coin toss."

"You're Coach Grimsley's *daughter?!* But you're so small!"

"My mom was four-foot-ten."

"Oh. Guess that explains it."

"My mom's smarter than you, Joe."

He grinned.

"She is. You're too big to be smart. My dad's big like you and he only makes half what my mom does and *he* didn't have to stop working for a year to have a baby." She paused long enough to stick her tongue out at Scott, who was sitting up in a daze. "See, Scott? Girls *are* better than guys."

"Huh?" Scott said. "No they're not."

"Yes they *are.* They're better 'cause they're smarter. My dad has an IQ of one-thirty-six. Know what my mom's IQ is?"

Scott rolled his eyes and went to use the latrine.

"One sixty-two," Monk said, as if she were a magician revealing an awe-inspiring trick.

Libby scoffed. "You're just saying that. You don't even know what an IQ is."

"Do too!" Monk cried, suddenly defensive. "If you have an IQ it means you're not gonna end up on TV."

Libby's face went blank. "What?"

"You won't end up on TV," Monk insisted. "Mom and Dad say the people on TV don't have enough IQ to figure out how to use toilet paper. That's why they're on TV."

"That doesn't make any sense," Libby said.

"Does too. My mom's got a lot of IQ and she's never been on TV. My dad has, though. He has to be on TV every time his team wins."

"That's stupid."

"It's what my mom said."

"Then your mom's a dumb bimbo who doesn't know her ass from her head."

Joe's head shot up and he gave Libby an irritated look. Libby, unabashed that she had copied his words, merely shrugged and yawned.

Monk got up and kicked Libby in the shin. "My mom's *not* a dumb bimbo! She's *smart. You're* the dumb bimbo, you stupidhead! You don't have any IQ at all. You're gonna be on TV and then everybody will know you can't use toilet paper, just like all those really tall supermodels who are so dumb they *want* to be on TV!"

Libby got up and, with a cold look at Monk, snapped a leg around and kicked her in the head with a perfect, powerful roundhouse. Monk's neck snapped back and she let out a small, startled sound. Joe felt his heart stop as he watched her crumple to the floor.

"Libby!" Joe shouted, in shock. "What the *hell*?!"

Then Monk began to scream.

Joe rushed over to her and dropped to his knees. Wailing, Monk climbed into his lap, holding the side of her head. Gently, Joe pried her fingers from her skull long enough to make sure she wasn't dying, then took a relieved breath. Her ear was bleeding where Libby's boot had cut it, but she was still moving her arms and legs, which meant she hadn't been paralyzed. Monk, meanwhile, shrieked like a banshee, her lungs gaining capacity with every breath.

"She kicked me!" Monk screamed. "*Joooe,* Libby *kiiiiiiicked* me!"

"I saw that," Joe said, scowling. Libby had sat back down and was non-chalantly picking at the bruise Monk had given her. "Looks like she was in karate."

"Taekwondo," Libby said, unconcernedly.

Joe felt his anger growing. "Then you should know you don't beat up on smaller kids. Apologize, Libby."

"Don't feel like it."

"Stay here." Joe set Monk aside, who was now sniffling quietly, watching Libby with a malicious anticipation. He walked over to stand over Libby and her eyes burned with challenge when she looked up at him.

"Apologize," Joe said softly.

"I didn't see you apologize when you beat up that kid who stole food at lunch," Libby said. "And he didn't even hurt you. You hit him first."

"I didn't beat him up," Joe said, prickling.

"You made him pee himself," Libby retorted. "That's worse."

Joe felt his knuckles cracking from the pressure in his fists. "Libby, you hurt one of your friends and you're going to apologize."

"She's not my friend," Libby said.

"You thought she was yesterday," Joe said. "That's why you don't want to go home. You want to stay with your friends."

"She hadn't kicked me yesterday."

"And you hadn't called her mom a dumb bimbo," Joe said.

Libby turned back to scowl at him. "You called *my* mom a dumb bimbo."

Joe could feel his jaw muscles work in frustration. "Fine. I'll apologize if you apologize for hurting Monk."

Reluctantly, Libby glanced at Monk, who now had little drops of blood crawling out from beneath her fingers where she was holding her ear. Her face softened and she guiltily glanced at the floor. "Sorry, Monk," she muttered. "I didn't mean to hit you so hard." Joe supposed it was better than nothing. He glanced at Monk, who was still sniffling, but looked somewhat mollified, if shaken.

Joe squatted in front of Libby. "I'm sorry for calling your mom a dumb bimbo."

Libby bunched her nose as if she smelled something bad, but still wouldn't look at him. "No problem, Joe," she whispered, her voice cracking.

Joe frowned, watching tears trickle down Libby's black cheeks. He turned to Monk. "Don't kick her again."

Monk's eyes got a little wide, like the very idea of kicking Libby was enough to evoke nightmares. She shook her head vigorously, still holding her bleeding ear.

"You okay, Libby?" Joe asked softly.

Libby bit her lip and shook her head, but didn't elaborate. Joe considered sitting down beside her, but when he scooted closer, Libby just got up abruptly and walked away.

Giving Libby one last, worried look, Joe went and sat down against the far wall, disturbed. It was the first time Libby had given any of them so much as a love-tap, and she had done it with such force she had almost taken Monk's head off. He had no doubts that Monk was lucky to be alive.

They're growing up too fast, he thought, watching them. *They're only learning what the Congies want them to learn.*

Which meant they were learning to kill.

14

GRACIOUS LORD KNAAREN

As soon as the rest of the recruits were awake, a dozen medics with varying sized golden circles emblazoned inside the silver borders of their rank insignias rounded them up and herded them outside. Their battlemasters met them at the door. The tense way the Ooreiki held their barrel-shaped bodies was Joe's first clue that something was wrong.

"Fourth platoon, get over here!" Battlemaster Nebil snapped. *"Chins, line them up!"* 'Chins' was Nebil's nickname for Sasha, in honor of her jutting lower jaw. Nebil's voice was sharper than usual and Sasha rushed to do as she was told, her usual superior look gone, her face anxious.

Apparently sometimes she can shut up and do what she's told, Joe thought. He was still frustrated that Battlemaster Nebil had not so much as even looked in his direction after giving him squad leader. No matter how well Joe did—and even an idiot could see he was *much* better than Sasha—Sasha remained Battlemaster.

It's not fair. It was supposed to be me.

Once Sasha had them lined up, *without* screwing up, for once, Battlemaster Nebil came to stand in front of them and fell into one of his long silences as he scanned their faces.

"Takki have delivered night-wear to your barracks," Nebil finally said. *"The sun will disappear in three hours and return in another four days. The*

ferlii branches trap in the heat and the spores act as insulation, but the dark side of the planet often drops below freezing anyway. As soon as the formation is over, you will don your night gear and continue wearing it until the night cycle is over.

"Until then, I want your minds sharp. Prime Commander Knaaren has decided to inspect you. He's finding all of our setbacks to be inconvenient and already suggested Congress sell Sixth Battalion to one of his brothers, so you Takki sootwads had better be on your best behavior if you want to stay out of a Dhasha's slave pens.

Libby's voice broke through the silence, loud and angry. "We're not slaves."

Nebil merely glanced at his protégée and Joe felt a pang of jealousy. If *he* had done that, Nebil would have pounded him flatter than a pancake.

"If you fail to learn, Congress has every right to sell you. Your species is still very new and very rare, so Dhasha will pay enormous prices for Humans. The Army can fund twenty ships for a year just from the sale of one dysfunctional battalion. You're a novelty, plus you have no scales, so you're easy to eat. That makes you high-demand, and the Dhasha hold a lot of sway in Congress. They've already had several bidding wars over which Dhasha planet gets the first load of Humans to fail training. If you want to avoid that, you need to—"

"I will take the platoon from here, Battlemaster." It was the first time Joe had seen Commander Tril since landing on Kophat, and his presence now seemed ominous.

Battlemaster Nebil stiffened bodily, then slowly stepped out of the way without looking at Tril.

Commander Tril moved to the front of the platoon and his eyes locked on Kihgl's *kasja*. *"You can't wear that, Zero. Bring it to me."*

"It's mine," Joe blurted. "Commander Kihgl gave it to me." That morning, Nebil had told him to wear it openly, that it deserved to be on the outside of his sleeve, not hidden under his clothing in shame. He knew he should be relieved Tril would take it from him, but after seeing the golden designs engraved on it after waking, the thing had grown on him. Besides, it was Kihgl's. Not Tril's. "Commander Kihgl gave it to me."

A look of satisfaction crossed Commander Tril's face. *"Commander Kihgl is being tried for treason,"* Tril said. *"I am now secondary commander of Sixth Battalion."*

Joe felt like he'd been punched in the gut. Nebil, too, looked similarly upset. The battlemaster looked away, his sudah flipping wildly in his neck.

Tril pointedly eyed the triangle on Joe's chest. *"You can give me the* kasja *or you can lose Squad Leader. Pick."*

Joe stared at Tril, feeling the beginnings of hatred. For some insane reason, he wanted to tell Tril to get stuffed, keep the armband, and lose his rank. The *kasja's* golden alien designs easily could have fit on the shelves beside the collection of Celtic armbands and neck ornaments that his dad had pounded out of silver at the base hobby shop. He opened his mouth to tell Tril where he could stuff his demands.

"Give it to me, Zero." Nebil stepped forward. *"I'll see you get it back."*

Tril stiffened. *"He won't get it back unless I give it to him, Battlemaster."*

Battlemaster Nebil ignored him, his sticky brown eyes holding Joe's. *"You'll get it back,"* he repeated.

Even after beating him and running him until Joe was puking like a dog, there was something about Battlemaster Nebil that Joe trusted. He reluctantly tugged the *kasja* over his bicep and lowered it into Nebil's open tentacles. Battlemaster Nebil tucked it under his arm and went back to formation.

"I'm turning it in to the Peacemakers," Tril snapped. *"Give it to me. It belonged to a traitor."*

"It belongs to Zero now," Nebil said, making absolutely no motion to obey.

Commander Tril's sudah were fluttering rapidly as he glared at Nebil. After a long silence, he snarled, *"Get them moving. We've got two hours to teach these furgs to march as a battalion. We're already underpowered and I don't want Lord Knaaren claiming any more of them than necessary."* Then he stalked off to another platoon, leaving Nebil once more in charge.

Under Tril's orders, the ten Ooreiki battlemasters gathered their platoons and formed them into a square five groundteams deep by thirty groundteams wide. A sense of urgency began to permeate the air as the Congies laid out the basics of marching in a battalion. Each recruit was to keep an arm's distance from the kid in front of him while keeping an eye on the recruits to either side in order to stay in perfect line, their boots landing in time to their battlemasters' orders—which were given in Congie, not English. Joe only knew half of them, and he had memorized every word that Tril had taught them on their trip here.

From the start, all of the Ooreiki turned their translators off, so it was left to the humans to decipher what they were trying to say fast enough to keep from getting singled out for stupidity. The battlemasters cuffed dozens of kids for minor errors, and the recruit battlemasters got worse. One was beaten bloody for stepping forward when the order was to stop. Another had her jaw shattered when she missed a step and sent her entire column out of sync. Sasha garbled a command, confusing the platoon, and Commander Tril broke her arm for it. Takki came to spirit her away and Battlemaster Nebil made Libby take over in her place. Though Joe was initially worried for her, Libby somehow managed to perform the drills perfectly, even in the alien language. It made Joe feel jealous listening to her smooth, confident commands. Again, he thought, *That should be me up there.*

The rest of the platoon was almost pissing themselves in fear. As the Ooreiki's orders grew more frenzied, the recruits' anxiety rose until all of them were shaking, unsure what to expect next.

It was the most nerve-shattering experience Joe had ever had. When Commander Tril finally called a halt, Joe felt the mass terror emanating from those around him, but their secondary commander either did not notice or did not care.

A horn reverberated across the glossy faces of the enormous buildings. Deep, resonant, it made everyone jump. Immediately, Commander Tril ordered them to march to one corner of the cleared parade grounds. Around them, black-clad recruits were flowing into the plaza in perfect, sharp formation. Joe glanced at Sixth Battalion's ragged columns and he felt a new wave of fear.

Their formation stood out amongst the others like a two-year-old's attempt at geometry mixed into an upper-division calculus assignment.

Their battlemasters stopped them at one end of the plaza and had them turn on heel to their left, leaving Joe in the front row with thirty other kids.

"Get your fire-loving eyes on the ground!" Commander Linin shouted. *"If a Dhasha's inspecting, keep your heads lowered and your bodies bowed like you gotta shit yourself. And* don't move. *His lordship Knaaren is a son of Prince Rethavn. That means he's a believer in the Old Pact. That means he can take you ashy furgs and make you pick his scales or eat you, whatever burning mood he's in. Whatever happens, don't move unless you're told to. And never look him in the eyes. Dhasha declare* ka-par *by looking each other in the eyes."*

Then Tril, Linin, and the battlemasters left them, moving to join the other Ooreiki standing in their own formation across the plaza.

This is bad, Joe thought. He stood as still as he could, despite the tremor in his limbs. Around him, a wild-eyed hysteria was spreading through the kids as they stood there, waiting. Most knew what it meant to be inspected by a Dhasha and they were so frightened they were trembling.

A commotion erupted at the far end of the plaza, but Joe kept his eyes down as Linin had told them. A girl beside him went pale, her eyes wide. "It killed someone."

Joe glanced down the rows at First Battalion.

A grizzly-bear-sized monster was strutting down the ranks, a screaming, armless girl thrashing on the ground in its wake, spreading blood over her stone-still, wide-eyed companions. A couple of the Takki trailing behind the monster stopped to bind up the girl's stump. Then one of them picked up her discarded rifle as they carried her away.

For the first time, Joe realized Sixth Battalion was the only battalion not carrying their rifles. He wondered what Tril had been thinking, making them march for hours when it would have been better to grab their rifles and take two hours to line them up perfectly before the Dhasha showed up. They could spend time on marching later. *Now* was the time they needed not to look like sootbags.

"She'll be fine," Joe said to the kids around him. "Everybody look at the ground." He hoped Tril's marching frenzy hadn't put the kids in a mood to bolt. He had the feeling the predator five battalions down would give chase and eat them alive.

Knaaren passed the rest of the battalions with only brief pauses at each. Then he was there, filling Joe's vision with a scaly rainbow of colors, his long black talons digging into the glittering gravel at Joe's feet as it moved. The thing was *huge*. It radiated a sense of power that made the back of Joe's throat slick with fear. Inwardly, Joe prayed the other children could hold still long enough for Knaaren to pass by, but he heard the gasps and strangled sobs just as well as the Dhasha. Joe felt sick when Knaaren came to a sudden stop in front of them.

A harsh, guttural snarl erupted from the Dhasha's enormous, shark-like mouth. All around Joe, children whimpered and cringed. *"So this is the traitor's battalion,"* the translator around its neck said. *"How pathetic. I saw you marching. You move like frightened Takki. You're an abomination! I thought the others were bad, but you are worse. It shames me to have you in my regiment. Are you afraid of me, Human slaves? You, are you afraid of me?"* Knaaren lowered its head so he was staring directly at the girl in front of him, his huge, gaping black mouth wide enough to engulf her.

The girl stared at the ground, too petrified to speak.

"Answer me!"

"K-k-kee," the girl whimpered.

"Good answer. You should be. I should sell you all to my father." The Dhasha continued down the row, stopping at Joe. *"What about you? Are you afraid of me?"*

Joe could feel the monster's rotten breath on his face. The bottom row of black, triangular teeth were only inches from his neck, the impossibly huge, egg-shaped green eyes boring down on him with the cold intensity of emeralds.

"Kee," Joe said, staring at his feet. *So scared I want to piss myself.*

The creature moved on. *"What about you? Are you afraid of me?"*

The girl in question snapped her head up, wide-eyed, and began to whimper an unintelligible garble of fear.

In an instant, the black jaws descended, snapping her in half. The lower body and some loops of intestine fell to the ground, knees first. For a moment, Joe wasn't completely sure he hadn't imagined it. Then the children around the torso began to scream and back away.

"Get back into your lines!" Nebil shouted at them. *"Return to your places or more will die!"*

The Dhasha, meanwhile, had wandered further down the ranks. Joe was watching him openly, now, fury rising in his chest. Knaaren relieved two more kids of limbs for minor infractions before circling around the back and returning to stand a few children away from Joe.

"My slave is right. You all smell like cowards. Where are your rifles? You dare come to a battalion inspection without your rifles? You sniveling Takki! I bet there's not one amongst you who will look me in the eyes."

Joe felt a cold tendril of fear curl in his gut. *Don't do it,* he thought. *Please don't do it.*

Apparently, the other kids were either too smart or too scared to look up. Everyone kept their eyes focused solidly on their feet.

Except Joe. He was too busy glancing around to make sure the other kids were keeping their eyes down.

"You." The Dhasha stopped in front of Joe. *"You're not staring at your feet like the rest of the Takki. You must enjoy being so big. Do you bully the other children? Do you take their food and steal their gear? Answer me!"*

"Anan," Joe said to his feet.

"Why not? Isn't that what Kihgl taught you? Take from your comrades instead of share? Pretend to clean their scales so you can drive a talon through their innards? The traitor contaminated you all. Look at me. I would see your face."

Heart pounding like a hammer in his brain, Joe tore his eyes from the ground far enough to look at the Dhasha's massive chest.

"I said look at me!"

"I am looking at you," Joe said, continuing to stare at the iridescent chest.

"What did you say, Human?"

"I said I *am* looking at you."

"The Takki has a spine. Look me in the eyes and tell me that." The Dhasha poised above him, waiting to strike.

Joe knew his next choice would mean either life or death. He kept his eyes down.

The Dhasha's colorful lips peeled away from its triangular black teeth and Joe saw pieces of the other children stuck between the razor rows. It began to bark in Joe's face, clacking its teeth together like knives. Sprayed with blood and saliva, Joe thought he was going to puke.

As quickly as it had begun, the Dhasha closed its mouth and moved on. *"I like the look of your fingers, girl. By the laws of the Pact, I claim you for my service."*

The girl the Dhasha had chosen stumbled out of line with an uncomprehending look at the purple Takki tugging her away from the rest.

"And him. He doesn't have the look of a warrior. He'll do well as a slave."

The Takki tugged the boy out of formation and Knaaren moved on. A new sort of anger filled Joe. The Dhasha was taking *slaves*. Right out in the open! And no one was going to stop him.

Knaaren made a barking sound of disgust. *"You're not warriors. You should all be slaves. Him. He's a fat one. I could use him tonight. Him. And her. And her."* The Dhasha made another full circuit, circling Tril's battalion once more, claiming over two dozen children. He stopped back in front of Joe. *"Him."*

Joe braced himself as the Takki rushed toward him.

But it wasn't Joe that Knaaren wanted. It was Elf. The Takki took him out of line and dragged him to stand amidst the whimpering, white-faced children following the Dhasha in a frightened mass. Joe could do nothing but watch, stunned and relieved, and shamed at his relief. Shamed to his core.

"There. That should suffice for now. If you continue to fail in your training, I'll take more. Until then, you may share the other battalions' day of liberty, even though you haven't earned it." At that, Knaaren padded toward the next battalion. The desperate look that Elf gave Joe as they led him away seared Joe's memory like a curse.

After another hour of terrifying the recruits further down the line, Knaaren departed, taking his slaves with him. He hadn't claimed a single recruit since taking the two dozen from Sixth Battalion. Once he was gone, the Ooreiki descended upon them. "You got off easy," Commander Tril told them. "He only took twenty-eight. We still have a chance."

"What about the ones he killed?" Sasha demanded, her voice rigid with anger. "Do I get a replacement?"

Tril glanced at the torso still splayed on the ground in front of her. "He only killed one. The other two will get prosthetic limbs. They should be back in a day."

"She was in my ground team," Sasha cried. "Now we're down to *four*."

"Do you wish to join them, recruit? Recruit Battlemaster does not make you immune. Far from it."

Sasha seemed to shrink in on herself and shook her head.

"Then do not argue. A Dhasha can always find a place for one more."

Joe stared at Tril. How could he threaten them like that after what they'd just been through?

"We are running out of time," Tril continued, as if he had said nothing out of the ordinary. "Lord Knaaren looks at you unfavorably because of Kihgl's treason. We will have to spend every free moment training, until you are better than the others."

The shock was beginning to wear off and many of the kids were starting to cry.

"Silence your recruits, Battlemasters!" Commander Tril snapped. "Anyone who makes any more noise will clean up the mess Knaaren made."

Joe felt a twist of rage in his gut, hearing those words. Knaaren's 'mess' included several partial bodies, bits of flesh, and gallons of blood.

"We'll use this day to practice," Tril continued. "Kihgl's trial is scheduled in eight days Standard. We must be ready by then." Tril paused. "And…I'm sorry. *Zahali*. Kihgl was deranged, and many of you will pay for it."

As he said the words, Nebil's sudah fluttered suddenly and he looked to the side, watching something in the distance. Joe noticed his boneless fingers tightening into ropy knots in front of him as Tril continued his explanation of what had occurred with their secondary commander.

A 'shame,' he called it. An 'unfortunate inevitability.' A 'tragedy that it was allowed to go on this long.' Most of the battlemasters—and even Small Commander Linin—seemed to follow Nebil's lead in finding something else to look at while Tril droned on about the expectations and responsibilities of a secondary commander in the Congressional Army, and how Kihgl had fallen short.

And why, once Kihgl's crimes were discovered, Tril had been granted his rank as a reward for bringing about the capture of a traitor. For, Tril declared proudly, it had been *he* who had discovered Kihgl's treacherous nature and *he* who had been responsible for making his corruption known to Peacemakers.

One of the battlemasters walked off suddenly, making Tril stop and give the Ooreiki's retreating back a narrow look. When he went on, it was to discuss the possibility that the ranks were filled with 'sympathizers' and 'collaborators' and to be alert for any symptoms of disloyalty to Congress. The Peacemakers, Tril added, were offering ten turns off the enlistment of any recruit who could provide information leading to the detainment and conviction of other defectors.

Joe felt goosebumps crawl up his arms at that, but somehow kept his eyes forward.

Once Tril finally finished and dismissed them, Nebil and the other battlemasters broke the battalion into their ten platoons and began marching them to separate areas of the plaza.

Thus began the longest day of Joe's life.

They marched until their feet were blistered and their calves ached, got their rifles and broke them down until they could see the individual parts every time they closed their eyes, straightened their rumpled lines, received glossy new helmets and learned about the onboard computers, gasped and retched as the battlemasters ran them in formation around the plaza, listened to Congie curses until their ears burned, and shouted *"Kkee nkjanii!"* until their throats were hoarse.

By the time Nebil led them from the plaza, they were barely able to put one foot in front of the other. They didn't realize their torment was over until they were standing at the base of a switchback black stair, facing the long climb back to the barracks.

"Get up there!" Battlemaster Nebil shouted at them in Congie. "You're not done yet, you soot-eating jenfurglings! Faster! Faster! *Run!*"

The battlemaster stopped them halfway up the six-story climb, telling them to do it again. The second time, they ascended the staircase even slower than the first. Nebil made them do it again. And again. They climbed stairs until Joe couldn't tell if he was going down or up, with the battlemaster pacing them easily every time.

Joe didn't remember reaching the top. Inside, Battlemaster Nebil had them check their weapons for diamond chips and stack them into a locker at the end of their communal beds. Then they had to undress together, on command, taking off each article of clothing and folding it as Nebil shouted out its name in Congie.

They stacked their clothing inside their lockers, under their guns. Their boots came last. Joe had thought they were too heavy for regular boots— and he was right. As their heads bobbed with exhaustion, Battlemaster Nebil had them break down their boots, uncovering the tools and weapons hidden within and going at length to describe their names in Congie and how each could be used on the battlefield.

Then, when they could barely keep their eyes open, Nebil made them stand beside their big round beds in a circle with their groundmates and say, *"I am a grounder. These are my groundmates. Apart, we are nothing. Together, we are a groundteam. I will never abandon my groundteam and my groundteam will never abandon me. I will live with my groundmates, fight with my groundmates, and when I die, my essence will be carried on by my surviving groundmates. I will obey the commands of my ground leader without question. I am a grounder."*

Only then could they crawl into bed. Joe's groundteam was down to five. Elf had not been replaced.

15

CALLED OUT

"**H**e's the one they predicted you'd save, isn't he?" Nebil's voice was soft from the dim hall outside his prison.

Kihgl was slumped against one wall of his cell, staring at the floor. He didn't lift his eyes. "They're recording everything about your visit. If they find anything they don't like, they'll try you as a traitor as well."

"I disabled it," Nebil said. "I got you into this mess with that damned *kasja*. Do you want me to get you out?"

Kihgl wanted it more than life itself. Yet he had to fight the urge to laugh. "I chose my path, Nebil," Kihgl said softly. "Don't twine your fate with mine. I'll only take you down the tunnel with me."

Nebil seemed to digest that a long moment. "Why didn't you kill him, knowing what it would mean?"

Kihgl looked up at Nebil. His old friend looked agonized. Softly, Kihgl said, "Would you have killed him, knowing what he'll do?"

Nebil took a long time to respond. "It was an honor to serve with you on Ubashin. I hope you can find peace with yourself before the end."

"No soldier does."

Nebil gave him a long, unhappy look, then nodded once and left.

• • •

As the eight days of intensive training before Kihgl's trial wore on, Joe drank up the information like water. That worried him. He had to remind himself that he wasn't going to become a soldier, that he was going back to Earth.

And yet, everything here was so *easy* for him. Marching was simple. Tactics were a breeze. And when he picked up a gun…

It was like the gun spoke to him, whispering its secrets, baring its faults.

Back in school on Earth, he had struggled through every class, just barely doing well enough to pass to the next grade. He went for the football and the friends, not for education. Here, he couldn't stop learning. His brain consumed every scrap of information like it was starving. He seemed to already have an innate knowledge of the Congressional military, like everything the Ooreiki told him was already floating under the surface of his subconscious and he just needed their words to unlock it. He soaked up the terminology, the strategies, the customs, the weaponry—and craved more.

I'm becoming one of them, Joe realized one night in horror. He pulled out his dad's Swiss Army knife and rubbed his thumb along the smooth red plastic, thinking about home, ashamed he had allowed himself to be brainwashed by the enemy.

The next day, Joe left others to answer the teachers' questions, deliberately made mistakes in the drills, and purposefully dropped his rifle when Battlemaster Nebil passed out the ceremonial weapons that they would need for Kihgl's trial, naming them *otwa.*

Though Nebil said nothing else about them, Joe knew that it was a design from countless years ago, one only used for important events. The gun felt old in his hands, a wizened thing of beauty. Its stock was formed from the same black rock that covered Kophat, and the metal held a blue-white sheen. He felt an instant respect when touching it, knowing that it meant something special to the aliens.

I'm not one of them, Joe thought suddenly, his admiration shutting off as if a switch had been flipped in his mind. *I'm not going to fight for them. I'm going home.*

The next morning, when Nebil showed them how the *otwa* worked, Joe pretended to be baffled. As an older model, it was more complex than anything Joe had taken apart thus far. It had over twenty pieces, all fitting together in odd and complex ways. Inside the outer layer of stone, strange interlocking pieces of different metals and compounds fitted together in ways that seemingly defied all logic. Faking ignorance was easy when the rest of the kids were completely bewildered by it.

Still, Battlemaster Nebil gave him an odd look when Joe struggled with every slide and pin, finishing only third from the last when he and Libby were always first. The next day, he did the same. It was on the third day that Libby confronted him about it.

"Why are you pretending you don't know anything?" Libby asked.

Joe had taken off his sweat-stained shirt, and now had it stretched out on his knee as he polished his rank. The rest of his groundteam was dead asleep, as they had been for the last two hours, ever since the rest of the platoon got to retire while Joe had to run laps because someone in his squad had screwed up the drills.

Joe gave her a tired look. "I don't know what you're talking about, Lib."

She narrowed her pretty brown eyes at him. "Yes you do. You're like me—you can see all the pieces in your head before you even touch them."

Joe went on polishing the silver triangle embedded into the fabric of his shirt. One thing Battlemaster Nebil required of him was that it held a perfect shine at all times, even after he'd been crawling through the diamond dust.

"Joe!" Libby poked his bare shoulder.

"Go back to bed," Joe muttered.

"What's wrong with you, Joe?" Libby insisted. "Are you sick?"

"I'm not gonna be a Congie," Joe said. "I'm going back home."

Libby's young brow furrowed instantly. "No you're not."

"Just because you wanna stay here doesn't mean the rest of us do." Joe flipped his jacket off his knee and held it up to inspect the silver triangle.

It should be a star, a rebellious part of him thought before he squashed it.

Irritated with himself, he folded his jacket neatly in his locker-niche and began unlacing his boots. "As soon as I get the chance, I'm out of here. I've figured out some of their writing, Lib. I got the barracks door to open for me on duty last night. Won't be long before I can do it every time."

Libby scowled at him. "You can't leave, Joe."

"I'm not fighting for some friggin' aliens, Lib," he growled back at her.

She stared at him long and hard. "Tril already hates you. You keep making Nebil mad and you're never gonna get battlemaster."

"*You* be the battlemaster," Joe said. "Nebil's never gonna give it to me. He hates me. You see how he treats Sasha. She screws up all the time and he doesn't find someone else. Then one recruit messes up in my squad and what does he do? He drills me for hours because I was responsible for him. Does he do that to anybody else? No. Does he make Sasha drill when *her* recruits screw up? No. It's just me. Why the hell does he do that to me?"

"Because you're better than them, Joe," Libby retorted. "You're gonna make the best soldier they've ever seen and Nebil knows it."

Joe laughed and slammed his boots into his niche, startling several sleeping recruits. "I'm getting out of here. Nebil can go screw himself." Without another word, he went to crawl in bed with the rest of his groundteam and go to sleep.

The next day, when Battlemaster Nebil had them check out their new weapons from the armory and disassemble them, Joe stalled. When Nebil had them reassemble them, Joe read the writing inscribed on the armory wall instead. He was going to need the writing to find a way off the planet. He'd never need the rifle.

Then, suddenly Libby's loud voice clearly rang out, "Battlemaster Nebil, Zero has put the barrel on backwards three times now and he's been playing with the trigger mechanism for twenty tics."

In the moment it took Joe to shoot Libby a scathing glance, Battlemaster Nebil was standing in front of his table. For the first time, the Ooreiki really inspected the parts arrayed before Joe. Apparently, he didn't like what he saw.

"*Get up, Zero.*"

Joe did.

"*Why are you not taking my class seriously?*"

Joe bit his lip, promising himself he would get back at Libby later.

"*Assemble your otwa, Zero.*"

Joe bent down and slowly started to fumble with the pieces.

"If it takes you more than a tic, I will take that little pocketknife you've been hiding from us in your gear and throw it into the waste system."

Joe glanced up sharply. Libby dropped her gaze and would not meet his eyes.

You little shit, Joe thought, utterly furious.

"Now, Zero," Nebil warned.

Furious, Joe assembled his weapon, the silence in the room shattered by the pops and clicks as he slammed the parts together. When he finished, he threw the weapon on the table in front of him, glaring at Battlemaster Nebil.

Instantly, Battlemaster Nebil had him by the throat in a stinging python grasp.

"The otwa is what we used to fight the first Jreet invasion, before we formed Congress. It comes of an era where our ancestors gave up their ideals to survive, and it will be treated with respect."

Joe held Nebil's brown gummi-bear eyes unflinchingly. *Why should I care about your ideals? It's not my history.*

The Ooreiki released him suddenly and peered down at the weapon. When he raised his eyes to Joe, his face resembled Kihgl's after Joe ran from him after the Choosing Ceremony. *"Am I making things too easy for you, Zero? Is that why you are insulting me like this?"*

Joe did not respond.

Battlemaster Nebil spun and disappeared inside the armory and returned toting a big gun Joe had never seen before. He slammed it down on the table in front of him. *"Disassemble that. You have one tic."*

Joe stared at it. It was like nothing he had ever seen before. "I don't—"

"Do it, Zero, or I'll find worse things to do to you than take a little trinket you're not supposed to have anyway." Battlemaster Nebil's voice was utterly cool, utterly furious. Joe had never seen him lose his temper like this. Swallowing, he picked up the weapon and turned it in his fingers.

It was completely foreign, the difference as great as that between the Congie guns and those he had watched his father clean a billion years ago on Earth.

Yet, somehow, Joe's fingers seemed to know what to do. They slid along the barrel, found the catch, and twisted it free. The cartridge came next, followed by the trigger mechanism and then the slide. It was more complex than the ceremonial weapon, much more. As each sleek blue part came off in his hands, Joe felt his confidence growing, until he had the entire weapon splayed out on the table in front of him. It had to be over a hundred pieces, some no larger than the tip of his thumbnail. Joe put it back together even quicker than he had taken it apart. He set it down in front of Battlemaster Nebil as one sleek, seamless piece.

Nebil stood before him in silence for so long that Joe began to shift uneasily.

"If you ever feign ignorance again, Zero, you will not eat for a week."

After the weapons class, Libby tried to apologize, but Joe ignored her. He managed to keep his cool through Tril's miniature hell, but when Linin lined them all up for an inspection and began berating them for arriving sweaty when Tril had not allowed them to wash off, Joe ended up in a shouting match with him. Afterwards, several battlemasters took Joe aside and took turns exercising him until he was too exhausted to move. They returned him to his room well into the night.

Libby was the only one still awake when the battlemasters shoved Joe into the barracks, doused in sweat and coughing up red phlegm.

"Sorry Joe," Libby whispered, trying to touch his arm as he passed.

Joe ignored her and stalked over to his gear to see if the aliens had taken his knife. They had. Furious, he went to the far corner of the room and lay down on the floor, his blanket wrapped around him. He was still wet—they hadn't allowed him a shower—and stank. The acne that had been bothering him had been rubbed raw and was stinging from all of the salt, but Joe couldn't sum up the energy to take a shower.

He was beginning to fall asleep when a cold hand touched his arm. Reluctantly, he looked over his shoulder.

Libby was squatting behind him, her face a picture of misery. She held out a fist. "They looked for it but couldn't find it." She dropped his knife into his palm. "I tried to get it all off, but it might still have a little spit on it—I had to hide it in my mouth."

Seeing his father's knife again, Joe felt his anger fade in a wash of total gratitude. "Thanks."

"I'm sorry, Joe," she said softly. "I should've left you alone."

"It's okay," Joe said. "No use worrying about it now."

"It's *not* okay," she whimpered, drawing her knees up to her chin. He could see tears glistening at the edges of her eyes.

Joe sat up and touched her shoulder. "It's okay. Really. All they did was run me around a bit."

She shook her head, biting her lip.

"Come here," Joe said. He dragged her into a hug. Her skinny body shook as he held her, but her tears were silent. When she was through, he held her at arm's length and looked her in the eye. "I'm not mad at you, okay? You were right. I shouldn't be blowing off my training. If we're—" Joe took a deep breath and let it out between his teeth. Starting over reluctantly, he said, "If we're gonna be here awhile, I should be paying attention. I don't take it seriously, I might miss something that will save my life later on."

The relief in her eyes as she looked up at him was immense. "How'd you take that gun apart, Joe? It wasn't in any of the pictures they showed us."

"I don't know," Joe said. "It was like you said. I just saw it in my head."

"There were too many parts. I couldn't have done that, Joe."

Joe ruffled her hair. "You're just eight, Libby. You might be growing like a beansprout, but you're still just a kid."

She straightened, her face serious. "I'll get better, Joe. I'll get so good they have to keep me here forever. I'm not going back."

Joe was taken aback by her vehemence. He wondered what her life had been like to make her this adamant about staying. He wished he knew if it were as bad as she claimed, or if it were simply an eight-year-old who didn't understand the pressures her parents were under. Not knowing quite what to say, he ventured, "Lib, it's not your mom and dad's fault the aliens took you…" When she didn't respond, he added, "They couldn't have stopped the aliens from taking you, Lib. None of our parents could. You shouldn't blame them for that."

"They never wanted me anyway," Libby said, obviously convinced of the fact. "I was the first one on the ship. My mom dropped me off early so she could go to a photo shoot. Why else do you think they called me recruit One?"

Joe frowned. "She did? You're serious?" He hadn't even bothered to learn Libby's number. When he looked at her armband, though, tiny numerals under the bold alien squiggle marked her as One. He lifted his eyes back to her sad face. "Lib, I didn't know—"

"It's okay, Joe," Libby interrupted. "I didn't like them anyway." She stood up. "I'll get better. Watch me. I'll get better than you, Joe. Then I'll never have to go back." Then she went back over to the bed and settled her head on Scott's arm, tugging a corner of a blanket over herself and closing her eyes.

Joe watched her, feeling a stab of pity. What had her home been like? His had been good, until the end. He flinched, remembering his mother's last words to him before the aliens caught him.

Go to Hell, Joe.

Minutes went by, Joe lost in thought. He started when he realized Scott was watching him over Libby's head.

"You gonna sit there all night, Joe?" Scott asked softly, so as not to wake the others.

"Thinking about it."

Gently, Scott levered Libby's head off of his arm and stood up. He came over to where Joe was sitting and squatted beside him. "She was really upset when they came looking for the knife."

Joe sighed. "Yeah, I know."

"You gonna forgive her?"

"I guess I have to, don't I?"

Scott glanced at the knife in Joe's hand, then shrugged. "You can do what you want. You're Zero."

Joe snorted.

Scott slumped against the wall beside him, sighing.

"You're not gonna sleep?"

"With you sitting there watching me?"

"I wasn't watching you. I was thinking."

"About what?"

"About home."

Scott absorbed that in silence. The minutes stretched out between them before he said, "Do you miss it?"

"Yeah." Joe felt his throat tighten, his eyes sting.

"Me, too," Scott said softly. This time, it was *he* who seemed to zone out, staring at the far wall in thought.

• • •

"Oh yeah? Well I bet I could hit that beer can over there."

Scott eyed the distance, then shrugged. Billy hefted the rock in his hand, then tossed it. It sailed past the can and landed in the dirt beyond.

"Want me to try?" Scott said.

Billy was still frowning after his last throw. He picked up another rock and tried again. It flew even further off course. He threw two more, neither of them even coming close.

"Want me to try?" Scott asked again.

Billy threw a pebble down in frustration. "We both know you can hit it."

"What about with my eyes closed?"

A sly look crossed his friend's face. "Eyes closed and I get to spin you around."

Scott felt a smile itch his lips. "But that's gonna be a lot harder than just throwing with my eyes closed. I should get your juice if I make it."

Billy eyed his juice box. "I don't know…"

"I'll give you the rest of my gum if I lose," Scott offered.

"Deal!" Billy cried. No one could resist an almost-whole pack of Big Red gum.

Scott tried to contain his grin as he picked up a stone. "Okay. I'm closing my eyes. Spin me."

"Bull!" his friend cried. "We need a blindfold." He glanced around and, finding nothing but dust, trash, and broken glass in the abandoned lot, he peeled off his shirt. "Here. Put this on."

Scott wrinkled his nose. "It's all sweaty."

"Well it's *hot* out. Now put it on. I'm not letting you cheat."

Scott sighed and took the shirt his friend offered. He tried not to inhale as Billy tied it around his forehead and checked to make sure it was secure.

"Okay," his friend said. "Here we go." He spun Scott around several times, stopping him in the opposite direction of the can. "There you go. Throw. You're facing the can."

Scott laughed and turned to face the can. He threw. Through the blindfold, he heard the tinny clatter as the pebble knocked the can over.

"How do you *do* that?!" Billy cried.

Scott left his blindfold on and turned. "Dunno." He grabbed Billy's juice box and unerringly poked the straw through the top, still blindfolded. He took a sip. Grape. Scott wrinkled his nose, but took another drink anyway.

"You don't even like grape," Billy muttered.

"I do now," Scott said. He was sipping through his straw, still showing off, when he felt something move overhead. He dropped the juice box and whipped the blindfold off.

"What?" Billy asked, following his stare. Nothing but perfect, blue sky.

Scott felt another presence follow the first. Just as he could point in a straight line to any place he'd ever been, from his grandma's home in Idaho to the gaming store downtown, he knew something was up there, moving above them.

Seeing nothing there, Scott felt waves of goosebumps electrify his arms and legs. "We need to get back home," he said, staring at the sky.

Billy frowned at him, then at the clouds. "You going crazy or what?"

"Something's happening," Scott said. He felt another presence slide overhead.

Billy crossed his arms stubbornly. "So now you got ESP too or what?"

"Come on, Billy," Scott said, grabbing him by the arm. The one above them had stopped, directly above the playground. "We need to go *now*."

"What about my juice?"

"Take it," Scott said, backing away. Whatever it was was sinking, getting closer. "I don't like grape anyway." Feeling the impending presence descending from above, Scott turned and bolted.

Billy, who knew Scott would never willingly give up the spoils of one of his bets, left the juice where it was.

16

STORYTIME

Battlemaster Nebil jolted them out of bed the next morning by upending their lockers over the floor.

"Get your gear!" he was screaming. "Get your fire-loving gear on *now!* Faster, faster! Do it *faster!*" The Ooreiki battlemaster's translator was turned off, as it was most of the time now.

Joe's groundteam stumbled over each other as they tried to pull their clothes from the jumble. They weren't doing it fast enough, however, and Battlemaster Nebil started kicking their gear around the room in a fury.

"You Takki sootbags would be dead by now! When you're fighting Dhasha, you have only three seconds after the first man screams before you're all dead! Hurry! No! The vest goes on the other way! Useless Human Takki! You're dead! All dead!"

All the while, the Ooreiki battlemaster was kicking clothes and boots around the room, upending lockers and throwing gear in all directions.

Joe managed to find a shirt big enough for him and put it on—it was tight around the chest, but as long as he didn't breathe too deeply, it would work. He found pants that pinched at the waist and, finding no better alternatives, forced his legs into them. He got a mismatched pair of boots, put them on, and struggled to find a vest that would fit. He finally had to coerce one of the smaller kids in another groundteam to give up a vest that was obviously much too big, getting into a fight with the kid's ground leader when he saw what was happening.

The battlemaster zeroed in on the disturbance like a hawk. "Zero, you Takki sootbag!" He let loose a string of Ooreiki curses, grabbed Joe by the neck of his shirt, and dragged him to the front of the barracks. "What were you doing, Zero?" he demanded, once Joe was out where everybody could see. "*Stand at attention*, you miserable furgling!"

Joe straightened, acutely aware that everyone was staring at him.

"Tell them your name and what you were doing!" Nebil shouted into his face, sudah fluttering on his neck in fury.

"I'm Joe and I…"

Battlemaster Nebil cuffed him. "You're a recruit! You have no name! Only a number! Remember that! What is your number, recruit?!"

"Zero," Joe said. *But my name is Joe.*

"Tell them what you were doing, Zero."

"I don't understand…" Joe began.

"Shut up, sooter!" Nebil snapped. "I don't want to hear your furgling voice unless I tell you to burning use it!"

"But you just told me to—"

"Did I tell you to tell us what you *understand?* No, I told you to tell them what you were *doing*. Do you know what you were doing? You were stealing from a fellow grounder. Stealing *gear* from another grounder. Do you know what the penalty is for stealing gear, Zero?"

"It was just a—"

Battlemaster Nebil cuffed him again. "Just a what, Zero? Just a vest? Just a piece of clothing? Just something that provides camouflage, just something to carry your gear, just something that keeps you warm when you're cold and hungry? Tell me, Zero, just what is it?"

"A vest," Joe muttered.

"It's your *life*, you miserable Takki. Every piece of gear you have can be used to save your life." Battlemaster Nebil leaned in close, until his huge gummi eyes were almost touching Joe's chin. "So why is your life worth more than the recruit you stole that vest from, Zero? Because you're a Squad Leader? That can change in a heartbeat, you Takki sootbag."

"I know," Joe said. "Our clothes got mixed up because you—"

"You took it from him and he didn't want to give it to you. You used brute force. You *stole* that vest, Zero."

Joe pressed his lips together, scowling down at the battlemaster. He was a foot taller than the Ooreiki, but the alien was a mass of muscle that could easily break every bone in his body. He waited.

"You shame me. You do not steal from other Congies. A squad leader gives everything he has to keep his grounders alive. He *never* takes from his own troops. *Never.*" Nebil broke into another string of Congie curses. Then, "Chins will deal with you later. Say the Groundteam Prayer."

Joe did, to the best of his ability.

"No good! Again!"

Joe did.

"Do it again! That sounded like Takki ashes! You are wrong!"

"I don't know what I'm—" Joe began.

Nebil hit him. "You do what I tell you! Say the Prayer. Again!"

Joe tried. Nebil told him he was wrong. He tried again. And got it wrong. Again. And again. Finally, the battlemaster recited it for him and made him repeat it six more times before he was satisfied.

Then Nebil shoved him out the door, vestless, rifleless, to march at the head of the platoon. He only tired of humiliating Joe when one kid started snickering at him as they went through rifle drills, Joe holding empty air. Nebil tore the rifle out of the snickering kid's hands and threw it to Joe, then proceeded to hound the snickering kid, shouting in Congie they didn't understand. The kid ended up wetting himself and running off to change through a hail of Congie curses. Then Nebil moved on to another unfortunate soul. Everyone got a taste of his wrath.

Their two food breaks were treasured moments, a full half-hour of peace where all they had to do was eat in silence. Then Battlemaster Nebil herded them back out to practice marching. They marched with gear, without gear, with rifles, without rifles, and one unfortunate boy got to march without boots when he complained that they were too heavy for him.

Not even the youngest kids were spared Nebil's attention. Maggie tripped and Nebil stood her up and shouted in her face until she was bawling. Maggie looked to Joe, who continued to stare straight ahead, knowing that Nebil was waiting for him to show a lack of discipline so he could punish his whole groundteam. Though it hurt to ignore her, Joe knew she needed to understand he couldn't always come to her rescue when she was in trouble.

In the end, Maggie stopped crying and started shouting back.

Nebil cuffed her, shoved her rifle back into her hands, and stalked away. Maggie scowled after him so long that Joe thought she would drop her rifle again. But she got back into formation and didn't look at Joe the rest of the day.

Later, Joe wished he could talk to Maggie, make it up to her, but between Sasha using his every spare minute to make him do pushups in front of everyone and the complete monopoly Battlemaster Nebil had on their time during waking hours, Joe didn't find the opportunity until that night, when Nebil left them sitting on the floor of the barracks cleaning their rifles before bed.

"What happened to Elf?" Monk asked once they were alone. It was the first time any of them had mentioned Elf's disappearance since Knaaren had taken him. "Where'd those lizards take him?"

No one wanted to answer her.

"Knaaren ate him," Libby finally said.

Monk's fingers whitened on her rifle. "He did not. Don't lie."

"I'm not lying," Libby said, continuing to clean her rifle without looking up.

"You're stupid. He *didn't* eat Elf," Monk said. "They can't because he's a *soldier* now." Like it was the Holy Grail or something. "Right, Joe?"

Before Joe could respond, Maggie said, "Joe doesn't know everything, you burning ashsoul." The last two words were perfect Congie, proof that Nebil had been teaching her something.

"Maggie!" Joe cried, glancing at the door. "Stop cussing!" The Ooreiki, he knew, considered 'ashsoul' to be an extreme insult, one of the worst verbal invectives someone could say to another.

"I don't have to," Maggie said. "The Ooreiki cuss all the time. I've got a gun. I'm a Congie now. Congies can cuss when they want to."

"Not in my groundteam."

"So make me stop, asher." Again, perfect Congie.

Libby, who was seated beside Maggie, swatted her in the back of the head.

Without warning, Maggie threw her rifle down and lunged at Libby, taking the bigger girl down with her tiny fingers gouging her eyes. Joe and Scott had to drag them apart to break them up.

"Let go of me!" Maggie cried, struggling in Joe's grip. "Let go! Let go, let go, let go, let *go!*"

"Mag, calm down! Calm—" Maggie kicked his thigh in a move that bumped his nuts just hard enough to hurt and ran from the barracks as he recovered, jumping over startled recruits still cleaning their weapons.

Worried Nebil might catch her in his rounds before lockup, Joe got up and ran after her. He caught her on the long, switchback stair to the ground.

"Maggie, stop!" he shouted, grabbing her around the waist. "You know what they do to kids that run off?!" She kicked him again in his knee for the trouble.

He twisted her around. "Mag, I'm sorry I didn't help you. I couldn't. We gotta be big kids now. We're soldiers. We can't cry anymore. We gotta dig in and get this over with, do what they tell us to do. You were doing great today...I was so proud of you."

Maggie wouldn't look up. "Sasha says I'm stupid because I can't hold my rifle."

Joe felt his irritation rise, remembering it. "I know." Sasha had also made Joe do pushups for taking the vest even after Nebil had forgotten about it.

"You should tell Nebil she's mean to us."

"I think he already knows," Joe said. "He doesn't care."

Maggie kicked at the stairs.

"Mag, I'm sorry I couldn't help you today," Joe said softly, squeezing her shoulder. "I won't always be there to help you. You gotta grow up and do things on your own."

"It was heavy," Maggie muttered, thumping her boot against the carved black stone.

"What?"

"The gun," she whined. "It was heavy. My arms hurt. And I tripped."

"I know," Joe said. "That wasn't your fault. You're small now, but you're getting bigger. Soon you'll be as big as the rest of us, and it won't be so hard for you."

She looked up at him, her tearful gray eyes seeking. "Is Elf really gonna get eaten?"

Joe opened his mouth to lie. Seeing her plaintive stare, however, his words died on his lips. "I don't know," he said honestly.

"I miss my guppies." Maggie's voice cracked, her eyes filling up with tears. She had the face and body of a teenager, but her mind...

Her mind was still a child's.

Joe hugged her. "I know you do, Mag."

"I can't remember what I named them," Maggie whispered. "All I remember is their spots. It's even getting hard to remember Mommy and Daddy."

Joe felt at a loss. He'd thought he was the only one. "I remember you called one of them Jabber."

Maggie's breath caught. "Can you help me remember the rest, Joe?"

"I can try," Joe said. *Oh yeah?* part of him demanded. *How, you dumbshit? You don't know anything about her. She's gonna grow up an alien because she's not gonna remember Earth.*

"You can tell me stories," Maggie said, taking his hand. "About Jabber and my parents."

"Okay. Sure, I can do that." *Oh, man, Joe, you idiot. You couldn't tell a story to save your ass.*

By the time they returned to the barracks, the others were already done inspecting their weapons and had turned out the lights. The day had been so exhausting that not even their own groundteam had waited up for them. Joe and Maggie finished with their rifles, folded their clothes, and Joe, hoping she had forgotten his offer, went to bed. Before he fell asleep, however, Maggie jerked on his sleeve and demanded her story.

Blushing, Joe made up a halting tale about a fish named Jabber and how her parents would feed him one pinch of food morning and night. It was hesitant at first, but as he talked, the words grew easier.

"But Jabber was getting lonely," Joe said, getting into it. "So he went out looking for other guppies."

"How did he get out of his bowl?" Maggie asked, fascinated.

"He put on a drysuit," Joe said. "You know, like a wetsuit, but one for fish."

Maggie listened, enraptured, as he put in all the details about Earth he could, trying to fix it in her mind so she didn't forget her home.

When he finished, he realized the entire barracks was sitting up in bed, listening to his tale. Softly, a little girl on the next bed over said, "Can you tell me a story tomorrow night? About my cat?"

"And my pet snake!" a boy cried, jumping up. "His name was Jax. Can you tell me about Jax?"

Joe scanned the hungry faces, feeling good for the first time in weeks. "Yeah." He grinned back at them self-consciously. "I can do that."

• • •

"Feed them as much as you want, Maggie. They deserve a treat."

Maggie gave the little cylinder of fish food a dubious glance. Her parents had been acting strange today. Maybe it had been Grammy and Pops showing up. They'd brought Maggie a lot of presents but didn't have any for Mommy and Daddy, so maybe they were mad she got to open everything and they didn't get any.

"Go ahead, Mag." Daddy smiled down at her, holding Mommy's hand. Their eyes were wet but Mommy and Daddy had gotten al-her-jic to the new sweater Grammy had given her and that's why they were crying.

"You feed them, Daddy," Maggie said, offering up the canister to her father. "Jabber likes you to do it."

"You should do it," Daddy said, making no move to take the fish food from her. "You need to, baby."

"As much as you want," Mommy added.

Maggie stared up at them, then down at the multi-colored flakes. She considered dumping the whole canister into the tank, then dutifully reached inside and drew out one pinch. This she sprinkled atop the water.

She giggled as Jabber raced the others to the top and sucked in three flakes before any of the others had one.

"You sure that's all you want to give them?" Mommy asked. "You can give them as much as you want, honey."

"But you said it would make them get sick," Maggie accused.

"Once in a while is okay, honey."

Maggie considered the surface of the water, which had been picked clean of food, and quickly put in another pinch. Then, feeling naughty, she twisted the cap back onto the canister and set it by the tank. She gave her parents an anxious glance to see if this had been some sort of test that she'd failed, but their faces held no disapproval. Her mother was being al-her-jic again.

"I don't have to wear Grammy's sweater," Maggie said, glancing down at the little yellow duck on the front. "I won't wear it if it makes you cry."

Mommy wiped her eyes. "No, baby. You're fine. Keep Grammy's sweater. She made it for you."

"But I don't like to see you cry, Mommy," Maggie said. "I'd rather you were happy."

Her mother ran from the room, leaving Maggie alone with Daddy. Maggie stared after her, feeling something wrench inside of her, but before she could start to cry herself, her father knelt in front of her and pulled her into a big hug.

"You've gotta be a strong little girl for Daddy, okay Mag? Grammy and Pops are going to take you on a trip for a while. You like to go on trips, right?"

"Do I get to see birds?" Maggie asked.

"You'll see all sorts of birds," Daddy told her. "Crows, blackbirds, seagulls—"

Maggie pushed her father at arm's-length so she could see his face. "If I'm really good, can we catch a little baby seagull so I can have it as a pet? I'd rather have a seagull than a parakeet."

Her father looked at the floor. "I'm sorry we never got you a parakeet, Mag. You like birds so much more than fish. We just thought—" He broke off and when he looked up at her, this time he was being al-her-jic. "Maybe Grammy will stop so you can get a seagull. You've got to ask her, though."

Maggie's heart soared. "Thank you, Daddy! I'll get you a seagull, too! It'll be the littlest, littlest seagull I ever saw and I'll give it to you so our seagulls can be friends."

"I'd love to have a seagull with you, Mag." Somehow, however, her father's smile didn't seem very happy. He hugged her again. "I love you, Mag."

"I love you too, Daddy."

17

KIHGL'S FALL

The morning of Kihgl's trial, Battlemaster Nebil did not knock over lockers to wake them up. He used a pocket-sized device that broadcasted his voice like a bullhorn.

"*Get your gear! Get your gear you useless Takki dogs! Ceremonial* otwa *and full regalia! Get dressed, furgs! Faster! Faster! Move your bony Human* asses *faster!*"

Joe scrambled to get his stuff on, but before he could finish, Nebil stopped them and made them take everything off again and start over.

"*Today is the* trial!" Nebil shouted. "*You will look* good *when Kihgl gets burned. Now do it again! Faster! Faster! You soot-eating furglings, move* faster!" All the while, he walked down the halls, shoving the alien bullhorn into people's faces and screaming at them if they weren't moving fast enough.

All of their ears were ringing by the time they finally got themselves meeting Nebil's standards. Then he had them spend an hour cleaning the *otwa* they had been drilling with the last week. Once they were pristine, he had them form up by groundteam on the black roadway below the barracks and marched them to the plaza, cursing at them all the way. There, they met up with the nine other platoons from Sixth Battalion and got into formation.

We look better, Joe thought with a bit of pride. Everyone was in step, and there was barely any jaggedness to their lines. That, and the painful process of taking off and putting on their gear had paid off—they almost looked professional. He even could see the other members of Sixth Battalion stand up straighter upon seeing the improvement.

Then he saw the other battalions marching up, every member adult-sized and utterly rigid in spine and step. As they took their places on either side of Sixth Battalion, Joe's heart sank. Whereas he had been proud of Sixth Battalion's straighter rows and crisper uniforms, the other battalions marched with enough force to shake the ground, their formations were confident and tight, and they carried dozens of streaming black banners bearing the symbol of Congress—eight small blue circles surrounding a large silver sphere—and the blocky squiggles of Congie writing.

Once again, they were going to look weak and unprepared. Joe saw Battlemaster Nebil eye the black banners and curse. Even Linin looked unnerved. He and the other Ooreiki of Sixth Battalion conferred momentarily, then Tril stalked over to the tertiary commander leading Fifth Battalion and spoke with him with increasing intensity, loud enough to be heard over the commands of the battalions still arranging themselves in the plaza.

Tril returned to Sixth Battalion with his sudah fluttering harder than Joe had ever seen before. Sharply, he shouted in Congie, "Battlemasters, are your platoons in order?"

"They are, Commander!" the battlemasters returned in unison, their voices booming over the plaza with an intensity that made Joe stare.

"Good. Retain them."

"Retain!" Nebil shouted at them.

That, Joe had learned, meant to stand with his heels together, his toes pointed at a forty-five degree angle, his arms held tightly down in front of him, one hand grasping the butt of his rifle and the other grasping the barrel. Sixth Battalion managed to do it quickly enough, though the sound of their boots slamming the ground were not as loud as the battalions on either side.

"Check arms!"

Joe quickly popped the rifle back, opening up the fist-sized bulbous chamber. Inside were a cluster of blue pellets inside a tight membrane resembling a sac of fish eggs. He snapped his rifle shut and winced at the way the snaps from Sixth Battalion's guns echoed unevenly, spread out between a ten-second interval. In the other battalions, the snaps roared as one, a crisp and even sound that left his hair standing on end.

Joe felt a rush of shame as they stood there, bannerless, feeling the other battalions' disdain like a hot poison in his chest.

It wasn't fair.

Sixth Battalion's battlemasters seemed to share his anger. All of their sudah were fluttering hotly as they stood beside their platoons.

Down the ranks, First Battalion's commander called out a question and they responded by lifting their rifles to their shoulders and, aiming over the heads of the recruit in front of them, fired into the sky. The *"Kkee Diinrok!"* that blasted across the plaza from nine hundred mouths made Joe flinch. He knew Sixth Battalion didn't sound that good.

Down the lines, each battalion fired their rifles in time, the echoing *burp* signaling they were ready. When it came time for Sixth Battalion's turn, Commander Tril lifted his voice over the plaza. "Is Sixth Battalion ready to serve?"

They lifted their rifles and fired on queue and shouted a ragged *"Kkee Diinrok!"* that was garbled from everyone starting at different times. Then a kid brought his weapon up and fired late, probably thinking that being late was better than not firing at all, and the sound of his gun cut off Tril's ceremonial reply. Joe was close enough to Fifth Battalion to hear several of them snicker.

"The Sixth is ready to serve!" Tril repeated, sudah whipping in his neck as he scowled at the child who had fired out of turn. Joe knew the poor kid would probably get run into the ground for his mistake. "We shall hear the accused." The rest of the regiment repeated the drill, then the entire plaza fell silent as everyone waited. Out of the corner of his eye, Joe saw bright-clad Ooreiki civilians watching from balconies like curious children.

Then he saw him. It was impossible to miss the Dhasha's iridescent rainbow scales silhouetted against the obsidian behind him. The beast rode in an elevator, descending one of the nearer buildings. He was scanning the formation as the machine bore him down the side of the Prime Commander's tower, his sharkish mouth open. Even from this distance, Joe could see the multiple rows of triangular black teeth, the egg-shaped crystalline green eyes focusing on them without pupils.

He was only a hundred feet from the bottom. Joe's heart began to pound. He wished the elevator would quit. He wished the building caved in. He wished the power would go out… Anything to keep it from reaching the plaza and releasing its cargo upon the recruits again.

His prayers went unanswered. As Lord Knaaren stepped off the elevator, a deep, resonant horn echoed across the plaza, vibrating in Joe's spine. Knaaren strutted toward them deliberately, trailing a handful of the twenty-eight children he had taken the week before. Joe could not tell if Elf was amongst them without turning his head to look.

Instead of stopping at each battalion as he had the last time, Knaaren stalked directly to Sixth Battalion. Commander Tril stepped out to meet him.

"Where are your standards?" Knaaren demanded. *"Every battalion has standards except yours."*

"I was never notified our standards were ready, Ko-Knaaren," Tril replied.

"So you are unprepared."

"I was busy securing battle dress and otwa *cartridges for my recruits."*

"So you're incompetent. That should have been done beforehand."

"I was working with Peacemakers until the last inspection, Ko-Knaaren. I'm still catching up."

The Dhasha snorted, and Joe felt the blast of rotting breath all the way from where he stood. *"So be it. The traitor's battalion does not need standards."*

"I'll find them as soon as we're done here."

"You don't need them. Your battalion is a disgrace. They'll be stored for the day you deserve to carry them."

All around Joe, the Ooreiki of Sixth Battalion stiffened. He could feel their anger like heat waves emanating from them, but none of them moved to object.

Tril bowed his head quickly. *"As you wish, Commander."*

"You will refer to me as Your Lordship, you stupid vaghi."

"My apologies, your lordship," Tril said immediately. "I'd forgotten you used a different ranking system." Joe had never seen an Ooreiki so subservient.

The Dhasha, meanwhile, appeared to be enjoying making the Secondary Commander grovel. "You forgot? You ignorant Takki. Dhasha spit on Congressional titles. Perhaps I should just take you back to groom me tonight so you don't forget again, eh, Tril?"

"I apologize, your lordship," Tril repeated. "It will not happen again."

"See that it doesn't. And see that your Humans learn the proper way to march. Their efforts are disgraceful."

"Of course, your lordship."

Lord Knaaren grunted and moved away, circling Sixth Battalion slowly, eying its recruits. Joe caught Elf staring at him from the knot of humans following the Dhasha commander. His eyes were red and puffy from crying, his face pale as death. Joe watched him until they moved out of sight, guilt scoring his chest.

"I want that one," Knaaren said, stopping.

Commander Tril stepped forward.

Battlemaster Nebil caught Tril by the arm and stopped him. "No, furg," he hissed under his breath, glancing to make sure Knaaren hadn't seen. "You'll only make it worse."

Tril's sudah were fluttering as he violently ripped his arm out of Nebil's grip. He stalked toward the Dhasha, who was slowly walking along the ranks, eying the rest of Sixth Battalion, his new slave walking behind him with the rest. Knaaren gave a startled snort when Tril stepped in front of him.

"I'm going to have to ask you do not take any more of my recruits, Ko-Knaaren. We are down twenty-nine as it is."

Knaaren jerked to stare at him, emerald eyes cold. "You dare tell me what to do, Ooreiki?"

Tril stood tall despite the way the Dhasha's rainbow lips were peeling away from his teeth. "It is a request, your lordship. Nothing more."

"Then I deny your request." Knaaren began choosing recruits from the ranks at random. He didn't stop until he reached twenty-nine. Bearing huge, sharklike black teeth, the Dhasha paused in front of a rigid Tril and said, *"Now you're down another twenty-nine. If you haven't improved them in a week, I will take twenty-nine more."*

"The battalion can't function in the—"

"It will function or it will perish," Lord Knaaren retorted.

Tril's body was as stiff with rage. *"Your lordship, the combined force exercises have minimum troop requirements for each battalion. You would put us below the standard if you take any more."*

Knaaren sprang at Tril, but landed short, his thousands of pounds of muscle making the ground shudder and spraying the front row of recruits with a shower of gravel. Commander Tril stumbled backwards, his sudah rippling in his neck.

"Then if I take any more," Knaaren growled, his slick ebony teeth brushing Tril's neck, *"I'll have to start with you, Ooreiki worm."*

"I'm sorry, milord. So sorry…" Tril fell backwards to the ground, cringing and babbling in terror.

Knaaren snorted and turned on the children behind him, Tril's groveling already forgotten. *"Take the whimpering Humans back to my quarters. They're making it hard to think."*

Bet that's not very difficult, you asshole, Joe thought.

Finished with Sixth Battalion, Knaaren moved to the front of the regiment and faced them. A Takki turned up the volume on the translator hanging from the Dhasha's thick neck.

"You all know why you're here," the translator boomed across the plaza. *"One of your battalion commanders is a traitor to Congress. We are here to give him the punishment he deserves."*

"You are here to give him a fair trial, Knaaren," Commander Lagrah said. Joe felt every Ooreiki in the plaza stiffen. Beside him, Battlemaster Nebil sucked in his breath and turned to watch their Ooreiki Prime Commander.

Knaaren twitched to stare at Lagrah. *"Do you wish to join him, Commander? Perhaps you'll share a cell on Levren. I hear a vkala is always welcome there."*

"Such is why the Dhasha are rarely elected to the Tribunal." The new voice came from above them. *"You have absolutely no tact."* Lord Knaaren looked up, digging his talons into the plaza beneath him. Representative

Na'leen sat enthroned on a huge haauk floating twenty feet off the ground, six Huouyt attendants clustered about him.

"Come down here and speak to me like that, you spineless Takki coward," Lord Knaaren snapped up at Na'leen.

Instantly, the pilot lowered the skimmer to the ground and Na'leen disembarked, striding up to Knaaren and stopping directly under his huge jaws. *"I said, your kind are too stupid to serve on the Tribunal. You have the thought processes of an Ooreiki niish that just crawled from its membrane. It would please me greatly to see you declawed and trained as beasts of burden."*

Knaaren tensed, and for a moment, Joe thought he would eat Na'leen. Finally, he said, *"You're filled with empty threats. The trial proceeds at my direction."*

Representative Na'leen peered up into the Dhasha's eyes, his electric-blue gaze cold. *"If I had threatened you, furg, you would be dead now."* He ignored the Dhasha's teeth as if they did not exist to him. *"I won't waste words trying to make a Dhasha see reason. I came to watch and advise. You will heed me, or Congress will have to find a use for your scales, once they tear them off your back."*

The Dhasha took a step toward the Representative, forcing him backwards with his massive, scaly chest. Immediately, two bus-sized Jreet materialized and jammed their glassy daggers into the Dhasha's chest, under the scales. Knaaren backed up, teeth clacking together in a laugh as deep violet blood began to leak from around the Jreet spearheads. The Jreet, in turn, yanked their spears free and vanished again.

Representative Na'leen continued as if nothing had happened. *"I did not come here to humiliate you, Knaaren."* He lifted a flat, paddle-shaped limb languidly, his cloth-of-gold cape shimmering about his shoulders. *"I came to observe your pathetic attempt at justice."*

"He'll get a fair trial," the Dhasha said.

Na'leen bowed, surprisingly elegant for a being that most resembled a squid. *"Then I leave it in your capable claws."* He moved in his awkward three-legged shuffle back to the skimmer and settled into the scoop-shaped throne in its center.

Knaaren turned his back to the Huouyt abruptly. In an angry snarl, he snapped, *"Bring out the prisoner!"*

Four black-clad Ooreiki emerged from the far end of the plaza, leading an Ooreiki dressed entirely in white. Joe realized, horrified, that Kihgl was missing his arms. Where the flowing brown tentacles had once been, two wiggling stubs remained. They looked like the tail of a lizard regrowing itself.

They tortured him. It left a tightness in Joe's chest as he watched. As much as Kihgl had scared him over the course of the last few weeks, he had still saved him at the Choosing and protected him from the Peacemaker. He had let Joe into his confidence. He had even tried to give him Battlemaster.

I'd be dead if it weren't for him, Joe thought, taking in the gashes that were still raw to the fact that one half of Kihgl's face was limp and drooping.

The tension in the air as Kihgl approached increased a thousandfold, and the sudah of every Ooreiki in the plaza was fluttering.

Kihgl's escort came to a halt in front of the Dhasha, then backed off several paces, leaving Kihgl standing alone before the predator.

"Cut yourself, Commander?" Kihgl asked, looking at the purple fluid leaking from the wounds the Jreet had given him.

The Dhasha stiffened, and for a second, Joe thought he would eat him. *"Battalion commanders, approach,"* Knaaren snapped.

Tril left Sixth Battalion to stand with the other eight, facing Kihgl in a grim line. The Dhasha towered behind them, resplendent and gleaming. A young, dark-skinned Ooreiki with an eight-pointed star on his dark blue uniform stepped in front of them. Unlike a Prime Commander, however, each point of the young Ooreiki's star had a tiny circle balancing upon it, each a different color. Several of the battlemasters stared at the symbol, their sticky eyes hard.

The strange Ooreiki unrolled a shimmering scroll and raised it in front of him as he spoke. *"Secondary Commander Kihgl of the Three Hundred and Twenty-Fifth Ooreiki Ground Force,"* the new Ooreiki read, *"you are charged with treason, conspiracy, sedition, and espionage. Myself and attending members of the Peace Force found forbidden volumes and artifacts hidden in your quarters. Further questioning revealed you have a vast knowledge of the Trith conspiracy. We have examined archives from your previous duty stations and found numerous occasions where your loyalties are questionable in your speech and actions. On these grounds, we have found reasonable evidence to* implicate you for the charges previously stated. What is your defense?" The Peacemaker rolled up the silky parchment and waited.

Joe held his breath with the others, willing Kihgl to say something that would spare him.

Kihgl's sudah remained utterly still. "I have no defense."

"You admit your guilt?" Knaaren demanded.

Kihgl continued to stare at the fluid dripping from Knaaren's chest. It was already starting to slow, now, becoming only a small trickle. Kihgl seemed to take a breath, steadying himself, before returning his gaze to the line of battalion commanders. "This trial has only two outcomes for me, and I fear them both more than death itself. Do what you will."

The line of Ooreiki stared at him in silence. When it was obvious none of the other commanders were going to question him, the Peacemaker insisted, "The ship's records indicate you questioned Congress's motives in making you train these recruits."

Kihgl remained motionless, sudah as though dead. "In the beginning, I didn't believe they were worth my time. I wanted to get back to my old regiment on Lakarat, not waste my skills trying to train Humans that would in all likelihood end up in a Dhasha's pens. Ooreiki are Congress's grounders. No other species has even come close to matching our success in the tunnels. Humans are so weak—I thought they should've been assigned to the Space Force or the Sky Force. I didn't understand how the bureaucrats on Koliinaat could be stupid enough to put them in biosuits."

On his haauk, Representative Na'leen made an amused snort.

"So you believed Congress was wasting your time?" Tril demanded pointedly.

Kihgl turned to face Tril directly. "Kkee."

"Proof of his guilt," Knaaren said.

"Please," Na'leen snorted from his haauk. "It's a common sentiment. If you'd ever sat through a Regency meeting over mineral rights, you would understand."

"Explain to me why you ran," Lord Knaaren said, ignoring the Huouyt. "If you are innocent, why did you flee?"

"I was afraid."

Joe blinked. Kihgl had actually tried to run?

"*You are a secondary commander of the Congressional Army. You fought my kind on Ubashin and survived. If you were innocent, you had nothing to be afraid of.*"

"*I am not innocent.*"

The Dhasha stiffened, its talons digging into the gravel. "*If you're not innocent, why are we wasting our time trying you?*"

"*I don't know.*"

Lord Knaaren's thick muscles tightened under his metallic rainbow scales. The rest of the formation was silent as they stared at Kihgl. "*Do you have anything to say in your defense?*" Knaaren snapped.

"*No,*" Kihgl replied.

The Dhasha growled, deep in its chest. "*Commanders, your verdict.*"

For a long moment, none of them spoke. Then, softly, Commander Lagrah said, "*Kill him.*"

Kihgl's sudah gave the briefest of flutters, then went still.

No, Joe thought. *Please don't kill him.* Guilt was settling over his shoulders like a moldy jacket. This was his fault. Kihgl had gone crazy over that stupid tattoo…

Joe glared at the other Commanders, feeling angry that Kihgl's own friends would betray him. Lagrah, in particular. Once, Joe had thought the ancient, drooping-skinned Ooreiki was one of the good ones, one of the ones that saved children who were slated to die. Now, he simply looked old. The pale, sagging skin that had once made Joe think of power and wisdom now looked washed out and used up. The black scars crisscrossing were no longer impressive. They made Joe hate him because they made him look like Kihgl. *They're nothing alike,* he thought angrily, looking from Kihgl's still form to Commander Lagrah. Each was motionless, staring at each other, saying nothing more.

A thin stream of neon-orange saliva began to drip from between the parallel rows of the Dhasha's black teeth. "*I hear no other opinions,*" he said.

"*Neither do I.*" As Kihgl said it, his body relaxed. He almost sounded relieved.

The Peacemaker stepped forward with his silken paper and two of his companions grabbed Kihgl by the white uniform he wore, forcing him to face the herald. *"Kihgl, we have determined you to be a traitor to the Congress…"*

The interesting part over, the Dhasha made a satisfied grunt and began to walk back to the elevator.

"…You are hereby stripped of all rank in the Congressional Army and shall be shipped to Levren for further questioning. Afterward, you shall receive Jreet poison through the chest until you are dead. Three days later, your oorei will be extracted and shipped to Poen for burial."

The Peacemaker lowered his silken scroll. *"Do you have any last words for the assembly before you meet your fate?"*

"Kkee," Commander Kihgl said. He was facing the Dhasha, who was walking away. *"I'm looking forward to the day someone puts you animals in your place."*

Lord Knaaren turned back, mild curiosity in his gemlike eyes. When he saw Kihgl staring at him, he let out an angry snarl and padded back. *"What did you say?"*

"Careful, Lord Knaaren," the Peacemaker said. *"This one belongs to us now."*

The Dhasha made a disgusted sound and swatted at Kihgl lightly—shredding one of the new limbs growing from Kihgl's side. Then he turned and began to walk away again.

Kihgl ignored his dangling limb like it didn't matter to him. *"You're abominations. Congress should've never let you crawl off that sootwad you call a planet."*

What are you doing? Joe's mind screamed. *Shut up, you dumbass.*

Lord Knaaren spun around on his haunches and launched himself at Kihgl, who stared him down. Lord Knaaren's basketball-sized emerald eyes were glinting like cold gems.

"Take him back to holding!" the Peacemaker snapped. *"Lord Knaaren, he is a Peace Force prisoner now. Killing him does us no good until we learn his secrets."*

Lord Knaaren was ignoring the Peacemaker, his emerald eyes locked on Kihgl's. He was utterly motionless, like a cobra about to strike.

As the other Peacemakers reached to take Kihgl away, Kihgl said, *"You're just helpless niish."*

"Silence that prisoner!" the Peacemaker screamed. His companions cuffed Kihgl and dragged his head backward until Joe could see a vibrating ball in his throat.

"Release him." Lord Knaaren's voice was crisp. Cold.

The two Peacemakers glanced at their leader, then reluctantly let Kihgl go.

"What did you mean by that, traitor?" Knaaren snarled. *"Who are helpless?"*

No, don't say it, Joe pleaded.

"The Dhasha," Kihgl replied.

Lord Knaaren stared at him for long moments, his emerald eyes glinting. Finally, he said, *"Are you calling me weak?"*

Kihgl gave the Dhasha lord an amused look. *"Without your Takki, you are nothing. Someday, they will grow tired of serving you and you'll all die, starving and rotting in your own filth. Until then, you should be returned to the pitiful rock you came from and used to pull plows."*

Lord Knaaren let out a roar and lunged forward. In an instant, he bit down on Kihgl's torso.

A rush of brown fluid spilled out over the rips in Kihgl's white clothing and out onto the plaza to soak into the crushed black diamond. Kihgl's lower half started to thrash and Joe could hear his former secondary commander screaming inside the Dhasha's jaws. Knaaren stepped on Kihgl's feet and jerked back, separating the upper half of Kihgl's body from his legs and groin, then snapped his head forward and swallowed.

"You petty, stupid beast!" the high-ranking Peacemaker screamed. *"He was not to be killed!"*

Lord Knaaren leapt at the nearest blue-clad officer and swallowed him whole. The survivors ran to hide behind Representative Na'leen's skimmer and Knaaren tore into the Huouyt on the ship, knocking two of its passengers to the ground. Even as the Huouyt cried out and changed colors like startled squid, he ate them. Then Representative Na'leen's haauk took to the air, pulling the Representative well out of range of the Dhasha's frenzy, while, simultaneously, three enormous ruby-scaled Jreet materialized in front of Knaaren, the plaza resounding with their rumbling *shee-whomp* battlecry.

Knaaren's rainbow plates were tight against his body now, however, and only one of the Jreet spears made it into his chest. One shattered with the force behind the Jreet's attack and another made a tortured, metallic sound as the scale deflected it. As the third slid against the grain and sank into his flesh, Knaaren let out a roar that made the gravel tremble and threw himself at the Jreet responsible. The other two Jreet disappeared as Knaaren slammed their companion to the ground, ripping it into long red shreds as if its body were made of lettuce.

Higher up, a dozen more haauk appeared, crawling with Huouyt. They did not land, but fired hundreds of plasma shots that harmlessly bounced off Knaaren's scales and into the spectators, dripping from his body like oil. Knaaren sneered at them, pieces of the Sentinel still clinging to his teeth. Then he went back to Kihgl's body and began to feast, ripping and tearing at the Ooreiki's torso with black razor claws.

The two larger Jreet used the opportunity to attack again. In an instant, they had both wrapped their long bodies around him, cinching down his arms and legs, drawing the Dhasha to the ground in a stranglehold. As Knaaren struggled vainly, one of the Jreet used its muscular red arms to pry up one of the scales guarding the Dhasha's back, preparing to stab it with the poisonous appendage in its chest.

"Leave him!" Na'leen snapped.

Immediately, the two massive Jreet vanished. Moments later, Knaaren was on his feet again. *"Cowards!"* he screamed, spinning and raking his talons at air. *"Come fight me, cowards!"*

All of it had happened in a matter of seconds. A dozen Huouyt and Ooreiki Peacemakers lay scattered in bloody pieces, their corpses mingled with the crimson strips of an enormous Jreet. Several children in Third Battalion lay dead or dying, body parts disintegrating under the blue goo coating them. When the two larger Jreet did not reappear, the Dhasha spun back to Kihgl's body in a rage, tearing the corpse to unidentifiable strips before he ate it, ignoring Na'leen's angry shouts.

Then everything went silent. A glowing yellow ball had slipped out of Kihgl's corpse and was rolling over the ground, tinkling across the rough black gravel. Around it, a luxurious golden fog was spreading, expanding with the pulse of a slow heartbeat.

Several Ooreiki rushed to retrieve the ball, but Knaaren swatted it out of their reach. The tiny sphere went tinkling across the plaza and stopped against a recruit's boot, the amber fog still pulsing around it. The startled child flinched, but managed to hold his composure until Knaaren stalked across the plaza to retrieve it, at which time the recruit had to jump out of the way to keep from losing a foot.

"Don't do it, furg," Representative Na'leen warned.

Knaaren lifted the small yellow ball in his mouth, the golden cloud spreading between the rows of black razors lining his jaws, caressing them. Knaaren's rigid, toadlike tongue stretched out and licked at the amber fog, spreading it around like tendrils of disturbed smoke. Then he squeezed his mouth shut.

Sparkles of gold cascaded from the Dhasha's jaws and the nearby Ooreiki gave a collective gasp. Several battlemasters stumbled out of formation in horror, eyes riveted to the glittering remnants of the oorei. The golden cloud spread over the fallen pieces, then slowly dissipated into nothing.

…like dust in the wind, Joe thought, his gut twisting in horror.

Still hovering above the plaza, Representative Na'leen's voice was calm. *"That's on* your *head, you ignorant savage."* At that, he wheeled his haauk around and flew away, his retinue of Jreet and Huouyt warriors following on a dozen ships behind him.

The Ooreiki closest to the shattered oorei pooled its lower body to the ground and began a deep, heart-rending cry that built as more voices joined it. They surrounded the scattered shards of Kihgl's oorei, pushing the Dhasha out of the way as they raised their sorrow in song.

Knaaren backed up, glaring at them. *"You are jenfurglings, to mourn over a traitor."*

The Ooreiki ignored him, their mournful voices rising in a growing tide.

Lord Knaaren snorted. *"I cannot bear these wretches' howling."* At that, he turned and departed, trailing his escort of Takki.

And it wasn't just the Ooreiki in the courtyard, Joe realized. The entire *city* was taking up the heart-rending wail. It was reverberating from every hollow cave, every skyscraper, bouncing off every wall, every crevice, a mournful sound that reached to the very soul. The kids stood in formation for another twenty minutes, but none of the Ooreiki made any motions to excuse them. They had gathered in a circle around the pieces of Kihgl's oorei and were ignoring them completely, their collective song loud enough to make the diamond jitter at their feet.

Once the Ooreiki screaming had lasted more than an hour, one of the recruits from the other battalions muttered he was hungry. His battalion disintegrated as its members went to go have lunch. Another battalion followed, and another, until Joe's and the Second Battalion were the last two remaining. Only the constant training of the past few days kept Joe and the others in place. After endless hours of Nebil's drills and Tril's attempts to trick them, one thing stood out in their minds more than anything else—they hadn't been dismissed yet.

After a while, Sasha made a disgusted noise and started to move, but Libby stopped her. "They didn't dismiss us," Libby said.

"They're just standing there howling," Sasha said. "Besides, I'm battle-master. I'll dismiss us for them." She gave Libby a condescending look and started to leave the formation.

"Stay," Joe commanded.

Sasha jerked, frowning at him like he'd just grown antennae. "*What* did you say to me, recruit?"

"Stay," Joe repeated, "Or I'll make you stay."

"*We'll* make you stay," Scott said.

"Yeah," Monk said. "*We'll* make you stay."

Sasha scowled at Monk, who was quickly becoming the smallest member of the battalion, and for a moment, Joe thought she would try to dismiss the battalion anyway. Then her gaze passed from Monk to Libby, to Maggie, to Scott, all of whom were staring her down with the obvious intent of pounding her freak jaw into oblivion.

Nervously, she turned back to Joe. She looked him up and down with a disdainful sneer and Joe watched her reach that split-second decision where she judged whether or not her five-five frame could win in a fistfight.

Sniffing loudly with disdain, Sasha returned to her place as recruit battlemaster. For the next hour, she sighed, rolled her eyes, and fidgeted as the Ooreiki song went on. Joe glared at the back of her head as she stood in front of them, pouting. *That spoiled brat doesn't deserve to be battlemaster*, he thought bitterly, watching her scuff at the diamond dust. All around them, all activity in the entire city had come to an utter standstill. All haauks had landed, their colorful passengers all facing the courtyard and its pitiful group of black-clad mourners.

Across the plaza, Second Battalion also remained where it was.

The Ooreiki did not stop wailing. Instead, their despondent cry continued to grow until the very air trembled and all of Alishai was ringing with the sound. The noise was so powerful it made Joe's knees and lungs shake. It was so unavoidably *strong* it felt to Joe like they were *inside* a violin or a set of bagpipes, and that the sound was seeping into every single molecule, of everything from his flesh and blood to the stone at his feet. Joe had to clench his fists together in front of him to keep from feeling his fingerbones vibrating against each other. The sound penetrated everything, right down to his marrow.

But still it continued.

Other cities took up the cry. Like the odd scraping sounds in the forest, the echoes of the other cities were a distant, softer tone that bounced against the ferlii and seemed to come from everywhere at once. It felt like it was going to rattle him apart.

"That sound's driving me crazy," Sasha said. "You guys are really stupid to make us stay here. Her angular face was strained, her hands clenched into fists at her side.

"My fingers are going numb," Scott said behind Joe.

"I'm hungry," Maggie whimpered.

And still the Ooreiki howled. On and on, until Joe thought he was going to lose his mind.

Then it stopped.

All at once, like a conductor had dropped his wand, every single Ooreiki on the planet stopped screaming. The echoing silence was enormous, filling his ears until they hummed. Then, like nothing had ever happened, the Congies all turned away from the shattered pieces of the oorei to face their recruits.

Sixth and Second Battalions got to sleep that night. The others did not.

18

CHRISTMAS SONGS

"Any of you know any Christmas songs?" Joe asked into an otherwise sullen silence. He had gotten all of his chores done and he was bored, looking for something to do. From what he could guess, it was sometime around Christmas, though he couldn't be sure. The Congies measured time differently, and had never given them a conversion of turns to years—they just expected the kids to pick it up as they went.

"I do!" Monk cried, "I know lots. Jingle Bells, Rudolph the Red Nosed Reindeer, Dashing Through the Snow—"

"That's Jingle Bells," Scott said.

"No it's not."

"Yes it is."

"No it's *not*. Joe, is it Jingle Bells?"

"I don't know," Joe admitted. "Not big on Christmas."

"So why do you wanna sing Christmas songs?" Scott asked.

"I think it's around Christmastime."

"That was last week," Libby said.

"Well soot. I mean damn. I mean crap. *Burn.* Mag, just close your ears, okay?"

"We missed Christmas?" Maggie asked in a tiny voice. Her eyes were wide, and her lip had started trembling.

Wincing, Joe said, "Maybe. It was close to Christmas when we left."

"It was last week," Libby said again.

"Well, Hell," Joe muttered, giving Libby an irritated look. She hadn't been wrong yet, but couldn't she just *fudge* it for once? "We can make our own Christmas."

"When are we gonna get our presents?" Maggie asked, with instant excitement.

"Aliens don't believe in Christmas," Monk said. "Mom says they're all heathens and Mr. Allen says they're all going to Hell. Why would they give us presents if they're all going to Hell?"

"*Santa* could bring us presents," Maggie retorted. "I don't want alien presents anyway. I want them from Santa. When is Santa going to bring us presents, Joe?"

Monk frowned. "There is no—"

"We don't have to have presents to have a good Christmas," Joe interrupted. He shot Monk a pointed look and pulled the top of his collar shut to retain warmth. The sun was on its dark cycle again, and they were all wearing heavy, heat-retaining jackets because the barracks weren't heated.

"How can you have Christmas without presents?" Maggie asked, perplexed.

"Christmas isn't about presents, it's about getting out of school," Scott said.

"It is *not!*" Monk cried. "Christmas is about making sure you give everyone a good gift so the Lord doesn't think you're stingy and send you to Hell."

Libby rolled her eyes and stayed out of the conversation. She was using Joe's Swiss Army knife to cut holes in her gear. Joe had already tried to stop her, but she had ignored him.

Joe rubbed the acne that was itching on his back, then sighed. "Let's hear Rudolph the Red Nosed Reindeer. I don't know anything else."

Monk joyfully broke out into *Rudolph the Red Nosed Reindeer* and he and Maggie joined in. It took a little bit longer for Scott, but soon enough half their barracks room was singing. Libby looked up with a frown and watched them over her gear, but didn't join.

Once they finished *Rudolph the Red Nosed Reindeer*, Joe started *Deck the Halls* and even more kids got into it, some of them learning the lines as they went. For the first time in months, Joe saw an entire roomful of kids grinning and laughing. He heard more of Sixth Battalion start up all around him, their voices reverberating off the honeycombed black walls and glassy ebony tunnels.

Joe thought Sixth Battalion was singing awfully loud when he realized that it wasn't just them. The level above them was singing, too. He actually stopped and listened, stunned, as kids on the other barracks levels took up the song.

They finished *Deck the Halls*, and Monk started singing *Frosty the Snowman*. This time, the sound was incredible. It echoed against the glassy walls, threatening to shatter them.

"You hear that?" Libby whispered after the last verse was over.

But by that time, the battalion below them had started singing *The Twelve Days of Christmas*. All around them, the stone was vibrating with thousands of voices. Joe went to the locked barracks door and quickly punched in the code he'd seen Nebil use to open it. After glancing both ways for battlemasters, Joe stepped onto the balcony. Libby followed him outside to listen. Standing still on the circular highways surrounding the other buildings, brightly-garbed Ooreiki civilians had stopped their daily activities and were staring at the barracks. Some had even boarded haauk and approached, their brown eyes alight with curiosity.

Once *Deck the Halls* was over, someone started *Old MacDonald Had a Farm*. Then it was *Row, Row, Row Your Boat*. Joe was dumbstruck. Eight thousand voices vibrating in the caves sounded like thunder. They stuck to kids' songs for a while, then someone started *Oh Say Can You See* and they went through a litany of patriotic songs loud enough to make the walls shake. They did every song Joe knew, and more he didn't. More Ooreiki gathered to watch, some even walking to the base of the barracks and climbing the stairs to get closer, but the songs continued.

"*You Humans have voices to make the ancestors cry,*" a translator said beside him, bringing on a full-body wash of goosebumps. Joe's heart stuttered like he'd been dipped in a bucket of icewater, the songs forgotten. He ducked, bracing himself for a blow.

"Battlemaster Nebil," he began quickly, "we were just—"

A brightly-garbed civilian stood behind him, his haauk sitting on the deck a few feet away. His skin was so dark it was nearly black, which, Joe had learned from observing his captors, indicated youth.

Scott and Libby, who had followed Joe to the door, backed away from the young Ooreiki nervously. Battlemaster Nebil had made it clear that any recruit caught talking to a civilian would be exercised until he could no longer feel his feet, and Joe had the door wide open when it was supposed to be locked.

"You look much different than I imagined," the Ooreiki said, stepping closer to Joe, his huge pupils dilating in curiosity. *"The images they sent back showed so little detail. Your eyes are actually different colors."* He seemed to find that fascinating, glancing from Joe to Scott and back. *"Is that natural or altered?"*

"We're not allowed to talk to you," Libby said, grabbing Joe's arm. "Come on, Joe. Let's go back before Nebil sees the door."

But Joe was staring at the Ooreiki in front of him with equal fascination. The alien wore long, graceful swaths of bright red cloth glittering with waves of colorful stones. As he watched, the cloth changed color, shifting from a deep scarlet to a bright orange, then yellow. Thousands of Dhasha scales the size of Joe's thumbnail gleamed like jewels in spiral patterns radiating outward from the Ooreiki's abdomen. Pebble-sized gems of all colors hung in silver tassels from his arms. Silver caps laced with the same Celtic-type knots as Kihgl's armband encased the tips of the Ooreiki's tentacles on the right hand, leaving only the left still functioning. Joe could not stop staring.

In the background, the children had switched to *Mary Had a Little Lamb.*

"What is the significance of their song?" the Ooreiki asked. He was taller than most of the Ooreiki Joe had seen, almost five and a half feet.

Joe hesitated, not sure he wanted to risk Nebil's wrath for talking to the civilian. And, at the same time, he was *dying* to talk to him. Maybe he knew things, knew ways to get them home…

"Come *on,* Joe. You're gonna get in trouble!" Libby had stepped back within the confines of the barracks, leaving him alone with the civilian.

The bright-clad Ooreiki looked from Joe to Libby and back. *"Your name is Choe?"*

"Kkee," Joe said reluctantly. "Joe Dobbs. Who are you?"

"Choe." The Ooreiki youngster's eyes began to gleam with excitement. *"Yuil."* He stepped closer and glanced inside the barracks. *"Ghosts,"* he said in astonishment, *"They make you live like the Jreet. Where is your art?"*

"I don't think the battlemasters care about art," Joe said. Around them, the last children's song was dying down and the barracks once more descended into silence.

"Every Ooreiki cares about art. We did not evolve out of the darkness of the lower canopy not to appreciate beauty." Yuil flourished his metal-tipped fingers toward the *ferlii* trees ringing the edge of the city. *"It's an abomination that Congress makes us give up so many young ones for the Draft. To wear black all day—"* Yuil's sudah began to tremble. *"It's unnatural."*

Joe stared at the Ooreiki. "You mean they don't *want* to be soldiers? Just like us?" He found it hard to believe Battlemaster Nebil and Commander Tril might actually desire to wear the bright cloth of the civilians.

"Only the Dhasha and the Jreet want to be soldiers. The rest of Congress is filled with lovers of peace. That's why there is a Congress. Without it, the Jreet would renew their wars with the Ooreiki and the Dhasha would eat us all."

"So why don't you just kill all the Dhasha and stop drafting people?" Joe asked.

Yuil glanced back to his friends. *"As much as I love a good conversation, this is not a subject I should be discussing in public. Especially not around Army property."*

"Then take me somewhere," Joe said. "We can talk there."

"Joe!" Libby cried.

The young Ooreiki hesitated, glancing at Libby. *"Perhaps another time, Choe. It is too dangerous now—everyone is watching because of their singing."* Yuil hesitated, then quickly got back on his haauk and floated away.

Joe felt the lost opportunity like a knife in his gut.

"Come on," he muttered, stepping back inside the barracks and entering the alien code to shut the door—it was remarkably easy, the same set of characters that meant 4-1-6, or Fourth Platoon, First Company, Sixth Battalion. "Let's go back to sleep."

• • •

Tril caught Commander Lagrah's arm as he approached Lord Knaaren's elevator. "Commander, a word?"

Lagrah nodded at his aides, who boarded the elevator and waited for him. "Commander Tril, I'm quite busy," Lagrah said, turning to him with a tired look. "Priests from Poen have come to collect Kihgl's remains, and my battalion is currently preparing for a hunt."

Tril felt his sudah quiver angrily. "That's what I wanted to talk about. Sixth Battalion has been overlooked in the drawings for the hunts eight times now. No one is acknowledging my requests."

"And I'll be surprised if they ever do," Lagrah said, body rigid. "You've doomed your Battalion, Commander Tril. There is much resentment for Kihgl's death."

Lagrah had confirmed his fears. Tril's unanswered messages and lonely meals weren't a mistake. The other Ooreiki were avoiding him.

"He did that to himself," Tril snapped. "If he hadn't taunted the—"

Lagrah held up a hand scarred by onen. "I am not arguing with you, Commander. If you hadn't turned him in, someone else would have. His lifestyle led to his demise. Still, Kihgl was loved. The regiment feels you bear the responsibility for his demise."

"*You* called for his death, Lagrah," Tril retorted, disgusted that the Ooreiki could not see his own hypocrisy. "Not I."

Lagrah snorted. "You furg... The *last* thing Kihgl wanted was for the Peacemakers to take him to Levren."

Tril frowned at him, having to take a moment to comprehend the inference. "You mean you *wanted* him to die before he could be questioned?" he blurted. Was the whole *regiment* filled with traitors?

Lagrah narrowed his eyes. "Regardless of his fascination with the Fourfold Prophecy, Kihgl deserved an honorable death. There are many who would see you disappear for what you did. And plenty of them are capable."

The symbol of Planetary Ops—a single sphere with a diagonal slash through its center, one half red, one half blue—stood out on Lagrah's shoulder where he had earned it from many years of tunnel-wars and special operations. From many years of killing.

"Is that a threat?" Tril managed, taking a reflexive step backwards.

Lagrah gave him a very long, cold look, then said, "I suppose the fact that Kihgl was a better friend—and *oorei*—than you will ever be crosses my mind often."

Tril just stared at him, unable to speak. The...*nerve.* "I could tell the Peacemakers—"

Lagrah just smiled at him, his pale, elderly eyes filled with disdain. "Commander Tril, there are fifteen Planetary Ops veterans who were brought in to teach this Human regiment alone. How long do you think you will survive if you betray another of your comrades to the Peace Corps?"

Tril blinked. He, a *yeeri*, was being threatened. By a *vkala*. It was so utterly beyond his comprehension he could only stare. After a long moment of trying to compose himself, he said, "I am formally requesting for Sixth Battalion to be included in the next hunt."

Lagrah just watched him a moment, then shook his head. "Commander, your recruits are not ready." He reached forward and touched his arm in a beseeching gesture. "Forget our personal differences for a moment and think of your charges. Do them a favor and wait."

"It's been three weeks!" Tril snapped, shrugging off the *vkala's* repulsive grip. "Three *weeks*, Commander."

"And they're not ready," Lagrah said. "You'll only humiliate yourself if you enter your battalion in a hunt."

Tril stiffened. He was a *yeeri*. He refused to be told he was inadequate by a Fire God. It was beyond humiliating. Forcing his body into rigidity, he growled, "Every day the Sixth wastes preparing for the hunts, your battalion is getting better, and we are being left behind."

"Commander Tril, you're not the commander Kihgl was," Lagrah said softly. "The other Ooreiki battalion commanders despise you. If you take the Sixth out to the hunts now, it'll become the weakling the other battalions rip apart. You're too inexperienced to keep your recruits from disintegrating under that kind of pressure. Had I to make the judgment, I would say only Battlemaster Nebil is worthy of the job."

Yet *another* mention of Battlemaster Nebil's supposed 'worthiness' made Tril want to scream. The impudent Ooreiki battlemaster had been a talon in his side ever since Kihgl's trial. "If Nebil were 'worthy," Tril growled, "he wouldn't have been demoted to battlemaster. Repeatedly."

Lagrah gave him a tired look and appeared for a moment as if he wanted to argue, then just shook his head. "Tril, withdraw your recruits from this cycle and wait for the next training schedule. You would have a better chance if you started with a new regiment. Bring your papers to me and I will approve your request." It almost sounded like…an *order*.

"My battalion will enter the hunts if I have to write the invitation myself," Tril said, fingers knotting in fury.

Commander Lagrah eyed the scars on Tril's right hand where he'd been forced to remove the *adpi* to enter recruit training. After a moment, he said, "The Army is not like *yeeri* academy, Tril. Failing here means death. If you subject your troops to hunts with this regiment, against commanders and battlemasters who had once been Kihgl's closest friends, your recruits will become like beaten Takki. Seeing that, the Dhasha will swoop down on them and eat what remains. They will all die for your pride."

"My pride is not the issue here," Tril snapped. "You just don't want a *yeeri* crushing your pathetic battalion against his boot, you bigoted old ashsoul."

Commander Lagrah stared at him long and hard. Then, softly, he said, "So be it."

• • •

This afternoon, like every day for the past week, Battlemaster Nebil was in a bad mood. He barked complicated commands in Congie, cursed them even if they did their tasks right, and ran them down the glittering black roads until kids began falling down puking. Halfway through the afternoon, in a particularly wrathful mood, he pulled out a white, arm-length switch that he began using on every recruit who dared to make a mistake in front of him.

Finally, Sasha made a minor misstep in her marching commands and Nebil laid the switch across her back. Instead of humbly falling back into place in front of the platoon, she turned on the Ooreiki and shouted, "Stop hitting us! It's not our fault he ate your stupid traitor friend!"

Nebil's entire body posture tensed and, without any other warning, the Ooreiki yanked Sasha out of line and began whipping her with a violence Joe had never seen before. His huge Ooreiki arms lashed out with full force, the white switch turning pink as it cut through the cloth of Sasha's cammi jacket and into her flesh. His wet eyes glinting with fury, Nebil continued beating her until her entire body was a mass of bleeding red welts and her Congie blacks hung from her limbs in gory strips. Even Joe, who had for weeks wished Nebil would do that very same thing, felt nauseous watching the flesh peel from Sasha's limbs and back.

After several minutes beyond the point where Sasha had finally stopped her piteous whimpering and wasn't even twitching anymore when Nebil hit her, Joe finally couldn't take it anymore. "Stop it, you asshole!" Joe snapped. He stepped out of formation and grabbed Nebil by the arm. "You're *killing* her, goddamn it!"

Nebil instantly spun and took Joe by the throat, his stinging grip tightening on his neck like a boa constrictor. Looking into Nebil's furious brown eyes, Joe knew he was going to die. His vision dimmed and he struggled for breath, his knees already going weak as his brain was denied oxygen.

Suddenly, Nebil stopped tightening his grip. For a long moment, he just scowled up at Joe, the gills in his neck flipping madly. Then he released Joe and shoved him roughly backwards. "Get back in formation, Zero."

Without another word, Nebil dropped the switch and turned back to face Sasha's limp and bleeding form. Looking irritated, he pulled a black box the size of a cigar case from his vest. He took out a silvery vial and a huge needle with a handle that kind of looked like a tiny screwdriver. Unstoppering the lid on the vial, he dipped the tip of the needle into the silvery solution. On the ground, Sasha was much too pale.

Nebil slackened the muscles in his lower body and pooled beside the girl. He rolled her onto her back and yanked her jacket apart, exposing her breasts. As her eyes widened and she feebly reached up to try and stop him, he stabbed her in the chest with the silvery needle. Every recruit recoiled in sympathy as Sasha's body jerked when the needle sank through her ribs, all the way to the handle. Then Nebil yanked it out, replaced needle and vial in their case, and returned the box to his vest and stood.

"Take your battlemaster to medical," Nebil said brusquely. Then, without another word, he turned and strode off, the switch still on the ground where he'd left it.

Libby immediately walked up and broke the switch in half over her knee, glaring after the Ooreiki.

"Come on," Joe muttered, stepping up to squat beside Sasha. "Scott, Libby, help me here." Joe grabbed Sasha's arms, his groundmates each grabbed a leg, and together they carried the unconscious girl to the front of the hospital. Ooreiki medics rushed out upon seeing them approach and began firing questions at them about her condition.

"*We* didn't do it," Libby snapped. "Battlemaster Nebil did it. Then he stabbed her in the heart with a needle and walked away."

The medics seemed to think that was perfectly normal, because they stopped asking questions and just relieved them of their burden.

Later that morning, Battlemaster Nebil returned. "Listen carefully, you Takki turds. I've got bad news—we're finally doing a hunt. That means your recruit battlemaster will be working closely with your squad leaders to conduct you through the exercise." Battlemaster Nebil once again carried a switch, though he seemed content with pacing along the ranks, scowling at them. "Squad leaders, this is where you shine. A squad leader is in charge of three groundteams. It's your job to know exactly what each groundteam is capable of and use them to follow your recruit battlemaster's orders. It is *not* your job to tell each grounder what to do. That is for their ground leaders."

Battlemaster Nebil stopped, glaring at Joe. "Tomorrow's only going to be practice, Company-on-Company, but we'll be getting the real thing here soon. That jenfurgling Tril's made sure of that."

Nebil sighed and looked down at the switch he carried, then collapsed it in a telescoping patty and stuffed it into his vest. "Zero, you're in charge until Chins gets back. Make sure they get some food and take them to Tril for drills." Then Nebil simply turned and departed, leaving Joe standing there, staring after him with his mouth hanging open.

Sasha returned to Nebil's platoon that evening and, upon seeing Joe standing in her spot at the head of the platoon, she gave him a look that could have cut through metal. She reclaimed her position rudely, barking at him to return to his groundteam. Joe did, unable to stop staring at her.

Sasha's face and arms were a mass of puckered pink scars. Half of her ear had been cut off, giving her a wretched, lopsided look, and apparently the medics had seen no need to replace it. Joe felt sorry for her, despite himself.

The next day, Battlemaster Nebil lined them up outside the barracks and handed everyone a blue cartridge for their rifles. Earlier that morning, Battlemaster Nebil had singled Joe out for screwing up and had stood on his back with one heavy, cylindrical boot while he made Joe do push-ups until his arms gave out. Joe got a fleeting rush of excitement as Nebil handed him the cartridge, thinking about how easy it would be to load it into his rifle and blow off the Battlemaster's foot.

Self-preservation, however, kept Joe's itchy fingers at his side. Ooreiki were fast. He'd only get a toe, at best.

"Load your cartridges!" Nebil shouted.

Ninety recruits hurried to do as he asked.

"Now," Battlemaster Nebil said, "Chins, you're leading them today. You know how to talk to the squad leaders on your headcom?"

Of course she doesn't, Joe thought.

"Kkee, Battlemaster," Sasha said.

"Good." Nebil swung around to face Joe. "Squad leaders, get your groundteams cleaned up and dressed in their full tunnel gear, then get them back down here in nine tics. The battalion's going on a hunt."

"You heard him, let's go!" Sasha said. "Upstairs! Get *up* there you use-less Takki worms! Pushups for the last one to the top!"

They climbed up the stairs to the barracks, stripped out of their dia-mond-encrusted clothing, and filed into the shower. The noxious vats of liquid were big enough to fit twenty at a time, though nobody stayed in them long enough for them to fill up. As Joe dunked himself, every scrape that he had endured in the last few days burned like fire, making the experience akin to throwing himself into a vat of needles. Still, the endless laps around the base of the barracks that Battlemaster Nebil dished out to recruits caught not bathing made the alternative even less pleasant.

Once he'd sluiced the diamond dust from his body, Joe hurried back into the hall, still unable to see or breathe. The fans on the wall activated at once, chilling him to the core as the alcohol evaporated from his skin. Once dry, he threw on a new set of clothes, shouldered his gear, and stumbled back down the stairs to where Battlemaster Nebil stood, waiting for them.

"You're late!" he barked, swatting Joe across the arm with his switch. "You call yourself a squad leader?!" Joe flinched at the sting, but held his composure while inwardly hating Sasha, who was giving him a smug look from the recruit battlemaster's position. She had been the first one back down the stairs and Joe *knew* she hadn't bathed. She'd taken too much time to harass the kid who'd made it up the stairs last.

Battlemaster Nebil marched them to the plaza, where a flotilla of large haauks waited for them. Other platoons were already boarding, the plaza a milling mass of confusion and shouting Ooreiki. Nebil loaded them all onto a giant haauk and pulled the gate up, locking out the other straggling platoons. The platform jerked as the Ooreiki pilot lifted off and began following the other haauk down the black diamond road.

"Shut up and listen," Nebil shouted, though no one was talking. "We're about to start an in-battalion hunt. It's a practice hunt for when they put us up against another battalion. Attackers wear black, defenders wear white. Second Company defends, First Company attacks. Defenders will be at the bottom, trying to keep us out. Somewhere underneath you'll find a Congressional flag, if you get that far. That's your goal. Reach that, and the hunt is over."

Joe's hands grew sweaty where they gripped his rifle, his focus suddenly narrowing to the battlemaster's every word. Somewhere…*underneath*? Were they sending them down *tunnels*?

"Any of you janja pellets have questions?" Battlemaster Nebil demanded.

Joe cleared his throat. "Is this live ammunition?"

"Does it *look* like it's live ammunition, jenfurgling?" Several kids snickered. A furg, as Linin's eye-opening Species Recognition classes had taught them the evening before, was a short, squat, very *hairy* alien that was as ugly as it was stupid. A furgling, a younger version of the same primitive beast, was shorter, hairier, and stupider. A *jen*furgling was an evolutionary offshoot of the same species that had lost a few brain cells along the way, and delighted in beating its hairy face against the ground and playing with its own excrement. The video clip of a group of them running in circles around a boulder, shrieking and flinging excrement at each other, had been the highlight of their capture.

Remembering the gun Kihgl had shoved into his face, Joe said. "Well… yeah."

A look of respect passed through Nebil's sticky brown eyes before it was hidden again. "It's not. It's full of marker shots. Real plasma will twist the light until it hurts to look at it. Even a soot-eating furg knows that."

"So what happens if we get hit?" Libby asked, giving her gun a nervous look.

"Don't get hit," Nebil growled. "You will not like it if you do. Any other questions?"

"Where are we going?" Libby asked.

"Practice Flats Ninety-Five," Nebil said, as if that answered her question.

Not to be outdone, Sasha said, "So what do we do when we get there?"

"You charge the tunnels. If you survive, you fall back and try again."

"That doesn't sound very smart." In horror, Joe realized the words had left his mouth before he had a chance to stop them.

The Ooreiki swiveled to face him. "Say that again, Zero?"

Joe bit his lip. "Why can't we just drop a bomb down there and blow them up?"

"Because, if it were Dhasha trapped down there, their Takki would just dig them out again," Battlemaster Nebil retorted. "Collapsing the tunnels is something they do to *defend* themselves, you furg."

"Oh." Joe kept his mouth shut for the rest of the questions.

Then, before they were ready, the haauk dropped down in the middle of what had once been a city, broken only by a few odd remnants of buildings and deep pits filled with white-clad recruits that were already firing at them. A blob of blue hit one of the attackers in the head and he collapsed with a scream, twitching and convulsing like a dying thing. Then he lay still.

Joe and the others stared at the body, their confusion quickly turning to fear as more blue shots whizzed over their heads like blue hail from the hundreds of defenders firing at them. Two more black-clad recruits went down in convulsions, blue goop moving on their bodies like it was alive. Everyone ducked, trying to shield themselves with the scant protection of the railing and their fellows' bodies.

The haauk's gate clanged open and no one moved.

"Out!" Nebil shouted. "Get out and fight, you gutless cowards!" Then Nebil was whipping them all, forcing them off the haauk and into the blue-painted Hell.

Five went down immediately, falling in a screaming, shaking heap. The rest hunkered down behind the bodies in a panic. Then Nebil and the pilot were lifting off, leaving them there, the sucking wet sound of gunfire coming from all around them.

The wall of bodies wasn't enough to protect them. One guy beside Joe had nothing but his eyes showing when a shot hit the body in front of him, sprayed, and a couple drops caught him in the face. He fell just as quickly as the rest. All around him, recruits were falling, screaming like something was ripping open their innards.

"Come on!" Joe shouted, grabbing Libby by the arm. He had no idea where the other members of his group had gone.

"Where?" Libby shouted back. "There's nowhere to go!"

A jagged block of diamond jutted from the ground a few dozen feet away. Joe ducked his head and ran. He heard heavy footsteps pounding the crushed diamond behind him, but he wasn't sure if it was Libby or someone from another groundteam.

Joe's vision narrowed to only the battlefield in front of him. He felt a few shots whoosh over his head as he ran, all high. He reached the block and fell into a prone position behind it, gripping his rifle with white knuckles.

Libby fell down beside him, as did two other kids Joe didn't recognize.

Back at the dropoff point, a few attackers were trying to make a stand, but the fire from the tunnels was destroying them. In minutes, they were all convulsing or still. A cheer went up from the defenders.

"That was fast," Libby said, eying the pile of bodies.

"You think they're dead?" a younger boy asked Joe. "They looked dead."
He was shaking all over, but he looked excited nonetheless.

Joe examined his three companions. Of all of Nebil's platoon, only the
four of them were still functioning.

Further away, on the other side of the city, they heard more sucking
burps of gunfire. Apparently, another platoon was meeting the same end.

"You think they forgot about us?" the other survivor, an older girl,
asked. "They're not shooting anymore."

"They're probably circling around," Libby said. "I saw tunnel pits all
over this place when we landed. They might be walking under us right
now."

"Then let's beat them to it!" the younger boy cried, hefting his rifle.
"Come on, Zero!"

Joe glanced at the pit closest them and swallowed down the fear in
his gut. The last thing he wanted to do was go down there. "It's too open.
They'd shoot us up before we even got there."

Libby frowned at him and edged her head around the block of diamond just enough to see the other pits. Immediately, one of the defenders fired a blast that bounced off the stone only inches above her head.
She jerked back and took a deep breath, staring at the blue goop crawling
across the stone where her head had been. "Yeah, they know we're here."
Behind them, more defenders were firing at their diamond block, keeping
them pinned.

Joe stared at the pit in front of them. *Come on you big baby. You're
gonna have to do it sooner or later.* "We're gonna need a distraction," Joe
heard himself say. "We aren't going anywhere until—"

"No," Libby said.

Joe glanced at her. "What?"

She shrugged out of her pack. "That's not the way. There's another pit
on the other side that's closer." She pointed. "It's just got little kids in it, and
they're bad shots. We can get to it before they shoot us. Gotta leave our gear
behind, though."

Joe gave it a split-second thought, then said, "Okay, everybody get your
packs off. When I say go, grab your rifles and run like hell after Libby and me."
He doubted the two kids with them would be able to keep up, but maybe they

could avoid getting shot. Both of them looked older than Libby, but Libby was getting tall—she was easily six inches taller than the boy and seven inches taller than the girl. She could almost keep up with Joe on the runs. Almost.

"Okay," Joe said, pulling his pack from his shoulders. "When I say go, I want everybody to throw their packs in that direction." He pointed in the opposite direction that Libby had done. "I don't care if you have to kick them or they only roll a little ways. As soon as they leave your hands, get up and run after me and Libby."

As they waited for the two smaller kids to get out of their gear, Joe eyed the pit directly across from them with increasing anxiety. He could *feel* the defenders creeping through the tunnels under them. Looking over, he saw Libby's grim stare was fixed in the same direction.

"We ready? Count of three. One, two, *three!*" They heaved their packs away from them and lunged up into a sprint toward three wide-eyed kids in the pit. The other defenders were already recovering and blue shots spattered the ground and flew past them as they tried to catch Joe and Libby in their sights. Behind them, Joe heard a scream.

Then they were in the pit, struggling with the defenders. They were forced to wrest the rifles out of the little kids' hands before they had a chance to fire at them. Diamond dust tinkled and crunched underfoot, scattered by their stomping boots. Libby finally got a weapon free and fired point-blank at the nearest defender. His agonized scream made Joe cringe, but Libby fired again, taking the second boy in the chest. Joe yanked free the remaining enemy's rifle and held it trained on the wide-eyed girl on the other end, who stared back at him in unconcealed terror. Libby shot her, too.

Joe lowered his gun and stared at her.

"They're the bad guys," Libby said, shrugging. "We're supposed to kill them."

"I guess," Joe said, feeling bad regardless. Joe tore his eyes off the three convulsing defenders and glanced over the edge of the pit at the two bodies lying out in the open. "Damn. The others didn't make it."

"They were too slow." Libby said it as if she couldn't care less. She began picking up the defenders' weapons and taking their charges to refill her own.

Joe found himself staring at her, glad he'd never pissed her off.

After looting the defenders, they fell back against the edge of the pit, staring down into the dark, diamond-encrusted tunnel. The opening was a full ten feet tall by six feet wide, and Joe felt his heart rate increase just by being near it. He had to grip his rifle tightly to keep his hands from shaking. "We're not in a very good position," he said.

"No flashlights," Libby agreed.

"No, I mean numbers," Joe said. "They've got us outnumbered."

Libby said nothing. In the distance, down the tunnel, they heard voices.

"Well," Joe said, "Let's get this over with." He took a deep breath. Sweat stood out on his face and his hands felt slick. He felt like he was going to vomit. Somehow, he made himself stand and led them into the tunnel.

It's not so bad, Joe tried to tell himself. *I can handle this.* He was standing erect, the ceiling another foot above his head. Still, he wasn't fooling anybody. He had broken out in a cold sweat, the damp earth sucking the warmth out of him on all sides.

It was almost a relief when he got shot. They were rounding a corner when a group of white-clad defenders opened fire. The bluish, gooey blast caught Joe full in the face. Joe's world collapsed to a blinding white fire that roared down his spine and tore through his limbs. It was the worst pain he had ever experienced.

Tortuous seconds later, he felt his heart stop.

19

A BATTLEMASTER'S FOLLY

Joe woke with an Ooreiki needle jammed in his arm. All around him, spread out in piles like fallen timber, hundreds of black-clad kids lay in silence. Some even had their eyes open, watching their Ooreiki caretakers.

Was he dead?

Joe tried to sit up, but couldn't. He tried to ask a question, but his mouth wouldn't work. All he could do was lay there, helpless, as an Ooreiki worked over him, his golden medic's circle almost pressed up against Joe's face. He was squeezing a bag of some sort of red liquid into his arm.

Joe's mind raced. Blood? Were they giving him blood? He couldn't remember losing any blood. For that matter, wasn't this supposed to be practice? Why did they need medics? And why couldn't he *move*?

The Ooreiki medic that was treating him did not seem to understand or care about Joe's increasing panic. He simply finished with what he was doing, removed the needle from Joe's arm, and moved on to the next person, bringing out a fresh bag of red liquid and using the same needle he had used on Joe.

A whole new wave of worry washed over him. What if one of the kids before him had had AIDS? Or some other horrible disease? Didn't they know they had to sanitize the needles before they used them? What if he was going to die of a cold like a drug addict, just because these Ooreiki bastards were too stupid to use fresh needles on their human victims?

For that matter, why was Joe even breathing? He had *felt* his heart stop, *felt* his body shut down. He had felt himself die. If only he could sit up and ask someone!

"Listen up, you soot-eating jenfurglings!" Battlemaster Nebil roared. "We lost! Not only did we lose, but we never even got inside their tunnels! I've never seen such a Takkiscrew in all of my time in the Army! You are pathetic! Worthless! We should send you worthless sooters home!"

Good, Joe thought. *You do that.*

Nebil continued to berate them disgustedly. "You're not warriors! You are worms! Small, terrified worms! *Niish* would eat you all alive, you fat-assed primates!"

The medics continued with their tasks, oblivious to Battlemaster Nebil's tirade. When they finished working with the humans, they packed up their supplies and boarded a haauk, leaving the kids behind.

Joe listened as their battlemaster ranted on and on, alternating between cursing at them, shouting at the ancestors for cursing *him*, and kicking up sprays of diamond dust in a rage.

Nebil finally ran out of breath, though his sudah still beat in a fury. "Grab your gear and find your own way home," he snarled. "Ancestors save your worthless asses if you don't make it back to the barracks before I lock it down." Then Nebil got on a haauk loaded with the nine other battlemasters, the medics, and a few Takki assistants and departed. Joe's anger turned to worry as he watched their skimmer slide out of sight, following the road back to the city.

Joe and the rest of the kids continued to lay there, helpless, as the light rapidly faded from the purple planet. Somewhere off in the distance, the fingernail-on-chalkboard sound filled the silence. Joe wondered whether or not the creatures making that horrible noise could acquire a taste for soft, helpless flesh, should they be given the opportunity. Joe's stomach churned at the thought of walking back to the city in the dark.

Apparently, some of the other recruits were having the same thoughts, because their eyes were wide as they stared at the deepening purple of the sky.

It's just a walk through the woods, Joe told himself. *Nothing to worry about.*

Half an hour later, after night had fallen completely, the paralysis wore off—for everybody, all at the same time.

Those bastards, Joe thought. *They waited until dark.*

Libby found him as soon as he stood up. "They're trying to scare us," she said, scanning the huge ferlii surrounding them. Even with nightvision, the upper canopy was too dark for them to see it. Likewise, they could only see parts of the forest around them—everything under the second canopy was obscured in shadows that even sunlight could not touch. With only meager amounts of starlight filtering down through the spore-thickened atmosphere and then the tight weave of the upper canopy, everything from the ground to the two hundred foot mark was completely black. They had to be really close just to make out the shapes of the huge ferlii root systems.

"Let's find the others," Joe said, once they'd found their gear amongst the recruit belongings the Ooreiki had graciously dumped into an enormous pile.

"You hear Nebil?" Libby said. "He said none of us made it into the tunnels."

"Maybe two out of four hundred doesn't count," Joe said.

Libby's face twisted, but before she could reply, Scott jogged up, panting. "Joe, you gotta stop them. They're going the wrong way. Monk, too. She wouldn't listen when I told her it was a trick."

"What's a trick?" Joe asked, glancing at the stream of people following the same road the Ooreiki haauk had taken. He thought he saw Monk's slight form amongst the walkers, but he couldn't be sure from so far away.

"That isn't the *way,*" Scott said. He turned a hundred and eighty degrees and pointed at a road that looked abandoned and dark, all away across the battlefield from where they stood. "*That's* where we need to go."

Joe and Libby peered doubtfully into the darkness, squinting.

"I saw them go that way," Libby said, pointing at the flood of humans. More than one platoon had already begun walking down the path after the Battlemasters.

"Me, too," Joe added.

"Look," Scott said, "Just trust me, okay? I'm really good at this. We've gotta go *that* way." He pointed at the empty road behind them.

"Why?" Joe asked, still unconvinced.

"Because that's the way we came in," Scott said.

"You recognize something over there?" Joe asked dubiously. Everything about the planet looked pretty much the same to him.

"I don't need to," Scott said.

"Why not?" Libby demanded, frowning.

"I just *don't*," Scott insisted, looking desperate, now. "You've gotta *stop* them, Joe. They're gonna get us in *trouble*."

Realizing that Scott was verging on panic, Joe lowered his gear to the ground and took the hyperventilating kid by the shoulder. "Okay. Dude. Tell me what you know, then we'll see what I can do, okay?"

"I know *direction*," Scott said. "My dad said I musta been a homing pigeon in a past life. Back home, I never got lost anywhere, not even in the city." He jabbed a finger at the departing group. "And that is the *wrong* direction. Home is *that* way." He yanked his thumb behind him.

Joe glanced at Libby, who shrugged. "So you want me to chase those other guys down and tell them they're all going the wrong way? They won't believe you."

Scott's impish face stretched in a grin. "They'll believe me next time, after we get home and they don't."

Joe gave Scott a long look, inwardly feeling like Monk had a bit of sense when she spoke of safety in numbers.

"Either way, we're gonna look like morons," Libby said, shrugging. "Or we get lost and eaten and never seen again. Maybe a few years from now somebody'll find a few pieces of our gear scattered over the upper canopy, or shards of bone stuck in—"

"You don't believe me," Scott said, his grin sliding from his face.

Seeing the kid's anguish, Joe felt something twinge inside. "I think I'm gonna give you a chance to prove it to me," Joe decided, to which Scott immediately started beaming again. "Let's go get Monk. Where's Maggie?"

They found the other two members of their team wandering amidst the exodus. Maggie was happy to be reunited with her group, but Monk stomped and screamed like a banshee when they tried to take her.

"But everybody's going *that* way!" Monk started walking again and Libby caught her roughly by the arm, yanking her back. Monk shrieked and tried batting off her grip, but Libby held fast, glaring down at her with impassive brown eyes.

Monk let her legs go limp and began an all-out tantrum right there in the road. Joe lost his temper. "We're going," he snapped. "And you're coming with us. All of Third Squad is."

Something in the tone of Joe's voice quieted Monk. She still held her chin in a pout, but at least she closed her mouth and followed them as they went to collect as many of their squad members as they could find. The others followed Joe willingly, gathering around him in an increasing knot until he had over a dozen children with him. He even saw a few faces that didn't belong, but since none of the other squad leaders were taking charge and forming up their own groundteams, Joe let them stay.

"What the hell are you doing, Zero?" Sasha had seen the disturbance and had come to investigate.

His back to her, Joe winced. He'd hoped to collect everyone and be gone before she noticed.

"Scott thinks we came in on the other side of the clearing," Maggie said, motioning the road at the far end.

"Nebil and the medics went that way," Sasha barked. "Let's go. *Now*, recruits."

"That's not the right way," Scott blurted. "I can feel the city we came from over there." He pointed.

Sasha snorted. "You *feel* it?"

"Yes," Scott said, dead serious.

Sasha frowned at Scott, then at Joe. "That's soot. Get moving, Zero. The others are getting ahead of us."

"We're going this way," Joe growled, shouldering his rifle where she could see it. He still had cartridges left. "And you can stuff it."

"Yeah," Monk said. "Stuff it."

Sasha narrowed her eyes. "It's safer if we all stay together. So you're *coming*."

"We're not gonna walk off a cliff just because the rest of you do," Libby said. "Joe's our squad leader. If he says we go, we go."

Sasha's smile faded, and her spine straightened proudly. "He might be a squad leader, but I'm *battlemaster*. Get back in the group."

"Just go burn off, Sasha," Joe snapped.

"Yeah," Monk said. "Burn off."

"I'll tell Nebil if you don't listen to me," Sasha said, glaring at Monk. More children were coming to stand around Joe, almost half a platoon, now.

"We *are* listening to you," Libby said. "And when Nebil promotes Joe to battlemaster because you're a dumb bimbo who doesn't know her ass from her head, we'll be listening to that, too."

"Fine. Go with *him*." She waved a disgusted hand at Joe. "I'll just make you all run laps around the barracks until you all puke," Sasha sneered. At that, she jogged to catch up with the rest of the battalion as it departed.

Within minutes, Joe and his group were the only ones remaining in the war-pocked city that was Practice Flats Ninety Five.

"Well, let's get this over with," Joe said, turning toward the other side of the clearing with a sigh. He knew Sasha would be as good as her word, regardless of who got back to Alishai first.

"You won't be sorry," Scott insisted. "I'm right. I know it."

"It doesn't matter if you're right," Libby said, sounding tired. "Sasha's in charge of us and we didn't listen to her. Nebil's gonna be pissed."

As it turned out, she was right.

Not because they went the wrong way—Scott's instincts had proven right and they were the first and only squad to appear at Alishai under their own locomotion. The other platoons arrived huddled on haauks, red-eyed and white-faced, their battlemasters still screaming at them in Congie. As they shuffled off the ships and directly into drill, however, Nebil descended upon Joe with even greater fury.

"You disobeyed your battlemaster?!" Nebil screamed at him. "Why?!"

"Because I believed my groundmate was right," Joe replied, cringing for a blow.

The blow did not come. "What?"

Joe hastily explained how Scott had pleaded with him to go the opposite direction. As he told his story, Nebil's sudah fluttered more and more rapidly until they were a blur down the sides of the battlemaster's neck.

"You said he *felt* the city?" Nebil demanded finally.

"Kkee," Joe replied.

"Tunnel instinct," Nebil barked. "Burning tunnel instinct. You lucky Jreet-loving sooter." Nebil shook his head.

"What is—" Joe began.

"Never mind!" Nebil snapped. He suddenly lashed out, lifting him off his feet by his jacket. "Listen up, you soot-eating asher. This is the only time I'm gonna tell you. You disobeyed a direct order. That is un-burning-acceptable, you get me? The commands of your battlemaster supersede anything you want, no matter *how* burning stupid she is." He released Joe harshly. "A hundred laps around the barracks. Once you finish that, go rake down the plaza. Alone." Then Nebil turned and stormed off to help the other Battlemasters yell at their platoons.

Joe took a deep breath and let it out slowly. The massive barracks tower had a base the size of a football field, and raking the plaza was usually a whole platoon's job. Apparently, Nebil had decided he wasn't going to sleep that night. Setting his shoulders and lowering his head, he began to jog.

As he passed the Prime Commander's tower, he caught sight of a dead-eyed human descending the stairs, one of the slaves Knaaren had captured the week before. The boy was so badly scarred that Joe missed a stride, almost falling flat on his face. Only the boy's hands were untouched, beautiful and slender, the hands of an artist. As Joe watched, the kid reached the bottom and entered one of the rooms at the base of Knaaren's tower.

That could have been me, Joe realized, guiltily. He bit his lip and pushed himself back into a run.

Well into the night, Sasha joined him. She was as full grown as she was ever going to get, with wide hips and a thin, wiry frame. Her face, however, reminded him of a pouting child.

"You told him," she accused. "You liar."

Joe, whose lungs were already struggling with the dual load of ferlii spores and running, had to pant. "What...are you...talking about?"

"You told him I didn't listen to you."

"You...didn't."

"You were the only ones who wanted to go that way!" Sasha shouted.

"But we...were right."

Sasha's eyes narrowed. "The battlemaster gave me a hundred laps and then I have to help you with the plaza."

"Good…luck," Joe said. "It's gonna…be time to…wake up…before you even…get done with your laps." Then he fell into silence because it was either that or pass out.

"You better listen to me next time," Sasha said, eyes glittering.

Joe rolled his eyes and ran faster. Even fresh, Sasha couldn't keep up with him, nor did she have the heart to try. She just settled into a lazy jog and waited for him to pass her on another lap. The longer they ran, the slower she went, until she was running slower than most people could walk. Then she stopped running altogether and sneered at him every time he loped past.

Joe was on his eighty-seventh lap when Battlemaster Nebil popped out of a door in front of him and nearly bowled him over.

"Zero! Why aren't you on the plaza yet?"

Joe doubled over, gasping. "Eighty-seventh…lap."

"What about your battlemaster? I sent her out here four hours ago."

It was too much. Joe started dry-heaving into the diamond dust.

Fortunately, Joe didn't need to explain. Sasha rounded the corner at a walk and by the time Nebil was finished with her, she was running as fast as Joe had ever seen her go. When Nebil returned, his sudah were beating in his neck. In a deft maneuver, Nebil snaked an arm under Joe's sweat-soaked jacket and pressed the metal ranking unit to Joe's chest. In an instant, the silver triangle on Joe's breast began to morph into a four-pointed star. "You're the new recruit battlemaster for Fourth Platoon," Nebil growled. "You'll also be the ranking battlemaster on the field, so you'll be in charge of all of First Company. Don't burn it up."

Joe's mouth dropped open. All he could say was, "I will?"

"No, that star on your chest is just for show. Now go finish your laps. The plaza can wait. We've got a hunt coming up tomorrow, and I won't have my battlemaster falling asleep in the middle of a raid."

Joe stumbled back into a run, but the prospect of being in charge of half the battalion on the next hunt gave him the extra energy to once again find his stride. He finished and, not even glancing at Sasha, climbed the barracks steps.

Sasha ran up behind him and grabbed his shirt. "Where are you going? We're not done with the plaza."

"Battlemaster Nebil said I could do it later," Joe said.

Sasha released him. "Well, if you're not gonna run, I'm not gonna run either."

The ridiculousness of the statement would have made Joe laugh if he weren't so exhausted. He just nodded and somehow found the energy to finish climbing the stairs to the barracks room.

20

YUIL

"Choe."

Joe was just cresting the stairs to Sixth Battalion's barracks balcony, his exhausted body feeling as if it were made of lead, when he heard the odd sound seemingly coming from a Takki tunnel near his feet. Ahead of him, Nebil had left the barracks door open for his return. The barracks room beyond was silent but for the snores of other recruits. Thinking he had imagined it, Joe kept trudging forward, so tired he was having trouble staying upright.

"Choe." A cold, metal-tipped finger brushed his arm, and goosebumps washed down his spine in a startling wave at the contact. Joe jerked and turned.

The young Ooreiki that had come to listen to their Christmas songs was standing in the shadows outside the barracks, glancing nervously at the open door. *"Do you still want to talk?"*

Joe felt his heart skip a beat and he instantly forgot about sleep. "Do you?"

"Kkee," Yuil said. *"But you need to come with me."*

"He's not going anywhere with you," Libby's voice said suddenly. She had stayed up late cutting holes in her gear and now stood near the barracks door, Joe's Swiss Army knife still clutched in her hand. She was scowling at Yuil, looking ready to use the knife on the Ooreiki.

Staring at the knife, the pupils in Yuil's huge, sticky brown eyes dilated until they looked completely black.

"I'll go," Joe interrupted, scowling at Libby.

Yuil was obviously reconsidering his plan. *"It is dangerous if she tells."*

"She won't tell," Joe said, giving Libby a warning glance. "Not this time."

Libby cringed, glancing at the Swiss Army knife in her fist.

Yuil hesitated, then he shrugged a long swath of brilliant blue fabric off of his shoulders and held it out to Joe. It changed colors in his hands. *"Wrap yourself in this,"* Yuil said. *"You'll resemble an Ueshi if you hunch down."*

Joe obeyed, ignoring the dirty looks Libby was giving him. The cloth felt unnaturally smooth in his hands and glided over his calluses like cool water, not even catching on the rough skin of his palm. It felt like something sultans and emperors would wear back on Earth. "I'll be back soon," Joe said to Libby. "Get some sleep."

"Nebil made you run all night," Libby insisted, scowling at the Ooreiki. "Aren't you tired?"

"I'll be fine," Joe said.

"What if Nebil comes in and finds you never came back from your laps?" she demanded.

"Tell him I lost something and had to go find it."

Libby wrinkled her nose, giving the Ooreiki a bitter look. "I don't like him, Joe."

Joe's chest clenched at his groundmate's lack of civility. Desperate not to lose their first real contact in this alien place to the manners of an eight-year-old, he gave Libby a pointed glare and said, "You just wanna talk, right Yuil?"

"Of course, Choe. There are many things that fascinate me about Humans."

"See," Joe said, following Yuil around the corner to a lavishly-decorated haauk. "He just wants to talk." Gems and ribbons adorned the sides, glittering and flapping in the alien breeze. Joe's cloak had shifted to canary yellow by the time the Ooreiki youngster began powering up the haauk.

"You don't know him," Libby pleaded, having followed him around the balcony. She grabbed Joe's arm. "What if he sells you to the Dhasha?"

Yuil grunted laughter. *"I think your friend is safe. Nothing could get me within a ferlii-length of a Dhasha."*

Libby released Joe and gave Yuil a cold glare. "If you don't bring him back I'll kill you."

Joe sucked in a breath. He knew enough about Congie society to know a death-threat against a civilian could get her executed.

The Ooreiki youngster stared at her, then lowered his head solemnly. *"I will bring him back, little one."* He plucked a smooth silver scale from his clothing and handed it to her. As it caught the light, it swirled with every color of the rainbow. From the delicate way the Ooreiki handled it, Joe guessed it was expensive. As Libby reluctantly took the Dhasha scale, Yuil said, *"It's a promise."*

Then the Ooreiki ushered Joe onto the haauk and maneuvered them into the air. In moments, they were out of sight of the barracks.

"We've gotta be careful," Yuil said as they flew. *"All Congressional property contains tracking devices, even soldiers. They insert them in places that you can't cut off, like your head or your chest."*

Joe stared down at himself, remembering the gun that the Ooreiki doctor had fired into chest on the ship. "So they'll come looking for me?"

The Ooreiki gave Joe a mischievous look. *"You don't grow up on Kophat without learning ways to bypass Congressional security measures."* He plucked a metal ring from under the rim of the skimmer's control panel and showed it to Joe. *"An akarit. All Congressional frequencies within three bodylengths are voided."*

Joe touched the thing and turned it in his hand. To all appearances, it was just a band of gold. It even felt heavy, like his dad's wedding ring. He returned it to the Ooreiki with reluctance. "Isn't it illegal to carry something like that?"

"How can it be, when so many use it?" Yuil demanded. The haauk soared skyward, leaving the ground behind with such rapidity that the crushed black gravel seemed to fall out from under them. Joe gasped and his fists spasmed reflexively around the railing.

The young Ooreiki seemed to enjoy Joe's reaction. *"I worked for six turns to save up the regard for this haauk. It's of special Ueshi design. Maybe someday I'll show you the things I can do with it."* He veered teasingly.

"That's okay," Joe said, feeling ill. "I believe you."

Yuil slowed near the edge of the city, proceeding towards a jagged roof that looked unfinished. The Ooreiki maneuvered the haauk up and under a lip of rock and a wide cave appeared before them, invisible from the outside.

Yuil set the haauk down and brought the akarit out from under the dash of the control panel. Then he stepped off the craft and began to walk back toward the entrance of the cave, motioning for Joe to follow him.

The view was frightening. This close to the edge of the city, the *ferlii* trees seemed too large to be real. From his vantage, Joe could see the red masses of spores atop the branches and immediately his lungs began to itch. He hacked up a red glob of mucus and glanced at the Ooreiki.

Yuil was watching him. He turned away quickly, pretending he hadn't been, but Joe had seen. He had the uneasy thought that maybe Libby was right, that he was simply bringing Joe here for a rendezvous with a slave trader.

"*I found this place when I was in* yeeri *academy*," Yuil said. "*Back when Alishai voted to commission a seventh ring. They abandoned it because* draak *could reach it from the ferlii branches. They'll finish it the next time they add a ring to the city.*"

"You go to school?" Joe felt a surge of hope, of kinship.

"*I went. I failed. My art was not good enough.*" Yuil made a disappointed sound.

"Your...art?"

Yuil held up his silver-encased fingers. The Celtic knots winding their way around the four tentacles on his right hand reminded Joe of Kihgl's kasja that Nebil had taken from him. "*I am of the yeeri caste. We are expected to either excel in art or devote ourselves to tending our ancestors' oorei. I will probably be shipping off to Poen soon, unless I can hire myself out to a foreigner. Even poorly-trained* yeeri *are in high demand in the newer planets. I might even be able to find work on Earth.*"

"We have artists on Earth," Joe said. "Good ones, too."

Yuil scoffed. "*Nothing in the universe can compare to a master yeeri. People will impoverish themselves simply to pay for the right to watch her work.*"

"Wait," Joe said, frowning at the Ooreiki. "You're a *girl?*"

"*I could be if I wanted to. The* yeeri *is the only caste allowed to reproduce. It helps keep the lines clear of Fire Gods.*"

Joe stared at the Ooreiki, trying to understand if she was telling him she *was* a girl or could get a sex change if she felt like it. Then something very pressing occurred to him. "Are my commanders all girls, too?"

Yuil looked as if he'd insulted her. "Yeeri *aren't drafted. It was written into the Ooreiki Pact. Your superiors are probably* hoga *or* wriit, *but one or two might be Fire Gods.*"

"You worship gods of fire?" Joe had not envisioned the Ooreiki, with all of their superior technology, to be pagans.

"*No. Fire Gods.* Vkala. *They're the descendants of the diplomats who signed the pact that made the Ooreiki one of the eight founding members of Congress. The Ayhi gave them the Jreet's ability to resist fire so they could visit Vora and sign the Pact. They would not go otherwise.*" Yuil gave him a funny look. "*Do you know* nothing, *Choe?*"

Joe ignored the jab. "Because Ooreiki hate fire," Joe said, thinking of what Kihgl had said.

"Kkee. *Fire. It is the greatest danger to an* oorei, *aside from maybe the* Dhasha." Her face twisted at the last. "*The gods are unjust, letting Knaaren survive after what he did. I hope the ghost sickness claims him swiftly, for your sake, Choe.*"

"What's a Fire God look like?" Joe asked, still thinking of the Ooreiki castes. He was pretty sure he could already guess.

Yuil pulled a wisp of gauzy fabric away from her chest, bearing a small, puckered mark on her stomach. "*They bear no* Shenaal *because their skin does not burn during the Niish Ahymar. The priests put them in cages or pits with immature onen. Most get ripped to pieces, but the ones who survive are given to the Army, marked by thousands of scars crisscrossing their bodies so every Ooreiki remembers what their ancestors did.*"

That meant Kihgl and Lagrah were both Fire Gods.

"Vkala *are the lowest caste,*" Yuil continued. "*They are still paying for their ancestors' sins.*"

"Back when they signed the Ooreiki up for the Congress," Joe said.

"Kkee," Yuil said, nodding.

Joe cleared his throat. "Wasn't Congress formed two million years ago? When will they be forgiven?"

Yuil's face instantly darkened. *"When Congress no longer exists."*

"So you guys hate Congress as much as we do."

"Kkee. Everyone hates Congress."

"So why don't you disband it?" Joe asked.

Yuil laughed. *"Do you realize how difficult it is to kill a Dhasha? Their only vulnerability is a tiny nerve center at the back of their head, under their horns. The only way you can hurt them there is if you hit them with a direct blast of energy fire. Then you've only got a few moments to get to it and tear out the nerve center, or cut away enough scales to give it a direct blast to its core. Either that or Jreet poison, but Jreet die before giving up their poison sacs and even if you had it, you'd have to get it past the scales to make it work."*

"You sound like you know a lot about being a soldier," Joe said.

Yuil glanced wistfully out at the city. *"I used to wish I was a hoga or* wriit *so I could help the Army bring the Dhasha under control. I'm more mature now, but I still want to be there when the Fourfold Prophecy is fulfilled."*

Joe's ears pricked up. "My commander mentioned that to me."

The young Ooreiki glanced back at him, looking excited. *"He did? He must have favored you greatly. What'd he say?"*

"Nothing much," Joe said, sighing. "He confused me more than anything."

Yuil looked disappointed. *"They say the Trith made it, that they've seen Congress's doom from the moment it was conceived."*

"And it means Congress is going to fall apart?" Joe asked, remembering Representative Na'leen's comment.

Yuil made a noncommittal sound. *"No one really knows. My guess, Choe, is someday it's going to meet a planet it can't conquer, and that planet will have a species that is going to rip it apart. They'll create a new peace, one not even the Dhasha can break."*

Joe contemplated that in silence as he stared out over the alien city. "I don't believe in prophecies."

"You should," Yuil laughed. *"You're living in the time of the foretelling, Choe. Everyone's saying it's gonna be sometime in the next hundred years. Some say it's gonna be the Dhasha Vahlin, but personally, I think it'll be a*

Huouyt to end Congress. *They can become any species in the universe, so why not one of them?"*

"I heard about that," Joe said warily. "They can change shape."

"Yes," Yuil said. *"But more than that. It happens at a genetic level. All that remains of them afterwards is their zora."*

"Huh?"

Yuil made a dismissive gesture. *"You've probably never even see a Huouyt."*

"I've seen one," Joe said, remembering Zol'jib and Representative Na'leen.

Yuil looked a little surprised…maybe even impressed. *"This is an Ooreiki planet. They're very rare, here. Still, you wouldn't see the zora. They keep that inside their heads."*

"The wormy thing," Joe said. "Is that what they use to eat?"

"Actually, yes," Yuil said, giving him an odd look, now. *"They use it to collect and assimilate genetic material. It's why they will rule Congress some-day. They can be* anything, *Choe."*

Joe bristled at that. "A Huouyt told me there were plenty of creatures they can't reproduce," Joe said. "So why not one of *them?"*

Yuil's sudah fluttered. *"It is true. Certain creatures…resist…the pat-tern. Turn the Huouyt into mush for trying to imitate their genetics. But the Jreet and the Dhasha have had hundreds of thousands of years to throw off Congressional yoke, and here they remain."*

"What about the Trith?" Joe asked, thinking of the fabled creatures everyone seemed to talk about like the boogey-man. "Could they take over?"

"The Trith are as indifferent to us as a mountain is to a grain of sand." Yuil had an almost…awed…tone when she spoke.

"Why?" Joe asked, frowning.

Yuil looked at him like he was stupid. *"If you ever see one, you'll understand."*

"You've seen one?" Joe asked, curious.

The young Ooreiki glanced around them, then put her silver-capped fingers on Joe's shoulder and pulled him back inside the cave. She took him to the far corner and pulled him down into a sitting position, with the Ooreiki seeming to pool on the floor from the waist down.

Yuil glanced both ways and pulled her translator from her neck and set it on Joe's knee so she could lean in close. *"From a distance,"* she whispered. *"It was walking across the commuter terminal orbiting Neskfaat."*

"Congress lets them walk around?" Joe demanded. "I thought they were traitors. Why don't they just kill all of them?"

"You can't kill a Trith," Yuil said, suddenly sounding irritated. *"They see every loophole, every mechanical malfunction, every lapse in security millions of years before it happens."*

"But if Congress—"

Yuil held up her silver-capped fingers, stopping him. *"We can speak more of Trith next time we meet. Tell me of yourself."*

Joe realized he had offended Yuil somehow and he began to worry that his conversation would be cut short. He looked at his knees a moment, then said, "I could tell you about where I come from," Joe said.

"Earth." The way Yuil said it, it sounded like, "Year-thuh."

"I lived in San Diego during the Draft," Joe said. "My dad stayed there after he got out of the Marines in Camp Pendleton. That's like the Army, but better. They're really bad-ass. I was thinking about joining up after I got out of high school."

Yuil sounded almost dreamy when she said, *"So you were* destined *to be a soldier."*

It was Joe's turn to be irritated. "I'm not a soldier. I'm a prisoner."

"Ah." An uncomfortable silence stretched between them. Then, *"It must have been nice to believe you were the only creatures in the universe."*

"Nobody really thought that," Joe said. "Not many of us, anyway. We just didn't think aliens would find *us*, you know? We always thought *we'd* find *you*."

Yuil snorted through her sudah. *"With your technology? It would have been eons before you left your solar system."*

"Hey, we'd been to the Moon," Joe said. Then he felt stupid, because the aliens had been traveling through space for three million years, if not more, and moons were no big deal.

"*It doesn't matter,*" Yuil said. "*As soon as you become a citizen, Congress will give you the technology you need to travel to other galaxies. You Humans will learn more in the next hundred turns than you learned since you started building fires in caves.*"

"At least we're not scared of fire," Joe retorted, feeling inexplicably defensive of his home. He *hated* the way everyone treated them like they were weaklings or morons or bacterial colonies under a high-powered microscope.

Instead of being angry, Yuil looked excited. "*You've seen it?*"

"What?" Joe asked, frowning.

"*Fire.*" Her huge eyes were aglow with interest, the pupils dilated so fully they appeared black.

Joe was a little stunned. "Yeah. All the time. My dad barbecues with his buddies on the weekends. He'll cook hot-dogs and bratwurst for us on his grill. Mom bought him one of those nice big ones with the lids that fold down that's got enough space inside to roast a pig."

Yuil cocked her wrinkled head. "*What are 'khot-doks' and 'bratweers'?*"

"Food," Joe said.

Yuil looked shocked. "*You use fire on your* food?"

"Hell, yeah!" Joe cried. "Have you ever tasted barbecued ribs? My dad makes some bomb-ass ribs." His stomach groaned with the memory. "It's a thousand times better than that scummy shit, I'll tell you that for *free.*"

The young Ooreiki stared at him. "*Scummy shit?*"

"You know. The stuff that tastes like something they scraped off the inside of an aquarium?" At Yuil's continued blank look, Joe said, "The green slime. Kids have been adding the salt buildup from their skin after runs, just to make it taste better."

Revelation brightened her eyes. "*You're talking about recruit food.*" Yuil laughed, a froglike croaking in her throat. "*Recruit food's never any good.*" She reached into a fold of her clothing and withdrew a bundled package. "*Try this. I can get you more, if you like it.*"

Gingerly, Joe took the bundle, afraid it was something alive. Up until now, he had never seen an Ooreiki eat. As far as he knew, they ate giant scorpions by the fistful and washed it down with glasses of arsenic.

At first, he thought the substance inside was a piece of ceramic. It detailed a solar system, with each planet a different color and pattern, some of which had moons and rings, all etched with delicate precision. It smelled lightly of mint.

"You recognize it?" Yuil asked. *"It's one of the new spices they found on Earth. I was told it was quite common..."* She gave the solar system a dubious glance.

Joe took a breath, allowing the smell to reach deep into his lungs. After the ever-present rotten stench of Kophat, it was decidedly a slice of heaven.

"You like the smell, don't you?" Yuil said. *"I can't stand it. The spicers were insane to bring it back with them. It's like the downwind side of a Dhasha."*

Joe glanced up. "Can I have this?" His heart was pounding, his fists wanting to tighten on the tiny morsel for fear she would take it away again.

"Take a bite. It's food."

Joe stared at the intricate detail. "You *eat* this?"

"Of course. The chefs enjoy making it as much as we enjoy eating it."

"I'd rather save it for the smell," Joe admitted. "This planet stinks like someone cherry-bombed a fucking outhouse at a shitting contest. This shit fucking reeks."

Yuil gave him a blank look. "That is something I never understood... I've done some research of your language and am puzzled. Why do you humans have such an obsession with orgies and bodily excrement? You are as filthy as the Jahul and the Dhasha in your speech, but even the Jahul don't have such a barbaric focus on reproduction and waste elimination."

Joe felt himself flush, because, for the first time since leaving his home, he had felt himself 'let loose' as he would have with other Earth teenagers. "Never mind," Joe muttered. "Can I keep it? To save it?"

"I can get you as many of those as you want, Choe," Yuil said. *"Don't worry about saving it."*

When Joe still did not move to eat it, the Ooreiki forcefully broke off a tiny moon and held it out to him. Joe reluctantly touched it to his tongue. It had a sweet-tart taste that diffused throughout his entire mouth, leaving it swimming in saliva. It was...different...than anything he'd tasted before, more complex and bitter. He knew that he would have spat the strange flavors back out on Earth, but here, he hadn't eaten anything so good in his entire life. His stomach screamed for more as he swished the last little bit around in his mouth, savoring it. He couldn't remember tasting anything so wonderful, partly because he couldn't remember exactly what food on Earth tasted like. Despite describing lasagna and chicken pot pies to the kids during storytime, his memories of those things were fading just as surely as the rest of it.

"I can't remember what food tastes like." Joe stared at the candy solar system, feeling as if he had failed his home somehow. How could someone forget what *food* tasted like? He was pretty sure, then, that whatever drug Congress was feeding them, it was intentionally wiping away their old alliances, like a wet rag cleaning off a chalkboard. The idea frightened him more than fighting the Dhasha.

"*I will bring you more,*" Yuil said. "*They have exotic foods in a little shop at the edge of the third ring. It's got a bunch of Human stuff right now. I can easily get more.*"

"I'll pay you," Joe blurted. Then he lowered his head. "Somehow."

The young Ooreiki's sudah began to vibrate in a laugh. "*You'll pay me nothing, Choe. Food is free here. The shopkeepers would even give you some if you ask. Everyone wants to see a Human close up.*"

"Thank you," Joe said, as he stared at the candy through tears.

Yuil stood up suddenly, whipping around to face the entrance. "*Peacemakers are nearby.*" She held up the akarit. It had changed from gold to black. "*Probably just a sweep, but I've got to hide this.*" She placed the akarit inside a small bluish metal box and shut the lid. "*If they come inside, there is a tunnel behind us. Run down it. It will take you a few days, but the tunnel leads all the way to the ground. Takki made it when they were hollowing this place out.*"

"What about you?" Joe asked, her obvious fear infectious.

"*Don't worry about me. I'll pretend I was sightseeing.*" She stiffened. "*They're getting closer. Go to the tunnel.*"

Joe, being the one training to be a warrior, felt as if he should somehow try to take the brunt of their elopement. "But I—"

"*Go now!*" Yuil snapped, shoving him towards the back of the room. "*If I'm caught with you, it'll be the end for both of us.*"

Biting his lip, Joe ran into the deepening shadows. He found the tunnel, but his body simply locked up as he stared at it. It was only about four feet high and four feet wide.

That's a Takki tunnel, he thought, panic swelling up from within.

"Get inside!" Yuil cried. *"Hurry, Choe!"*

Joe couldn't do it. He tried, but his limbs started shaking as soon as he ducked his head to enter. He felt like he was going to puke as he backed out again, shame weighing down his chest like a tumor.

Yuil scowled at him, then went to the entrance to the cave. After a few long moments outside, she walked back to him, sudah fluttering in a hum. *"They're gone. What is the matter with you? Why didn't you go down the tunnel?"*

"I'm scared of tunnels," Joe said.

Yuil blinked at him as if he'd said Dhasha had fins. *"You're afraid of tunnels?"*

Joe swallowed bile. "Yeah."

Yuil was giving him a strange look. *"But you can't—"* Then she looked away. *"Never mind. We must get back before they find you missing."*

"Will you come back tomorrow?" Joe asked.

"Maybe," she said, looking uncomfortable.

Which meant he had disgusted her and she wanted to get rid of him.

Shoulders slumping, Joe followed her to the haauk. "Thanks for the food."

Yuil said nothing and gestured for him to board the hovercraft. Once he was settled, she flew him back to the barracks in silence.

Once he unwrapped the now-green cloth from his shoulders and handed it to her, the Ooreiki wordlessly guided the haauk off the balcony and back out over the plaza. Joe was turning to go back into the barracks when she called his name from above. She was holding out the akarit box. *"Here. Take this."* She dropped it into his hands. *"You might need it someday."*

Joe stared at it. Despite wishing earlier she would do this very thing, Joe didn't want it. "You don't have to," Joe said. "You probably need it."

"I have others." Saying nothing, Yuil turned off and was gone.

Joe stared after her in shock. He didn't understand. She acted irritated, upset with him, but had given him the akarit…

…Then she had flown away without a word. He glanced down at the little box. It felt cold in his hands, dangerous. He had to fight off the impulse to throw it over the balcony.

What's wrong with me? I should be happy. This could get me home.

Yet, the longer he held the akarit the more he didn't want it. Deciding to hide it until he found a safe way to get rid of it, Joe reluctantly took it inside the barracks.

Maggie was awake and sitting up in bed when Joe stepped into the sleeping quarters. She watched him enter with an accusing look, following him with her eyes as he undressed and hid the akarit in the bottom of his clothes chest. When he stood up to get under the covers, she was still scowling at him over the other sleeping recruits.

"What, Mag?" Joe demanded, so tired he was near-delirious.

"Libby told me you left with some Ooreiki."

He frowned. "Yeah, so? It was only for a couple hours."

"You missed storytime," Maggie said. Her eyes added, *Asshole.*

"Oh." Joe grimaced. "Uh. Sorry, Mag."

"Yeah whatever." Maggie rolled over and went back to sleep, leaving him feeling like a jackass.

21

SLEEVES

"Did you give him the akarit?"

"Yes."

"But?"

"But what? I gave it to him."

"There's something you aren't telling me."

"There is, but I doubt you want to hear it."

"Say it."

"He almost got us both killed. I realized Peacemakers had followed me and tried to get him to hide in a tunnel, but he was too afraid. I had to kill them both."

"He's afraid of Peacemakers?"

"He's afraid of tunnels."

"*Tunnels.*"

"You see our problem."

"But the signs clearly point to—"

"A grounder is useless if he can't fight underground."

"We could pay to have him treated."

"And risk a recurrence? I've seen things like this before. It might be too deep to treat. It could come back at any time."

"What will the Army do?"

"He's hidden it well enough until now, but when they find out, they'll get rid of him. They'd have to add a hundred turns to his enlistment to make it worth their while to treat him, and a grounder's projected lifespan is only sixteen."

"They'll cut their losses? Sell him?"

"Yes."

"That makes things simpler."

"If you still believe he's the one we want."

"He is."

• • •

Despite his exhaustion, Joe woke early, a thousand different worries racing through his head. He and Yuil had evaded Peacemakers. He was now Fourth Platoon's recruit battlemaster. He had to lead a hunt. In tunnels. Knowing he wasn't going to get any sleep with *that* thought on his mind, Joe finally pulled his exhausted body out of bed and tried to find something productive to do.

His eyes caught on Libby's gear. She had finished modifying her pack. It now had a third strap, one that tied across her middle. Joe frowned at it, wondering how much trouble it would get them into.

He sighed and pulled out his jacket to look at his four-pointed star. He finally—*finally*—had battlemaster. He would no longer be watching on the sidelines. *He* was the one Nebil would yell at when things went wrong.

What if I screw up and he puts Sasha back in charge?

That was an unpleasant thought.

Joe folded his jacket and was putting it away when the cause for the nagging wrongness that had plagued him since first trying the garment on finally dawned on him.

It's the sleeves.

They were baggy and cumbersome, getting in the way when he was trying to move his arms.

Joe tentatively took a cuff and folded it back on itself. It looked horrible. He winced and tried again, folding it carefully, smoothing the wrinkles out with his hands. He made five folds, smoothing it tightly each time, creasing the upper bicep area over itself to keep the roll skin-tight. Then he tugged the jacket over his head and pushed his arm down through the narrow opening he had created with the sleeve roll.

The material fit around his bicep like Kihgl's *kasja*. It felt good. *Real* good. Joe tugged his jacket off and laboriously did the other side. He was just putting it on again when Battlemaster Nebil unlocked the barracks and stepped inside. Instantly, the entire barracks came to life as kids jumped out of their beds, trained to wake at the sound of their battlemaster's footsteps. Joe quickly buttoned his jacket back in place and turned to face the Ooreiki.

Nebil stopped halfway down the rows of round, six-person groundteam bunks, peering at him like a wary cat.

Joe glanced down at himself and immediately felt a rush of pride at how good he looked. Almost like his dad before he stepped out into the swirling chaos of the Draft.

"Zero, what in the fire-loving *hells* do you think you're doing?"

The other recruits paused in the middle of dressing to stare at Joe's sleeves.

Seeing their confusion, Joe flushed and blinked down at his arms. What *had* he been doing? He'd known Nebil would only make him undo them. "I modified my uniform. See? It moves better with the sleeves rolled up like this." He swung his arm for Nebil's perusal, then held his breath, watching Nebil's reaction.

Battlemaster Nebil stared at him as if he had grown purple scales and big sapphire eyes. "Zero, you sooter, fix it."

"It *is* fixed," Joe said stubbornly.

Battlemaster Nebil glanced from Joe to his sleeves and back. "Now."

"No," Joe said, even as he thought, *What the hell are you doing? You just got Battlemaster and you're about to blow it!*

Battlemaster Nebil walked up and cuffed him. "All right you stupid furg. You'll run later. Eighteen laps a night for as long as you insist on looking like a sootbag. In the meantime, get your platoon together. We've got another hunt today."

Then their battlemaster turned and began striding down the length of the barracks, throwing fistfuls of white clothes at the bunks.

"Get dressed! Get your gear! *Not* your blacks! You're defending today, you soot-eating furglings! Get *up!* Don't think I won't march you till you bleed if you don't move fast enough! Get *dressed!*"

Everyone, of course, was already out of bed and trying to make sense of the piles of clothes he had thrown at them, but Nebil was running around the room and screaming as if they were still sleeping soundly, ignoring him.

Joe shrugged into his new white garments and made it to attention faster than half the rest of the recruits. Unfortunately, they were the slower, dumber half. He was still tucking in his shirt when Nebil stalked by and saw him.

"You're not finished, Zero? And you think you're fit to be a battlemaster? Get on the ground! Two hundred pushups. No, *one* arm. What do you think you are, a spacer?" Nebil started walking around him as Joe dropped and started doing his pushups. "Keep your back straight!" he ranted on. "This isn't Second Battalion. Take some *pride* in yourself, you jenfurgling Human. Each time you fall on your face, you run a lap. And you! You think that's funny? Get down there with him. Ah, burn it! All of you get down! Two hundred pushups! You females can use two hands, if you weaklings feel you have to. *Now*, recruits!"

Everyone got to the ground, glaring at Joe as they did so. Libby and Maggie were two of the only girls who used only one hand. Maggie fell on her face more often than not, but Nebil did not seem to notice. Sasha, on the other hand, used both hands and still finished dead last. It didn't earn her much respect, and she got as many nasty looks as Joe had for getting them into the mess in the first place.

"That's enough!" Nebil snapped. "Get your Jreet-loving rifles and get outside. Battlemaster, get up here to get your extra rounds."

Joe started forward, but Sasha brushed past him to take her usual place in front of Nebil. He hung back, waiting.

"What are you doing?" Libby whispered, coming to stand beside him. She had her rifle against one shoulder. "He made you battlemaster, didn't he?"

Joe took a deep breath and walked up to where Sasha was waiting for Nebil to notice her. When Sasha looked up at him with a poisonous scowl, he calmly said, "I'm battlemaster now. Go get your *groundteam* together."

Sasha ignored him. Her face fell, though, when Battlemaster Nebil loaded the spare rounds into Joe's arms and not hers. Sasha's eyes fell on Joe's burden and stayed there. The single line of a ground leader seemed pathetic on her chest.

"Go, Sasha," Joe said gently.

Eyes brimming with hatred, she turned to leave. Libby caught her arm.

"Told you," Libby said.

Sasha ripped her arm away. "My daddy said even Congo gorillas can play the stock market and be right a few times."

Libby stiffened, every muscle taut. Joe tensed, wondering if he was going to have to wipe Sasha's brainless face off of Libby's boot.

Libby, however, shrugged and went to form up. In the ranks, a Takki was passing out prepackaged tubes of green slime, which the recruits were sucking down like ice-pops as they listened to the plan for the day. Then Nebil gave the order and Joe took a deep breath. In his best Congie, he shouted, "Fourth Platoon, follow on your left foot! March!" Then he counted, "Left, left, left-right-left, left, left…" When they reached the main plaza, the battlemaster took over and loaded them onto a huge haauk.

As they lifted off, Commander Linin shouted, "All right you Takki pukes! Tril's got us on another practice run. Same idea as last time, except this time you're trying to keep the other half of our battalion from reaching your flag. You have an extra thirty-six tics to arrange yourselves before they drop off the attackers. Zero's got command of this one. Third, Fourth, and Fifth platoons on surface duty. First and Second stay in the tunnels. Keep in mind that Second Company's already been down those holes and they know them better than you do. You're gonna have to be on your toes. Squad leaders and above, your headcom mics have been turned on. Speak loud—the sets weren't made to pick up your gutless Takki whimpers."

Commander Linin scowled at the five recruit battlemasters. "And just so you know, Second Company put a bounty on battlemasters. Each one the attackers kill gets them an hour of free time."

"What about us?" Maggie asked.

Linin scoffed. "Burn that. Each battlemaster you lose, you run for an hour."

Then they were landing, spilling from the skimmer like a flood of cottonballs.

As the almost two hundred children in First and Second platoons descended into the tunnels, Joe tried to find a high point to survey the situation. He ended up climbing one of the ruined diamond mounds, feeling the jagged crystal try to cut him even through his thick Congie gloves.

"This is a good spot," Libby said, coming to stand beside him. "They're gonna enter from that side and we'll be able to shoot them before they make it to cover."

"Just like they did to us," Joe muttered, jumping down. "All right." He glanced at the three platoons waiting for his orders. "Split up," he ordered. "I want three recruits to a hole. Squad leaders, make sure you stagger them so not all the youngest ones go to a single hole. Maggie, go with that team. Libby, you stay here. I'll go over there, so we don't have all our spare ammo in the same place."

No sooner had they taken their positions than Second Company was arriving—with armored skimmers.

"*What the Hell?*" the recruit battlemaster of Second Platoon demanded in Joe's headset. "*They've got armored plating!*"

Not only that, Joe was seeing, but the skimmer was lowering them directly over an unguarded tunnel and they were exiting through a special door in the bottom of the skimmer.

"They're inside!" Joe said into his headset.

"*Which tunnel?*" one of the battlemasters below asked.

Joe grabbed his Planetary Positioning Unit. The symbols were in blockish Congie squiggles, not English. "Can anyone read the PPU?" Joe shouted back. He was clambering down his tunnel, seeing if there was a connection to the one that the enemy was using to infiltrate. There wasn't. He would have to double back. "What does North look like?"

"*I don't know, but I can hear them!*" Joe's onboard computer identified the speaker as Number 424, a squad leader from Fifth Platoon.

"*Everybody retreat to the flag!*" Third Platoon's battlemaster shouted. "*They're in. We've gotta fight them off inside!*"

Up on the surface, Joe could hear the skimmer lifting off. He stuck his head out of the hole to look. No enemies were in sight. The damage was done. Even now, their full force was descending to reach their flag. They hadn't even left a guard.

"Fourth Platoon, get out of your holes!" Joe shouted suddenly. "Meet me on the surface!"

"*What the hell are you doing?*" the battlemaster of Fifth Platoon demanded. "*They need us at the flag!*"

"*Burn it, asher,*" came Maggie's hot response. "*Zero can do what he wants.*"

Damn it, Maggie, Joe thought. But into his headcom, he said, "Hurry up!"

"*You're going to the surface?!*" Second Platoon's battlemaster cried. "*We need your help!*"

"You're getting it!" Joe shouted, jumping out of his hole. Libby was already leading an assault on the enemy tunnel. The rest of Fourth Platoon fell in behind him, eyes wide with excitement and fear.

"Just slow them down until we can reach them," Joe said into his head-set. He and Libby charged down the tunnel, with only a handful of the squad able to keep up. Ahead, he heard the wet, sucking sounds of gun-fire. His stomach roiled, remembering the last time he had gotten shot, but adrenaline was coursing through his system, making the fear bearable. He barely even noticed the tunnel walls closing in around him.

They found the enemy clumped together behind a wall of bodies, a mass of hundreds of black-clad recruits firing at the defenders. Black and white corpses littered the floor and the noise was so loud it was hard to think. The voices of the other four battlemasters were clamoring in his head, shouting for help or more ammo. One was screaming.

Joe fell to one knee and started firing. Libby, Scott, Sasha, and the other big kids from Fourth Platoon did the same, spattering the attackers with blue bile from all sides.

In three minutes, it was over. Pinned in place, caught in the crossfire from above and below, the attackers didn't stand a chance. They collapsed in shrieks, their muscles spasming in agony. A couple that hadn't been hit dropped their weapons, cold terror showing in their wide eyes as they surrendered.

"Are we supposed to take prisoners?" the leader of Second Squad asked, standing beside Joe. She was a twiggy imitation of Libby, except she came from Mexican roots. In the headset, the other platoons still hadn't realized they had won and were still calling wildly for backup. Joe ignored them, his gun sighted on one of the two captives. All the recruits around him were waiting for his answer.

"Maybe Linin won't make us run for losing a battlemaster if we have captives," the Mexican girl suggested. He was pretty sure her name was Tina.

"Take their headcoms," Joe ordered. "So they can't talk to anyone we missed."

"Put their headcoms *on*," Libby said. "So *we* can talk to anyone they missed."

No sooner had one of Joe's squad members pulled the helmet from another boy's head and slipped it onto his own did he fall down in a dead faint. Everyone stared at him, confused.

"Did he step on some goop?" Tina asked. "What's wrong with him?"

"What the hell is going on? Why'd the shooting stop? Where are you, Fourth?"

"We're standing over the bodies of all the bad guys, asher," Maggie said.

Joe scowled at her, but he couldn't take the time to correct her. Something about the situation was bothering him. "Someone else get that helmet. This can't be all of them. There's more out there somewhere."

"What if they're booby-trapped?" Monk asked.

Joe frowned, watching someone from First Squad grab the helmet. Booby-trapped? If they could bring people back from the dead and mend bones in a few hours, they probably had the technology to incapacitate an enemy who was trying to use Congressional equipment.

Before he could say anything, however, that girl slumped to the ground, the helmet still stuck to her head.

The owner of the helmet was clearly as surprised as they were. His eyes were showing whites all around and he was obviously wondering whether or not he would be blamed for their companions' mysterious unconsciousness.

"Leave the helmets," Joe ordered. "Monk says they're booby-trapped." He nodded at his groundmate, making her stand up straighter with pride. "First and Second Platoons, stay at the flag. There's more coming." He glanced at the eighty-some children standing in the tunnel with him. "The rest of you are gonna help me find the rest of Second Company." He was only now beginning to feel the pressure of the earth above him, and it was making his hands sweat.

I've got to get back to the surface, he thought, with growing anxiety.

The rest of Third and Fourth Platoons were only now creeping around the corner, crawling over the pile of corpses with their guns raised. They hesitated when they saw the two prisoners. It took Joe a moment to realize they were all looking at him, waiting for something.

"We should shoot the prisoners, Joe," Libby prodded.

Joe grimaced. "They surrendered." He knew she was probably right. It would take at least four recruits just to guard these two. Still, they had surrendered. It didn't seem like the honorable thing to do.

"Hey!" Joe demanded of their 'prisoners.' "You two swear to stop fighting?"

They both nodded vigorously, relief and gratitude flashing across their faces.

"Okay," Joe said, "Third Squad will keep watch on them. Libby, your groundteam will be in charge of guarding them. Everybody else reload. We're going back to the surface."

The second wave of attackers fell in the same way. As soon as they were offloaded, Joe had Fourth Platoon attack their tunnel and follow them down. They took half the second wave prisoner, leaving them with over a hundred captives after all the attackers were either corpses or disarmed.

They spent the next couple hours huddling in the pits, sucking on slime-sticks, the captors playing tic-tac-toe with the captives. When the Takki arrived to drag the corpses out, they paused to give the captives an odd look before retreating with their burdens. One even paused to whisper to Joe in Congie, "Shoot them. Do them a favor."

Joe ignored the lizard. Moments later, Commander Linin's voice boomed in their helmets, *"Everyone out of the tunnels for a battalion formation."*

When they got to the surface, the prisoners' battlemasters descended upon them in a flurry of wrath. As Joe and the other defenders were ushered into ranks, the survivors in black were led to a separate formation facing the main one. The black-clad 'corpses' that the Takki had dragged from the tunnels were now quickly being revived by an army of Ooreiki surgeons. Revival, this time, was practically instantaneous upon the feeding of the solution into the recruits' veins, now that their commanders didn't want to make the kids walk home in the dark. As soon as they woke, they were allowed to join Joe and the other defenders in the main formation.

Once everyone was standing and accounted for, the battlemasters handed the Battalion over to Secondary Commander Tril, who paced in front of the prisoners with a cold, merciless stare. The few days he'd been in charge of Sixth Battalion had lightened his eyes by several degrees. His skin was also beginning to lose its rich brown-orange color, dulling noticeably by the week.

"Apparently, you are unaware of Congress's policy on surrender," Tril said. The tone he used was so icy that Joe got goosebumps. "The First Rule of a Congressional soldier is to obey any and all orders that his superiors give to him without question. Do you know what the Second Rule is?" His voice was ominously quiet, his snakelike gaze never leaving the fidgeting group of black-clad prisoners.

"It's never surrender." He said, his voice a whisper of rage. "How *dare* you surrender?! This is just a *game!* We are not even in a real battle and you have the audacity to disgrace me and your battlemasters with *surrender?!*" He turned and retrieved a small black handheld device from his vest. It reminded Joe of the circular gadget the Ooreiki used to promote them, but this one was thicker, stockier.

"I suppose I should be grateful this happened now, before you ashy furglings did it while Lord Knaaren was watching. For that, I'll only give you the weakest punishment available to me." He held up the small black gadget. "I'm sure you all remember the day back on the ship when the doctors lodged a small device into your chest. It has several purposes, but one of them is to give Congress an effective means of punishing its soldiers without causing lethal damage. It is the most absolute pain you will ever experience, because it releases small impulses upon command that allow you to feel nothing else."

Joe stiffened. Some of the prisoners in the front row were beginning to cry.

"This," Tril said, touching the black gadget, "is the controller that every battalion commander carries around with him. It's indestructible, so don't any of you furgs get any ideas. It has nine settings. The lowest—what you are about to experience—will leave you dazed for a few hours afterwards. It also makes you release your bowels, so it would be in your best interest to undress before I use it."

The children glanced at one another tearfully, unsure what to do.

"He said strip!" one of Second Company's battlemasters snapped.

Still, only a couple obeyed.

"Suit yourselves," Tril said. "By the authority given to me by the Universal Congress as your Commanding Officer, I hereby sentence you to the First Degree of perceptual punishment." At that, he touched the black pad in his fingers.

A hundred kids fell to the ground, shrieking. It was worse than anything Joe had seen in the mock battles. This was long, unyielding agony. At least the blue goop killed them quickly. Tril's little black device gave them no quarter, and did not allow them the relief of a fake death. Joe grew sick watching and had to close his eyes. As he stood there, the stench of excrement filled his nostrils and still they screamed.

In that moment, watching the kids writhe on the ground, Joe knew that he would always hate Congress. No matter what came in his future, no matter how many rewards they gave him, he would always hate them. Shaking, Joe had to turn away. When he did, he saw Battlemaster Nebil standing stiffly to one side, sudah whipping silently in his neck. He wasn't watching the screaming children like everyone else—he was watching Tril.

Exactly twenty minutes after it began, Tril ended their torment. The kids on the ground gasped and stared blankly at the sky. They lay like the dead, only the rise and fall of their chests indicating they were still alive.

"Battlemasters, tend to your platoons." At that, Tril turned and walked back to his haauk. Without another word, he flew away.

"Come," Battlemaster Nebil said, sounding tired. "You owe me an hour for losing Sixth's battlemaster." He paused. "And Zero, you get eighteen laps for your sleeves."

22

CAPTURE THE FLAG

Joe wore his sleeves rolled up proudly the next morning, and caught more than one strange look from other battlemasters and Ooreiki from other Battalions. Nebil had said absolutely nothing about them since he'd run his laps the night before.

"Where'd you learn to do that?" Maggie asked as soon as she saw them that morning. She ran a fascinated finger along the band of cloth around his arm. "I wanna do that, Joe!"

"You can't," Joe said. "Nebil will make you run."

"I don't care," Maggie whined. "I want to have my sleeves rolled, just like you, Joe."

Joe put his foot down, however, and had to endure Maggie's pout for the rest of the day. That night, when they formed up in the plaza for their nightly inspection, Commander Tril saw Joe's sleeves for the first time.

"Battlemaster Nebil, have you lost your mind?" Tril demanded, coming to a stop in front of Joe.

"Zero chooses to run eighteen laps each night to keep them, Commander," Battlemaster Nebil said with a shrug. "There's nothing I can do."

"Nothing you can—" Commander Tril broke off in the middle of his sentence, gaping at Battlemaster Nebil. To Joe, he said, "Fix your uniform, recruit."

"It is fixed," Joe said stubbornly.

"You see?" Nebil said. "Nothing I can do."

Tril's sudah were fluttering wildly in his neck. "Nebil, you will see me in my quarters tonight."

"I will be sleeping in *my* quarters tonight, Commander," Nebil replied. "If you want company, you should go back to *yeeri* academy and apply for motherhood."

Tril stared at Nebil so long that other battlemasters started to fidget. Nebil met his eyes unflinchingly, his sudah utterly calm, hands twined casually behind him around his switch. Seeing that, Joe got the distinct idea that Nebil was a moment away from using the weapon on Tril.

Apparently, Tril saw it, too. Sudah fluttering madly, he spun and, without another word, their secondary commander stormed off, leaving Nebil once more in charge of his platoon.

"Well," Nebil said. "Now that *that* unpleasantness is over, how do you pukes feel about a little shuteye?" His eyes caught on Zero. "Except for you, you fire-loving Jreet sooter. You run laps."

Joe felt a surge of triumph that his battlemaster had the balls to stand up to Tril. A lot of the other battlemasters did not, and their platoons often didn't get enough to eat because Tril ordered them to do more drills than they could reasonably fit in one day. Joe found himself proud of the fact that Nebil, despite Tril's orders, made sure his platoon got three meals and a full night's sleep each night—as long as his recruits weren't stupid enough to want to run eighteen laps at bedtime to prove a point.

Joe ran his eighteen laps that night grinning, finding this small means of rebelling to be exhilarating instead of exhausting. Each lap left him with more energy, until he was running all-out, his head up proudly as he served his penance.

When he finally charged up the stairs an hour after the other recruits had gone to bed, Battlemaster Nebil was waiting by the door.

"Looks like a member of your groundteam will be joining you tomorrow," Nebil said as Joe stepped inside. Without another word, he touched the control pad and the door dripped shut between them.

Joe turned and saw Maggie with her tongue stuck in the side of her cheek, rolling up her sleeves in big, childish bunches. The other children in the barracks were watching her silently, though they had enough sense not to follow her lead.

Joe groaned. He knew Maggie would pass out before the tenth lap. "Mag, what are you doing?"

Maggie wiped her face and Joe realized she had tears in her eyes. "They don't look as good as yours, Joe," she said. "I can't make them look that good."

Joe took her jacket and frowned at the crude little wads of sleeve she had made. He started to unroll them.

"*No!*" Maggie cried. "Battlemaster Nebil said I could have them!" She wrenched the jacket out of Joe's hands and cradled it in her lap. Soon she began to rock back and forth, crying.

Joe glanced at Libby. "Did he?"

Libby shrugged. "He said she could if she wanted to run."

"Damn it," Joe muttered. "Mag, what are you *doing?*"

"I want to be a soldier like you, Joe!" Maggie wailed. "I just want to have *sleeeeeves.*" She threw herself down on the bed, sobbing.

Joe took a deep breath and squatted beside her. "Mag. Listen to me. I'll roll your sleeves for you tonight, okay? But I'm not rolling them again after that. If you take them out because you don't want to run anymore, I'm not rolling them back up again. Got it?"

Maggie stopped sobbing and nodded vigorously.

Sighing, Joe pulled her tear-stained jacket out of her clutches and gently tugged the sleeves loose. "Now watch how I do this, okay? You don't just roll them up. You've gotta fold them and smooth out the wrinkles. And up here near the top of the arm, you gotta pinch the sleeve shut as you roll it so it's not baggy on your arm."

Maggie's face contorted with concentration as she watched him work. Joe felt like he was a horrible person, giving an hour of nightly running to a five-year old, but he reminded himself that she didn't have the *body* of a five-year-old anymore. She could have been fourteen or fifteen, back on Earth. In fact, some of the twelve-year-olds had been giggling under the covers at night, and Joe had a pretty good idea they weren't discussing the Bible.

That reminded Joe of the way his own body had changed, and how some of the oldest girls caught his eye at the most awkward moments. It was becoming embarrassing—mentally, he knew they were all still kids, but physically, he really, really needed a girlfriend.

"There you go," Joe said, handing the jacket back to Maggie. "Try that on. If the arms are too tight I can loosen them for you."

"They're *perfect,* Joe!" Maggie squealed and danced on the bed, showing her new jacket off to all the other recruits in delight. "Thank you Joe! I *love* them!"

"You're not gonna love them when you're running tomorrow night," Libby said dryly.

Maggie stuck out her tongue and turned to let Scott inspect them, giggling like a little girl.

She is a little girl, Joe reminded himself again. *She just looks older.*

When he finally got Maggie calmed down enough to sleep, he couldn't stop thinking about the way Libby's leg was touching his where she slept beside him. Off in a far corner of the barracks room, he heard two of the older kids murmuring as they fumbled under the blankets. Joe felt a hard-on coming on—he hadn't had a chance to get off since the last time he'd stolen a peek at his father's Playboy collection back on Earth—and he was painfully aware of how his balls were beginning to ache. He quickly tried to think of something else.

Libby, however, wasn't helping matters. She was sprawled out right beside him and her childish body had grown athletic and leggy, her lithe form as perfect as a model's. Even her face, which was always serious while she was awake, was soft and delicate as she slept, her exquisite features only a few inches away.

Like he usually did when he couldn't sleep, Joe rolled onto his back and began to wonder what it would be like to get laid. The thought stuck in his brain and, added to his body's hyped-up energy level from his run, he found himself wide awake for several hours.

Desperate for some rest, he moved as far as he could toward the edge of the bed, but he could still feel where his leg had brushed Libby's. It had been as smooth as silk, so feminine it sent shivers through his body. For the first time since getting abducted, he realized that he was sleeping next to three almost-naked girls. He got rock-hard despite himself, and spent the next hour wondering if there was a safe place to jack off without the other kids seeing him.

The sounds of the other couple making out eventually ended and the entire room fell silent. Still Joe waited, listening. He was only going to get an hour or two of sleep, at most. Finally unable to stand it any longer, he got up, snuck to the far wall, and began to beat his meat into a chamber pot.

When Monk spoke beside him, he almost pissed himself. He scrambled to put everything away before turning to face her.

"Joe?" Monk asked again.

"Yeah," Joe said, his face blushing so hard it felt like it would explode. "What is it?" He backed away from her, feeling like he was going to die.

"You okay?" she asked, moving closer. She was still only a few inches taller than she had been when they first met, but her body was developing in ways that he hadn't noticed until now. She was so close she was almost brushing against his thigh. He jerked away and closed his eyes.

She's still a kid, Joe thought. *She's a kid.* Suddenly very disgusted with himself, he cleared his throat. "I'm fine, Monk. Go back to bed." His balls were aching bad, now. He needed some relief, even if it meant half the barracks watching him jack off.

"Are you sure?" Monk insisted. "Why are you still awake? Aren't you tired?"

"Damn it, Monk, I'm fine," Joe growled. "Please, leave me alone."

"What are you doing over here?" Monk asked, glancing at the chamber pot. "Is something wrong with you? I saw you trying to pee."

"I'm not trying to—" Joe cut off abruptly, realizing that his sarcasm would be lost on her. "Look, Monk, just go back to bed."

"I don't like Libby," Monk said. "Do I have to sleep next to her?"

"Yes," Joe said. "Just go, okay?"

"The battlemaster says we're gonna be doing the fighting game again tomorrow. We get to wear black this time, though."

Joe leaned against the wall in despair. "I know, Monk. Please, go."

In the darkness, Monk made a face. "Libby's being mean. She keeps saying Elf is dead. That's why I don't want to sleep with her."

Joe looked up sharply. "Elf is alive." Then it hit him. The dead-eyed human climbing down the staircase outside the Dhasha's tower... It had been *Elf.*

"What?" Monk said. "Why are you looking at me like that?"

Joe swallowed hard. He was remembering Elf's skin, all those scars… Only his hands had been unaffected. He had been completely unrecognizable, like those pictures of guys mauled by bears. Quite abruptly, Joe's hard-on was gone.

"Monk, promise me something."

"What?" she asked, instantly wary.

"If you get picked by Knaaren, kill yourself as quickly as you can."

She wrinkled her nose at him. "You're weird, Joe."

Joe sighed and moved away from the wall. "Yeah, I know. Let's get to bed."

He had no problem falling asleep, though his dreams were filled with nightmares of perfect, unscarred hands dragging him down a tunnel towards something horrible waiting to rip him apart.

• • •

"You publicly disobeyed me, Battlemaster."

"So I did." Nebil sounded amused. "On a full night's sleep, too. Fancy that." He had arrived *after* breakfast with the commanders—who had taken to shunning Tril to the point that Tril now ate alone in his room—still eating a spore-cake from the chow hall.

Tril tried to ignore the boredom in Nebil's voice, but knowing a *battlemaster* was enjoying the morning revelry at breakfast with his peers, taking a spot that rightfully belonged to *Tril*, made his fists clamp down on his desk in fury. He took a moment to size the other Ooreiki up. Nebil had seen over four hundred turns. His skin was shamefully loose for a battlemaster. Any other Ooreiki would have taken his last four-rank penalty and begun climbing the ladder again, but Nebil had stubbornly refused to leave battlemaster after his command had cut him down from Prime. Repeatedly.

"How long have you been a battlemaster, Nebil?"

The question seemed to catch the older Ooreiki off guard. He gave Tril a long, analyzing look, then said, "In all?"

Tril nodded.

"Eighty-five turns."

Longer than Tril had been alive.

Trying not to look surprised, Tril carefully pried another black growth from his new *ferlii* plant with the grooming tool. One thing about ship air—at least it didn't contain the spores that caused *ferlii* to try and grow on other *ferlii*. In the wild, draak would scrape them off and eat them, but here in the barracks, Tril had to do it by hand.

"How long were you a Prime?"

"Forty-three." He said it immediately, without hesitation.

"Don't you want to regain the ranks you lost, Nebil?" That he'd lost... three times, now. That still boggled Tril's mind. Promoted to Prime...only to bungle it to ashes and get kicked back to battlemaster. The *wriit* had to be some sort of jenfurgling.

"No."

Tril frowned at him. "Then why re-enlist? Why not resign? Why stay forever trapped in a pathetic rank like battlemaster?"

Battlemaster Nebil laughed. "What do you want, Tril?"

Tril eyed Nebil a moment before putting down the grooming tool. "Why do you let Zero keep his sleeves?" Nebil stiffened and Tril held up an arm. "I'm not telling you to get rid of them—you wouldn't listen to me anyway. I just want to know why."

"Zero is a recruit battlemaster," Nebil said. "It helps his platoon to iden-tify him quickly."

"If his recruits can identify him, Lagrah's recruits can identify him." Tril retorted.

Nebil's face stretched in an evil smile. "Exactly."

• • •

Sixth Battalion was dressed in black, clutching guns loaded with the poi-sonous blue solution as Commander Linin discussed the plan of the day. Linin had noticed Joe's rolled sleeves but, as Nebil had done, he ignored them, acting as if they didn't exist.

"Listen up!" Linin shouted. "Commander Tril's got a slug up his ass to go challenge the other battalions, so today's our first real hunt. We're up against Lagrah and Second Battalion, so unless you all learn how to unclog your sudah in the next couple tics, we're all gonna look like wriggling white *niish* out there today. Lagrah spent fifty turns in Planetary Ops before he started training recruits. He's almost got more experience at this soot than Nebil. With me so far?"

The kids on the skimmer gave Linin wide-eyed looks that were more terror than understanding. Joe could sympathize. As the attackers, it was horrifying to know that, if they didn't retrieve the flag, they would all have to get hit with the goop by the end or they would get punished with Tril's little black box. Everyone on the skimmer was nervous, their grips on their rifles tight as they waited for Linin to offload them from the haauk.

Commander Linin made a frog-like grunt into the silence. "Commander Tril says you Takki get an hour of free time for every squad leader you take down, three hours for every Battlemaster. If he wants to pamper you pussies, that's fine. I'm not gonna question that Takki ashsoul, but I am gonna add something of my own. For every recruit that dies within the first nine tics, the entire company will run for eighteen tics."

Which, Joe was pretty sure, would negate any battlemaster or squad leader kills they gained. "So what do we get if we capture the flag?" he asked.

Linin snorted. "You get the pride of knowing you're the first Human company in the history of Congress to successfully infiltrate an enemy battalion's tunnels, you worthless Jreet bastard." Linin croaked out an Ooreiki laugh. "Anyway, you wriggling Takki sooters aren't gonna get the flag. Tril's pitted us against Lagrah, so unless you all learn to grow hahkta in the next couple hunts, we're all gonna be writhing around in our own shit until they decide to pull us from the regiment. Just try to stay alive past the first nine tics, then we can talk about burning flags." He turned to open the gate at their feet.

"Wait," Joe said, holding up the Planetary Positioning Unit. "Can you show us how these work?"

Linin frowned at the unit, then at Joe. "You're not gonna learn the PPU until your second year."

"We could use it now," Joe said.

Commander Linin snorted. "A good fifty percent of you weren't even literate when you were drafted, and you ashpile Humans take extreme repetition to learn even the most basic tasks." He gave Joe and his sleeves a pointed look. "Dressing yourselves, for instance."

"I can read," Joe said, desperate, now. He could *feel* the tunnels down there, under the ship, and his heart wouldn't stop hammering at the thought of getting lost in them.

Linin snorted. "They say you sooty furglings wrote in *lines*." He shook his turd-shaped head, making the hahkta slap against the sides of his face. "They're sending specialized linguists to deal with you furglings next turn. Until then, I don't have enough time to teach you slugs to read." He wrenched open the gate to the haauk. "Figure it out yourselves." In the tunnel underneath, Joe could see movement in the shadows.

"They're waiting for us!" Joe shouted into his headcom. To Linin, he said, "We need another tunnel."

"Burn that," Linin said. "You get the tunnel we give you."

Frustrated, Joe started firing at the movement in the shadows. "Fourth Platoon's got cover! Second and Third jump in there!" Libby squatted beside him and opened fire.

"*Burn it, Zero. Take your own platoon down there.*" Joe recognized the speaker as Third Platoon's battlemaster.

"You know, the nine tics doesn't start until you get off the haauk," Commander Linin said casually, leaning against the skimmer's armored side.

"*Someone's* gonna have to get in there," Joe shouted.

"We could sure use some grenades," someone muttered.

"That would plug the tunnel," Commander Linin commented behind them.

Joe frantically tried to figure out what to do. Two attackers had already been hit and the game hadn't even started yet. He peered into the darkness of the tunnel. There couldn't be more than two defenders down there. The attackers had them outnumbered, but none of them wanted to climb out of safety and go press their advantage.

Joe surveyed First Company. They had pulled away from the hatch in the massive haauk, huddling down and to the back to avoid the spray of goop. Several of the kids were watching him, and not all of them were from Fourth Platoon, either.

Joe took a deep breath. The longer they waited, the more time the defenders would have to reinforce their tunnel. Steeling himself, he said, "Libby, Scott, Maggie, Monk, down the hole!" He got up and lunged through the open gate, down into the dark pit, firing as he fell. Libby was right behind him. Seeing more attackers pouring in after them, the defenders pulled back, shouting for help from their companions.

Libby started to follow the retreating defenders, but Joe grabbed her arm. "No," he said. "Fourth Platoon stays at the surface." She gave him an odd look, but stayed.

Behind him, the rest of First Company was pouring from the skimmer, swarming the tunnel. "Fourth Platoon hang back!" Joe shouted. "We'll protect our ass!"

If the other Battlemasters heard, they were too busy shouting orders, pushing their own platoons deeper into the warren. Soon thereafter, one of them started screaming. In minutes, only Fourth Platoon was still in the entryway.

"I'll go keep watch," Libby said, moving toward the rim of the pit.

"Wait," Joe said. "Maybe if we make it look like the tunnel's empty, they'll come to get us."

Which is exactly what happened. One entrepreneuring squad leader rushed his recruits across the surface, thinking to take them by surprise. Joe and his squad surprised them and disabled all eighteen without losing a single recruit. Then they waited, hunkered down in their pit, surveying the abandoned landscape for any signs of another attack. There were none. They were alone.

Still, Joe couldn't bring himself to lead them back to the fight.

"They're all down below," Scott said. Like everyone else, he could hear the fighting taking place over the headcom. "Why're we still up here, Joe?"

Joe tensed, wondering if his groundmates had any suspicion of his fears. He'd been afraid Libby had begun to catch on, but when he looked at her, she said nothing.

How are you gonna lead these kids if you're goddamn claustrophobic?

Joe glanced at his friends' faces, his hands sweaty. They looked irritated for the lack of action, but they didn't appear to notice he was procrastinating. That wouldn't last long, though. They were glancing at each other, then out across the pitted clearing, obviously noticing the fact that there was no one here for them to fight. In his ear, the other battlemasters were demanding that Joe get down there and help them. Joe pulled off his helmet and took a deep breath. He was letting everyone down. He had to do something.

And yet, the idea of leading them down into the darkness below made his guts clench up in terror. He already felt like he had to take a massive liquid dump, just from the sheer proximity of the dark hole in the ground. "Listen up, everybody," Joe managed, his voice cracking. His hands, he noticed, were shaking badly. "We're changing tunnels—there's too much fighting blocking the path to the flag with this one. We're gonna change to a different entry point, but first I need a volunteer, someone to go out there and see if anyone shoots at you."

Several recruits' faces soured at that, but Maggie immediately raised her hand and said, "I'll do it, Joe!"

Joe gave her a relieved grin. "Okay, Mag. Give your spare ammo to somebody. Then run out that way as far as you can until I tell you to come back. Act like you're running scared." Joe pointed toward the other side of the clearing.

Maggie beamed and handed her ammo to Monk. Then she got up and crawled out of the pit. When nobody shot at her, she broke into a run. Libby watched her as she crossed the surface, her face unreadable.

"She's not getting shot," Libby said finally.

Joe called her back, and when Maggie returned, she was flushed and panting. She hacked up a lump of red from her chest and took her ammunition back from Monk.

"What'd it look like out there?" Joe asked.

"Nobody out there," Maggie replied. "I even looked down a few holes. Everything's empty."

Joe slipped his helmet back on. "Okay everybody, let's go." He got up and led them sprinting across the landscape, ignoring the other platoons' shouts in his headcom. He found a tunnel entrance on the other side of the battlefield and Joe only hesitated a moment, eying the height and width of the walls before hurrying inside.

Almost immediately, they got lost.

"I can't see anything," Monk muttered, after they'd been wandering for hours. The space was dimly lit with the glowing blue light of their guns, all the tunnels looking the same in the underground maze. "Where are we, Joe?"

"We're lost, stupid." Sasha, who had been demoted to a grounder after her walking episode three days earlier, was haphazardly gripping her rifle with one hand, leaning against the tunnel wall with the same air of casual indifference she had borne ever since losing her rank to Joe.

"Just shut up, Sasha." Joe had finally given up on trying to get to the flag in the center chamber and now just wanted to get them back to the surface. He slumped against the wall. His hands were shaking outright, now. He was using every spare ounce of self-control trying to keep himself from panicking in front of the little kids and he felt himself dangerously close to a breakdown.

"Maybe they ended the hunt," Libby said. "I haven't heard anything in a while."

"Me, neither," Joe said. "But that could just mean the rest of the platoons are dead." He cleared his throat, glad to have a distraction to take his mind from the fact that he had spent the last several hours trapped and lost under the earth. Into his headcom, he said, "Hey, any other battlemasters out there? This is Zero, Fourth Platoon. Can anyone hear me?"

There was no reply.

"Well, soot," Joe said. "If I could make this stupid thing work, I could tell you where we are, but I can't read Congie." Joe flipped his Planetary Positioning Unit away in disgust. In the gloom, Libby bent to pick it up. The unit was surprisingly sturdy, made from some sort of metal composite that refused to scratch, dent, or bend.

She handed it back to him. "Nebil said we run laps 'til our feet bleed if we lose anything," she reminded him.

"Thanks," Joe muttered. He stuffed it back into his cargo pocket in disgust.

"Last time the hunt ended, we heard it in our helmets," Scott said. "I haven't heard anything like that."

"Maybe we're out of range," Libby said.

"Out of range?" Sasha scoffed. "These things work in outer space."

"There's a lot of diamond dirt above our heads," Scott said. "Maybe it's blocking the signal."

Joe's skin grew slick and cold with the thought. He closed his eyes and took a deep, steadying breath. "If the hunt was over, they'd send Takki after us," Joe said. "So we're still supposed to be trying to find the flag."

"Then let's find the flag," Libby said. "It's gotta be down here somewhere."

"Scott, which way's the way we came in?" Joe asked, able to only really think about the surface at this point. His hands hadn't stopped shaking in hours.

Scott sheepishly pointed to a wall of dirt.

"Fat lot of good that does us!" Joe snapped, losing it. Then, at Scott's cringe, he caught himself and took a deep, steadying breath. The walls hadn't closed on him yet. He was doing fine. All he had to do was keep his cool. He let his breath out slowly. "Can you get us out of here, Scott?" he asked.

Libby shot him a glance and said, "Can you get us to the *flag?*"

Monk sniffed. "Maybe we're at the bottom already. We went down a *long* ways, Joe. Like my Uncle George in the mineshafts right before they collapsed and they gave Aunt Susie that huge check."

Oh God, Joe thought, his fingers reflexively clutching his rifle. *Oh God oh God oh God…*

But the other kids went on as if Monk hadn't said anything out of the ordinary.

"Seriously?" Scott said. "A check? Like how much of a check?"

"A big house and new car and llamas check," Monk replied. "She bought llamas. They spit."

"No they don't," Maggie said.

"Do *too*," Monk retorted. "One of them spat in my hair. It was green and gooey."

"My grandmother had llamas," Scott said.

"The *flag*, Scott," Libby reminded him.

"Oh." He winced guiltily. "Yeah, I dunno."

"Well, how did you get us back home?" Libby demanded. "Can't you do the same thing and get us to the deep den? You said you felt the *city*, Scott."

Scott grimaced. "Yeah, uh, okay. If I knew where it was, I could get us there, but right now, all I can do is guess. Like, I can feel there's a tunnel directly underneath us, but that's like twenty feet down."

Twenty feet down... Joe felt his face break out in sweat and his heart start to hammer. The flag, he knew, was always in the deepest section of the tunnels. They had to go *deeper*...

"Joe, maybe we should let Scott lead." Libby was looking at Joe, eying him a little too carefully.

"I don't wanna lead," Scott said, eying the empty black tunnel ahead of them. "The ones who lead get shot."

"Try, okay?" Joe managed. "We've tried marking our path and turning left at every intersection. That just got us even more lost. Maybe you should see what you can do, okay? We can't get any worse off than we are right now."

"Second Battalion could find us," Monk reminded them.

"Right now, I'd *love* it if Second Battalion found us," Joe retorted. "At least if Lagrah's recruits found us, we could all get shot and we won't end up having to explain to Tril why we ran away."

"We didn't run away," Maggie said, frowning.

"I know, Mag," Joe said. "But you gotta admit it looks pretty damn bad. Scott, how 'bout it? Think you can get us out of here?"

Scott straightened, looking increasingly irritated. "You want me to get us out of here or find the flag? Which is it?"

"The *flag*," Libby snapped.

"Too bad!" Scott snapped back. "I can't do either. It's a burning *maze*. A sense of direction doesn't mean jack shit if I can't go where my head's telling me to go."

"Don't be an asher, Scott," Joe muttered.

"*Libby's* the asher," Scott screamed. "We're *stuck* down here and we're not getting home and it's her fault because she wouldn't *listen* to me when I kept telling her she was taking the wrong tunnels!" He sat down and crossed his arms over his knees.

A hand touched Joe's shoulder. "Excuse me," a kid said quietly.

Joe rounded on him. "What?!"

The kid nervously pointed at Scott. "Is that the kid that got your groundteam back to Alishai before all the others?"

Joe frowned at the newcomer. "Yeah. Why?"

The kid blushed and dropped his eyes. "I played a lot of video games before the Draft. Pyramid PI was almost exactly like this. It was a huge Egyptian maze with the Pharaoh's tomb at the end. I'm the only one I knew who could get all the way to the tomb and then all the way out again without using the magic transporter at the end. If I can use Scott as a…a…" The kid swallowed and looked at his feet.

"Use him as a what?" Joe barked.

"Compass," the kid squeaked. "I think I can get us out if I had a compass."

Joe peered at him. "What's your name?"

"I'm Carl, Zero."

"My name is Joe. And if you think you can get us out of here, Scott will help you out." He turned to glance at groundmate. "Scott, help him out."

Scott ignored him, sniffing. Joe kicked him. "Be his compass."

His groundmate snorted and rolled his eyes. Joe kicked him again, harder.

Scott lunged to his feet. "Goddamn it, what the hell do you want me to do? Hold his hand?!"

Carl twined his fingers and stared at the ground. "Back on the game, "I always had a compass in the corner of the screen."

"So?" Scott said, glaring.

"Just do what he says, Scott," Joe warned.

Carl looked like he was about to have some sort of death-by-shyness. He swallowed and glanced at Joe, then finally found the courage to look at Scott. "I can navigate a maze no problem, as long as I have a compass. I just have to be able to see you all the time."

"You mean walk in front."

"Yeah." Carl blushed.

"I hate walking in front."

"He'll walk in front," Joe and Libby said at the same time.

Scott sighed deeply. "That's it?"

"No. I'm gonna need you to…to…" Carl turned as red as a beet. In the bluish light of the guns, he looked purple.

"Oh spit it out," Scott muttered.

Carl's next sentence came out all in one breath. "I need you to hold out your arm and point toward the entrance all the time."

Scott stared at him. "You're kidding." He glanced at Joe. "He's kidding, right?"

"Just do it," Joe said.

Sulking, Scott lifted his hand and pointed at the wall.

Joe nodded. "Go ahead, Carl."

"And get us to the *flag*," Libby added, still giving Joe that odd look. "We go back to the surface now, Tril will give us perceptual punishment."

Joe bit down the urge to contradict her and instead nodded.

Still red as a beet, Carl said to Scott, "Okay, so start walking. As soon as you come to an intersection, stop."

"Do I have to hold my arm up the whole time?" Scott whined.

"Yes," Libby and Joe said as one.

"Oh *man*," Scott muttered. "What if someone shoots me in the back?"

"Libby will watch your back," Joe said, gesturing at her.

Libby obediently started down the tunnel, gun up. When Scott just crossed his arms and pouted, she frowned, stalked back, grabbed him by a hand, and tugged him deeper into the darkness. Though Scott technically weighed more than she did and probably could have put up a fight, Libby was taller, and she had the reputation of wiping grins off faces with her combat boot. Everyone in the battalion was terrified of her, some even more than they were of the legendary 'Zero.' Probably wisely, Scott went utterly meek in her grip, trudging along and rolling his eyes, one arm held up in disgust.

For what seemed like an eternity, they walked, Libby and Scott leading the way, Carl staring at his arm in rapt attention. When they reached a four-way intersection, immediately Carl told them to turn left. Then Scott was walking backwards, complaining even more loudly.

They made six more turns over another hour, then Libby suddenly brought them up short. She released Scott's hand abruptly and grabbed her rifle. Scott, who had been leaning on her as a form of noncompliance, fell onto his ass. As soon as he started to curse, Libby kicked his arm. "Shhh. Does anyone hear that?"

Voices? Joe held his breath, trying to pinpoint the source.

"Nice going, asher," Scott muttered, getting back to his feet. "You led us to the bad guys."

"Shut up, Scott," Libby snapped. "That's what we told him to do."

"It only sounds like a couple," Maggie whispered.

"Could be a lot more and only two's talking," Libby said.

"Okay, get ready for a fight, guys," Joe said, "I want my best shooters in front. Libby, Scott, Carl. If it's more than two, Sasha, you and your best groundmate are gonna help us out. If it's more than four, everybody just start firing. Got it?"

Everyone nodded.

"And cover up the cartridges on your guns," Joe added, shielding the blue glow with his palm. "I want to surprise them."

The two defenders who came wandering through their tunnel didn't even have a chance. Joe wrestled one to the ground while Scott tore her rifle out of her hands, and Libby and Carl took the other. While Joe was working on holding the kid's mouth shut, however, he heard the wet thwap of gunfire. Wincing, he turned, thinking one of his own had been shot.

Libby and Carl stood over a screaming body, the muzzle of Libby's rifle still giving off a blue glow.

"Shut him up!" Joe said, furious that they had shot the boy without asking. "Hurry!" He glanced back down the tunnels to make sure they hadn't been heard.

Silently, Libby placed her boot on the boy's chest to hold him steady while Carl held a hand over his mouth until his thrashing ceased.

"Why'd you *shoot* him?" Joe demanded once it was over. "We could've got him to lead us out!" Libby gave him a blank look.

Taking a deep breath, Joe said, "Never mind. We've still got the girl."

The prisoner in question was wide-eyed and panicked, hyperventilating through Joe's fingers. She, like everyone else in Lagrah's battalion, was fully grown, though Joe could tell she was Maggie's age.

"I guess that answers our question," Scott said, frowning confusedly down at the terrified girl. "The hunt's still on."

"Yeah," Joe said. "And she's gonna tell us exactly where to find that flag before we kill her."

The girl's eyes opened until the whites were visible all around and she shook her head wildly, nostrils flaring.

Libby squatted in front of the girl, casually leaning her rifle against a knee. "You tell us, we'll make it quick. You don't tell us and maybe we won't kill you. We'll just leave you here for the Takki to find. Alive."

At that, the girl stiffened, her entire body rigid.

Libby looked bored. "So where is it?"

The girl tried to say something through Joe's fingers, but it came out as a garbled mess. Libby glanced at Joe and Joe scowled down at the girl. "You do *anything* except tell us exactly where the flag is and I'll beat you to a bloody pulp. You got me?"

"K-kkee, Zero." The girl was crying softly, trying to keep her choking sobs silent, her tears glistening blue in the muted glow of their guns. Joe and Libby glanced at each other. *She knows who I am?* Joe mouthed to her.

Libby didn't miss a beat. "You better tell us before Zero gets any more pissed than he already is."

The girl couldn't have looked more terrified if she had told her that they were about to tear her apart and eat her flesh to stay alive. She shivered and nodded her head quickly. Joe actually felt sorry for her.

"First off," Libby said, "Tell us how many defenders are still alive."

"Most of the battalion," the girl blubbered. "You guys fight like Takki."

At Joe and his groundteam's scowls, however, she flushed and quickly looked away.

"Tell us how to find the flag," Libby ordered. "Which tunnel did you come from?"

"Please, Commander Lagrah will punish me if I tell you!"

"Lagrah will punish you worse if he finds out you surrendered," Libby said.

"Tell us!" Joe barked, when the girl hesitated.

The girl gulped, blue eyes fixed on him in horror. "Down the way we came, there's a crossroads. We marked the right path with a little X on the floor."

"How many tunnels until we reach the flag?" Joe pressed.

She frowned at them in confusion. "Just one."

"How many defenders on the flag?" Libby asked.

"You mean you guys didn't know where you—"

"Shut up and answer the question!" Libby snapped.

"Five," the girl whimpered. "A battlemaster and the rest of our groundteam."

"*Just* five?" Joe demanded.

She nodded. "Everybody else is on the surface. We thought you were all dead."

As promised, Libby shot the girl in the chest. As soon as she opened her mouth to scream, Joe clamped his hand back down over her face. When her body stopped spasming, Joe stood up and examined his platoon. Almost eighty in all.

"You guys hear that?" he demanded. When everybody nodded, he said, "All right. The groundteam at the flag might be wondering where these two went, so let's go in there and get it. She said there's a battlemaster, so we're gonna have to be fast in case he decides to call for others. Libby and I will be in front. Everyone behind us make sure you're quiet. It's not gonna help us if half of Second Battalion's waiting for us at the flag because we made too much noise getting in there."

Once he was sure they all understood, he and Libby covered their guns and moved down the tunnel.

They crept to the crossroads the girl had mentioned and crouched, listening. After a minute went by without hearing anything, Joe uncovered the cartridge long enough to find the X that the defenders had scratched into the floor. Then he cut off the glow again and led them deeper.

The light at the other end of the tunnel was the first sign that the girl had been telling the truth. Joe felt a rush of excitement and crept closer, until he could clearly see the five defenders sitting around a black standard with eight Congressional circles. Two were playing rock, paper, scissors and another looked like he was dozing.

"Now!" Joe jumped up and charged, followed by the rest of his platoon. He hit the biggest kid head-on and both of them went sprawling to the ground. The others followed his example and soon they had all five wrestled to the ground, helmets off, their faces pressed into the dirt. Libby went around and shot each one, and once their convulsions had stopped, they had the room to themselves. In the center, the flag hung from the ceiling, motionless.

Scott walked up and touched the flag, running his fingers along the smooth red and black designs. "So now what?" he asked, sounding almost in awe

Joe wasn't sure. "They probably all heard the battlemaster screaming in his headcom. They'll know something's up." He glanced around. The chamber had four tunnels leading out of it, giving any attackers an advantage. "We've gotta get out of here."

"I thought the hunt ended if we got the flag," Maggie said, walking over to stand by Scott and frowning up at it. "Don't we have the flag?"

"Maybe we need to take it with us," Joe said. "Back to the surface. Mag, grab it."

Maggie was pulling the flag down when Sasha snatched it and yanked it from Maggie's grasp. The ripping sound that followed made everyone in the room flinch.

Unconcerned, Sasha was stuffing the flag into her pack when Joe grabbed her arm and stopped her. "I told Maggie to carry it."

"She's not big enough to defend it," Sasha said, picking up her rifle.

"He said give it back to her," Monk said, eyes dangerous.

Slowly, lip curled in disgust, Sasha pulled it from her pack and threw it at the ground at Maggie's feet. "Fine. Take it. Didn't want to carry the stupid thing anyway." Maggie, sniffling, gingerly picked up the torn black cloth.

"Carl, Scott, get us out of here," Joe said. "Everyone else, be ready for a fight."

They had been moving through the tunnels for another two hours, groping their way through them at a crawl, afraid of letting the defenders seeing the glow of their rifles, when Joe finally brought everyone to a halt.

"I think we're far enough away to use a little light," Joe said. He pulled the rag from over his gun and several recruits breathed a sigh of relief when the blue glow filled the tunnel. For Joe, however, the light reminded him of the walls surrounding him. He took a deep, irritated breath and fought down the urge to yell. "Carl, you don't know where we're going, do you?"

Carl bit his trembling lower lip, on the verge of tears. It was disconcerting, coming from what was, to all appearances, a full-grown man.

"Don't worry about it," Joe said. "We've got the flag. We won."

Libby frowned at him in the gloom. "Then why haven't they come to get us?"

That very same question was running through the back of Joe's mind, nagging at him. "Nebil said you capture the flag, you win. That's it."

"What if a whole side has to be dead before they'll let us go?" Libby said.

"Then we'll get some sleep," Joe said. "I'm tired of walking in circles."

Scott and Carl looked away and he felt instantly bad.

"Hey, guys, it's not your fault," he told them. "It was dark and you couldn't see."

"He can see now and he still doesn't know where he is," Scott muttered.

"Everybody relax," Joe insisted. "Take a break, catch a nap, whatever you want to do. We'll just wait for the hunt to end." He sat down against a tunnel wall and brought out his PPU again in desperation. He stared at the screen, trying to make sense of the blocky Congressional squiggles. He could read some of the numbers, but numbers by themselves meant nothing to him.

"You already tried that," Sasha sneered. "Didn't work last time either, remember?"

Joe scowled at Sasha and stuffed his PPU back into his vest and went back to waiting.

But the hunt didn't end. Eventually, Joe had to admit that they weren't coming. "Okay, everybody. Let's get moving. Carl, just make your best guess. We can have as much light as you want this time. Just get us back to the surface." *Before I lose my mind down here.* He'd managed to control himself so far, avoiding a serious attack, but he knew if he was down here much longer, he was going to come totally unglued in front of an entire platoon of kids.

Libby started moving around the camp, kicking everyone awake like Nebil liked to do. Joe nudged Maggie with a toe to spare her the rougher treatment, and she started, blinking up at him like an owl. "Hunt's over, Joe?"

"We're still trying to figure out where we are," he admitted. "Listen up! Everyone keep a good eye out for X's or any other markings that look out of place. I want as much light as possible, so uncover your cartridges. Maggie, take the safety off your rifle. Let's move! Everybody follow Carl."

"Like that's gonna help," Sasha sneered. "He's been walking us in circles."

"Go, Carl," Joe said, glaring at her. "You're doing great."

Reluctantly, Carl obeyed. Four intersections later, they were staring down at a well-defined arrow in the entrance to one of the tunnels, pointing down it.

"Does an arrow mean In or Out?" Libby wondered aloud.

"Let's say it means Out," Joe suggested. "Come on, everybody. If it's the wrong way, we can always turn around and go back."

They followed the tunnel until they abruptly came to a dead-end with a tight, one-person passage leading into the darkness. Joe got on his knees and shone the light of a spare cartridge into the hole. It was so small he'd have to crawl on his hands and knees to get through it…and a fetid breeze hit his face the moment he got close to it. Immediately, he stepped back, his heart rate climbing.

"Looks like Out meant the other way," he said. "Let's turn around."

"Wait a minute," Libby said, squatting near the entrance. "Can't you smell that?"

"Smell what? I don't smell anything," Joe lied. He swallowed, hard. His hands were shaking all over again.

"The *air*," Libby said, frowning at him. "I can smell ferlii. This is a way *out*, Joe."

"It's too narrow," Joe blurted. "We gotta backtrack. He immediately turned to go.

Libby grabbed his wrist as he turned. Her eyes were hard as she looked up at him. She was only a few inches shorter than him, now, and she hadn't stopped growing yet. "Joe." The word was as much a command as anything.

"This is the way out," she said, low enough that only he could hear. "Do you want to get out of here or do you want to stay trapped?"

Joe swallowed convulsively and the word 'trapped.' "It's *tiny* Lib. We don't know if anybody can even *fit* through there."

"I can!" Maggie cried, stepping forward. Joe winced. He'd already made Maggie run across the battlefield. He couldn't bear to see her pinned in a tunnel in his place, suffocating, unable to wiggle free. "Not you. You've gotta carry the flag. You'll go last. Scott?"

Scott wrinkled his nose and peered into the hole. "I can see claw marks in there. Do I have to?"

"I'll go!" Maggie cried again. "Here, Libby. You take the flag." She shoved it enthusiastically into her groundmate's hands.

Libby took the flag from Maggie and stuffed it under her belt. "Come back whenever you figure out what's on the other side."

Excitedly, Maggie crawled into the dark burrow. Ten minutes later, she was back, dirty and excited.

"I found it! The tunnel comes out on the inside of one of those broken buildings. There's a couple narrow spots, but I think even you can get through, Joe."

"You *think*, Mag?" he asked, more harshly than he wanted.

"Well, yeah," Maggie said, "it was easy for me, but you're a little bigger than me, so you might have to crawl a little."

He sure as hell wasn't about to stake his life on a five-year-old's estimate. Just how good *was* Maggie at determining proportions? He remembered stuff being a lot bigger as a kid. What if she was wrong?

Then he realized everyone was staring at him, waiting for some sort of signal.

Joe cleared his throat nervously. He had to do it. He couldn't just stand here. He couldn't let them down.

Still, he couldn't bring himself to lead them into the tunnel. He'd rather sit there and starve to death. Joe bit his lip and glanced at the tunnel entrance. He could feel Libby watching him, gauging his reaction. Reluctantly, he said, "Maybe you guys should go first."

"Maybe *you* should go first, Joe," Libby said, watching him way too carefully.

Joe could feel his entire body trembling. Libby was right, as much as he hated her for it. He couldn't wait for the others to go. If he did, and was last, he knew he would never find the willpower to crawl into the tunnel by himself. "Guess maybe I should, huh?" A nervous laugh built in his throat and he choked it back down. *You're acting like a baby. Not even Sam acted like this when the aliens caught him, you big pussy.*

Feeling his groundmates' eyes fixed on him, Joe reluctantly pulled off his pack and dropped it into the entrance. He hesitated, taking a deep breath. He caught Maggie giving him a strange look and he forced a smile. "Never been a fan of tight spaces," he said. "Keep getting this idea I'm gonna die." *Say it, you coward. You're afraid you're gonna bleed to death. In a tunnel. Where the sharpest things are little bits of stone. You fire-loving furg.*

"We'll be right behind you," Libby assured him. Her face had softened a little, and she almost looked like she sympathized with him now. Joe quickly looked away. Someone else's sympathy would give him the excuse he needed to back down.

"Don't follow me too close," Joe said, eyes fixed on the dark maw of the tunnel. "If I get stuck, I'll have to back out."

"Ten minutes enough?" Libby asked.

Joe swallowed, hard. Ten minutes. Alone. In a body-fitting tunnel. "Yeah. I can do that." He got down and started crawling, pushing his gun and his pack through the tunnel in front of him. Almost immediately, feeling that cold, lifeless stone swallowing him, he felt as if the world had suddenly shrunk to a pinpoint above and behind the back of his head. His breathing grew more rapid and sweat sprang out on his brow, worsening the already hot conditions of the tunnel, making it almost impossible to breathe. He had a sudden urge to stand up and run, but crammed into the narrow passage as he was, he could barely even crawl. Up ahead, he even saw a place where he would have to get down on his belly.

Suddenly, an overpowering image of blood on the floor of the tunnel made him jerk away, slamming his back against a rough spot in the roof above him. The pain only panicked him further, making him *convinced* something had punctured his skin. All the way down here, they had no way of getting him to a medic. He lost it, then, and thrashed, his legs churning up the tunnel floor, the ceiling raining down more sandy blackness from where he was trying desperately to stand up.

I'm gonna die. That's blood and I'm gonna die. He backed up until the back of his shirt caught on the tunnel ceiling and held him in place. In a panic, Joe lunged forward and wedged himself into a tight spot, and between the shirt and the narrow passage, he was suddenly unable to move. He choked back a scream, his lungs sucking in ragged, panting breaths of stale tunnel air.

After several minutes of futile, mindless struggling, a voice of sanity broke through the terror. *Calm down! That's not blood. That's just a darker layer of dirt. Maggie must've brushed it off the ceiling when she crawled through here earlier. Stop freaking out!*

Joe blinked repeatedly, trying to cement in his mind that the stain on the floor wasn't blood. It was difficult. He actually had to reach out and press his hand into it, brushing his fingers through the dry sandy layer in order to dispel the image of red wetness. He gave a desperate laugh and lowered his head to the dirt, his entire body shaking.

Just sand. It's just sand, Joe. Get a grip, man. Come on and get moving. They're gonna be behind you any minute now.

That was the wrong thing to think. Joe started breathing harder, thinking about how he was going to get stuck in here, trapped by a line of kids behind him. He swallowed several times, staring at the two-foot-tall space up ahead. Cavers wouldn't have any problem at all getting through that. He'd seen documentaries where they crawled miles through spaces much smaller than the one in front of him.

And they never freak out like a burning pussy, either.

Joe closed his eyes and pushed one shaking limb forward. Once that was in place, he forced his leg to follow it. Soon afterwards, he was on his belly, staring at a narrower spot in the passage ahead. His every joint and muscle was tingling and felt like gelatin and his fingers wouldn't stop shaking.

He took several deep, ragged breaths, then lifted his head to once more eye the path ahead of him. What if it got too tight? What if he couldn't squeeze through? What if he got *stuck*? Somehow, Joe found the will to push himself forward on shaking limbs. When he reached the tight spot in the tunnel, he reluctantly lowered himself to his belly.

You can do this. Maggie did it twice. *How's that feel, furg? You've got less balls than a five-year-old girl. That's something to write home about. Hey, Dad, I'm a soldier that pissed himself in front of ninety little kids. What an accomplishment, huh? Just close your eyes and get it over with, you damn pussy.*

Taking a deep, unhappy breath, Joe forced his shaky body to move forward. His back brushed the ceiling and Joe gasped, trembling all over.

Closing his eyes, he pushed his rifle deeper into the tunnel and pulled himself forward again. He did it again and again, his eyes squeezed shut, forcing himself to just keep inching along. Ten minutes later, he stumbled out of the black honeycombed tower and fell to his hands and knees, gasping. The ferlii-tainted air had never smelled so good to him, and he couldn't get enough of it, sucking in deeper and deeper lungfuls into his chest. Panting, he lowered his forehead to the ground and tried to force himself to stop hyperventilating.

One by one, the members of his platoon piled out of the honeycomb behind him. Distantly, he knew they were giving him odd looks, but he couldn't bring himself to get up, so relieved was he to be in open air again.

"Joe?" Maggie said, coming up to him. She squatted and touched his shoulder where it touched the ground. "Are you okay?"

"Yeah," Joe lied into the dirt. His whole body, however, betrayed him. He was shaking all over, his limbs weak and lifeless. He knew his actions baffled the other kids, but he didn't care. He was so glad to be out of the tunnel that nothing mattered to him anymore. A Dhasha prince could have walked up to him in that moment and Joe wouldn't have noticed.

After taking a long moment to steady himself, Joe reluctantly sat up to survey their surroundings. All of his platoon had made it safely out of the tunnel and were clustered around him expectantly. They were on the far side of the clearing, almost touching the enormous, twisted rootstalks of first row of cream-colored ferlii. Towards the middle of the clearing, he could see a group of Lagrah's white-clad defenders sitting along the edges of a pit, talking. They had their backs to them, but Joe urged his platoon back behind the rocks, out of sight, should Second Battalion happen to glance their way.

"Is everybody here?" Joe asked quietly. "Squad leaders, count up your grounders."

They did, and everyone was accounted for.

Suddenly, Libby's face went slack. She tore at her belt, patting it wildly. When she looked up, she was pale. "Joe. The flag. I lost it."

Joe jerked around. "What?"

Libby patted down her belt, swallowing. "I don't know what happened."

Joe stared at her. "You can't be serious." He hadn't meant to be so harsh, but he wasn't feeling very charitable at the moment. That flag was all that really stood between them and enough manual labor to make them doing chores in their sleep. As it was, it already looked really bad that they were the only platoon from their entire battalion that hadn't been killed yet.

"I was the last one out," Libby said quickly. "It's in the tunnel somewhere, Joe. Don't worry, I'll go find it." Without another word, she ducked back into the honeycombed tower and disappeared.

Half an hour went by and Joe was thinking about sending Maggie in after her when Libby returned empty-handed.

"I went through it twice," she said, coated with black dust and looking miserable. "I couldn't find it, Joe."

"Let me look," Maggie said quickly. "I'll find it. Mommy said I was good at finding stuff." She dove back in after Libby, but twenty minutes later, she, too, came back empty handed.

"It's a *tunnel*," Sasha sneered, upon Maggie's crestfallen return. "How do you lose something in a *tunnel?*" She laughed, looking Libby lazily up and down. "I knew we couldn't trust an ape like you."

Libby raised her rifle and shot Sasha in the face.

"Damn it, Libby!" Joe cried, dropping to cover Sasha's mouth with her jacket as she began to scream. "She was one of our best shots!"

Libby shrugged. "She deserved it." She casually threw her gun over her shoulder. "Besides, I'm better."

Joe gave her an irritated look and got back to his feet. "Okay, look, the damn thing has to be back there somewhere. Monk, you're the smallest, can you go back and take a look real quick?"

Monk grimaced, but did. She came back dirty and shaking her head. "Not back there," she muttered. "Someone must've grabbed it after we came out. They're never gonna believe we got it." Her pert chin was quivering with devastation.

And, as Joe looked at his friends' faces, he felt their disappointment like a knife to his chest. After all that, they were still going to fail. It wasn't *fair*.

"Look, if we can't find the flag, we sure as hell better do our best to take out as many of Second Battalion as we can before they get us. We gotta finish this. Okay?"

Maggie frowned at him. "But we got the flag, Joe. We shouldn't have to die, right?"

Hearing her plaintive words, Joe felt another pang of guilt. He almost went back through the tunnel looking for the flag himself. Almost.

"We've gotta kill as many as we can," Joe muttered, fisting his hand to keep his fingers from shaking at the idea of again entering the tiny space. "It's the only way they'll let us get this over with."

His entire platoon grimaced. Carl went back looking for the flag, and came back another twenty minutes later, empty-handed. "I don't understand," Libby muttered. "I *had* it, Joe." She frustratedly threw a chunk of diamond aside and glared at the tunnel.

Joe shook his head. "Who knows what happened, Lib. Look, we're just wasting daylight sitting here. What do you guys say we go assault those dweebs over by that pit? Maybe get a few more kills under our belt before they put us down?"

"Ugh," Monk said, gripping her rifle.

"Well soot," Scott added.

"This is *furgsoot*!" Libby cried. "We *had* it. We shouldn't have to die."

"Yeah, but Nebil's gonna eat us alive if it looks like we were hiding here all day," Carl added.

That was true enough. Joe grimaced. "Come on, guys. Don't shoot until I give the signal." Taking one last look at his grounders' solemn faces, he led them across the pocked landscape to where the defenders sat around the rim of their pit, their backs to them. Before they were quite ready, Libby opened fire. She knocked two off their perches and hit two others before they began to fight back. With a shriek, Libby stood up and ran at them, firing ahead of her, screaming Congie curses.

It was the first time Libby went down before Joe. Joe watched her fall, feeling guilty. If he hadn't been such a Takki, he would have been the one to carry the flag through the tunnel and losing it wouldn't be on her head. Grimly, he settled down to take out as many defenders as he could before Second Battalion overpowered them.

In the end, the defenders flanked them. It was only minutes before Joe's entire platoon was having seizures in the dirt. Joe took a shot to the arm, then, as his convulsions began, he got shot again. His heart struggled for a few more seconds, then spasmed and gave up.

23

SECOND BATTALION

"**Y**ou failed."

Joe opened his eyes to see Battlemaster Nebil standing over him, sudah fluttering angrily.

"You *had* the flag in your useless Human hands and you *failed*." Nebil looked and sounded like he was on the verge of taking his switch to Joe for the offense.

"You should be happy we got it at all," Joe muttered.

"*Happy*?!" Nebil roared. "You had the tunnels to *yourself* and a whole platoon of recruits to defend it and you lost the flag. You'd beaten Second Battalion and you *lost* it."

"It was an accident," Joe said. He sat up. All around him, recruits in black were laid out in rows, waiting to be revived.

Battlemaster Nebil grabbed him by the jacket and yanked him closer, his gummy eyes almost touching Joe's face. "An accident, Zero? Or you having a mental breakdown?" At Joe's flinch, Nebil's eyes narrowed. "I monitored your bio signs during the whole hunt. I saw what happened when you had to go in that tunnel. Kihgl's a cursed furg. By the ninety Jreet hells, you're just a Takki coward!"

"But we got the flag!" Joe shouted.

"You *lost* the flag." Nebil stood up suddenly. "You made me the laughingstock of the whole regiment. My recruits are such Jreet-kissing furglings they can't even hold onto a flag. I won't be able to enter the chow hall without hearing about it. And Commander Tril—" Nebil's snakelike pupils narrowed. "Best you avoid Commander Tril. He'd already made the call to Second Battalion to brag when he found out you'd lost the flag."

That…was not good. Nebil was already turning away in disgust.

"So teach me how to use the PPU!" Joe cried, grabbing the Ooreiki's arm. "None of that would've happened if I could've figured out where we were."

Nebil scoffed, though there was a flicker of interest in his wet, gummy eyes.

Joe leaned forward. "You teach me how to use that thing and I'll get that flag back next time we attack."

Battlemaster Nebil stared at him long and hard. "You fail and I swear to Poen you'll wish you'd never been born. Understand, Human?"

Joe nodded, hope beginning to make his heart hammer.

The Battlemaster took a deep breath through his sudah, still glaring at him. "I've signed you up for phobic conditioning. Keep it quiet. So far, Lagrah and I are the only ones who know the truth of what happened to you down there, and I want it to stay that way. Tril would send you to the Dhasha in a second if he knew you were afraid of tunnels." Nebil snorted. "That's like having a pilot that's afraid to fly."

Joe felt a chill. "Lagrah knows?"

"He figured it out, the fire-loving bastard. Didn't even have to see your brainwaves. Pray Tril's not that smart."

Gingerly, Joe said, "What is phobic…conditioning?"

"Regulated overexposure. You'll keep it between the two of us, though. I'll log your absence as a broken bone you received in the tunnels. Tril will not find out, you understand? Even with treatment, there's a high chance of recurrence. He's not going to want to take the chance."

Joe swallowed hard, having a pretty good idea what 'regulated overexposure' meant. "Can I skip it?"

Nebil gave him an amused look. "After Lagrah already made the arrangements? No, I don't think so. You'll earn me back every credit I spent on you if I have to butcher you and sell your parts to Knaaren."

Joe's throat constricted as he thought again of Lagrah. "And he's not gonna tell Tril? Even after…what I did…back home?"

Nebil snorted. "The Takki turd owed me a favor. A big one. He's even chipping in for your conditioning."

"You could give me another rotation," Joe said hastily. "You don't have to send me in now. I can work on it. You know, like meditate or something. Besides, once you train me with the PPU, I can spend all my time learning it. You can tell Lagrah I'll use it to—"

"No," the Battlemaster said immediately. "Nobody's gonna know about the PPU, either, especially not Lagrah. It's against regulations to teach recruits how to use sensitive Congressional equipment until they've completed two turns of training. They figure you're indoctrinated enough by then to not find a way to mail it back to your home planet with an instruction booklet."

Joe frowned. "Then you're gonna teach me how to use it?"

"Yes," Nebil muttered. "Later. Right *now*, I've gotta go deal with Tril and finish cleaning up your mess. Oh, and convince the Jreet-sucking lunatic not to execute your whole platoon. Lagrah will be here soon to take you to medical. The doctors want to get a head start because from those burned-up brainwaves of yours back in the tunnel, you're gonna be one tough piji shell to crack."

With that, Battlemaster Nebil turned on heel and departed with all the force of a freight train. Medics with small golden circles inside their silver borders got out of the way to let him pass, then went back to injecting the red stuff into the kids' arms. Reluctantly, Joe got to his feet and eyed the approaching haauk. Already, he felt his cold sweat returning.

This was what he wanted, wasn't it? All his life, every time he broke down into a sobbing wreck because a friend tried to show him his snow-cave or his uncle tried to get him under a car to look at the oil pan, wasn't that what he wanted? Back on Earth, with two kids and a mortgage, his parents hadn't been able to afford sending him to a shrink to figure out what the hell was wrong with him. Here, they would do it for free.

The thought was not comforting.

The pilot of the skimmer had the pale, drooping skin of an older Ooreiki. When it grew close enough, Joe could see the black scars criss-crossing its body. He tensed, wondering if Lagrah remembered him from the streets of San Diego, the colorful explosions going off all around them. Steeling himself, Joe moved toward the haauk.

Once he landed, the Ooreiki Prime looked him over with an unreadable stare. "You Zero?"

"Yeah," Joe said, tensing.

"Get on." Lagrah showed absolutely no recognition.

Joe did as he was told, but the Ooreiki never took his eyes off him. Joe's skin prickled under the stare. *Oh please don't let him remember me...*

Lagrah made no move to take the haauk off the ground, just looked Joe up and down in obvious appraisal. "You're afraid of tunnels."

Joe felt his throat tighten and started to inch back towards to edge of the haauk. "Maybe a little."

Lagrah snorted. "A little." He continued to stare, analyzing Joe with his pale brown eyes. Finally, once Joe was ready to leap over the railing and run, the old Ooreiki said, "Nebil's lost his mind."

Saying nothing else, Lagrah turned back to the haauk console and lifted them off the ground. Once they were in the air, Joe relaxed a little. *He doesn't remember,* he thought, relief flooding through him as he thought of how he had rescued Sam and the hundreds of other kids destined for the Ooreiki ship. *If he remembered, he'd kill me.*

Prime Commander Lagrah was silent as he guided them back into Alishai. "Well done, getting the flag. My battalion will do laps for that. Are you military-trained, boy?"

Joe glanced at the Prime nervously. "My dad was in the military on Earth."

Lagrah glanced at him. "Ah. Makes sense. A soldier begets a soldier." He turned back to guiding the haauk between the massive ferlii trees.

Makes...sense? Joe frowned at Lagrah, wondering if the Prime was giving him some sort of compliment, but Lagrah never clarified.

"We still haven't found the flag," Lagrah said. "And our Takki combed every inch of the area you were in. Any ideas?"

Joe remembered the diamond dust in the crawlspaces and said, "Uh... probably got buried?"

"No." Lagrah gave him another odd look. "You didn't hide it?"

Joe frowned. "*Hide* it? Are you cra—" He caught himself quickly. "No, sir."

Lagrah gave him a snort of laughter and said nothing else until they entered the manicured outer ring of Alishai. "You're supposed to be injured," Lagrah reminded him, as they neared the hospital. "To get in the front doors without suspicion."

Taking a hint, Joe slumped against the side of the haauk, favoring one leg.

Lagrah brought them to a hover a hundred feet above the medical center, then left it there. "We're here," Lagrah said. Joe glanced over the edge. In the walkway underneath, several medics were standing around, chatting, looking like tentacled brown mice. When Joe glanced back up, he froze at the look on his Prime's face.

The Ooreiki's eyes were cold and hard, reminding him of frozen clay. "You can't fake injuries where you're going."

Joe paled. "Oh, uh…" He grimaced. "What are you gonna break?" He knew all-too-well how much it hurt to break bones, and he was not looking forward to the experience.

"Probably most of them," Lagrah said.

…*most*? As Joe's startled mind was stumbling through that, Lagrah took him by the front of his jacket and hefted him off his feet. Into his face, Lagrah said, "This is for robbing us of an extra battalion, you crafty Jreet prick." At that, the Ooreiki hurled Joe over the railing, at the awaiting medics below.

• • •

Several days later, Joe walked out of the hospital feeling numb. His broken bones had healed, but his mind was still ragged where they had ripped it apart. He no longer feared tunnels, but Joe wondered if he would ever be able to sleep again. 'Regulated overexposure' had turned out to be just that. Locking him in a coffin for hours on end while an Ooreiki shrink monitored his brainwaves in a separate room and talked about his feelings over the intercom. His throat was still raw from screaming.

He found his groundteam eating at a table in the chow hall with the rest of Fourth Platoon. As he approached, he saw that Maggie was no longer the only one with her sleeves rolled—Libby was the only one of his groundteam that wasn't. Even some of the other recruits in the Fourth had bared their arms, including a few squad leaders. Joe was stunned. He had thought that, with him being gone for almost a week, Maggie would have lost interest.

He got his food and sat down beside Maggie, who wasn't lifting her gaze from her scum soup. "Tired, Mag?" Joe asked her.

Maggie jerked and looked up at him with a gleeful expression. "Joe!" she squealed. She jumped up and hugged him, wrapping her not-so-little arms around his neck and touching his chest with what he was pretty sure were breasts.

"What happened while I was gone?" Joe asked in an attempt to get her to release her hold.

Maggie dropped back into her seat and began to pick at her scum soup again.

When no one offered anything else, Scott sighed and said, "They didn't count it."

"Commander Tril made it sound like we were running away the whole time," Maggie sniffled. "But we weren't. We *had* the flag. Libby just lost it."

"It's not fair," Monk agreed. "They're acting like we never even *had* it."

"Nobody would believe us," Maggie continued. "Even First Company hates us. They blame us for losing the flag."

Joe did not know what to say. He cleared his throat and nodded at Maggie's sleeves. "So Nebil stopped making you run?"

Maggie frowned down at her sleeves, still tightly rolled from the night he'd done it for her. "No, he makes us run."

"Us?" Joe's brow went up and he glanced at the others at the table with their sleeves up. "He's making *all* of you run?"

"Eighteen laps a night," Scott said with a mock sigh. Despite his sarcasm, his sleeves were rolled as tight as the ones Joe had done for Maggie. He must have helped Monk, too, because hers looked just as good.

Joe's eyes caught Libby's questioningly. He didn't want to *ask* her why she was the only one who hadn't put her sleeves up, but he was curious. She sniffed and looked away, picking at something under her thumbnail with her military knife.

"Sasha keeps saying you were scared, Joe," Maggie said. "She's telling everybody that's why you were gone for a week. She's—"

"Shut up, Maggie," Libby said. "We all know he was scared sooty."

"He wasn't scared!" Maggie shouted. "He was just…" She hesitated, seeking the right word. "He was just tired. He'll be better next time."

"Stop defending him!" Libby said, slamming her empty bowl on the table and standing. "Joe doesn't know everything. He *was* scared back there, so scared he was shaking, and that's why he was at the hospital. They were unscrewing his head so he doesn't get the rest of us killed in a real fight." She looked up. "Isn't that right, Joe?"

Joe hung his head staring at his soup.

"They fix it or not?" Libby demanded.

"They fixed it," Joe whispered.

"They better've fixed it. If you ever do something like that again, I don't want you as my battlemaster. You weren't thinking back there. You weren't even *trying* for the flag. It's like you were all doped up just like my—" Libby caught herself suddenly. Then, without explanation, she took her bowl and left the table.

"Don't know why *she's* mad," Monk said. "*She's* the one who lost the flag."

"Yeah," Maggie said, "Don't listen to her, Joe. We still want you for our battlemaster, even if you *were* scared. I'm scared of gummi bears. I got one stuck in my ear and had to go to the hospital. They had to pry around in there and it *hurt,* so I don't eat gummi bears anymore."

"Gee," Scott said, "You ever think maybe you shouldn't shove them in your ear?"

"I could sure go for some gummi bears," Monk said.

Joe suddenly remembered the delicate candy solar system that Yuil had given him. He had hidden it under his gear with the akarit and hadn't thought about it in days. He decided to share it with them that night.

Joe opened his mouth to tell them about it, then frowned. "What is that?" He pointed to the new patch on Maggie's shoulder, on the opposite side from her names, just above the edges of her rolled sleeves. They all carried them. The Congie symbol was bright blue on black, a blockish squiggle that almost looked like a D with a dot following it. Joe knew it meant the numeral 6. He'd woken up from his last screamfest wearing one as well.

"It stands for Sixth Battalion," Scott said. "I think it's a promotion. Commander Tril said if we continue to be good, we get to wear the symbol of Congress, too."

"I didn't see any other recruits wearing them on my walk over here," Joe said.

"It's just Sixth and Second Battalions that get them," Carl said. "Nobody else has come close to getting the flag."

Joe stared at them, surprised.

"Secondary Commander Tril's making us go on a hunt against Second Battalion again," Monk said, lowering her eyes. "Battlemaster Nebil says they're so much better than us we don't even deserve to be in the same regiment."

"They're beginners, just like us," Joe said.

"But have you seen them *march?*" Carl asked. "They look like machines."

"We look like machines, too," Joe said, but he knew he was fooling himself. Second looked better than any other battalion in the regiment. If they graduated them all right now and made Second fight Sixth, Sixth would scatter like rabbits just from the sound of Second's boots on the march over.

Sherri, another ground leader from Fourth Platoon, looked worried. "The battlemaster says it should be Fifth or Third Battalion going up against Second, not us. He says we couldn't even find our own asses if we knew how to use our PPU's."

"He always says that," Joe said dismissively.

"What scares me," Scott said, "Is that Tril makes it sound like we're way ahead of everybody else because we had the flag. But we're not. We really suck. It was an accident, you know? What happens next time the Dhasha sees how bad we are?"

"We aren't that bad," Joe said. The silent faces at the table, however, told him they thought otherwise. He scooped up a handful of goop and began eating in silence.

"We're really glad you're here," Maggie said. "We need you. The last hunt we went on, Second Battalion really beat us up."

Joe knew the first time was a fluke and they were gonna get stomped, no matter who was on their side. He opened his mouth to say it, but Nebil's shout interrupted him from the front of the chow hall.

"Zero!" Battlemaster Nebil called. "Collect the platoon and bring them to the obstacle course! No rifles or gear, just what you're wearing. You have five tics!"

When they got to the course, another platoon was already there, waiting for them on one edge of a circular pit of fine black sand marked off with huge black chunks of rock. A female recruit stood sharply at their head, and none of them even blinked as Joe led his platoon up to stand on the other side of the pit. They looked *good*. Too good to be from Sixth Battalion.

A little knot of dread settled into Joe's stomach as he brought his platoon to a halt beside Battlemaster Nebil.

"All right, you Takki bastards," Battlemaster Nebil shouted, "Sixth got paired with Second, so you are looking at your training cohort. I'm Battlemaster Nebil and that's Battlemaster Gokli. Fourth Platoon, meet Fourth Platoon."

"We will be working together from now on," Battlemaster Gokli continued. "You will still conduct hunts with other Battalions, but for martial arts and platoon drills, these are the recruits who will be challenging you for the rest of training."

Joe heard someone in the other platoon snicker and their battlemaster rounded on them with a vengeance. The kid who had laughed got laid out with one heavy blow. "You think it's funny, recruit?! Get up! Nebil, pick your best recruit."

Joe stiffened in anticipation, but when Nebil turned to his platoon, it was Libby he ordered out of line.

The boy laughed again when Libby stepped into the pit with him and Joe's chest clenched with worry. Libby's opponent was a big kid, probably an inch or two taller than her and outweighing her by thirty pounds.

"Battlemaster Nebil," Joe said, "I can—"

"Shut up, Zero," Nebil said, even as Libby glanced back to give him an acid scowl. Unhappily, Joe went back into the 'retain' position. He wasn't sure, but he thought several other recruits in the other platoon perked up at his name, and he itched under their stares.

"Put these on," Battlemaster Gokli said, throwing padded gloves into the ring. Libby and her opponent did as they were told, cinching them tight before settling back to eying each other.

"This," Battlemaster Nebil said, "is your first day of confined combat instruction. As you may have found during your experiences in the tunnels, sometimes you find yourselves in situations where your own hands do you more good than your rifles. As much as we work your bodies in runs and drills, they will still be weak in one-on-one combat unless you have a chance to practice. Congressional soldiers are never completely without weapons, so this is our chance to show you how your short-range armaments work. Recruits, hold up your hands."

Libby and her opponent obeyed, lifting their gloved fists into the air.

"These gloves have been equipped with systems that mimic the effect of a recruit's biosuit on non-suited opponents in hand-to-hand combat," Gokli said. "But before we give you ashy furgs your biosuits, you're gonna learn how to use them. The effect will depend on the positioning of the fingers inside the gloves. Going through the different combinations will take too long and you Takki furglings wouldn't remember anyway, so you'll just have to learn as you go. Recruits, begin the demonstration."

The big boy seemed to have been waiting for this. He charged Libby, tackling her before she had a chance to get her guard up. His momentum threw her off her feet and she landed on her back in the sand, the bigger recruit on top of her. As she struggled to get up, he slammed a fist into the side of her head.

Libby jerked like she'd been shot with blue goop. She lay there, paralyzed, and the bigger kid laughed and stood up. Then, as Joe watched in fury, the kid spat on her.

"As you can see," Nebil said, seemingly not noticing the boy's behavior, "a fist produces a temporary stun, very useful if you are looking to take captives."

The boy turned his back to Libby and started to walk back to his platoon.

Libby suddenly leapt to her feet, a deadly look in her eyes. She tore off her gloves and threw them in the sand. As her opponent turned to look, she took a running step, swiveled, and slammed the heel of her foot into the side of his head. Then, as he fell, she followed through and rammed the side of her naked hand into his neck and another underneath his ribs. The boy collapsed like a rag doll, utterly motionless. Then she calmly turned, gathered up the gloves she had discarded, and handed them to Battlemaster Nebil on her way back to her place in the platoon.

"Unfortunately for many a furg," Battlemaster Gokli said, "The paralysis is very short lived. Rat, get him out of here. Have the medics check for internal bleeding."

The girl in the recruit battlemaster's place at the head of Gokli's Fourth Platoon moved suddenly and directed two grounders to carry the unconscious recruit off to medical.

Rat? Joe thought. *They call her Rat? And I thought* Sasha *had it bad.*

One by one, they each got a chance to fight in the ring. The various effects of the practice gloves ranged from paralysis to actually slamming the unfortunate recruit backwards ten feet. The battlemasters thankfully tried to pair them by size, but Monk, still at only four and a half feet, had to fight someone almost twice her weight. She lost.

The recruit battlemaster they called Rat got paired with Scott and, to Joe's dismay, massacred him so badly that Joe suspected she'd practiced with the gloves long before this. She made no extra motions and, like Libby, simply left the ring once Scott had given up.

Joe was one of the last ones to go, and he was paired with the strongest, most freakishly huge boy in the other platoon. Joe stared up at him when they got into the ring, wondering if the aliens had made some sort of mistake and drafted Bigfoot.

"I'm Tank and I'm gonna kick your butt," the boy taunted in a singsong voice. If it weren't for the heavy rumble in his chest, he sounded like a five-year-old.

"I'm Zero and I have the feeling I'm about to get my butt kicked," Joe said, peering up at him. He had to be like seven feet tall.

The boy grinned widely, a huge smile that filled his whole head.

"Begin," Nebil said.

Tank swung at Joe with a fist—the favored mode of attack that day. Joe ducked easily and jumped back, eying the bigger kid. He had an advantage over the other children in the regiment because, unlike them, he had had time to grow into his size, which left him relatively agile, compared to the others. He still banged knees and elbows into things when he wasn't paying attention, but at least he didn't bang his *head* into things.

Tank's grin faded when he saw Joe dart out of the way. He rushed Joe again and Joe dodged, trying to decide how to approach this fight. He didn't want to hurt the kid—he reminded him too much of Maggie. He decided to go with the flow and use a fist, even though while he'd been standing on the sidelines he'd been itching to try the technique that sent his opponent flying backwards like getting struck by a wrecking ball.

Tank, however, did not seem to have the same reservations. When Joe continued to dance out of his way, he let out a frustrated roar and leapt forward, both hands flipped upwards in a shove. Joe couldn't get out of the way fast enough. Instantly, he felt his entire midsection compress as the gloves' pressure released. His breath rushed out of him in a *whoosh* and Joe flew backwards like his body no longer obeyed gravity.

He landed in a heap about fifteen feet away, his chest and guts on fire.

"And that," Nebil said, "is what is called a compact force compression. Good against bigger foes, better-trained foes, or multiple opponents. Next!"

Wincing, Joe started to struggle back to his feet, feeling weak and disoriented. He was stunned when Tank reached down and offered a big hand. The big kid actually looked remorseful.

"Sorry," he said. "I didn't know it would do that."

Despite the pain in his abdomen, Joe grinned at him, pleased to discover that Second Battalion wasn't completely filled with ashers. After Lagrah tossing him off the haauk and the kid spitting on Libby once she was down, he'd had his doubts.

"No problem, Tank," he said, getting to his feet. He winced, feeling like someone had taken a sledgehammer to his insides.

Tank gave Joe a long look, still holding his hand. "Are you really Zero?" he asked, peering down at him curiously.

Joe frowned. "Uh, yeah. Last time I checked."

Tank continued to peer at him like an exotic bug. "Huh. Thought you'd be taller." Then he turned and went back to Gokli's platoon, leaving Joe staring after the seven-foot-tall monster, mouth hanging open.

All he could think was,

He thought I was…taller?

• • •

Tril seethed as he watched Fourth Platoon march by, Battlemaster Nebil at its head. Zero was leading, and his corruption was everywhere. Over half of the recruits in the Fourth wore their uniforms in Zero's style, their soft flesh exposed to the air, mocking him.

They love him.

The thought infuriated Tril. He knew the recruits hated him. It was only fair—he had hated his own battalion commander in recruit training. But to have the *battlemasters* back Zero, against his direct orders… It was outright *treason*, and no one was doing anything about it. The one time he had mentioned it to Lagrah, the Prime had given him a long look and had said, "I'm sorry, are you making a formal complaint that you can't control your own Battalion, Commander Tril?"

And it had ended at that. Because Tril, despite what the bastards thought, was not that stupid. So now his underlings were rebelling, and there wasn't a damn thing he could do about it because of Kihgl's demise. Tril had made several formal petitions to the Ooreiki Internal Affairs division claiming segregation and caste prejudice against him, but the OIA had responded by saying that the actions of his peers were 'not unjust.'

Damn Kihgl. That wasn't his *fault*. It was *Knaaren's* fault for *eating* him.

Watching Fourth Platoon march past, Tril tightened his grip on his pen, snapping it in half. After he had tried so hard to bring Sixth Battalion to the forefront of the hunts, after he spent his every waking minute thinking about their training, worrying whether it was enough and agonizing how to keep them out of Knaaren's claws, all Zero had to do to make them love him was put a few wrinkles in his uniform.

Someday, Zero, they're going to hate you.

He would make sure of it. And, when it happened, he would laugh.

• • •

Joe, as it turned out, didn't fare as well from Tank's compression attack as he had thought. When he started vomiting blood two days later, Nebil sent him to medical, only to find that Tank's glove-powered shove had caused massive internal damage that would require *another* turn added to his enlistment in order to patch up.

Once the Ooreiki doctors finished with him, they had two Takki carry him back to the barracks. The purple lizards carried him in silence, eyes forward and bodies slack, apparently not thinking anything at all. Joe, still drugged and a little loopy, surveyed the scaly creatures from his position on the gurney, finding them remarkably beautiful to hold such a bad repu-tation amongst the Congies. Their eyes, especially. They were a deep, end-less azure, like huge, egg-shaped sapphires that had been polished smooth and set into the sides of their heads. Like the Dhasha, they had no pupils that he could see.

Joe was alone in his bed, waiting for his groundmates to return so he could share Yuil's candy with them, when Battlemaster Nebil strode into the barracks. He stopped at the base of Joe's bed and scowled at him so long that Joe thought he was about to be punished.

"Here," Nebil muttered finally, thrusting a silvery pad into Joe's hands. "Lessons in writing basic Congie. It's all automatic. It will pronounce the sound and then draw the symbol, which you must then repeat with the little pen on the side. Until then," Nebil pulled out the PPU and pointed out a squarish symbol in the lower left. "Touch this to rotate through your options. Whenever you want to look something up, just draw the symbol on the lesson pad and it will tell you what it means."

"Okay," Joe said, a little overwhelmed. "How long am I—"

"You've got three days to study," Nebil interrupted briskly. "The medics put you on light duty until we've got to take up black against Lagrah. You can spend the time working on learning to use your PPU."

Joe's jaw dropped. "I'm out of the hunt tomorrow?"

Nebil's sudah gave a dangerous flutter. "They *wanted* to put you out of service for two entire weeks. He turned your insides to *pudding*, Zero. And you, you fire-loving Jreet, kept going for *a day and a half.* Two of the medics told me you should've died from that, you jenfurgling sooter. I'm going against their orders letting you fight at all."

"But my groundteam *needs* me!" Joe cried, starting to scramble out of bed. He'd thought they would take him off duty for an *afternoon*, tops.

Nebil held up a tentacle, stopping him. "They need you to figure out how to get Lagrah's burning flag. Right now, Tril's made Sixth Battalion the laughingstock of the regiment. The only way Knaaren's gonna leave the Sixth alone is if we hold our own against the best. It's gonna be hard. Lagrah's almost five hundred turns old—he should be a Corps Director by now. The only reason he *isn't* is because he turns down his promotions so he can stay at the battalion level. He's one of the few commanders out there who's not in it for the titles. He's got a long history of taking his recruits into battle when they graduate, and they love him for it. Beside him, Tril doesn't stand a chance. He's young and inexperienced and is pushing us too hard in the wrong directions. He's a pampered *yeeri* ashsoul who doesn't understand the Ooreiki military isn't like the society on Poen. We're like a pack of Jreet, Zero. We sense a weakness in one of our own and we tear it apart. A platoon can hold up against that kind of assault for only so long before its recruits start to fail their training. You get Lagrah's flag again and the other battalions are gonna take us seriously. I don't give a fire-loving pile of ashes what Tril regurgitates up at the front of formation, the only way we're going to graduate Sixth Battalion is if we make the other battalions believe we're better than them. We need to be more visible, more dangerous, more arrogant. That's what we're gonna need to survive, Zero. That's what's it's gonna take to keep you out of Knaaren's pens. And *that* is why you're going to spend the next three days figuring out how to use that PPU."

Joe stared, a deep, gnawing anxiety beginning to build in his gut. He'd already failed Elf. They *had* to graduate. He couldn't let Maggie and Monk fall into the hands of that creature.

Nebil's sudah were still fluttering as he turned his head away. "Listen, Zero. I think you're our best chance. After you went in for surgery, your platoon almost killed the recruit that wounded you. It took six battlemasters to break up the fight." Nebil snorted. "Your recruits respect you, Zero. That's why I'm giving you the reader. If the Training Committee found out I did that, they'd take another rank and put me on Neskfaat to inspect Dhasha draftees." Nebil paused, glanced at the low ceiling, then back at Joe. "Sixth is in serious trouble. Tril doesn't see it, but I do. The battlemasters and commanders are already turning on us. They hid our standards from Tril when he went to retrieve them. They're giving us the worst time slot to eat—earliest in the morning and latest at night. Repair orders and supply requests fail to go through. We've got the worst haauk in the regiment, and we end up having to bunch all of our recruits up into the same vehicles on the hunts because half of them aren't working at any given time."

Nebil looked tired. "I saw the same thing happen twenty turns ago. A battalion in my regiment failed in a mission to retrieve a group of prisoners that enemy Huouyt had captured. Their failure wasn't their fault. The Overseer in charge of the mission had given the battalion a bad dropoff location and they got massacred before they even got off their ships. Still, the other Ooreiki in the regiment took their retreat personally. It started with insults. Words quickly turned to actions and for eight rotations, their fellows picked at them, giving them bad assignments and withholding gear until every single soldier in that battalion was either dead or transferred. Then, once the soldiers were gone, they renumbered the battalions and pretended it had never even existed."

Nebil leaned forward, intense. "It's happening again. A stray comment here, a changed keycode there… Tril thinks the turning is just a myth, but if we don't stop it now, it's going to get worse. For all their beautiful creations, Ooreiki can be…dark…creatures sometimes, Zero. We need to put an end to it now if we're going to keep you Humans out of the crossfire."

"Were you one of the ones who got transferred?" Joe asked.

Nebil's pupils narrowed. "No. I was Prime Commander of the regiment. They took away four ranks when I abandoned the Takki ashsouls out of shame."

Joe stared. Nebil was a Prime Commander?

"Since then, I've never trusted Ooreiki nature. Commanders, especially. They're always struggling to gain favor, to make the one bold move that will catch their superiors' attention and get them promoted to Overseer. Lagrah's the one exception, and that just makes the ashy furnace we're in all the worse because he makes Tril look like a janja slug in comparison."

Joe glanced down at the silvery pad Nebil had given him. "I'll try to get his flag."

"Do more than try, Zero." Nebil gave him a long, silent look, then turned and left him alone in the barracks.

Joe spent the next four hours deciphering the symbols of the PPU with the help of Nebil's lesson pad. He was actually making good progress when he heard voices on the balcony outside the door. He hid it away under his pillow as his groundteam returned, sweaty and covered in black dust.

"Joe!" Maggie cried, breaking into a run. She looked stunned he was alive. They all did.

Frowning, Joe asked, "Where were you guys?"

Maggie made a face. "Nebil had the whole platoon raking the plaza because we got in a fight with the other platoon."

Joe glanced at Libby, instinctively knowing she had started the fight. "You didn't hurt that kid, did you?"

Libby looked away, confirming his suspicions. Joe felt a rush of pride—and shame—that he was the cause. "Libby," he began, "you know it's not cool to—"

"He deserved it," she interrupted. "Tank cheated."

"He didn't cheat," Joe said. "I was stupid. I didn't get out of the way fast enough."

Libby shrugged and he knew he would get no more out of her on the subject. "They fix your guts?" she asked, giving him a dubious look.

"Tril said you were *dead*," Monk added, wide-eyed.

Joe sighed and gently patted his stomach. "The jenfurgling medics said they couldn't heal everything without putting six more turns on my service, so I told them to go burn themselves. As it was, they still gave me a turn."

"You gonna be with us tomorrow?" she asked softly.

Wincing inside, Joe held up his PPU. "Guys, look at this. Battlemaster showed me what a few of the symbols mean." Libby's gaze sharpened, but Joe blundered on, trying to ignore her scowl. "This one means Acquire, which beams out a signal and maps out the terrain around you. This one is

Zoom, and you can pull back so far you're looking at the whole planet. This one's Orient, which twists the map around until it's facing the same way—"

"Somebody said Second Battalion really kills kids on the hunts," Maggie said. She hadn't been paying attention. None of them had.

Joe reluctantly put his PPU away. "They don't."

"Yeah, but they're bigger than us," Monk said.

"We eat the same green crap they do," Joe said.

"Yeah, but…" Libby glanced again at his bruised torso. "If you're not there… Things could get really bad. Sixth Battalion looks up to you."

Joe snorted. "You said yourself I almost pissed myself trying to crawl through a tunnel. They don't look up to me."

Libby looked dumbstruck. "They do. You're older than they are."

"There's nobody in the regiment better at this than you, Lib."

"Yeah, but Joe, it's *you* they like," Libby insisted.

"Just keep Second Battalion from getting your flag tomorrow," Joe said. "I'll be there to help you next time. Promise."

His friends grimaced and muttered under their breath, but in the end, he managed to convince them it would be worth it…if only to see the shocked expression on Second Battalion's faces when they stole their flag right out from under them, making them look like unprepared Takki. That seemed to make his friends happy. They actually went to bed grinning, obviously seeing it in their dreams.

24

CONTRABAND

Joe spent the next day in bed, scowling at the little symbols on his reader. A Takki brought him food and water, and Joe ate it while he worked. He was so focused that his friends startled him when they returned.

"We held it," Monk said, jumping up into bed beside Joe, not noticing as he hurriedly tucked his reader out of sight. "They didn't get our flag!"

"See?" Joe said. "You guys were worried for nothing."

At that, everyone sobered.

"They set up command posts," Libby said. "They were organized. They attacked from one side, then, when we went to defend, they attacked on the other. They are *good,* Joe. Better than us. The only reason they didn't make it to the flag was they didn't know where it was. They invaded three of the five deep dens. It was just dumb luck they didn't get the one with the flag in it."

Joe grimaced. "What time is it?"

"Past bedtime," Libby said. "We were fighting all day. We only ate once because it took so long to kill them all off."

"We're tired," Maggie added. "And hungry."

"They didn't feed you?" Joe glanced at the other groundteams filing into the barracks, all of them looking like the walking dead.

"Commander Tril was pissed," Scott said. "He told us losers didn't need to eat."

"You didn't lose," Joe said, his brow furrowing. "You kept your flag."

Libby shrugged and began getting out of her gear. Joe, who had been noticing her sleek, feminine curves more and more by the day, quickly decided he had a couple more hours to decipher the PPU. He hastily gathered up his devices and got out of bed. "I'm gonna go study the PPU. If you guys are hungry, there's something you can eat in my locker." Then, before Libby could unbutton her jacket, he left the barracks.

Carefully descending the stairs outside, his abdomen still sensitive from the Ooreiki medics' attentions, he passed two patch-wearing recruits. Unlike the blocky D of Sixth Battalion, the writing on these patches was diamond-shaped with a dot and half-circle inside. So far only Second and Sixth ranked patches.

Apparently, the recruits realized the same thing.

"Hey!" one of them shouted. "You're one of those charhead pussies we wasted on the hunt today! How's it feel to be a loser, sooter? You run home to mama and tell her all about it? How badly we spanked you soot-bag furgs?"

Joe hurried to hide the reader as he turned to face the two recruits. He recognized them immediately. The speaker was the same kid who'd paralyzed Libby, and the one standing beside him was Tank. The grinning, soft-faced five-year-old was now scowling at Joe through a mass of bruises, his ham-sized hands bunched in angry fists at his sides. Joe instantly felt bad. He'd never meant to get the kid hurt.

"Well, look who it is," the shorter of the two jeered. Joe realized it was the same kid Libby had dropped with a kick to the head. "You're the one who got Tank beat up for whipping your ass." The speaker stepped toward him, eyes dancing. "What's the matter, Zero? Gotta get others to do your dirty work? Too much of a pussy to do it yourself?"

"Bailey!" someone roared. For a startled moment, Joe thought it was one of the battlemasters, then he realized it was a recruit bearing a Second Battalion badge—as well as the four-pointed star of recruit battlemaster. I took him a moment to realize it was the same girl that Battlemaster Gokli had called Rat. Despite being fully grown, she was as flat-chested as an ironing board and had arms made for wrestling. Even her voice had sounded male.

"Get your ass back to the barracks, Bailey! You're already in enough soot with Gokli for spitting on that girl. You start getting Tank in trouble and I'll make your life a Jreet hell." She paused and held Joe's gaze a moment, her gray eyes almost purple in the reddish light. "Stop screwing around. Zero's got things to do and so do you."

The boy snorted. "They only thing I saw him doing was crying for his mama."

"Too bad she didn't show up because she would've whipped your ass," Rat retorted. The girl glanced at Bailey's companion. "Tank, take Bailey back to the barracks. I don't want to see him out here again before lockup. He tries to run off, you beat his jenfurgling face in. Get me?"

Tank nodded and silently plodded back down the stairs, dragging the smaller recruit behind him.

The girl gave Joe one last look, obviously summing him up—and finding him lacking—then turned and left him there.

So, Joe thought, *That's the competition.* The way the girl walked reminded him of Libby. That connection worried him.

Once she was gone, Joe found a quiet corner on the stairway to sit down and research the symbols on his PPU. He was concentrating intently on trying to memorize the difference between Scroll, which looked like a box with wings, and Mode, which looked like a box with flexing arms, when he realized somebody was watching him.

Joe hurriedly pushed the lesson pad aside and looked up.

It was the old, pale-eyed commander of Second Battalion.

Burn me.

Joe felt himself freeze up just like the first time he'd been under that cool, unreadable gaze. Joe had been staring up at him from the ground, two Congies holding his face into the concrete, guns trained on his head, their owners waiting on Lagrah's command to let him live or die.

"Where did you get that, boy?" Lagrah asked. He was looking at where Joe had hidden Nebil's lesson pad.

"I stole it," Joe said. "I'm gonna sell it for some food that doesn't taste like soot."

"Really." The Prime Commander held out a hand. "Give it to me. I'll check the register to see who held it last."

Joe's heart began to pound. He didn't want to get Nebil in trouble. Nebil had taken the brunt of Tril's fury after losing the flag to protect Joe. If everyone found out he had tried to cheat to help his battalion win…

"No." Joe pushed the lesson pad behind him, wedging it between a corner of the stair and the building.

"No." The droopy Ooreiki limb did not even twitch. "Do you realize what I could do to you for disobeying me, Human?"

"Probably something pretty crummy," Joe muttered. This was not going well. Not well at all.

With the speed of a striking snake, Lagrah lashed a stinging tentacle around Joe's neck. Despite Lagrah's ancient appearance, his grip was just as powerful as any other Ooreiki Joe had managed to piss off. He held Joe to one side as he reached for the lesson pad.

Then Joe remembered what Lagrah had said about checking the reader's register. If Lagrah checked the register, Nebil could lose his command. If Nebil lost his command, that left no one with the balls to stand up to Tril, and Sixth Battalion would end up being sold to the Dhasha by the end of the year.

I've got to stop him, Joe's panicked mind shrieked.

Joe let his legs go slack, choking himself as he slumped low enough to grab the lesson pad. As soon as he had it, he started bashing it against the side of the building as hard as he could. Even as his vision was darkening around the edges, Joe realized with dismay that the device wasn't suffering even the slightest bit of damage under his assault.

Just as he was about to pass out, Lagrah pulled his arm back. "Interesting. What's your name, Human?"

Joe stepped back, gasping. The underside of the Ooreiki's arm had ripped his skin with its tiny suction cups, leaving a burning red streak around his throat. He touched his neck warily, surprised he wasn't bleeding to death. "Zero."

"Your real name."

Joe froze. Was this some sort of trick?

Lagrah waited.

"Joe," he said quietly. It was the first time any of his commanding officers had asked.

"You're the one from the alley." It wasn't a question. "The son of that rebel."

Joe bit his lip and nodded.

Lagrah's eyes caught on Joe's chest and stayed there. "And you're Recruit Battlemaster now."

Joe nodded.

"Maybe Tril's not as stupid as I thought." At that, the old Ooreiki turned and left him gaping after him like an idiot, one foot still crushing the lesson pad into the staircase.

Cautiously, Joe bent down and retrieved the lesson pad. Aside from a couple of cosmetic scratches, it was in the same exact condition it had been when Nebil had given it to him.

Joe climbed the stairs to return to the barracks.

He jumped when a voice above his head said, "Choe!"

Joe glanced up. Yuil stood on her haauk, her sudah fluttering with worry.

"Choe! Did he hurt you?"

"No, I'm fine. How's it going, Yuil?"

The Ooreiki teenager scrunched her face disgustedly. "You make my name sound like something a Jreet would eat." She glanced at the staircase above him. "Are you busy, Choe? You want to drive my haauk? I just got it upgraded. I found an employer here on Kophat, so I don't have to go back to Poen to tend oorei."

Joe knew he had an obligation to his platoon to learn the PPU, but the thought of learning to drive the floating platforms was too tempting to resist. Joe climbed on board and, as Yuil croaked in amusement, he fumbled through the steps of flying a haauk.

He was actually doing pretty well, skimming over the tangled red treetops that looked like masses of veiny muscle, when Yuil suddenly took the controls away from him and lowered them into the canopy. For the first time, Joe was standing amidst the monstrous branches, perched on a limb big enough to be a highway back on Earth.

Yuil turned off the haauk and stepped onto one of the branches. "We must walk from here."

Joe, suddenly realizing how vulnerable he was all the way out here, away from the city, frowned at her. "Why? Where are we?"

"Nowhere," Yuil said. "At least you won't find it on any maps of Kophat."

"What do you mean?" Joe asked, his wariness increasing.

Yuil's eyes were alight with excitement. "It's a secret storage facility. Everybody on Kophat knows it's here, but the government pretends we don't."

"Storage for what?" Joe remained on the haauk.

"Weapons," Yuil whispered, her pupils fully dilated. "Horrible weapons. Weapons that would mean the end of Congress if they were set off on Koliinaat."

Joe felt a prickle of nervousness itch at his spine. Yuil's excitement seemed strange, a little off-pitch. Was this some sort of test? Was he supposed to tell her he didn't want anything to do with the end of Congress and demand she take him home?

"Come," Yuil insisted, gently wrapping her metal-encased fingers around his arm. "I'll show you."

"They just leave it open for anybody to walk into?" Joe asked in disbelief. Even if Kophat was a training planet, he doubted Congress would leave a weapons stash completely unguarded.

Yuil tapped the little golden band she now wore on a finger, right above the metal casings that looked like Celtic knots. Another akarit.

"Something you learn in *yeeri* academy is that akarit aren't just good for privacy." Yuil leaned close conspiratorially. "Congress has no creativity. All government buildings open with codes related to what they are used for. It only took my friend and me eighteen tics to figure out that the code was the initials of Kophat's Prime Overseer. The akarit kept the lock from alerting Peacemakers of our attempts."

Joe felt a cold tingle tracing up his back. If Congressional security was so lax that an Ooreiki teenager could break into it, what was keeping rebels from storming the compound and using the weapons against Congress?

Then again, Yuil might not be any teenager. Even on Earth, there were geeks who could crash half a country with a click of their mouse. Like Sam.

Who was to say Yuil wasn't some sort of Wunderkind who had discovered a glitch in the system?

"Someday you gotta show me how to do that," Joe said. Though, if it was anything close to as complicated as some of the stuff Sam had shown him, back on Earth, he knew it was out of his league.

But Yuil just nodded. "Follow me."

Yuil led him along the branch highways, hopping down and changing *ferlii* when it pleased her. Every once in a while, Joe caught a glimpse of the ground through the branches and his muscles threatened to seize up at the dizziness that followed.

Eventually, they came to a nondescript door set into the side of a *ferlii*. Joe stared at it, stunned by its simple appearance. *This* held a weapons-storage facility that could destroy Congress?

Yuil stepped close to the door's control pad and Joe glanced both ways, nervous.

Amazingly, as soon as Yuil entered the code, the door dripped open. No sirens, no alarms, no bombs going off. Just a gaping hole in the side of the *ferlii* and a row of red lights leading them inside.

Joe stared, his mouth ajar. If this was how easy it was to break into top-secret government installations, maybe he did still have a hope of getting back home. Excited, he followed Yuil inside and was only a little worried when the door shut again behind them.

"So what do you think?" Yuil asked inside, her eyes almost completely black from her widened pupils.

"It's really cool," Joe said. His voice echoed down the empty corridor. He peered down it nervously. "You sure nobody's here?"

"There's never anybody here," Yuil said. "Congress has got a tenth of its army hovering around Kophat. They don't need to guard it."

"I don't know…" Joe began.

"Don't worry. We're safe." Yuil motioned at the corridor. "Where do you want to go first?"

"What do you mean?" Joe asked.

"They've got rooms filled with bombs, rooms of guns, rooms of tanks, artillery… There's even an *ekhta* in here. The top of the ferlii folds over so it can deploy."

"Ek-ta?"

"Planet-killer. Target a species giving you a problem and *boom*. Problem eliminated."

Joe bit his lip, glancing at the rows of doors. The place was making him nervous. He couldn't believe Congress would just leave a stash of weapons and never come back to check on it. "I think I should be getting back."

Yuil gave him a sharp look. "Why?"

"I don't think it's a good idea to be here," Joe said. "I mean, who in their right mind would just leave all these weapons here and not guard them?"

"Congress," Yuil said matter-of-factly. "The politicians grow old and stupid. The whole Regency is too cocky. Kophat is in the Old Territory, so they automatically assume that nothing can touch them here. Come on." Yuil pulled Joe further down the corridor. "I'll show you the guns."

Joe followed her a little ways, then paused again, glancing at the floor. Below him, the surface was darker than that around it. He touched it and his hand came back slick with light brown fluid. He quickly wiped it on his leg, wondering if it had leaked from a canister of poison. "What's that?"

Yuil frowned down at the splotch. "Nothing. A leak."

"What kind of leak?" Joe asked. The corridor was beginning to remind him of the Takki tunnels. A few yards away from the smudge on the floor, an Ooreiki military flashlight lay forgotten against one wall. Joe rubbed at the goosebumps in his arms, eying it. "Look, I really think we should leave. Back home, we'd get in real deep soot for sneaking into a place like this. Like we wouldn't see the light of day for fifty years, that kind of stuff. I can only imagine what the Peacemakers would do to us."

"Peacemakers wouldn't care," Yuil said, waving off his concern and continuing down the corridor. "We're just kids."

Still, something about the place was setting Joe's nerves on end, and refused to follow. "I'd just like to go home, okay? I've got stuff I need to study for the next hunt."

Looking extremely irritated, Yuil complied. By the time they had gotten back to the haauk, however, she had cheered. She even let him drive.

Joe pulled the haauk up through the scarlet ferlii branches and hovered above the house-sized clusters of crimson spores, uncertain. "How do we get home from here?"

"The city is due west," Yuil said, pointing to a dial on the haauk's controls. "It's nine *ferlii*-lengths out. See those cuts in the canopy on either side? The highways converge on Alishai. Just follow them back."

Joe followed her instructions and eventually they arrived at the barracks.

"Thanks, Yuil," Joe said. He was flushed with adrenaline—on the way there, Yuil had showed him how to do a roll, and how the gravity of the haauk kept their feet on the floor even if they were hovering upside-down.

"Next time I will show you how to activate your commanders' haauks," Yuil said, a huge Ooreiki smile bunching the skin of her face. "It's a lot like opening doors."

Joe watched her fly away, though something was nagging at him. He was sure Yuil had been lying about something. His gut was telling him that the government compound had been too easy for them to access. Further, he just simply could not believe they would leave it unguarded all the time. From what she told him, an ekhta only a few minutes from Alishai was basically the same thing as leaving a nuclear bomb unguarded in the middle of Washington DC. Debating this, he turned to go back inside.

He ran into Libby, blocking the entryway. She had been standing behind him, her arms crossed. She wore only her underwear. She just scowled at him.

"Hi," Joe said, acutely uncomfortable. Behind her, the door was unlocked. Libby must have opened it herself.

"They said enemies of Congress might try to buy our loyalty."

Joe felt suddenly cold. "Nobody's tried to buy me."

Her flat stare told him he wasn't fooling anybody. "Where'd you get that candy, Joe?"

Joe swallowed hard. "Good night, Lib."

25

GETTING READY FOR WAR

"**H**ow did you get that rash, Zero?"

Joe blinked, unsure what Battlemaster Nebil was talking about. All morning, he had been preoccupied with the fact that the little silver lesson pad—the pad he had planned on using during the hunt tomorrow—was gone. He realized Nebil was looking at the mark on his neck from Lagrah's tentacle. He lifted a hand to cover it reflexively.

"I had a problem with an Ooreiki, sir."

"Commander Tril?"

"No, sir." Joe tensed, dreading the battlemaster's next question.

"Who?"

Joe grimaced. "Lagrah, sir."

Battlemaster Nebil grunted, then turned away from him to survey the rest of the recruits. He raised his voice and shouted, "The hunt's tomorrow, and I'll be damned if Tril's gonna starve you again. Everyone get your canteens and fill them with food at the chow hall. I don't care if you all die in the first tic, Fourth Platoon *will* eat."

Battlemaster Nebil guarded the end of the food line as the entire battalion filled their canteens with the green goop, scowling at any other Ooreiki who dared to give his recruits a second glance. Then he made them give double servings for that morning's meal and sat them down in the center of the chow hall as if they owned the place, even though they were using Fifth Battalion's time-slot.

As Fifth Battalion crowded into the tables that were left, Nebil took a bowl for himself and acquired his own serving of pond scum. He then sat down at the table with his platoon and wordlessly began to scoop the food into his mouth. It was one of the first times Joe had ever seen an Ooreiki eat, and it was not a pleasant sight. The alien's face distorted and stretched until it surrounded its tentacle like a balloon and sucked the pond scum free. Then he repeated the process.

Everyone else in the chow hall stared with him, their eyes wide with fascination. Even Fifth Battalion was riveted with Nebil's performance. For several minutes, no one said anything, listening to the odd sucking sounds the Ooreiki made as he ate.

Finally, Battlemaster Nebil shoved his half-eaten bowl aside and stood. "You're right, Zero. The food here tastes like Takki ashes. You guys get the flag tomorrow and I'll find you some real food."

Every kid in the cafeteria sat up.

"Another thing," Nebil said, lowering his voice so that only his platoon could hear, "About these ashsouls with the other battalions. I've had three recruits kidnapped and beaten in the past two days. Until we wring the soot out of Second on a hunt, it's gonna get worse. I don't want any of you walking around the city alone. Everybody travels with partners. I'm instigating the Rule of Three. Whenever you're three yards away from the rest of the Battalion, I want there to be three of you. I don't want any of you soot-eating furgs getting caught alone again. If you are, I'll make you regret it."

He paused, waiting for the recruits to shout their acknowledgement.

"Also. Whoever beat the soot out of that Second Battalion punk yesterday..." The battlemaster scanned their faces, stopping twice on Joe. "Keep up the good work. Show those ashy furgs we mean business. Every time *you* are out there and *you* catch one of 'em alone, I want you to burning destroy him. Get me? Put as many of those janja pellets out of commission as you can. Let's see how well Lagrah can hunt with half his force at medical. Now finish up and meet me in the plaza in eighteen tics." Then, giving his half-eaten bowl to Maggie, Nebil left.

Joe immediately glanced at Libby. "Was it you?"

Libby shrugged.

"Who'd you beat up, Libby?"

She shrugged again.

"Make sure the rest of us are there next time, okay?"

A slow grin spread over her face. "How about tonight, after the hunt?"

Joe snorted. "We're not going looking for a fight."

"They're doing it to us," Monk said, coolly logical. "You heard Nebil. They're not gonna stop unless we make them stop."

Joe grabbed her by the arm. "Listen to me. It's not a game, Monk," Joe said. "One of these days, someone's gonna get killed, and there's no fixing that. We should ignore them. Eventually, they'll get tired of harassing us."

"No they won't," Libby said. "You're wrong. The rest of the regiment is trying to bully us. What do you do with a bully? You wipe his nose in the dirt and make him run back home."

"They aren't gonna run home," Joe said, frustrated. "They're gonna run back to their battalion to get more people. Believe me, it's not gonna be much fun when things get going. People will get hurt."

To his frustration, Scott shrugged and said, "We either get hurt here or we get hurt on some other planet, fighting aliens we never heard of. I'm with them. We might as well have a little fun before they send us off to war. My Grandad was in a war. I stayed up one night listening to him tell my dad about all the bad stuff he seen. If I'm gonna die, I'd rather die here than—"

"*Nobody's going to die!*" Joe said, standing. He slammed his palms on the table, making everyone in the cafeteria jump. "You four better not try to do anything against the other battalions. That's an order from your *battlemaster*. You understand?!"

Libby grimaced and bent her head until she was staring directly into her soup. Scott and Maggie looked chastised, but Monk simply looked away.

"Monk..." Joe warned.

"Fine!" she said. "I'll stay with you and I won't have any fun!"

"You won't get hurt, either."

Monk pouted.

"If I was battlemaster, I'd let you all go ambush them," Sasha said loudly.

Joe turned to scowl at her. "It's not a burning vote, Sasha."

"If I'd been in charge, we wouldn't have lost the flag."

"You never would have *had* the flag," Joe said. "Sherri, see she does a hundred pushups before she goes to bed tonight. I'll be running my sleeves laps." *Or trying to.* Hobbling around the base of the barracks with his guts jostling against his spine and ribcage didn't involve much running.

"I wouldn't have chickened out in the middle of some tunnel," Sasha continued.

Joe gripped the table with anger. "Two hundred pushups."

She lifted her head and sneered. "Don't worry. When I get battlemaster, I won't make you run like you deserve."

"Three hundred."

"I'll only make you a grounder and put Libby in charge of your team. She's better than you, you know."

"*Four* hundred," Joe snapped. "Do you want any more?"

Sasha gave him a smug look. "It doesn't matter. I'm not doing them anyway."

Joe narrowed his eyes. "Yes. You are."

And she did. Though he had to stay up much of the night to see her finish, Joe convinced Nebil to leave the barracks door open while he counted out every single pushup down on the plaza, pushing her back down when she tried to stand up. Sasha had cried herself dry by the time she stumbled back into the barracks.

When Joe reached his bed, he realized his groundteam was gone. Or mostly gone. Monk lay under the blanket, awake and watching him.

"Where are the others?" Joe demanded.

"Libby took them out to hunt other battalions while you were busy with Sasha."

Joe felt a rush of fury. "Where'd they go?"

"I don't know. I didn't go."

Joe took a slow, deep breath. "Get out of bed."

Monk gave him a wary glance. "Why?"

"We're going after them."

"I'm tired and we've got our hunt tomorrow."

"You should've thought about that before you didn't come get me while the others were sneaking out."

"I said I wouldn't go," Monk retorted. "I didn't say I'd rat on them."

"Get dressed," Joe growled. "Now."

"But I've still got a few hours of sleep," Monk whined.

"Not anymore."

"We've got a *hunt* tomorrow," Monk complained. "Against Second Battalion! We won't do any good if we're all tired."

"We're not gonna do much good if half our platoon is dead, either," Joe retorted.

"They won't die," Monk snorted. "*Libby's* leading them." As if that solved everything.

"Get out of bed *now!*" Joe roared, waking up the other half of the platoon.

"You sound like Battlemaster Nebil," Monk muttered, getting out of bed.

"Good!" Joe said. "You charheads need a little more discipline in your lives."

"Well, soot," Monk said, getting her clothes on, "If I knew you were gonna be such an asher about it, I would've gone with them."

Joe ignored that. "Meet me outside."

At the door, Monk motioned at the other beds. "Look at that, Joe. Half of them are empty. You're the only Nazi who's keeping his groundteam from having some fun. You should just leave them alone."

"No," Joe said, shaking with rage and fear. He worried about Maggie. Most of the other kids in the regiment were muscular, fully-grown freaks, some as big as Joe. Maggie was petite, small, her bones delicate. And she was only *five*. "They disobeyed my orders. They're gonna wish they hadn't."

"You sound just like Sasha," Monk muttered.

Joe felt something twist painfully inside of him. He had to look away to keep from screaming at her. Softly, he said, "Just show me where they went."

"You know, Sasha was right about something," Monk said, descending the stairs.

"I don't want to hear it, Monk."

"Libby's a better leader than you."

Coming from one of his own, that sentence hurt more than anything else. Tired, near-delirious from lack of sleep, Joe paused on the stairs. "Why?"

"Because she took them out tonight."

Joe opened his mouth to argue, then closed it again. "Let's go back," he finally said. "Let them lose sleep if they want to. I'll talk to them later."

Monk made a disgusted noise and went back inside. Joe almost followed her, but then sat down on the stairs to wait. Somewhere along the line, he fell asleep, because he woke to the sound of laughter.

It was Maggie.

"...tied him up like that," she was saying.

"Wish we could tell Joe about it," Scott complained.

"Joe will find out tomorrow when they try to find out who did it," Libby replied.

"Joe will find out right now," Joe said, standing from the shadows. "Nice night for a walk, huh, guys?"

All three of them stopped dead in their tracks, several steps down from him. It was Libby who regained her composure first. "Hey."

"Libby." Joe glanced at the other two. "Scott. Maggie. Hope you enjoyed it out there tonight."

"We did," Libby said. Standing tall, she almost matched Joe in height. He had the uncanny feeling that she was going to keep growing.

"Good," Joe said. "Next time, warn me before you leave."

"Why?" she snapped. "So you can make us do pushups?"

"So Monk and I can go with you."

"Oh." Libby blinked at him.

"You're coming with us?!" Maggie shrieked. "Joe, it was so *cool*. We saw three guys from Third walking around, so Libby had us hide and we all—"

"Tell me later," Joe interrupted. "Scott, Maggie, go to bed. I want to talk with Libby for a few minutes."

Maggie's face lost its exuberance and quickly turned into a worried frown. "She's not in trouble, is she?"

"No," Joe assured her. "Get upstairs. We'll be in soon."

Scott gave Joe a searching look, then sighed. "Come on, Mag. We got a hunt tomorrow." At that, he turned and led her up the stairs to the barracks.

After they were gone, Libby braced herself, her face grim.

"Libby—" Joe began.

"We're not gonna stop," Libby blurted. "Nebil *told* us to, Joe. He said we need to stand up for ourselves. You don't let bullies *walk* on you, Joe. You fight *back*. And you kick their asses while you do it, so they stop picking on you."

"—do you want to be battlemaster?" Joe finished.

Libby jerked. "What?"

"You heard me," Joe said. "Do you want it? If you do, it's yours. Sasha's right. You're better at this than I am."

"No..." Libby took a step backwards, like he was trying to give her the plague. "Joe, I'm sorry. I didn't mean to make you mad." She looked panicked.

"I'm not angry," Joe assured her. "I'm a little frustrated and a lot tired, but I'm not angry. Come on, Libby. You saw how I screwed up the other day in that tunnel. If it wasn't for me, we would've kept that flag."

"But now you've got that little translator for the PPU," Libby said quickly. "That won't happen again."

Joe took a deep breath. "I lost it."

"What?"

He let his breath out in a huge sigh of frustration. "It wasn't in my gear this morning. Lagrah saw it earlier. I think he took it, or maybe a Takki when it was switching out my clothes."

He saw her face flicker with disappointment. "But you already know most of the symbols, right? You know how to position the map. That's enough to get us out of there next time we've got the flag."

"I'll talk with Nebil about getting you Battlemaster," Joe said. "Monk's right. You deserve it more than I do."

Libby grabbed his arm. "That's *furgsoot*. Every recruit out there knows who you are. You almost got us out of there with a *flag*. All of us look up to you. You're a hero."

Joe snorted. "A hero that starts crying like a little baby when he has to crawl through a hole." Joe yanked his arm away, narrowing his eyes at her.

"If you don't want to be battlemaster, that's fine," he said softly. "Just stop burning patronizing me." At that, he stormed back up the stairs, outraged that she would try to manipulate him like that.

Joe felt Libby hang back on the stairs, watching him go.

When the battlemaster woke them the next morning, Libby was gone.

26

THE PUNISHMENT FOR
FAILURE

"**W**here in the Jreet hells is your groundmate, Zero?!" Nebil demanded.

"I don't know." Joe blinked at the looks of horror Maggie and Scott were giving him. *They think I hurt her,* he realized, stunned. "Guys, I didn't—"

Battlemaster Nebil ripped his head back to face him. "Do you know the penalty for desertion?!"

"She didn't desert," Joe said quickly. *She'd never desert. This is her life.*

"Then where is she?!"

"I don't know."

"A battlemaster is responsible for an entire platoon and everyone in it. If you can't manage your recruits, Zero, I'll hand it over to someone who can."

"I saw her run off toward the east side of the city," Sasha offered. "She'd just had a fight with Zero and she was all alone."

Joe narrowed his eyes at Sasha, but said nothing.

"Find her," Nebil barked. "You have an hour while we get ready for the hunt. I want her back here before Tril finds out she's missing, you understand?"

Joe took his groundmates and ran.

They found Libby sitting against a wall, beaten bloody.

She looked up, both eyes swollen and her lip split and bleeding. As Maggie and Scott looked on in quiet fear, Joe knelt in front of her. "Libby? Can you walk?"

Slowly, she shook her head back and forth. Joe looked down and saw that both legs were bent in odd angles. The offending length of metal lay a few feet away, spattered with clotted blood. It almost looked like a crowbar, except blue instead of black. The whole area was covered with blood.

A little ball of fury began to build in Joe's gut. "Who did this?"

Libby made an odd, choking sound.

"Libby?"

Blood leaked from the corner of her mouth.

Joe swallowed down a spasm of terror. "Hold on. I'm gonna lift you onto my back."

Libby pushed him away and closed her eyes, making the same snorting sound in the back of her throat. More blood spilled out over her chest. A snake of dread wormed through him when Joe realized all the blood soaking the diamond chips was hers.

"I'll get her torso. Maggie, Scott, you get her legs. We've gotta carry her."

Against the wall, Libby thrashed her head back and forth. She made another weird, animal sound. Both Maggie and Scott stared at her, wide-eyed, as Joe hesitated.

"What did they do to you?" Joe asked, carefully peeling her vest away from her chest. The skin underneath was unbroken. He pushed her forward until she made a moaning cry, then did the same for her back. Nothing. Not even a bruise.

"I think there's something wrong with her mouth," Maggie said quietly.

Against the wall, Libby made a pathetic, hopelessly wry sound.

"Lib, open your mouth."

She refused.

"Burn me. Joe, is that her tongue?" Scott pointed at a bloody, gravel-encrusted lump in the dirt.

Joe's gut twisted in horror, spawning something entirely new and dangerous. He squatted beside the piece of flesh and, as Monk and Maggie shied away, gingerly picked it up. It was a tongue. He could even see taste buds on the pale, lifeless meat.

"You guys stay with her," Joe said, standing. "I'm getting some help."

"But the Rule of Three…" Maggie began.

"*Burn* the Rule of Three. Stay with her. Anyone tries to stop me, I'll make them wish they were never born." At that, Joe ran at a dead sprint back to the medical center. He brought the medics back to Libby and could only watch helplessly as they dosed her with the silvery solution and carried her away.

Joe returned to the barracks riding a wave of fury. He did not even remember gathering up his gear and going to the plaza. When the battlemaster got in his face, demanding to know where Libby was, Joe snapped.

"She's in the hospital," Joe snarled at him. "They broke her legs and cut out her burning tongue because *you told us* to pick fights with Second."

Battlemaster Nebil stared at Joe for several moments before saying, "Stay here, you Takki-ash furgs." Then, while the rest of Sixth Battalion boarded the attack haauk, he hurried off in his waddling alien gait. Joe closed his eyes and felt the full weight of his responsibility descend upon him.

It's my fault. I made her run off.

When Battlemaster Nebil returned, he was oddly subdued. "She's going to be fine. They'll be able to fix her legs. She'll earn her tongue back later, after she's worked a few years for Congress."

Earn back…her *tongue*? Joe was stunned. "She's not gonna be able to *talk?!*"

It was Commander Tril who said, "Recruits don't need to talk. They need to follow orders. She'll have a headcom that reads brainwaves so she can report while she's in combat."

"What about the rest of the time?" Joe demanded, furious.

Commander Tril ignored him. "Nebil, get them loaded on the haauk. We're wasting time."

Joe felt his fury carry him through their first fight with Second Battalion, but it wasn't enough. Second was better than Sixth—at everything. He managed to take down several white-clad defenders, but with

Libby gone and them pitted against Lagrah's recruits, most of his platoon went down within minutes.

Commander Tril was particularly unhappy with the day's events.

"This was our chance!" he shouted out at their formation once the medics had revived everyone. "This was our chance, but what happened?! Second Battalion starts attacking *us!* They burning left their tunnels to attack *us!*" Tril paced, his alien features twisted in fury. "Everyone who died within the first hour, step forward."

Two thirds of the battalion stepped out of formation and made a nervous line in front of him, Joe amongst them.

Commander Tril pulled the black device from his vest and held it up. "I've put it at the second setting. All of you undress. Now!"

Battlemaster Nebil stepped forward. "Commander, this was only their second attempt…"

"Be silent or I'll target you, too."

The battlemaster's pupils narrowed and he stepped into the line with his recruits.

"So be it," Tril said, scowling at Nebil.

The tight coil of rage that had awakened in Joe's gut over Libby's beating continued to grow. Slowly, he removed his vest and set it far behind him, out of the way. Then he followed with his shirt, his boots, and his pants. After cold deliberation, he removed his underwear, too. Then he stood there, waiting, the chilly breeze tightening his balls. He did not even look at the secondary commander, did not listen to the rest of what he said. All he felt was a deep, animal rage, a hatred for Congress and everything they had done to him. Not even their battlemaster's gesture eased the anger in his soul.

When the pain came, Joe sucked in a sudden breath. The spore-choked air inside his lungs was the last coherent sensation he felt. Then it was all a mash of agony. His entire world devolved into searing, mind-numbing pain. Endless pain, from which there was no escape careened through his body, missing nothing, hurting everything. Joe could think of nothing but how bad it hurt, how bad he just wanted to die…

When the agony finally ended, Joe was no longer standing. He was lying on his side, a pool of green vomit under his face, his heart skipping and pounding like he'd had a heart attack. His limbs would not work. All he could do was lay there and stare at the ground under his face, unable to think.

Near him, Commander Nebil was standing, pulling his Congie blacks back over his pale brown skin, an unreadable look on his face.

"Get them up!" he heard Tril shout.

After a moment, Ooreiki arms were grasping his shoulders, lifting him to his feet. Joe fell back to the ground, unable to hold himself upright. He thought he landed in a smear of shit, but he couldn't be sure.

"Now everyone understands the consequences of failure!" Tril shouted, once their battlemasters had dragged them all back to their feet. "Do any of you think I was unfair? That I was not within my rights as your commander? If you do, step forward again and say so. I will show you what it means to feel pain."

Battlemaster Nebil stepped forward. Commander Tril glanced at him, but returned his scowl to his recruits. They all stayed where they were. Joe fisted his hands at his sides, wishing he could use them. *Nebil shouldn't be up there alone.*

"You Takki sootbags," Tril ranted. "You better burning stay where you are. Just like you better *burning* get Second's flag next time. You humiliate me again and I'll set this asher to nine and watch you all sizzle."

Joe felt himself take a step forward. And another. Some insane rage was powering him, now, moving his body like he was on wires. He stepped past the last row of recruits and stepped beside Battlemaster Nebil, staring down at Tril in cold, wordless fury.

Nebil wrapped a tentacle tightly around his arm. "Get back, Zero." he said. "I'll handle this."

But Tril had already noticed him. "Battlemaster, step away from that recruit."

Nebil stayed where he was.

"You have something to say, recruit?"

Slowly, forcing his numbed mouth to form the words, Joe said, "When we get our first flag, you and your little black box aren't gonna have anything to do with it. You're just a sad dancing monkey who thinks he's a

Prime. You got Kihgl killed so you could take his place. That's why every-one hates you."

His speech was slurred from his last experience with the black device, but a collective silence swept through the ranks, even the battlemasters holding their breath. Beside Joe, Battlemaster Nebil's sudah were whipping the air, but he never took his eyes off of Tril.

"Watch carefully," Tril said, his voice amicable. Slowly, lazily, he twisted the dial on the black device. Then he held it out for Joe's inspection. "See that? That's the ninth setting. As soon as I push this button, you won't func-tion for a week."

Joe's stare never wavered. "Go ahead and do it, asher."

Tril's slitted eyes glimmered with malice, but before he could push the button, Battlemaster Nebil slammed a balled tentacle into Joe's solar plexus. "You poison-flinging Jreet!" Nebil screamed. "How dare you humiliate me in front of my secondary commander?!" He smashed a heavy tentacle into Joe's head and Joe's face exploded in a crunch of pain. Blood trickled from his nose and spattered onto his chest.

"Come here!" Nebil shouted, wrenching Joe off of the ground. He began dragging him through the putrid gravel surrounding the other naked recruits.

"Battlemaster Nebil," Tril said. "Where are you going?"

"This one's been a troublemaker from the start," Nebil snapped. "I'm taking him to Knaaren, trading him for one of the other recruits he took two weeks ago."

Tril's face twisted. "They won't be any good as soldiers."

"They'll be better than this mouthy jenfurgling."

Tril eyed the battlemaster for a long moment, then nodded. "With any luck, he'll eat him."

Without another word, Battlemaster Nebil dragged Joe away from the formation and onto his haauk. "You stupid sootbag furg," Nebil said, lifting the haauk off the ground. "I can't burning believe you did that."

"You did it too," Joe said.

"I did not force a young, insecure secondary commander to prove his power over his recruits in front of his entire battalion."

"Don't take me to Knaaren," Joe said. "Let Tril punish me. I can handle it."

"You're a soot-eating furg!" Nebil snapped. "Tril had that thing set to nine! It would have hotwired your system until your muscles gave up and you died. Tril's only read the literature. He's never seen it in action. I have. If he hit you with a Ninth Degree, it would kill you."

"So you're giving me to the Dhasha, instead?!" Joe cried. "Why can't you just tell him it would kill me?!"

"I'd already pissed him off," Nebil replied. "If I'd said anything other than what I did, he would have activated the unit and you wouldn't be here now."

Joe took a desperate grip on Nebil's arm. "Let him kill me. I'd rather be dead."

"Keep your eyes down and your mouth shut," Nebil said. "Do exactly what you're told and you might make it out of this alive."

Joe's anger left him suddenly to be replaced with cold, stark fear. "Please, I don't want to go to the Dhasha."

"You don't have a choice."

Joe panicked as they approached Knaaren's tower. "Then let him kill me!"

"I can't do that." The battlemaster lowered the haauk to the ground outside Knaaren's tower. "As stupid as you are, Kihgl would still haunt me if you died. At least this way, you have a chance of surviving." He shoved Joe toward the Dhasha's tower. "Get onto the elevator. Now." Behind Nebil, the rest of Sixth Battalion was offloading onto the plaza and Joe saw his groundmates watching him, their faces twisted in concern.

Joe swallowed hard, determined to remain strong in front of them.

He stepped onto the elevator.

Battlemaster Nebil followed him inside and the Takki controller shut the gate. Immediately, the machine started speeding them upwards, towards Knaaren's penthouse at the top. Joe glanced over the railing several times as they ascended, wondering if Congressional medicine was strong enough to bring him back from the dead if he jumped.

"I'm sorry," Joe said, trying not to let his voice shake.

"Shut up, Zero."

"I was stupid."

"Enough. You won't change anything by begging."

"Give me a second chance."

"It's too late."

Joe was panicking, now. "Let me talk to Tril. I'll apologize. I'm one of the best runners in the regiment. I can carry more gear than most. I led the only platoon to get its hands on a flag. I'll convince him."

"Are you going to whine all the way up?"

Joe slumped against the railing, all of his fight suddenly leaving him. He caught a look of satisfied amusement on the Takki's reptilian face before turning to slump over the banister and stare out at the huge, winding stair wrapping around the honeycombed tower.

The elevator passed over several badly-scarred Takki on the switch-backed stairs, each with unreadable sapphire eyes. They never looked up from their tasks. The humans were worse. The ones he saw had dead eyes, their bodies riddled with half-healed gouges that had ripped their skin into wrinkled valleys of scars. Only their hands were unscarred—beautiful, working hands that showed not a single scab.

Joe glanced over the railing at the ground below. They were at least a thousand feet in the air. Nobody could survive a fall that far.

Briefly, Joe thought of the skydivers he had read about whose para-chutes never deployed and they ended up alive on some parking lot some-where, with only a few broken bones to show for their mile-high plunge. He felt sick as he thought about it. Maybe if he jumped head-first…

Battlemaster Nebil lashed a tentacle around Joe's throat and dragged him away from the edge. "Don't even think about it." Joe endured the Ooreiki's painful grip for the rest of the ride. When the elevator stopped, Nebil dragged him onto the roof and into a tank-sized opening cut into the ebony stone.

On the other side, the hallway widened into the balcony of an enor-mous amphitheater. In its center, a handful of humans were gathered around Lord Knaaren, whose iridescent body twitched in time to his sleepy groans. The humans tending the Dhasha were prying up scales and using blue metal sticks to dig out huge flakes of skin from underneath. These they were piling in baskets, which a Takki was collecting.

"Stay here." Without another word, Nebil descended into the Dhasha's chambers. All of the children looked up as he entered, then glanced up at Joe as soon as he spoke. Slowly, haltingly, one of the boys stepped away from the rest. With a start, Joe recognized Elf.

The Ooreiki led Elf back to the top of the stairs, where the battlemaster paused for a moment to look Joe up and down. Finally, he said, "Good luck, Zero." At that, Nebil turned and walked out the door, gesturing for Elf to follow him. Elf stayed for several long heartbeats, looking at Joe with an anguished look of pity and relief. Then, like he was afraid to lose the opportunity, Elf turned and hurried after the Ooreiki, leaving Joe alone.

At least I saved Elf. Joe felt a ridiculous laugh forming in his chest. Turning, he stared down at the pathetic figures scraping filth from under the Dhasha's scales. He watched the meek, scuttling slaves for several moments before, out of nowhere, a Takki grabbed him roughly by the shoulder and spun him around. If an Ooreiki was solid muscle, a Takki was solid steel. As easily as lifting a doll, the Takki threw Joe against the stone railing overlooking the sleeping Dhasha. His six armored fingers were tipped with blunted purple talons that dug into Joe's skin as he held him.

"Why were you standing here?" the Takki demanded. "Humans are not allowed beyond the den." He pulled Joe down the stairs, until he was only feet from the twitching Dhasha. There, it shoved a blue metal scratching stick into Joe's hands, then pushed him toward Knaaren. When Joe did not immediately squat and begin cleaning with the rest, the Takki casually raked purple talons along his back, opening up the hide there and shoved him to his knees.

Joe stared down at the basket of stinking skin flakes beside his thigh. He saw tiny, red alien insects crawling through the mess, four sets of mandibles ripping at the dead skin, each the size of a large water-beetle. They snapped at the humans when they came too close. He saw a kid flinch when he was bitten by one of the invertebrates, a welling of blood beading on his wrist. Then the Takki ruthlessly grabbed Joe by the back of his head, its wrought-iron arms shoving his face towards the Dhasha's sleeping body.

Joe whipped around and slammed the metal stick over the Takki's glistening purple muzzle.

The Takki's pained howl woke Knaaren. The Dhasha was on his feet instantly, bowling his attendants aside as he sought to locate the source of the noise. As soon as his eyes found the whimpering Takki, he knocked the creature to the ground and ripped off its head. Then it turned to Joe.

Joe dropped the crowbar.

27

THE TROUBLE WITH TAKKI

"I recognize you," Knaaren said, purple scales stuck between his rows of black teeth. "You're the big one who claimed he wasn't a bully." The Prime Commander glanced up at the railing where Nebil had disappeared. "Looks like you lied, doesn't it?"

Joe made a split-second decision. Standing before the monster, all Joe's self-righteous thoughts about death before slavery fled him and, in that instant, faced with those razor-filled jaws, all he wanted to do was live. He lowered his head and waited.

Knaaren gnashed his teeth together, grinding bits of purple flesh and scales between them. *Chewing*, Joe thought, disgusted. He heard the sharp crunch of bones as the Dhasha crushed the Takki's skull in his jaws. Then, swallowing, Knaaren said, "Why are you here?"

Joe felt all his courage drain out his feet. "I questioned Commander Tril in front of his battalion," he managed.

The Dhasha snorted, filling the place with a blast of fetid breath. "Really. That's unsurprising. What did you say?"

"I think I said he was a sad dancing monkey that didn't deserve to lead the Sixth," Joe said.

Lord Knaaren bared his rainbow lips and clacked his inky black teeth together, then snatched up the rest of the dead Takki and swallowed it. Joe endured several minutes of the sick crunching of bones only a few handswidths from his neck before the Dhasha languidly returned to his place amongst the brightly colored pillows, apparently not in the mood to kill Joe after all. "Tell me of Human females. What's the best way to get them to breed?"

Joe stared. "What?"

Knaaren watched his reaction like a hungry cat. "Every Human I've asked so far has clearly not known what I was talking about. Somehow, I think you might."

Joe cleared his throat, face reddening. "Well, uh, I hear they like flowers. Candles. Dinner and a movie. My friend told me a poem worked for him."

"Dinner?" Knaaren's attendants moved forward and began picking purple scales and flesh from between his teeth. "I've not been withholding their food."

"They…uh…" Joe didn't know how to say what followed without inciting the Dhasha's wrath. "I think the Ooreiki made them all sterile anyway."

"Do you think I'm stupid?!" the Dhasha snarled. "Of course I'm not using former recruits. I ate those useless creatures immediately."

Joe glanced at the other human slaves. For the first time, he realized all of them were boys. He felt a fearful twisting in his gut. *He ate all the girls.*

"I paid for a shipment from Earth," Knaaren continued. "Nine females. I tried to vary the colors, to create more interesting stock, but most are your dull pink."

Joe felt a sick feeling rising in his stomach.

Knaaren eased backwards on his pillows, still watching him. "The recruit I put into their stable has done nothing more than eat and sleep."

Immediately, Joe understood the problem. Most of the recruits had been far too immature when they were Drafted to know anything about sex. Whoever Knaaren had chosen, he was probably more interested in bedtime stories than reproduction.

"So what must I do?" Knaaren insisted. "Must I buy these things you speak of and bring them here for the male to use?"

"Yeah, probably," Joe said.

The Dhasha snorted. "Useless creatures. How is it your species survived, if the male cannot impregnate the female without help?"

"We've always had it, I guess," Joe said, flushing.

"That will mean another two rotations before I can start breeding them, even if I send my fastest ship," Knaaren growled. "You Humans are turning out to be more trouble than you're worth."

Joe kept silent, not sure what the Dhasha wanted him to say.

"You taste good, though," Knaaren continued. "No scales at all. Very tender. You're even better than farmed Takki. At the farms, they de-scale them and keep them in one spot until their muscles grow soft and they can't even hold themselves upright and still they are tougher than a Human could ever be. Humans are much more palatable, even with their bitter aftertaste. That's why I bought those nine from Earth. I want to start a farm." He gave Joe an interested look. "You're larger than most Humans, aren't you?"

Joe felt his gorge rising. "No," he lied. "About average."

"Pity. I need a good stud. This one I have is useless."

Joe kept his mouth shut.

The Dhasha closed his double-lidded eyes. Joe waited for him to say something else, but the Prime Commander had fallen asleep.

When he no longer had Knaaren's attention, several Takki came forward and dragged Joe away to receive his first beating upon arriving in the dens. He quickly realized that, despite the terrible force behind an Ooreiki thrashing, their punishment did not hold a candle to the cruel efficiency of a Takki slave.

• • •

"Nebil, why do you continue to allow your recruits to disfigure their uniforms? Zero is gone, and your entire platoon is dangerously close to following in his footsteps."

Battlemaster Nebil had barely said a word to Tril since he had included him in the perceptual punishment. Curtly, Tril's battlemaster said, "Commander, my platoon is my business. As long as it performs well in the hunts, I expect you to leave it alone."

Tril felt his sudah give a quick flutter at the word 'expect.' No one under his command had ever dared to speak to him like that. An array of punishments for Nebil drifted through his mind, immediate demotion and transfer topping the list. He quickly had second thoughts about both of those, however, because Nebil's platoon far outstripped the others in efficiency and hunting skill. Tril didn't like to admit it, but Nebil was one of the best battlemasters he'd ever seen, and he knew that when Sixth Battalion finally brought Second to heel, it would be Nebil's platoon that led the charge.

Still, Nebil's disrespect had to be dealt with. With all the dignity he could muster, Tril said, "I've ignored your disobedience until now, Battlemaster, and every day I see more of your recruits with their arms bared. That did not concern me overly much—if you wish to distinguish your platoon from the others as a sort of friendly competition, that is fine. However, this morning I saw three recruits from another platoon with their arms likewise bared."

Nebil looked amused. "Perhaps you should transfer them to Fourth."

"I had their battlemaster withhold two days' worth of food for the infraction."

Nebil's face hardened.

"So, Battlemaster, tell me. How should I run Sixth Battalion? You're only one of ten battlemasters I have to deal with each day, each of whom wants something different for his platoon. If I allow Fourth Platoon to make its own dress code, how do I make it fair for the other nine platoons in my battalion? Should I allow Second to paint their jackets orange? Should I let Seventh go without boots?"

"Do what you want," Nebil said coldly. "All I know is that when Fourth marches through the plaza, people turn their heads to watch. When we come after another platoon in the hunts, they know who we are. Fourth is the only platoon in the regiment that has its own table at the chow hall. When it goes to sit down, everybody else moves out of the way."

Tril's sudah were whipping in irritation. "I've heard about that, Nebil. You purposefully left Fourth Platoon's time slot and now go to eat whenever you please. The other commanders are furious."

Battlemaster Nebil looked completely unruffled. "Those Takki pussies are trying to make Sixth choose between food and sleep. A battalion can't function long that way before it cracks. I'm not letting them push my recruits around. You shouldn't, either."

At that, Nebil turned and left without another word.

• • •

From the very first moment in the den, the Takki methodically shattered Joe's dignity. It was everything he could do to remind himself he was a human being. For the first few days, until Knaaren commented on it, they refused to clothe him. They gave him the nerve-shattering jobs—like picking rancid strips of flesh from between the Dhasha's teeth—and made sure he crawled like a dog between the Dhasha and the refuse heap to deposit his piles of rotting skin and parasites. When he was too slow, they ruthlessly added their claw marks to his skin.

Joe only left Knaaren's den a few times, but during each outing, he realized with a sinking gut how hopeless his situation was. The platoons continued to drill and the battalions continued to hunt, still functioning efficiently despite the missing recruit called Zero. Unlike the other humans, who hoped for a miracle upon seeing their old comrades, Joe always opted to stay behind if he got the chance. He didn't want Libby and the others to see him as he was—a bent-necked, rubber-spined, teeth-picking slave.

Knaaren, however, gave him no choice. The Prime Commander was getting increasingly odd—sometimes shouting at thin air as if someone was standing there, shouting back. The Dhasha's dreams were also becoming more restless. Almost as soon as Knaaren closed his eyes, he began to quiver and shake, snapping at the air with his huge jaws so often that the most dangerous task for the slaves became grooming the Prime Commander while he was sleeping.

On those rare occasions when Knaaren decided he wanted certain slaves to accompany him out onto the drill plaza, even the slightest suggestion that Joe wanted to stay behind was enough for the Dhasha to order the Takki to hurt him.

Knaaren himself couldn't touch the humans without causing irreversible damage. His claws, as Commander Linin had demonstrated, were wedge-shaped and as sharp as razors. Instead of simply tearing flesh like claws on Earth, these cut. And, with the human slaves dressed in nothing except flimsy purple robes, even a light bat from a Dhasha paw was enough to cut them in half. Therefore, he had the Takki do his dirty work for him.

And they excelled at their job. They gave Joe a new scar at every opportunity, and the two times Joe dared to fight back, they showed him just how weak he really was. It took no effort at all for a Takki to beat him senseless. Unlike the Ooreiki, the lizard-folk didn't even have to put much energy into it. They simply had to slap him and Joe felt like he'd been hit with a Mack truck.

Joe eventually discovered his treatment was not special. The Takki dealt with all the other humans with the same amount of cruelty. To the Takki, all slaves who had to wear purple robes to symbolize their servitude were considered lesser creatures than they, who had been the loyal companions of the Dhasha for millennia. Joe quickly realized that the Takki were *proud* of their station. They were even angry that Knaaren had decided to grow humans as food. That was *their* place, they figured, and the humans were trying to usurp it.

Insanity. Joe found that they had no concept of Self, no sense of purpose other than to live and die serving the Dhasha. He never heard any of them use the word 'I.' As far as he could tell, they all thought of themselves as a single being with different jobs to do. If any of them failed in their duties, they were ostracized by the whole until the stress became too much and the victim made a fatal mistake in front of its master. This lack of compassion made them quick to snitch on the other slaves, human and Takki alike. And, Joe quickly found when Knaaren calmly ate one Takki in front of its uncomplaining mate, they had not an ounce of courage.

Joe hated the Dhasha, but he hated the Takki even more. Knaaren was thoughtless and brutal, but it did not even compare to the Takki's cold, methodic cruelty. The more he served with them, the more he realized that, without the Takki, the Dhasha never would have evolved past a stinking, mindless predator. It was the Takki who gave Knaaren the ability to send summons to his subordinates. It was the Takki who kept dead skin from rotting away his scales and his teeth from falling out. It was the Takki who manipulated objects and carried delicate instruments. It was the Takki who opened doors and operated haauk.

Knaaren took it all for granted, too. Several times, Joe glanced up at the door locking them inside the den and wondered what would happen to Knaaren if he suddenly went on a rampage and killed all of his slaves. His powerful forequarters were too stubby to lift higher than necessary to run, and his paws were too rigid to press individual buttons. His sharklike face was too wide to do anything but mash the keypad and his tail was too small and stiff to use it as another limb. In short, he had absolutely no way of getting himself out of the den, should the Takki lock him in there forever.

And yet, for some reason, they never did.

They're cowards, Joe thought, hating them. *All this time, they could be free and the Dhasha couldn't stop them, but they don't even try.*

What made him hate them even more was that the Takki were treated even more poorly than the humans and still they did nothing to help themselves. Knaaren cuffed and batted them daily, sometimes scoring deep furrows in their scales, sometimes breaking through and dipping into skin. He ate them often, usually for a slight infraction. Those that he ate were always replaced, their fresh scales and bright eyes indicative of transfer from some Dhasha slave colony. Those were usually the first to make mistakes and become lunch. The older ones, the ones bearing the most scars from Knaaren's rages, had somehow clawed their way to the top of the Takki food chain and spent all of their time outside the den, managing their master's affairs.

Once Knaaren was clean and groomed, he only seemed to care about making Joe and the other humans do his bidding, watching their movements with an interested air. Joe could not help but shudder when those green, egg-shaped eyes were fixed on him, feeling like a trapped rodent pinned under a cat's cold stare.

Knaaren delighted in singling out a human and forcing him to lean into his mouth to retrieve some stubborn bit of rot that lay between his sharklike fangs. When they finished, he would insist that they did not get the right piece of flesh, telling them that they were worthless and command them to do it again. If they were too shaken to go in a second time, he had the Takki punish them. If they said there was nothing left between his teeth, he had the Takki punish them. If they whimpered and cried and begged, he had the Takki punish them. Then he would move on to the next human and start the process all over again.

Knaaren was in one of these moods when an Ooreiki messenger summoned him to the drill field to oversee the punishment of an attempted escapee. Knaaren chose Joe, who had just been about to start the nerve-wracking process of crawling inside the lion's jaws, to accompany him.

Out on the plaza, Joe kept his eyes away from the sharp black rows of recruits, staring instead at the ground. The last thing he wanted to do was recognize somebody he knew. He slumped to hide his height and kept the Dhasha between him and the regiment.

Still, he knew instantly which one was Sixth because it was still the only Battalion without the symbol of Congress flapping above it. As much as Knaaren enjoyed playing mind-games with his slaves, he enjoyed it even more with his subordinates. Tril probably wouldn't get his standards until the day his recruits were to graduate.

"Carry this," an older Takki ordered, shoving an alien notepad into his hands. "Master will need it to log his discipline choice in the escapee's record." Joe recognized some of the symbols, but immediately shifted his eyes back to the ground. The Takki would return for it later, once Knaaren needed it.

The unfortunate kid who had attempted escape was standing at attention in front of Sixth Battalion, pale and wide-eyed. He, of all the kids in the plaza, was wearing white. Joe felt a breath of relief when he did not recognize him, but knew that another black mark against Sixth Battalion was bringing it dangerous attention it didn't need.

Joe realized upon examining the boy that the growth hormones had been working on some better than others. The kid was as large as Joe and as beefy as a steer, with biceps the size of small turkeys. Looking at him, it was easy to imagine that humans were related to apes. Joe had the feeling that if the drugs hadn't gotten rid of their hair, the boy would be sprouting a rug from his belly-button to his sternum.

Tertiary Commander Tril stepped forward, as stiffly as ever. "My lord, this recruit is charged with abandonment of his duties, failure to return to his post upon request, and assaulting the soldiers who brought him in."

It took Joe a moment to realize that the Mexican kid bore a bruised face and a split lip. He was also shivering uncontrollably under Knaaren's stare, but at least he had the good sense not to run. Joe felt sorry for him, but knew that at least whatever punishment they gave the kid would end. The only way Joe was getting out of Knaaren's clutches was if he screwed up and the Dhasha ate him.

"A Sixth Degree of perceptual punishment is common for desertion," the Dhasha said. "Why are you wasting my time?"

"We punished him, sir. After my punishment, he ran away again. This time, he assaulted two soldiers who were sent to retrieve him."

"He assaulted an Ooreiki?" Knaaren asked. The Prime Commander was in a good mood—he had eaten a Takki that morning and his stomach was full. It was surprising to Joe that he was actually staying awake to hear out this case.

"Two of them, my lord."

Knaaren snorted. "We both know a Human can't hurt an Ooreiki."

"This one did," Tril said. "It took nanorejuvenation to keep them both from dying."

"What did he use as a weapon?"

"His hands and a chunk of rock."

The Dhasha glanced over at the Ooreiki lining the battalion. "Sounds to me like your underlings are incompetent, commander."

"The boy used tactics he learned in the hunts to lure them both out of hiding, separate them, and ambush them."

"Sounds like you should be promoting him, not punishing him."

"He is uncontrollable. He killed a fellow recruit and hurt another before we found him the second time. She is still undergoing treatment for mental trauma."

"What sort of mental trauma?"

"He utilized her reproductive capabilities against her will."

Lord Knaaren, who had been boredly scanning the regiment, swiveled. "He did?"

Joe stiffened as he stared at the ground. *Don't let him do it.*

"It's a severe crime amongst Humans. Mentally, they are unprepared to handle unwanted partners. Physically, they can only birth one child every year, so it's in their best interest to make sure they only breed with accept-able mates. It's an evolutionary side effect, sir."

The Dhasha's eyes were fixed on the Mexican boy. "I want him."

Commander Tril's sudah gave a startled flutter. "This is just a routine punishment, sir. My recruits have earned their first badge. You no longer have the right to take them from us."

"What do you want for him?"

"He is here for punishment, not sale."

"And I will see to it he receives his punishment," Knaaren retorted. "What do you want for him?"

Tril's sudah were almost invisible, they were moving so fast. "To avoid further psychological damage, I believe we need to institute a few rules before things get out of hand."

Knaaren snorted. "I don't think so."

"Several other regiments have been experiencing the same problem," Tril insisted. "In order to stabilize their recruits, they've written up several differ-ent sets of laws. It would help if you read them and drafted a standard of—"

"I do not cater to cattle," Knaaren barked. "If you really believe he has done wrong, hand him over to me and be done with it. I could always use another slave."

"The boy is one of the younger ones, sir."

"So?"

"These Humans do not mature like normal creatures. He's still a child with an adult's body, with new hormones assaulting his system. He does not have the mental development to understand the psychological reper-cussions of his actions."

"*I want him*," Knaaren roared.

Tril balked. "The boy did not understand. Even Dhasha hatchlings are given allowances when they murder fellow soldiers…"

Knaaren bared his teeth. "Of course they are given allowances. They have natural urges. It is not their fault they are drawn to blood."

Joe stared at the back of the Dhasha's head. *You sure are one stupid son of a bitch, you know that?*

Tril, seeing that he was going nowhere, straightened. "I cannot give you the recruit, my Lord. We are already well below acceptable battalion numbers. Second Battalion has a full fifty-eight recruits more than we do. Almost an entire platoon. I cannot afford to lose any more. Whatever punishment the recruit receives, I must request that it is non-lethal and does not remove him from his duties."

The Dhasha swung around to stare at Joe. "What if I trade?"

"Excuse me?"

"A trade," the Dhasha said. "This one behind me for that one of yours. They're both large, fleshy. Either one would make a fine soldier. This way, your recruit receives his just punishment and my slave can replace what you lost."

For the first time, Tril looked at Joe. Immediately, his sudah gave an angry quiver. "That recruit was more of a problem than this one."

Joe felt like he had been stabbed. He was more of a problem than a rapist and a murderer? The injustice of it made him want to hurt something, but he kept his cool and his head down.

"This one is reformed," Knaaren said. "Look at him. He has no more rebellion left in him."

"And if you're wrong, the Sixth will be weighed down with a useless recruit. I want something else. Something to make it worth my while."

Knaaren moved toward the Tertiary Commander until he was staring down at him. "Don't you dare to presume to tell me what to do, Commander." Orange saliva had begun to dribble from between his teeth. "Your battalion is just a mongrel mishmash of Kihgl's leftovers. It will never be battle-ready. You're lucky I haven't decommissioned it yet."

Tril straightened. "We have the highest attacker success rate of any of the Battalions, and our overall score is second only to Second Battalion."

Knaaren laughed. "You're proud of your pathetic, molting Takki, aren't you? You don't even have your own standards!"

"That is your fault, my lord."

Joe glanced up, stunned. *When did he grow a set of balls?*

The Dhasha opened his mouth slightly and stared down at Tril for long moments. Then he said, "It's your fault, for not deserving them. Your battalion has the highest rate of rebellion and insubordination than any of the others. You yourself are new to the job. I wouldn't put a single Takki down on you and yours surviving a real battle."

"Time will prove you wrong, my lord."

Knaaren paused, the only sound that of the whoosh of air entering his gigantic lungs…and the dribble of saliva on the plaza between his feet. After a long consideration, he said, "Very well. Your standards for the Human."

"That still leaves me one recruit short, my lord."

"Your standards *and* my slave for the Human."

Joe's heart caught in his chest and he found he couldn't breathe in the tense silence that followed.

In that eternity, Tril met Joe's eyes, a look of disgust on his face. After weeks with the Takki, Joe reflexively dropped his gaze.

Lord Knaaren made an angry guttural barking sound and regurgitated bits of slimy meat in a wave over his innermost row of teeth. "I'm done bargaining." He turned to walk back to his tower.

"You can have him," Tril said suddenly. "For the standards and the slave."

Knaaren turned back, rainbow lips peeled back. "Then do it. Renounce your claim to him. Make it official."

"That's hardly necessary…" Tril began.

"I don't want the Training Committee suggesting I stole one of your recruits. I want him to be mine. Not just a Congressional slave serving me, but *mine*. I don't want to give him up to the next Dhasha commander that's posted here."

All over the plaza, Ooreiki sudah were fluttering madly, and some of the Battlemasters looked outright furious.

Stammering, Tril said, "It's against policy to turn a slave over for personal—"

"Don't preach to me about policy. Either do it or you won't see your standards at all. I'll destroy them myself."

From his place at the head of Second Battalion, Commander Lagrah moved forward. "Commander Tril, I will give you my own standards before seeing you dishonor—"

"Silence!" Knaaren snapped, whirling. "Get back in formation, Lagrah, or I will crush your *oorei* like I did Kihgl's."

Lagrah's droopy face scrunched in an alien smile. "Then I'd enjoy haunting you along with him. Enjoying the ghost sickness, Knaaren? You look ill. Haven't been getting enough sleep?"

Knaaren's entire body stiffened and he did not respond.

Lagrah turned back to Tril. "Commander, you don't need your standards to be an honorable opponent on the battlefield."

Tril stood rigidly, sudah flapping like hummingbird wings. "Be it known to everyone gathered here that, as guardian of this recruit—"

Lagrah made a disgusted sound and left, taking his battalion with him.

"Continue!" Knaaren snapped.

"As guardian of this recruit, I have decided he is no longer any use to the Army. I hereby renounce Congress's claim on him." In front of the gathered battalion, the Mexican kid was crying.

"Good!" The Dhasha moved toward the Mexican kid. "Human, I find you unaffiliated with Congress, unprotected by its laws. I hereby claim you as my personal slave. Serve me, or die."

The Mexican kid wet himself. Joe could not dredge up the compassion to feel sorry for him. Not after what he knew Knaaren had planned for him. Joe knew the kid would probably think Knaaren was giving him some sort of reward. He wished he could stop him, do something, but none of Joe's options ended in anything other than his death—and Knaaren doing what he wanted anyway.

"Follow." Lord Knaaren turned, leading the way back to his lair.

"What about my standards?" Tril demanded.

The Dhasha turned back, exposing row upon row of glistening black teeth. "You have my slave. Be happy with that."

The Takki took the notepad from Joe and shoved him towards the battalion.

"But—"

"If it upsets you, go complain to the Training Committee that I didn't give you your standards in exchange for expelling one of your own. Perhaps next time you will be quicker to accept my offer." At that, he left, the terrified Mexican kid trailing after him.

Joe stood in the Dhasha's wake for several minutes, unmoving. Then Sasha's voice echoed across the plaza like a shot.

"Get in formation, Zero! You'll have time to look stupid later."

Sasha stood amidst a sea of bare arms, though she herself kept her sleeves down. She and Libby were the only two that had.

"Now, Zero!"

Joe somehow made his feet move, though he still couldn't believe what had happened. He kept his eyes straight ahead as he fell into line, unwilling to let his groundmates see how the Takki had broken him.

Other formations were breaking up around them, but Tril stood there staring at Knaaren's rising elevator with the silence of the dead. When he turned, his sudah were fluttering with fury. "Battlemaster Nebil," Tril said, his voice cold, "be sure that your newest recruit gets a good workout today." Joe actually saw hatred in Tril's eyes. "Look at him," Tril sneered. "He's been spending too much time with Takki. You will have to break him back into our routine, work his slave-laziness out of him. Don't bother letting him change. He can run in those robes. If he can't keep up, he doesn't eat. I don't need weak recruits."

"Kkee, Commander," Nebil said. He sounded stiff. "I'll make sure he keeps up."

Tril gave Joe a cold look. "You can start now."

28

FINDING THE FLAG

Commander Tril used the next seven hours to make Nebil parade Joe around in Takki robes, making sure everyone in the city knew he had just come from peeling rotten skin out from under the Dhasha's scales. When he finally got bored and handed the platoon back to Nebil, Joe's robes were sweat-soaked and his knees and wrists were bloody from continuous tripping.

Upon regaining command, Nebil immediately dismissed them with, "Everybody but Zero, get the hell out of here. *Move!*" Filled with shame, Joe stayed where he was, staring at his feet. Joe felt his groundmates give him unhappy glances as they and the other recruits dispersed for the barracks at a run.

When Nebil approached him, Joe's body was quivering with humiliation. He couldn't meet his battlemaster's eyes. He couldn't even hold the 'retain' position. His fingers were curled into fists and his arms shaking at his sides.

"I see you survived," Nebil said softly.

Joe couldn't speak. He turned his head away to stare at the crushed gravel of the plaza.

"If it makes you feel better," Nebil said, "if I had any doubts before that Kihgl was right in saving you, they're gone now."

Joe's brow furrowed and he turned to look, despite himself.

Nebil was regarding him with something akin to respect. "No one comes out of a Dhasha's service alive, Zero. The ancestors must love you, you wily Jreet bastard."

Dressed in the robes of Takki, bleeding and doused in weeks of fear-soured sweat, Joe could only drop his eyes again.

"Go sleep," Nebil said, nodding at the barracks. "I'll make sure the cooks give you double rations tomorrow."

Joe nodded silently at Nebil's kindness and turned to go.

Nebil grabbed his arm, pulling him up short. "I can't make you battle-master again," he warned.

Joe stared at his feet. He hadn't expected anything else.

"But I can give you squad leader." Nebil told him. "You lucky sonofabitch."

Giving another wordless nod, Joe waited for Nebil to release him, then followed silently after his groundteam. He ascended the six flights of stairs and stepped inside Sixth Battalion's barracks room with a wave of old familiarity.

Gathered just inside the door, his groundteam was waiting for him.

Maggie reached him first, and threw her arms around him, despite the fact he stank and was drenched in sweat. Monk also hugged him, but the other three stayed back, waiting for the younger girls to finish.

"Hey guys," Joe said. It was all he could do to keep his voice from cracking. His eyes caught on the youngest boy. "Hey Elf," he added, quieter than he meant to. Elf lowered his gaze and looked away. Around him, everyone fell into an uncomfortable silence. The youngest kids began to fidget. Elf wouldn't meet his eyes.

"Was it bad?" Scott finally asked.

"Yeah." Joe choked, feeling tears threaten. He looked away. "But it's over. How's it been for you guys?"

But Scott wasn't finished. "You're so scarred up I didn't recognize you until Maggie pointed you out. What'd they *do* to you?"

"I can't tell you anything Elf hasn't already told you."

"He doesn't talk about it," Maggie said, giving Elf an accusing look. "He doesn't want to talk about anything."

Silently, Elf turned and went back to bed without even glancing back.

"He doesn't have to if he doesn't want to," Joe said, watching him. Elf's body was worse off than his own, the Takki's claw-marks covering every inch of skin, leaving puckered pink valleys everywhere except on his hands. Elf picked up his boots and began cleaning them, and did not look up again.

Joe turned to Libby, since she was the only one who wasn't staring at him like he was some sort of ghost. Clearing his throat, he tried again, "So what happened while I was gone?"

Too late, he remembered the lifeless lump of flesh on the ground beside her feet. He bit his lip as she merely shook her head.

"She can only talk on the headcom," Maggie said.

"I'll help you pay for surgery," Joe said. "As soon as we get out of here."

"Me, too!" Maggie said.

"And me," Scott said.

"How much will it cost?" Monk asked.

"Does it matter?!" Maggie cried.

"Yes," Monk retorted.

As they were arguing, Joe peeled off his sweat-soaked layers of purple robes and threw them into a soggy pile in the corner of the room. Briefly, he wondered if somewhere in his gear the Congies had given him a lighter. The robes, just like everything else about the Takki, deserved to burn.

"Does anyone know where I can get some matches?" Joe asked.

It was then that Joe realized that the barracks had fallen into a deathly silence. When he turned, everyone was staring at his scars with mixed looks of horror and pity. Joe swallowed and quickly shrugged into a black Congie shirt. "It's nothing," he said. "Don't worry about it."

"The *Dhasha* did that?" Maggie whispered.

"Nah, it was Takki," Joe managed. "Knaaren couldn't touch us without killing us, so he had his lizards do it for him."

"Didn't they give you nanos?" Monk demanded.

Joe grimaced wryly. "Knaaren doesn't like the way nanos taste."

Scott was the first one to speak. "We'll make sure you don't go back."

Joe felt embarrassed and grateful at the same time. He just nodded.

"You look like a tiger danced on your back," Maggie said.

"With its claws out," Monk added. "Tigers have retractable claws."

"Shut up, Monk, they do not."

"Do *too!*"

Libby elbowed Scott, who cleared his throat.

"Joe, things got real bad while you were gone. Tril put Sasha back in charge. Knaaren's acting really weird—he ate another Ooreiki a few days ago. That got all the Congies mad and the battlemasters are being ashers to everybody."

"Tell him about the boys," Monk said.

Scott stared at his feet, looking embarrassed. "At night, some of the boys from other battalions are getting together looking for girls. The youngest kids are acting really weird." Scott let out his breath between his teeth. "It's scary, Joe."

"The drugs made their bodies too big and their brains too small," Monk explained. "You saw Escobar. He's five and a half and he just now realized he had a cock. They're usually the ones running around at night, and if they catch you out there, you're in trouble."

Maggie nodded, looking genuinely frightened.

Joe was sad at how fast they were being forced to grow up. "Then nobody's leaving the barracks after lights-out. Any idea who's leading them?"

"Sure," Monk said, then she went on to describe Bailey perfectly, right down to the cleft in his chin. Toward the end, Joe noticed that Libby was watching Monk with a slight frown.

"I'll deal with it," Joe said. "Until then, get some sleep." He led the way toward the huge, circular bed.

Libby caught his arm as he moved toward the bed. Joe looked up—disconcerted by the fact that they were almost eye-to-eye. Libby hugged him. When she pulled back, her gaze promised they would talk later. Then, ignorant to his sudden, rock-hard boner, she slid into bed with the others.

When Joe turned toward the bathing chamber, Maggie called out, "I thought you were going to bed, Joe!"

"I need a bath," Joe said, which was the truth. He spent the next twenty seconds jacking off in the relative privacy behind the door. He couldn't actually *shut* the door because Battlemaster Nebil had promised horrible consequences to anyone who got caught inside with it closed. Then he spent a good half an hour getting clean, rubbing the accumulated grime from his skin until the alcohol burned and his eyes were watering.

When he finally returned, his skin was red and stinging and he smelled like a medical sterilizing pad, but at least he felt clean. As he approached the groundteam's bed, he saw that everyone was already asleep. He breathed a sigh of relief and stripped off his shirt.

"Nice," a voice said behind him.

Joe flinched and turned. Sasha sat on one end of her groundteam's bed, holding something silver in her hands. She was grinning at him, her smile full of contempt.

"Congratulations on getting battlemaster again," Joe said stiffly.

"Couldn't have done it without you." She held up the lesson pad that Nebil had given him.

Instantly, Joe felt a flash of rage, realizing why he hadn't been able to find it. "*You* took it?"

"It's mine now." She tucked it under a leg. "*I'm* battlemaster. *I'm* the one who needs it."

Joe took several steps toward her. He meant to quietly tell her what he thought of her so he wouldn't wake the rest of the recruits, but Sasha immediately reached for something hidden between the folds of her blanket. Joe froze, watching her.

Sasha gave pause, hand on whatever it was between her blankets. When he did not move any closer, she gave another nasty grin and pulled out the knife Congress had issued her. "Afraid I'll add another scar to that pretty collection of yours, Zero?"

"That's what you were gonna do, wasn't it?" Joe stayed back, wary. "Why are you sleeping with that thing? Nebil's got the door locked. Second can't get in here."

Sasha snorted. "It's not them I'm worried about. It's the ones already in here."

"You mean Sixth?" Joe was baffled. "Nobody's gonna—"

"Mario did," Sasha spat. "He grabbed Katie out of her bed and raped her in the showers while everyone else was asleep."

Joe felt a reflexive rise in his gorge. "It won't happen while I'm here."

Sasha's smile was malicious. "I saw how hard you got when Libby hugged you. Does she know you want to screw her brains out? Maybe I should tell her."

Joe's face darkened. "I'd never do that." *Bitch.* "Ever."

Sasha gave a careless shrug. "Maybe. But you can't control your cock and I'm gonna get you neutered."

She's just a child, Joe thought. *She doesn't know what she's saying.* He turned his back on her.

"I could plant this blade right between your shoulder-blades," Sasha said. "Right in your spine. Not even the Congies could help you, then."

"You do that," Joe said, walking back to his own bed. "Commander Tril would probably give you a medal." Without another word, he crawled in under the blankets with his groundmates, as far from Sasha as he could get.

Sleep came slowly. His body was still on constant, Takki-inspired alert. After Tril's exhibition on the plaza, it took him hours to wind down, hours of staring at the ceiling and jerking at the slightest noise around him.

Most of the noises came from Elf. Even in sleep, his groundmate's scarred brow pinched in a frown. His body twitched continuously and small, tiny sounds escaped his lips.

He was with Knaaren a lot longer than I was, Joe realized, feeling a stab of pity for his friend. *But he won't go back. He's got his whole life to heal.*

· · ·

As the next few weeks went by, Joe gradually eased back into the life of a recruit. He even found himself opening his mouth to give his platoon a command, only to shut it again when he realized Sasha was back in charge. He felt at a loss, marching in formation after he had led it from outside. Watching Sasha give bad commands was even worse. The hunts especially. Sure, she sometimes came up with new and interesting ways to baffle the enemy, but only because someone whispered it into her ear. And usually *that* came from Libby or Joe, both of whom were on Sasha's permanent shit-list and had to run their ideas through Maggie or Scott before Sasha would take them seriously.

Joe, frustrated, usually did something that Sasha could punish him for, so he spent all of his free time at work with chores Sasha had assigned him.

It was the same this afternoon. When the rest of the platoon was enjoying a half-day from a successful inspection with Lord Knaaren, Sasha had ordered Joe and Libby to rearrange the barracks until they were spotless, every item in its place, every fold crisp, every blanket perfectly aligned. Libby was at work near Sasha's locker and Joe was on the other side of the room, neatening a group of rifles, when Libby made a strangled sound and held up a deep den flag.

Joe frowned at her, his first thought that, should an Ooreiki come in and see it, they would be accused of trying to cheat in the hunts. Then, when he drew closer, he realized it belonged to Second Battalion. He hadn't seen a flag like that since losing one in the tunnels.

"Where did you get that?" Joe asked.

Libby's face was a thunderstorm as she pointed to Sasha's locker.

"Where'd she get it?" Joe asked. "We haven't had our hands on a flag since—" A tiny frown came over his face as he moved forward to inspect the flag. The little tear it had undertaken from Sasha and Maggie tugging on it was still visible in the fabric, along with a thick coating of tunnel dust.

Libby nodded at his look, her lips compressed in fury.

"Now wait a minute," Joe said, taking the flag from Libby and holding it up. "We don't know how she got this."

Yes we do. She stole it. Just like she stole my reader.

Apparently, Libby thought the same thing, because she threw down her cleaning rag and stormed out of the room. Joe hesitated, staring down at the material in his hands.

Everything would have been different if she hadn't taken it. Hot rage began to make his intestines burn. What kind of person would steal something that would mean a reward for everyone if they had kept it safe? Something that would actually get an entire platoon into trouble if they didn't have it?

A psychopath bitch, that's who. Joe's fingers fisted in the flag and he went to find Libby before she killed her.

That night, as the platoon was getting together for storytime, Joe and his groundteam approached Sasha's bed and tossed the flag down in front of her.

"How could you be so burning stupid?"

Sasha's eyes lit up with anger. "You can't call your battlemaster stupid."

"You're not my battlemaster."

Sasha drew her knife and held it between them.

In one effortless motion, Libby disarmed her and threw her to the floor, twisting the knife backwards by the blade like she was about to throw it.

"Libby, no!" Joe shouted.

Libby made a disgusted snort and slung the knife across the room. Sasha was crying on the floor, holding her wrist. No one moved to help her.

"No one's gonna help you ever again, you bitch," Monk said.

And it was true.

Everyone in the platoon watched coldly as Sasha picked herself up, her expression changing from fear to anger. Thankfully, she didn't waste her breath trying to make them all do pushups. She simply gave them an acerbic glare and returned to her groundteam.

Joe watched her hobble away. *She's never going to have anyone's respect after this,* Joe thought. Her groundteam, upon Sasha's return, turned away and found other places to sleep, leaving her utterly alone.

Joe tore his eyes from the lonely figure on the bed. *Not that she ever did.*

• • •

The next day, Battlemaster Nebil took them through a bout of training that left everyone gasping for air, hacking up chunks of red ferlii spores that had lodged in their lungs. Their next offensive against Second Battalion was tomorrow, and Commander Tril had ordered his battlemasters to step up their training to prepare. It felt ludicrous to Joe, since it only left them weak and tired when the actual hunt dawned, but he dared not risk Tril's wrath a second time by mentioning it.

After Nebil had dismissed them, Sasha gave the groundteams tasks to finish before they could return to the chow hall for the evening meal. Joe's groundteam bore the responsibility of wiping down the entire barracks room before they could go to eat. While the others began cleaning around the beds, Joe began wiping down the bathing chamber. It was the most unpleasant part, since the alcohol fumes were suffocating and the air made his eyes burn.

Sasha's voice from the entrance surprised him. "Be sure you get that corner behind the door. All sorts of…" she hesitated, looking at his crotch, "…*disgusting* stuff winds up back there."

Joe clenched the rag in a fist, eyes glued to the knife in her hand. The familiar rush of adrenaline began etching his veins.

Seeing his nervousness, Sasha grinned at him. "I sent the rest of them to chow. So we could talk."

Joe had a pretty good idea what her idea of 'talk' was going to entail, and he surreptitiously began wrapping the rag around his fist, in case he needed to grab the knife.

Sasha stopped two yards away from him, but didn't get any closer. "Did it feel good to tell everybody about the flag, Zero?"

Joe waited. Even with a knife he doubted she could overpower him. Still, he wanted to avoid getting stabbed if he could help it. Getting stabbed hurt.

"You think you're so great," Sasha said. "Bigger than me, stronger than me…you took battlemaster from me and then you thought it was funny watching me do all those pushups. Well, I'm the battlemaster now. Start doing pushups."

Joe eyed the knife. "No."

Sasha gripped the weapon more tightly, looking both angry and exhilarated that he had not obeyed her. "You have to. I'm your battlemaster."

"I haven't done anything wrong."

"You did too. You disobeyed me today in front of Battlemaster Nebil."

"And I'm paying the price for that right now." Joe turned his back to her and went back to cleaning the walls.

"I'll tell the battlemaster you wouldn't do pushups," she said lamely.

Joe sighed deeply. "I might if I didn't think you'd try and stab me as soon as I got on the floor." Her flinch made him realize that she had planned to do just that. He grimaced. "Just go find someone else to screw with, all right, Sasha? I'm too tired for your gutless furgsoot right now." Joe went back to cleaning the walls.

For a long time, Sasha said nothing. Then, "You're such an asher."

"Yup." He was not even listening.

"I gave you back your knife and asked for your help, but I was just a girl and you were a big, bad, fourteen-year-old boy who could kick anybody's butt on the ship. I thought we were gonna starve 'cause I only had one boy in my team and you didn't care."

Joe flushed and turned back to her. "If I'd thought you were in trouble, I would've helped."

"But not just if I ask, right?" Sasha demanded, eyes glittering. "You're gonna wait until you can be the hero. That's what you think you are. A hero."

Joe felt himself clench the rag. "That's where you're wrong." He tugged up the front of his shirt to show her his scars. "Would a hero have these? Would he have let a Dhasha take him as a *slave*, Sasha? No. A hero would've fought them. He would've died before picking dead skin from under that monster's scales. Sasha, if I wanted to be a hero, I wouldn't have spent two weeks looking at the floor and hoping they didn't kill me."

Sasha's eyes flickered across the puckered scars crisscrossing his chest, then looked away.

Joe dropped his shirt. "Bad things are happening to all of us. I didn't deserve to go to Knaaren and you didn't deserve to be ignored when you were most scared. But believe me, stealing from people and threatening them with knives isn't gonna solve things."

Sasha would not meet his eyes.

"I'm here if you need a friend," Joe said. "That's what you want, isn't it?"

Her head came up suddenly, eyes bright. She almost looked…hopeful. And desperate. She opened her mouth, and for a split second, Joe thought she'd say yes. Then her face darkened. "Just stay away from me," Sasha said. "Or I'll cut off your burning dick like you deserve." She spun and left him alone again.

Watching her go, Joe felt something tugging on his soul.

He was almost done by the time his groundteam found him. Joe felt a swelling of gratitude as every one of them grabbed a rag to help him.

When they were finished, Maggie brought Joe his helmet. Joe stared at it, uncomprehending.

"So we can *talk*," Maggie insisted, pointing at Libby. The others had already put theirs on.

"Oh…" Joe took a moment to fasten the straps over his ears, then cleared his throat. "Can you hear me?"

"Loud and clear." Joe recognized Libby's voice and turned to her, startled. She was smiling, but her lips weren't moving.

"Nebil got her one that reads her mind," Maggie said, obviously in awe. *"Isn't that cool, Joe?"*

Joe felt another stab of gratitude to his battlemaster. "So these things are accepting all frequencies, now?" he asked tentatively.

"Yeah," Scott replied. *"After the first couple of hunts, they activated all ground leaders' helmets, then a couple of hunts after that, they did everybody's. It's a lot better when everybody can tell everybody else what's going on."*

"Gets frustrating, though," Libby said. *"Not everyone knows when to shut up. The frequency gets pretty blocked up with stupid soot. Sometimes you just wanna strangle some of them."*

Joe felt himself smile. "So are you guys looking forward to the hunt tomorrow?"

"Tril's gonna blow up again," Libby replied, grimacing. *"He always does."*

"He gave sixty recruits the Fourth Degree last time," Maggie said. *"They accidentally let a squad from Second Battalion sneak into the deep den they were guarding. If it wasn't for Libby, we would've lost our flag, but he punished her, too."*

"He did?" Joe glanced at Libby. "And you saved the flag?"

Libby shrugged, but Joe saw the anger in her face. *"Saw group go down hole near edge of clearing. Didn't hear for time, so figured they moving in on den. Took groundteam, went to closest one, hid in far tunnel. Showed up minutes later, deep den. Kept pinned. Reinforcements arrived."*

"She talks like that because it's hard for her to concentrate when she's angry," Maggie explained. *"You can't use a headcom good if you're angry. If you can't understand her, tell her to slow down and think harder."*

"*Thanks, Maggie,*" Libby said. "*Remind me you said that next time you get your tongue cut out.*"

"*See?*" Maggie said. "*That sounds a lot better.*"

Across the room, Libby made a disgusted noise, but Joe was disquieted. Tentatively, he said, "*Libby, who did that to you?*"

The tone in the room immediately became sullen.

Libby's face twisted. "*Nobody, Joe. Don't worry about it.*"

"Was it Second Battalion?"

"*Who cares? It's over with. My legs healed and I can walk as good as new. A few years from now, I'll go buy myself another tongue. Soot happens.*"

"Not to my groundteam," Joe said. "Not soot like that." He wondered if something else had happened to her that day, something her assailant had cut out her tongue to keep secret. He felt a ball of disgust and rage building in the pit of his gut. *Someday, I'll find the bastard and kill him.*

Libby snorted. "*We're going to war, Joe. Get over it.*" At that, she lifted the helmet off her head and left the room.

"She say anything about it to you guys?" Joe asked, once she was gone.

"No," Maggie admitted.

"I wonder why she won't tell us," Joe said, frowning after her.

Elf suddenly threw his headcom on the bed and followed Libby out.

"Elf!" Joe called. Elf ignored him.

"He hasn't said more than four words to anyone since Battlemaster Nebil brought him back from Knaaren," Scott said, sounding irritated. "He came back a little crazy, Joe. A couple times, I caught him hiding in a corner, saying something about a ship over and over."

"He talks about ships in his dreams, too," Monk said. "Did Knaaren put you on a ship, Joe?"

"No," Joe said, frowning. "I barely left the tower."

"Well, *something* happened," Scott said. "He's been acting really funny. I caught him hiding scum soup in the pockets of his vest three times now. Just shoving it in there, covering everything else in the pockets. Said he was saving it for later."

"Maybe he's not getting enough to eat," Maggie suggested.

Joe remembered the nine women Knaaren had brought over from Earth and wondered if Elf had seen them come off the ship. Maybe Knaaren had even tried putting Elf in with them. Anything could have happened in those days before Joe and Elf switched places.

Joe mulled over that as he and the others finished the bathing chambers in silence.

Back in the barracks, Joe paused before undressing for bed. Sasha was gone, and she had taken several of the other groundteams with her. Joe just hoped she got caught before Nebil came to lock up.

"We've got to get her to stop doing that," Joe said. "It's only going to make things worse."

"I hate her," Monk muttered. "Let's just hope someone catches her and screws her brains out so you can lead the platoon tomorrow."

"Hey!" Joe snapped, disgusted with Monk. "She's your battlemaster! Show a little more respect."

"Why?" Monk asked, obviously puzzled. "You don't." The others were looking at him, clearly wondering the same thing.

"She's just a kid," Joe said. "She doesn't deserve anything like that."

"Yeah she does," Monk said. "She's asking for it every time she goes out at night."

"She just needs a few years to grow up," Joe said.

"She needs to die," Monk said. "That would help her."

Joe sighed. There was no arguing with a six-year-old. He tugged off his shirt and climbed into bed. He caught Libby staring at his scars again before he hid them with the blanket. He cleared his throat. "Don't worry about it, right?" he said softly.

Libby's brown eyes flickered up from his chest. She was scowling.

"Who cares?" Joe gave her a weak smile. "Soot happens."

The corner of Libby's mouth twitched. She nodded.

• • •

"Look, it's the Elf."

"Don't call me Elf."

"Why not? Don't like it? Too bad, because you look like you just stepped out of a mushroom. Where's your fairy dust, Elf? Still don't have it?

Guess we'll have to take your Fruit Roll-Up, instead." Greg reached forward and yanked the paper bag out of Eric's hand. He peeked inside. "Another peanut-butter sandwich? Doesn't your mom love you, Elf?"

"She does!" Eric cried, jumping for the bag. The other boys hooted and Greg lifted it out of reach.

"Then what's with the peanut-butter and bananas? You an elephant or something?"

"Elephants eat hay," Eric said. "Not peanut-butter."

"Oh, that's right. Your mom works at the *zoo*, cleaning up animal crap. Guess she would know what to feed you, huh? What you figure he is, guys? A monkey? Monkeys eat bananas, right? Act like a monkey, Elf, and I'll give you the rest of your lunch back."

Eric bit his lip, peering up at Greg. The older boy had freckles, but did not have the happy face Eric normally associated with freckles. From the first day he met Greg Riley, freckles would always be tainted in his mind, combined with cold blue eyes and a cruel sneer.

"You won't eat lunch today unless you do it," Greg warned.

Eric ignored him, turning away.

"Fine," Greg said. He threw the paper bag on the ground and stomped on it.

"Leave him alone, you little dickweed." It was a girl's voice, someone a lot older. Eric looked up. She towered over both him and Greg, looking like she could drop-kick either one of them without even an effort. Eric stared up at her in awe.

"We were just having fun," Greg muttered, looking up at the girl. "Later, Elf."

"*My name's Eric!*" he screamed after them. They laughed and kept walking. Limbs trembling, Eric bent and picked up his paper bag. It was damp where the banana had smashed on the inside. The sandwich was no better off. It had a big footprint in the center, where Greg's shoe had flattened it.

"You know, if you didn't let it bother you, they'd stop."

Eric glanced up at the girl behind him. She was watching him with a mixture of pity and concern. He sniffed and stuffed his squished lunch back inside the bag.

"I think Elf is a cool name. You ever thought about having a nickname?"

Eric stared at her. "That's what the bullies call me."

"So? In the stories, elves have magical powers. If you were a real elf, you could work a spell to give Greg a third leg."

"I'd put it right on his face, where his nose would be."

The girl smiled and ruffled his hair. "There you go. Think about that every time he calls you Elf. See, he's actually giving you a compliment. He thinks you could have magic."

Eric felt his eyes widen. When she wasn't working, his mom read him stories about magic towers and knights who rescued pretty princesses and dragons and witches and good wizards and enchanted kingdoms. He felt himself grow stronger, almost like he could lift twice as much as he could before. He glanced down at the mashed remains of his lunch and smiled anyway. *Elf. I could be an elf. Like in Mom's stories.*

Someday, when he was older, maybe he would see dragons.

29

NIGHT TERRORS

The hunt the next day ended in humiliating defeat. Sixth Battalion was too exhausted from Tril's drills the day before to mount much of an offense, and Second was bright-eyed and quick to pick off careless attackers, doubtlessly due to a good rest beforehand.

Tril, as expected, called out a huge portion of recruits for real or imagined failures and punished them in front of the battalion. Then he sent them all to the barracks without that evening's meal.

That night, the mood in the barracks was sour.

"We're not gonna have the energy to run down the tunnels if he won't even feed us!" Carl said. "What's he expect us to do? Starve *and* win the hunts?"

"Second Battalion had it easy," Scott said. "All they had to do was hole up in the towers and pick us off. How were we supposed to know there were gonna be snipers?"

"We weren't," Joe muttered. "Lagrah was planning on ambushing us all along."

"I hear Second gets double rations and two hours of liberty every time they beat us," Carl said. "What do we get? More pushups."

"They're eating our food?" Maggie whimpered. "That's not fair."

Joe added his agreement to the others sitting around his bed. It had become a sort of rebel hotspot—over the last three hours, at least thirty recruits had voiced their disgust for their commander and for the Second Battalion pansies in general. Aside from Sasha, who was sulking in her own bed, the general consensus was that Sixth was the better battalion, but they were being worked too hard to prove it.

"So why don't we go *show* them?" Maggie demanded. "You can open the door, Joe. I've seen you do it."

"Yeah!" Scott cried. "Maybe some haven't been locked up for the night. We could ambush them!"

"Who says we can't just invade their barracks?" Joe asked. "Do this right, instead of sneaking around half-assed?" When they just stared at him, he said, "Come on, guys, think about it. Why should we hunker down *hoping* to catch maybe one or two kids, when we could take out a whole *platoon*?"

Every kid in the room went silent, staring at him, their mouths open.

"Their battlemasters sleep on a separate level," Joe went on. "I can get us in. We could have the whole barracks to ourselves."

"The *barracks*?" Maggie asked, wide-eyed. She was the first to regain her composure. "But if we get caught in the wrong barracks, they'd make us run…"

"We already run," Scott pointed out. "More than we should. I heard one of the medics tell Nebil that he should watch for heart failure."

Heart failure? Joe frowned at that. What kind of sane commander would put them on a routine that could produce heart failure? And none of them were over fifteen!

"They call us the Sick Battalion from hacking up spores," Scott continued. "They'd stop laughing at us if we captured one of their platoons."

"If we're gonna do this," Joe said, "Why stop at just one platoon? If we can sneak into one, why can't we sneak into all of them?"

"So you want to get the rest of Sixth involved?" Scott asked, sounding excited.

"No," Joe said. "Let's do it ourselves. Just Fourth Platoon. We'll take them on one barracks room at a time. Tie them up in their sleep, draw a big X on their forehead, maybe take their clothes. Show them who they're dealing with."

"Not an X," Maggie cried, delighted. "It should be a Zero!"

Joe immediately winced at the idea of putting '0s' on faces, pretty sure he knew who would be doing the running, then. Then again, an X could mean anything…

"The *whole regiment?*" Monk whispered.

"No," Joe said, deciding. "That would take too long. Just Second Battalion. They're getting too proud of themselves."

"So you'll go with us, Joe?" Maggie asked, gleeful.

"After today? Hell yeah," Joe said, still fuming that Tril had withheld their food. "Those pricks need to be taken down a few pegs."

"What about Commander Tril?" Monk asked. "He'll be pissed."

"I'm tired, hungry, and Commander Tril can kiss my ass," Joe replied.

"I'll tell him if you go anywhere," Sasha said, her voice ringing out loud and clear. When they turned, she cast them a sweet smile from her bed. "We're not supposed to leave the barracks, *remember*, Zero?"

Libby and Joe glanced at each other.

Joe cleared his throat. "But this could really work, Sasha."

Sasha sighed and began trimming her nails with her knife. "You know the rules, Joe. I'm your battlemaster. I say you stay, you stay."

Joe gave Scott and Libby a pointed look. "We could really use your help in this," he told Sasha.

"I said no," Sasha said. "You keep begging and I'll go right now and tell him. Tril will have you all running laps for days if he finds out you want to—" She let out a sudden squeak as Libby sprang forward and grabbed her knife wrist. In one swift motion, Libby disarmed Sasha and stuck the blade under her belt.

"Well," Joe said, amused by the startled look on Sasha's face, "If you're not with us, you're against us. Maybe you can help us practice."

Sasha's wide-eyed look flickered to him, then back to Libby. "Give it back."

Libby shrugged and turned away. Sasha tried to jump on her, but Joe got between them. Monk and Maggie were on her in an instant, and as Sasha struggled, they bound their recruit battlemaster hand and foot, gagged her, and tucked her beneath the covers. When they were finished, only her head was above the covers, her eyes filled with murder.

"Hey," Monk said, "Whaddaya know? She's actually kind of cute when she's not acting like a bitch." She leaned forward and tweaked Sasha's nose. Everyone laughed.

"Leave her alone," Joe said. "We're in enough trouble as it is."

"Well," Monk said, "If we're already in trouble…" She pulled an indelible black marker from her vest and leaned forward long enough to draw a mustache on her disabled battlemaster. The entire barracks burst out in laughter at Sasha's feeble struggles.

"Quiet!" Joe ordered. "You want Nebil to hear us? Monk, stop it. Save your ink for Second Battalion."

Monk tucked the marker back in her vest and admired her handiwork, apparently oblivious to the smoldering look of hatred Sasha was giving her.

"Let's go," Joe said. The way Sasha was staring at Monk was making Joe's skin prickle. "We've only got another six hours before wakeup."

Joe opened the door for them and they quietly snuck from the barracks and down the stairs, walking lightly upon the stairwells to avoid waking the Takki sleeping inside the honeycombed hollows. They stopped at the second level of the barracks and circled around the huge balcony wrapping around the building to the sleeping chamber of Second Battalion's First Platoon. The other kids waited nervously as Joe entered the code—1-1-2, or First Platoon, First Company, Second Battalion—then they stepped inside the first of Second Battalion's ten platoon barracks rooms unimpeded. Everyone inside was sleeping. They hadn't even bothered to post a guard.

Not that we ever post a guard, either, Joe thought. They would have to consider that after their prank was over, in case Second Battalion thought to retaliate.

Disabling them was almost too easy. With all of Second Battalion's recruits sleeping, Joe's platoon went bed by bed, stifling their victims' shouts with hands over mouths as they gagged and bound them. Monk and Maggie did the honors of drawing a big '0' on the forehead of each of the recruits they subdued. Looking at the bedfuls of 'dead' recruits, Joe knew his platoon was going to be in trouble in the morning. Right now, however, he didn't care.

He was having too much fun.

Like wraiths, Fourth Platoon filed out of the room and padded out onto the balcony. There, they threw down all the boots and clothes they had collected from their victims, leaving a pile of black on the stone that a handful of their group spirited away.

"Okay, the next one," Joe whispered, once they'd completely ransacked their victims' barracks.

Second Platoon, too, went off completely without a hitch. And Third. And Fourth.

By the time they got back to the barracks, they'd successfully visited all ten of Second Battalion's platoons and it was only minutes before Battlemaster Nebil was due to wake them that morning. Joe led the other recruits back to their own barracks still riding the rush of excitement and adrenaline, feeling like he'd slept all night. He actually felt a rush of pride as the rest of Fourth Platoon deposited their last armloads of stolen clothes in the bottom of the baths and went to crawl into bed. Everyone was grinning and chatting with pent up enthusiasm, telling stories and giggling. Nobody, Joe knew, was going to do any sleeping. He stopped at Sasha's bed.

"I'm gonna untie you," Joe said.

Sasha's eyes burned with malevolence.

"But," Joe said, "I want you to think long and hard about whether or not you're gonna tell Battlemaster Nebil about this. Do you really want to admit to him that your entire platoon—even your own groundteam—tied you up and left you here while they went to fight Second Battalion?"

Monk came to stand beside him and grinned down at Sasha. "In case you're too stupid to get it, you don't want that, because as soon as he finds out what a crappy leader you are, he'll put Joe back in charge."

Sasha flushed a deep red, then looked away. Joe cut her loose, then handed her knife back to her, handle-first. She took it slowly, and for a second, Joe thought she might try to use it on him, but she tucked it back under her pillow, instead. Then she gave them a cold sneer filled with hatred. "You're all gonna be sorry."

"Nice mustache," Monk said.

"Get to bed, Monk," Joe said. "She won't tell." He crawled under the covers and lay there, waiting for Nebil to arrive. Despite the sleepless night, he couldn't lie still. He saw the other recruits were having the same problem. Everyone was grinning and laughing about the night's adventure, the whole platoon in an entirely different mood than eight hours before. Lying there listening to it, Joe felt a swell of pride that he had been able to help restore their spirits so thoroughly.

When Nebil arrived, everyone jumped out of their groundteam beds immediately, fully dressed and wide awake.

The battlemaster hung back in the doorway, his eyes wary. "What's going on? Why are you all awake?"

"Just happy to see you," Joe said, grinning, feeling like himself for the first time since stepping out of Knaaren's den.

Nebil eyed the other recruits, then his gaze fell back to Joe. "Furgsoot. What did you charheads do?"

He found out soon enough. A frantic Battlemaster Gokli came up to them in the middle of marching drills, asking if Nebil had seen any extra cammies lying about.

"Cammies?" Nebil asked, giving the other battlemaster a quizzical look.

"Some thieves crept into the barracks last night and stole some of our gear," Gokli said. "Just a minor inconvenience, that's all."

"They crept *into* your barracks?" Nebil asked. "You didn't lock up?"

"They unlocked the door," Gokli said briskly.

"To steal gear?"

"They tied up a few recruits, too," Gokli said. "Graffitied on Congressional property… Nothing major."

"What kind of graffiti?"

Gokli's sudah looked like they were going to fly away. "They drew on our recruit's faces. Indelible ink. The kind issued for marking on maps in hostile climates."

"Really?" Nebil asked calmly. "How many recruits?"

"We think an entire platoon was involved in last night's crimes," Battlemaster Gokli growled.

"No," Nebil corrected. "How many recruits were graffitied?"

The other battlemaster made a grunting sound. "If you see any spare gear lying around, let us know. Right now, we've got our recruits wearing defenders' whites."

"How horrible."

"Yeah. Uh. You didn't happen to notice anything strange with your recruits this morning, did you? My recruits all agree that the attackers wore their uniforms in your…unique…manner." He nodded at Fourth Platoon's rolled sleeves.

Battlemaster Nebil replied with a deadpan look that he had seen absolutely nothing out of usual that morning, that perhaps some other platoon was imitating them in order to get them into trouble. Then, as soon as Battlemaster Gokli left, Nebil turned on them in a fury. "You stupid self-molesting furgs! Was the whole Battalion involved or just you sootbags?!"

"Just us, Battlemaster," Joe said.

Battlemaster Nebil's slitty eyes homed in on Joe in an instant. "You. Zero. You sootwad. What did you do?"

"We assaulted the enemy's barracks and detained them for questioning, sir," Joe replied, finding it hard to keep a straight face.

Battlemaster Nebil gave him a flat look. "You what?"

"We tied them up and drew on their faces."

"How many of them?" Nebil demanded.

"All of them, sir." Several recruits around him snickered.

For a moment, Nebil stared at him as if he had not heard. Then, slowly, he said, "Where are their clothes?"

"Submerged in the baths in our barracks, sir," Joe replied.

Nebil glanced at the sky. For a long time, he simply watched the reddish clouds, looking like he was counting. Then, dragging his head back down to face them, Nebil said, "You furgs better pray they're too stupid to look there. If they don't catch you before tonight, I want all their clothes dumped inside the chow hall and left there. If anyone sees you, I'll skin your fire-loving hides. Until then, you earned yourselves an extra hour of free time. Get out of here."

• • •

After their assault on Second Battalion, Joe began leading a nightly raid on the enemy, sparing no one. Every morning, several more platoons were found with a '0' scrawled across their foreheads. As long as Joe and the others were back in their beds by wake-up, Nebil quietly ignored their nightly excursions. He even supplied them with new markers when they ran out of ink.

Joe and Sasha came to a sort of understanding after the first night. As long as Joe followed her commands during the hunts, she kept her mouth shut and sometimes even went with him on the night raids. The other members of Joe's ground team—notably Libby and Monk—refused to speak with him on these occasions, of the opinion that they should leave her behind, but Joe was determined to mend the rift between them and let Sasha come anyway.

Joe was having more fun than he'd ever had in his life, and for the first time, he felt like he really had a purpose. For their part, Fourth Platoon followed him religiously on the raids. Even during the daytime, battlemasters from other platoons asked his advice on the deep den hunts. And, for the first time since coming to Kophat, Joe felt like he really had a purpose in life.

To *lead*.

He was good at it. The way the kids followed him made Joe's chest swell with pride. Each night he took them on a raid, he fantasized about leading them into the deepest, darkest Dhasha tunnels to root out a rebel prince and win the war. Even the thought of small spaces didn't quell his fantasies.

For the first time, Joe realized he *wanted* to be a soldier. He *wanted* to lead a squad on some rebel planet. He *wanted* to secure the win that turned the tide of a battle.

He wanted to be a hero.

30

ELF'S RELEASE

Tril stifled a chuckle at seeing Lagrah's assistant. The girl had apparently been sleeping in the barracks when Nebil's platoon had struck. A fading '0' stood out on her forehead in a childish scrawl.

Lagrah's recruit turned beet red under Tril's stare, though she continued to hold her message out for Tril to accept. As expected, it was another invitation to a hunt. Lagrah's pride had been wounded and only blood would ease his fury.

Excellent.

Tril nodded at the recruit battlemaster, who hurried from the room.

"It's burning hard to miss, isn't it?" Commander Linin asked. "Who do you think is leading them?"

"Zero," Tril said reluctantly.

"Thought so. Everywhere the Fourth goes, heads burning turn," Commander Linin said, nodding. "It's like every other battalion out there turns into Takki pussies when they go by. They stand out like a Jreet hit squad."

Tril felt his sudah flutter excitedly. "Really?"

Commander Linin grunted the affirmative. "Makes me burning proud to see it, I tell you."

As Tril watched the recruit battlemaster hurry away, an idea began to form...

Joe was resting against a glistening black wall, enjoying one of the first moments of true free time he'd had since the hunts with Second Battalion started. He had finished his task of unloading a haauk laden with prepackaged scum soup and was now taking the moment to close his eyes and give his aching body a break.

That morning, Commander Tril had made the announcement that all of Sixth Battalion was now required to roll up their sleeves. Fourth Platoon, Joe included, believed *they* had earned the sleeves, not the rest of the battalion. The complaining that followed had gotten them neck-deep in extra chores, with no end in sight.

Further, Tril's stepped-up training had been taking its toll. Even with the green slime Congress was feeding them, Joe was now feeling a constant, underlying exhaustion in everything that he did. He had even been forced to cut back on the number of nightly raids in favor of more sleep.

Everyone in Sixth was near the end of their resources, even the battlemasters. Joe didn't know how much more training they could take.

Joe was in the middle of a blissful, impromptu nap when he heard Elf's whisper.

Joe lunged up, glancing around to see if anyone had caught him sleeping.

"Joe." Elf crouched under a stone staircase, his scarred face twisted and almost unrecognizable in the shadows. An Ooreiki rash spread over half his head from someone's rough handling. His sturdy Congie shirt was ripped at the neckline and he was bleeding from several cuts along his jaw and cheek.

It was Elf's fear that caught Joe's attention. He was afraid for his life—Joe recognized the look from his time with Knaaren. Elf was disheveled, insanity shining in his eyes. He was a totally different person than Joe had seen earlier that morning, when Sasha sent him and Maggie off to rake gravel somewhere deeper in the city.

"What's wrong?" Joe asked, getting to his feet.

Elf licked his lips. His eyes darted to the side, then he said, "You remember how you said you'd take me home if I got you a ship?"

Joe stared, uncomprehending. "What?"

"A ship," Elf said. "You told me to get a ship."

"What are you talking about?" Joe asked. "Did you leave Maggie alone?"

"I found one," Elf said.

"Elf, why aren't you with—"

"I killed her," Elf interrupted.

Joe felt a stab of dread. "What?"

"I killed her. She had this egg sac on her back. Like a burning spider. I could see them wiggling around in there, trying to get out." Elf's eyes were wild, pleading with Joe to understand. "I saw them and I snapped. I couldn't take it anymore. You know what the Takki did to you. They're all aliens, Joe. *Aliens*. Congress doesn't need any more of them. We're the good ones, Joe. Not them. They don't deserve to live."

Slowly, Joe said, "Elf, did you just say you killed Maggie?"

Elf's wild-eyed look grew frustrated. "No, the *pilot*. I killed her and the guard outside. Rammed my knife in her neck and crushed all her maggots with my rake. Now we can all go home."

Joe stared, aghast. "You killed an Ooreiki?"

"Lots and lots of them," Elf said, bobbing his head up and down happily. "Now we can all go home, just like you said, Joe. We've got a ship."

"A ship? What are you burning talking about?"

"Back when we first met. You said you'd take me home if I got you a ship."

Joe did not know what to say. He opened his mouth several times but couldn't find the right words, knowing he was talking to a dead man. Finally, "I don't know how to fly a ship, Elf. None of us do. You know that."

Elf nodded, smiling

"*Elf*," Joe said sharply, "Get out of here. Go hide in the woods. Okay? I'll see if I can find Yuil. Maybe she can help you."

Elf's eyes darkened. "No."

"Elf…" Joe started, moving toward him.

"No," Elf said, backing out of reach. "I'm going on the ship. I need you to fly it for me like you said you would."

Joe stared at Elf in helplessness, wondering how much sanity remained behind his feral eyes. Slowly, he said, "I can't fly a ship, Elf. Only the aliens know how to fly the ships."

Elf jerked, his expression turning to disbelief. "But you said—"

"I never *meant* it," Joe snapped, desperation and fear pushing him over the edge. "I never thought you'd actually *try*. Elf, you've gotta hide."

Elf suddenly sprang from the shadows, his torn lip quivering. *"You were supposed to take care of us!"*

Joe glanced around them to see if anyone had heard. "Elf, listen. Let me take you to the edge of the city. You can hide in the woods…"

"No! Help me, Joe," Elf shouted. "You said you would fly the ship if I found one for you. Now I found one and they're gonna catch me if we don't leave right now! We have to *go*!" Elf reached out to grab his arm. "Maggie ran off, but you can still come."

"You're crazy!" Joe shouted. "I can't help you!"

"Please get me off this planet, Joe," Elf said. The insanity in his eyes was replaced with a shot of fear. "They're gonna kill me."

"You need to hide, Elf." Joe felt a burning in his chest. "I can't fly a ship."

Elf stared at the ground. "I know." The whisper was almost too faint to make out. "I knew it when I killed them. I just couldn't stop. I thought…" He looked up, his hazel eyes bloodshot. "I thought maybe you could help me, Joe."

"I can't," Joe said. "I never could."

"Yeah," Elf said softly. He wiped tears from his eyes. "I learned that when Lord Knaaren took me away. Nobody tried to help me. Everyone was too afraid." He hesitated. "I don't know why I killed them. I just…" His voice cracked and he glanced at the ground. "I'll go now. I don't want to get you in trouble, too." He turned.

"Elf."

His groundmate turned, his hopeful expression that of a little boy's.

"Let me help you hide, Elf."

His friend's face collapsed and he nodded.

It wasn't until he'd left Elf inside the abandoned building at the edge of the city that Joe realized he was shaking. He had no idea how to find Yuil.

• • •

Elf did not return with Maggie that evening and Sasha was punished for it. She, in turn, blamed Joe and gave him pushups, which he did quietly and without complaint.

Joe did not sleep that night. After he had helped Elf hide at the edge of Alishai, he had spent the night hours wandering outside the barracks, doing everything he could think of to catch Yuil's attention. Yuil had never showed.

The next morning, instead of going to the hunt that was scheduled that morning, Battlemaster Nebil told them to leave their guns behind.

"Chins! Form them up outside and march them to the plaza. Prime Commander Knaaren will be there in an hour to inspect you. He's ordered all Ooreiki to stay behind, so pray to your heathen Human gods that you don't catch his attention." He said the last looking at Joe.

Monk tugged on Joe's shirt, her face fearful. "You think Elf—"

"Fourth Platoon!" Sasha interrupted, scowling at Monk. "Get down the stairs, you ignorant furgs!"

As Sasha marched them to the plaza, awful scenarios played through Joe's mind. Any human on the planet was either a slave or a recruit, and either one would be punished for hiding. Still, Joe had given Elf the akarit, and as long as he kept his head down, he should be able to survive until Joe could find Yuil.

Second Battalion was already waiting, looking crisp and professional— as long as one didn't pay too much attention to the fading 0's scrawled across their foreheads. Sasha brought Fourth Platoon into Sixth Battalion's place several yards down the plaza and made a show of making sure none of her charges had untucked shirts or poor stances. Then she fell back into her spot at the head of the platoon and they waited as the rest of Sixth Battalion arrived, their sleeves crisply rolled. Bannerless, with their sleeves rolled, Sixth Battalion stood out sharply amongst the others, giving the impression they didn't follow the rules. Joe caught several recruits from other battalions staring at them as they formed up.

Lord Knaaren appeared much later than he had scheduled. He trotted out in front of the battalions almost two hours past due, his talons throwing diamond gravel into the air. He held a slim black Congie rope between his teeth, dragging something big in his wake.

It took Joe a moment to realize the bundle at the end of the rope was Elf.

Lord Knaaren dropped the rope. Two Takki lifted Elf to his feet. His whole body was covered in welts and scabs, and he had lost his ear and most of his left cheek to alien claws. Both eyes were masses of puffy, bruised flesh, his fingers dark from where the ropes around his wrists had cut off the circulation. Joe suddenly found it hard to breathe.

"I knew the taint stretched beyond Kihgl," Knaaren said. "This Human scum killed a pregnant Ooreiki on her way to Poen to give birth, then stayed out of sight using an extremely rare, highly illegal device while we searched for him. Then, despite carrying an akarit of the highest caliber, he was stupid enough to leave it behind when he went searching for food and water. The Kophati government wants him for murdering the *yeeri*. The Peacemakers want him because of the akarit. But none of that interests me. He is my recruit. They can take their weak, toothless threats and feed them to my Takki. The boy will not be punished."

He's letting him go? Joe felt a brief pang of hope.

Knaaren's rainbow lips peeled away from triangular black teeth as he surveyed Sixth Battalion. "*All* of you will be punished. After you watch him die, the entire regiment will receive the Black Pain of the Sixth Degree... unless one of you comes forward and tells me something that makes sense. Why did this recruit kill the *yeeri*? Where did he get the akarit?"

Joe's hope became despair as the Dhasha's emerald gaze swept over the regiment.

"Release him," Knaaren said.

The Takki moved away from Elf, who swayed on his feet without the support. Knaaren moved up to him and gazed down at him with cold emerald eyes. "Do you have anything to say in your defense?"

"I just wanted a ship," Elf whimpered. His eyelids were sunken into his skull, despite the bruised puffiness of his face.

Seeing that, bile surged in Joe's throat. They had cut out his eyes.

Knaaren cuffed Elf. It was a light blow, but Knaaren's black talons cleaved through the flesh of Elf's shoulder and his left arm fell to the diamond gravel, clinging to his other wrist by the length of rope still binding them together. Elf's mouth formed an O and he stood there for a moment, as if unaware of what had happened. Then he screamed and slapped his hand over his shoulder while shying away from the heavy limb dangling from his wrist. The damage was too much. No sooner had Elf tried to save himself than his skin began turning a deathly pale. He slid to the ground, still gripping his bleeding stump between rigid white fingers.

"Fix it," Knaaren said.

A Takki rushed forward and jammed a needle of the silver stuff into Elf's chest. Almost immediately, the bleeding stopped. Elf lay on the ground, panting.

"Just…wanted…ship. Just a ship."

"I want to know who else is involved in this conspiracy," Knaaren said. "You could not have gotten an akarit on your own. You do not have the resources to pay for one, let alone the connections to find such an item. Who gave it to you?"

Elf tried to stand, but Knaaren stepped on him, razor claws sinking into Elf's chest like it was warm butter. "Answer me," Knaaren said. "Who helped you?!"

"No one," Elf whimpered, his uplifted arm dwarfed by Knaaren's massive leg.

Almost delicately, Lord Knaaren bit off his remaining hand.

Knaaren allowed Elf to scream for a while, then said, "Fix it."

A Takki rushed forward and gave him another dose of nanos.

"I will not allow you to die until you tell me," Knaaren rumbled, his sharklike teeth hovering only inches from Elf's contorted face.

"Please. He didn't help me."

"So there *was* someone!" Knaaren roared. "Who was it? *Who?*"

"I want my mommy," Elf sobbed.

"Answer me, you miserable beast! Who was helping you?!"

"No one helped me," Elf said. "No one."

Joe felt a spear of agony lance his chest. He couldn't watch, but he couldn't look away, either. Half of him wanted to rush forward and confess. The other half feared what Elf would say.

"Slave, punish him."

A Takki standing nearby twisted the dial on a black device resembling Tril's. Elf began to scream.

"Stop."

Sobbing, Elf rolled in the dirt, begging for his mother.

"Tell me who helped you," Knaaren said. "It won't end until you do."

"Nobody helped me!" Elf screamed.

"Punish him. A higher setting."

Joe shuddered at his friend's screams. *I gave him the akarit.* His fingernails bit into his palms and his jaw ached. His chest was a throbbing mass of agony. He took a step forward.

Libby grabbed his arm. She gave a slight shake of her head, eyes hard.

Joe shuddered and closed his eyes as Knaaren's frenzy continued.

"Are you ready to talk? No? Punish him. Stop. Punish him. Stop. This will go on as long as it needs to. *Who was helping you?* Punish him. A higher setting."

"Stop it," Maggie whimpered. "Somebody stop him."

The Dhasha paced around Elf as his Takki hurt him, saliva frothing around his teeth, staining the ground orange. His muscles were twitching as he stalked back and forth, his insane emerald eyes fixed to Elf as he moved, ordering his Takki to hurt him. It continued for almost half an hour, until Commander Lagrah crossed the plaza and stepped into the formation.

"That's enough, Knaaren," Lagrah said. "Even if he knew, he can't answer you now."

By that time, Elf's pleas had devolved into unintelligible, animal babbles.

Knaaren swiveled and rushed the Ooreiki, spraying black dust across the plaza.

Lagrah never moved. He stared fearlessly up into the Dhasha's open maw, his sudah not even flickering. After the Ooreiki met and held

Knaaren's insane gaze for several heartbeats, he said, "He'll haunt you until you die, Knaaren."

The Dhasha made a grating bark of laughter. "Humans have no soul. They cannot haunt me."

"Not him. Kihgl."

The Dhasha took one step backwards, baring its teeth.

Lagrah continued, unperturbed. "You see him, don't you? Where is he right now? Standing over your shoulder? Over mine? Do you hear him whisper to you when you're trying to sleep? What does he say?" The Ooreiki took a step toward the Dhasha. "Because he will *never* go away. He has all of eternity to whittle away at your mind."

For a split second, Joe thought that the Dhasha would eat Lagrah. Instead, with a cold, merciless fury, Knaaren spun on Elf and tore his groundmate apart until all that was left was strips of twitching meat and severed bone. Then he abandoned the corpse and returned to his tower, his Takki trailing along behind him.

I failed him, Joe thought, watching the rainbow figure rise toward the top floor in his elevator. *I was supposed to take care of him and I let the monster eat him instead.* Joe was left in shock.

"Fall out!" Commander Lagrah shouted to the regiment. "Go back to your barracks rooms. Your battlemasters will meet you there. All hunts are cancelled for today."

Joe had to tear his eyes away from the spot at the top of the tower where the Dhasha had disappeared. When he turned, he caught Libby watching him intently. Joe quickly looked away. His gaze returned to the plaza behind them where medics were picking Elf's remains from amongst the diamond bits.

I failed him. The single, powerful thought overwhelmed everything else. Maggie and Monk were crying, but Joe remained silent.

He didn't deserve to cry.

He knew, beyond any doubt, he'd gotten Elf killed.

31

MOURNING THE DEAD

Joe gathered the group together that night to say a small prayer for Elf. "I didn't really go to church," Joe said, clearing his throat, "But we say the Groundteam Prayer every night, and he was one of our groundmates, so I didn't think it would be right not to say something about him…" He cleared his throat miserably.

Maggie came to his rescue. "Dear Lord, please take good care of our friend Elf. I know you don't like the stuff he's been doing lately, but please take him to Heaven anyway. Elf was a good kid that got captured by aliens. He liked toy soldiers and peanut butter sandwiches and hated gummi bears so he couldn't have been so bad. Amen."

"Amen," everyone agreed. Libby nodded.

When Joe couldn't sleep that night, he got out of bed and began sharpening his knife. He knew it was a stupid thing to do, that half the creatures in Congress wouldn't even blink if he stabbed them to the hilt, but it made him feel better. He wanted to do nothing more than to plunge it into Knaaren's big, perfect eye.

He had been sitting like this for several minutes before he realized Libby was watching him.

"Go to sleep," Joe said. "I'm just not tired."

Libby slid out of bed and put her hand on his shoulder.

"I don't feel like raiding tonight." Growing uncomfortable under her unyielding gaze, Joe got up and moved off into the baths, where he sat down beside a stinking vat of alcohol.

I failed him, he thought. *He trusted me and I failed him.*

How could he have thought he was a good leader? How could he have been *enjoying* himself? He'd gotten someone *killed.* A friend. Someone who trusted him. Someone who'd followed him. Someone who *needed* him. He was *dead.*

And it's my fault.

Libby slipped into the baths and sat down beside him. She touched his arm, then, before Joe realized her intent, she leaned over and kissed him. On the lips.

Joe got so hard so fast that he experienced physical pain. Thoughts of Elf vanished, replaced by instant panic. He pulled back quickly. "What do you want?"

Libby gave him a look of utter consternation. He could almost read her mind. *What do you* think *I want, furg?*

Joe cleared his throat. "I...uh...I just wanted to sharpen my knife." *Great. You Grade-A furg, that's just what she wants to hear. Joe Sex Master Dobbs. First time any woman shows even the least bit of interest in your sorry ass and you tell her you'd rather polish cutlery. She's gonna hate you forever. You can still save it though. Just—*

But Libby was already up, her graceful legs removing her from the baths at a run. Joe stared after her in despair.

• • •

"I heard what happened, Choe. I'm sorry."

Joe refused to look up at the haauk hovering above him on the plaza.

"It's always hard to lose a friend."

"Go away," Joe said softly. "I know what's going on. You're a rebel. You're trying to turn me into a spy."

Yuil didn't even blink. "So? Do you really want Congress to survive? It killed your friend."

"*Knaaren* killed my friend," Joe said. "Congress didn't even know he existed."

"Exactly," Yuil retorted. "We're all insignificant to them, Joe. We're all pawns to do as we're told. We don't even have the freedom to choose membership. They force us to pay tribute, send children off to die on strange planets, and have Peacemakers kill anyone who objects. We need to destroy them, Choe."

Joe gave Yuil an irritated glance. "What the hell can I do? I'm just a kid."

"I'm not sure yet," Yuil said. "But Kihgl told me to help you."

Joe stiffened. "He did?"

"Kkee. Take this." Yuil held out another akarit, complete with black shielding box. Joe hesitated, then reluctantly took it from the Ooreiki's metal-tipped tentacles.

Yuil looked satisfied. "Next time you find yourself in trouble, come to the abandoned *ferlii* I showed you. Take the first stair you see up three levels and circle the building until you find a tunnel entrance that is more circular than the rest. Inside, there will be a small diamond etched into the floor—this is the symbol of the resistance. Take that tunnel up and you will find a room fitted with weapons and communications equipment. Say anything at all in that room and I will hear you. Just be careful—it is fitted with enough explosives to wipe out half of Alishai, should the authorities discover it."

Joe tucked the akarit into his vest. "They won't. Not from me."

Yuil's face bunched in an Ooreiki grin. "Kihgl said we could trust you."

• • •

"Hey Chipmunk. Can you reach that ratchet for me?"

"Okay Dad. Which one's the ratchet?"

Her dad laughed. "The one with the ratchet on it."

Carol frowned at the set of tools, then handed him the one that looked the best.

"That's a screwdriver." Her father sighed and slid out from under the car. His big hands set the screwdriver back in place and plucked one of the tools from the set. "See this here? Listen." He twisted the knob, making a clicking sound. "That's a ratchet. You can change direction with this little lever here. See?"

Carol nodded, though she really didn't see at all. "How does it change direction? It's not going anywhere, Dad."

Her father laughed—a liquid, happy sound that filled her chest with joy every time she heard it. "Come under here, my little Monk. Lemme show you something."

Carol eyed the greasy underbelly of the car, then her new pink pants. "Mommy told me not to."

"Mommy wouldn't let me buy you coveralls, either. Get under here. I'll deal with Mommy."

Squirming with glee, Carol inched her way under the car, staring up at the unidentifiable masses of dirt and grease that seemed to make sense to her dad.

"Watch that nut right there," her dad ordered. He put the open end of the ratchet over it and started yanking on the handle. The garage echoed with its quick, efficient clicking sounds. Then he pulled his hand away. "See it now?"

"It's coming off," Carol said, fascinated.

"Right," her dad replied. "Now watch what happens when I set this baby in reverse." He flipped the lever, and the clicking sounds returned. When he lifted the ratchet away a second time, the nut was back where it had started.

"Wow!" Carol exclaimed. "Cool, Dad."

"One of the many marvels of modern technology. If we've got time tonight, I'll show you that new air compressor I bought at—"

"James."

Both Carol and her father jerked at her mother's hard tone. Carol quickly skidded out from under the car and did her best to brush herself off. Her hands, greasy from touching the underside of the Toyota, left black smears across her pants. She bit her lip and watched her dad, hoping he wouldn't get in trouble. She liked it when he let her work on cars with him.

"I need to talk to you, James. Our visitors."

Carol frowned. She hadn't seen any visitors, but her parents were constantly talking about them. They probably slept in the den, with the TV. Neither of them had allowed her to watch TV in days, and Carol was beginning to miss Sesame Street.

"Now, James."

"All right, Kate." Her father's voice was soft, as it always was, though Carol could tell he was irritated. He picked up a greasy blue rag from the floor and began wiping his hands with it.

"Stay here, Monk." Then, giving Carol a wink, he followed their mother back inside the house.

• • •

Two weeks later, while they were tending the plaza after drills, Maggie walked up and yanked Joe's rake from his hands. "What's the matter with you, Joe?"

Joe stared at his rake. He had been lost in thought, thinking on what Yuil and his companions had taught him the night before about biosuits. Yuil had introduced him to other rebels, and as Joe was accepted deeper into their society, they taught him things about fighting Congies that had never come up in Battlemaster Nebil's discussions—like how to get a Congie out of his biosuit for questioning. "What are you talking about?"

"That!" Maggie cried. "You're not saying anything and you let Sasha bully you around. You haven't led a raid in weeks."

"I don't want to talk about it," Joe said, taking his rake from her.

A few feet away, Libby was watching him. Though they had been neck-and-neck on their growth spurts, she had finally stopped growing. Now she stood at six-foot-three, all leg and waist. She could have been a model, back on Earth. Here, she never left the barracks without her black utility vest, heavy Congie boots, and her rifle—yet somehow even with all her gear she looked as sexy as anything out of Playboy.

Joe ignored them both and continued to rake in silence.

Petite as she was, when Maggie grabbed him by the shoulder and yanked him around to face her, it hurt. "What's *wrong* with you?! Sasha's been getting us all killed on the hunts. Pretty soon, they're gonna pair us with some other battalion because Second keeps kicking our ass. Why won't you *say something?*"

"Just leave me alone, okay?"

"Is it about Elf?"

Now everyone in the platoon was looking at him. Joe stared at the base of his rake. Even a *rake* looked alien here. Only three prongs that looked like fat fingers, slightly curved and black as coal. It reminded him of the instrument the rebels had shown him that was good for cracking open a Congie's biosuit for interrogation.

"It is!" Maggie cried. "It's about Elf!"

"Mag, leave me alone, okay?"

"I'm the one who couldn't stop him from killing those Ooreiki. If I had, he'd still be here."

Joe just shook his head.

"It's not your fault, Joe!" Maggie cried. "Can't you see that?!"

"It *is*." Joe took a deep breath. "He tried to take that ship because of me. I told him I'd fly him home if he could get me a ship. I *said* that. And now he's dead. Because he trusted me."

Libby turned abruptly and stalked off toward the chow hall. Joe felt an ache in his chest as he watched her go. She'd hate him if she knew what Yuil was. She loved everything about the Army. If she found out Joe was meeting with rebels, she'd probably kill him herself.

Maggie wasn't finished. "Elf was crazy, Joe. You didn't do it. Knaaren did. It's a miracle you're not crazy, too."

"Maybe I am," Joe replied, thinking about his excursions with Yuil. He started raking again, but Maggie stepped on it.

"We need you, Joe. Sasha's gonna get our flag captured, then we'll all be screwed. We need you to *lead*."

Joe snorted. "Who gives an ash about Congress and their games?"

Maggie made a disgusted noise and released his rake. Glaring at him, she said to the others, "Come on, guys. Let's go get lunch." She and Scott followed Libby across the yard.

Monk watched them go. Once they were out of earshot, she turned to him and said, "You know, you should stop being a Takki."

Joe rolled his eyes. "Look, I don't need this. Maggie already—"

"It's not fair making Libby beg," Monk went on. "She already got in a fight over who gets to pop your cherry. Come on, Joe. All you have to do is look at her and you get a hard-on."

Joe sputtered, his face catching fire. "Where did you—" He stopped himself. He didn't want to know where she was getting her information. He still preferred to think of the others as little kids because, even with their grown-up bodies, that's what they were.

What did it matter if Monk knew about sex, anyway? It wasn't as if some sootwad could knock her up and ruin her life. Hell, a little good-natured nookie probably did wonders for morale. Too bad he was too much of a fumbling furg to get any.

"You should just get it over with," Monk continued. "If sex would make her stop being so moody, I'd pay you for every night. Lately, she's been such a bi—"

She broke off suddenly as a group of black-clad Ooreiki waddled past them. English was now forbidden to the recruits. Any time they were caught using it by the battlemasters, they were given new and heinous chores as penance. The last kid had been given the job of cleaning the eastern windows of one of the civilian towers—clinging to a rope dangling a thousand feet above the ground.

Once the Ooreiki had passed, Monk continued in Congie.

"Really, Joe. You need to get your priorities straight. Elf's dead and Libby's horny as hell. She'd screw a light-post if it was wearing your clothes." Then she turned and walked off, leaving him standing there, mouth agape.

Before Joe could follow her, a horn blasted across Alishai, announcing an immediate regiment formation. Sighing, Joe put his rake aside and followed the others to the plaza and got in line.

Several minutes went by without any sound except the thick flapping of banners in a heavy ferlii spore-wind. All except for Sixth Battalion's—Lord Knaaren still hadn't given Tril his banners. To make up for it, every single recruit in Sixth Battalion, even Libby and Sasha, wore their sleeves rolled above their biceps. To Joe, seeing the rolled sleeves looked even better than if they'd had banners. It gave him a sort of pride to be the only battalion allowed to have them.

Then he remembered what he was going to be fighting for and reminded himself that sleeves, banners, hunts, and formations were all a way of the Congressional Army to control them, to blind them to their real purpose. They encouraged the recruits to spend so much time squabbling and testing each other that they lost sight of the truth of their situation. Congies were the enemy, and the last thing Joe was going to do was become one of them.

A flash of color blazed across the courtyard in front of them, the Dhasha's rainbow body at a full charge, then was gone.

Half an hour later, after their Prime Commander still hadn't reappeared, even the battlemasters began to get impatient. In the battalion beside his, Joe heard two commanders discussing whether they should stay or go.

Almost an hour after that, a lone Takki waddled out from the Dhasha's tower and handed an electronic note to the nearest tertiary commander before hurrying away. The Ooreiki stepped forward and activated it.

Immediately, Prime Commander Knaaren's voice boomed out over the plaza, but his tone was hushed and calculating. "...*seen them train. They can't fool me. They try to hide him, but I see his taint. I see everything. They rot inside just like Congress. I must root out his evil.*"

The tertiary commander of First Battalion continued to hold the device above his head for another two minutes, until it was obvious nothing else was forthcoming. He lowered it with a puzzled grimace.

"He's lost his mind," Nebil muttered.

"Ghost sickness," Prime Commander Lagrah agreed.

Just then, Knaaren came barreling from the base of his tower, sharkish mouth wide and gasping, head swinging in all directions at once. Without warning, he leapt forward and bit down on one of Third Battalion's battlemasters. Brown fluid gushed out from between the rainbow lips and spread in a pool in the diamond dust. Knaaren viciously shook the Ooreiki between his powerful jaws until the lower half of his body went flying off into Third Battalion. Then Knaaren spat the rest of the carcass aside, half-eaten, and stared blindly around the ranks.

"Who else?!" Knaaren screamed in Congie. "Who else holds the taint?!"

The Dhasha's eyes caught suddenly on one of the recruits in First Battalion and stayed there, riveted. He spent the next three minutes like that, absolutely motionless. Then he threw himself backwards, landing in a sprawl, howling like a possessed thing. The recruit he'd been staring at made a miserable, confused whimper.

"I see him!" Knaaren screamed, clawing his way back to his feet, casting chips of diamond in all directions. "I can see into your heads! All of you! He's in you! I can see his corruption! I know he's…" The Dhasha shuddered and backed up three steps. "You!"

He was staring at the air above his head.

"Leave me alone!" Knaaren screamed. "No! *No…*" His last words degenerated into an alien roar as he tore at the air with his talons then crumpled in a panting, twitching heap on the plaza in front of them. His Takki slaves calmly knelt and began grooming him as if it were the most natural thing in the world for their master to have thrown a tantrum and collapsed in front of his entire regiment.

"Get the recruits out of here," Lagrah said, watching the Dhasha. "It's *oorei* sickness. It's only going to get worse from here."

Nebil and the other battlemasters were quick to comply. Joe and the rest of the recruits spent the next five hours doing weapons drills on the other side of the city while Knaaren terrorized the plaza, stalking back and forth and talking to thin air. The battlemasters only allowed them to return to the barracks to sleep when a black-clad Congie brought word that Lord Knaaren was once again ensconced in his high tower.

Over the next several days, Nebil kept them locked in the barracks, having Takki deliver food to them at the appropriate times. Through brief visits by their battlemaster, Joe learned that Knaaren was currently eating his way through his slaves—all of them. The Training Committee had ordered all Ooreiki and human personnel to stay indoors until they could send a replacement. Because of this, the recruits had hereto unknown hours of free time, which most of them spent giggling under the covers.

Joe, however, made sure to sit over by the chamber pots, pretending to clean his rifle, until Libby went to sleep. Only then would he go to bed.

As he was starting to undress, Monk grinned at him and whispered "Takki."

Irritated, Joe left his clothes on and retreated to the baths.

"Jacking off isn't gonna help!" Monk called after him.

Joe's ears burned. Behind him, many recruits laughed.

Slowly, rigidly, he returned to the bed and grabbed Monk by the wrist. Even as her eyes widened and she tried to resist, he jerked her out of the bed and dragged her with him to the baths. Inside, he slammed the door shut and blocked it with his body.

Monk made a nervous giggle and gave him an apprehensive look.

"This," Joe said, "has got to stop."

Behind him, Sasha banged on the door. "Zero?! Open the door!" Sasha shouted. "I'm your battlemaster and Nebil said you can't shut the door! You leave her alone and open the door. *Now!*"

Joe crossed his arms, his eyes never leaving Monk.

"Come on, Joe," Monk said. "Everybody knows you want each other. Libby beat some girl senseless when she said you had a nice back."

Joe's arms unfolded in astonishment. "She did?" On the other side of the door, Sasha's shouts were getting angrier, the pounding more violent.

"You're the two best soldiers in Sixth," Monk said. "You're perfect for each other. Everybody sees it."

"She's *eight*, for ashes' sake!" Joe said. "And what are you? *Six*?!"

"I'm as big as either of my parents," Monk said.

Before she could flinch away, he reached out and tapped her bald skull. "You're still a kid in here, though. Just because you shoot guns and swear doesn't make you an adult."

Monk pouted. "You think we're all still babies, but we're not. We've seen stuff that would make our parents piss themselves, and we're still here."

She had a point. Joe sighed. "All right. Fine. What's it gonna take for you to stop pushing it?"

Monk shrugged. "Just do something about her," she said. "Yesterday, she asked Nebil to transfer her to another platoon."

Joe's mouth fell open in shock.

"Nebil told her to deal with her own burning problems," Monk said, "But Joe, she's really determined. I think she might go talk to Commander Tril." She paused, eying him narrowly. "Did you say something to her?"

Joe flushed and blurted, "She tried to kiss me. I told her I just wanted to sharpen my knife."

Monk pursed her lips. "Wow. Here I thought neither of you had the balls to make the first move… No wonder she hates you. She must think you didn't kiss her because she has no tongue."

Oh soot. Joe swallowed, hard.

"Now you have to do it," Monk said.

"Huh?" he said, unable to hear over his pounding heart.

"Now you have to make the first move. It's the only way she'll stop hating you."

"Monk," Joe managed, "sorry to say this, but I don't need relationship counseling from a six-year-old. Besides, I never said I wanted a relationship in the first place."

"Yeah you do, otherwise you wouldn't spend all your free time staring at her."

Joe's blush deepened. "I don't stare."

"Sure you do," Monk retorted. "You look at her like she's the centerfold of a sex mag."

Joe's brow creased. "Do you even know what that is?"

Monk shrugged. "Scott told me. He's the one who said it first."

Joe groaned. "Fine. Okay? I'll go apologize. Will that get you off my ass?"

"Sure," Monk said. "Now maybe you should open the door. I think Sasha went to get the battlemaster."

The thought of Nebil catching them with the door closed made Joe wrench it open immediately. Sasha was poised outside, one fist hovering over the metal, the other fist gripping her knife. She gave Joe a look that could have scorched stone, then peered behind him at Monk, who grinned and gave a cheerful wave.

"A hundred pushups," Sasha ordered. "Both of you."

"Burn you," Monk said, pushing past Joe. "Do your own burning pushups."

Sasha's face reddened. "I'll tell the battlemaster you didn't listen to me."

"Good. Maybe when he sees how you complain about everything like a spoiled brat, he'll give Joe his job back." Monk returned to her bed, ignoring Sasha completely.

Sasha was shaking as she turned back to Joe, her eyes glittering with outright hatred. "Go make her do pushups. Five hundred of them."

Joe snorted. "I don't think so."

"Three hundred, then." Sasha almost looked desperate, and soon Joe understood why. By now, their commotion had woken everyone in the barracks, and she had an audience. The entire *platoon* was watching. If she didn't make them accept some sort of punishment, she would look incompetent.

When Joe didn't move, Sasha turned to two other ground leaders. "Grab them. Help me punish them."

Carl and Sherri hesitated.

From the bed, Monk laughed. "The only person they're ever gonna listen to is Joe. You're just a crazy bitch with a knife."

In that instant, Sasha lunged at Monk and landed on top of her, trapping her under the cover. Then, almost like in a dream, she drew her knife across Monk's throat, the blade biting deep. Even as Monk's eyes widened in a scream, blood gushed out over the metal and onto the silvery covers, more blood than Joe ever thought possible.

Libby wrenched Sasha off of Monk immediately, but it was too late. Monk's eyes were already dulling, her life spilling out over the blanket.

Libby tore her eyes from Monk and turned to Sasha, who suddenly looked scared. Taking three purposeful steps forward, Libby ripped the knife from Sasha's hand and stabbed her in the neck. Sasha collapsed with a strangled gurgle.

Then she stood there, staring pitilessly down into Sasha's white face as she collapsed on the floor.

It all happened in a matter of seconds.

"Scott!" Joe roared, suddenly breaking out of his paralysis, "Get the medics! Maggie, press down on Monk's neck! Carl, go get Nebil. *Does anyone have nanos?!*"

That night they found that, despite their great advances, Congress still couldn't bring somebody back from the dead.

32

KA-PAR

L ibby, for her part in Sasha's death, received the Eighth Degree. Commander Tril had actually ordered the Ninth Degree, but when Battlemaster Nebil returned to his platoon to mete out his punishment, Joe saw that he used the setting one notch below.

Not that it mattered much for Libby.

This time, Joe could not keep his eyes free from tears as her low, unintelligible wail pierced the barracks. They all stood lined up at the ends of their groundteam bunks, Libby's naked form struggling against invisible agony on the floor in front of them.

When it was over, Nebil put the black device away and stood silently for long minutes, sudah fluttering. Finally, he said, "Zero, take care of your groundmate. She'll be dazed for the next week or so. She might have trouble eating."

"Shouldn't we take her to medical?" Joe asked.

Nebil's gaze remained on Libby's body. "Perceptual punishment is not an ailment Congress allows its doctors to treat. If they did, it wouldn't be a punishment." Nebil turned to go, but stopped. "Zero, get your platoon under control. Anything else happens and I'll hold you responsible."

"I thought you couldn't give me battlemaster," Joe said, stiffening.

"No ash like this happened on your watch," Nebil barked. "You're it. Tril can go complain to the Training Committee if he doesn't like it."

"I don't want it."

Nebil's snakelike pupils narrowed. "What?"

"I don't want it," Joe repeated. "I don't want ground leader, I don't want squad leader, I don't want anything to do with your burning Army. My friends are *dead*!" The last came out as a scream.

"You don't have a choice." Nebil's voice was almost a whisper. "None of us do." He rounded and left them gathered around Libby's body.

Joe was gritting his jaw so hard that it hurt. Very slowly, he turned to the other recruits. "What the ashes are you standing around for?! You heard him. Get some rags and clean her up. I want the smell of shit out of this place in the next thirty seconds or you're all doing jumping-jacks until you puke."

Joe went to the far wall and sat down in a brooding silence. Once Libby was clean, Scott and Maggie wrapped her in a blanket and carried her to the bed—the same bed that was still crusted with Monk's dried blood. He averted his eyes back to the spot where Libby had struggled ineffectually moments before. He was still staring at the same place when Maggie sat down beside him.

Neither of them said a word.

They sat like that for hours, until Maggie finally got up and went to join Scott and Libby in bed. None of them slept.

The next morning, Nebil came back early. "Grab everything and get to the plaza. We're getting inspected. Our new Prime wants to see you."

Indifferent, Joe gathered his equipment with the others and halfheartedly marched them to the plaza, where an enormous Dhasha sat alone at one end, easily twice as big as Knaaren. His gut clenched reflexively and he swallowed down a spasm of instinctive fear. Along the other side of the clearing, twenty much smaller Dhasha sat amidst a swarm of Takki, their emerald eyes alert and curious. A huge pile of black bricks sat beside them.

"Eyes forward!" Nebil snapped.

Once they were all in formation, the plaza was utterly silent except for the *thwapping* of the other battalions' standards. After a few moments, Joe heard the clicking scrape of Dhasha talons on diamond chips. Soon a blur of color filled the corner of his vision and he felt the inevitable surge of rage.

"Commander," the massive Dhasha said in a precise, yet heavily-accented Congie, "Why does your battalion not bear its own standards?"

"Lord Knaaren withheld them from us, Prince Bagkhal."

"Oh? Why?"

"He decided we were not worthy."

"Then he was a furg." He turned to one of Sixth's battlemasters. "Go retrieve them from the armory. If the clerks refuse, tell them I'll get them myself." As the Ooreiki bowed and hurried off, the Dhasha paused, huge egg-shaped emerald eyes scanning the gathered recruits of Sixth Battalion. "Did Knaaren also force you wear your uniforms differently?"

"It is our choice, my lord," Tril said, bowing low.

"I see. What else has been withheld from you?" Prince Bagkhal asked, pacing. He seemed almost naked without an entourage of slaves, but aside from the mass grooming the younger Dhasha off to one side, Joe could see no Takki in sight.

"Their bio suits," Lagrah said. "They were supposed to get them after the first rotation of training."

"As you can see, I have already remedied that problem," the Dhasha said, gesturing with his huge head towards the piles of black bricks. "What else?"

Tril stepped forward. "He took forty-seven of my recruits as slaves. Several of them were squad leaders."

"That cannot be helped."

"Some must still be alive."

"No. They are not."

"Then perhaps you might consider giving me some recruits from another battalion?" Tril insisted. "We are undermanned."

"No, Commander."

Tril lowered his appendages in acquiescence.

Prince Bagkhal clicked his teeth together and went to the next battalion. He circled the plaza, stopping at every other battalion to speak with its commander, then returned to the Sixth.

"Commander Tril, I have need of a personal assistant. I was called too quickly to bring my own with me. You are not obligated, but I thought I'd give you the honor before offering it to someone else."

Tril's sudah began fluttering. "The…honor, sir?" All around them, the Ooreiki were stiffening, as if Bagkhal had deeply insulted them.

"Not you," Bagkhal snorted. "One of your recruits. Lagrah tells me you have several that are quite talented."

Tril relaxed. "We had one, but she killed another recruit in a fight yesterday. I gave her the Ninth Degree."

Prince Bagkhal spun. "You killed a *recruit?*"

Tril looked baffled. "No. I only gave her the Ninth—"

"You stupid ashsoul!" Bagkhal raged. "How did you manage to become a secondary commander?"

The entire regiment was so silent they could hear the wind in the ferlii branches. Tril's sudah began fluttering rapidly. "She's alive. My battlemaster reported so to me earlier this morning."

"That's because I only used the Eighth," Nebil said.

Both Tril and Prince Bagkhal turned to look at Nebil.

"What is your name, Battlemaster?" the big Dhasha said.

"Nebil, my lord."

"You disobeyed an order from your secondary commander?"

"I wasn't about to kill my best recruit for avenging her groundmate," Nebil replied calmly.

The Dhasha pulled back and began to pace, his great weight crunching the diamonds under him. "I am not liking this, Commander Tril. If you don't command the respect of your battlemasters, why should your recruits take their training seriously?"

"They do," Tril said quickly. "Even with nearly a tenth of its recruits missing, my battalion has kept up with Second Battalion throughout training. One of my squads managed to capture a flag."

Prince Bagkhal turned. "Really? Who was the battlemaster of that squad?"

Tril flinched as if he had been struck. "Nebil, my lord."

"The same one who ignored your command to kill a recruit."

"I didn't order him to kill a—"

"Battlemaster Nebil, you are the new head of Sixth Battalion."

Tril stumbled forward. "He's just a battlemaster! The Training Committee—"

"From what I've been told," Bagkhal interrupted, "There are plenty of things going on around here the Training Committee would not approve of." As Tril recoiled, he continued, "I already scheduled your departure, Commander Tril. Go pack."

For a long time, the Ooreiki did not move. Prince Bagkhal cocked his huge, sharklike head at him, watching. Then, stiffly, Tril turned.

"Before you go," Bagkhal interrupted, "I want your perceptual unit."

Tril slowly retrieved the little black device from his vest, his sudah fluttering madly.

Bagkhal snorted his amusement. "I'm not going to use it on you, furg. Put it on the ground and get out of here."

Tril dropped the unit on the ground and, looking numb, walked away.

The huge Dhasha nudged the device at Nebil with a rainbow-scaled toe. "Do you want it?"

Nebil didn't even look at it. "No."

"Good." Bagkhal stomped on it, slicing through the metal with his claws. Joe let out a pent-up breath, unable to believe what he was seeing.

"Unfortunately," the Dhasha said, once the thing was utterly destroyed, "Tril is right. The Training Committee will take umbrage with a battlemaster commanding a battalion. I hereby promote you to—"

"Roast them," Nebil said.

The Dhasha hesitated. "Excuse me?"

"Roast them," Nebil repeated. "I'm not taking another point. Been there three times already. Not doing it again."

The Dhasha peered at Nebil for several breaths, then said, "Very well. The Committee can take its complaints up with me." He turned to scan Nebil's recruits. "Now. If you really gave that recruit the Eighth Degree, she won't be useful for another week. Do you have another recruit that might be able to assist me?"

"Zero," Nebil said.

Joe felt like he'd been punched in the gut. Nebil was offering him up as a *slave*?

Prince Bagkhal twitched his head. "Zero? Is that the name of a recruit?"

"Kkee," Nebil replied. "He's the one who led the offensive that captured the flag."

No, Joe thought, his whole body stiffening. He fisted his hands against his sides. *No. I won't do this. Not again.*

The Dhasha cocked his huge, sharklike head. "I was under the impression that Draft rolls began at One."

"They do," Nebil replied. "He was an Unclaimed who Kihgl added under Zero."

Prince Bagkhal clicked his teeth together. "Very well. Bring him to me."

Battlemaster Nebil turned to Joe. "Zero, get out of formation."

Betrayal raking his insides, Joe did not move.

For one long moment, Nebil stared at Joe and Joe ignored him, staring straight ahead as rigidly as a statue. Then the Ooreiki stalked forward, grabbed him in his stinging tentacle grip, and threw him at the Dhasha's feet.

"No!" Joe shouted, jumping back. "I won't do it again. I'd rather you killed me first, you burning asher!"

"That can be arranged," Nebil said coolly.

Prince Bagkhal observed the exchange with a quizzical tilt to his massive jaws. "What does he mean, 'again'?"

Joe turned to stare directly into the Dhasha's eyes, hoping it would get him killed. He was *not* going back. The Dhasha grunted and flinched slightly, like someone fighting down a sudden reflex, then just stared back, looking almost…curious.

"I gave Zero to Knaaren rather than see Tril use the Ninth Degree on him," Nebil growled, "the ungrateful furg."

The Dhasha jerked. "He was a *slave?*"

"For two weeks. Knaaren traded him back to Tril for another recruit."

Joe continued to meet the Dhasha's gaze, deciding to pull Kihgl's maneuver and get eaten for it. He would *not* be a slave again. *Never.*

Clicking his black rows of teeth together, Prince Bagkhal said, "It doesn't appear he learned any manners while in Knaaren's care. Unless he is deliberately trying to provoke me." The Dhasha leaned closer to Joe, filling his vision with a single emerald eye. "*Are* you trying to provoke me?"

"I'm not a slave," Joe gritted. "I'll die first."

The Dhasha seemed to digest that a moment. "Take off your shirt, Human."

Joe ignored him and returned to his groundteam.

"You Jreet-loving sootwad, *do* it!" Nebil roared, yanking him back.

"I won't wear those burning robes again," Joe snapped. "Go burn yourselves." Joe turned around and started to walk away.

"Battlemasters, detain him," the Dhasha said. Three Ooreiki swarmed Joe and dragged him back to the Dhasha's feet. They held his face in the gravel until Bagkhal gave them the command to release him. Slowly, fury burning in his chest, Joe righted himself.

"I'll repeat, Human. Take off your shirt," the Dhasha said. "You would not like it if I did it."

Taking a step away from the Dhasha so he could look up into his eyes, Joe said, "And I repeat, asher, go burn yourself."

The Dhasha clicked his teeth together again. "Battlemasters, take off his shirt."

"Get off of me!" Joe shouted, trying to struggle out of the Ooreiki's burning grip. When he refused to raise his arms over his head, they ended up ripping the shirt off of him. When they released him again, Joe picked up a chunk of diamond from the ground and got ready to clobber one of them with it.

"Zero!" Nebil snapped, "Put that down, you soot-eating furg! He's not looking for a burning slave!"

Joe paused uncertainly. "What?"

"I'm going to need to document that," Prince Bagkhal said.

Joe realized the Dhasha was staring at his chest.

"Is this the only survivor?"

"As far as I know," Nebil replied.

"And he was still under Congressional protection?"

"Kkee."

"Destruction of Congressional property. Send clips of it to the Committee for Knaaren's trial. Let them see what he did when he wasn't eating them."

Joe dropped the rock, confused.

Prince Bagkhal clicked his teeth together in amusement. "I'd tell you to put your shirt back on, but it seems you can't." He turned to Nebil. "Battlemaster, you're sure I can have this one?"

Joe stiffened again. "I'm not going anywhere with you."

The Dhasha stared down at him, his scaly alien face lit up with amusement. "Then we are at an impasse, because I'm not leaving until you do."

Joe laughed. "What kind of furgsoot is that?"

The Dhasha waited.

Joe's amusement died in his throat. "You're just going to *stand* there?"

The Dhasha said nothing.

"I'm not going anywhere with you," Joe repeated uncertainly.

"Zero, I will beat you until you're a bloody—" Nebil began.

"It is just as well, Battlemaster," Bagkhal replied. "My sons and I had a good fight with Knaaren and I have nothing more to do today. The rest of you may go acquaint your battalions with their biosuits."

"Perhaps we should have kept the perceptual unit," Nebil said, his scowl giving Joe the idea he wanted to strangle him. "He's one stubborn sooter."

"So am I," the Dhasha said, staring down at Joe like a cat watching a mouse.

"You're declaring ka-par?" Lagrah demanded, from a few yards off. His pale brown eyes went from Joe to the Dhasha and back. "With a *recruit?*" He sounded shocked.

"I'm considering it," Prince Bagkhal said, still fixated on Joe. "This one intrigues me."

"No need to waste your time, milord," Nebil growled, reaching for Joe's neck. "I'll deal with the fire-loving Jreet."

"Go attend to your battalion, Battlemaster," Bagkhal ordered, his tone allowing no complaint. "I will handle this."

Battlemaster Nebil gave Joe a look promising a few thousand laps around the barracks, then turned and went back to Sixth Battalion, leaving Joe standing in front of the enormous Dhasha alone.

As the spore-breeze whipped across the plaza, tinkling the diamond chunks disturbed by Bagkhal's taloned feet, Joe found himself stunned that the Dhasha hadn't ordered anyone to drag Joe back to his den for him, let alone batted him in half.

Still, he knew that it could be a ruse, a hoax, a cat playing with its mouse... The last thing he was going to do was go back to a Dhasha's den.

Once he was there, Bagkhal could do anything he wanted to him, anything at all, and Congress would simply turn its head.

"Whenever you're ready to follow me to my quarters," Bagkhal calmly said into the silence that followed, "let me know."

"I *won't* serve you," Joe growled. He started to back away.

"I didn't dismiss you," Bagkhal reminded him.

Joe felt a flush of anger. "Like I give an ash." He turned his back to the Dhasha, fully prepared to be eaten, rather than taken as a slave to Dhasha again.

"What you are doing is insubordination," the Dhasha reminded him calmly.

"Damn right, it is," Joe said, still walking towards the barracks.

"You're not afraid of me," Bagkhal commented.

"I just know I'm gonna die," Joe retorted, without turning. "Don't really care, at this point." He kept going, waiting for the jaws to descend upon him.

"Do you know what ka-par is, Zero?" Prince Bagkhal rumbled, at his back.

Joe hesitated. He could feel the huge predator watching him. Frowning, he turned. "Let me guess..." he snapped, with more disdain than he intended. "Some obscure new way to claim a slave?"

"It is an ancient ritual amongst the elders of my people," Bagkhal said serenely. "A way to settle arguments and determining the better warrior without the inconvenience of shredding each other. Though with lesser species, it is often a way for a Dhasha to legitimately claim dominance, yes. When declared, even Congress recognizes the results of ka-par, and other Dhasha will enforce the result, which is why it is not offered often."

Joe snorted. "Burn you." He turned to go again.

"I haven't dismissed you," Bagkhal repeated calmly.

"So eat me," Joe said, still walking.

"I could," Bagkhal said. "But I'm more interested in fixing the mess that my ignorant furg of a predecessor left for me. Thus, I would like to offer you ka-par."

Joe hesitated at the word 'offer.' He stood there for several moments, staring up at the barracks, feeling the Dhasha's piercing green stare at his back.

Knaaren had never *offered* him anything.

With that thought nagging at him, Joe turned back slowly, suspicion heavy in his soul. "What do you mean?" he muttered.

"Ka-par," Bagkhal said, cocking his huge head, "is a contest of wills. Instead of using tooth or talon, which, with Dhasha, rapidly depletes the fighting force, the two warriors duel with their eyes until one backs down. The first one to surrender submits completely to the victor. Much more important than physical brawls—it is how princes are made."

Joe narrowed his eyes, still fighting the urge to walk away. "And if I lose?"

"You will do whatever I tell you to do, without question, from now until your training is complete," Prince Bagkhal told him.

Yeah, *that* wasn't going to happen. Still, Joe was curious. "What if I win?"

"Like I said," Prince Bagkhal said, cocking his shark-like head, "Congress recognizes the results of ka-par. If you win, you would find yourself in command the Eighty-Seventh Regiment of the Fourteenth Human Ground Force, and I would serve you, if that was your wish."

Joe's heart stuttered at that. Warily, thinking it had to be some sort of trick, he looked the Dhasha up and down. "A staring contest."

"A *ka-par*," Bagkhal replied.

"You want me to beat you in a *staring* contest."

"I don't *want* you to beat me," Bagkhal said, clicking his teeth together in a Dhasha chuckle. "I want your service, after all."

Joe's pulse was beginning to hammer in his ears. "You're serious, aren't you? I'd command the *regiment*?"

"If you accept my ka-par, and win, you would command the regiment, yes."

Licking his lips, Joe said, "How?"

"You watch your opponent with the intensity of a hunter. You cannot back up or lower your gaze. The goal is to make him nervous enough to break his concentration and make him back down. It is the test of a warrior."

Feeling a rush of suspicion, Joe growled, "And you'll, what, jump at me? Snarl at me? Shove me over? What?"

"I will wait," Bagkhal replied. "And watch. It is not about sudden movements or distractions. It is about spirit. A Human has the capability of winning. It is why it is a duel, not a slaughter."

Joe could not believe it. *A staring contest. He wants me to duel him in a burning staring contest.* Nervously, he glanced up at the barracks, wondering if his groundmates were watching. Turning back, he scowled at the Dhasha. "I won't be your burning slave."

"So," Bagkhal said, tilting his great head, "ka-par?"

Joe narrowed his eyes. Though the stubborn part of him was screaming at him to back down, to stalk back to the barracks or get eaten for insubordination, it was the rash and reckless part of him that had gotten him captured by aliens that said, "You're on."

Bagkhal made a satisfied grunt, and Joe felt a little spasm of panic, realizing he couldn't take it back. "Ka-par rak'tal. I accept." Immediately, the Dhasha prince took three steps towards him, until they were little over an arm's-length apart, then settled a comfortable position and leveled him with a bone-deep emerald stare, focusing on Joe with complete predatory intensity. "Mahid ka-par," Prince Bagkhal said. "May it begin."

After the first hour passed, Joe realized Bagkhal was utterly serious. The Dhasha never twitched, his gaze never wavering from Joe the entire time. Joe, meanwhile, became more and more uncomfortable. He was standing bare-chested in front of a gigantic killing machine that was frozen only a few feet away, staring at him with all the intensity of a predator.

After the second hour, the group of smaller Dhasha and their Takki caretakers got bored and wandered back to the Prime Commander's tower. Everyone else had already left the plaza, leaving only Joe and the Dhasha. Staring at each other.

Joe, you idiot, his mind ranted at him. *You just declared a staring contest with something that doesn't* blink.

Indeed, the hard, green, crystalline eyes showed neither pupil nor flicker of movement. Joe wasn't even sure they *did* move, looking more a feature of the Dhasha's skull than anything with mobility.

Later that day, several battalions formed up on the plaza and began to run through drills, marching around Joe and his opponent as if they were simply immobile physical obstacles in the terrain. As they passed, Joe caught several curious looks from recruits and Ooreiki alike.

Prince Bagkhal's complete focus never wavered, giving Joe the unnerving feeling of being a rabbit having the full attention of a tiger.

When Joe's head turned to watch a battalion enter the chow hall for dinner, however, feeling the ache of hunger like a knife in his gut, Bagkhal said, "Generally, looking away is a symbol of submission, Human. Are you submitting?"

Joe snapped his attention back to Prince Bagkhal immediately. "No," he blurted, his face flushing with fear and embarrassment.

"Then ka-par," the Dhasha told him, as utterly motionless as a sphinx.

Another hour passed. The nagging discomfort of being the sole focus of a deadly predator was beginning to wear at him. Joe had to concentrate on the scales on the Dhasha's nose to keep from looking at the unending rows of triangular black teeth. His feet hurt. His legs itched to move. He was hungry. He could *feel* the coolness coming off the Dhasha's scales, just a few feet away. Shirtless, the spore-breeze was giving him goosebumps. His back itched. His acne had gotten worse, and it was even then covering his arms, legs, and chest.

The unlucky platoon that had been given the task of raking the plaza that night approached them warily. Their curious stares made Joe's shoulder-blades itch as they tentatively raked all around them, keeping a twenty-foot swath around the Dhasha. Feeling their eyes on him, it was all Joe could do not to turn and look at them.

Prince Bagkhal, for his part, hadn't so much as twitched since their contest had started.

He could do this all day, Joe realized, with a pang of terror. *Oh burn me, I'm going to lose.*

Then, *I'm never going back. Never. I'll make him kill me first.*

"I'm not your slave," Joe growled.

"Then I'd say it's in your best interest not to lose the ka-par," Prince Bagkhal replied. Throughout the exchange, Bagkhal never stirred. He just…watched.

After the twelfth hour, when everyone else was asleep, Joe was beginning to nod off on his feet, but he forced himself to stay where he was, staring into the Dhasha's cold green eyes. Joe remembered how Knaaren had claimed the Mexican kid, and how he'd led him off the plaza. His hackles lifted. That wouldn't happen to him.

"I'm *not* gonna be your slave, you stubborn asher," he growled, peering back up at the beast.

If anything, he thought he saw amusement flash across his opponent's emerald eyes. "It is custom not to speak during a ka-par," Bagkhal said. "Speaking is a sign of fear. Only Takki and children try to talk their way out of ka-par, once it's started."

"I'm not trying to talk my way out of it," Joe growled, his pride prickling. "I'm just stating a fact."

"Then don't lose," Prince Bagkhal replied, utterly motionless.

Joe's hunger became a dull ache in his gut. He grew dizzy with exhaustion. Pinned under the Dhasha's predatory stare, he fought down the urge to fidget. It was becoming more and more uncomfortable, feeling as if his vulnerabilities were rising to the surface, evaluated and analyzed by this creature that could kill him with a casual swipe of his paw.

I can't lose, he thought, in anguish. *I can't lose…*

Joe had to start distracting himself from the uncomfortable itch of Bagkhal's attention. The Dhasha's scales seemed to be a baseline color of silver, he noted, with the odd, shimmering colors moving across his body like motor oil across the surface of water. Even with the time to examine it, he still wasn't sure if it was tiny movements on the Dhasha's part that made the colors swirl, or if they just randomly shifted on their own.

As the hours went on, Joe noticed that the Dhasha prince didn't stink. Not like Knaaren. While Joe did occasionally catch the stale smell of old skin on the breeze—much like a combo of sweaty feet and used jockstrap—Bagkhal didn't have the pervasive reek of rotten flesh.

And, when Joe looked, he couldn't see any pieces of corpses clinging to his rows of teeth.

What if Dhasha don't need to eat? Joe thought, on a flush of panic. Just how long *could* he stand there, without food or sustenance? How long could he go without sleep? Already, Joe was weaving on his feet, light-headed with exhaustion. He could barely hold his head up, whereas Prince Bagkhal had shown absolutely no change whatsoever.

And, now that Joe had thought about it, could he *really* expect a Dhasha prince to serve him, when it was so much easier to bat him in half?

I can't win, Joe thought. *Soot soot soot, I can't win this...*

With the thought, Joe felt his palms slicken and his heart start to pound. His every instinct started to scream at him to back away, to retreat from this monster's striking-distance. In that moment, Joe realized he was cracking.

"I'm not your slave," Joe managed, sweating. What would Bagkhal do with him, if he won? Eat him? *Breed* him?

I can't lose, Joe thought. *I can't...*

Prince Bagkhal said nothing, as inert as a statue.

Breakfast came and went, and Joe's knees started trembling with the effort of holding him up. Battalions arranged themselves on the plaza for morning formation, and it was all Joe could do not to return their curious looks.

Not your slave, Joe thought, lifting his chin and meeting the creature's eyes stubbornly. *Not your slave, goddamn it.*

The Dhasha remained utterly stone-still, waiting.

It was as battlemasters began leading their platoons to the chow hall for lunch the next afternoon that Joe finally buckled. He bit his lip and looked away from the monster in front of him, trying to ignore the shame in his soul. "Fine. Whatever. I'll just find a way to kill myself later."

"Good," Bagkhal said, his huge body suddenly coming alive again. "By the rules of ka-par, I accept your surrender. Come with me." He turned and started stalking across the plaza as if nothing had ever happened.

Bristling, Joe did as he was told. As soon as the Ooreiki manning the elevator began its ascent, the battalion commanders began shouting orders on the plaza below, organizing the morning inspection. Joe felt an ache of resentment as he watched. That should have been *him* down there. Except Nebil had betrayed him. Given him to the Dhasha. As a *slave*.

"You'll return to your Battalion as soon as I'm finished discussing your new post with you," Bagkhal said. At least twice the size of Knaaren, he took up so much room in the cramped elevator that his jaw brushed Joe when he talked. Joe flinched back, revulsion drawing bile into the back of his throat.

Then his words registered and Joe glanced up. "Wait…I *will*?"

"Of course. Contrary to what Knaaren believed, the fact that you Humans make good pets does not give him license to claim slaves. You'll have to forgive his indiscretion," Bagkhal said. "This always happens during a species' first Draft, especially if that species is as dexterous as yours. Therefore, I'll be subtracting twelve turns from your contract for the wrongs you suffered under Knaaren. If you choose to add the duties of my assistant to your training for the next three turns, then I will subtract another six."

Joe blinked at him. All he could manage was, "But…you won."

"Winning the ka-par means only that I get to choose what to do with you. I choose to subtract twelve turns from your enlistment and offer you a place as my assistant."

Joe felt a brief welling of gratitude, which he quickly squashed. "You're lying."

"I will do it as soon as I get to a terminal."

Joe wanted to believe him, but he shook his head and stared out over the plaza. *I'll never trust a Dhasha.*

"You don't believe me," Bagkhal noted. He didn't sound surprised. Just…curious.

Joe ignored him.

After a moment of silence, the Dhasha said, "You aren't by any chance older than the rest of these recruits, are you Zero?"

His head jerked back to the Dhasha, wary. "Maybe."

The Dhasha's eyes glittered. "Thought so. Since you so graciously gave me a chance to study you, I noticed your rash. Classic example of post-puberty hormone conflict. How old were you when they Drafted you, Zero?"

"Fourteen," Joe said, his voice a whisper. His heart had once again begun hammering in his ears.

"I'll have them change your rations. Tril's a jenfurgling not to let Nebil change your diet. I noticed he'd filed several petitions, but until now I hadn't realized why. Next time you eat at the chow hall, the problem should be fixed. If it's not, come talk to me."

"Shouldn't you be offering to send me home?" Joe demanded. "You guys took me off my planet illegally."

"Wrong," the Dhasha said, clicking his teeth together. "You assaulted an Ooreiki ground team back on Earth. They lost all the recruits they'd been transporting. For that alone, you were a legal draftee. Further, you embarrassed Lagrah, lost us an entire battalion. By all rights, they *should* have used you as an Unclaimed. That they didn't still amazes me. *Vkala* usually aren't so kind."

Joe grimaced and looked away.

"Why *did* you attack Lagrah's collection team, anyway, Zero?"

"He had my brother," Joe managed.

"Ah." Bagkhal was quiet a moment. "Is he here now? In one of the other battalions, perhaps?"

"He escaped," Joe said, his throat getting tight. "I distracted them and he ran."

"So you took his place," Prince Bagkhal said thoughtfully.

He *had* taken Sam's place, and now he was a slave again and he hated his brother for it. Joe swallowed and nodded.

"Sometimes," Prince Bagkhal said, "when the Mothers weave their tapestry, the needs of the many replace the needs of the one."

"Or sometimes you're just stupid," Joe muttered.

They rode the rest of the way to the top in silence, Joe staring out over the city, wondering what it would be like to leap over the balcony and swan-dive to his death. The Dhasha, for his part, said nothing more.

As soon as the elevator came to a stop, Bagkhal stepped onto the rooftop and went over to a boxlike object built into the wall under a wide overhang.

To the box, he said, "Access the file of Recruit Zero, Sixth Battalion, Second Brigade, Eighty-Seventh Regiment, Fourteenth Human Ground Force."

Immediately, an Ooreiki voice said, *"File accessed, Prince Bagkhal."* It was the same computerized voice that Joe had heard each time Tril had taken him over to a terminal to observe as he added more time to Joe's service. Joe tensed, realizing this was where Bagkhal erased him from the system entirely, to start his penance as a Dhasha slave.

"Remove twelve turns from Zero's current enlistment term."

"Twelve turns have been removed, Prince Bagkhal. Updated enlistment term is fifty-eight turns."

Prince Bagkhal made a startled grunt and glanced over his shoulder at Joe. "Jreet gods, boy… Whose scales did *you* crawl under? Enlistments start at thirty-three!" He glanced back at the box. "For what cause was Recruit Zero's enlistment lengthened?"

"Recruit Zero's enlistment was lengthened for sixteen counts of disobedience to superior officers, twenty-one counts of disrespect for superior officers, seven counts of severe injuries, eighteen counts of minor injuries, twelve counts of—"

"Remove another twenty turns."

"Twenty turns have been removed, Prince Bagkhal. Updated enlistment term is thirty-eight turns."

"That's more reasonable," the Dhasha said. "Seal that, and put a lock on it. Altered by overseer or above only."

"Recruit Zero's file has been sealed and locked, Prince Bagkhal," the Ooreiki computer said pleasantly. *"Further alteration requiring approval of Overseer or above."*

Prince Bagkhal again glanced over his shoulder. "Believe me now, Zero?"

Joe's heart was pounding like a jackhammer. He had been mentally adding up the extensions to his enlistment in despair over the last weeks, knowing that, at the rate he was going, he would never actually be able to leave the Army.

Without another word, Bagkhal turned and disappeared into the gaping door set in the wall.

He just reset my enlistment term, Joe thought, utterly stunned.

Still, Joe held back, his chest aching in terror, remembering the last time he had gone through those doors, and how he had almost not come back out. Perhaps Bagkhal just wanted to lull him into complacency...so he could eat him later.

"The elevator will not go down again unless I request it," Bagkhal said from inside the den. "You might as well come inside, Zero."

"I could jump," Joe said. "Flatten myself on the ground out there. Medics wouldn't have a chance in hell of saving me."

"That's true," Bagkhal agreed. Then he left Joe alone with the baffled Ooreiki elevator-operator.

Though he swore to himself he wouldn't follow, several minutes later, Joe swallowed his pride and stepped into the monster's lair. Immediately, he noticed that the lavish cushions Knaaren had spread around the place had been removed. Now, only stark, bare stone remained. In one corner, a single metal desk stood over a utilitarian Ooreiki chair. Prince Bagkhal sat beside it, watching him. There was not a single slave in sight.

Joe hesitated at the top of the stairs leading down into the den. "What's all this waiting ash about, anyway? You trying to burn my head or what?"

"Obedience broke down because of a breach of trust," the Dhasha said. "I am attempting to repair that trust. Is it working?"

Joe cleared his throat embarrassedly. "Maybe."

"Good. Are you planning on staying up there all night?"

Joe peered over the railing anxiously. Just an empty room and a really big burning Dhasha. Tensely, he descended the stairs halfway, then paused on the staircase, poised to bolt back out to the elevator at the first sign of aggression. "What do you want?"

"Come sit," Bagkhal said, indicating the scoop-shaped chair with a swipe of his claws.

Joe eyed it, then eyed the Dhasha. Bagkhal just waited in silence. Warily, Joe descended the rest of the way into the lion's den and sat in the proffered seat.

"As you know, Dhasha civilization has depended much upon the hands of our slaves," Bagkhal said. "We do not have the dexterity to manipulate small objects." Bagkhal lifted one rigid, clawed paw a few inches off of the ground to illustrate his point. "For that reason, most Dhasha take slaves. I'm one of the few who does not. I favor having a friend help me, instead."

Joe curled his lip. "I am not your friend."

"Not yet."

Joe lurched from his chair, making the chair scrape against the diamond floor with a metallic screech. "I'm not burning grooming you."

"I didn't ask you to."

Joe stared at him a long moment, then reluctantly sat back down. "So what *do* you want?"

"Your hands," Bagkhal said simply. "Manage my files for me, manipulate devices, open doors, carry objects… Everything you take for granted. In return, I will take six more turns off your enlistment."

"You want a secretary."

"*Kkee.*"

Joe chewed on that a moment. "You're not taking me away from my battalion? Out of the hunts?"

"You will still participate in all of your responsibilities as a recruit battlemaster. You will be included in all the same training and exercises. Instead of going to sleep with the others, you will simply come here to help me."

"Wait. I won't be getting any *sleep?*"

"I will provide you with drugs to keep you alert."

Joe felt himself staring, his heart pounding in his chest. Was Bagkhal really serious? Another six years off his contract?

"Okay," Joe agreed. "But I want it in writing."

A wry look passed over Prince Bagkhal's sharklike face. "Dhasha don't put things in writing. It is meaningless to us, since we are never the ones to write it. However, I will give you my word."

"A Dhasha's word is soot to me."

Prince Bagkhal lunged to his feet, black rows of triangular teeth bared. "What did you say?"

Joe stood up to face him. "Go ahead and eat me. Show every one of your commanders out there just how good your burning word is."

For a spit second, Prince Bagkhal tensed and Joe looked Death in the eyes. Then, seemingly for no reason at all, the Dhasha relaxed. "If this is how you acted around Knaaren, it's amazing all he did was give you a few scars."

"I was too much of a coward back then to stand up to him."

"Or maybe you sense I'm not going to eat you," Prince Bagkhal said thoughtfully. "However, I've already suffered enough insubordination from you for a thousand recruits. Any more and I'll find somebody else."

Joe glanced at the desk, feeling oddly ashamed.

Bagkhal sat again. "Your first task as my assistant will be to deliver the list of rules in front of you to every battlemaster in the regiment. Return here once Nebil dismisses you for the night."

"List of rules?" Joe glanced at the electronic device in front of him. The symbols on the screen were much more complex than the simplified characters on the PPU. "What does it say?"

The Dhasha cocked a sharklike head at him. "Are you going to make a habit out of questioning me?"

"Probably."

"Then you should also make a habit out of being disappointed. Go do as you were bid, Zero. Come back when Nebil is finished with you."

Joe picked up the electronic unit and started toward the stairs. Then he hesitated, turning.

"Kkee?" Bagkhal asked.

"I've got a friend," Joe said. "The one Tril tried to kill with the perceptual unit."

"I warn you, if you're about to ask me to send her back to Earth—"

"No," Joe said quickly. "She loves it here. I think she actually likes it better here than she did back at home." He hesitated. "Someone cut out her tongue. Medical fixed her broken legs, but they didn't replace her tongue."

Prince Bagkhal gave him a long look. "Technically, a tongue is not necessary for a recruit's function."

"You said you'd take six years off my contract if I helped you," Joe pressed on grudgingly. "Would you give her a new tongue, instead?"

"Now?"

Joe nodded.

The Dhasha cocked his head at him. "You're asking me to reward you for work you haven't done yet."

Joe flushed. This was where the Dhasha questioned his honor, as Joe had done to him a few moments earlier. He lowered his head, ashamed.

"Very well. Tell Nebil to send her to medical. I might as well have them cure her of the aftereffects of the Eighth at the same time. No use having a valuable recruit waste a week of training in a coma."

Joe's head jerked up and he stared, and this time he couldn't stop the wash of gratitude toward the alien, mingled with grudging respect. "You fix her," Joe said softly, "and I'll help you as much as you want."

"Thank you," Prince Bagkhal said, with genuine relief, "I'm helpless without an assistant." He sighed when Joe looked startled. "I don't delude myself, Zero. I'm old. I've seen enough of this world to know that my people can't survive on our own. In a normal evolutionary process, we would have ended up as the Takki's mounts, possibly their soldiers. By all rights, the Takki should have exterminated us long ago. They still can, in an instant." He shook his huge head. "Yet somewhere the natural evolution failed and here we are." He turned, his emerald stare boring into Joe's. "And, somehow, when I look into Humans eyes, I see our future."

Joe bristled immediately. *What's he trying to say?*

Bagkhal clicked his teeth together. "No, I'm not saying Humans will replace Takki. Unless your people do something incredibly stupid, Congress will not let the Dhasha have your planets. I was merely saying that, despite our great strength, there is something within you Humans that makes me even more nervous than the Takki. Something that makes me wonder why Congress didn't destroy Earth as soon as it was found."

Joe felt his skin tingle with goosebumps. "What do you mean?"

Bagkhal seemingly shook himself. "Never mind," he said abruptly. "My fight with Knaaren left me exhausted and rambling. Go tend to your tasks. I'll send an Ooreiki to deal with your friend."

Joe hesitated. "Thanks. And…I'm sorry. I shouldn't have insulted you."

"You're right," Bagkhal said, sounding amused. "But I accept your apology."

• • •

Bagkhal was as good as his word.

The next day, Libby was seated with Scott and Maggie in the chow hall, tentatively scooping green slime into her mouth and moving it around with her new tongue. Just back from the medics, she was the only one in the entire cafeteria not wearing white from their last hunt against Second Battalion. Joe, having only then finished writing and delivering a post-hunt report for prince Bagkhal, grabbed some food and sat down across from her.

"How is it?" he asked.

"Ith a lithle thore," she admitted.

"You sound like you just got back from the dentist," Joe laughed. "My dad sounded like that when he got a root canal."

"You should hear her say jenfurgling," Maggie giggled.

"Thuth up."

"Tell him about how you were chewing and you thought you had your mouth closed but you didn't. See her vest?"

"I will beath you thilly."

"How long until you can talk normally?" Joe asked.

"Docthor thaid three or four dayth." She hesitated. "Thank you, Thoe."

He blushed and looked at his food. It resembled runny baby crap. "You're welcome."

"Maggie thayth you're working for thath Dhatha. Thath how you paithe for ith."

Joe shot Maggie an irritated glance, then shrugged. "It's nothing. I said I was going to help and I meant it."

Libby glanced at the table. Her cheeks flushed. Then, to his amazement, she began to cry.

Joe reached out and touched her hand. "Libby? You okay?"

Libby jerked and her eyes found him, looking startled. To his surprise, she stood up suddenly. Without another word, she left.

"What'd I do?" Joe asked, glancing at Maggie and Scott.

Scott shrugged, but Maggie was staring after Libby. Sighing, Joe went back to eating. Maggie turned to him after a moment. "Do you like her, Joe?"

The question caught him mid-spoonful and a spray of baby-crap brown spewed across the table in front of him. "What? What kind of question is that? I like all of you. You're my friends." He felt himself blushing so hard his head felt like it would pop.

"You know," Maggie said. "Like a girlfriend. A lover. You think she's sexy, right? Don't you know she wants to get you in bed?"

All around them, conversation had stopped, and Joe could feel the attention of a hundred nearby recruits, waiting for his answer. Joe's mouth opened and closed, to no effect. He made a little strangled noise in the back of his throat. Finally, with a little whimper, he stood up and said, "I have to go to the bathroom."

"You just went," Maggie pointed out.

"I think there's something wrong with my food."

"It's the same exact stuff we're eating."

"I have to go."

"Just answer the question, Joe. Why's it so hard? You're the oldest person here and you act like you're just a shy little kid. If you want to bang her, just say so."

"It's none of your damn business!" At the sudden silence in the hall, Joe realized he had shouted the last loud enough to be heard back on Earth. Every gaze in the place was on him, and he heard several kids snicker. Feeling like he was about to throw up, Joe turned and left.

By the time he'd taken three steps, he was running. Behind him, he heard half the cafeteria break out in laughter. He hit the doors at full tilt, barreling into an Ooreiki Battlemaster on his way inside. He caught the startled Ooreiki by surprise and they went down together in a heap, to more laughter.

His cheeks flushing crimson, Joe thought he was going to die.

Then he saw the look on Battlemaster Nebil's face.

"Zero, what the burning ashes was that? And why the burning hells are you jenfurglings laughing? You think this is burning funny? Get your furgling asses up. All of you! Burning giggling Takki ashpiles! Push-ups! Three hundred! Let's go! You, too, Zero, you charhead. Everyone! *One! Two! GET YOUR STOMACHS OFF THE GROUND!* Three..."

More kids laughed, and by the time Nebil was finished with them, Joe was ready to die. He quickly escaped to Bagkhal's tower to 'lend further assistance,' then just sat outside the Dhasha's front door, trying to sort through the Takkiscrew that was his life.

A sound from within the Dhasha's chambers startled him. "Zero," Bagkhal grunted. "Thought I smelled you. What the hell are you doing sitting out here? I dismissed you for the day."

Joe swallowed hard, the shame still leaving him sick. "Girls," he managed.

Bagkhal made a clicking laugh. "Come inside. Let's talk."

33

NEW RULES

"Rule One," Battlemaster Nebil said, holding the electronic device Joe had given him. "You self-molesting furgs had better keep your burning dicks in your pants, cause if a girl so much as whispers a suggestion of rape, Bagkhal'll cut them off. Got me?"

Several of the boys suddenly went pale.

"Rule Two," the battlemaster continued. "Females, with one examination, medical can determine who you copulated with, how many times, and when...*and* whether or not you were distressed at the time. Bagkhal has ordered that any false accusers will be locked in a room for a day with their accused. Inside, normal Rules will no longer apply. Do *you* get me?"

This time, it was the girls who went white.

"Rule Three," the battlemaster said, "One you're already familiar with. There will be *no* killing. Congress values you as fighters, not as corpses. Any murderers will spend a day with Prince Bagkhal. Any repeat offenders will be executed."

"What if we kill two at one time?" a boy asked stupidly.

The boy shrank back from the battlemaster's slitted gaze. "Rule Four," Battlemaster Nebil said pointedly. "No more infighting between battalions. That means *you*, Zero. Bagkhal's sons will patrol the city every night. Anyone they catch outside the barracks after curfew will be considered a troublemaker and will be punished—since they don't seem to enjoy their sleep, they can spend the next week running instead of sleeping."

"That's not possible," someone snorted.

Battlemaster Nebil gave the boy a long, hard look.

The kid swallowed, hard.

"Rule Five," Nebil continued. "No lying. Lying seems to be an unfortunate trait you Humans share with the Huouyt. For each offense, you will spend a day emptying chamber pots and scrubbing the baths.

"Six. No stealing. Another trait you and the Huouyt have in common. The next time one of you is caught taking something that doesn't belong to you, you'll be stripped naked and marched at the front of the battalion for a week.

"That's all for now," Nebil said. "Battlemasters, resume biosuit training."

Fourth Platoon's new battlemaster, Battlemaster Aneeir, stepped forward, looking much younger and more nervous than anyone else. Even his voice sounded jittery. "Fourth Platoon! Grab your biosuits and meet back here!"

While the other recruits had already unpacked their biosuits from the tight black bricks they had come in, Joe had to start from scratch. He fumbled with the odd alien clasp that released the lid of the lightweight chest, then struggled to pull the heavy black bundle from inside.

Instead of being a single piece, like a wetsuit, the biosuit came in two parts; one for the front of his body, one for the back. Joe just stared at it dumbly.

"You have to take your stuff off first," Maggie said. "It won't seal if you're wearing anything."

Joe sighed. He supposed being naked wasn't a big deal anymore. Aliens, it seemed, did not put much stock in modesty. He stripped.

"Now put it on like this," Maggie said. She spread one half of her suit out on the ground, laid down, and, starting at the feet, she touched the edges of the two halves of the suit together. They sealed immediately, molding to her body as tightly as some weird sort of living spandex. As soon as the feet sealed, the rest of the suit followed in a wave, like an invertebrate convulsing. Maggie didn't even have to have her arms arranged perfectly for the suit to grab them and swallow them whole. The suit stretched over her skin like glossy black glue. Underneath, Joe could see the outlines of her body as clearly as if she were wearing nothing at all. Joe winced, trying to avoid recognizing how good she looked. Then he wondered what would happen to him if he did the same thing. The way the suit contracted hadn't looked very gentle.

"So how do you get it off?" Joe asked, tapping Maggie on the shoulder. He yanked his hand back when his finger hit solid, rocklike rigidity. Tentatively, he touched it again, and found himself touching a piece of stone. Cold stone.

"You can still move?" Joe asked, marveling at the suit. "It's like you turned into some sort of statue."

Maggie giggled. "Isn't it cool?" She turned around to show him her back. Along her back a long, wrist-thick bulge followed the indentation of her spine from the top of her buttocks all the way to the base of her skull. Two more ran on the outside of either leg and, when he looked closely, along the backs of her arms, as well.

"Now you try," Maggie ordered.

Joe hesitated, giving the two halves of his suit a nervous look. "How do you get it off?"

"All you've got to do is *want* it to come off." Maggie saw his look and laughed. "Don't worry, Joe. It feels great. I bet you could sleep in this thing."

"We're probably going to," Joe muttered. Sighing, he followed her lead. The key to getting inside, he learned, was to make sure the seam at the toes was in the right place. As soon as Joe touched the seams together at his feet, the entire suit convulsed on him, catching him still half-seated. It did not crush his balls, as he half-expected, but it still delivered a brief jolt of panic, especially as it closed around his mouth and nose. Even as Joe was reaching up to claw at his face, the passageways opened and he sucked in a startled breath of air. He touched his face, stunned at the metallic *tap* when the suit came into contact with itself. Blinking felt odd—a layer of the suit actually melted to the surface of his eyelids.

Still, the comfort of the thing was amazing. It was heavy and made him have to exaggerate his motions, but as a whole, it actually felt a part of his body. It was also the perfect temperature…at least on the inside. On the outside, it felt like he was made of refrigerated steel. Glancing down at his hands, Joe was further amazed to see that, despite his fingers being covered with a thin layer of the black substance, he could still feel everything that his hands came into contact with. For that matter, his whole body continued to have sensation. He could feel the sharp gravel under his feet despite the fact that the suit was rock-hard on his soles.

The suit was, Joe realized, delivering normal sensations to the wearer without the normal consequences. Standing there, feeling yet not feeling the air around him, he felt awed and a little frightened of Congressional technology.

"This is the Human Biocasing I," their new Battlemaster Aneeir told them once they were all fitted and standing back in formation like sleek black ants. "Obviously, since this is the first model, there will be improvements as Congressional engineers come to understand your body structure more completely. Until then, this is what you've got. You can eat, sleep, piss, and shit in this thing. Some of you furgs will probably even try to mate in it."

Joe winced at the thought of that, but some of the other recruits gave Battlemaster Aneeir looks of fascination.

"Though the suit feels heavy to you, it is not. In fact, you will find that you are approximately eighty-one percent stronger. It feels clumsy because the suit is still adjusting to your body. Once you have spent three days in it, the suit's biomechanisms will be fixed and, like your helmets, it will be so well adapted to your body that only you will be able to wear it."

"Now," Battlemaster Aneeir said, "As you can probably tell, these suits are very complex. What you *don't* know is how complex they really are. For instance, to stop feeling the gravel beneath you, all you have to do is decide that you no longer wish to feel those stones and the suit will pick up your thoughts and desist. Try it right now."

Joe did. As soon as he thought negatively of the sensations the suit was passing on to him, the feelings abruptly stopped.

"Cool!" Scott cried.

"As grounders, this suit is designed to save your lives in more ways than one. It takes over sixteen thousand pounds of pressure to crush the outer shell. The material itself is resistant to brief laser attacks, projectiles, some plasma, and even electricity. Of course, if a Dhasha attacks you, all bets are off."

"So their claws can rip through this stuff?" Joe asked, surprised. The suit felt harder than anything he'd ever felt before.

"Like you were wearing nothing at all," Battlemaster Aneeir replied. "Now, if an attack makes it through that does not cause instant death, the suit can save your life in several other ways. First off, it will seal itself over the wound. This does not necessarily help in a plasma attack, but it does with most other injuries. If something over sixteen thousand pounds lands on you and crushes a leg, then the suit will support you enough to walk, though it will probably hurt like hell. If you have taken a mortal wound, the suit will shut down and put you into a state of hibernation to give you time to reach a medical station. The suit protects against all types of chemical attack, but if something nasty somehow gets past your other gear, it will instantly put you out of commission until medical personnel can evaluate your situation."

"That doesn't sound smart," Joe said. "Putting us out in the middle of a battle? What happens if we can still fight, even with a lungful of gas?"

Aneeir gave him a wry look. "Believe me, Human. You get a lungful of the stuff Congress's enemies have in their arsenals and you will not be breathing, let alone fighting."

"Oh."

"Now," Aneeir continued, "Caring for your suits: Congress supplies its ground soldiers with two types of meals. When you are not wearing your suits, it's the green stuff you're already acquainted with, also called RHCI, or Rudimentary, Human Class I. When you are using your suits, it will be called BNHCII, or Biocasing Nourishment, Human Class II, janja shit for short. Janja shit is a slightly yellowish color and it has a metallic taste to it. While on the battlefield, at least one meal a day should be of the Class II format. It will provide the sustenance your suit needs to survive."

To survive? Joe glanced anxiously down at the thing covering his body. *What the hell is it?*

"Of course, this requires that you eliminate your wastes while still wearing the suit. It might feel uncomfortable, but believe me, you do not want to wind up buck-ass naked squatting out behind a rock when the enemy finds you."

Joe grimaced at the image, knowing all-too-well how that could turn out.

Aneeir stopped and scanned his new platoon. "Any questions?" Once again, his sudah began fluttering nervously. Joe guessed this was probably his first time as Battlemaster, possibly promoted on the spot just for the occasion.

"So the ammo we use in the hunts won't hurt us anymore?" Maggie asked.

Aneeir gave her an amused look. "No. These are just training suits. Real ones are immune to the poisons in the fake rounds. No more questions? Then everyone get to the barracks. You will need to wear your suits continuously for the next three days, including during sleep. Zero, you may begin your duties with Prince Bagkhal. *Haagi.*"

Joe looked down at himself and realized he looked like an onyx statue. A *well-defined* onyx statue. Rippling abs, outstanding pecs, biceps the size of grapefruits… At that revelation, he felt a tiny spark of satisfaction. If Congress had done one thing for him, it had certainly made him look good. Glancing up, he saw that several nearby girls had realized it, too. One of them was staring at his crotch with unabashed interest.

Blushing, Joe cleared his throat and covered himself. "Hi," he mumbled, groping for his clothes with one hand. "Nice to meet you."

They giggled and walked off.

You are a goddamn furg, you know that?

As he pulled on his pants, he noticed that Maggie was scowling after the trio with a look of Death. When she turned back, it was to give him an accusing glare.

"Don't worry," he said, grinning. "They only want my body."

• • •

Joe was going to his first meeting with Bagkhal when he saw Libby sitting alone in the shadows behind the chow hall, staring into space.

"Lib?"

Libby jerked, getting to her feet in an instant. She wasn't wearing any gear over her biosuit and Joe felt himself blush like a beet. Her long, lean body was outlined to feminine perfection, right down to her small, pert breasts and the subtle lines leading down to her groin.

He tore his eyes away from her.

"How's that new tongue working out for you?" he asked, staring at his feet.

Sex Master Dobbs strikes again. Oh my God. Kill me now. "How's your tongue working out for you?" Why not just ask her how her gun's been firing lately? Or if her boots still fit. How did Dad do it? Mom must've taken pity on him. It's the only way a guy in my family could ever—

"I could show you," Libby said shyly.

Joe's eyes jerked back to her face. Then, *That's not what she means you furg. You friggin' wish. She's just—*

Libby's biosuit peeled off and fell to the ground.

Oh.

• • •

"This is really stupid, Joe."

"Just shut up and watch, okay? That's your sister down there, too."

"Yeah, but… Joe, they've got guns. They killed your da—"

"Stop being a pussy, Eric. You weren't pissing yourself back when we came up with the idea in your living room."

"I was just fooling around, Joe."

"I wasn't. I'm getting him back. You don't wanna help, I'll tell Katie when I see her that you didn't think she was worth it."

"That's not fair! They've got guns, Joe. Your stupid idea isn't gonna work."

"It will. Watch it."

"Well I wanna be the one to light them, then. You can be the one to go down there and get killed."

"Fine. Be sure you don't light them all at once."

"My dad was the pyrotechnic, Joe. Not yours."

"Just do it. When I hit them with the truck, I want them looking up, not at me."

"*This is such a stupid idea. What makes you think they'll care about fireworks?*"

"*You really think they've got fireworks on alien planets?*"

"*Well, yeah.*"

"*Let's hope they don't.*"

"*You're leaving?*"

"*Yeah. Gotta talk to the guys with the trucks before the aliens get here.*"

"*Good luck, Joe.*"

"*Just be ready to run. As soon as they figure out what's going on, they're gonna come after you.*"

"*Get my sister back. That's all I care about.*"

"*I will. Promise.*"

"*Joe?*"

Joe opened his eyes. His skin was prickled in goosebumps where it was exposed to the air, but the ground beneath him was cushioned by his biosuit. Libby lay beside him, her elegant body partially covered in one half of her suit, her head nestled against his shoulder. Joe took a slow breath, praying he wasn't dreaming.

"Joe?" Libby stroked his chest.

I'm in paradise, Joe thought, shuddering.

"Weren't you supposed to meet Bagkhal, Joe?"

"Oh, *ash!*" Joe leapt to his feet so fast that Libby tumbled out of his arms, onto the ground. He froze, horrified.

Instead of spitting curses at him, she giggled. "Go on. You don't wanna piss him off."

Joe helped her to her feet and gently embraced her. "Thanks, Libby." He hesitated, staring into her soft brown eyes. *What else are you gonna say? We should do this again sometime? You furg.*

He kissed her, blushing, then dove into his suit.

• • •

"You're late."

Joe winced under Bagkhal's accusatory stare. He cleared his throat uncomfortably. "I was working out a problem with a member of my groundteam."

"You stink of hormones, Human," Bagkhal growled. "Don't lie to me."

Joe flushed furiously and bit his lip. "I didn't."

Prince Bagkhal gave an impressed snort. "*That* problem?"

Intensely embarrassed, Joe began to thoroughly scrutinize the claw-marks in the floor near his feet. He nodded.

"Well, good for you." Moving to the table, Bagkhal nodded at the red-dish-brown vial lying on the table beside him. "Your drugs came in. Drink that."

Grateful for the distraction, Joe went to examine the vial. "Looks like coffee sludge," he noted.

The big Dhasha returned to his gelatinous mat nearby, the gaping 'wounds' that his jet black claws left in it quickly sealing shut after a couple seconds. "It's a powerful mental stimulant that commands ridiculous prices on the open market from politicians and businessmen throughout Congress. We'll have to monitor your consumption and make sure you don't form an addiction."

"So...coffee sludge." Joe uncapped the vial and took a whiff. Immediately, he recoiled. "This smells like pig vomit!"

"Then perhaps Congress should invest in some pigs," Bagkhal said flatly. "This stuff costs three thousand credits a batch. Drink it."

Joe took another whiff and wrinkled his nose. "Am I going to have to do this every night?"

"Only every six or so. You'll know when it's time—you usually fall asleep where you stand."

Grimacing, Joe said, "So this stuff is induced narcolepsy?"

"Only if you don't dose yourself fast enough."

Joe grunted and scowled at the vial. *I can't* not *drink it. Not after he already helped Libby.* Closing his eyes, he put the vial to his lips and tipped it back.

It burned on the way down, but other than that, he felt fine.

Then he felt *more* than fine. Everything suddenly came into focus. The leftover exhaustion from his constant running fled him in an instant. He was as wide awake as he'd ever been, and not the least bit jittery.

"I think it works," Joe said, staring at the vial in astonishment. "Whoa. You know, if I had this stuff in school, I probably would've been able to read Shakespeare without passing out."

"Excellent. Just for safety's sake, though, pick up that ring and slip it on a finger. Medical would like to monitor your life-signs for the next day or so, as you're the first Human test subject."

That didn't sound good.

Nervous, Joe went to the table and slipped a rubbery orange ring over a gleaming black finger. It reminded him of the akarit and he winced, feeling a little guilty for his duplicity. He kind of liked the Dhasha.

Prince Bagkhal was watching him. Something in the Dhasha's gaze made Joe blush and look at the floor. "So how do you like your suit?" Bagkhal asked.

"It's okay," Joe said. "It sucks we're gonna have to wear them for three days."

"Something I see you're already having problems with." The Dhasha shifted, leaning one shoulder against the wall. "So, what did the recruits think of my new rules?"

"We honestly should've had them a long time ago," Joe said.

"Good."

Joe gingerly looked around. He couldn't *see* any slaves or grooming bars or hook-shaped tooth picks. "So what's my job for the day? Err... night? Hell, this place has got ashy daylight cycles anyway. How am I gonna tell night from day anymore if I can't sleep?"

"Keep track of the time," Bagkhal said. "As for your duties, I have an errand for you to run. I would like you to arrange a meeting between myself and the Huouyt Representative. He's been on this planet much too long and it's making me suspicious. The first thing a wise soldier learns is never trust a Huouyt. The second thing he learns is to never trust a Huouyt on a planet with an ekhta. They are spies, assassins, saboteurs, thieves, and very, very good liars. The whole species should be destroyed."

Coming from a Dhasha, that was saying something.

Then Joe realized what Bagkhal had said, and felt himself pale. "You mean Na'leen's still here?"

Too late, Joe realized a recruit should have no knowledge of a Representative's affairs. It was the same as an amoeba knowing the comings and goings of an eagle. Apparently, Bagkhal realized that, too, because the prince cocked his head at him and was silent for too long. "How do you know of Representative Na'leen, Zero?" His words were much too casual.

Joe swallowed hard, pinned by that predatory stare. "He…wanted to…interview me…about Kihgl."

The Dhasha continued to give him a long, piercing look. "And why would you know anything about Commander Kihgl?"

"Ummm," Joe managed.

Bagkhal got off his mat and took a step forward, head lowered, so that their eyes were almost on level. "I chose this regiment because I heard what Knaaren did to my old friend. I got here as fast as I could. Knaaren was shipped to Levren without his talons or scales. I removed them myself. You understand what that means, for a Dhasha?"

Joe could guess. He swallowed, hard.

"Why," Bagkhal rumbled, lowering his head further, until his lips were almost touching Joe's abdomen and their eyes were level, "would Representative Na'leen wish to interview *you* about Kihgl?" The intensity of the ka-par was back.

Joe cringed. "He gave me his kasja. Before he…died."

Bagkhal twitched. It seemed like an eternity that Bagkhal just stared at him. Then, very slowly, Bagkhal said, "You're the reason he's dead." There was no malice to his words, but Joe's guts twisted in fear anyway.

Bagkhal examined him a moment longer, then twisted to glance up the stairs at the exit of the room. A moment later, he once again pinned Joe with his gaze. "Na'leen approached you. When?"

Though he knew his very life danced on his next words, Joe found it impossible to lie. "The night after the Tribunal's inspection," he said

Bagkhal's gaze sharpened. "What did he want?"

Trying not to tremble, Joe said, "He wanted to know if Kihgl said anything to me about the Fourfold Prophecy."

"*Did* he?" Bagkhal barked.

Though his every instinct screamed at him to lie, Joe whispered, "Yes."

Bagkhal gave him a long, piercing look, then swiveled and stalked across the room. He paced for several minutes, with no sound except the grinding-tinkle of his claws sinking into the floor, breaking chunks of stone loose in his passage.

Finally, Bagkhal swung back to face Joe and said, "It was not your testimony that condemned him. Your name was never even mentioned in the Peacemakers' logs. How much did you tell Na'leen?"

Joe swallowed, remembering Battlemaster Aneeir's warning about Dhasha talons ripping through biosuits. "I told him that Kihgl said that nobody tells the Fourfold Prophecy more than once."

Bagkhal froze, giving him an acute look. "That's all?"

Joe nodded.

"Was he satisfied with that?"

Remembering the cold way the Representative had dismissed him, Joe shook his head.

Sharply, Bagkhal snapped, "Was there *more* Kihgl told you, boy?"

"He said…" Joe swallowed, so scared he was shaking.

"*Tell* me!" Bagkhal barked.

"That it was my life or his oorei," Joe whimpered. Something about the Dhasha prince did not allow for evasion or half-truths.

"And he chose for you to live. Why?"

"He said he had hope the Trith was right," Joe whispered. "Something about the fall of Congress."

Bagkhal gave him a long, piercing look. "Well, at least you're not a total furg." He let out a huge sigh and lowered his head disgustedly between his front legs. "Damn."

"What does that mean?" Joe asked, hating the way his voice cracked.

Bagkhal snorted. "It means nothing. The Trith make everyone else dance to their whims like puppets on a string. They never give the whole prophecy, and their words are self-fulfilling." He gave Joe another long, hard look. "Have you told anyone else what you just told me?"

"Not exactly."

"Not *exactly*?" Bagkhal roared.

"I think Nebil knows," Joe cried. "He asked me in private one day if Kihgl had talked to me about the Trith."

"*When?!*" Bagkhal demanded. "How recently? *Where*?!"

"Back on the ship," Joe whimpered.

Bagkhal seemed to hesitate. "What ship?"

"Coming from Earth," Joe managed. "Please, I'm sorry."

"The *troop*ship," Bagkhal clarified. "*Before* you met Na'leen."

"Yes," Joe managed, the Dhasha's harshness returning him to the instinctual terror that Knaaren had etched into his being.

Bagkhal seemed to relax entirely. He gave Joe a long look, then softly said, "Calm down, Human. I'm not going to hurt you." He almost sounded...apologetic.

Joe let out a sob of relief and clung to the table, his legs going weak. He could only nod in gratitude.

"Sit down," the Dhasha prince commanded him gently. He padded to the far wall and sat down, facing him. "I'll keep my distance. Tell me the rest."

Joe gratefully sank into the chair. "It was a stupid mark on my arm. One of my groundmates got bored and started drawing on me with markers. It looked a lot like the image the Trith had given Kihgl."

"*Looked* like or *was*?"

Joe swallowed hard, remembering. "Was," he admitted softly.

Bagkhal grunted. "What else?"

There wasn't much to tell. Joe shakily recounted everything he knew. "...When we got to Kophat, Kihgl took me out to the practice flats to kill me. But he decided not to. Gave me his kasja, to show Nebil his decision. Nebil made me wear it, instead."

"And where is the kasja now?" Bagkhal demanded.

"Nebil has it," Joe said. "Tril made me take it off."

"As he should have," Bagkhal growled. "You didn't earn it."

"Nebil made me," Joe babbled, sweating inside the biosuit. "I didn't want to, but he wanted me to—"

"Recognize Kihgl's sacrifice," Bagkhal interrupted. "I understand." He snorted deeply and turned to stare at the far wall, seemingly lost in thought. Eventually, he turned back to Joe and said, "You realize it is my duty to kill you, right, Zero?"

Joe swallowed convulsively. "Why?"

"Because," Bagkhal growled, "apparently the Trith are interested in you. If they've tied you to the fall of Congress, that's bad. A Trith cannot lie—because of what they are, it destroys them." He sighed and idly began raking up bits of gravel with his talons. "They *don't*, however, have to tell the whole prophecy. Which allows them to *make* the future, because idiots like Na'leen get involved, led around by their snouts like a harnessed Takki."

Joe lowered his head, the slick heat of his sweat warming his skin under the biosuit.

"Don't worry," Bagkhal said. "Kihgl went a little insane after the Trith's visit and I decided to do some research of my own. After all, who can tell a Dhasha prince what to do?"

Not very many, Joe thought. He still felt like pissing himself, just from the alien's proximity, all the way across the room.

"As it turns out," Bagkhal continued with a grunt, "the future is not a stagnant image, as everyone assumes. It's all probabilities. Computers could guess the future to extreme degrees of accuracy, if we ever made one powerful enough. Yet each sentient creature our Creator put in this playground we call Life maintains its free will. He can *choose*. Even a damned Takki has free will. They just *choose* not to use it." Muttering, he continued gouging stone from the floor. "But the future is just that—*probabilities*. It can *change*. That the Trith have tied you to the fall of Congress merely means that the *probability* is that you will have a hand in it. Which means it's coming in your lifetime."

Eventually, Bagkhal stopped and got back to his feet. "The Trith are going to visit you, Joe. When they do, punch them in the face for me." He made an irritated snort. "Until then, go schedule that meeting with Na'leen on my behalf. His continued presence is annoying."

Joe flinched. "I don't know if I should do that..." *What will he do when he finds out how Na'leen tried to claim me?*

"Your very first day and you tell me to get somebody else?" Prince Bagkhal demanded, irritation thick in his voice.

"I'll do it," Joe said quickly.

Bagkhal grunted. "While you're there," he continued, "tell him I know why he's been making friends on the Training Committee. Now go. All this talk of Trith and Huouyt is making me angry."

Indeed, drops of neon orange spittle were spattering the ebony floor.

All the way to the Representative's tower, Joe wondered what Bagkhal would do to him if he found out about Kihgl and Yuil's rebels. The great Dhasha had claimed to have been a friend of Kihgl, yet something told Joe that Bagkhal would slaughter him, Yuil, and every other rebel in an instant, the moment he found out what Joe had been doing in his off-time. The thought was enough to make his palms sweaty on his walk to Representative Na'leen's tower.

At the base of Na'leen's edifice, a lone Huouyt stood guarding a single elevator. At Joe's approach, he didn't even appear to show any interest at all.

"I have a message for Representative Na'leen," Joe said, once he got within talking range.

The Huouyt looked him up and down. "From who?" The disdain in the alien's words was enough to make Joe bristle.

"Prince Bagkhal," Joe said.

The Huouyt showed no reaction whatsoever. The downy white cilia covering his body remained as stagnant as death. For a long moment, the Huouyt said nothing. Then, "Climb on." He backed into the elevator and allowed Joe to enter.

Joe stepped onto the platform and the Huouyt pressed the button. For what must have been close to thirty minutes, Joe rode from the base of the tower to the top-floor penthouse overlooking the city, enduring the Huouyt's flat, fishy stare the entire way. Two more Huouyt met them at the top, and they escorted Joe from the top of the elevator to the blessedly fresh air inside the first set of heavy doors. The masses of treasure had been removed, the remnants tastefully used to decorate the outer chamber. Only the golden statue of the Representative remained in place.

Then invisible hands grabbed Joe by the back of the shirt and dragged him through the lavish passageways, back to the room with the pool.

"Speak," Representative Na'leen said once Joe had been shown to his chambers by the rough hands of Jreet. He was in his water-bath again, the wormy red appendage blossoming under the surface.

"Prince Bagkhal would like to meet with you," Joe said.

"Would he," Representative Na'leen said, sounding completely uncon-cerned. "How interesting. Tell him I'm busy." He plucked another gelatinous disc from his dish and dropped it into the wriggling worms in his head. "Take him away, please."

Immediately, invisible Jreet hands grabbed him again and started to drag him from the pool. The exchange had lasted no more than fifteen seconds.

"He knows why you've been making friends on the Training Committee!" Joe cried, terrified that his very first task in Bagkhal's service would end in total failure.

"It's a politician's job to make friends." As the Jreet hesitated, the Huouyt sat up from his bath and stared at Joe with its huge, eerie, electric-blue eyes. The wormy appendages in his forehead immediately began retracting back into his head. "Tell him that. Also tell him that a member of the Tribunal does not caper to the whims of a mere Secondary Overseer and his Human pet."

Joe stared. *Bagkhal's an Overseer?*

"Why is he still here?" Na'leen demanded. "Get rid of him."

Joe bit his lip. Bagkhal was not going to like his message. As the Jreet began to tug him away, the Huouyt said, "Wait. You are the recruit they call Zero, aren't you?"

Grimacing, Joe nodded.

"Have you remembered anything about Kihgl's prophecy yet, boy?"

Joe swallowed, hard. "No sir. I told you what he told me."

The Huouyt gave him a flat stare. "On second thought, tell your Prince I will meet with him." The Representative stood, his metallic clothing dripping into the vat beneath him. "I hear Bagkhal is as much of a loyalist as they come. He personally executed the last traitor he found in his ranks. Him, and all of his friends." He flipped a wet, paddle-shaped tentacle at Joe. "But I'm busy for the next week or two. I'll have one of my assistants meet him with the date and time sometime tomorrow."

Joe forced himself to smile. "He'll be glad to hear it."

He was shaking on his ascent back to Bagkhal's tower. How much did Na'leen know? Had he been here the whole time, investigating? Had he had one of his assassins follow Joe when he went with Yuil? Is that why he hadn't had Joe killed yet? Because he was leading them deeper into the enemy's ranks?

He was in a cold sweat by the time he got back to Bagkhal.

"Well? What did the *vaghi* Huouyt have to say?"

"He'll meet with you," Joe said. "He'll send one of his assistants to discuss the date tomorrow."

"Assistants." Bagkhal snorted. "You have a lot to learn, Zero." He indicated the table with his head. "Now, grab the infopad and take a seat. I have dictations."

Joe spent the rest of the night aiding Bagkhal in reviewing information from the regiment and taking notes on training expectations. These he delivered to the Battalion Commanders, who were as wide awake as he was in their apartments, writing reports on little pads. When Bagkhal was finished with him for the night, Joe wanted to go to Yuil's meeting-place and tell her to be careful, but knew, after the day's events, he'd only be putting her in more danger.

Joe's heart began to pound as he stared out toward the empty building on the edge of Alishai. If they found Yuil, they'd arrest Joe. Unless they were using him to get at someone bigger. Who was Yuil working for? As of yet, the Ooreiki hadn't said.

"I wish I could help you," Joe said to the empty sky. If Yuil got caught, it would be Joe's fault. Joe had led Na'leen to the Ooreiki. Just like Elf.

With no response except the eerie howl of ferlii-wind on the buildings around him, Joe returned to the barracks.

• • •

It was a stalemate.

With Joe leading them, Sixth Battalion was finally holding its own. But then, so was Rat. Neither battalion, when it was on offense, could get past the tunnel entrances.

Everyone was getting frustrated.

Joe was sitting outside the barracks, picking at the inside of his headcom as he waited for Battlemaster Aneeir to bring his groundteam down for breakfast, when Nebil stopped beside him.

"What are you doing, Zero?"

"Bagkhal's finished with me for tonight," Joe said. "I'm waiting for Aneeir to wake up the platoon for today's hunt."

"I meant with your headcom."

Joe glanced down at the thing in his hands and he winced. As he'd been sitting there, he'd absently pried up some of the padding. He quickly mashed it back down. "Nothing, sir."

Nebil turned to go.

The thought that had nagging at Joe for days broke to the surface and he cleared his throat. "Battlemaster?"

Nebil turned back. "What?"

"Is there some way to make a headcom broadcast to someone not on my team?"

The Ooreiki's gummi eyes narrowed instantly. "Like who?"

Joe bit his lip. "Like Second Battalion?"

Battlemaster gave him a cold, hard look. "Now why in the ashy hells would you want to talk to the enemy, Zero?"

"I don't wanna talk to them," Joe said. "I want them to hear *me* talk."

For a long moment, Battlemaster Nebil simply stared at him and Joe knew he was about to get clobbered. Then, without another word, Nebil simply walked off.

In formation that afternoon, Nebil surprised them by telling them that, starting that afternoon, recruits would vote for their recruit battlemasters. The ceremony turned out to be relatively simple, except when the kids forgot who was in their platoon.

"Anyone says Zero again and I'm going to choke the living soot out of him!" Nebil screamed. "Pick someone in your *platoon,* you Takki bastards!"

Maggie was grinning when Nebil stormed up to her. "You! Are you *amused* by this, recruit? Is there something *funny* about this situation that I somehow missed?"

"No, Battlemaster!" Her words came out in a giggle.

"Really? Because I thought I saw you with a big, stupid grin on your face. *Did* your groundmate have a big, stupid grin on her face, Zero?"

"I didn't see one, Battlemaster!"

"Then that makes you a liar, doesn't it, Zero? Unless I misunderstood my lessons in Human anatomy, a big, stupid grin means that she thought something was funny."

"Must have misunderstood your lessons, sir," Joe said, deadpan.

Nebil's pupils narrowed to slits. "You must enjoy emptying chamber pots."

Joe winced. He was pretty sure Congressional technology had ways to disintegrate bodily waste, but no. The Ooreiki saved it to use as punishment.

Nebil went back to haranguing the platoons into choosing their leaders. When their turn came, every single recruit in Joe's platoon voted for him. As he stood there, stunned, he realized that Libby and all of his groundmates were grinning.

When the ceremony was over, Nebil returned to the front of the battalion. "We've got another hunt tomorrow! Second Battalion's defending, so you Takki have the black. Bagkhal will be watching again, so make it look good! For the rest of the day, I want all of you to rest up for the hunt. Let's show our new commander what we can do, for once! Dismissed. Except you, Zero. You stay."

Grimacing, Joe waited while rest of the battalion departed, wondering which set of chores it would be tonight.

"Tomorrow," Nebil said, shoving a headcom at him, "you're going to try something different with that fire-loving Jreet Lagrah. We're upping the ante, boy." Nebil and Lagrah, Joe had discovered, were both former long-term Planetary Ops veterans, and the two of them had begun a gentlemen's game of 'Screw The Other Asher' and Second and Sixth battalions were quickly becoming pawns in a superior-officer grudge-match.

"We...are?" Joe asked, gingerly taking the headcom.

"Something I learned in Planetary Ops," Nebil said. "All headcoms have the capacity to transmit on all frequencies. It's an internal governor and battery limitations that keep them in check. Your PPU, on the other hand..." Battlemaster Nebil brought out an utterly demolished PPU and handed it to him, "...has a battery that could power a cruise-ship."

Staring down at them, Joe realized that he was looking at *his* PPU and *his* headcom. He felt a cold wave of dread.

"Lagrah rigged the haauks to fail on our last hunt and we got dumped a mile off course, so we didn't have enough time to fully entrench ourselves before Second arrived," Nebil said.

Joe frowned. He had been *wondering* why the Ooreiki had made them all walk to the tunnels.

"He wants to use dirty tricks?" Nebil went on. "Two can play at that game. Everything you say will now be heard by *both* Sixth and Second Battalions. If anyone asks, your PPU *accidentally* got smashed and certain parts *accidentally* wound up on the internal workings of the headcom." With that, he turned to go.

"Wait!" Joe cried. He stared at the headcom in his hands, suddenly feeling like it was a poisonous, fire-breathing snake. "They can *hear* me? *Everything*? Isn't that a *bad* thing?" The *last* thing he wanted Second to do was to hear him give all of his commands. "I meant just something I could turn on and off, you know?"

Nebil gave him a long, flat stare.

"What am I supposed to do with this?" Joe demanded. "How am I supposed to lead the battalion if they can *hear* me?"

"Figure it out," Nebil said. "I'm supplying accidents. Not a replacement for a small simian brain." Then he turned and left Joe there, anxiously staring at his dismantled gear.

That evening, after Aneeir locked up the barracks, Joe brought out his headcom and showed it to his friends. "Nebil said Second would be able to hear me tomorrow," Joe said, after they had hissed at the damage done to it. "Maybe we could use that."

Libby gave his headcom a dubious look. "You *want* them to hear you giving commands on the hunt?"

"I dunno," Joe said, still perplexed by Nebil's all-out ruining of his helmet. "Maybe you could lead this hunt, Libby. I could be a decoy. Give them all the wrong ideas."

Libby snorted. "Rat's not stupid. She'll see nobody's listening to you."

"You got a better idea?" Joe demanded. "I'd like to make it count, 'cause I think they're gonna take the headcom from me as soon as they figure out what Nebil did to it, and Aneeir's gonna really thrash me for that PPU. Take a look. Nebil ripped it apart."

Libby fell into a mournful silence when Joe brought out the ruined PPU. "Damn," she muttered. "So how the hell do we fight like this? We *need* you, Joe."

It was Scott who said, "Well, soot, I got an idea, Joe." He was still frowning at Joe's headcom. "Why don't we make the whole *battalion* a decoy?"

• • •

The plaza was alive with the roar of bored recruits. Sixth Battalion wore black and nearby, dressed in white, Second was waiting for its pickup.

"You ready, Joe?" Scott whispered.

Joe nodded. He slipped his headcom over his skull and said, "...well, sure, but girls don't really know what a guy wants in bed. I'd take guy-on-guy action over a girl any day."

The plaza suddenly went silent.

Joe blundered on, "Besides, guys are just downright sexier. That Tank guy, especially. He's a burning stud. Have you <u>seen</u> those pecs? Who'd you rather be lookin' up at, I mean really?"

"I dunno," Libby said. "I kind of like Rat."

Joe froze, trying to figure out if she was serious. Libby winked.

Clearing his throat, Joe said, "Yeah, I guess she's okay. We're gonna kick her ass today, though. I've got it all planned out. They'll totally never-goddamn, this thing's been giving me a headache ever since Maggie threw it off the balcony. Ash. Thanks a lot, Mag." He wrenched his headcom off and glared down at it. Behind him, Second Battalion was riveted in place, staring in his direction. Rat was leaning forward, waiting for him to say more. Joe sat down and rested his headcom on a knee.

"I think it's working," Scott said, grinning as he sat down beside him. "They're all staring at you, Joe."

"Yeah." Joe could feel them. "My back's itching like hell."

The defenders left first to go prepare the tunnels for invaders.

When Aneeir came to get the platoon with the attackers' haauk, Joe and Libby held back, waiting to board until very last. Then Aneeir lifted off and they were skimming down the road, toward the hunt. Scott and Carl stood directly behind Aneeir, so when they got into a shoving match, they almost bumped him off the haauk.

"What in the Jreet hells?!" Aneeir snapped, rounding on them. "What are you sootbags doing?!"

Scott was amazingly red-faced, considering they had planned it out the night before. "I want a different squad," Scott said. "I can't stand being in the same one with this redneck asher any longer. I saw him screwing a Takki the other day, just like his dog back when he lived in Alabama."

Carl threw down his headcom and the two of them got into an all-out brawl, assisted by half the platoon. Caught in the middle of it, Aneeir never saw Libby get on her stomach. Then, with a grin at Joe, she rolled under the gate and off the back of the <u>haauk</u>, alone. When the Ooreiki finally got the platform moving again, he was furious, cursing them with a mastery of Congie that even Linin would have found impressive.

"Main force is following at a run," Libby said, once they were out of sight.

"All right," Joe said. "Everyone stick to the plan. The decoy will attempt to draw their attention while the main force makes a tunnel incursion. The decoy's gotta make it look real, though, so don't do anything stupid. Got it?"

Every kid standing on the haauk nodded while Aneeir drove on, oblivious.

"Okay," Joe said, seeing the clearing ahead of them. "We're coming up on the dropoff. Everyone get ready. Decoy, get ready to do your thing."

When Aneeir set them down, they all hurdled the railing of the haauk, having long ago learned that to wait to file out the back was to get shot by Second Battalion snipers. While Joe and the rest of Sixth Battalion secured a corner of the battlefield, Scott, Carl, Maggie, and four other members of their squad crept across the field, keeping low to avoid being seen. When they were in position, Scott said, "Ready."

"How are we doing?" Joe asked.

"Main force selected a tunnel," Libby said. *"Waiting on decoy."*

"Go, Scott," Joe said. "Main force is waiting on you."

Moments later, Joe heard the sucking *thwap* of gunfire. He waited several minutes, then said, "Main force, go!" He lunged up and raced across the battlefield, jumping into a deep den tunnel and opening fire on the defenders inside. The rest of Sixth Battalion followed, and they pushed deeper, allowing Second Battalion to close them in from behind.

"They've got us surrounded," Joe said. "Everyone dig in. Main force has still got a chance."

"*Affirmative,*" Libby said. "*They haven't seen me yet.*"

Joe had the rest of Sixth Battalion make a wall of bodies blocking either end of the tunnel and they hunkered down inside. There they sat. For hours.

"Real brilliant plan, Zero," Rat called from somewhere deeper in the tunnel. "A burning frontal assault. How stupid can you get? Your decoy's all dead and your main force is pinned. You might as well give up now."

"*Main force needs a distraction,*" Libby said. "*Looking at the flag and two defenders right now. Rest of groundteam got called back. Rat's going to blitz you.*"

Hunkered against the wall of bodies, Joe nodded at the remnants of Sixth Battalion. "All right, main force, here we go." He leapt up and led Sixth Battalion in an all-out charge toward the deep den, screaming every command he knew.

Despite the confusion Joe broadcasted over the headcom, the fighting was intense. His comrades began dropping all around him, and Joe began to worry that he'd been premature in making his charge. The attackers kept dwindling, with white hitting them from both directions.

Then Joe and Rat were face to face. Rat was grinning. She raised her rifle. Joe was grappling with another defender, unable to lift his weapon. "You're such a furg, Zero," Rat laughed. "Next time bring your diapers."

Then Libby said, "*Main force is on the surface. Got the flag in my hand.*"

Joe grinned as Rat shot him in the face.

• • •

When the medics revived them, Nebil immediately gave the entire battalion two whole days off. Halfway through the second day, when they entered the chow hall, their tables were laid out with hot platters of roast beef and turkey, still steaming from the oven. Buckets sat beside the trays, filled to the brim with mashed potatoes and gravy. Macaroni and cheese lay piled behind those, and milk and apple juice shared table space with more alcohol and candy than Joe had ever seen in his life.

Before he allowed them to sit down, Battlemaster Nebil made them recite the Groundteam Prayer. Joe held hands with the others and recited it with the others, his eyes as wide as theirs as he stared at the feast before them.

"I am a grounder. This is my groundmate. Apart, we are nothing. Together, we are a groundteam. I will never abandon my groundteam and my groundteam will never abandon me. I will live with my groundmates, fight with my groundmates, and when I die, my essence will be carried on by my surviving groundmates. I will obey the commands of my ground leader without question. I am a grounder."

"Enjoy, you Takki bastards," Nebil said. "Prince Bagkhal thought you should have a reward for whipping Second. It was a real pain in the ass to get it, too. The Training Committee wouldn't pay for it, so your overseer provided it out of his own pocket. I'm not going to even try to explain to you how much that costs."

Battlemaster Nebil started to leave, then turned back with a dubious look at the vodka and whiskey. "Oh, and watch how much of that stuff you drink. It is *said* that this is what Humans use to celebrate, but from everything I've read, it has some extremely undesirable aftereffects. So imbibe your spoils in moderation. I'm putting you back to work tomorrow whether your head hurts or not. Got it?!"

Nine hundred kids shouted, "Kkee, Battlemaster!"

"Keep them in line, Zero," Nebil snapped.

"Kkee, Battlemaster," Joe replied.

Grunting, Nebil gave them all one last, long look, then left.

The next morning, Joe could barely move without vomiting. It had been his first taste of alcohol and Joe, like every other kid there, drank himself stupid before he'd realized what he'd done. He had taken a brief detour on his way to the chow hall to puke in privacy when a shadow made him glance up from the diamond gravel. Joe swallowed down bile, hoping it wasn't a battlemaster.

It wasn't. The creature had tiny limbs, its spindly legs looking utterly incapable of holding up the rest of its mass. Its skin was pale and gray, its head impossibly huge and egg-shaped, its mouth a tiny button in an invisible chin. It was the eyes, though, that made Joe stop breathing. They were utterly black, showing not a gleam of wetness. Peering into them was like peering into the night sky, one swept clean of stars, leaving just the void.

It's a Trith. His skin became awash in hard, painful goosebumps. Joe scuttled backwards on his hands, staring up at the thing in horror.

The Trith took a step towards him, focused on his face. *Joe Dobbs. Son of Harold, brother of Sam. As all creatures dance on the strings of Fate, so shall you.*

Joe's mouth fell open. The thought had not been his own.

Your future has been written. The Trith's midnight eyes continued to hold his, drawing him in like black wells of gravity. *Your life will follow the path it was given.* Joe felt himself losing his sense of self, becoming a part of the creature in front of him, completely helpless to stop it. *Eventually, you must face your destiny.* The gravity wells of the Trith's eyes tugged him deeper, surrounding and crushing him on all sides, reducing him to a pinprick of light in a mass of inky blackness. *For Fate decided you will shatter Congress, Joe.*

As the endless black pits of the Trith's eyes became Joe's whole world, he had the utterly humbling knowledge that he was just a tiny speck in a universe, his existence insignificant in the face of the bigger picture. *Fate decided you will shatter Congress, Joe,* the Trith repeated, like a gong going off inside eternity. Joe felt the Void closing in on him, assailing him from all sides, its sheer vastness threatening to stamp out the tiny speck that was himself.

Heavy silence reigned absolute after the Trith's final words, and Joe panicked, lost in the unyielding, inky depths that surrounded him. For long moments, Joe felt nothing, saw nothing, experienced nothing but his own terror. Then, into the darkness, the Trith spoke again.

You will try to fight it, but invariably, your path will lead to the same end.

Then Joe's paralysis broke and the Trith was gone.

34

VISIONS OF TRITH

Weeks later, on his way to Prince Bagkhal's chambers, Joe glared up at the brightly-clothed Ooreiki going about their business in the *ferlii* towers. Not a single one wore black. Instead, they wore Dhasha scales, long strings of glittering beads, flowing red and yellow and pink cloth, elegant fringed scarves and sashes, ornamental headdresses, spined blue plumes, runed bones, vibrant silken gauzes, crystals, precious metals, and even peacock feathers.

I'll bet they have flushing toilets, Joe thought disgustedly as he walked. *The pampered bastards.*

Staring up at them, Joe realized Yuil wasn't any different. *She doesn't know what we have to go through. She's got her plush room, her fancy equipment and her soft clothes... She doesn't know what it's like to breathe diamond dirt while trying not to get shot, or what it's like to die every other day, just to be brought back to life so we can do it again the next time. She's like all the rest—she's soft.*

Then a small, logical voice reminded him, *Yes, but she's the only one who wants to help you get out of here.*

Just that afternoon, Yuil had laid out her plan to get Joe off of Kophat. Three rotations from now, he had to rendezvous with Yuil's companions in the abandoned *ferlii*. Yuil had said Joe could bring his groundteam, but Joe was still debating that. Maggie seemed to be enjoying her new life, especially now that Nebil was in charge. Scott was the type of person who could be happy whether he was living the high life in a fancy hotel ballroom or digging dirt out from under his thumbnails after a hunt.

Libby was the real problem. He knew nothing in the world would get her to go with him, and he suspected that, despite their budding relationship, she would turn him over to Nebil the instant she caught a whiff of what he was really doing with Yuil.

Prince Bagkhal was in a foul mood when Joe entered his den. Joe recognized the Dhasha's body language and immediately felt a spasm of fear. This was what Knaaren had looked like right before he began eating slaves.

"Come in," Bagkhal barked. "Sit down."

Joe swallowed hard and obeyed. Then he stiffened, remembering. The prince had met with Representative Na'leen that morning. What had Na'leen told him about Kihgl? Did Bagkhal know about Joe's relationship with Yuil? Bagkhal said nothing about it, and instead frothed and panted as he dictated his notes, digging his talons into the stone floor like it was made of wet clay. His fury was a palpable thickness in the air, one left Joe sick with terror as he sat there, trapped. Even in the biosuit, his hands were shaking.

Prince Bagkhal stopped suddenly, leveling his cold emerald gaze on Joe. For the first time since meeting the Dhasha, Joe lowered his eyes.

Bagkhal deflated suddenly. "I'm sorry. I didn't realize I was frightening you."

Joe said nothing, wondering if it was a trick. The Dhasha's anger still permeated the room and he didn't dare glance up.

Bagkhal gave him a long look, then let out an explosive sigh. His breath, unlike Knaaren's, did not stink of rotting meat. When Joe had asked, beating around the bush for a full hour before he was able to delicately make his question clear, Bagkhal had simply laughed. "I eat nutrient cakes. Much less messy." At the time, Joe had found himself unable to believe it. He could not conceive of a Dhasha eating anything other than living, breathing beings that could at least scream before they were bitten in half. Now, though…

"The Training Committee put our regiment under observation despite our recent successes," Bagkhal said, with a rumble of frustration. "Any more screw-ups and they're commissioning a Jahul auction-house to sell the entire regiment."

As Joe stared, the Dhasha began to pace again.

"Further, it seems that Ooreiki ashsoul I had deported somehow knew a Corps Director. He's been installed as Prince Rethavn's replacement."

"Prince Rethavn?" Joe asked. "Knaaren's father?"

Bagkhal grunted. "Kophati Peacemakers finally found their teeth and raided Rethavn's den. They're shipping him to Levren for questioning—they believe the furg was involved in an insurgent movement here on Kophat, and that the rebels are actively recruiting amongst our ranks."

Joe felt his face flush with guilt under his biosuit.

Prince Bagkhal let out another massive sigh. "If I'd known Knaaren was the son of that slime, I would've killed him instead of wasting the time dragging him out of here for detainment. Traitors breed traitors. It's in the blood."

Traitors breed traitors. Joe glanced down at his hands, remembering a swirl of smoke and darkness, the sound of rifle fire. *Dad wasn't a traitor.*

Once he'd calmed himself, Bagkhal resumed dictating progress reports to the Training Committee and the Human Overseer of Kophat, now the same Commander Tril that had once run Sixth Battalion. Bagkhal said nothing about his meeting with Na'leen and Joe began to suspect that the Representative had indeed told him something damning. It was a gnawing fear that ate at him until he finally had to ask how the meeting had gone.

"Representative Na'leen?" Bagkhal asked, giving Joe an odd look. "Why would you care?"

"Just curious," Joe said quickly. "He seems like an asher."

Prince Bagkhal clicked his teeth in amusement. "He is. It went poorly." The Dhasha made a grunting noise. "The furg tried to impress me with his pet Jreet and I had to show him I'm not Knaaren." Bagkhal snorted. "He's convinced the Training Committee to order a mandatory gathering of all Congressional personnel working with Humans so we can share our experiences and offer advice."

"Sounds like a good idea," Joe said.

Prince Bagkhal snorted. "It's typical bureaucratic crap. They always feel they have to sink their claws in things, meddle where they don't belong.

The Congressional Army has been fully functioning for over two million turns now. There's nothing some self-important politician is going to come up with that we haven't already considered. Not only do I already correspond with the other commanders daily, but we share all Human training statistics and have a database on training methods versus end results. But the Kophati Training Committee is so starry-eyed that a Tribunal member has shown an interest that it'll give him anything he wants." Bagkhal snorted loudly. "He wants us to *meet* with each other? And do what? No one will be able to get a word in, there are so many of us. Where do we start? Will they sort us by species? If not, half the gathering is going to end up killing the other half. I hear a contingent of Jreet has been training one Human regiment, while the Huouyt have taken another. It's going to be a huge bloodbath."

Joe finished taking his dictations with an increasing feeling of dread lumping in the pit of his stomach. He thought of the Trith's prophecy. He knew, without a doubt, that Bagkhal would kill him if he ever discovered Joe was meant to end Congress.

A Trith never gives the whole prophecy, Kihgl's words returned to him. Maybe it was a ploy. Maybe it was a lie, a half-truth…

No, Joe thought, once again thinking of Elf, of Monk, of the millions of children that had been kidnapped to become alien slaves…. He felt hot anger rising in his gut. He *would* end this. And Yuil was going to help him.

Joe was lost in thought when Scott caught him on the way back to the barracks. "Hey, I was looking for you."

"You in trouble?" Joe asked, worried by the paleness of Scott's face.

"No, I…" Scott bit his lip and gave a nervous laugh. "This is gonna sound really stupid, Joe, but I think I had a Trith visit me."

Joe felt his blood run cold.

"Yeah," Scott said, running his hand over his bald head nervously. "Weird, I know. What he said was even weirder. At least I *think* he said it. Soot, it's so crazy. Like I was floating in space—" He broke off, giving Joe an anxious look.

"Tell me," Joe said.

Scott's eyes were full of fear. "He said you're gonna destroy Congress, Joe."

35

IT'S IN THE BLOOD

The day before Joe was supposed to meet with Yuil, he found it hard to concentrate on anything. He fumbled his orders during drills and spaced out to the point that Battlemaster Aneeir sent him to medical to receive another dose of Bagkhal's drug and take the rest of the day off.

Joe spent the next three hours lying in bed, staring at the low ceiling. He was not tired in the least, and sometimes missed being able to close his eyes and fall asleep. Still, he was finding his time with Prince Bagkhal enjoyable, especially when the Dhasha told stories of his long life in the military.

Bagkhal's company was enough to make Joe begin to regret telling Yuil he would leave with her. He was learning so much—the Dhasha was opening up whole new worlds for him, discoursing for hours in politics, science, history, war, philosophy...

And there was much to learn. Bagkhal had lived a full nine hundred and sixty turns, ancient for a Dhasha. Despite the fact that they could continue to grow indefinitely, like the Jreet, Bagkhal's species tended to kill each other off long before they could meet that potential—also like the Jreet. That Bagkhal had lived almost a millennium was...amazing. Even more chilling was the fact he had declared ka-par with over five thousand worthy opponents, won them all, and every bested foe continued to serve him to this day, making him one of the most powerful Dhasha princes in

Congress. Further, he had helped fight down six Dhasha rebellions and quelled further resistances in all corners of the known universe. Bagkhal's war stories were as good as his father's.

It was the stories of Dhasha uprisings that left Joe with a wash of dread, though. From what Bagkhal described, they were terrifying things, all-out slaughters that decimated the numbers on each side, leaving enormous swaths of the galaxy annihilated, whole prosperous, high-tech planets thrown back into their dark ages for centuries to come. A Dhasha prince would have his Takki dig a deep den on a planet, and with that as his base, the prince and his sons would carve out all resistance from the planet in a matter of weeks.

"There's going to be another one soon," Bagkhal said one evening, while Joe was busy copying notes.

Joe looked up. "Another what, sir?"

"Rebellion." Bagkhal heaved a huge sigh. "The problem is a prophecy, Joe."

Joe felt his heart skip. Swallowing, he said, "Sir?"

Bagkhal sighed. "There is a legend amongst the Dhasha, something that has been with our people for many hundreds of thousands of years." He swung to give Joe a long look. "It is the prophecy of a great leader, one who will unite and liberate the Dhasha. The Vahlin."

Joe's heart began to pound, but he managed to nod.

"The Dhasha Vahlin is foretold to free the Dhasha of their mass servitude to a tyrannical, archaic system," Bagkhal growled. "It is said He will be the greatest mind the Dhasha have ever seen, and that He will lead our people into the greatest war that the universe has ever endured, followed by giving us the greatest peace our world has ever imagined."

Joe's heart hammered at the parallels between this and what the Trith had told him. Was he supposed to...lead the Dhasha? Wasn't that like a rabbit leading a horde of wolves?

Prince Bagkhal was pacing, now. "The problem is that the prophecy gives no clan name, no place of birth. It says He will be dark of color. And alone. And forgotten."

Joe didn't *need* to glance down at his biosuit to know he was, at the moment, pretty damn dark. He swallowed, hard.

Bagkhal, however, went on as if he didn't even see Joe's inky black bio-suit. "The legend of the Vahlin has been tearing our society apart at the seams for eons. Rethavn is not the only Dhasha with aspirations. I can only pray the next rises up near the Outer Line. If Kophat had rebelled..." He swiped wicked black talons at empty air. "It contains over two thousand deep dens carved out for training sessions. Koliinaat would have been forced to destroy the entire planet. Thirty billion Ooreiki, nine billion Ueshi, two billion Jahul...dead because some Takki-fucking furg decided he wasn't making enough off of his protection fees."

Bagkhal slumped to the floor with a clatter of metallic scales. "Sometimes I am ashamed of my kind. Truly ashamed."

"Would they really destroy the entire planet?" Joe asked.

Bagkhal leveled his unreadable emerald stare on Joe, making his spine itch. "I don't know if you have been told this yet, Zero, but Kophat is a storage center for weapons designed to work against every species known to Congress. It is one of six such planets, and if any one of these planets ever falls into enemy hands, protocol gives the Army three days to get it back under Congressional control or it will be destroyed, along with everyone on it."

Joe felt a cold chill crawl down his spine. "An entire planet?"

"The alternative is worse. With the weapons Congress has stored in these depots, rebels could eradicate a thousand planets just like it. And they would, too. Most rebels are mindless zealots who simply want to do as much damage as they can before they are found and killed. They don't realize that Congress is the glue holding the universe together. They just want to destroy."

Remembering his date with Yuil—and how Yuil had excitedly talked about doing exactly that—Joe stared at his hands.

"It's not too late to change your mind, Joe."

At the Dhasha's calm, matter-of-fact statement, Joe's head snapped up. "Change my..." Then, in that moment, looking into Bagkhal's emerald eyes, Joe knew that Bagkhal knew about Yuil. His breath caught in his throat and his face flushed with panic. He found it impossible to deny it and a thousand excuses rose to his lips, but he just lowered his head and waited for the Dhasha to finish him.

Instead of condemning him, Prince Bagkhal leaned forward and said, "You are one of the most gifted warriors I have ever met. You lead your recruits like you were born to do it, and, if one was to believe some of my comrades, you were."

Joe just shook his head.

"It's true. It's why the rebels want you."

Joe's chest tightened and he hunched further in on himself, the words hovering out in the open like a headsman's axe.

"I know it's a difficult decision," Bagkhal said. "When I was first Drafted, I hated Congress. If someone had given me a button to annihilate it all, I would have pushed it. It got easier, though. A few turns after graduation, I realized that ours is the most important job in the universe. The universe is highly unstable—a delicate ecosystem constantly teetering on the verge of collapse. The Army is the net that binds Congress together. Should we fail in our duties, everything in it will collide with such force that, once the dust clears, there will be nothing left."

Joe sank in on himself further, misery overwhelming him. "Sorry," he whispered.

Bagkhal huffed. "I must cater to the whims of politicians tomorrow. The Kophati Training Committee dances to Na'leen's demands like an Aezi puppet. I'll be gone for two days. If you're still here when I return, I will ask you to help us dismantle the rebel hive that has been wooing you and about fifty other recruits from our regiment. If you are gone, I'll add your name to the list of known traitors and send all of your friends to Levren for questioning. But Zero—" Bagkhal paused, waiting for him to look up.

"You'll be here when I get back."

Joe felt so ashamed to have betrayed Bagkhal that he could barely breathe. The Prince's lack of anger made it worse.

"Do you want to know why?" Bagkhal said.

Joe couldn't lift his eyes off of the ground.

"You'll stay because Knaaren was just one of trillions," Bagkhal said. "Each one of those would love to own their own planets and populate them with slaves. When Peacemakers captured Rethavn, it took three thousand Ooreiki lives to roust one Dhasha prince and his three youngest children from a single tower, not even a deep den. Nine thousand more Ooreiki were badly injured in the fight." The Dhasha paused, giving Joe a long look. "You'll stay because a pathetic, ragtag group of Ooreiki teenagers might have grand plans for a universe without Congress, but they forget the Dhasha."

Joe swallowed, hard.

"Only Dhasha can control Dhasha, Zero," Bagkhal told him. "For that, we need Congress."

Joe just nodded.

Bagkhal gave him a moment to digest that. Eventually, he went on, "I can always judge a soldier's character. I look at Tril and see a misguided idealist, but one with good intentions. He will make a good leader in twenty or thirty turns, as soon as he realizes there's a difference between life and a classroom. Nebil is too honorable to retake Prime, despite how much good he would do the Army if he did. He's an excellent soldier, but due to his inability to bend, he is unsuited to anything beyond a battalion command. You know what I see when I look at you, Zero?"

A traitor. Joe stared at his hands in shame.

"I look at you and I see myself, eight hundred turns ago," Bagkhal said. "You're a Congie, Zero. I hope you realize that before they force you to decide."

Joe still couldn't speak, so deep was his disgrace.

Bagkhal got up and started walking towards the exit. At the base of the stairs, he stopped and turned back. "I have no doubts in my mind that there *will* be a Dhasha Vahlin," Bagkhal said. "Until the true Vahlin makes Himself known to us, though, it is our duty to keep His usurpers from destroying the universe that rightfully belongs to Him."

Then, with a parting look at Joe, Bagkhal climbed the steps and left him sitting there, staring at his lap.

• • •

That afternoon, Bagkhal boarded the shuttle to take him to the mandatory training meeting, taking all of the ranking Ooreiki commanders and battlemasters with him. Out of all of Sixth Battalion, only Battlemaster Aneeir remained. Instead of battalion drills, Aneeir gave every platoon a different task to do, then assigned free time after that. Joe spent the first half of the day raking the plaza with his friends, then found a quiet place to sit and think.

Yuil was expecting him that night.

This was his chance. Bagkhal had said that the Trith couldn't lie. If Joe helped the rebels, he could put an end to the Draft. He could go home.

But Bagkhal's words haunted him. What would they do about the Dhasha? Just the mere thought of fighting on the opposite side as Bagkhal made the hairs on Joe's arms raise. He didn't want to betray his friend. Were there really trillions of Dhasha out there? Had Yuil and her friends *thought* about that?

The more Joe considered it, the more he realized Bagkhal was right. Yuil, despite her startlingly vast knowledge on military workings and tactics, was just an alien dropout. Against an organized force like the Congressional Army, they would be annihilated.

Dad would want me to fight.

That single thought made everything Joe knew come to a crashing halt. Even now, his father's words came back to him as he stood over the ironing board, his arms moving in slow, deliberate motions as he ironed his sleeves. *Sometimes you've gotta stand up for yourself, even when you know you ain't got a chance.*

I've gotta do something, Joe realized. *Congress doesn't do enough to stop Dhasha like Knaaren from hurting people. There had to be a better way.*

And there was. With Yuil. Shattering Congress, like the Trith had foretold.

…right?

What would *happen* if they shattered Congress? That nagging sense of unease disturbed him. Bagkhal had lived *centuries.* He'd fought on dozens of planets. If *he* didn't think there was a way to control the Dhasha, what hope did Yuil and her friends have, really?

But how will I know if we don't try?

Perhaps it was that very mentality that kept the Dhasha secure on their pedestals. Perhaps everyone was just too *afraid…*

It was the memory of Elf's scream as Knaaren ripped him apart that decided him.

Joe was trying to figure out how to get Libby to go with him when Scott found him sitting against the haauk depot.

"Kind of weird without the battlemasters here, isn't it?" Scott said. He grinned. "Maggie and Carl are talking about writing a thank-you note for that Tribunal guy. It's the most time we've had off since we got Second's flag." Scott hesitated, his smile fading as his gaze flickered across Joe's face. "What's wrong?"

Joe took a deep breath. "Battlemaster Aneeir's planning a night raid against Second Battalion tonight. One groundteam only. We're supposed to capture their battlemaster and bring him back."

Scott frowned. "Which one? That Rat girl?"

"No," Joe said, shaking his head, "Their *battlemaster*. Gokli."

Scott's eyes widened to the whites. "Gokli? He'd kill us all."

"The battlemasters made a bet or something," Joe said, shrugging. "Anyway, it won't be hard. He'll be traveling outside the city all alone."

Scott glanced both ways and crouched in front of him. "You're *serious*? What do we do with him once we have him?"

"Beats me. Aneeir will give him soot, I suppose."

"Wow," Scott said, shaking his head. "Wow." He gave Joe a curious look. "Does this mean we get to use our biosuits?"

"Hell, yeah," Joe said, relieved Scott was buying the story. "You think I'd let you guys tackle an Ooreiki without them?"

Scott rubbed the back of his neck and shook his head. "I don't know, Joe. That sounds pretty damn stupid. Isn't Gokli like, so far above Aneeir on the food chain he could kill him by taking a crap?"

"You don't want to do it, I'll get somebody else," Joe said.

"No, I'll do it," Scott said quickly. "It's just a little crazy, that's all."

"That's why he wants us," Joe said.

"Yeah," Scott said, his face stretching in another grin, "Makes sense."

"Meet me outside the barracks after chow," Joe said. "Don't tell *any-body*. I don't want it getting back to Gokli."

"Sure," Scott said. "I'll be there."

• • •

"They're letting you use a haauk?" Maggie whispered, her eyes round with awe. "I didn't know they'd taught you to drive one of these, Joe."

"Bagkhal taught me so I can deliver messages faster," Joe lied. He hot-wired the haauk and gave a little sigh of relief as it lifted off the ground. Nervous, Joe reached up to wipe the perspiration from his brow. He froze when he realized Libby was watching him. She hadn't said a single thing all night.

"So," Joe said, clearing his throat, "Here we go." Joe brought the haauk off the ground and Maggie let out a gleeful squeal.

"*Quiet*, Mag," Joe said, glancing anxiously at the barracks. "It's a *secret* raid."

"Sorry," Maggie whispered, looking like he'd slapped her.

In minutes, they were skimming over the veiny red masses of *ferlii* branches, circling around the road where Joe was supposed to meet Yuil's companions. Up ahead, through the tangled limbs, Joe saw a haauk sitting on the road, its pilot standing beside it. Joe brought them down upon a *ferlii* branch. He took out his spotting scope and trained it upon the Ooreiki in the road.

"Is that him?" Maggie asked excitedly.

"No." It was the first thing Libby had said since Joe had told them about the raid. She looked away from the pilot and fixed her gaze on Joe once more, her brown eyes hard.

Joe lowered his scope, trying to stay calm. Where was the pilot's companion? Yuil had told him at least two rebels would meet him on the road. Joe didn't want to approach his contact without at least two Ooreiki to help subdue Libby. He was pretty sure Maggie and Scott would do whatever he wanted, but Libby would fight. He knew it as well as he knew anything, and he loved her for it. He would have left her behind, but he knew Bagkhal would give her to the Peacemakers if he did.

"What are we waiting for, Joe?" Libby asked. Her brown eyes were piercing, as if she knew his purpose and was just waiting for him to confirm it.

Joe shook that suspicion out of his mind. "This looks like a good place to ambush Gokli. I'm just wondering what that Ooreiki is doing just standing down there."

"He doesn't look like a civilian," Scott said. "He's wearing black. What if he knows we're not supposed to be out of the barracks and gets us in trouble?"

"He's right," Libby said. "This is a bad spot. He looks like he's heading out of the city, so we should move closer to Alishai."

"We'll stay a little while longer," Joe said. "Maybe he'll move." What he was really hoping for was for another rebel to show up to help him keep Libby from killing them all, but he couldn't tell them that.

Two hours passed without another rebel appearing, and Joe could tell the Ooreiki on the ground was getting anxious. Scott and Maggie retired to catch some sleep stretched out on the *ferlii* branch, but Libby stayed awake to watch the road.

"He's not moving, Joe," Libby said. "Maybe he knows we're coming after Gokli. What if he's a Peacemaker?"

For the first time in ages, Joe heard a hint of fear in her voice. He frowned at her, then back down at the Ooreiki rebel. "He's not a Peacemaker. He's just some guy whose haauk broke down."

"He's waiting for something," Libby insisted. "Look at the way he's standing. If his haauk broke, he would have called for help. He's watching the road. What if Aneeir set us up? What if he's a Peacemaker?"

"Why would he be a Peacemaker?" Joe demanded. "That doesn't make sense."

"It does," Libby whispered. There was real fear in her eyes now. "A Trith visited me that night Bagkhal bought us the feast."

Joe's breath caught in his chest.

Libby looked into his eyes. Tears formed on her cheeks but she held his gaze. "He said—" She shook her head and looked away.

Joe caught her arm, blood thundering in his ears. "He said what?"

The hurt in Libby's eyes was enough to tell him the truth. "I can't say it, Joe. I don't believe it."

He told her I'm going to shatter Congress. She thinks I'm a traitor. Joe glanced down at the Ooreiki on the road. *Well, you are, aren't you?*

Dad wasn't a traitor. That solid realization made his gut twist. He didn't know who he owed his loyalties to anymore. Was it Earth, who had handed over its kids without a fight? Or was it Congress, who stood between Earth and the Dhasha? Or was it the aliens in the Army who helped him, kept him alive, given him guidance? Aliens like Nebil and Kihgl and Bagkhal? If it was them, did he stay with Nebil and Bagkhal, who seemed to believe the Army was the only way to keep the Dhasha at bay, or did he go with Yuil, who had Kihgl's confidence before he died?

Joe's eyes fell back on Libby.

Or did his loyalties lie somewhere else entirely?

Quietly, Libby said, "I thought I was dreaming, but Maggie saw him, too."

"She did?" Joe croaked. *Not Maggie, too.*

"Haven't you noticed how weird she's been acting lately? She threw that girl off the second floor balcony for getting in her way."

Joe had been wondering about that. "What did the Trith tell her?" Joe asked softly.

"She wouldn't tell me," Libby said, eying him. "He say anything to *you*, Joe?"

Fate decided you will shatter Congress, Joe.

"No," Joe said. He turned and looked down at the Ooreiki rebel on the road.

You will try to fight it, but invariably, your path will lead to the same end.

Joe watched the Ooreiki fidget nervously in the dark. The haauk was there, the offer open. He could leave at any time. He could be free. He could return to Earth and see his family again. All he had to do was show himself.

"I'm gonna go talk to Maggie. Watch the road a sec." Joe got up and found Maggie and Scott sitting together, trying to stay awake.

"Is Gokli here?" Maggie asked.

"Not yet." Joe sat down beside them and took a deep breath. Quietly, so Libby could not hear, he said, "Guys, if you had the chance to go home, would you take it?" He was staring down at his father's Swiss Army knife. He had pulled it out of his vest and had started rubbing it unconsciously.

"You mean back to the barracks?" Maggie asked.

"No," Scott said, yawning, "I think he means Earth."

Joe nodded.

Maggie laughed. "We're not going home, Joe."

"But if you *could* go home…would you do it?"

Maggie's amusement faded. "You mean leave the Army?"

"Yeah."

Maggie stared at him darkly, saying nothing.

"So? Would you go?"

"Sure," Scott said.

Joe felt himself relax a little.

"...as long as you could give me my old body back. My friends back home aren't grown-ups and my parents won't recognize me like this."

Joe was surprised. "You'd stay because of that?"

Scott shrugged. "They'd expect me to be a kid again. I'm not."

Joe realized he was serious. Guilt lanced through him. He'd simply assumed he'd want to go. The Trith had told him he'd shatter Congress, but he hadn't said his friends would have to help. He could just send Scott back to Alishai with Libby and take Maggie with him.

"What about you, Mag?"

"My friends are here," Maggie said. "I don't even remember what my mom looked like."

We're everything she's got. Joe wrapped his father's knife in a fist.

Burn the Trith. They don't know everything.

"Let's go," Joe said loudly, standing. "You're right. Gokli's not coming."

36

WAR WITH THE HUOUYT

Joe was lying in bed, unable to sleep due to Bagkhal's drugs, when a horn sounded suddenly outside the barracks, loud enough to vibrate the stone.

"What's *that?*" Scott asked, sitting up in bed.

"I don't know," Joe said. "Never heard anything like it before."

"Sounds like the call to regiment formation," Libby said. "Except it's still going."

"The Ooreiki are all gone and our barracks are locked," Joe said. "How do they expect us to get to formation?"

"Maybe they think everybody knows how to open the doors now," Maggie said.

The sound stopped suddenly, leaving the entire barracks in a wave of whispers.

Outside, an explosion sounded, rattling their rifles in their lockers. Two more followed, one right after the other.

"What is it?" Maggie whispered.

"I don't know," Joe said. "But everybody get your biosuits on. Right now."

They heard no more commotion while they suited up, but as they were gathering their gear, an explosion knocked them off their feet. It was followed by a deep, powerful rumbling. Joe's heart skipped a beat. He'd heard that sound before, in school. His teacher had spent the week studying the Andes Mountains and she'd shown them a film documenting the perils of mountaineering. The sound outside was the sound of an avalanche.

Joe ran to the door and punched in the code to open it. As soon as he did, he stepped outside onto the balcony and froze.

Half of the barracks was missing. It had sheared off from Joe's half and lay in an enormous black jumble on the ground. Below, over the jagged edge of the balcony where it sheared off beneath his feet, Joe could see an arm sticking out from the debris.

"Everybody out!" Joe screamed. "Get down the stairs! *Move!*" He ran back inside and grabbed his rifle and his gear. As Libby ran out and took in the situation below, he went to the closest barracks door, Ninth Platoon's, and opened it.

The kids were still in their big circular beds, trying to sleep.

"Get your biosuits and get out of here!" Joe shouted. "The barracks is caving in!" He continued his circuit around the remaining half of the barracks, opening those doors that remained on his level. Some of the kids were ready, waiting to be released, but most had simply gone back to sleep. Joe got them all up and ushered them down the stairs, stopping when he reached the jagged edge of the other side. Fifth through Ninth platoons had collapsed in the explosion, along with dozens from other Battalions.

"Zero! Get the recruits off of the seventh level!" a familiar Ooreiki voice shouted behind him. "I'll get the eighth!" Joe had just enough time to see Commander Lagrah before he disappeared up the stairs at a run. Below him, he heard the wet *thwap* of gunfire and hesitated.

Libby can handle it.

As soon as he had the thought, he charged up the stairs to reach the next battalion. More of them were awake than the last battalion, some already dressed in all of their gear. Joe rushed them down the stairs and went back for more.

"It's falling!" Lagrah shouted at him, wrenching him away from another door. "Zero, get down the stairs!"

Joe hesitated and Lagrah bodily dragged him down the switchback stairway. Immediately, wet plasma rounds smacked into the stone behind their heads. Joe flinched and looked back.

Instead of simply staining the wall a glowing blue, as recruit rounds would do, the side of the wall was dissolving under the plasma, disappearing as if it had never existed. Lagrah grabbed him by the arm and yanked him down behind a pile of rubble.

"That's *live fire*," Joe cried, still unable to believe it.

"It's a war, Zero. As soon as the commanders got together for their meeting, the Huouyt blew up the space station and everyone in it. Nebil and Bagkhal are dead and that Jreet-loving Na'leen has taken control of the weapons stores."

Joe's first thought was of anger. *They were my friends.* Then a cool, simmering rage began to build in his stomach. "What do you want me to do?"

"I know you were associating with the rebels, Zero. Where are they?" Lagrah gripped his jacket, his pale brown eyes narrowed to dangerous slits. "Tell me or I'll kill you right now, damn what Kihgl said."

What Kihgl said?

"The abandoned *ferlii* on the edge of the city," Joe whispered.

"They wouldn't have their command post so close to Alishai," Lagrah snapped. "Where else?"

Joe thought back to the hidden weapons cache Yuil had tried to show him. He remembered the wet stain on the floor, the Ooreiki flashlight. "There's a spot in the forest. A small black door set in the side of a *ferlii*."

Lagrah released him suddenly. "Did you see them enter this place, Zero?"

Joe nodded.

Lagrah's sudah began to vibrate. "And you didn't tell anyone?"

He shook his head.

"At least now we know where they're getting their weapons. Get your platoon. Grab a haauk and take what you need from the armory. Gokli's inside. Tell him you need Jreet poison rounds and *fahjli* grenades. Find that door again, Zero. Get inside, whatever it takes. This is *real*, you understand? Bagkhal was wrong. This isn't a few furgling teenagers. The one you called Yuil was Na'leen's assassin, Zol'jib. They're *Huouyt*, Zero. Every one of them. They're making a grab at this sector of space. Na'leen's been planning it for turns."

Joe nodded, feeling ashamed and angry.

"Go!" Lagrah shouted, shoving him. "If you're anything close to what Kihgl thought you were, you'll find a way inside that depot. You've got to do it fast, while they're still distracted with the takeover. I'll follow with whoever I can find."

Joe ducked his head low and hurried between the debris piles, trying to ignore the bodies buried underneath. He found Libby with the rest of his platoon, holding their position behind a sheer wall of half-crumbled diamond with their recruit rounds as the rebels fired back with real plasma, slowly dissolving their cover out from in front of them.

"Did you see Lagrah?!" Libby cried. Behind her, the barracks let out another explosion and the rest of it imploded, sending up a cloud of black dust that blotted out all sight of the enemy.

"He told me to find you," Joe said. "We need to go attack their base."

"Who *are* these guys?" Maggie cried. She was holding her gun tightly, hiding behind a chunk of rock, stark terror in her eyes.

"Is this a drill?" Scott said, peering through the black dust. "Is that real plasma?"

"It's real," Joe said. "Don't let it hit you."

"Why do *we* have to attack their base?" Maggie cried. "Joe, I'm scared."

"This is just like the hunts, Mag," Joe said. "Now let's go get a haauk before the dust clears."

Maggie whimpered, but followed him and Libby as they charged through the smoke to the haauk depot. In the dust behind them, a kid let out a startled scream that turned into an unending, agonized shriek.

He's dying, Joe thought, terror creeping into his veins. *That's real plasma and he's really dying.*

Joe grabbed a haauk big enough for the entire platoon, one with armored plating used to drop off attackers in the hunts, and made everyone get on board.

At the armory, Battlemaster Gokli and his platoon were holding off a group of attackers. Rat was firing from the roof, picking off rebels with a laser rifle while Tank and Bailey fought them off on the ground. As soon as Joe landed, he ushered his group inside.

"Zero! Get rid of those recruit toys and man the walls. Send your best snipers to the roof with Rat, your skirmishers outside."

"I'm not here to stay," Joe said.

"Furgsoot! This is a real firefight and you'll—"

"Commander Lagrah said we'll need *fahjli* grenades and Jreet poison rounds," Joe interrupted. "We're going after their base."

Battlemaster Gokli narrowed his eyes at him. "Where is that bastard? I thought he got blown up with the others."

"He's directing the surviving platoons on the ground," Joe said. "They're fighting rebels over by the barracks."

"Then he'll be here soon and I can hear it from him," Gokli said. "Until then, take up positions to guard the armory."

"We have to go *now*," Joe said. "I know where to find Na'leen."

"You're recruits," Gokli snapped. "Lagrah's insane to send you off by yourself."

"My platoon's got the best rankings on the hunts," Joe said stubbornly.

Gokli gave him a long, piercing glare. "You realize this isn't a game, right Zero? They will kill you and all of your friends and not even blink."

"I know," Joe said.

Gokli swiveled and led him deeper into the armory. "*Fahjli* grenades," he grunted, shoving handfuls of little black discs that resembled bottlecaps into his arms. "Twist the two halves in opposite directions and toss it at the fire-loving Huouyt. It stuns them like a flash grenade, except it only works on Huouyt."

Joe passed the grenades to the other members of his platoon, then followed Gokli further down the endless rows of weapons.

"Jreet rounds," Gokli said, shoving packs of bright red canisters at him. "Use it like your fake plasma, except this stuff will really kill you. It's the only poison a Huouyt bastard can't neutralize with a shape-shift." He began taking the stuff off the shelves, handing packs of it to Joe and his groundmates. "Didn't exactly plan on fighting a war with the Huouyt, so there's a limited supply. Good thing is, though, it only takes one hit to kill them. Even a spatter will do."

Once he was finished, Gokli hesitated, scowling at Joe. Finally, he said, "Take Rat and her squad. I can fight off the rebels with the rest."

"I don't think—" Joe began.

"Do it, Zero. You'll need the help."

Joe collected the others and passed out the new rounds to Rat and her friends. Joe caught Libby's cold look when she handed Bailey his portion of the new weaponry, and an image of Libby sprawled in her own blood, a lump of dirty flesh laying in the dirt beside her returned to Joe's mind. Bailey, in turn, gave her an anxious glance as he snapped the chamber closed over the new rounds.

He did it, Joe thought, suddenly furious. *He's the one.*

"Get out of here," Gokli shouted. "Before the Huouyt blow up your haauk!"

Joe and the others clambered aboard the haauk as the remnants of Second Battalion covered their retreat. Then Joe fired up the haauk and they were soaring above the chaos, shooting eastward, looking for a needle in a haystack.

Three hours later, they had still not found the door. Back in Alishai, silence had descended upon the city. For hours, they had anxiously listened to the battle, jerking at every explosion. Now, the stillness seemed ominous. Lagrah still had not appeared with his promised assistance.

"So where is it?" Rat demanded. She had been angry that Gokli had made her leave the fight, even angrier to find out Joe didn't know where he was going.

"It's somewhere around here," Libby said. "Just shut up."

"I'm a burning battlemaster. If I want to know why I'm riding around with this loser when my friends are dying, I'm gonna find out." She turned her hawkish gaze on Joe. "So why *do* you know where this place is, anyway?"

"Lagrah showed me once."

Rat gave Joe a narrow look. "Right. Find that door or I'm going back."

"Then you're gonna have to find out some way to fly, because Joe's the only one who knows how to use the haauk," Maggie said. Her tone of voice added, *Bitch.*

"Listen!" Joe shouted. "It's around here somewhere. The last thing I need you guys to do is fight. Rat, if you wanna go back, I'll put you on the ground, but I'm not flying us back. Commander Lagrah told me to find this place, and I'm going to."

Mention of the Prime Commander made Rat's face sour. "Just hurry up."

They found the entrance twenty minutes later, the door wide open. Three dozen dead Ooreiki lay on the *ferlii* branch outside, their brownish faces contorted in pain.

"Soot, Joe," Scott whispered to him. "I think there's something big moving down there."

Joe drew closer, frowning at their blue Peacemaker uniforms. One of the closer ones held a scaly, cream-colored lump of flesh in a death-tightened tentacle. Beside him, almost falling off the branch, a small Jreet lay with its cream-colored throat torn open, the fanglike appendage in its chest unsheathed.

One moment, Joe was staring at the dead Jreet, the next a recruit behind him cried out and fell, convulsing. His biosuit was even then sealing over a puncture wound in his chest.

"*Jreet!*" Joe shouted. "Look out for Jreet!"

Rat dropped to a knee and raised her rifle at the same time Libby jerked, then flipped around and smashed a boot into thin air. Around them, the *ferlii* suddenly vibrated with an ear-splitting *shee-whomp,* the sound of an aircraft engine gone awry. A huge reddish figure shimmered in front of her, then slammed a fang-tipped appendage down at her leg with all the strength in its powerful central limb. Joe's heart stopped.

Libby's biosuit deflected the fang and reddish poison spilled over her leg, dribbling onto the branch beneath them. Unfazed by her brush with death, Libby slammed the butt of her rifle into the Jreet's diamond-shaped head.

The Jreet snapped around like a whip and slammed its upper body into Libby, knocking her clear off the *ferlii* branch. Joe heard a startled cry as she fell over the edge. The Jreet made another eardrum-piercing *shee-whomp* cry and found another target.

Recruits everywhere were running from the monster in their midst. The Jreet was nearly half the length of a school bus, built like a massive python with a nearly humanoid torso. It lashed out again, jabbing its spear-like shaft into another recruit's back. She fell and curled into a ball on the ground, never uttering a sound.

Rat had retreated fifteen feet and was back on one knee, aiming her rifle at the Jreet's flickering head. It disappeared again before she could fire.

Joe backed away, heart pounding in his ears, knowing he wouldn't be able to see the thing until it struck again. "Everybody keep your eyes open!" he shouted, hoping his command would draw the Jreet's attention to him.

"He's right *there!*" Scott screamed, spinning and pointing at thin air. A kid that had taken refuge in the entrance suddenly collapsed in silence, a red shape disappearing as quickly as it had appeared.

"There's two of them!" Rat shouted at him.

"Yeah," Scott shrieked. "*Two!*" His head was swinging back and forth, like he was watching two different grim reapers stalking towards them. He brought his rifle up and fired, coating something invisible in red Jreet poison.

Joe was busy twisting the *fahjli* grenade, activating it. He threw it at the spot where the Jreet had disappeared. It hit something in the air and bounced to the ground, closer to Joe than he would have liked. He ducked, flinching.

There was a brief blue flash, then nothing.

"They don't work!" Joe shouted.

"Rifle rounds aren't working either!" Rat shouted. "I've hit that asher twice and he keeps on going!"

"Are Jreet immune to Jreet poison?" Joe cried.

"How should I burning know?!"

Joe bit his lip as another recruit crumpled, her biosuit punctured by the Jreet's powerful strike. "Keep your rifle pointed at him, Scott!" he shouted, running back to the haauk.

"Where the ashes are you going?!" Rat demanded.

"I'm getting rid of them!" Joe climbed onto the haauk, raised it off the branch, and twisted it around to the spot where one of the Jreet was whipping its tail through the recruits, slamming them to the ground. An unfortunate few went careening over the edge, screaming.

Scott continued to point out the Jreet with his rifle, though he was backing up, now. "It's coming at me, Joe!" Scott cried.

"Just hang in there!" Joe shouted, then he sighted down Scott's line of fire and crammed the accelerator forward.

The haauk hit something invisible head-on and a Jreet flickered into being, snapping its fang against the armored plating of the ship. It tumbled a couple yards, its crimson-and-cream body whipping back and forth like an angry earthworm. Joe held on and rammed the haauk into its middle with all the speed the ship could muster.

Both ship and Jreet went sliding down the ferlii branch, leaving a blue streak of Jreet flesh and blood along the way. Screaming its shee-*whomph* cry, the Jreet wrapped its body around the haauk's bow and held on, bluish fluid leaking over the *ferlii* branch beneath it. Joe was maneuvering the haauk and its unfortunate victim over the edge of the *ferlii* when something like a hammer slammed into his back.

The second Jreet had found him.

The Jreet grabbed Joe by the head and threw him out of the haauk. Joe hit the ground in a roll, the edge fast approaching.

Someone caught him and jerked him to his feet.

"You okay?" Maggie asked. "I saw him hit you with his fang."

Joe felt his back. "I'm all right. Where's Rat?"

Maggie pointed to the haauk. Rat was wrestling the Jreet inside, ramming her combat knife into its throat over and over. The Jreet had long since stopped fighting. The Jreet trapped under the haauk's bow was being similarly dismantled by Carl and the rest of Fourth Platoon.

Joe jogged over to Rat and helped pull her out from under the alien's body. "You okay?"

"Fine," Rat snapped. She looked him up and down with disdain. "You?" The old rivalry was back.

"Dude," Carl said breathlessly. "Guys, I think we just killed two *Jreet*."

"They were little ones," Rat grunted dismissively, at the same time Joe said, "Don't get cocky, those were babies." He turned to the haauk. "Help me here. We need to block the door."

With Rat's help, he pushed the Jreet corpses over the armored railing and moved the haauk to block the entrance. Once they were sure no more Jreet were going to sneak up on them, Joe took a moment to stare at the devastation. No less than twenty kids lay dead on the *ferlii* branches, with a dozen more missing.

"Now what?" Rat demanded, eying the haauk. "How are we getting home?"

"We're not. Lagrah told us to go in."

"*Burn* that," Rat spat. "Are you crazy? We'll all die."

"If Zero says we go in, we go in."

Joe turned at Libby's voice, unable to believe it. She was alive, and standing over the flagellate body of the dead Jreet. "Libby, how—"

"I hit another branch, about a hundred feet down." She stood, shouldering a dead recruit's rifle. "I had to find my way back."

Even Rat looked impressed.

Libby scanned the branch and her confident smile suddenly faded. "Oh no."

Joe's eyes caught on Maggie, who was sitting by a body, her knees up to her chin, rocking back and forth. "Maggie, get over here."

Maggie shook her head and continued rocking.

Still, it took Joe a moment to realize the body was Scott's.

37

INTO THE LION'S DEN

"No, Joe, *please*. Don't make us go in there." Maggie was sobbing, hugging him. "What if you and Libby die, too? I'd be all alone, Joe."

"Grow up, Mag," Lib said. Her face had hardened after her initial shock, and now she only looked angry. "We're not gonna die."

"Joe," Maggie sniffled, ignoring Libby. "Please. I'm scared."

Joe winced. First Elf, then Monk, now Scott. Maggie was watching the only family she had ever known drop like flies. "We have to, Mag. Lagrah will bring more."

Maggie looked up at Libby, then tugged Joe's arm, pulling him away from the others. Joe stiffened, thinking she was going to try and act cute to get out of the fight, but once they were alone, she simply stared at him. "Are you really gonna ruin Congress, Joe? Is that why we're fighting?"

Joe suddenly felt like he couldn't breathe. He glanced at the door, his eyes raking in all the dead recruits, the dead Jreet, and the dead Ooreiki Peacemakers.

"No," Joe said, taking a breath. Saying it hurt and at the same time was a relief. He knew what he had to do, but he also knew that doing it would mean giving up on getting home. "I'm not. *That's* why we're doing this. We've got to stop Na'leen."

"But the Trith said—"

"Forget about the Trith!" Joe snapped. "I'm fighting for Congress."

"No," Maggie wailed. "You're lying."

Joe stared at her. She was his *groundmate* and she didn't believe him?

Maggie clung to him. "Don't go in there, Joe. *Please.*"

She was making a scene and Joe knew he had to end it before her fear spread to the rest of the recruits. Sharply, he said, "Libby's right. Grow up. You're a soldier, not a baby. Start acting like it. This is what we *do*. If you don't like it, sit out here and cry. The rest of us are going in." At that, he wrenched her arms from around him and stalked toward the haauk.

In front of it, Libby, Bailey, and Rat dropped to a knee, preparing to fire into the entrance. Joe climbed into the haauk and, once he was sure the others were ready, moved it away from the door. Immediately, Libby tossed a smoke grenade inside and they waited.

"Nothing," Libby said as purple smoke issued from the hole. "Or if there is something in there, it's not moving."

"All right, everyone get ready."

"Joe…" Maggie whispered, the whites of her eyes showing under her biosuit.

"Stop your whining, recruit!" Joe snapped. He tried not to look at her, knowing how much his words would hurt. It lanced his soul just to say them. "Let's go."

• • •

Joe stopped in the crossways, his every muscle tense and buzzing with adrenaline. Behind him, his comrades came to a reluctant halt. Their small group was breathing hard, panic from the last Jreet attack still hot in their lungs.

"This isn't a good idea," Libby said, staring down the four-way corridor in the dim red light. "We should go back and wait for Lagrah."

Their group was huddled together in the convergence, their rifles jerking from spot to spot as they nervously scanned the tunnels before them. They had encountered two more Jreet and seven Huouyt. Only a third of their original number had survived. Those that had now used plasma pistols they had taken off the Huouyt. The Jreet rounds, they had confirmed, did not work on Jreet.

"We've gotta do our best without him," Joe said.

"Everyone's *dying*," Bailey said. He, Tank, and Rat were the only three that Gokli had given them that had survived. Their friends had all fallen. "She's right, Zero. We should go back."

"You *scared,* Bailey?"

Bailey scowled at Libby. "I wasn't scared when I was crawling through sewers in San Diego with Rat and I'm not scared now. Are *you* scared, bitch?"

Joe slammed the muzzle of his plasma pistol between Bailey's eyes, pushing him into the wall. Into his face, he shouted, "You burning shut up or I'll cut out *your* tongue, you fucking ashsoul!"

Bailey's eyes went wide under the biosuit.

Quietly, Joe added, "You touch any of my friends again and you'll be puking out your own guts. I should kill you right now for what you did, in front of everybody."

"She started it," Bailey whispered.

"Furgsoot!" Joe roared, shoving the gun further into Bailey's face.

"Stop threatening my recruit," Rat snapped. "He's right. This is stupid. What the hell are we supposed to do down here, Zero?"

Joe lowered the pistol, still glaring at Bailey. "Lagrah told me to come." *But they're right. It's crazy. We're just recruits. We shouldn't be here.*

"Lagrah's a sootbag furg," Libby said.

"He is not!" Rat snapped. She looked ready to throw down her rifle and fight Libby for insulting her Prime. "If he said to do it, then he must've had a reason." Still, she looked unsure as she gazed down the four long corridors.

"Like what?" Libby demanded. "There's an entire *planet* rebelling. How's one little hidey-hole gonna make the difference between—"

The plasma shot hit her rifle head-on and splattered over the two closest recruits. Libby dropped her rifle and stared down at herself, stunned. Somehow, the plasma hadn't hit her.

"Get your biosuits off!" Joe shouted at the two panicking recruits. Libby picked up one of their rifles and began spraying the corridor with

Jreet poison. Along with what seemed like a hundred moving shapes in the far corridor, they saw predatory aliens on six legs with way too many teeth. Several kids around Joe let out little whimpers and began to bawl even as they fired their rifles.

"Careful!" Joe shouted. "At least they're not Jreet. We can kill them!" He threw a *fahjli* grenade down the corridor and watched the monstrous-shaped Huouyt scatter. Several got hit with the blue flash and their bodies reverted back to their squid-like form with a colorful flutter. They fell to the ground and remained motionless as the children around Joe pelted their bodies with Jreet poison.

Then they saw a real Jreet—its head held almost fifteen feet off the ground, hunched over in the low corridor like some monster in its dungeon—and barely had time to flinch before the massive thing was on them, bowling them over like they were made of cardboard. It caught Bailey and pinned him against the floor with a huge tail, and only his biosuit kept it from crushing his chest. Its poison-tipped appendage unsheathed under its head and it reared back to slam it into Bailey's chest.

Libby picked up another recruit's plasma rifle and fired it point-blank at the Jreet's torso. The Jreet forgot about Bailey. It made another *shee-whomp* sound as it swiveled and slammed its fang into the recruit standing beside Libby.

The girl crumpled instantly, the plasma rifle falling from her hands. Joe dodged under the Jreet and picked it up, then tumbled out of the way as the Jreet launched itself at another recruit and disappeared again. Joe's eyes fell to Bailey.

Bailey was still pinned by the Jreet's weight on his biosuit. Joe lifted his rifle, making Bailey's eyes widen. "I'll kill you later," Joe promised him. As Bailey gave him a look of horror, Joe shot directly at his chest.

The Jreet uncloaked and slammed its lower half into Joe, sending him sprawling. Joe scrabbled for his rifle and began firing at the creature's throat. The massive Jreet screeched another defiant battle-cry and continued killing until the plasma ate its lower half away from its torso and its head fell from its neck. It died with its fang sunk deep into a boy's biosuit, a pile of dead recruits scattered around it.

They were down to eight.

Libby and Rat were leading the others at the front. They were shooting down the hall, trying to hit the Huouyt who were holding their positions from behind the doors Joe did not have the codes to open. Joe fell in beside them.

Out of the corner of his eye, Joe saw Tank take a plasma round full to the chest. Tank's eyes opened wide and he dropped his rifle in terror.

"*Get your suit off!*" Rat screamed.

Tank ignored her and reached into his belt. He took out a *fahjli* grenade and activated it. Already, his face was contorting in pain. As he threw it, his chest became an open purple wound where his biosuit should have been. Instead of bouncing down the corridor, the grenade hit the corner of the wall and bounced back at them. Libby bent down and swept it up, deftly twisting the two halves back in place before stuffing it into her boot. Tank was already dead.

"There's too many, Joe," Maggie said. "Take us back!"

"So they can follow us back out?" Joe demanded. "No. Everybody follow me. We'll take a different corridor."

"You want to go *deeper*?!" Bailey demanded.

"It's either that or get shot!" Joe shouted. "We don't have any cover and they do. Now everybody *run*."

They found a corridor perpendicular to the last and took it, delving deeper into the enemy warren. Libby frowned as they retreated down the hall. "It's almost like they're herding us. Those Huouyt are shooting the walls more than anything."

"Maybe that means we're close to the bottom," Joe said. "They could be bad shots because they're Representative Na'leen's secretaries, not warriors."

Libby scowled at him. "Representative Na'leen has *assassins*, Joe. And Jreet can kill *Dhasha*. I don't like this. We should fight our way back out, wait for Lagrah."

Peering down the endless rows of red lights illuminating the corridors, Joe had to agree with her. His heart sank. With so few of them left—only seven, now—fighting their way back out would get them killed just as quickly as staying.

"We can't go back," Joe said. "We've got to keep going and hope Lagrah will show up with reinforcements."

"Maybe we should surrender, Joe."

Libby swiveled on Maggie and hit her hard, knocking the shorter girl to the ground. She was standing over Maggie in an instant, her rifle in her face, her finger touching the trigger.

"No!" Joe snapped.

Libby made a grim face, but moved away.

As Maggie stood, Joe stepped in front of her, putting his back between her and the rest of the platoon. Watching her gray eyes light up with hope, he said softly, "Mag, if you say something like that again, I'll kill you myself."

"But—" She looked startled, betrayed.

"Just get moving, Mag," Joe said.

He led them on in silence, the only sound that of their boots on the hard black diamond. Every face in the group had grown older in the last two hours, and even Rat had stopped questioning him, resigned to their fate. At their backs, they heard several mechanical *shee-whomps* in rapid succession, spurring them forward.

We're dead, Joe thought. *I should've never taken us in here alone. I should've waited for Lagrah.* All of Joe's friends were going to die because he'd tried to prove the Trith wrong. He hesitated, wondering if he still had some way to save them.

"There's a door open up here!" Rat cried. "Zero, a door!"

Joe jogged with Libby to inspect it. The opening was narrow enough for one person to pass, and it had an exit to another room out the back.

"Looks like a crypt," Libby muttered.

"So we should keep going?" Joe demanded. Behind them, the Jreet were getting closer. They could hear their scales scraping on the floor.

"It might be a good place for a last stand," she said, shrugging.

"Screw that," Joe snapped. Still, when he looked at the straight, never-ending tunnel in front of them, he said, "Everybody get inside." He ducked his head under the doorjamb as he ran. "Libby, watch that end."

He was jogging to the back of the room to check to see where it led when the door began to drip shut ahead of him. A black-clad Ooreiki stood on the other side, tentacles still touching the control pad.

"No, wait!" Joe said, upon seeing the Congie uniform. The door dripped shut and stayed shut.

He wheeled at a run. "Everybody get out! They're locking us in!"

"But—" Maggie began.

"Ash!" Bailey shouted. "Libby pushed me and ran out!"

Joe felt a flutter of fear in his gut. What if Libby had been fighting for the other side all along? Then he realized that she probably hadn't survived the fall off the *ferlii*, after all. A Huouyt could have mimicked her and then come back to take her place.

Joe felt bile rising in his throat at the thought of her dead. *No,* he thought frantically. *That was her. I'd know an impostor.* So why had she abandoned them?

Violet-colored steam began seeping out of the ceiling and Joe jerked. *Our own side is gassing us.* "Shoot the doors!" Joe cried. "Cover your faces!"

The ragged remnants of their group huddled along the edges of the walls and fired their weapons at the two locked exits. Plasma ate the heavy material of the door, albeit too slowly to do them any good. His shirt wrapped over a hand and pressed to his face, Joe tried fiddling with the control pad on the door. Nothing worked. Yuil's tale of simple locks and easy codes could not have been further from the truth—every door required an eighteen-digit PIN, plus a rank-scan of Overseer or higher.

Around him, his recruits were slumping over, dead or unconscious.

After repeated denials from the control panel, Joe ripped his shirt from his face and slammed his fist into the controls. *"We're on your side you son of a bitch!"*

Joe thought he smelled oranges before he collapsed.

38

LOYAL TO THE END

"How many of them are there?!"

"I only see the one!"

"Well where's the rest of them?"

"Is anyone injured?"

"Stop looking at the sky you furgs!"

"What are they firing at us?! Poison gas?"

"Suits aren't registering it. Either he's a kamikaze or its just smoke and lights."

"It's coming from that rooftop. Send someone to investigate. The rest of you, round up as many of the recruits as you can find."

"What do we do with this one, sir?"

Stinging, python limbs reached through the broken window and tore Joe out of the bashed-in driver's door of the Ford pickup, throwing him down on the pavement in front of one of the aliens. Joe, still stunned from colliding with the side of an apartment building without airbags, hit the concrete and he stared at the creature's glossy black boot in a daze. He could feel the alien in charge staring down on him, could feel the other alien's gun brushing the back of his head, waiting to blow him away.

"Commander Lagrah?"

"How old do you think it is?"

"Sixteen, is my onboard's guess, Commander Lagrah," one of the glossy, black-suited aliens said. "Maybe fourteen, with growth irregularities."

There was cruel purpose in the alien's pale brown eyes as he said, "I'm sorry, Gokli. What did you say his age was?"

There was a long pause. "Twelve, sir."

"Go find his friends. I want them all."

"Yes, sir."

"No," Joe groaned. He tried to pull himself to his feet, but the alien in charge slammed a foot into his back, sending him back to the ground. It peered down at Joe through the obsidian suit, looking like a cold, calculating wasp. Joe groaned and closed his eyes.

"Sir? He had no accomplices, other than the one on the roof. We're still looking for him, but the residents in this area are not cooperating."

"He got away?"

"Yes sir."

"They all got away? All nine hundred?"

"Yes, sir. They had some sort of locomotion planned. Hundreds of them. They scattered in all directions. High speeds." Joe felt a wave of relief that his high school buddies had followed through and pressed his face back to the concrete. He didn't care that the alien in charge was glaring down at him, his gun shaking as it hovered over his head. Sam was safe.

"Take him."

"Kill him, sir?"

"Take him back to the ship."

"To use as an Unclaimed?"

"We'll see."

"Why don't you take them both, my lord?" The new voice was high-pitched, musical. Nothing at all like the raw fury in Lagrah's voice as he ordered Gokli to take him away. Joe groaned and opened his eyes.

Representative Na'leen stood above him, though he was looking at something across the room. His cloth-of-gold cape was still in pristine condition, with the eight circles of Congress embroidered in precious metals on his chest.

"Only one has a destiny to fulfill, Zol'jib. Only one will come with me. I will not spend the rest of my life wondering which it is."

"That won't be long, traitor."

Joe flinched and turned. Battlemaster Nebil hung against the wall along with a dozen other Ooreiki. His head had collapsed into his neck, leaving a shapeless brown mass protecting his eyes. Sharp hooks driven through the meat of his tentacles kept him from reaching the ground. The delicate tips, those used for grasping and manipulating objects, had been cut off. The four-pointed silver star of a battlemaster stood out on his tattered black uniform. His boots had been cut away, revealing for the first time the crude lumps of flesh Ooreiki had for feet. The pale skin there was dripping brownish fluid from numerous cuts. The Jreet responsible stood nearby, his lower body coiled beneath him, yellow eyes fixed mercilessly on Nebil.

"Your stubborn bravado is getting irritating, soldier," Representative Na'leen snapped. "Help us or you'll die here."

"I'd rather lose my *oorei* than help a Huouyt find water."

"That can be arranged, you stupid creature."

Representative Na'leen was scowling at Nebil. Several Huouyt stood with him. One of them held Libby. Like Joe, they had removed her biosuit. She looked half-dead, bruised and bloody from head to toe. If her captors hadn't been holding her up, she would have fallen. Joe felt his throat constrict upon seeing her limp and helpless in their arms. Then he realized one of her eyes was open slightly. She was *watching* him!

"Then arrange it and stop wasting my time."

At Nebil's unfavorable response, the Jreet casually lashed out, slashing a taloned claw across his chest. The four-pointed battlemaster star fell to the ground along with a strip of cloth. Nebil shuddered, but said nothing.

"Think very hard, Battlemaster," Na'leen said. "One of these two will aid us. One of them is expendable."

"The female is the better fighter," one of the dozen disabled Ooreiki hanging from the wall said. The Ooreiki's voice was familiar, one that Joe had heard a thousand times before in long, idiotic speeches. He could not believe it. Commander Tril.

"Possibly," one of Na'leen's assistants said. "It took six of my men to bring her here alive. She actually killed a Jreet who was not trying to be killed."

"So take her and let us go," Tril retorted. "We're on your side. We hate Congress just as much as you do."

"Tril you fire-loving Tak—" Nebil's words ended with a grunt as the Jreet slashed him again, adding more cuts to his pale brown flesh. He was, by far, the worst off of any of the Ooreiki hanging on the wall, yet somehow he still had enough energy to curse his Jreet tormentor. Joe's heart gave an anxious twinge.

Representative Na'leen motioned at the room. "What loyalties do you have to Congress? Were you not stolen from your home like the rest of them? Don't you want to see Congress fall?"

"Fall where? Under Huouyt dominion?" Nebil made a throaty, toadlike laugh. "I spent forty-three years as a Prime. One of the first things I learned was to never trust a Huouyt. They have as much conscience as Takki have courage."

Representative Na'leen's electric-blue eyes were flat, but Joe saw the unrepressed ripple of his snowy-white cilia. "We want to create a new society," Na'leen said.

"You want to *rule* a new society," Nebil retorted. "How many of us will you care about once you reach your goals? Zero. It's wrong. Whatever you were told, a Trith never gives the whole prophecy."

Joe frowned at Nebil. It had almost seemed like he had been talking to Joe.

Na'leen's downy white cilia began to move in waves across his black skin. "Those who sit around waiting for Congress to fall apart will never see it happen. You make your own futures, and damn the Trith. We've spent so much time waiting for their prophecies, running their little errands, praying for them to deliver us from this snare we've woven for ourselves that we've never taken the time to reach out and untie the knot."

"And then what?" Nebil said. "You think the Jreet will follow you forever? You think the Dhasha will let you rule?"

"The Dhasha are simple," Na'leen said. "We destroy their planets with the ekhta." He glanced at the Jreet warrior standing beside Nebil. "As for the Jreet, they will follow whoever has the courage to lead them to victory."

"They will follow you until you win, then they'll abandon you to resume their old wars. The Jreet don't need you, Na'leen. They don't need anything except the blood of their enemies."

"Which I will give to them, in rivers."

"And when you become one of their enemies?"

Na'leen's silence stretched over the room, casting it in a cold chill.

"That one will not help us," one of the Huouyt said. "Kill him." Joe recognized the Huouyt who had tried to claim him for Na'leen back in the barracks. His white-blue eyes were fixed coldly on Nebil.

"No, Zol'jib." Representative Na'leen matched Nebil's stare. "That's what he wants. Unfortunately for him, I am not Knaaren. I do not intend to have a repeat of Kihgl. We have nanos enough to keep him alive through whatever torture we need to inflict. You may gag him if his noise bothers you."

Joe's heart began to pound as he watched Nebil stiffen.

He's protecting me. Joe felt a rush of gratitude and shame. *He's protecting me and I'm just sitting here.* His stomach began to ache with fear. Hadn't the Trith warned him against fighting his destiny? Wasn't that why Scott was dead? Because he didn't go talk to the rebel in the road when he was supposed to? Hadn't fate simply twisted things around so he was right where he would have been even if he *had* boarded that ship, except now most of his platoon was dead? What choice did he have, if everything he ever did would bring him the same result? He *had* to help Na'leen or more of his friends would die.

"It's me. The Trith said so." As soon as he said the words, Joe knew he could never take them back. He looked away from Nebil's searing glance and faced Na'leen.

"So." Representative Na'leen gave him a weighing look. "Perhaps he finally remembered his conversations with Kihgl?"

"A Trith visited me. Told me I would shatter Congress."

Every alien in the room stiffened, Huouyt and Ooreiki alike.

"And what," Representative Na'leen said very carefully, "*else* did the Trith tell you, boy? What were your four prophecies?"

Joe frowned. "He only gave me one."

Several of the Huouyt went utterly still and glanced at each other, and the Ooreiki prisoners' sudah fluttered rapidly in their wrinkled brown necks. No one said a word.

"But it doesn't matter, because Bagkhal and Commander Lagrah are going to rip you ashers apart," Joe added.

"Bagkhal and Commander Lagrah are dead," the Huouyt holding Libby said. "Bagkhal is a pretty new comet and I killed Lagrah myself, before he ever had a chance to board the shuttle. I left the body in an air duct. They'll find it a few days from now, when it begins to stink. Not that it will make any difference. We'll be controlling Kophat by then." As Zol'jib spoke the last, he touched something to the wormy red appendage in his face and his body began to darken and shift, the coating of cilia tugging inward, his body growing stockier and more compact.

A moment later, Commander Lagrah stood where the assassin had been, his scarred chest and shoulders still loosely draped with the cloth-of-silver of Representative Na'leen's staff. Joe was looking upon the same creature who had urged him to take his friends down this dungeon in the first place.

Joe felt like he'd been punched. "You never let those platoons out of the eighth level, did you?" Joe asked quietly.

"Of course not," the assassin in Lagrah's body said. "They were still loyal to Congress. We'd just have to kill them later."

Seeing how perfectly he imitated Lagrah, right down to his drawling Ooreilian accent, something snapped into focus for Joe. He felt a coldness pool in his guts, remembering that Na'leen had wanted his cooperation that first day he'd summoned Joe to his opulent chambers high above the city of Alishai. And Joe had refused. Swallowing, he whispered, "Were you Yuil, too?"

The Huouyt smirked and gave a slight bow, his Ooreiki face wrinkling in smug satisfaction. "There is more than one tool to declaw a Dhasha," the assassin said. "Especially when dealing with such..." he looked Joe up and down in disdain, "*simple* minds."

"Negate the pattern," Na'leen ordered. "Our goal is not to antagonize him."

Immediately, Zol'jib inclined his head and went to a vat of water in one corner of the room and submerged himself. When he stood, rivulets running down his metallic clothing, he was once more in the shape of a Huouyt, his body crawling with writhing white cilia.

Joe felt hot fury scraping the inside of his veins, watching the transformation. *They didn't get me the first time, so they made me come. That's why Scott's dead.*

"Ignore him." Na'leen waved a dismissive arm at his assassin. "Don't you want to return to Earth, Zero? Don't you miss your family?"

You're holding my family. Joe looked at Libby. She was still faking her exhaustion. *She thinks I'm trying to distract them so she can attack.* He felt a surge of affection. However, with no weapons nor a biosuit, against a Jreet and almost a dozen Huouyt, Libby didn't stand a chance. He glanced behind him and located Maggie in the group of children huddled against the wall. They were all still wearing their biosuits, though the Huouyt had removed their gear and piled it against the wall. The Ooreiki hung beside them, their Congressional uniforms tattered and their bodies limp and defeated. He took a deep breath. "You let them go and I'll—"

"Kihgl didn't give you his *kasja* because of a Trith prophecy, Joe."

Joe jerked to look at Battlemaster Nebil. He had hung in silence the entire time, watching him. *He used my real name,* he realized, in shock.

Battlemaster Nebil met his gaze and held it. "He gave it to you because he knew you'd make one hell of a Congie."

Joe felt a rush of gratitude for his battlemaster. He ached to tell Nebil his problems, wishing he had done it sooner. Looking into the old Ooreiki's eyes, he knew that Nebil could help him. *I don't know what to do. The Trith said—*

"*Now* you may kill him," Na'leen said. "We have what we need."

An arc of fire shot through Joe's being as the Jreet struck his battlemaster with his sheathed chest-fang. "No!" Even as he rushed forward, Nebil's sudah gave a brief flutter above the point where the Jreet's fang entered his chest, then his body went limp, his tattered corpse hanging from the hooks in the wall like a drooping pile of loose meat.

A deep, burning hatred ate at Joe's lungs, making it hurt to breathe. In that moment, he knew what he had to do. Dad fought for Sam. Joe would fight for his friends.

Instantly, the Trith's words replayed in his mind. *You will try to fight it, but invariably, your path will lead to the same end.* Joe took a deep breath and ignored them.

Please let this be the right decision.

"Libby, you remember Sasha?"

Na'leen frowned as Libby mumbled something in response. "What did she say?"

"Remember how Sasha died?" Joe said.

"How could I forget?" Libby's exhausted façade dropped away and she jammed a fist into Zol'jib's throat. His white-blue eyes looked startled as she whirled, slammed a foot into the side of his head, and lunged away from him as he fell. She spun around Na'leen, jumped under a Huouyt's grasping arm, and yanked a plasma rifle from his belt. She started firing into the Huouyt and they let out startled cries and tried to shield Representative Na'leen.

Joe's guard tightened its paddle-like arm around Joe's bicep. Joe jammed his other elbow into the Huouyt's face, wheeled, and kicked it over as it reached to protect its eyes. Then he turned back to help Libby. Out of the corner of his eye, he saw Zol'jib pull something the size of a small pen from his pocket. Joe lunged at Zol'jib, taking him down as a Jreet uncloaked behind Libby.

"Jreet behind you!" Joe shouted.

Libby swiveled and hit the Jreet in the throat with plasma and it began to thrash, bowling Huouyt over with its tail. More Huouyt screamed, their bodies spattered with the plasma from Libby's gun. Na'leen's assistants were ushering him from the room, leaving several Huouyt behind to fight.

"Release me!" Zol'jib snapped, trying to wriggle his wet arms from Joe's grip.

"Not a chance, asher." Joe held on tight, keeping the Huouyt's slick, paddle-like arms pinned tightly to his sides so that only the tips could move.

The Huouyt's electric-blue eyes radiated fury. "As you wish." Joe felt a pinprick on his side where it touched the Huouyt, like a bee sting. Then, suddenly, all of his muscles went limp. Joe could feel everything, but could control nothing. Nothing except his voice.

An interrogator's weapon, he realized. It left him in the most terrifying state of paralysis he had ever experienced. He could only listen helplessly as his groundmate continued to struggle behind him. "Watch out, Libby! They're using poison!" he screamed.

Zol'jib shoved Joe off him and stood. "Libby! Behind yo—" Joe's words ended with a grunt as the Huouyt's powerful leg knocked the air out of him.

As Joe fought for breath, Zol'jib stalked toward Libby. Before he reached her, another Huouyt grabbed her from behind and kicked her knees out from under her. Without her biosuit to protect her, she collapsed, the Huouyt wrenching her stolen rifle from her white knuckles with one paddle-like tentacle as he wrapped the other around her neck. Though he couldn't raise his head to see, Joe could hear her choking as the Huouyt strangled her.

"Don't hurt her," Joe desperately said to the floor. "You need me as a friend, not an enemy."

Apparently, they released her, because the choking sounds stopped.

"My boot, Joe!" Libby shouted.

Her boot?

Joe glanced to his left. Libby's gear lay stacked in a pile on the floor in front of him. Her boots stood off to one side. Only her rifle was missing. Suddenly, he remembered Libby disarming Tank's *fahjli* grenade and stuffing it beneath her laces. His eyes caught her left boot. The dull blue surface of the grenade peeked out at him.

"My *boot*, Joe!"

Doesn't she realize I can't move?

"Libby, I can't—" Zol'jib interrupted him as he hauled him to his feet.

Libby was giving Joe a look that pierced his soul. Glowering at him, she drew her knees to her chest and threw her long arms around her legs. She had bruises on her neck and arms where she'd struggled with the Huouyt.

Joe ached to help her, to hold her, but he couldn't even wiggle his pinkie finger.

"We'll take them both," Na'leen said from the doorway. "Even if she is not the one we need, she will do well in our army."

"I'll never fight for you," Libby said, her eyes fixed on Joe. "I am not a traitor."

Joe felt a stab of fear, realizing she had misunderstood. She thought he had given up! She thought he had surrendered. "Libby, I—"

"Shut up," Zol'jib snapped. "No more code." The Huouyt's downy tentacle brushed his neck. Joe felt another pinprick and all powers of speech left him.

Representative Na'leen had noticed Libby's scowl. "You have no idea who he is, do you, girl?"

Only reluctantly did Libby's eyes leave Joe's face. To Na'leen, she said, "Who is who?"

"Your friend. Zero. He's what every Congressional citizen has been waiting for since our society was spawned. He is the one the Trith have foretold will destroy Congress."

No!

Libby jerked as if she'd been struck and gave Joe a wounded look. "You will?"

No, no, no! It felt like his body was floating outside his body, watching from afar, utterly disconnected from the controls.

"The Trith came to you that day too, didn't he, Joe?"

After countless hours in the tunnels, Joe knew she could read his eyes, just as he could read hers. She knew Na'leen was telling the truth, just as Joe knew she hated him for it. He felt an ache of despair and closed his eyes, wishing he could explain.

"And he said you would destroy Congress?"

Joe could only listen miserably, unable to even twitch his head in the negative.

"You're a rebel, Joe?"

No! I'm standing next to a burning assassin and I'm paralyzed, can't you see that?!

Libby's face hardened. "Well you know what the Trith told me, Joe?"

He said I was a traitor. But I'm not. I've got an assassin's poison in my veins and I can't. Burning. Move!

Like a panther rising from its nap, Libby stood, her gaze fixed on Joe. "He said I'd have to kill you to save Congress."

Joe's eyes jerked open. At the same time, Libby hurled a knife at him.

The blade hit home. Joe felt the air rush out of him as it slammed into his chest in an arc of wet fire. He reeled, staggering backwards. He heard a commotion, a Huouyt screaming, and the soggy *burp* of a plasma rifle going off. Then, nothing.

Joe was on his back, staring at the ceiling, his vision fading to a red haze. His heart was slamming in his chest, slicing itself on the blade, driving the agony deeper into his body. He grew weaker, unable to even call for help.

She hit me in the heart, Joe thought. His mind felt as clear as ever, utterly logical. *I'm dying. Not even nanos can work fast enough to save me.*

He knew he should feel hurt, betrayed, but all he felt was frustration. It was all a misunderstanding. Libby didn't really hate him. She did what she thought she had to. If only he could *explain!* Then, as his vision faded, taking his thoughts with it, he saw a slender black shape crumple to the ground. Something about the way she fell sent another jolt of adrenaline lancing his shattered veins.

Oh God. Libby!

39

THE TUG OF FATE

"**D**ad didn't come home last night, Joe."

"What? How do you know?"

"I stayed up on the sofa waiting for him. I heard Mom calling the hospital this morning."

"Why would she call the hospital? Where's Dad?"

"I don't know, Joe, but the aliens are saying they killed a bunch of Marines last night. I hacked into their waves. They laid a trap for them."

"Shut up, Sam. You're lying."

"I'm not lying, Joe! Get out of bed! Mom wants to talk to you."

"We've got to go find him."

"Dad? Mom told me not to leave the house. She wants to talk to you."

"So let's go out the window, okay?"

"Sure, okay. You know where he is, Joe?"

"Probably pinned down somewhere. You know where they laid their trap?"

"By the river. Pushed them into the water. It was on the news, Joe."

"I think Mom heard us. Your door just slammed."

"Run, Sam! We've gotta check the river."

"But Mom's gonna—"

"Just run, Sam!"

"Joe, what's that up there? Why are all those kids—"

"Shit, Sam, hide!"

"They're behind us, too. Joe, they saw me."

Stay away from my brother you assholes!"

"Joe! Help, Joe!"

"He's breathing."

"It's an improvement. Brain damage?"

"Possibly."

"Will it impair his functions?"

"I don't have the proper equipment, so it's completely up in the air. Your dose was the best Congress has to offer, but he wasn't breathing for several minutes. I think the drug I gave him kept him sedate enough to avoid too much damage, but I'm still not sure he's completely stable. The antidote showed no change at all."

"He can't die. The Trith told him he'd be the one."

"We don't know that. He could've been lying."

"The girl tried to kill him for it. Possibly did kill him."

"So what should we do? We're losing time."

"Can you move him?"

"Not sure. Humans are delicate."

"Representative, Commander Pur'wei is having problems in the third Alishai ring, near the shuttle launch. He wants to talk to you."

"If it's not important, I'll pull his *breja* out myself."

"Representative Na'leen?"

"Yes, Commander, what is it?"

"You were supposed to kill all the Dhasha, sir."

"Excuse me?"

"There's a Dhasha ripping apart my regiment out here. Biggest one I ever saw. He's leading a small Ooreiki contingent against our positions. Rousting them every time. He's pushing through Alishai, headed straight for you."

"Curse him to the ninety Jreet hells. Fine. We'll move things forward. Destroy all the haauks you can find, force him to walk as far as possible. *Jreet hells!* I'd like to know how that janja slug survived space. Zol'jib, is he awake yet?"

"No, Ko-Na'leen."

"Then stay here with him. Meet me at the main control hub once he wakes."

"You're firing the ekhta?"

"Bagkhal gives me no choice. If he finds a usable haauk, we only have eighteen tics before he tears open the door and finds his way down here."

"What did you do, Joe?"

"I'm sorry, Mom."

"What did you do?! Where's your brother?"

"He's... He..."

"The aliens got him, didn't they? You let the aliens take your brother, didn't you?! Answer me, Joe!"

"I'll help Dad get him back. I'll go with them tonight and get him back."

"Your Dad is dead, Joe. All of his friends are dead. There's no one to help your brother now. They're both gone. I told you not to let him leave the house and you took him anyway and now he's gone!"

"I could go find Dad, Mom. We could get Sam back together."

"You're just a stupid kid, Joe. A stupid kid who gave his brother to the aliens."

"I'll find Sam, Mom. I'll get him out, I swear."

"Oh just go to Hell, Joe."

"Hey asher. Thanks for getting my platoon killed. I knew Lagrah would never make us do anything this stupid. Libby had the right idea when she tried to gut you. Too bad they killed her."

Joe's eyes flashed open. Rat stood by his arm, sneering down at him.

"Shut up, girl." A Huouyt pushed her out of the way and beamed down at Joe. Joe recognized Zol'jib and felt bile burning his throat.

"You killed Libby?"

"She acquired another plasma weapon and was going to use it on you."

No. Joe let his head fall to the side, away from Rat, away from the Huouyt. He found himself staring at Libby's empty boot.

You will try to fight it, but invariably, your path will lead to the same end.

What if Nebil was wrong? What if he had to help Na'leen? What if everything he did only prolonged the inevitable? What if he'd just gotten Libby killed?

No. The voice within him seared through his veins like fire.

The Trith never said how *I would shatter Congress.* The sheer truth of it resonated within him, extinguishing his doubts. *I'm a Congie. Bagkhal was right. I don't have to help them.*

Joe clenched his fist, reveling in the strength he felt there.

Zol'jib noticed the movement. "He's weak. Gather the other Humans. They'll carry him."

"Like Hell." Rat spat at Joe and backed away, throwing off the Huouyt's grip.

"Rat," Joe said. She hesitated and frowned down at him. "I'm gonna need your help."

"I'll never help you again, traitor," Rat said.

"I'm not a traitor," Joe said, eyes falling once more on Libby's boot. He thought he could see a naked human form sprawled on the floor beyond it, but couldn't make his eyes focus on it. *I never was.*

You will try to fight it, but invariably, your path will lead to the same end.

Joe sat up and tore the *fahjli* grenade out of Libby's boot. As the Huouyt watched with startled white-blue eyes, he twisted it and set the grenade down on the ground between them. "Take the ones along the wall," Joe said to Rat. "I'll get these."

As Zol'jib bent to retrieve the grenade, Joe grabbed the knife Libby had thrown at him and rammed it into the creature's tubular, downy white chest. It reeled backwards in surprise, forgetting the grenade. Instead of pulling the knife free, Joe twisted it and yanked down, eviscerating him from neck to legs. Several egg-shaped orange lumps gushed from the wound on a wave of clear mucus. Zol'jib let out a terrified, musical wail and Joe kicked him backwards off his knife.

When the *fahjli's* blue flash went off, Joe descended upon the others. The startled Huouyt could only watch in horror as he slaughtered them. Joe killed five before the flash wore off and they began reaching for their weapons.

"Put it down, Zero!" one of the Huouyt snapped, its mirror-like eyes staring back at him in calm disdain. "You are outgunned. I don't care what Na'leen said. Fight us, and you won't get out of here alive."

Joe glanced back at Rat, who had another plasma pistol in her hands. A group of four terrified recruits were huddled behind her, eying the Huouyt in terror. Like Joe, all of them were naked, their bodies bared to the dozen guns aimed on them.

Sometimes you've gotta stand up for yourself, even when you know you ain't got a chance.

He spun and slammed his knife into a startled Huouyt's throat. As his opponent fell, something carried him onward, a culmination of every bit of anguish, every bit of rage, every bit of terror he had endured in the past months. He leapt over the body and dove into the startled throng of defenders. Something deep within was powering him, now, pushing him, electrifying his limbs as he sliced through his opponents with a detached grace. More Huouyt rushed into the room and grappled him, but they couldn't find a secure hold and their bee-stings didn't work on him.

"He's had the antidote too soon!" one of them cried. Joe rammed his knife into the speaker's slit of a mouth, then pulled the blade up and through the brain. The room echoed with plasma fire and Huouyt screams. Behind him, he heard the *shee-whomp* of a Jreet. Earlier, in the tunnels, the very sound had been enough to push a sheet of adrenaline through his body. Now, it only gave Joe another target.

Sometimes you've gotta stand up for yourself, even when you know you ain't got a chance.

Now he knew what his Dad had meant.

The Jreet was huge, almost forty feet, one of Na'leen's personal guard. It circled Joe, sliding through the bodies of the Huouyt, hesitating to use its poison.

It still thinks I'm going to help them, Joe realized.

"Joe, get out of the way!" Rat cried, from behind him. "I can't get a clear shot!"

But something had taken a grip on his soul, and Joe walked forward, so that he was almost touching the point of the fang jutting from the Jreet's chest. It hovered above his forehead, its dark tip glistening red in the hazy light. It would have only taken a twitch on the Jreet's part to end Joe's life right there. Yet, as massive and ancient as the warrior before him was, it did not strike. Looking past it, Joe saw the indecision in the Jreet's tiny golden eyes. And, in that moment of clarity, Joe understood.

Kill me and I won't fulfill the prophecy, he thought, looking up into its face. *And you don't want to fail.* He could understand its dilemma, and respected it on a deep inner level.

Joe lifted his knife and the Jreet slid backwards, away from him. It dropped the tip of its translucent spear between them, keeping him at a wary distance.

"You're going to have to kill me." The words Joe spoke were neither Congie nor English. He wasn't sure how he knew them, but he did. "My blood or yours, brother."

The Jreet gave him a startled look, the tip of its spear wavering minutely.

Joe stepped forward, until his chest was touching the spear. He felt the tip sink into his chest, up and to the right of Libby's scar, before the Jreet started to pull back, preventing him from impaling himself. Warm blood began to slide down his skin as he moved forward, dripping onto the ground between them. Joe's eyes never left the Jreet's.

The Jreet tentatively lowered its spear.

Joe jammed his knife into the vital area in the Jreet's throat, above the poisoned fang. The fang twitched once, stopping only a hairsbreadth away from Joe's skin before it retracted. Dropping its spear, the massive Jreet slid into a corner and collapsed.

With no more enemies to fight, Joe's fury drew him back to Zol'jib's corpse. The Huouyt who had taken Lagrah's form. Na'leen's assassin, who had poisoned him so Libby thought he had betrayed her. The same Huouyt who had pretended to be Yuil, to make him betray his friends. Joe buried his knife into the corpse, dismantling the body bit by bit, stabbing the hated blue-white eyes out.

"He's dead, Zero."

Tril's voice cut through the haze. Joe glanced up. The Overseer was watching him from the wall, along with the rest of the Ooreiki survivors. The other kids in the room were staring at him in open fear. Rat looked startled, her lips parted, the plasma gun half-hanging from her limp hand. Joe realized he was covered in sticky Huouyt blood, the transparent slime glistening upon his body from head to toe.

Joe's eyes found Maggie. She was standing beside Libby's corpse, her usually adoring gaze containing something Joe had never seen before. He got goosebumps.

"So it was all a trick?" Rat demanded. "That thing with Libby and the Trith…it was a *trick?*"

Maggie's eyes never left him and Joe realized that she had come to the exact opposite conclusion.

"Very clever." Tril twisted on the wall. "Where'd you learn Voran Jreet, Zero? It's a very rare dialect."

Joe dropped his knife and stood, suddenly feeling every spatter of alien blood as if it were acid. He stared at his palms. "I didn't."

Tril frowned at him a moment, then said, "I knew you Humans had a talent for languages. You've done the work of a fully-trained Planetary Ops squad. Congress will reward you well. Now hurry and release us. This structure is rigged as an Overseer's bunker. There should be a command center nearby where I can call for help."

Joe ignored the Ooreiki and stood. "Come here, Mag." He held out his gore-encrusted arms.

Maggie ignored his gesture, her eyes locked on his face. "You're a traitor. That's why you didn't help Libby."

Joe's arms dropped. "Mag, I couldn't—"

"*Now,* Zero!" Commander Tril snapped. "Do you want Na'leen to return with more of his Jreet? The same trick will not work more than once."

Joe hesitated. He could see Maggie needed him to deny it, to assure her there was nothing he could have done to save their friend. But there would be time later to explain and unless he wanted Maggie to die, too, his comforting words would have to wait. He moved to help Tril, ignoring Maggie's searing look.

"Mag, help me here," Joe said, hefting Tril's weight. "Unhook his arms."

Maggie sat down beside Libby and began stroking her arm, humming.

"Bailey," Joe snapped. "Help me."

The boy jerked. He tore his eyes from Libby's body and hurried to help slide the hooks from Tril's tentacles. Once Tril was on his feet, he hurried from the room, leaving them the option of following or staying behind for the Jreet. Rat turned to follow. Joe glanced at the other Ooreiki hanging from the wall. They would be useless in a fight, but he couldn't leave them behind.

"Bailey, help me get the others." When Bailey hesitated, looking like he wanted to follow Rat, instead, Joe screamed, *"Now! Or I swear to God I'll gut you for what you did to Libby!"*

Bailey flinched and his eye went wide. "Joe, I never cut out Libby's tongue. I never broke her legs, neither. The Takki did that."

Joe frowned. "The Takki?"

"Yeah. Six of them were walking across the yard and Libby insulted them. Right out of the blue. Like she wanted to pick a fight with them. When that didn't work, she started insulting Knaaren. That made them attack her. She fought them off as best she could—killed a couple, I think. I started throwing rocks at them, shouting for Rat. That scared them off. But by that time, Libby was hurt real bad. One of 'em had got hold of her tongue and cut it out, sayin' she didn't deserve it."

Joe stared at Bailey, uncomprehending. He remembered the crowbar-shaped stick that had lain in the dust beside Libby and the connection jolted him. "Takki did it?"

"Yeah. I thought she told you."

Of course she didn't. Beaten by Takki. God, Libby, I'm sorry. Joe felt a tired rush of despair.

"Yeah. I would've helped her sooner, but she—"

"Just help me," he said, drained to the core. "You can tell me the rest later." Brushing past Maggie, they released the other six Ooreiki. They beamed and congratulated him, increasing Joe's discomfort. He wasn't the hero. Libby was. If she hadn't thrown the knife and made them give him the antidote to whatever Zol'jib gave him in order to keep him from bleeding out, he couldn't have activated the grenade.

Then a cold chill settled in the marrow of his spine. What if the Trith knew that? What if that's why the Trith had told Libby she'd have to kill him? To make her do it? To make her trade her life for his?

"Here, Zero." Bailey shoved a gun into Joe's lifeless arms. "We've gotta go. The Huouyt are coming back. Rat's waiting for us in the hall."

Joe stared at Bailey dumbly.

"Let's *go*, Zero!"

Numb, Joe followed the Ooreiki survivors out into the hall.

Libby died because of me. Because of that Trith. He felt the beginnings of hatred burning his intestines.

Maggie ignored Bailey's order to follow them and he had to bodily pull her away from Libby's corpse. Joe watched in solemn silence as she fought, screaming.

Finally, Bailey rounded on her. He dragged her close and into her face he shouted, "Libby's *dead*. You wanna die too?!"

Maggie ignored Bailey, her eyes locked with Joe's. "Why didn't you help her, Joe?"

"I couldn't, Mag," Joe whispered. "I wanted to."

"But you didn't," Maggie bit out. "It's your fault she's dead." She pronounced it with all the finality of a jury's verdict.

"I know, Mag."

"Hey." Bailey drove a finger into Maggie's shoulder. "He's a hero. He killed a Jreet by himself with just a *knife*. I didn't see *you* do anything to save Libby. You're just a whining little coward, you know that?"

Maggie's chest shuddered in a sob. Whimpering, Maggie spun and fled down the opposite corridor.

"Maggie!" Joe cried.

The plasma shot took Maggie in the neck and chest, knocking her off of her feet. Two massive Jreet rounded the corner beside her, their *shee-whomp* battle cry ringing down the corridor. Seeing Joe and Bailey, they cloaked. Joe could hear the rapid scraping of their bodies on the floor as they slithered toward them. Behind the Jreet came a dozen armed Huouyt, their powerful tentacle legs working awkwardly against the floor as they ran.

Joe's eyes fixed on Maggie's body, his breath burning in his lungs. He felt the beginnings of a sob in his chest.

I can't fight it. The Trith was right. I fought it again and Maggie died for it.

"Get out of here, Bailey." Joe lifted his rifle, aiming at the nearest Huouyt. He didn't have anybody left to lose but himself.

"Joe, come *here*." Bailey threw an arm around Joe's throat and dragged him backwards down the hall. Joe tried to struggle free, but Bailey had put on his biosuit—it was like fighting a statue. Cursing, Bailey threw him into a control room filled with maimed Ooreiki and followed him inside, blocking his escape.

As soon as they were in, Rat touched the control panel near the entrance and the door oozed shut. Joe stared at it, wondering why he wasn't on the other side, fighting.

"Is he here?" Tril demanded.

"Here, sir." Gokli shoved Joe in the Overseer's direction.

"Zero, you were given the Overseer's stimulant drugs, right?"

Joe frowned.

"And Nebil illegally taught you to read?" Tril demanded.

…*Taught me to* read? Joe nodded, frowning, still unable to understand why he wasn't fighting.

"Get over here," Tril ordered. "I need you to hit some buttons for me. We've got to seal off this section of the compound before Na'leen can get to the main control hub and fire an ekhta at Koliinaat."

Joe stared at the glowing, multi-layered, three-dimensional map of the bunker hovering over the central table. Na'leen and his companions were bright red dots moving down the staircase closest to them. Gokli, Tril, and all the other Ooreiki were standing beside the map, waiting for him, their tentacles reduced to short, useless stubs.

Seeing what they expected him to do, Joe hesitated.

Maggie was dead. Libby was dead. Scott was dead. Nebil and Lagrah were dead. What if the Trith was right?

What if more would die if he fought Fate?

And what if they had all died because the Trith wanted them to die? What if the Trith fed them lies to make them act the way they wanted them to act? To produce a desired result?

But then, something about the Trith's eerie stare left him with the undeniable impression that a Trith's prophecy was more than smoke and mirrors.

So what do I do?

Joe noticed for the first time the other recruits watching him. He knew Na'leen wouldn't make the mistake of letting Rat and the others live a second time.

Fate decided you will shatter Congress, Joe.

"Burn fate." Joe walked up to the map and, acting as Tril's hands, attempted to close off Representative Na'leen's route. Each time they had the Representative and his staff trapped in a section of the bunker, Na'leen somehow found a way to continue, working his way deeper into the *ferlii* with each passing minute, growing closer to the core and the ekhta inside.

"He outranks me," Tril cried, frustrated. "He's overriding my commands."

"Let me try," Gokli said. "Zero, start activating these." He pointed a truncated tentacle at the purple self-destruct buttons littering the map.

Tril pushed Joe's hand away from the screen, glaring at Gokli. "This building is rigged to explode in an emergency. He could set off a chain reaction and kill us all."

Gokli gave Tril a level glance. "So?"

Sudah fluttering, Tril took a deep breath and nodded. "Try collapsing the tunnels around him. Just don't hit one that's too close to the rest."

"He'll realize what we're doing as soon as we start," Gokli said. "We've gotta work fast or he'll start avoiding those halls."

"Fast but careful," Tril added.

Joe felt sweat beading over his face as he worked, his entire focus narrowing to the little red dots that were Na'leen and his companions. *You aren't getting away.* The *ferlii* rocked with successive explosions each time he touched the screen, making everyone in the room tense, eyes fixed to the shuddering black walls.

Joe barely noticed, so intense was his concentration. *For all my friends, for everything you've done and everyone who's died. I'm gonna stop you.*

With Gokli's help, Joe cornered Na'leen in a section of the *ferlii* that had no exits to override, no staircases to climb, no means of escape other than the hallway that Joe had collapsed behind them. Joe stepped away from the controls and Tril opened up a communications link between himself and the Tribunal member. Representative Na'leen's electric eyes were sizzling as he appeared on the screen.

"Looks like you killed the wrong one, Na'leen," Tril jeered. "Idiot."

Joe watched the Huouyt's eyes focus on him over Tril's shoulder. "Appears I did. How irritating."

"'Irritating' is hardly the word to describe your situation, Na'leen. Peacemakers are going to make you sing for turns on Levren for your crimes."

Na'leen was still looking at Joe. "My secrets die with me, Tril."

"*Overseer* to you, prisoner." Tril snorted. "And to think that Huouyt are known for their ability to spot a lie. You were looking right at Zero when he told you about his visitation from a Trith."

"Was I?" Na'leen eyed Joe calmly. "How odd. I was also under the impression Huouyt could detect a mistruth."

The tiny hairs on the back of Joe's neck stood on end before he crushed the reaction. *No. The Trith is wrong. I'm not one of them. They killed my friends. They killed Libby and Scott and Maggie. I'm a Congie. I'll never fight for them.*

Holding Na'leen's gaze, Joe said, "I'm loyal to Congress. I swear it." *I swear it for Libby. And Scott. And Maggie. I'll never let my groundmates down again. Never.*

Na'leen's electric-white eyes blinked in surprise. "You're telling the truth."

Tril laughed, the toadlike croaking of an Ooreiki. "A myth, then, just like your Regency seat will be. Congress won't let a Huouyt near the Tribunal for a million years."

"Congress won't last another million years," Na'leen said, his eyes still fixed on Joe. Joe turned away, ignoring him. From the screen behind him, Na'leen let out a long breath that sounded like the tinkling of wind chimes. "I was so sure this was the time."

"They all think that," Tril said. "Congress can't be beaten, Na'leen. Of all your time on the Tribunal, you should've known we would crush you."

It's not unbeatable, Joe thought, turning back to glare at Tril. *All I'd have to do is finish what the Jreet started, you stupid prick.*

Apparently, Na'leen was thinking the same thing. "Somehow I doubt the accuracy of your statement. Congress came within a hairsbreadth of falling apart this day. You can thank your recruit that it still stands, though

I wonder for how long." Representative Na'leen made a formal flourish to Joe with his paddle-like arms. "I wish you luck in the future, Joe Dobbs. In *all* of your endeavors."

Then, as they watched, he took a cylindrical capsule from beneath the golden folds of his cloak and held it up. Joe could have sworn the Huouyt was looking at him as he inhaled the hissing vapors. Na'leen collapsed, leaving the video feed blank.

Joe felt a rush of relief, staring at the body. *I beat it. I beat the prophecy.*

"Damn," Tril said. "The Peacemakers would have sold their *oorei* to have him alive on Levren." He slapped his severed tentacle against the screen, cutting off the feed. "Get out of here, Zero. Find us some weapons. And get yourself some clothes—Bagkhal will be here soon. Take some off the dead recruits if you can't find your biosuit. And for the sake of all that is colorful, clean yourself up. I don't want you looking like incompetent Takki when they come get us."

Narrowing his eyes, Joe went to do as he was bid.

40

LOYALTIES

"Tell your story again so the Overseer can hear."

Tril watched as the recruit's face twisted in disgust.

"Joe was hanging out with rebels," the recruit said. "Every night, whenever he could find time after working for Bagkhal."

"How did he get out of the barracks?" Tril demanded. "We changed the codes on the locks."

"Monk helped him figure them out."

"The rebels taught him to read," the Peacemaker added.

The recruit frowned. "No, Battlemaster Nebil gave him a lesson pad."

"Impossible. It is against regulations to give a first turn recruit an advanced—"

"Battlemaster Nebil is dead," Tril interrupted. "Arguing with the only surviving witness is pointless."

"Tell him about the akarit," the Peacemaker insisted, giving Tril an irritated look.

"The first day, Yuil gave Joe some candy and a little black box he hid in his gear. He never talked about it, kept it hidden, but I looked. It had a little gold ring inside."

"We found the akarit," the Peacemaker said. "Right where she said it would be."

Tril found himself growing irritated with this recruit who would so easily betray her groundmate. "Why are you turning on him now?"

"She almost didn't make it. We had to resuscitate her when we stormed the depot. She was put in a different groundteam. Zero doesn't even know she survived."

Tril held the recruit's eyes. "So why are you betraying him?"

She returned his gaze coldly. "My friends all went back to Earth in bodybags because of him."

"Zero also had this," the Peacemaker said, handing a small red object to Tril. "Contraband from Earth. Possibly a symbol of his true leanings."

Tril took the knife, remembering that Commander Linin had been furious when they hadn't been able to find it in his gear after his screaming-match with Zero. He wondered briefly how he had managed to hide it all of this time.

"It's a symbol of nothing," Tril said. "A memento, nothing more."

"Still, it is forbidden," the Peacemaker insisted. "We could hold it against him in a trial. Until then, we told his battlemaster to give him double chores for a turn for having it. We also told him to make sure Zero wears his uniform correctly from now on."

Tril gave an indifferent grunt.

"Overseer, this matter deserves a formal investigation. Normally, I would simply take it up with his superiors and would not involve you, but I realize the sensitive nature of this particular case, since Zero was the one who rescued you in the—"

"No one rescued me," Tril snapped.

The Peacemaker bowed. "Then I shall attend to the matter myself, sir." He turned to leave.

"Stop," Tril commanded. "What exactly do you plan to do?"

The Peacemaker hesitated. In that instant, Tril knew that it was only a matter of time before Zero wound up in a cell on Levren.

"Well?"

"We must test his loyalties, sir."

"He helped to squash the rebellion," Tril retorted. "He took *untrained recruits* against Jreet and Va'ga-trained Huouyt and won a fight only

Planetary Ops had any right to win. What more proof of his loyalty do you need?

"He carried an akarit," the Peacemaker said. "I'm sure that as soon as we begin questioning him properly, he would collaborate his groundmate's story."

"No."

"Sir, he knew exactly where to find Representative Na'leen and the other rebel leaders. If that is not evidence of guilt, then I am in the wrong profession. I *know* that I need only test him and the lies will start pouring out."

"No," Tril heard himself repeat. "Test him, but do it here, in my office, while I watch. I will not have you abusing a Congressional hero so that you can wring a phony confession from him."

The Peacemaker's eyes hardened in anger. "Sir, I can't work under those conditions."

"You will," Tril said, "Or I will draft some letters suggesting that Kophati Peacemakers are wasting their time chasing ghosts and that's why Na'leen was able to build his rebellion under your noses."

The Huouyt's eerie electric-blue eyes fixed on him. "And if I prove this Zero is not a loyal and willing soldier of the Congressional Army?"

"You may have him."

The Peacemaker gave Tril a bitter nod and left, taking the recruit with him.

Tril turned the Earth artifact in his sensitive, newly-grown fingers. The surfaces of the object were gleaming smooth in patches and the white cross had been rubbed almost completely off. Falling rubble had gouged deep marks in the sides and bent the corkscrew slightly out of place.

Tril set it aside. *Something brought you down into Na'leen's lair, Zero. Pray it was your desire to help save Congress, not your desire to destroy it.*

• • •

"No."

"Zero, you have half a tic to take them down or I will do it for you."

"You can try," Joe snarled, gripping a sleeve with tight fingers. "My last battlemaster let me wear them."

"I am not Nebil," Battlemaster Gokli said, his voice cold. "Do not make me prove it."

Joe glanced from Battlemaster Gokli to the other three Ooreiki he had brought into the barracks with him that morning. Behind him, his platoon waited. They'd been together just over a turn, now, and they best kill rate in the regiment. Joe had been about to take them to breakfast when Gokli came to demand they take down their sleeves. Not one member of his platoon had complied.

Gokli was pissed.

"So who ordered it?" Joe demanded. "Was it Tril? Well you can tell that *vaghi* to go burn himself."

"*Overseer* Tril had nothing to do with it," Gokli said. "Zero, you have used up my patience." His battlemaster nodded at the other Ooreiki and they began to surround him.

Without his biosuit, Joe didn't stand a chance against three Ooreiki. Still, he couldn't will himself to do as they ordered. It felt like a betrayal.

"Back off," Joe warned. "I'm not doing it." He tore a clothes chest off the ground, ready to throw it at the first Ooreiki to come at him.

Gokli stopped, staring at the chest in his arms. "Disobedience in a soldier is punishable by death, Zero."

"Then kill me," Joe snapped, "And stop wasting my time."

The four Ooreiki converged on him. Joe threw the chest, knocking that Ooreiki back, but the three others grabbed his arms before he could dodge out of the way. Joe struggled and Gokli tightened his grip until he cried out. Then another reached out to rip off Joe's cammi jacket. Joe slammed his heel into the third Ooreiki's abdomen, a young battlemaster that reminded him of Aneeir. The Ooreiki stumbled backwards, cradling the sensitive spot protecting his *oorei*. Joe kicked him again, this time in the head.

The Ooreiki fell over.

"*Zero!*" Gokli wrapped a stinging tentacle around his neck and jerked him back until he was bent over almost double. "That was your last mistake, recruit. You've caused me enough trouble for a whole platoon. The Peacemakers can have you."

Joe struggled for breath, his vision darkening around the edges, blood pounding like thunder in his ears.

Not even the roar of his pulse, however, could drown out the sound of his grounders swarming the Ooreiki. In a panic, Joe tried to call them off, but couldn't make out more than a strangled groan. His last thought before he passed out was, *Oh soot. They'll kill us all.*

• • •

Joe stepped into the cool, well-kempt Ooreiki office and immediately felt a bitter taste in his mouth when he saw Overseer Tril sitting behind a desk. "What do you want?"

A brightly-dressed Ooreiki immediately moved toward him from across the room. "Are you the recruit battlemaster that led your untrained platoon into Na'leen's den to help bring Kophat back under Congressional control? The recruit named Zero?"

"My name is Joe."

Joe caught the flicker of a glance between the civilian and Tril. He tensed.

"Were you groundmates with a recruit One? She was in Kihgl's battalion with you, I believe."

"She's dead."

"She's alive," the Ooreiki corrected. "She was unfortunately permanently crippled, though, despite our best attempts at rejuvenation. We fixed her wounds to the best of our abilities and sent her back to Earth on our fastest ship. She's got a full pension and lives in style, as befits a Congressional hero."

Joe's heart began to hammer. "You sent Libby home?"

The Ooreiki smiled. "It is always much more beneficial to us to send our heroes back to their home planets so they can serve as examples and recruit more of their species for the army. That's why we're offering to send you with her."

I can go home. Joe found it hard to breathe. *They're offering to send me home.*

"What about the others?" he heard himself ask. "Did you save anyone else?"

The Ooreiki gave him an apologetic look. "She had her spine severed by a Jreet's ovi, which we caught in time. She was the only one. Nothing in the universe can stop plasma or Jreet poison once it has entered its target."

Joe drew a shaky breath. He had hoped someone had lived, but he had never guessed it would be Libby. He was relieved and saddened at the same time. "Is she happy on Earth? She really wanted to be a soldier."

"Every recruit says that, but doesn't really mean it," the Ooreiki said. "She's relieved to be back, I assure you."

Joe swallowed hard. "And you want to send me back, too."

"With full pension and benefits," the Ooreiki replied. "Since Earth's economy is still adjusting to Congressional trade, Congressional credit is worth more than ruvmestin. Considering your record… You'd live like a king, Zero."

"Joe."

The Ooreiki civilian's smile broke for an instant, showing a flash of irritation, but it was quickly smothered. "Joe. What do you say? You can leave the Army behind forever, never have to lift a weapon again in your life. It's entirely your choice, of course, but it would be in our best interest to make sure you live in style back on Earth." He tilted his head, giving Joe the Ooreiki version of a wink. "Good PR, you know?"

Joe barely heard him. "You'll take me to see Libby?" Joe asked. His heart ached to explain things to her, to apologize.

The Ooreiki's face wrinkled in a broad smile. "Absolutely."

Joe's pulse was thudding in his ears. He could see it now. His return, his mother's weeping, Sam's happy shouts. They could have fresh bread and fruit and lasagna and all the other foods he'd gone without for the past year. He might even be able to convince Libby not to hate him. Maybe she could even like him again. He doubted any other girl would understand him, after everything they'd been through.

Joe's eye caught on the small bit of red on Commander Tril's desk. He remembered his dad, stepping into the darkness.

Then he thought of Battlemaster Nebil, hung up on the rack like meat in a butcher's shop. He thought of Elf and Scott and Maggie and Monk. He thought of Prince Bagkhal, who owned no Takki, who had dug him from the rubble of the ekhta's tower with his own claws.

"No."

The Ooreiki civilian's sudah began to flutter. "What?"

"No," Joe said, turning to the door. "I'm staying."

"Wait," the civilian snapped, "I've already scheduled a ship. Your account has already received its first pension payment. Your family is expecting you. Here." The civilian popped a small chip into the vidscreen embedded in Overseer Tril's desk. Instantly, his mom's picture appeared, her face beaming in a smile. She'd gotten a new perm and the bags were gone from under her eyes.

"Joe!" she said, then blushed embarrassedly. "They say this is gonna get to you, but I feel kind of stupid talking to a little box. It's like two inches tall, Joe. It's so hard to believe it's—Anyway, are you really coming home, Joe? They say you're a hero. Sam can't wait to see you. We got a new dog. A lab. Cute little chocolate thing. Named it Harry, after Dad. Oh, Joe, I'm so excited you're coming home! I just wish your father could be here to see it. We had a service for him a week after you left. Mom came down with Aunt Caroline. They made a collage of his time in the Marines that was really nice. Sam—"

"I told you no," Joe said, cutting off the rest of the feed himself. The civilian seemed startled that he knew how to do so, but quickly recovered.

"We have everything arranged, Zero. All you have to do is climb on the ship. You're a Congressional hero. We treat our heroes like kings."

Joe was still scowling at the vidscreen. "Can you send a message for me, like you did with my mom?"

The civilian blinked at him, and it was Tril who said, "Of course."

"Good. I want to tell Libby I'm sorry. I disappointed her. I almost got her killed. She probably went back to Earth because she hates me. To get away from me. I don't blame her, but there was a mistake. She didn't understand. Tell her I couldn't move."

"Excuse me?"

"Tell her I couldn't move. When Zol'jib had me beside him, he'd used some drug on me. Paralyzed me. She'll understand."

The civilian glanced at Tril, who nodded.

"I always thought Libby'd be the last of any of us to go back willingly." Joe stared at his feet, wondering how it turned out this way, why he couldn't just let them take him home. He tried to find the desire to tell the Ooreiki he'd changed his mind, but it wouldn't come. "I guess if she was crippled, though…" He glanced at the Ooreiki anxiously. "Was it bad?"

"She can't use her legs."

"Oh," Joe whispered, not sure what to say. He took a deep breath, then let it out through his teeth, trying to imagine Libby without being able to kick something in the head if it looked at her funny. The thought brought tears to his eyes, which he quickly wiped away. "Tell her it should've been me, okay? And that she was the better Congie."

The Ooreiki civilian's sticky eyes sharpened. "What do you mean by that?"

"Nothing," Joe said softly. "Just that she was right. I didn't try hard enough, and I got everybody killed. I should've paid more attention in class, listened more…" He took a shuddering breath and looked away before that train of thought slammed him right back to those wretched, miserably lonely weeks after Bagkhal had dug him from Na'leen's command center. It had taken him almost nine rotations to get to the point where the simple thought of losing everyone didn't make him a weeping wreck. Clearing his throat, he said, "Can you tell my mom I'm sorry? She won't understand, but I can't come back. I can't leave the Army. I'm a Congie, now. I just wish—" Joe took a deep breath, closing his eyes. "Is there much more on that tape?"

"Kkee," the civilian replied. "At least thirty-six tics."

"Can I have it?"

The Ooreiki nodded, looking a bit stunned.

"Thanks." Joe took the chip and turned to go.

"Zero. Stay for a moment."

Joe turned to glance at Overseer Tril. The civilian gave him one long look, then brushed past him on the way out the door.

"Here," Tril said, holding an object out to him.

Joe took it, staring down at the red surface uncomprehendingly. His fingers recognized it before anything else, and his breath left him. "Dad's knife." It was scraped and battered from the collapse of the barracks, but still functioning. His fingertips automatically found the patches he had worn smooth over his long, homesick nights and he felt a wave of relief so strong it left him dizzy. "I thought I'd lost it."

"Peacemakers found it and recognized it as an Earth artifact. They were going to have it destroyed, but I figured you'd get more use out of it."

Joe nodded, speechless with gratitude.

"And here." Tril handed Joe Kihgl's *kasja*. The golden markings on it glowed with Celtic beauty. At Joe's stunned look, he said, "If they ask, it's Nebil's, not Kihgl's. They survived Ubashin together. But, even if it were Nebil's, he wouldn't object. Nebil thought you were his best student."

Joe took Kihgl's *kasja* gingerly. "He did?" His throat felt tight. His vision was blurring. Joe wiped his eyes viciously.

"He wanted you to have battlemaster from the beginning. I told him no. He gave it to you anyway. Twice. He was a Prime once, you know. Once they get that eighth point, there's no going back. It was Hell having him under my command."

Joe stared down at the *kasja* and nodded, overwhelmed.

Tril's eyes caught on Joe's sleeves, now fully extended down to the cuffs. Joe had lost battlemaster over the episode. Again.

"I'll inform your commander you can wear your uniform any way you like from now on. Congress *does* appreciate its heroes, Zero."

Joe could not speak.

A long silence hung between them. Then, Tril said, "You made the right decision."

"I know," Joe whispered.

Tril's sudah gave a surprised flutter. "You do?"

Joe nodded and somehow found his voice. "I'm like my dad. He was a Marine before he—died." He felt his vision blurring again and did nothing to stop it. "I've got a new groundteam. Not like my old one, but they survived the war and they're pretty smart. They need me, too. Most of them lost everyone when the Huouyt blew up the barracks. I can't leave them. I can't leave the Army."

Joe glanced down at his knife and forced himself to laugh. "Besides, I'm not about to go through a whole turn of this soot not to graduate."

"You'll graduate," Tril assured him. "They've lost too many soldiers not to graduate even their most…problematic…recruits."

"Thanks," Joe said. "For everything."

Tril nodded once. "Good luck, Zero."

41

THE CONGIE

Joe graduated, as Tril predicted. The ceremony was a full regiment formation where every battlemaster went down the lines to give each recruit a circle and personal congratulations, along with the first alien recognition of their real names since the Draft.

Joe was one of the ninety recruit battlemasters who got their ranks from the Prime Commander himself. Along with their circles, the new soldiers got warnings that depended on how they had managed their recruits during the last two turns. "Battle is not a game to brag about, Pete," the Prime said to the boy three ranks down from Joe. "You're still soft. You'll learn that when you face a real foe." Only then did he place the ranking device against the recruit's chest. When he reached the next one, he said the same thing. "Your training's not over, Jessica. You're soldiers now, but you aren't Congies until friends die under your command." The girl beside Joe received a similar warning. "Spend more time talking with your platoon, Mary. Get to know them. Sometimes saving lives must override strategy. Once you leave here, their deaths are always on your conscience." The girl in question blushed and looked at her feet, for it had been she who had intentionally killed her entire platoon to retrieve the last flag.

When Prime Commander Weriik stopped at Joe, the drooping-skinned Ooreiki took a long breath and said, "Joe, no one has lost battle-master so many times, only to get it back a few weeks later. You are the most frustrating, yet uniquely talented recruit I've ever seen. Sometimes I think you should've been graduated a turn ago, and sometimes I think a hundred turns won't be enough. You—"

A deep, gravelly Dhasha voice interrupted the Ooreiki. "I'll graduate this recruit, if you don't mind, Commander."

Joe's breath caught in his lungs. Prince Bagkhal was on the plaza, moving towards them. He was the first Dhasha they'd seen since the Training Committee had called him to Koliinaat to testify against the Huouyt, the testimony of which had officially removed the Huouyt from their Tribunal seat, ending the 1293rd Age of the Huouyt.

…And ushering in the 215th Age of the Dhasha.

While on Kophat, you will enter Congress into a new Age…

Fighting goosebumps, Joe forced himself to look straight ahead.

Prime Commander Weriik bowed low and moved to one side, allowing Bagkhal to step in front of Joe. He stopped several feet back, a courtesy so Joe didn't have to stare at endless rows of triangular black teeth. "I see you made it." His voice was like a liquid rumble that made the gravel at Joe's feet shudder. "You have no idea how much that pleases me. Congratulations, Joe. I'm sorry I wasn't here to see you train. I'm sure I missed quite a show. Rank him, if you will."

Around him, Joe felt humans and Ooreiki alike openly staring. Prime Commander Weriik stepped between them and touched the ranking device to Joe's chest. As soon as he lowered Joe's jacket, the silver circle began to form around his four-pointed star.

"No one will ever take that away from you," Bagkhal said. "You've earned it, Joe. More than anyone knows." Then he nodded at Prime Commander Weriik to continue and removed himself to the sidelines to watch the rest of the ceremony. Joe could feel his eyes throughout, though he managed to keep from looking. He couldn't wait to talk to him—so many unanswered questions milled through his mind.

"You are all now full soldiers in the Congressional Army," Prime Commander Weriik said, once he'd finished with the last recruit battlemaster and returned to the front of the regiment. "Starting tomorrow, you will have thirty-three days of liberty and three turns worth of credits to your accounts. Your battlemasters will give you further instructions on how to access your funds once the ceremony is over. Commanders, you may dismiss your battalions."

Before they did, the battalion commanders gave long speeches on how proud they were to see this day, and then allowed every battlemaster to do the same. Joe waited impatiently throughout, wishing they'd hurry so he could talk to Bagkhal. When it was finally over and Joe turned to find him, however, the Dhasha was gone.

"He came to see you graduate," Gokli said, noticing his search. "After his testimony, Koliinaat sent him to patrol Eeloir. He had to go back—it's almost open rebellion now that the Dhasha have the Huouyt Tribunal seat."

Joe nodded numbly, though he still scanned the crowds with his eyes, hoping for a glimpse of the Dhasha's rainbow reflection. He should've known Bagkhal had other things to do.

Though his entire platoon offered to buy him Earth food, Joe did not partake in the festivities afterwards. Thinking of Libby and his dead groundmates, he sought out a small alien restaurant specializing in exotic foods and used some of the credits he had earned over the past three turns to buy himself six Earth meals. The waiter gave him an odd look, but filled his order anyway and soon Joe was seated at a table with six hot meals steaming in front of him. As he sat there, the four-pointed star of Battlemaster felt cold against his chest.

All around him, newly-graduated grounders sat in groups, laughing, eating.

"Wish you guys could be here," he whispered, locating each of the five empty chairs with his eyes. He planned the meal for weeks, trying his best to get the foods they liked, but it had been difficult to remember. That was the worst part, the part that meant they were slipping away.

I'd do anything to bring you back, he thought, tears welling in his eyes. *I'm so sorry, guys.*

"Sir?"

Joe glanced up. The Ooreiki waiter that had been eying him all night was standing beside him, a note in his hand.

"A Congie wanted me to give you this. Said it came from a Dhasha." The waiter dropped the filmy slip of paper in Joe's hand like it had been doused in fire. "This too." The waiter tugged a small black box from the folds in his flowing, brightly-colored robes. Joe nodded his thanks and set it on the table in front of him. He returned his attention to the uneaten plates and sat there in silence, the food growing cold around him. *My first groundteam and I failed them all.*

After the juices had congealed around Maggie's steak, he unfolded the strip.

In the neat handwriting of a scribe, it said, *I was right about you, Joe.*

Joe folded the strip of paper and lifted the top of the box. It was a simple construction, though more ornate than he was used to seeing. Still in Congie black, it had woven bands of black metal winding around the edges and sides, reminding him of something Irish. A second note covered what lay inside.

The politicians said you couldn't have this until after you graduated. I see you still wear Kihgl's. It would do you well to have one of your own.

Swallowing, Joe peered into the box. His breath caught. A *kasja* lay in a velvety cushion, golden bands knotting the outside. Gingerly, he lifted it.

For Bravery and Valor Despite All Odds. Joe Dobbs. Huouyt Rebellion. Kophat.

Joe's chest ached as he tucked the *kasja* back into the box. He felt tears threaten, then break free. It was several minutes before he could fight them back down. Taking a slow, steady breath, he closed the lid and stared at it for several minutes, until a motion beside him reminded him of the waiter's presence.

The Ooreiki was staring at him. "You're Zero? The one that stopped Na'leen?"

"No," Joe said, giving the uneaten meals one last look. His eyes lingered on Libby's. "That's someone else."

He pushed the box across the table, until it rested between his friends' uneaten plates. "This is for you guys."

Then he paid the baffled Ooreiki and went to find a quiet place to wait out the celebrations.

A rotation later, after the other graduates had used up all their liberty and their credits, Joe boarded the shuttle to take him into space, where he would be assigned to his new unit. He was sorted into a battlemaster wing of the new station, where organizers were calling out roll and coordinating their departures to all ends of Congressional territory.

Joe was one of the few who got assigned to Torat for Planetary Ops training. It would be another two years of crawling in the dirt, getting bruised and screamed at by angry, merciless Jreet, but by the end he would be able to lead a special unit through the worst Hells in Congress without batting an eye.

Joe was looking forward to it.

And, since the Huouyt had long memories and were still disgruntled over the death of their influential Representative, the Army was expecting another war in the near future. His extra training would put him at the forefront of the fight, leading elite teams of grounders in life-or-death hunts in parts of the universe he'd only dreamed about.

Unfortunately, it was going to take him even further from Libby.

Torat was one of the first planets entered into the union, located in the very center of Congress, deep in the Old Territory. Earth, which had just recently been discovered with the expansion of the Outer Line, was many weeks in the opposite direction.

That disappointed Joe. Of anybody he knew, only Rat would be going with him. Once more, he was losing his groundteam. He wished he could have seen Libby again, just once before he left.

Joe strengthened his resolve. Libby would understand. She, of all people, would want him to stay with the Army.

Joe had his bags over his shoulder and was milling in the congested station waiting for his flight when he thought he recognized a face in the crowd.

"Maggie?!" He pushed his way through the other grounders. "Mag? That you?"

The soldier turned reluctantly.

Joe's heart leapt. "Mag! God it's you! Mag, how did you—Where *were* you?! Mag, I saw you *die!*"

"Hey Joe."

"How—"

She gave him a cold look, and it gave him a full-body wash of goosebumps. "The Huouyt picked up one of the recruit rifles by mistake. Shot me with a training round."

Joe's jaw dropped open, his chest surging with joy. "How have you been?"

"Fine."

"You got battlemaster!" Joe cried, forcefully rubbing away the goosebumps. "That's great, Mag!"

"Yeah." She peered up at him, her once innocent eyes dark.

"Mag, did you know Libby survived, too? She's back on Earth, recruiting more people for the Army. They offered to let me go, but I told them I wanted to stay."

"You should've gone."

"I don't belong there anymore. I mean, I grew up here. I wouldn't know what to do on Earth. I mean, can you imagine us doing anything else? Just look at us. They'd probably treat us like we're aliens. Jeez, it's hard to believe Libby decided to go back. I thought she would've stayed."

"She didn't go back. She's dead."

"No, I talked to a guy who worked for the PR department. He said she's back on Earth. They resuscitated her."

"No they didn't. They resuscitated me, after you left me to die with the Huouyt."

Joe blinked. Her words were so cold, so hard—they felt icicles, aimed at his soul. Libby was dead? He'd sent her letters, video... After regaining his breath, he whispered, "Mag, I'm so sorry. I didn't know—"

Maggie brushed the comment aside. "I hear you commanded the best recruit platoon in the Force. They're sending you to Planetary Ops. That's really something, Joe."

"Thanks," Joe said, feeling wary, now. Something about the way Maggie was acting wasn't right. "What about you?"

"Going to Eeloir. Huouyt are causing trouble there now the Dhasha have their Tribunal seat."

"Eeloir. That's where Bagkhal is." He felt a pang of jealousy.

Maggie wasn't listening. She was peering up at him, weighing him with her eyes. "Was the Trith right, Joe?"

Joe's heart hammered convulsively. "What?"

Laughing, excited graduates passed them on both sides and Maggie lowered her voice until only they could hear. She grew so close that Joe could smell her perfume. She carried the scent of roses, but there was something cruel in her face.

"Because I've been thinking," Maggie said softly. "Planetary Ops is the *last* place I'd send somebody like you, if I was Congress." She smiled, but her eyes bit like razors. "Don't think I won't tell them, Joe. Don't think Bagkhal won't come back to kill you, once he finds out you murdered Libby. Just like you murdered Scott and tried to murder me."

He stared at her, confused and hurt. "I didn't murder them."

"Yes you did." Maggie's eyes burned with hatred. She clearly believed he'd killed their friends.

Anguished, Joe whispered, "Mag, I beat the prophecy. I don't know what the Trith told you, but he was wrong."

She narrowed her eyes at him. "A Trith's never wrong, Joe. Don't you know that by now?" Then she turned her back to him and worked her way through the crowd of black-clad grounders, leaving him there alone.

But I beat the prophecy, Joe wanted to shout at her back. *It's over.*

Yet the Trith's nagging warning echoed once more in his skull. *You will try to fight it, but invariably, your path will lead to the same end.*

Unable to form a reply, Joe stood sweating in the congested terminal, watching Maggie go.

Only when an attendant began announcing the last call for his flight did he go search for his departure gate.

Two hours later, he was on a shuttle to Torat, with nothing to do for the next three weeks but pace his room, play simulated battle games, and check his messages. Within the first two hours, Joe got a note from his former groundteam, which had been given a new ground leader and was being shipped to Eeloir to fight the Huouyt. They wanted to know how his new Planetary Ops training was going—as if Joe had even reached Torat yet. Joe replied that he was doing fine and wished them luck.

The next three messages were much the same—old friends excited about their new assignments, bored like he was, trying to keep in touch. Joe responded to them as he had the first, pacing as he dictated the familiar reassurances.

Joe's fifth message made him stop pacing.

It was Sam.

On a secure, Congie feed.

"Hi, uh, Joe." Sam cleared his throat and made a nervous laugh. He was almost sixteen now. Older than Joe when Joe took his place. "I, uh, I bet you're wondering how I got in the system. Well don't freak out or anything. I didn't join up—I just hacked it, is all. They wouldn't let me talk to you otherwise. Mom's actually trying to pretend you died. When she got that last message from you, she kinda cracked. Like, a serious case of denial. Goes around talking like I never even had a brother..." Sam paused, clearing his throat with acute, teenage embarrassment. "So I had to find out, you know? I had to go look, 'cause there's something I really need to tell you. Turns out, there's this guy called Zero who saved some people on this planet you were going to. Ko-fat or something. Real smart, pissed a lot of people off, got time added to his enlistment for being a dumbass. Kind of sounded a lot like you."

Joe stared at Sam's image, his heart hammering. Put side-by-side, nobody would know they were brothers. Sam had grown taller than Joe, maybe six-seven, and he didn't have the freakish Congie muscles. Further, Sam's eyes were blue, not brown, and his hair was an unkempt near-black where Joe was utterly bald.

Yet, standing there in a tie-died T-shirt and khaki shorts, Sam looked so much like Dad. Joe felt himself gripping his chair so hard his knuckles hurt.

"So here goes: I'm not gonna forget you, Joe," Sam went on. "I know what you did for me. And I wanted to say thanks." Sam cleared his throat again and glanced nervously down at his hands. "Well, that's all I really wanted to say. That, and I'm a sophomore in college. MIT's paying my way. They didn't really care if I finished high school. Funny, huh? But I'm not bragging. No way. I'd be dead if you hadn't taken my place. I'm such a chickenshit when it comes to guns...I'm not like you or Dad at all." Sam cleared his throat again. "Anyway, let me know if I found the right Joe Dobbs. If you wanna send me a message, I set myself up an alias under Slade Galvin Gardner in the Congie database. I'll check it every week or so. Oh, and I think I can help you disappear off Congie radar if you wanna come back home. That's it. Peace out."

Joe was trembling by the time the message ended.

When he could finally make his stunned mind think long enough to reply, he said, "Hi Sam. MIT, huh? That's awesome. Make some robots for me. No, I don't wanna disappear. I know it sounds stupid, Sam, but I think this is what I'm supposed to be doing with my life."

He added other stuff, too.

For the next week, Joe added to the letter, detailing all the interesting things that had happened to him over the six years since he had been kidnapped under the brilliant glow of professional-grade fireworks, all the friends he'd made, all the deaths, all the training.

But, once he finally had his letter composed, Joe hesitated in sending it.

Sam was going to MIT at fifteen. He had a bright future. He could do anything he wanted. He didn't need to be weighed down by guilt for some Congie grounder who was never gonna see Earth again.

Mom's right, Joe thought. *He doesn't need to know.*

Joe opened the letter, held his breath, and pushed DELETE.

He was a Congie now.

END

Get the next book, *Zero Recall*, Today!

ABOUT THE AUTHOR

My name is Sara King and I'm going to change the world.

No, seriously. I am. And I need your help. My goal is simple. I want to champion, define, and spread character writing throughout the galaxy. (Okay, maybe we can just start with Planet Earth.) I want to take good writing out of the hands of the huge corporations who have had a stranglehold on the publishing industry for so long and reconnect it to the people (you) and what you really want. I want to democratize writing as an art form. Something that's always been controlled by an elite few who have (in my opinion) a different idea of what is 'good writing' than the rest of the world, and have been feeding the sci-fi audience over 50% crap for the last 40 years. (To get my spiel on character writing and what it is, jump to the Meet Stuey section of this book.)

To assist me in my goals to take over the world (crap, did I say that out loud??), please leave a review for this book! It's the first and easiest way for you guys to chip in and assist your friendly neighborhood writer-gal. And believe me, every review helps otherwise unknown books like mine stand up against the likes of the Big Boys on an impersonal site like Amazon.

Also, I have an email! (Totally surprising, I know.) Use it! (Don't you know that fanmail keeps writers going through those dark times when we run out of chocolate???) I love posting letters on Facebook—gives me something fulfilling to do with my time. ;) Shoot me a line! kingnovel@gmail.com

You can also fill out the little form to sign up for my mailing list at http://www.parasitepublications.com/authors.php (I'm second on the list).

And, for those of you who do the Facebook thing, check me out: http://www.facebook.com/kingfiction (personal) or http://www.facebook.com/sknovel (my author page) or stay up to date on continuous new ZERO publications with The Legend of ZERO fan page: http://www.facebook.com/legendofzero

AFTERWORD

In case you hadn't guessed, this is the first book in a (very) large, sprawling sci-fi world. More ZERO stories are coming out very soon, if they haven't already, and I will very likely write more novels in this world, simply because I've been told to. Repeatedly. By people with that crazed, hungry look in their eyes. (Shudder.) While I'm working on them, be sure to check out these great books, short stories, and additional ZERO materials on Amazon:

The Legend of ZERO: Zero Recall. (It's a play on Forgotten.) 53 turns after Forging ZERO, Joe Dobbs is recalled to fight a war the likes of which Congress has never seen.

The Legend of ZERO: Zero's Return. 20 turns after Zero faces off Forgotten in Zero Recall, he returns to Earth to fight a new kind of war—the kind that will determine the future of the Human race.

The Legend of ZERO: Zero's Redemption. Continuation of Zero's Return. It's a race to capture the greatest telepath the Human race has ever produced, and two of Humanity's greatest warriors find themselves on opposite sides.

The Legend of ZERO: Zero's Legacy. After preserving Earth's most precious resource from the hands of the Huouyt, Joe and his friends must now work together to survive this new post-apocalyptic world—and find the People a home.

The Legend of ZERO: Forgotten. A Sacred Turn after Zero returned to Earth, his descendants seek out his ancient nemesis with a bargain Forgotten cannot resist: Remove Earth from Congress without a single death, and Humans will give him his freedom.

<u>The Complete ZERO WorldBuilder</u>: A complete(ly massive) glossary, fun facts, timeline, illustrations, and cool details that I couldn't pack into the books.

The Moldy Dead: A story about the Origins of the Geuji, one of whom plays a dominant role in books 2 and 4. The Moldy Dead is easily one of my best short stories.

Opening Night at the Naturals Preserve: A story about Congress' discovery of the Baga, one of whom plays an important role in book 2.

Planetside: A fun story about how the Ueshi earned the right to fly.

The First Gods of Fire: The story of how Congress was formed.

Breaking the Mold: How the Geuji were betrayed by Congress (again).

Beda and Shael: A Jreet love story, a la Romeo and Juliet. Except this time, it's Vorans and Welus. Yeah, sparks fly. And blood. And scales…

Parting Gift: The Vanun struggle to escape the Huouyt, both of whom evolved on the same planet. (Vanun on land, Huouyt in the sea).

Syuri: Everybody loves lackeys. Here's how Forgotten got his. ☺

And keep your eyes open for more, as I will keep putting them up whenever I have time. Just search "The Legend of ZERO" on Amazon. Also, if you liked ZERO, you'd probably like Outer Bounds: Fortune's Rising. It's another character sci-fi that'll rock your world.

And guys? Thanks. You are freakin' awesome.

MEET STUEY

Meet Stuey. He's our mascot here at Parasite Publications. Stuey is a brain parasite. Stuey burrows into people's heads and stays there. He takes over your body. He shuts you away from your senses. He talks to you in the darkness. He makes you do things you would never do while you can only watch in horror.

But he's an understandable little monster.

Imagine your favorite action-adventure story. Your favorite romance. Your favorite epic sci-fi. Your favorite thriller. Each one of them is going to have a character that left you breathless, one that had you at the edge of your seat, rooting for, screaming at, and pleading with. Those are the *only* stories that Parasite publishes.

Our goal at Parasite Publications is twofold: First, we want to produce memorable, sympathetic characters that readers will still be thinking about years after finishing our books. Second, we want to create a team of creative minds whose work can be trusted by readers to produce the same kind of character stories they love, time and again. We're forming a club. A logo. A place for readers to go to read books about *people*, not places or machines. A place for character writers to band together and create a brand that means quality to readers. Readers of Parasite books will no longer have to wonder if they're throwing their money away on novels that, even in 150k words, never really get into a character's head.

They never have to wonder, because that's what we're *about*. Getting into the character's head. And, if we do our job right, Parasite will get into your head and stay there. Just like Stuey.

Check us out on Facebook at http://www.facebook.com/ParasitePublications/info to read more about Stuey's mission to change publishing for your benefit.

OTHER TITLES
BY SARA KING

Guardians of the First Realm: Alaskan Fire
Guardians of the First Realm: Alaskan Fury

Millennium Potion: Wings of Retribution

Outer Bounds: Fortune's Rising

Terms of Mercy: To the Princess Bound

ZERO: Zero Recall
ZERO: Zero's Return

COMING SOON

Guardians of the First Realm: Fury of the Fourth Realm ~ Sara King
Guardians of the First Realm: Alaskan Fiend ~ Sara King
Guardians of the First Realm: Alaskan Fang ~ Sara King

ZERO: Zero's Redemption
ZERO: Zero's Legacy ~ Sara King
ZERO: Forgotten ~ Sara King

Terms of Mercy: Slave of the Dragon Lord ~ Sara King

Aulds of the Spyre: The Sheet Charmer ~ Sara King
Aulds of the Spyre: Form and Function ~ Sara King

Outer Bounds: Fortune's Folly ~ Sara King

MINI GLOSSARY
(I.E. THE SO-YOU-DON'T-LOSE-YOUR-MIND TINY VERSION)

DHASHA-SPECIFIC

Ka-par (ka-par) – The predatory game of wills that older Dhasha play with worthy prey creatures or other ancient Dhasha. A stare-down until one contestant submits.

Ka-par inalt (ka-par in-alt) – 'I submit.'

Ka-par rak'tal. (ka-par rak*tal) – 'duel accepted.' *is used to denote a guttural, back-of-throat, almost hacking sound.

Mahid ka-par (ma-heed ka-par) – 'may it begin.'

Vahlin (vah-lin) – the legendary leader of the Dhasha, prophecized to be 'dark of body' and lead them to independence from tyranny.

HUOUYT-SPECIFIC

Breja (bray-shjah) – the quarter-inch long, downy white cilia covering a Huouyt's entire body. Extremely painful to be pulled or mutilated, as it is basically raw nerves.

Zora (zoh-rah) – the red, wormlike, many-tentacled appendage that exits a Houyt's forehead. Much like a fleshy form of coral in appearance when fully extended. It is the zora that allows a Huouyt to digest and analyze genetic material to take a new pattern.

OOREIKI-SPECIFIC

Adpi (ad-pee) – Three ceremonial ruvmestin caps on the tips of the fingers of an Ooreiki's right hand that signify an Ooreiki of the yeeri caste. Silver caps laced with Celtic-type knots. Must be removed in order for a yeeri to join the military.

Ash/soot – a disgusting, unclean substance

Ashsoul – the most extreme insult in the Ooreiki language. Also translates to 'lost one'

Ashy – shitty/gross/disgusting/awful

Burn/burning – used much like Human fuck/fucking

Charhead – dumbass, someone stupid, alternatively: someone with an unclean/dirty mind

Furgsoot – bull, bullshit, horseshit, crap, yeah right

Hoga (ho-ga) – An Ooreiki caste, one of 4—yeeri, wriit, hoga, vkala. Hoga are the Ooreiki upper-middle class. They consist of scribes, scholars, and scientists. The intellectuals and inventors, second only to the yeeri.

Niish (nish) – Ooreiki child, also used to describe a form of larvae.

Niish Ahymar (nish ay-a-mar) - An Ooreiki ceremony to determine caste where a red-hot brand is pressed into a child's skin. Vkala do not burn, and are then cast to onen. The traditional Ooreiki ceremony of adulthood.

Oorei (oo-ray) – the Ooreiki term for 'soul.' It is the name of the crystalline sphere carried within every Ooreiki and removed by Poenian yeeri

priests at their death. Emotional/psychological experiences throughout life change color of crystal. Considered to be the highest crime of
Ooreiki society to harm an oorei.

Asher – much like 'asshole,' but with an aggressive, fighting connotation

Shenaal (She-nahl) – Mark of the Pure. The burn left when Ooreiki niish
are tested during the Niish Ahymar.

Sootbag – someone disgusting, unprepared, unequipped

Sooter – disgusting, unclean person; bastard, dumbass. Less aggressive
connotation than 'asher,' though similar use.

Sootwad – degrading, denotes disrespect, a useless person

Vkala (vah-ka-la) – Fire Gods, the lowest caste of Ooreiki. Considered
unclean, are generally killed in adolescence during the Niish Ahymar.
Some Ooreiki vkala children survive their bouts with the onen, though
never without great scarring, which forever marks them as the lowest class of Ooreiki. Vkala gained their ill repute in the formation of
Congress on Vora, when the Ooreiki delegates were genetically modified to withstand fire in order to attend the peace-talks on the often-
fiery Jreet home-planet. All *vkala* are direct descendants of the original
Ooreiki delegation that helped form Congress, and whom returned as
heroes and were offered many breeding opportunities. Unfortunately,
the peace-loving Ooreiki, expecting the formation of Congress to lead
to a permanent end of war, were appalled when their new nation discovered its first heavy resistance and had to institute the first Draft.
Once hailed as heroes, those who now carry the genetic modification protecting them from fire are despised as having ancestors who
betrayed the Ooreiki race. (See The Legend of ZERO Additional
Materials.)

Wriit (wri-it)– An Ooreiki caste, one of 4—yeeri, wriit, hoga, vkala. Wriit
are the Ooreiki craftsmen, workers, and artisans; the Ooreiki middle
class.

Yeeri (yee-re) – An Ooreiki caste, one of 4—yeeri, wriit, hoga, vkala. Yeeri
are the Ooreiki's artists and priests, renowned throughout congress as
the creators of the most magnificent art in the universe. The highest
Ooreiki caste, very pampered and educated. Yeeri are also the priests
who attend the oorei in temples on Poen.

UNIVERSAL WORDS

Akarit (Ack-are-it) – Expensive, golden ring-shaped signal-scrambling device used by insurgents and assassins.

Ekhta (ek-tuh) – Planet-killer. The most destructive bomb in the Congressional arsenal, one of the many great inventions of the Geuji during the Age of Expansion. Like all Geuji technology, the manufacture is so complex that it is un-reproducible by any other mind, and Congress simply follows the steps outlined by the Geuji to create it. (For more info on the Geuji, check out 'The Moldy Dead' and 'Breaking the Mold' in The Legend of ZERO Additional Materials.)

Ferlii (fur-lee) – The massive alien, fungus-like growths covering Ooreiki planets whose reddish spores turn the sky purple. Used as a unit of measurement: One ferlii-length is similar to a human mile.

Furg – A short, squat, very hairy alien that is as ugly as it is stupid. A tool-user, but too primitive to use anything other than sharpened rocks. Think a stocky, 2.5-foot-tall Neanderthal who breeds fast enough to replace numbers lost to stupidity. Darwinian law does not apply.

Furgling – A younger version of a furg. Shorter, hairier, and stupider than its parents.

Haauk (hawk) – skimmer, the floating platforms used as personal planetary transportation

Jenfurgling – One of the most blatantly stupid creatures in Congress. An evolutionary offshoot of furgs arriving on an island where the population underwent a severe bottleneck and had no predators. They delight in beating their hairy faces against the ground and playing with their own excrement.

Kasja (kas-jah) – Highest congressional war-medal. Awarded to a very few, very highly esteemed.

Kkee (ca-ca-ee) – yes

Ninety Jreet Hells – The ninety levels of pain and unpleasantness that a Jreet warrior must pass through upon death in order to reach the afterlife. (See The Legend of ZERO Additional Materials.)

Nkjan (naka-john) – war; also: "Evil"

Nkjanii (naka-john-ee-ay) – "Evildoer" – battlemaster

Oonnai (oon-nigh) - hello

Oora (oo-ra) – "Souled one" - sir

Otwa (Aht-wha) – A ceremonial rifle that the Ooreiki used to fight the first Jreet invasions, before the formation of Congress. To the Ooreiki, it represents a time when they gave up their ideals to survive. Now considered the ceremonial rifle of Congress, used for important gatherings, presentations, and parades.

Peacemakers- the governmental, semi-military authorities who are autonomous in judging, monitoring, and policing the populace. Their main task is to make sure nobody has seditious thoughts, symbol is an eight-pointed star with a planet balancing on each tip. Their base planet is Levren, but they also maintain the Sanctuary on Koliinaat, which is the only place on the planet that is inaccessible to the Watcher.

Planetary Ops (also: PlanOps) – symbol is a single sphere, half red, half blue. Tattoo is of a green, single-moon planet with a headcom, a PPU, and a species-generic plasma rifle leaning against the debris ring. The tattoo glows slightly, a cell-by-cell gene modification that causes the tattooed skin to bio-luminesce.

Ruvmestin (ruv-meh-stihn) – A whitish, extremely heavy metal with a greater density than gold. The most valuable metal in Congress. Used in Geuji technologies, esp. nannites, like biosuits and spaceships. Does not oxidize in air. Mined on the government planets of Grakkas, Yeejor, and Pelipe. Once ruvmestin is discovered on a planet, Congress immediately claims the planet for the common good, removing it from the Planetary Claims Board queue.

Sacred Turn – Time period. 666 turns.

Tribunal – The three members of the Regency chosen to represent and make judgments for the whole of Congress. The Tribunal are the power-members of the Regency, usually occupied by members of the Grand Six. Aliphei is First Citizen, and has maintained a seat on the Tribunal for the entire duration of Congress. The symbol of the Tribunal is three red circles inside a silver ring, surrounded by eight blue circles formed into two sides facing off against each other.

Zahali (za-ha-li) – I'm sorry

SPECIES

Dhasha (Dah-sha) – One of the Grand Six. Very dangerous, violent beasts with indestructible metallic scales that shine with constantly-shifting iridescence. Big, crystalline, oval green eyes, long black talons, stubby bodies, sharklike faces with triangular black teeth. Their nostrils are set beside their eyes. Females are golden instead of rainbow, males have two layers of scales, indestructible metallic on top, gold underneath. Gutteral, snarling voice. Laugh by clacking their teeth together. Grow continuously throughout their lifetimes.

Huouyt (sounds like: White) – One of the Grand Six. Three-legged, ancestrally aquatic shape-shifters. Bleed clear mucous. *Breja* - Downy white fluff covering body. Tentacle legs and paddle-like arms. Cylindrical torso, enormous, electric-blue eyes, and a triangular, squid-like head. *Zora*- red, wormy gills in upper center of Huouyt heads that allow them to take the genetic patterns of another creature. Huouyt have a bad reputation in Congress. They are cunning, sneaky, adaptable, and excellent mimics. Considered to be psychopathic by most species in Congress.

Jahul (Jah-hool)– One of the Grand Six. Sextuped empaths with greenish skin and a chemical defense system of releasing their own wastes over their skin.

Jreet (Jreet) – One of the Grand Six. Red, gray, or cream-colored serpentine warriors who guard the First Citizen and the Tribunal. Have the ability to raise the energy level of their scales and disappear from the visible spectrum. Believe in ninety hells for cowards, and that each soul splits into ninety different parts so they can experience all ninety hells at once. Their rravut within their teks is the most powerful poison in Congress. Bluish blood. Short, engine-like *shee-whomp* battlecry. Cream colored bellies. Diamond-shaped head. *Tek*- the talon protruding from their chests.

Ooreiki (Ooh-reh-kee) – One of the Grand Six. Heavy aliens a lot like boneless gorillas. Five hundred pounds on average. Four tentacle fingers on each arm. Big brown ostrich-egg sized snake-eyes, brown legs, skin turns splotchy when frightened. Huge mouths. Wrinkle their big faces to smile. Grunting rattle of speech. Five feet tall on average. Laugh by making a guttural rapping sound in the base of their necks like a toad croaking. Average age is 400. Outnumber humans ten thousand to one. Only the Ueshi are a more populous species.

Shadyi (Shad-yee) – The species of the First Citizen, Aliphei. There is only one surviving member of this species. Shaggy blue alien, walks on four feet, elephant-sized, black tusks, red eyes.

Takki (Sounds like: Tacky) – The ancestral servants of the Dhasha. Reviled throughout Congress as cowards and betrayers. Purple scales, very dense bodies, upright humanoid lizards. Crystalline, blue, ovoid eyes.

Ueshi (Oo-eh-she) – One of the Grand Six. Small blue or blue-green aliens with excellent reflexes and rubbery skin. Aquatic ancestry. Headcrest.

MEASUREMENTS

ST – Standard Turns 9 standard rotations (1.23 years, 448.875 Earth Days to a Standard Turn)

SR – Standard Rotation 36 standard days (49.875 Earth Days to a Standard Rotation)

SD – Standard Day 36 standard hours (33.25 Earth Hours to a Standard Day)

SH – Standard Hour 72 standard tics (55.42 Earth Minutes to a Standard Hour)

St – Standard Tics (1.299 tics to an Earth Minute, .7698 Earth Minutes to a Standard Tic)

Standard Dig- approx. 1 foot
Standard Rod- approx. 9 feet
Standard Length - approx. 4,000 feet
Standard March- approx. 9,999 rods (90,000 feet)
Standard Lobe- approx. 2.5 pounds

RANKS

Multi-Specieal Galactic Corps – Prime Corps Director

18-unit Galactic Corps – Secondary Corps Director

3-unit Galactic Corps – Tertiary Corps Director

Single-Species Sector Corps – _____(species) Corps Director Single solid silver eight-pointed star with a solid black interior.

Sector Unit – Prime Overseer. Silver eight-pointed star and four inner circles of a Prime Overseer

Solar Unit – Secondary Overseer. Silver eight-pointed star and three inner circles of a Secondary Overseer

Planetary Unit – Tertiary Overseer

Force – Petty Overseer

Regiment (8,100)- Prime Commander - eight-pointed star

Brigade (1800)- Secondary Commander - seven pointed star

Battalion (900)- Tertiary Commander OR Secondary Commander -six pointed star OR 7-pointed star

Company (450)- Small Commander - five-pointed star

Platoon (90)- Battlemaster - four-pointed star

Squad (18)- Squad leader (Squader) - triangle

Groundteam (6)- Ground Leader - line

Grounder - point

And here's a brief glimpse of ZERO #2,
Zero Recall:

THE LEGEND OF
ZERO

ZERO RECALL

SARA KING

2

ZERO RECALL

"**H**ave you seen this man?" Joe held up the age-progression photo of his brother to the dirty glass window.

The hollow-eyed man behind the booth scratched his greasy beard and said, "A man like that don't come cheap. You a cop?"

"I'm his brother."

The man looked him up and down and snorted. "Yeah. Right."

"*Look* at him, damn it," Joe said, pointing at the picture. "We're obviously related. Same chin. I'm just trying to find him. I haven't seen him since the Draft. He could be going by the name Sam or Slade, okay?"

The druggie's hollow, skull-like gaze sharpened on Joe, for the first time taking in the rash that had developed around the newly-activated hair follicles of Joe's face and scalp. Immediately, distrust tightened his features. "You're a Congie?"

Joe closed his eyes to keep from putting his fist through the glass and strangling the doping bastard. "Not anymore. I was forcibly retired a couple months ago. Please. I'm just trying to find my brother. I hear he's still alive. Some sort of rejuvenation technology or something."

The druggie's face darkened. "Thought you sounded funny. Get out of here 'fore I get my gun."

"Listen, you sootwad," Joe snapped. "I've gone through eight other furgs just like you, all of whom said the same thing, and all of whom ended up telling me exactly what I wanted to know. Think about it. I was a Prime Commander in the Congressional army. Been working in Planetary Ops for fifty turns. It was my job for a good number of those turns to make ashers like you sing like canaries. You *really* wanna piss me off?"

The druggie eyed him sullenly. "You weren't in no Planetary Ops."

Joe slapped his right palm to the window, displaying the tattoo of a green, single-moon planet with a headcom, a PPU, and a species-generic plasma rifle leaning against the debris ring. The tattoo glowed slightly, a cell-by-cell gene modification that caused Joe's skin to bioluminesce. It was a government nannite tat, and no ink in the world could duplicate it.

Even as the druggie's eyes were widening with shock, Joe once more pressed his brother's picture to the window.

"Oh, shit, man." The addict behind the window looked paler than ever. "You're asking the wrong person. He's a big-timer. I'm just a wanna-be, man. I ain't got no idea where the Ghost is."

Joe had to fight back the frustration he had felt ever since returning to Earth to find his mother twenty years dead, his brother vanished into the world of crime. As of yet, every single person Joe had interviewed had responded in the same maddening way. They recognized his picture, but didn't know anything else about him. It was like Sam really was a... ghost.

"So tell me what you know of him," Joe said, as calmly as he could. "Everything you can remember."

"Shit, man. Shit. I ain't never *seen* him before, man. Just heard of him. Shit, I shouldn't even be sayin' nothin'." The guy swallowed and looked around like he expected the very walls to be watching them. "Don't care if you *are* his brother, he wanted to talk to you, he would've found you already."

"I've only been here a week," Joe growled.

The druggie nodded emphatically. "Yeah, man. If the Ghost had wanted to talk to you, he *definitely* woulda talked to you by now."

Joe was fed up. The last seven days of civilian life had been hell. Not only did they question him, but sometimes they outright refused to talk to him—something that had blown Joe's mind the first time they did it. People were rude to him, especially when they realized he'd been a Congie. His PlanOps tattoo tempered that a little bit, but the hostility was still there. While he got along with every alien species even better than a Jahul, Humans, his own kind, hated him.

Once more, Joe wondered if he'd made a mistake in going back to Earth instead of settling on an Ueshi pleasure-planet like Kaleu or Tholiba. On Kaleu, he would've been treated with the same welcome and respect as any other of the three thousand, two hundred and forty-four sentient species in Congress. Here, he was just one of those kids that got brainwashed by aliens. Here, he *was* the alien. He might as well have Ooreiki tentacles or a Huouyt's breja for the nervous looks and outright sneers he got. Earth simply didn't want him.

And yet, the Ground Force didn't want him, either. Not anymore.

Not after Maggie's final bitch-slap in front of half of Congress.

Thank you for your latest reenlistment application, Commander Joe Dobbs, but the Congressional Army is over-capacity and is no longer in need of your services. We've scheduled your shuttle back to Earth for tomorrow morning...

Bitterly, Joe said, "Just tell me what you know about him, okay?"

"They call him Ghost," the druggie said. "Not because he's hard to find, huh-uh. Because he—"

"—bleached his hair white and wears contacts," Joe interrupted. "Yeah, I know. What *else*?"

The druggie's greasy brow wrinkled. "No, man. Who told you that?"

"Look," Joe snapped, "Do you know *anything* that might be helpful? As I see it right now, you're just wasting my time. Just like I told all the other assholes I've come across, I grew up with the little shit and he's got *blue* eyes and *brown* hair. Even if he went all the way and had his eye color permanently changed—which, if he's really as smart as everyone says he is, he didn't—his eyes don't fucking *glow*. How stupid *are* you people?"

The guy raised his hands in surrender. "Man, I just know what I been told."

"Really?" Joe barked. "Then who told *you*? Maybe I'll get some answers from him."

"I don't know, man," the guy said, rapidly shaking his head. "I know a lot of people. I was prolly stoned at the time. Karwiq bulbs, you know? The one good thing Congress brought with 'em. You get a good one and it's like you died and went to heaven."

Joe narrowed his eyes and leaned in close to the glass. "You wanna find out what that really feels like?" Joe growled. "I'll show you, you Takki piece of shit."

The druggie sobered, really looking at him now.

Joe tensed, realizing that this could be the break he'd been looking for.

"Gum," the druggie said finally.

Joe waited, then when that was all that was offered, he blinked at him. "Gum."

"Yeah, you know." The druggie made exaggerated chewing motions. "I hear he likes gum."

Joe stared at him for several moments, then his face tightened in a scowl. "I should break your stupid neck."

"Hey, man, you asked."

"I asked for something I can *use*," Joe growled.

"You never know. Maybe the Ghost owns a gum factory or something."

Joe stared at the druggie for several moments before turning and stalking from the building. In the parking-lot, he took out the picture of his brother and threw it aside. He slipped inside his civilian *haauk* and pressed his head to the climate-controlled steering panel.

The hasty plans he had made of reuniting with his family and returning to his roots had crumbled to dust over the past week he'd been on Earth. Fifty-five turns after Joe had been Drafted, everyone was dead except Sam, and Sam did not want to be found.

Joe had spent over fifty turns—over *sixty-one years*—hunting down people who didn't want to be found, and yet somehow he hadn't even got a whiff of the little druglord shit's whereabouts.

"Damn this place," Joe muttered. For seven days, he'd been wandering the planet, wasting his retirement money, getting no more than four hours of sleep at a time, trying to pin down a ghost.

Joe gave a tired scoff and wondered what his groundteam was doing on Falra. It had to be more interesting than trying to find a career criminal who probably didn't remember him or even care he existed.

Joe lifted his head and glanced at the list of contacts he still had to visit. Six names, none of which he recognized, all of which had been given to him by the same unsavory sorts that in the last seven days had tried to murder him, rob him, drug him, rape him, and in one case, harvest his organs.

Joe had known from the beginning he wouldn't get a hero's welcome upon his return to Earth. What he had experienced here, however, left him feeling numb.

They hated them.

They hated every one of them. As if the Congies were responsible for Earth's woes. As if the kids who had been Drafted sixty years ago were to blame for Congressional rule.

They didn't understand. None of the Earth-bound furgs would ever understand. Congress was the only thing protecting them from something far more dangerous—the Dhasha, the Jreet, the Jikaln, the Dreit, the Huouyt, and all the other warlike creatures Congress had found along the way.

Sighing, Joe wiped the rest of the destinations from his *haauk* memory. He set it on autopilot and told it to take him home.

"You're back early," the smiling young receptionist at the desk of the hotel said as he stepped inside, "You find your brother, Mr. Dobbs?"

"No," Joe said.

Her smile faded. "Oh. I'm sorry, sir."

"Don't be," Joe said with a sigh. "He sounds like a prick anyway." He passed the ornate receptionist booth and took the plushly carpeted stairs to his room—Human buildings still hadn't fully adapted to the introduction of the *haauk*, with the older ones still requiring ground-level entry. Joe had had the poor sense to choose one of the more archaic hotels, longing for the memories of his childhood. At least the locks were reasonably high-tech.

They were biometric, forcing him to scan both eyes and a thumb before the door would open for him.

Not that Joe had anything to steal on the other side. He would have disabled the security measures altogether, because they weren't necessary. All his belongings—what little he'd acquired after a Spartan life in Planetary Ops—were still in transit, carried on a much slower freighter. He was due to pick them up in just over a turn—sixteen months, in Earth-time—and until then would have to get his apartment ready without them.

Sighing, Joe stretched out on the bed and stared up at the ceiling. He felt lost. It had been almost three rotations since he'd held a gun or worn his biosuit. Three rotations since Maggie finally got what she'd been aiming for, ever since Kophat.

Now, without his job, without his gear, without his *life,* Joe felt as if he were missing something. It was a burning ache in his gut, almost like the homesickness he had felt as a kid fresh off Earth. Congress could have chopped off an arm and he wouldn't have felt the same pangs of longing he did now without his rifle and his biosuit.

He felt lost.

Joe rolled over on the bed and squeezed his eyes shut. He wasn't going back. Maggie had seen to that. After fifty-three turns of completely screwing him over at every turn, she had finally won. *Might as well get over it, Joe. You're stuck on this heap.* As he mulled over that, the lack of sleep finally caught up with him. Joe unwillingly began yet another disturbing dream about his inexplicably bitter former groundmate.

The phone rang.

Joe jerked awake, at first thinking it was an invasion siren going off. When he realized it was the blocky device on his nightstand, he frowned. Back at the front desk, the receptionist could have seen he was sleeping. He'd paid top dollar for all the amenities, and she had said herself that the staff would divert all calls when his heart and respiratory functions indicated he was sleeping.

Joe picked up the phone, trying not to sound groggy, pouring through the list of possible emergencies in the back of his head.

"Yeah?"

"Joe Dobbs?" It was a woman's voice, girly, almost teen.

Joe checked the clock. It was 3:03 AM. "Let me guess. The freighter crashed and my stuff's missing."

"This is Samantha," the girl said, then giggled. "But you can call me Sam."

Joe's brows furrowed. "Do I know you?"

"You want to," the girl said happily. "I can make all your dreams come true."

Joe rolled his eyes and hung up. He was taking off his shoes so he could go to bed properly when the phone rang again.

"Look," Joe snapped, "I didn't give out my number so I could get propositioned by every whore in the East Side."

The girl on the other end giggled. "You couldn't buy my services if you wanted to, Joe."

"Then I won't." He hung up again.

When the phone rang the third time, Joe was just starting to fall back to sleep. He considered turning the ringer off. Instead, he yawned, lifted the receiver, and said, "I tell you, lady, you're starting to get on my nerves."

"And you're starting to get on mine."

Joe blinked. It had been a man's voice. "Who the hell are you?"

"Who the hell do you think I am, Joe?"

"I don't know…that little girl's pimp?"

"Oh my God, you have the mental density of a block of ruvmestin, don't you?"

Joe blearily glanced at the clock again. "Look, buddy, it's almost three-twenty in the morning. I'd be a lot more likely to buy whatever you're selling if you weren't fucking pissing me off."

"I take it being a Congie wasn't very stimulating."

"What the hell are you talking about?"

"The last sixty years of what would have been my life, before I saw the light."

"So you decided not to join the Army. Good for you."

"There were hundreds of them. All different colors. Sounded like bombs going off overhead. I remember them because they scared me just as much as they scared the ugly fucks I was with."

As Joe's sleep-starved mind tried to make sense of this, the caller added, "So did you ever end up in that cave killing dragons? 'Cause mine pretty much came true."

He's crazy.

Joe started to hang up again, then an ancient memory tickled the back of his mind. A fortune teller, telling Sam he'd grow up to be a drug-dealer, and that Joe would grow up to slay dragons. With that memory came the memory of the fireworks Joe had used to distract the Ooreiki that had been kidnapping his little brother for the Draft—and of Joe getting captured in his place. Joe brought the handset back to his face in a panic, his exhaustion-haze vanishing. "Sam?"

The line went dead.

Joe's heart pounded like a hammer as he set the handset back onto the receiver. He sat at the edge of the bed, staring at the phone, willing it to ring again. He stayed up the entire night. It didn't ring.

Not that night, not that week, not that rotation.

The next time Joe spoke with his brother was nine weeks after Joe had moved into his permanent apartment.

It was a rainy afternoon in September when Sam called.

"Yeah?" Joe said curtly, trying to get a foot into one of the new tennis shoes he had bought the day before. He was late for his morning run.

A girlish voice giggled. "Do you always answer your phone like that?"

Joe dropped the tennis shoe, his heartbeat quickening. "Sam?"

"How bad do you want to meet me, Joe?" Her voice had a flirtatious ring to it, like a cheap, mail-order hooker.

Joe hesitated. "That a trick question?"

"No. It's a warning. You might not like what you see. I'm probably not what you've been picturing in your head." Her voice lowered, sad and seductive at the same time.

"Fuck that," Joe said. "I want to see you." He held back all the things he had wanted to say to his brother over the turns, respecting Sam's wish for privacy.

"Thursday. I'll be working at the Hungry Kitten in Nevada. Talk to Mindy. She'll set you up with something."

"Sure," Joe said. Then, sensing his brother was about to hang up, he said, "Lookin' forward to it."

There was a pause on the other end, then, "Me, too."

The line went dead before Joe could say any more.

Joe had to fight the impulse to hop on the first flight to Nevada. Instead, he forced himself to put on his other shoe and step outside for a jog.

Two five-foot-tall Ooreiki Peacemakers were waiting for him on his front steps, dressed in Congie black. Their long, tentacle arms were twisted politely in front of them, their huge, sticky brown eyes mournful, their fleshy rows of air-exchanges in their necks flapping as inconspicuously as possible, the way they always did before giving bad news.

Upon seeing him, the brown-skinned Ooreiki flinched. They had obviously been waiting on his steps some time, and yet neither had dredged up the courage to knock.

"Commander Zero?" one of them managed. "*The* Commander Zero?"

Joe's heart began to pound, his mind returning to the conversation he had just had with his brother. "What?"

The Ooreiki who had spoken glanced to his partner, who continued to stare at the ground, mute. The first one turned back to Joe. His huge oblong eyes were filled with humble brown apology. "I'm sorry, Commander, but you've been re-activated."

It took Joe a moment for that to register. "On whose order?"

"Prime Overseer Phoenix, sir."

Joe ground his jaw and twisted his head away. Even retired, Maggie was going to screw with him. "Look, if this is a prank, I'm not falling for it. Phoenix would rather lube up her ass with a plasma grenade than put me back into Planetary Ops. She's the one who *retired* me. Just walk your happy asses back to headquarters and tell the Overseer I thought it was very funny and she can go fuck herself."

"It's not a hoax, Commander." The sincerity in the Ooreiki's sticky eyes was plain. "You...didn't hear?"

Joe stiffened at the outright fear in the young Ooreiki's wrinkled brown face. "What happened?"

"The Dhasha declared war, sir."

Joe's breath caught. Every Congie knew it was going to happen, and every Congie prayed it wasn't within their lifetime. "Fuck," he muttered, his breath leaving him. He thought of all of his friends and groundmates who were going to die. Billions. "How many of them?" he finally asked. If it was just one prince, like last time, perhaps it wouldn't decimate the Corps.

The Ooreiki that had been speaking glanced again at his partner. The second Ooreiki hadn't taken its sticky eyes off the ground.

It was the second one who finally spoke. In a whisper, he said, "All of them."

END SNEAK PEEK

29219736R10320

Made in the USA
San Bernardino, CA
16 January 2016